MARGARET TRUMAN

THREE COMPLETE MYSTERIES

MARGARET TRUMAN

THREE COMPLETE MYSTERIES

MURDER AT THE NATIONAL CATHEDRAL

MURDER AT THE KENNEDY CENTER

MURDER IN THE CIA

WINGS BOOKS

New York • *Avenel, New Jersey*

This edition contains the complete and unabridged texts of the original editions.
They have been completely reset for this volume.

This 1994 edition is published by Wings Books,
distributed by Random House Value Publishing, Inc.,
40 Engelhard Avenue, Avenel, New Jersey 07001,
by arrangement with Random House, Inc.

Random House
New York • Toronto • London • Sydney • Auckland

Printed and bound in the United States of America

Library of Congress Cataloging-in-Publication Data

Truman, Margaret, 1924–
Margaret Truman : three complete stories.
      p.   cm.
Contents: Murder at the National Cathedral—Murder at the
Kennedy Center—Murder in the CIA.
ISBN 0-517-11823-8
I. Title.
PS3570.R82A6   1994
813′.54—dc20   94-17809
                                                                    CIP

8   7   6   5   4   3   2   1

CONTENTS

MURDER
AT THE
NATIONAL
CATHEDRAL

To Wesley Truman Daniel
with love
from Gammy

"This church is intended for national purposes . . . and assigned to the special use of no particular Sect or denomination, but equally open to all."

Pierre L'Enfant
1791 Plan for the City of Washington

". . . a national house of prayer for all people."
The Congress of the United States—1893

"Here let us stand, close by the cathedral.
Here let us wait. Are we drawn by danger?
Is it the knowledge of safety, that draws our feet
Towards the cathedral? What danger can be . . . ?"

T. S. Eliot
Murder in the Cathedral

"Someone has been murdered in the cathedral."
The Right Reverend George St. James,
bishop of Washington

1

The National Cathedral, Washington, D.C.—
A Very Hot Morning in August

"DEARLY BELOVED, we have come together in the presence of God to witness and bless the joining together of this man and woman in Holy Matrimony."

Mackensie Smith, contented professor of law at George Washington University, formerly discontented but preeminent Washington, D.C., criminal lawyer, told himself to focus on what was about to happen. He'd been thinking moments before about what an ambivalent structure a cathedral was, even this relatively new addition to the world's cathedral population. So much majesty and awe—so much stone—so much bloodshed in the older ones over centuries. How inspiring these Gothic monuments to the simple act of believing in something greater and good, and how dangerous, as with all religion, when in the hands of creatures who get carried away and misuse the potent metaphor of faith.

Those thoughts banished, Smith glanced to his left. The stunning, mature woman who would become his wife in a matter of minutes turned to him and smiled. Annabel Reed had reason to assume that his thoughts at that tender moment were only of his adoration and love for her. She was largely correct, although her husband-to-be had room in his capacious mind for less romantic contemplations. He was also wishing that the priest conducting this ceremony in the Bethlehem Chapel of the National Cathedral weren't compelled to be quite so formal. Smith understood, of course, that there was a certain amount of religious boilerplate that had to be indulged. Still, he would have preferred something a little less stiff, perhaps something between an elaborate high mass in the cathedral's nave, and a last-minute midnight, minimal, bread-and-butter ceremony in an Elkton, Maryland, justice of the peace's home.

The priest, Paul Singletary, paused after intoning the tender words from the Book of Common Prayer, and smiled at Smith and Reed. The couple had known him for a time; Smith went back six years with him. Mac Smith was a close friend of the cathedral's bishop. George St. James was out of town that week, which was not the reason Smith hadn't asked him to officiate. It had more to do with what Smith termed "a reasonable level of modesty." Asking the bishop to marry them would have smacked of a certain overkill. Just a priest would do fine, thank you, especially one known to them.

Smith again looked at his bride. A tiny drop of perspiration was proceeding on a slow but steady descent down the right side of her lovely aquiline nose. Should he reach over and remove it? An affectionate gesture certainly, but probably not good form, so he didn't. Outside, the final days of August in the nation's capital had turned, characteristically, viciously hot and humid. It was cooler here in the chapel below ground-level, but even God's natural stone air-conditioning was wilting under the meltdown that Washington called summer. Carved figures of King David with his harp and Ruth with a sheaf of wheat looked down from their niches on the south wall as though they, too, might begin perspiring at any moment. The Bethlehem Chapel, one of four in the cathedral's substructure, was the first to be completed. Since 1912 it had been the site of many services, and was the church home over the years for the services of various denominations—Polish Catholic, Jewish, Russo-Carpathian, Serbian, Greek Orthodox. A *national* cathedral.

Reverend Singletary looked once again at the Book of Common Prayer. Smith looked into the priest's eyes. Was he amused at something? He seemed to be, Smith decided. Marriages made later in life always had a different aura from that accompanying the ritual of officially coupling the young for the first time.

Smith was widowed; his wife and only child, a son, had been slaughtered on the Beltway by a drunk driver. Annabel Reed had never married, although, God knows, more than a few attractive and successful men had energetically pursued the idea. That she had decided upon Mac Smith was flattering to him. But not humbling. No false modesty here. Smith was a handsome man by any standard, slightly taller than medium, stocky and strong, hair receding slowly and within acceptable limits, face without undue deficits.

Annabel's beauty was even less debatable. Playing the whom-do-you-look-like game, which Smith detested (his least-favorite version of it being "Which of us do you think the baby looks like?"), it was inevitable that Rita Hayworth was mentioned. Yet Annabel was more beautiful than any actress, at least in Smith's eyes. She was, to put it simply, the most beautiful female creature he'd ever seen, not much at acting, for she never put up a false front, and rather nice to boot. By virtue of the ritual being performed here today—all day?—she would be his wife. Let's get on with it, he thought. Enough.

Though any clergyman could make a determination as to whether the lawfulness of a proposed marriage was in question, Smith was surprised when Singletary chose to invoke that medieval section of the marriage ceremony. "If any of you can show just cause why they may not lawfully be married, speak now or else . . ." he said, allowing scant time for the clearing of a questioner's throat, much less speech, "forever hold your peace."

There was a silence that Smith hoped was not pregnant. The

Bethlehem Chapel seated 192 people; thirty of their close friends, including a few former members of Smith's law firm who had forgiven him for closing it down following the deaths of his wife and son, were clustered up front.

Mac's thoughts were on only one person, however—Tony Buffolino, a disgraced and dismissed former Washington MPD vice-squad cop whom Mac had once defended, and who'd become an unlikely friend in the best odd-couple tradition. If anyone pretended to raise an objection to the marriage just for kicks, it would be a character like Buffolino. Mac turned his head slightly, saw Tony, who winked at Mac, started to raise his hand, brought it down, and lowered his head.

Paul Singletary smiled at her as he said, "Annabel, will you have this man to be your husband; to live together in the covenant of marriage? Will you love him, comfort him, honor and keep him, in sickness and in health; and, forsaking all others, be faithful to him as long as you both shall live?"

"Oh yes, I will," she said with unmistakable cheer in her voice.

Singletary repeated the vow to Smith, who replied, "I will," in a surprisingly gruff, emotional voice.

Smith looked to the choir loft, where four members of the cathedral's boys' choir—the few who preferred music to baseball in August—had gathered to sing. Later in the service they would perform Annabel's favorite hymn, "Wilderness," the choice of which had pleased Father Singletary because of its humanistic, contemporary theme.

Singletary read the verse beginning "Love is patient; love is kind" from I Corinthians, and the four boys got through "Wilderness" rather quickly; the usual tempo seemed to have been accelerated by a third. Mac Smith approved. He was also impressed, as was everyone else in the chapel, with the strong, bell-like voice of one of the boy sopranos, whose tones rang out above the others.

Soon, it was time to exchange rings. Annabel had virtually no family. She had friends, of course, but her hectic schedule as an attorney-turned-art-gallery-owner and almost constant companion to Mac Smith had severely limited time to cultivate and nurture friendships. She was being given "away" as a wife by his mother, Josephine Smith, as spry and sparkling as a split of champagne, a tiny woman who lived in the Sevier Home for the Aged in Georgetown, a facility operated by the Episcopal church, and who often said that she considered Annabel as much a daughter as she did Mac a son, and sometimes more. Smith's best man was the new dean of GW's law school, Daniel Jaffe. Josephine Smith and Jaffe handed the rings to their respective charges.

Mac and Annabel Smith slipped the gold bands on their ring fingers, and Singletary blessed them, concluding with the familiar "Those whom God has joined together let no one put asunder."

"Amen," said their friends.

As Mac and Annabel knelt (It's always the knees that go first, Smith thought), Singletary intoned the final blessing of their union. They stood. They kissed. Eyes met eyes.

"The peace of the Lord be always with you," said the priest.

"And also with you," came the reply.

After the ceremony everyone went outside, where friends took quick point-and-shoot photographs, delivered quick point-and-kiss greetings to Annabel, and grasped the groom's hand, with an occasional teary kiss for him, too. Properly, they congratulated Mac, who said in mock modesty, "It was nothing," and added, "Just a four-year chase."

"Going on a honeymoon?" one of Smith's colleagues at the university asked him.

"London, but not right away. Somehow it seems you don't take an instant honeymoon at this stage in your life."

Another professor laughed. "You two have been on a honeymoon for years."

"I suppose we have," Smith said, not precisely caring for the innuendo in the comment.

Tony Buffolino came up and extended his hand. He was accompanied by his third wife, Alicia, a waitress he'd met at the Top of the Mark in San Francisco, where he, Smith, and Annabel had gathered while solving one phase in the murder of a presidential aide at the Kennedy Center. Afterward, Smith had got Buffolino a job as a security guard at the university. But Alicia came along with grander ideas. They now owned what Buffolino fondly referred to as the only Vegas-type cabaret in Washington, minus slot machines, of course.

"You did good, Mac," Buffolino said, in his best congratulatory style. Alicia kissed them on their cheeks. "Such a beautiful couple," she said.

"Frankly, I'm glad it's over," Smith said. He looked at Annabel. "You?"

"Frankly, I'm glad we've begun. Besides, I love weddings," Annabel said. "Maybe we could do this every couple of months. Don't forget, Mac, I've never been a bride before."

Father Singletary joined them. It was said that many women in the parish were in love with him. He was a tall, fine-looking man with a shrewd gentleness to his eyes and a wide, smiling mouth that women naturally responded to, a man self-assured without much—though with just a touch of—vanity. Singletary seemed, as Ralph Waldo Emerson had written, created of "God's handwriting." He took Smith's and Annabel's hands and grinned. "I was certain somebody would protest this marriage," he said.

"Who would protest it?" Smith asked.

"Me. I've been mad about this woman ever since I met her." Singletary smiled down at Annabel. "I suppose the fact that you've chosen a lawyer rather than a man of God says something about you."

"In God we trust, all others pay cash," Annabel said.

"If this distinguished legal beagle doesn't work out, Annabel, call me," the priest said.

"Don't wait by the phone, Paul," said Annabel, laughing. "And thank you for making us one."

"My pleasure. Well, excuse me. I have a funeral to prepare for. The cycle of life."

"Birth and death," Tony Buffolino said, pleased that he was able to contribute to the conversation. He always felt awkward around clergymen.

"Yes," said Singletary. "And marriage and . . ."

"Divorce?" said Smith.

"Fortunately, the church doesn't have a ceremony for divorce," Reverend Singletary said. "Maybe someday. Or the rite of blessed separation." He laughed.

"Not for us, thank you," Annabel put in.

"Better not be," said Singletary. "If you do, find another priest."

"No divorce," Smith said. "No separations. Just ordinary, routine bliss." He hugged his wife.

"All best," Singletary said. "I'm off to do the funeral. Then London tonight. I have to go there often."

As the man who had married them walked away, Smith's thoughts returned to where they'd been at the beginning of the ceremony. Odd. He looked up at the graceful portal above the flight of broad steps leading to the cathedral's south entrance. The carved, dominant figure of Christ stood with His disciples at the Last Supper. Death? Resurrection? Fact or fiction? No matter, not if one believed—or didn't.

A black cloud crossed the sun.

Mac was glad they'd eschewed any suggestions of a party following the ceremony. He wanted them to be, as the song says, alone together.

"Come on, Mrs. Smith," he said, "let's go home."

2

Lambeth Palace, London—
Two Months Later. A Windy, Cold, and Wet October Tuesday.
"Decent Day," the Locals Said.

THE REVEREND CANON Paul Singletary looked up at the library's hammerbeam ceiling, then to a faded, coarse beige-and-red tapestry that covered much of one wall. On the tapestry was the inwoven cross of the archbishop of Canterbury—*primus inter pares,* first among equals —whose seat of power as head of the worldwide Anglican Communion was the medieval Lambeth Palace, to which Singletary had come this late October afternoon.

A window on the west wall afforded a view across the Thames to Westminster and its Abbey, and to the Houses of Parliament. A twelfth-century primate had bought the land on which Lambeth Palace sat in order to be close—but not too close, God forbid—to the Crown.

Towering fuscous cumulonimbus clouds over Westminster unleashed a brief, brilliant shaft of white lightning as the door to the library opened and the Reverend Canon Malcolm Apt entered. Nice timing, Singletary thought. He sat in the chair and scrutinized Apt as he approached, not because he didn't know him, but because he always found Apt's face to be interesting. It was as though Apt's features had been pasted on the flat plane of his face slightly off-center, which created the effect of eyes, nose, and mouth out of alignment, pointing in a slightly different direction than the face itself. He wore a white surplice over a purple cassock; the cassock reached the floor. Apt was a short block of a man whose salt-and-pepper hair was the consistency of wire; he'd lost few wires in his fifty years.

Singletary stood without energy. "I didn't expect to be kept waiting this long," he said.

Apt ignored the comment and the tone in which it was delivered. "Come," he said, "we'll talk in the archbishop's study." He led Singletary along the Great Corridor, where portraits of all the archbishops from Victorian times hung, then into a large, comfortably furnished room. Apt went to the windows, looked out over the river as though to assure himself it was still there, and drew on a cord that caused heavy drapes to slide closed with a soft whoosh.

"Well?" Singletary said.

"He won't be able to see you, I'm afraid."

"Are you serious?"

"Some people think I'm too serious."

Singletary looked at his watch; it was seven o'clock. Seven peals of a church bell confirmed it. "I've wasted my time then."

"If you choose to view it that way, Paul," Apt said. "Sit down. The archbishop asked me to discuss certain aspects of this with you."

Singletary was not interested in discussing anything with Malcolm Apt. He'd wanted to see the archbishop of Canterbury himself. Apt was the archbishop's suffragan bishop, or VP in charge of . . . well, public relations. At least that's what his title would be in the secular, business world. His official title was director of church information.

Apt sat behind a highly polished cherrywood table. Singletary sat across from him. Although dusk was starting to fall outside, the open drapes had permitted some light to enter. With them closed, the efficacy of the study's interior lighting seemed to have been diminished by half.

"Paul, the archbishop is growing increasingly concerned about this Word of Peace thing."

Singletary laughed crisply enough to make his point, but not enough to indicate disrespect to the archbishop of Canterbury. Apt continued, and Singletary knew that he was speaking words that had been carefully considered, perhaps even written prior to his arrival at the library. "You must understand that when the archbishop gave his support to Word of Peace, not a great deal was known about it. Frankly, I tried my best to dissuade him from involving us in it." Apt smiled—not much of a smile, but because it tended to stretch his mouth slightly, it enhanced the feeling that the paste-up job had been hasty. "I must admit that you were very effective when you presented the Word of Peace program to the archbishop. How long ago was that, Paul, a year?"

Singletary shrugged.

"Of course, there was the weight of the others with you, especially the African bishop. What's his name?" Apt asked it with seeming sincerity, but Singletary knew that Apt was well aware of the African bishop's name. He'd seen Apt do this before, degrade someone by pretending to have forgotten the name.

"Bishop Eastland."

"Ah, yes, Bishop Eastland. Certainly one of our high-visibility bishops. Nasty mess, that apartheid. We'll all be happy when that's resolved. How is Bishop Eastland?"

"Fine, and still fighting apartheid, according to what I read in the press."

"A most impressive man. As I was saying, the archbishop's enthusiasm for Word of Peace has waned, although he has not withdrawn his support. Has your Bishop St. James's enthusiasm back in Washington been sustained, or has it waned, too?"

"Heightened might be a more accurate way to describe it," Singletary said flatly.

Apt sat back and clasped his hands on his belly. "Heightened. Interesting."

"Malcolm, you said the archbishop wanted you to discuss something with me about Word of Peace. Is this it, that his enthusiasm has waned?"

"In a sense, yes, although there is more behind it. He is, of course, not only charged with the administration of the church; he is equally responsible for how we are viewed by others. That is also my particular responsibility, one I take very seriously. You will admit that some of those who have become involved with Word of Peace seem self-seeking, or political, and many are controversial at best, including yourself."

Singletary laughed again; this time it was more genuine, and with less concern for the archbishop. "Controversial? We pray each night to a highly controversial figure."

"Prayers are our leveling factor, Paul. What we do between prayers is another matter."

"You mean, of course, to what extent we become involved in . . ." He thought before finishing. "To what extent we become involved in things not very *churchy.*"

"I'd rather not be told what I mean, Paul, although that is your prerogative . . . and bent." Apt smiled.

They'd had this conversation before, especially since Singletary had become a conspicuous leader of the worldwide and nondenominational Word of Peace movement, in which the world's clergy were to use their collective weight and individual pulpits to spread the word of peace. Apt, and the archbishop of Canterbury, whose religious philosophy Apt shared (genuinely or because it was good for tenure? Singletary often wondered) were advocates of the Anglo-Catholic division of the church —the "Oxford movement"—archconservative (he was not called "*arch*bishop" for nothing, Singletary thought in a whimsical moment), rigid, authoritarian, puritanical, and intolerant of the more liberal wing that did not, in Anglo-Catholic eyes, adhere strictly enough to *Catholic* doctrine, of all things. They were *for* peace, to be sure, but not for disturbing it.

Singletary, on the other hand, was very much part of what was called the Broad Church (in political jargon, the Episcopal "liberal party"). There was also the so-called Evangelical movement, claiming to represent a middle ground of philosophy but firmly sin-based, Luther- and Calvin-influenced, and without much respect from either the conservative or the liberal wing of the church.

Word of Peace was a distinctly liberal movement, aggressively intermixed with Singletary's widely publicized work with drug addicts, runaway teens, the homeless, and a score of other social causes back in D.C. And nationally. Truth was, it was not those social causes but politics that prompted criticism of the Word of Peace movement. The movement stood for boycotting South Africa until it rid itself of apartheid, and for getting out of Ollie North's Central America and dissociating from its so-called freedom fighters. The olive branch in place of the B-1. Politics!

Singletary looked at his watch again. He said, "You know, Malcolm, you and I are both canons because we serve bishops and cathedrals. I will give you that your boss holds higher rank, but mine, George St. James, is not exactly, as some of my friends would say, 'chopped liver.' I would also remind you that in both Luke and Matthew Our Lord calls for the church to feed the hungry, clothe the naked, heal the sick, be the harbinger of comfort and caring and hope."

"I am familiar with Matthew and Luke."

"Wasn't it from the gate I entered this afternoon that the Lambeth dole was practiced?" Singletary frowned as he pulled from his memory the words " 'Every Friday and Sunday, unto every beggar that came to the door, a loaf of bread of a farthing price.' "

Apt stretched another thin smile.

"And you're also familiar with what Canon Casson told the executive council," Singletary said. "That the Gospel isn't believable unless the church relates to its neighborhoods—including the larger neighborhood called the planet."

"So endeth the lesson!" Apt stood. "I have another appointment."

"So do I. I'm already late."

"Safe journey home, Paul."

"Yes. Please tell the archbishop how disappointed I was not to be able to see him on this trip."

"You didn't come to London just to see him, did you?"

"You know I didn't. Still, first things first . . ."

"You'll be staying a few days?"

"One more day. I have a meeting tomorrow in your limpid country-side. Then back to Washington on Thursday."

Singletary picked up his black raincoat from the chair. Apt opened the study door. And began to accompany him. Singletary said, "It's okay, Malcolm, I know my Luke, Matthew, and the way out."

Singletary had been provided a car and driver by the London Word of Peace Committee for his visit to Lambeth Palace. It was at his disposal for the evening. He climbed in the back of the navy-blue Ford and gave the driver an address in Mayfair, near Berkeley Square. When they reached it, the driver slowed to read numbers. Singletary said, "This will be fine."

"Shall I wait?" the elderly British driver asked.

Singletary wrinkled his brow and pursed his lips in thought. "No, Bob, I think I'll be here awhile. I'll take a cab back to the hotel or walk. It isn't far. Thank you very much for your courtesy."

Singletary waited until the car had been driven away. Then, after looking left and right, he walked back to the corner of Charles Street and went up Davies Street. At number 418 he climbed the short set of steps and announced his arrival with three brisk raps of the brass knocker on the red door.

"Paul?" a voice asked from behind the door.

"Yes."

The door was opened by a tall and slender, broad-shouldered woman of thirty-one. Clarissa Morgan possessed what Singletary considered a rare combination—black hair and eyes with milky-white skin. She wore pink silk lounging pajamas. "Come in," she said, her accent edged with a touch of Welsh clarity. "I was about to become worried."

Singletary stepped into the foyer, and she closed the door behind them. "He kept me waiting, didn't even see me," he said.

"Poor dear," she said, taking his coat. "Hardly the sort of behavior one would expect from the archbishop of Canterbury."

"Exactly what one would expect of *this* archbishop of Canterbury, considering the fact that he's to the right of Thomas Cartwright." Realizing that she didn't understand the reference, he muttered, "Another puritanical right-winger of the faith."

He walked into a small, tastefully decorated parlor and went directly to a cupboard, opened its doors, and pulled out a metal bottle of Danska. Clarissa came to his side carrying a bucket of ice. "You?" he asked as he put ice and the vodka into a glass and removed his jacket.

"I prefer wine."

They touched glasses and sat on a very contemporary-looking leather sofa, a jarring note in the midst of the room's antique furnishings. She touched his cheek with slender fingers tipped with nails the color of dusty roses, smiled, and said softly, "You look older when you're angry. Don't be angry, at least not tonight."

He managed to smile, downed half of his drink, and removed his clerical collar. "Where are we eating?"

Her voice now had a softer quality. "I thought we'd eat right here. If that's all right with you, of course." She looked into his eyes. "It *is* all right that we stay here, isn't it?"

His face said that the anger he'd felt since leaving Lambeth Palace was fading fast. "Yes, it's all right with me. Very all right. What are we having?"

She smiled and stood. "Cold tarragon chicken, a simple salad with raspberry dressing, rolls and butter, and a peach tart for dessert. How . . . hungry are you? All of it will keep nicely. But will you? Will I? Do you know how sinfully handsome you are?"

He stood and embraced her. The smell of her hair and perfume filled his nostrils as he touched his lips to her neck. His hands slid slowly down her back. The only words spoken between them as they entered the bedroom came from Clarissa. "If you'd like to unleash a little bit of that controlled anger now, Reverend," she said, "I'd love it."

*   *   *

As the Reverend Canon Paul Singletary communed with Clarissa Morgan, the driver called Bob pulled up in front of the Red Lion pub in Mayfair. He told the barmaid that Mr. Leighton's car was waiting. She disappeared into the back dining room while Bob returned to the Ford. A few minutes later a tall, gray-haired gentleman with a Burberry raincoat neatly folded over the sleeve of his brown tweed suit left the pub. He carried an umbrella, and walked with an odd slight leaning to the left, as though too many years of toting a heavy briefcase had bent him that way. Bob opened the back door of the Ford, and the man got in.

"Home?"

"Yes."

After driving a block, Brett Leighton asked, "Well, did you take our clerical friend someplace interesting?"

"To the house in Mayfair with the red door. Actually, to a nearby address—but he walked to his final destination."

"Yes." Leighton smiled to himself. "A most beautiful altar at which to pray."

Bob said nothing.

"His plans?"

"He said he would be going out of town tomorrow."

"Out of town. You'll be driving him?"

"Not likely. The dispatcher said nothing about it."

"Let me know if you do."

"Of course, sir."

Bob dropped Leighton in front of a white townhouse in Belgravia. "Thank you, Bob," Leighton said.

"My pleasure," said the driver. "Will there be anything else tonight?"

Leighton handed Bob a sealed envelope, which, after Leighton had disappeared inside his house, the driver opened. He put the hundred-pound note in his pocket and drove to the Lamb and Flag on Rose Street in Covent Garden, a pub formerly known as the Bucket of Blood, where he ordered a clanger and a Directors bitter and joined his friends at a round corner table.

"Good day?" Eddie asked.

"A bloody bore 'cept for the traffic. I swear it gets worse every day," Bob said. "Can 'ardly see where you're going. Have to keep your eyes open for sure. Bloody Americans everywhere. No idea how to drive."

After eating his pastry roll of bacon, onion, and herbs, Bob considered leaving. His wife would be angry that he was late again, but what did she know? He deserved his relaxation, with the important work he did. Couldn't tell her. Just as well.

He bought the next round. And another. And the hundred-pound note became smaller in proportion to Bob's growing expansiveness.

3

The National Cathedral, Washington, D.C.—
The Next Night, Wednesday

J OSEPH K ELSCH IDLY pulled sheet music from a large pile on the table in front of him. The choirboy knew there really wasn't any need to refile the music. Ordinarily, the cathedral's vast collection of religious music was meticulously maintained; Joey had been assigned the unnecessary task as punishment for having disrupted that afternoon's rehearsal of the boys' choir. What was especially annoying to him was that he was ten years old, it was nine o'clock at night, and he'd been told by the choirmaster, Canon Wilfred Nickelson, that he was to continue with this make-work until eleven, after which he'd surely be twenty years old, and which also meant he would be unable to participate in the Ping-Pong contest that was going on at that moment back in the boys' dormitory. Joey was one of the better Ping-Pong players in the school and had advanced to the final round, the winner to be decided that evening. Canon Willy Nickelson had caused him to lose his opportunity to be the winner.

If Joey Kelsch, the boys' choir's finest young voice and biggest cutup, had been honest with himself, he would have admitted that the worst thing about his punishment was having to be alone in the choir room at night. He'd turned on all the lights. Still, there was something murkily forbidding about being here alone, about being alone *anywhere* in the vast cathedral after dark. Every sound was magnified and caused him to stiffen. His eyes darted from window to window. Thoughts of the tournament took his mind off his fears for a moment. That nerd Billy would probably win, now that Joey couldn't compete. A series of black thoughts about choirmaster Nickelson filled Joey's head as he lazily shuffled another piece of paper onto a pile. He was *better* at Ping-Pong than Billy. This wasn't fair. He hadn't done anything terrible during rehearsal, just talked too much after Nickel-Pickle had twice told him to stop.

As he sat at the long table in the choir room, Joey heard voices a few times when people passed in the hallway outside the door. He recognized Bishop St. James's rumble on one occasion, and he considered going into the hallway to voice a complaint to the bishop about his punishment. "The punishment doesn't fit the crime," he would say to St. James if he went into the hallway. He didn't; Bishop St. James was a nice man, but he would say, "I suggest you take this up with Reverend Nickelson."

Joey sighed and looked at a clock on the wall. Another whole hour and a half to go. Though he wasn't always on the side of the angels, in the soft, subdued light he resembled one. "Crap!" he muttered.

Across the hall from the choir room, behind the altar in the Bethlehem Chapel, which had been Mac and Annabel Smith's wedding site, a man stood in the shadows. He cocked his head at the sound of footsteps on the hard stone floor. They became louder, then stopped. A figure appeared at one side of the altar, paused, looked down at the vault in which the Right Reverend Henry Yates Satterlee, first bishop of Washington, and his wife, Jane Lawrence, had long ago been interred, looked up at an alabaster tomb bearing a recumbent likeness of Bishop Satterlee, and then, through narrowed eyes, peered at the man in the shadows. They began to talk, their tones low, their anger soon evident. The one who'd been second to enter the chapel closed the gap between them; they were only a few feet from each other now, their voices rising in intensity and volume, their words coming back at them in fragments off the hard walls.

"Sssssssh, keep your voice *down.*"

"You won't get away with this."

"How dare you . . . ?"

". . . too far. You went . . ."

The tall man who'd been in the shadows made a sound of disgust and began to walk toward the small door at the front of the chapel that led to the hall. The other quickly turned to the Satterlee vault. Two large, heavy brass candlesticks used during Communion services had been left there by a member of the Altar Guild; they would be polished the next day by another of the guild's devoted, reverent women.

A hand grabbed one of the candlesticks by its top. A few quick steps after the man from the shadows. The candleholder was raised in the air, then swung down and around in a wide, vicious, and accurate arc. As the base of the candlestick caught the man in his left temple, there was the sound of bone being crushed, followed by a low, pained moan when the man hit the stone floor as if driven into it like a flame-hardened nail.

Joey Kelsch stiffened as the noises from the chapel reached him. The choirboy had been listening, had heard only one voice, but not the other. He hadn't been able to make out the words, but he knew the speaker was very angry. Other people's anger was always frightening. Besides, he had heard enough of it from the choirmaster. Still, Joey went to the door that led to the corridor and pressed his ear to it, heard footsteps in an irregular pattern, heard laborious breathing, heard what sounded like something being dragged along the floor, a large sack of flour, maybe, or a big cardboard carton. The sounds faded in the direction of the stairs that led up to the north entrance to the cathedral, where the tiny Good Shepherd Chapel remained open twenty-four hours a day.

Joey carefully pushed the door out an inch; its hinges made some noise, but not much. He continued opening it until there was room for him to poke his head into the corridor. Looking to his left, he saw empty corridor. Looking to his right, he saw a figure, nothing more than a black shroud really. He thought it a statue until he saw that it was about to turn the corner and go up the stairs with whatever was being dragged behind.

Joey closed the door, felt his heart threatening to beat through his chest wall. He waited, unsure of what to do. Then he heard footsteps returning. The door was open just enough for him to peek through the crack. Now it was not just a form in the distance. There was, for a split second, a face. The hands belonging to the face were carrying two red hand-crocheted kneeling pads from the chapel, their faded renderings celebrating Bethlehem and the birth of the Baby Jesus.

The face returned to the Bethlehem Chapel and disappeared from Joey's field of vision.

Joey quietly pulled the door closed, tiptoed across the choir room, left through another door leading to the outside, and ran as fast as he could to his dormitory. Other students were finishing the Ping-Pong tournament in the room, but Joey didn't stop to join them. Trembling, he raced up the stairs, went into his room, quickly got into his pajamas, climbed into bed, panting, and pulled the covers over his head.

Until then, he hadn't cried.

4

The Next Morning,
Which Would Be Thursday

ALTHOUGH THE SUNRISE was only a suggestion, the Right Reverend George St. James, bishop of Washington and dean of the National Cathedral, had already completed his daily contemplative stroll, had ridden his stationary bike, and had said his morning prayers. Now, as he stepped from the shower and vigorously began drying himself, he focused on the day ahead.

The major event was to be the funeral of Adam Vickery, a former attorney general of the United States, scheduled for nine o'clock in the cathedral's nave. Vickery and his wife, Doris, had been active in cathedral affairs for many years. Vickery had sat on the cathedral's chapter—its "board of directors"—for the past seven years, and as head of the building fund had received deserved accolades for his deft handling of it. His death had been sudden and unexpected. Seemingly in the best of health, he'd been found slumped inertly over his desk three nights before, the victim, apparently, of a massive coronary.

Now toweled dry, the bishop looked at his naked image in a full-length mirror in the rectory's second-floor master bedroom. The enticing aroma of coffee drifted up from the kitchen. St. James heard his wife, Eileen, singing along with a popular song of another decade that came from a radio, a song the bishop began to hum although he couldn't put a title to it. His wife would know the title *and* the words and carry the tune. He looked at himself in the mirror again and smiled; God had a reason for everything, even personal tragedy and sociological disaster, but what could possibly have been on His mind when He—okay, or *She,* the bishop reminded himself—decreed that in middle age weight must settle in the midsection? St. James was the same weight he'd been while attending the Yale Divinity School almost thirty years before, but the same number of pounds had found an unwelcome redistribution center between his chest and his hips. Maybe I'd better start riding more of it off—or up—on the bicycle that goes nowhere, he thought.

He dressed, joined Eileen in the kitchen, kissed her cheek, and ate the scrambled eggs and dry toast she'd set before him. *The Washington*

Post was beside his plate at the table. No need to look for the Religion section; it wasn't Saturday. Then again, politics was the city's religion, and there was always plenty of *that* in the *Post* each day. Which was not to say that religion—the spiritual variety—didn't play a role in the nation's capital. Lord knows there were enough prayer breakfasts every morning in Washington to save a regiment of souls. Prayer breakfasts in the White House were very much in vogue with the new administration, and the Cabinet, the House, the Senate, myriad governmental agencies, and even the military kicked off their days with a few words to a Higher Authority.

St. James had once delivered a sermon based upon the theory that religion played less of a role in Washington than in almost any other city in the world. He used the numerous guidebooks to Washington as an example, pointing out that they scarcely mentioned the city's religious life, and suggested that an interdenominational committee be formed to encourage better coverage in future editions. Nothing ever came of it, which did not surprise him.

What really bothered him (although he did not give a sermon on this) was that Washington's churches were usually better known for *whom* they attracted rather than for the quality of salvation being offered. President John F. Kennedy virtually put St. Matthew's Cathedral "on the map" because of his frequent attendance there, and because it was where his funeral Mass had been conducted.

Directly across from the White House, on Lafayette Square, stood St. John's Episcopal Church, known as the "Church of the Presidents" because virtually every American president showed up there at least once, including Gerald Ford, who privately and understandably asked for divine wisdom while contemplating a pardon for Richard Nixon. Nixon, of course, enjoyed having the church and clergy come to him at the White House, as opposed to Presidents Carter and Truman, who frequently prayed at the First Baptist Church, only a few minutes' walk from the White House.

Teddy Roosevelt had worshiped at Grace Reform Church, but his wife and her family went to St. John's Episcopal. Grace Reform rewarded TR's allegiance by creating a collection of memorabilia from the Roosevelt White House. St. John's did not create such a memorial for the rest of his family.

The Eisenhowers preferred worshiping at the National Covenant Presbyterian Church, which lost its location to a modern office building and was moved to new ground near American University, where tourists could browse its Chapel of Presidents.

Of course, there had been the snide references to *Christian* Dior, cattily referred to as First Lady Nancy Reagan's religion. St. James had thought that a cheap shot, but had laughed when first hearing it.

Churches everywhere, he mused, but only throwaway mentions of them in the guidebooks. A pagan city, if one used the travel literature as one's criterion.

He scanned the *Post*'s front page, was more thorough as he went through the Style section, finished his second cup of coffee, and kissed his wife good-bye on the other cheek. "I'll be home this afternoon," he said. "I need some quiet time to work on the presentation." He was to address the National Association of Asphalt Contractors that night—he gave many such speeches in the continuing process of raising money for the cathedral's building fund. What had begun for him as a quest for God too often translated into a quest for checks. It seemed never to end, this need for money. The cathedral, sixth largest in the world, was an insatiable devourer of cash, its completion so near yet so far away; just another ten thousand for an additional gargoyle, forty thousand to reinforce a corbel in the north entrance, a hundred thousand to repair water damage in the Children's Chapel. Adam Vickery would be missed, St. James reflected. Despite his unpleasant demeanor, Vickery knew how to shake money loose.

The bishop strode with purpose across the fifty-seven-acre close and looked up at the Gloria in Excelsis Tower soaring more than three hundred feet into the cerulean October sky. Given its supporting hill, the tower was the highest structure in Washington, so inspiring, so majestic, and so expensive. St. James felt good, but he always felt good in the early morning. Morning was the time his internal clock ticked at optimum speed. By the time he addressed the asphalt contractors, his clock would have slowed, and he'd have to wind it up a little to make it through. How much he disliked having to ask for money! Praying for it was one thing; asking was another.

A group of men milled about the south entrance. One of them, Idris Porter, chief of the Washington Cathedral Police, was leaning against his white Ford Bronco talking to a man whom the bishop didn't recognize. The man was bulkier than Porter, and wore a gray suit.

"Good morning, Idris," St. James said. "Ready bright and early I see."

"Yes, Bishop," Porter said with a smile. He was a very dark black man with sparse, unruly gray hair. "Bishop, this is Agent Lazzara, Secret Service."

"Good morning," St. James said, extending his hand. Security at the cathedral for events such as Vickery's funeral necessitated the involvement of other agencies besides the cathedral's small security force. Which agencies, and the number of personnel assigned, depended upon many factors—anticipated crowd size, the deceased's position and level of controversy, rumors, threats. There hadn't been any threats regarding the funeral as far as St. James knew. When attorney general, Adam Vickery had been controversial, as most attorneys general are, considering that they're appointed more for past political favors and fundraising than for legal insight, but controversy hadn't followed him into private life.

"Nice day," Lazzara said.

For a funeral, St. James suspected Lazzara was thinking. "Yes," the bishop said. "How many agents will be here?"

Porter, who was always a little disgruntled when his domain was intruded upon by other officials, answered with curt, controlled precision: "A dozen from the Secret Service uniformed force, four plainclothes, nine MPD officers. FBI is supposed to have six men assigned, too."

"Well, it looks like with you all, including the Metropolitan Police, we're all safe for another day," the bishop said, a chuckle in his voice. "Glad you're here." He bounded up the steps and entered the cathedral's south transept. To his immediate right was the War Memorial Chapel, dedicated to the men and women who'd lost their lives in defense of the country. St. James entered it, looked for a moment at a huge needlepoint tapestry called "Tree of Life" on which the seals of the fifty states were done in petit point, then continued through another door leading into the Children's Chapel, his favorite of the cathedral's nine chapels.

"Suffer the little children to come unto me," he said softly, looking at a reredos of carved wood overlaid with gold portraying Jesus when he'd spoken those words. Children and small four-legged animals, the most vulnerable and dependent of all creatures. Everything in the Children's Chapel was child-size—a small organ, scaled-down seats and low altar, miniature needlepoint kneeling pads featuring family pets and wild beasts, including those that had boarded Noah's Ark. A statue of the Christ Child stood near the entrance, its arms open wide in welcome. St. James did what he almost always did upon entering the chapel. He took the Christ Child's extended bronze fingers in his own and squeezed, as thousands of visiting children did each year. The statue itself had burnished with age, but the rubbing of so many tiny hands kept the fingers bright and shiny, a glow from children to Child. The bishop went to the altar, genuflected, gave thanks for the glory of another day of service, and crossed the cathedral to the narrow, winding stone steps just inside the north entrance and across from the Good Shepherd Chapel. A sign at the foot of the steps said CLERGY; an arrow pointed up. Good direction, he thought once again, and took the steps two at a time.

He'd no sooner entered the bishop's dressing room and closed the door behind him when there was a knock. He opened the door to admit one of his canons, Jonathon Merle. "Good morning, Jonathon."

"Good morning, Bishop," Merle said dourly, in a tone which mirrored his general personality. The canon was considerably taller than the bishop, his body lean and angular. His face matched his body; hawklike, eyes sunken and ringed with putty-like flesh, nose a bit of a beak. His face had an overall grayness to it that went perfectly with the rest of him. A sincere man but, sadly, a somewhat sour one.

"Everything in order?" St. James asked, referring to preparations that would be taking place downstairs for the funeral.

"Yes, I think so." The Bishop would be present during the ceremony, but Father Merle would conduct the service.

"Is Father Singletary back?" St. James asked absently.

"He's due tonight, I think," Merle said.

"I wonder how his meeting with the archbishop went." St. James said it not so much because he wondered what the answer would be but because he knew any mention of Paul Singletary nettled Jonathon. That these two canons disliked each other was no secret, and while St. James did what he could to keep their mutual animosity from getting in the way of cathedral business, there were times when he took a certain private delight in the conflict. The truth was that he, too, disliked Father Merle, a failing for which he often asked forgiveness during his prayers. He was confident that Merle had no inkling of his feelings, thank the Lord. The canon's devotion to God and to his priestly duties at the cathedral were indisputable. If those criteria were ever foremost in the bishop's mind, it would be Singletary's devotion he would question, not Merle's. The problem with Canon Merle was his personality, or lack of it. A rigid, dogmatic, and humorless champion of the church's conservative element, he had little patience with those who did not embrace his views. Heading that list was the Reverend Paul Singletary.

"What did you think of the article last Saturday?" St. James asked as he disappeared behind a folding screen. The article in the Religion section of *The Washington Post* was an update about the Word of Peace movement, to which Bishop St. James and the cathedral had pledged considerable support. There was no answer from Merle. "Did you hear me, Jonathon?"

"Yes. I didn't think very much of it."

"Really? What did you find lacking?" He knew the answer; a considerable portion of the article dwelt upon Singletary, and a picture of the handsome liberal priest dominated the page. The photo had been taken in an AIDS hospice in the Adams Morgan district that had been established through Singletary's untiring fund-raising efforts.

"It misrepresents the purpose of this church," said Merle.

"Interesting," the bishop said as he came out from behind the screen. "What *is* the mission of this church?" He was instantly sorry he'd asked. These conversations usually went nowhere; Merle would deliver a sermon on the spot. The bishop sometimes thought he himself had become a missionary cause for Merle, a potential convert to the canon's view of the Anglican role in the world.

Merle said, "You'll forgive my impudence, Bishop, but it has been my concern from the beginning that the lofty and holy purposes of this cathedral could be tarnished by overinvolvement with the Word of Peace."

"Why would I consider you impudent, Jonathon, for raising such a thought this morning? You've been saying it with some regularity for over a year."

"My concerns grow each day," Merle said gravely. "I find some of the leaders of the movement to be distasteful. I find the movement itself, despite its professed aims, to be distasteful." His usual pinched voice became more so.

"You find seeking peace in this world to be distasteful?"

There was silence, and St. James realized he had gone too far. He smiled broadly and said, "It is to my benefit and this cathedral's as well that we have Father Jonathon Merle to keep his eye on the till and his hand on the tiller. Perhaps we should discuss Word of Peace in a less busy, more contemplative atmosphere. In fact, I would be delighted to have dinner with you this evening, Jonathon, just the two of us. I've been thinking a great deal lately about China. More specifically, I've been craving Chinese food for a week. We can indulge my craving and spend some quiet, focused time discussing this." He clapped Merle on the arm.

The canon did not smile or respond to the invitation. Instead, he said in the same sober voice, "I think it's time for the reins to be pulled in on Father Singletary."

St. James had heard this comment before, too. "Could be you're right, Jonathon, although you must admit that Father Singletary's seemingly inexhaustible energy when it comes to helping the sick and the poor invites a rather positive image of our ministry. Wouldn't you say?"

"He seeks only his self-grandiosity, not the glory of the church."

St. James laughed and said, "I know, I know, Paul Singletary has a remarkable gift for—and interest in—self-promotion. He *is* grandiose at times, and seems to have a great deal of trouble practicing the sort of humility that we are expected to demonstrate. Still, as Hooker said, let us not attempt to unscrew the inscrutable. Tonight, Jonathon, I'll treat you to hot-and-sour soup and General Tsao's chicken. Shall we make it the Oriental Gourmet? My goodness, even talking about it has my mouth watering. Eileen has a meeting and—" He slapped his forehead. "Oh, sorry, I can't do it tonight. I have to talk to a business group. A raincheck? Meanwhile, Jonathon, let's get on with the business of the day—namely, to bury Adam Vickery. I think it's fitting that you conduct the service. You and he were quite close, shared common views."

"Well, not close, but we saw many things eye-to-eye."

"I'll see you downstairs," said the bishop.

Merle left, leaving St. James to put on a purple cassock, over which he slipped a white rochet with embroidery at the bottom. A black silk chimere with white lawn sleeves and cuffs came next; his stole hung straight down from his neck, befitting his status as a bishop. A pectoral cross rested comfortably on his chest. As he donned these holy garments, his thoughts were less than holy. There was no escaping politics, not even in the house God built. Even early in his career, when he was a simple parish priest, there had been the squabbles between parishioners, some seeking God, some seeking ego-gratification, others looking for the enhanced possibility of salvation through increased influence in church matters. As he rose through the ranks, political considerations had increased proportionately. He'd become the National Cathedral's bishop and dean after serving as suffragan, or assistant bishop, to the previous bishop, John Walker, a brilliant and passionate black man who seemed to walk easily between the lofty demands of his position and the humbler demands of using the nation's house of worship to feed the hungry, clothe the poor, and minister to the sick in the ghettos of the capital. A simple devotion to Christ was not enough, not in the nation's church in the most politically fueled city in the world, Washington, D.C. Politics! The least pleasant aspect of his duties, although he knew he was good at it; St. James had learned much about the art of negotiation and diplomacy from Bishop John Walker.

The bishop frowned as he gave himself a final check in the mirror, not because of what he saw but because of the invitation he'd extended to Merle. Now he'd have to go through with it another night. An evening with Jonathon over a Chinese meal was like the old joke, he thought, a contest in which the winner received one week in Philadelphia, the second-place winner two weeks. He looked up, crossed himself, and said with a wry smile on his face, "I do this only for You." *And because I do like hot-and-sour,* he added silently. Come to think of it, that describes my two canons.

As he opened the door and prepared to descend the steps, he thought of a dinner he'd had a month ago with Mac Smith and Annabel Reed, now Mr. and Mrs. Mackensie Smith. He'd been away from Washington when Paul Singletary celebrated Mac's marriage to the beautiful redheaded woman with whom Mac had been intimately involved for some years. The first thing St. James had done upon returning was to call and invite them to dinner. He wished Smith would be willing to take on a more active role with the cathedral chapter now that Adam Vickery was gone. Smith, like Vickery, was an attorney, which gave him a unique way of looking at problems. As the bishop started down the stairs, he realized he'd never met anyone who had Mac Smith's innate ability to be involved with so many people and so many things, yet maintain a safe distance from all of them. A lawyer. A very good lawyer —and, oh yes, a professor.

St. James had rounded the final turn and was about to step into the north entrance's foyer when the scream erupted, reverberating off the cold stone walls, ceilings, and floors. He stopped and felt his stomach tighten. Screaming again; a woman, close by. St. James swung to his right; the shrill, piercing voice seemed to be coming from only a short distance away—from the Good Shepherd. He went to the door and looked in.

Three two-person pews were empty. He stepped inside and looked left, to the small altar upon which a tiny vase of wilted flowers stood in front of the Salisbury pink granite sculpture of Christ cradling a lamb in His arms. Standing there was a woman, her eyes wide with fright, her screams now reduced to smaller sounds of anguish and pain. She was trying to speak, but the words were caught in her throat. She turned and stared down to a pew just large enough for one person, and almost hidden from St. James's view from the door. The bishop saw an arm. Another step and he saw more of the figure slouched in the pew. A crude sign taped on the stone wall directly in front of the body said PLEASE NO SMOKING.

The woman started to scream again. St. James held up his hand against the noise, put his hand on her shoulder, and took a final step that allowed him a full view of the occupied pew.

"My God," he said as his eyes fixed upon the crushed skull and lifeless body of the Reverend Canon Paul Singletary.

5

That Same Morning—A Splendid, Sunny, Temperate October Day

MAC SMITH RETURNED from a brisk walk with Rufus. He steered the Great Dane into the kitchen and set about squeezing two glasses of orange juice, heard the shower going, heard Annabel singing "When You Wish Upon a Star," which seemed to have become her favorite tune to lather by since their wedding. Prior to that she'd been partial to Gilbert and Sullivan and the Beatles. Good: he preferred the Disney song.

Smith was about to take a sip of juice when the phone rang. He glanced at the kitchen clock—7:10. Early for a casual caller. He headed for his small study at the rear of his—their—house in Foggy Bottom, which he'd shared until recently only with Rufus.

"Mac, it's George St. James."

"Good morning, Bishop," Mac said. "You're doing God's work early. What prompts a call at this hour?"

St. James sighed before he said in a low, breathy tone, "Mac, a terrible thing has happened here this morning." Before Smith could ask, St. James said, "Paul has been murdered."

"Run that past me again, George."

"Paul Singletary has been murdered. Right here in the cathedral. I found his body a half hour ago."

"Christ! I just saw him . . . well, no, it was August, but he married us."

"I know, Mac. It's a dreadful shock. I can't begin to tell you how terrible, to, find his body . . ."

"Where?"

"In the cathedral. In the Good Shepherd Chapel."

"The tiny one."

"Yes."

"How was he killed? How do you know it was murder?"

"The side of his head is bashed in. Someone struck him a wicked blow."

"*You* found the body?"

"Yes. Well, a woman actually did."

"What woman?"

"I don't know her name. She's distraught, beside herself. I have her here with me in my dressing room."

"Have you called the police?" Smith asked.

"No. I wanted to speak to you first."

"George, I think the police should have been first on your list."

"Please, Mac, can you come here right away? I want to explore things with you before I call the authorities."

"What about the cathedral's legal counsel?"

"They're money lawyers, Mac. You've had experience with criminal matters. I know this is an imposition, but . . ."

"I'll be there as quickly as I can. Annabel and I were getting ready for breakfast before coming to Adam Vickery's funeral. I'll tell her."

"Don't mention this to her, Mac. Not to anyone until we've talked."

"George, this can't be kept a secret." Smith didn't want to sound annoyed, but his voice reflected what he was feeling at that moment. "Who else have you told?"

"No one. I pushed a piece of furniture up against the chapel's door."

"The body is still in there?"

"Yes."

"You'll be in your office?"

"Yes, I . . . no. Can you meet me in the Bishop's Garden?"

Smith looked at a clock on his desk. "I'll be there in twenty minutes. But you should call the police."

He hung up and stuck his head into the bathroom, where Annabel was drying her hair, a huge pink towel wrapped around her nakedness. "Who called?" she asked.

"George St. James. I'm heading for the cathedral now to meet with him. We'll have to scrap breakfast."

"Why?" she asked.

"There's been a . . . an accident at the cathedral. George wants to discuss it with me . . . from a legal point of view. I said I'd meet him in twenty minutes."

"What kind of accident?"

Smith looked into her large green eyes and had a sudden burst of recognition, which had been happening with some regularity since the wedding. They *were* married. She *was* his wife. No secrets. Right?

Right! "Look, Annabel, this will be a shock, but Paul Singletary is dead."

She slumped back on a stool, the hair dryer blowing hot air on her feet. "Paul? How? What happened?"

No secrets. "He's been murdered. Somebody hit him in the head, at least according to George. He's . . . he's dead."

"I'll be ready in ten minutes," she said, standing and redirecting the hot air at her thick, wet red hair.

"No. Right now, George is concerned about people knowing, for some reason. It's got to come out, of course. I'm meeting him privately, in the Bishop's Garden. You hang out here, take any other phone calls, and meet me at the back of the cathedral at quarter of nine, near the statue of George Washington."

"Mac, I . . . You're not going to get involved in another—"

"Please. I've told you all I know. I'll do better at quarter of nine."

Smith drove his blue Chevy Caprice up Wisconsin Avenue and stopped at Church House Road, the first small access road to the cathedral close. He saw the gathering of security people, and decided to continue on Wisconsin until reaching another road that would take him to the north side of the cathedral, where there should be less activity. He parked in a designated visitors' space and walked briskly around the North Cloister and the administration building, turned right, the College of Preachers on his left, and followed the road south past the library and the deanery until reaching the Norman Arch, the main visitors' entrance to the lovely Bishop's Garden. He paused and looked back; a Cathedral Police white Ford Bronco, its yellow lights flashing on top, sped by. Had the bishop changed his mind and informed the authorities? Smith hoped so.

He didn't know where in the gardens George St. James would be waiting, but decided to head for the Rose Garden, where floribundas and hybrid tea roses would be in full bloom in Washington's mild October weather. His hunch was right. St. James, now dressed in simple clerical collar and black suit, stood at the end of the Rose Garden beneath an old pear tree. Next to him, surrounded by rare Kingsville dwarf box, stood Heinz Warneke's statue of the Prodigal Son. The scent of roses hung thick in the still morning air.

St. James spotted Smith and waved him over, as though directing the relocation of a piece of heavy furniture.

They shook hands. What had happened that morning was written all over the bishop's face. It was drawn and sallow, a pleading quality in his ordinarily bright blue eyes. "Thank you for coming," he said.

"I saw some activity," Smith said. "Did you change your mind, notify the police?"

St. James shook his head. "I told you I wanted to wait until—"

"All right, tell me again what occurred this morning."

St. James quickly recapped the events, culminating with the discovery of Singletary's body in the Good Shepherd Chapel.

"Who is the woman who found him?"

"I don't know her name. Eileen is with her in my dressing room."

"Eileen knows?"

"Yes, I had to tell her. I mean, she is my wife."

"Of course. . . . I understand. When did you last see Paul?" Smith asked.

"A few days ago, just before he left for London." St. James stopped, as though having been struck by a revelation. "He wasn't due back in Washington until today."

"Looks like he cut his stay short. George, you do know that we must advise the authorities and do it now."

"Can't we wait a few hours, at least until the Vickery funeral is over?"

"Why do that? What would that accomplish?"

St. James let out an exasperated sigh and turned away, took a few steps, then turned again. "I don't know, Mac," he said, "it just seems to me that a few hours wouldn't matter. A funeral is about to be held here of a man who has been important to this cathedral. Does it have to be interrupted by police sirens and television crews?"

Smith jammed his hands in his pockets and looked at the ground before saying, "One, there is always disruption when someone is murdered, whether it's in this cathedral or elsewhere. Two, it is illegal to withhold from the police the fact that a murder has been committed. Three, to postpone notification not only puts you and the cathedral in a bad light, it could have an adverse influence on the eventual investigation. No, George, the time to tell them is now."

St. James's mind seemed to wander into a less tangible realm. He spoke not to Smith but to an unseen person: " 'Puts the cathedral in a bad light.' That's what I want so desperately to avoid."

Smith said brusquely, "The light is going to shine here whether you want it to or not, George, and it's going to be a lot hotter if you don't do the right thing and do it now."

Smith's hard words snapped the bishop back to the garden. He nodded. "Yes, of course you're right, Mac. That's why I called you. I knew you would know the right thing to do, and would see to it that I did it. Is it possible . . . well, I also wondered: would *you* call the police and ask them if they could be as discreet as possible while the funeral is going on?"

St. James's concern for the funeral irritated Smith, but he didn't vent it. He simply said, "Yes, I'll call them now."

Smith followed the bishop across the gardens, through the Norman Arch and into the cathedral and the hallway outside the door of the Good Shepherd Chapel. A large armoire had been pushed against it. A scribbled sign hung from it: CLOSED FOR REPAIRS. Smith stifled a wry smile. What could possibly have been running through the bishop's head to go to this trouble? Confusion, obviously, and some well-meaning fear—more likely *hope*—that the reality of it could be postponed indefinitely. But sealing off the chapel would help the investigation.

"He's in there, exactly as you found him?" Smith asked, his eyes fixed upon the armoire.

"Yes. Maybe you should take a look before you make your call, Mac."

Mac silently debated it, then decided to do it quickly. "You said the woman screamed. Didn't anyone else hear her?"

"Yes, a parishioner looking for a bathroom, but I said someone had fallen, twisted her ankle."

"And with Security people within earshot, no reaction?"

"Not that I know of. They were all outside, at some distance. Sound sometimes travels here; sometimes it's, well, buried."

Smith looked left and right, pushed the armoire, and slid it far enough so that he could squeeze through into the tiny chapel. St. James stayed outside as Smith took the few steps to the pink granite altar. A window was open; Smith looked out onto the garth and its flowing fountain before turning and looking down on the body of Paul Singletary. "Jesus," he muttered, glancing up quickly at the sculpture above the altar of the Good Shepherd holding the baby lamb. Feeling sickened and saddened, Smith forced himself to do what he perceived at that moment to be his duty. He looked once again at Singletary, leaned forward to more closely examine the wound on the side of the slain priest's head. It hadn't been a flat object that killed him. The murder weapon obviously had a sharp and heavy edge to it, judging from the way the skull was cut open.

Smith came out of the chapel and joined the bishop in the hallway. "Horrible. Shall I call from your office?"

"No, upstairs, right above here. My dressing room."

Eileen St. James was nervously pacing the floor when they entered. "Eileen, Mac Smith is here," St. James said.

She spun on her heel and had the look of someone reacting to a very loud and sudden sound. "Oh, Mac, yes! George said he had called you."

St. James said, "Where is the woman?"

"She left."

"Left?" St. James and Smith said in unison.

"I couldn't stop her. She kept crying and moaning. I went to get some towels and cold water. When I returned, she was gone."

"Damn!" Smith said.

"Did she ever tell you who she was?" the bishop asked.

His wife shook her head.

Smith sat at the desk, his hand poised over the telephone. He looked up at the bishop and his wife and said, "Now look. No matter what happens, you must promise to be totally honest with the authorities. Whatever problems this may cause the cathedral can't be helped and will soon pass."

"The press will have a field day with this," St. James said. "One of our own, probably our most visible priest, murdered right here in the National Cathedral. I can't believe it."

"I had trouble believing it, too, until I saw the damage done to Paul's head." Smith's hand rested on the telephone. He looked at them before picking up the receiver and putting it to his ear. Before he could punch in the number of Washington's MPD Homicide Division—a number he'd never forgotten from his days as a lawyer who had handled many criminal cases—the sound of sirens was heard outside.

Smith slowly lowered the receiver into its cradle. "I think someone beat us to it."

6

Minutes Later—Clouds Moving In

MAC SMITH WENT OUTSIDE. Six Washington MPD squad cars had arrived; they'd parked in pairs outside the three main entrances to the cathedral, their uniformed officers fanning out over the cathedral close. An unmarked car had also arrived, and Smith recognized one of the men getting out of it. Chief of Homicide Terrence Finnerty was a lean-cheeked, wiry little man with a nasty cast to his face, and once-yellow hair discolored with age. He wore a cheap green raincoat, and black shoes sufficiently scuffed to make you notice them. The two other detectives who followed were bulky, heavy men. The black man carried a two-way radio, the white man a notepad. As Finnerty came up the steps leading to the south entrance, he spotted Smith and said in what could pass for a near-falsetto, "Mackensie Smith. I didn't know you were a daily communicant."

"Only on special occasions," Smith said. "The funeral of a friend of mine is taking place this morning." It wasn't true that Adam Vickery was a friend. Smith and Vickery had certainly known each other well enough when Vickery was attorney general and Mackensie Smith was Washington's most respected and successful criminal attorney. But it wasn't friendship. Smith had found Vickery to be shrewd, tough, and unpleasant. Compounding that evaluation was Smith's conviction that Vickery was not the most honest of men, and that the conflict-of-interest charges leveled at him had sufficient substance to ensure that had they been aggressively pursued, the result could well have been a finding of actual conflict, not just the appearance of conflict that had become a popular rationale for the sleazy behavior of some public officials. Still, Mac Smith had his reasons for attending the funeral, including the adages "Once you're dead, all bets are off" and "Everyone is entitled to be remembered for his best work."

Smith glanced at the squad cars and their uniformed occupants. "Heavy artillery, Terry?"

"Got a call about a murder here. Know anything about it?"

"Yes."

Smith's abrupt answer caused Finnerty's face to tighten. A muscle in his right cheek pulsated, and his small black eyes narrowed. "Tell me about it. Why didn't you call?"

"We were about to. Who called you?" Smith asked.

"Anonymous female."

"What did she tell you?"

"Hey, Mac, I ask, you answer. Who got it?"

Smith motioned for Finnerty to follow him up the steps and into the cathedral. The other two detectives followed. Smith stopped and said to Finnerty, "Have them wait outside for a few minutes." Finnerty obviously wasn't sure whether to honor Smith's request, but he did, holding up his hand to halt the progress of his colleagues.

Smith led Finnerty through the transept and into the empty War Memorial Chapel. "What the hell am I about to get, confession?" Finnerty asked.

"Not unless you need it. Look, the funeral of Adam Vickery, the former attorney general, is about to start. A priest, named Paul Singletary, has been found murdered. Somebody put something heavy to the side of his head."

"Singletary? The do-gooder?"

"The same. The bishop is concerned that this place not be turned into a zoo while the funeral is going on. Can you give orders to your officers to be less conspicuous? I'll take you to the body and to the bishop. Once the funeral is over, the place is yours."

"Give me a break, Mac. You're telling me that this priest gets wasted here in the Washington Cathedral, and I'm supposed to ice it until Vickery gets planted?" His laugh was silly. "Vickery ain't going to know what's going on."

"But his family will. Look, Terry, do what you want, but if you find it necessary to play war games for the TV cameras, count me out. I'm just a parishioner grieving at a friend's funeral. I know nothing about murder. Nice to see you again." Smith started to walk away.

"All right," Finnerty said, "as long as you and I move on this now. Wouldn't look good to sit through a funeral while a murdered priest lays around, but I'll do my best to keep things quiet until the funeral's over. It ever occur to you that the murderer could still be here?" Smith pointedly ignored the question, and Finnerty sensed his annoyance. "Okay, Mac, we'll move as quiet as possible. But we have to move."

"Good. This is, after all, a place of worship," Smith said, not proud of himself.

Finnerty went back and told his detectives to brief the uniforms while they began to look around and to guard exits. He then fell in with Smith and they walked across the nave toward the north transept and Good Shepherd Chapel. They'd almost reached it when a television crew—a cameraman with a large VTR on his shoulder, a sound man wielding a microphone, and a black woman reporter, Rhonda Harrison, with whom Smith had been friendly since she arrived in Washington eight years before—came through the north entrance. Rhonda flashed Smith a large, warm smile. To Finnerty she nodded: "Detective Finnerty." The smile was gone.

"Hello, Rhonda, how are you?" said Smith.

"Who was murdered?" she asked. A powerful light on top of the VTR came to life and flooded Smith, Finnerty, and Rhonda in blinding white light.

"Turn that thing off," Finnerty said.

"Can't talk this minute, Rhonda," Smith said.

"Come on, Mac, what's going on?"

"Later, Rhonda. Sorry. Come on," he said to Finnerty.

Two of the cathedral's uniformed security police had just entered through the north doors. Smith stopped them. "I'm Mac Smith, and this is Detective Terry Finnerty. There's been a problem here this morning, and I'm representing the bishop in this matter." He turned and saw the television crew approaching. "Keep those people out of this area until you're told otherwise." He could see ambivalence on their faces. One of them said, "I'll check with Captain Porter."

"Go ahead, but one of you keep that crew out of here."

As the remaining cathedral cop moved to block the TV crew, Smith led Finnerty past the armoire and into the Good Shepherd Chapel. "There he is, Terry. We were friendly. He married my wife and me a couple of months ago."

Finnerty glanced at Smith and smiled. "I didn't know you got hitched."

"It was time," Smith said.

"So she said, I'll bet."

Finnerty approached Singletary's body and bent down. He screwed up his face as he leaned to within inches of the wound. "Didn't bleed much," he said, more to himself than to Smith.

"I noticed that, too," said Smith.

"Any idea how long he's been here?"

"No. The body was discovered by a woman an hour or so ago."

Finnerty looked up from his kneeling position next to the body. "An hour ago? Jesus! What woman?"

Smith shrugged. "She came in here, probably to pray, discovered the body, and started screaming. The bishop heard the screams and came in. He took her to his dressing room upstairs and called his wife to come over and stay with her. She's disappeared."

"Who?"

"The woman who discovered the body."

"Wonderful. How come?"

"The bishop's wife went to get some . . . It doesn't matter. She's gone."

"Wonderful."

Finnerty touched Singletary's eyelids and lower jaw. "He's pretty rigid. He didn't get it this morning, more like last night. We'll get a better fix on it at the autopsy." He stood and stretched. "Who has access to this chapel?"

"The world, I think. It's open twenty-four hours a day."

"It is? Just this chapel, or the whole cathedral?"

"I think just this chapel, although you can confirm that with the bishop."

Finnerty shook his head and looked out the open window onto the garth and its large, abstract, siliconed bronze fountain. "Where is the bishop?" he asked, his words mingling with the gurgling water from the fountain and the faint, sweet sound of choristers rehearsing.

"Upstairs with his wife."

"Let's go, before she disappears," Finnerty said.

Smith led him up the narrow stone stairs to the clergy's rooms and into the one reserved for Bishop St. James. After Smith made the introductions, Finnerty said, "Mac told me you wanted to keep this quiet for a while, Bishop. I can't do that. I got to move my men in right now, get Forensic over here. There may be a funeral for a dead big shot, but my concern is the dead guy—sorry, Reverend—downstairs."

St. James nodded. "Yes, of course, I understand. I just thought—"

"Yeah, yeah, I know what you thought, but it can't be. Smith asked us not to make a circus of it, and we'll try. What about this woman who found the body?"

Eileen St. James explained that the woman had disappeared.

"You spent some time with her?"

"Well, yes, a little."

"I'll have somebody get a description from you."

The bishop vacated his chair behind a desk and pointed to the phone.

Finnerty shook his head. "Thanks, but I'll coordinate this from downstairs. I'm going to need a list of everyone who was in this building last night and this morning."

"Last night?" Mrs. St. James said.

"Yes. Can you get me that list right away?"

"I suppose so. I'll assign someone," the bishop said.

"Good." Finnerty turned to Smith. "You coming with me?"

"I'll walk down with you, but I'm attending the funeral. My wife is probably here by now."

"Check in with me later."

"If you want."

"Yeah, I want. Looks like you're in the middle of this mess, a friend of the corpse, here before we get here, delayed notification."

Smith looked at Bishop St. James as Terry Finnerty left. He certainly hadn't intended to be in the middle of anything. His plans for that day were to attend a funeral and work on some lecture notes for class. St. James's call had changed all that.

"Mac, what do we do now?"

"Concerning what?"

"Concerning the murder and the service for Adam Vickery. Do I mention during the service what's happened here?"

"I don't think you have any choice, George. You've got marked squad cars all over the place, and the TV crew we ran into downstairs will only be the first of many. You have to say something and do it right up front. It may be shocking news to the congregation, but speculation and rumor are worse."

St. James's expression was one of abject despair. He knew Smith was right, yet making such an announcement was anathema to him. He looked into Smith's eyes and said, "Of course, you're right. I'll announce it early, get it over with. Thank you, Mac."

Smith patted his friend on the shoulder and managed a weak smile. "I'll look in on you later," he said glumly, his concern not for St. James's difficult task but for the dilemma into which he himself had suddenly been thrust. Annabel would not be happy.

Annabel was indeed waiting downstairs when Smith arrived. So were hundreds of people who had gathered for Adam Vickery's funeral, members of the press, and police everywhere. "Is it true?" Annabel asked. "Murdered?"

"Yes."

She gasped, her eyes flooded. "I can't believe it."

"Believe it, Annie. I saw his body."

They joined others in the pews. The bishop, accompanied by Reverend Jonathon Merle and other members of the cathedral's clergy, slowly ascended to the high altar, known, too, as the Jerusalem altar because the stones of which it was constructed had come from quarries outside Jerusalem. St. James climbed up to the Canterbury pulpit. He surveyed the faces before him. A closed casket containing the remains of Adam Vickery stood alone on one of the risers leading to the altar. "Ladies and gentlemen, this is a sad day in the history of this cathedral. Not only have we come to mourn the death of a man whose record of public service to the nation and dedication to the goals of this cathedral were exemplary, we must also mourn the sudden and brutal death of a man of God who was loved by all, a man of God who reached out to the disenfranchised of our society in a way that our Lord Jesus intended, a man of God who served mankind and his church with vigor and sensitive devotion." His voice broke. "I speak of the Reverend Paul Singletary."

Annabel's earlier gasp was now a chorus echoed by many in attendance. Suddenly, it was clear why so many law-enforcement officers and press were milling about in the outer aisles. Most mourners had assumed they represented normal security precautions and press coverage of the Vickery funeral. Now they knew better.

St. James continued, "Unfortunately, we live in violent times. Not only has our dear colleague and friend Paul Singletary been brutally murdered, but it has happened right here in this House of the Lord, in the tiny Good Shepherd Chapel that is open day and night for the bereaved and troubled to seek solace through silent prayer. The shock, which you share, is considerable. Yet, in the cycle of life, we must continue. The life of our departed friend Adam Vickery must be celebrated here today, and his transport to a gentler place, carried there in the hands of Our Lord, Jesus Christ, must not be delayed. I ask all of you to do your best to concentrate on this solemn and necessary ritual. I can tell you nothing else about the death of Father Singletary. That is in the hands of the proper authorities." He swallowed, blinked his eyes, and said, "Let us pray."

The mood of most people following Vickery's funeral was more soberness at the news of Singletary's murder than grief for the former official whose obsequies they'd just attended. A hearse and a dozen long black limousines were lined up outside the south entrance. Smith and Annabel went up to Vickery's widow, Doris, and extended their condolences. If Mac had never particularly liked Vickery, Doris at least had a fairly pleasing and open personality.

Vickery had once approached Smith about taking a job in the Justice Department as an assistant attorney general for civil rights. Smith had turned him down. Vickery—the Justice Department itself, for that matter—had come under considerable pressure from civil-rights groups to modify his views and policies. Gains in civil rights for minority Americans, which had been hard-won over the years, stood in jeopardy during Vickery's time in office. Smith knew that his appeal to Vickery lay in his record and reputation as an attorney concerned with defending the rights of minorities, which would have given Vickery and the administration something—someone—to crow about. Smith was not about to give them that. Besides, Mac Smith had always been impatient with bureaucracies.

It was Doris Vickery who'd managed to bring Mac closer to the family. It happened in the midst of her husband's troubles over his alleged influence peddling. Doris had called Smith at home. She sounded distraught, which Smith assumed was the result of the pressure on her husband. He reluctantly agreed to meet with them. When he did, he was told it was their daughter, Pamela, who was the focus of their concern.

Pamela Vickery was a beautiful, bright, and rebellious young woman who'd begun running with "the wrong crowd," according to her father. She was with her friends in California when the house in which they lived was raided by local drug-enforcement agents. Adam and Doris Vickery swore to Smith that Pamela did not use drugs, and was a victim of circumstance, in the wrong place at the wrong time. It had been a minor-league drug bust—some marijuana, Quaaludes, small amounts of both—hardly destined to pique vast media interest. But it did, of course, given that Pamela was the daughter of the nation's attorney general.

Adam Vickery's initial reaction was to let her take the rap: "Maybe it's what she needs to straighten herself out," he told his wife. But Doris Vickery was not about to see her daughter, troublesome as she might be, have a serious mark against her in her young life for something Doris was convinced Pamela had had little to do with. That's why she called Smith, to ask him to intercede with the right people in California legal circles and try to extricate Pamela from the ramifications of the incident. Adam Vickery could have done so with ease, but his intercession would not have been viewed as an appropriate action by America's number-one attorney.

Smith promised merely that he would look into the situation. He did, became convinced that Pamela's parents had accurately characterized the level of their daughter's involvement, and worked through a California lawyer to see that charges were minimal against the young woman. Smith had one conversation with Pamela Vickery, after she was put on probation. He suggested to her that she return home and pursue her education. She told him three thousand miles weren't nearly far enough away from her father. No thanks, she'd stay in California.

Now, outside the cathedral, Doris Vickery squeezed Smith's hand. "Thank you for coming, Mac. How horrible about Father Singletary." She turned to Annabel and managed a tiny smile. "Congratulations on your marriage."

"Thank you, Mrs. Vickery," Annabel said. "I'm so sorry about your husband."

Doris Vickery sighed. "Yes, thank you. How ironic that Adam's funeral should occur on the same morning that a priest is slain in the cathedral. It's probably just as well that Adam wasn't here to experience it. He loved this place, Mac, put his heart and soul into it after leaving government service. It gave him . . . a new lease on life, a fresh start. We needed that."

"Yes, I know, Doris," Smith said. She was right; Adam Vickery, despite his previous personal shortcomings, had done a remarkably good job for the cathedral and its building fund. That's why Mac Smith had said to Annabel, "Cloud over his head or not, we go to the funeral.

Washington is like the Mafia. I shoot you dead, but I turn up at the church." To Doris, he said, "He'll be missed."

They were joined by Jonathon Merle, whose conduct of the service had been in his usual colorless, matter-of-fact style. Doris Vickery said to him, "Thank you, Father Merle, for your kindness. It must have been very difficult for you, knowing what happened to Father Singletary."

"Yes, very upsetting. I suppose it's only just begun, the scandal, the publicity, the nasty reports."

"It may not be as bad as you think," Smith said. "We can hope that they'll find who did this and put it quickly to rest."

Merle grimaced. "I've been saying for years that Good Shepherd shouldn't be open night and day. We have the dregs of society coming in here at all hours—addicts, alcoholics, criminals. This is the result I feared."

They were joined by the talented choirmaster, Wilfred Nickelson, whose boys' choir had performed ably during the funeral service. "Excuse me," Nickelson said to the others. He asked Merle, "Have you seen Joey Kelsch?"

"No."

"He didn't show up this morning. I was worried." Then to Mac, Annabel, and Doris Vickery he said, "Our best young singer, flighty but extremely talented. Not like him to simply not be here." He turned again to Merle. "Well, I thought I would ask. I'll call his parents. Perhaps he took ill and went home without informing anyone. A breach of the rules, but Joey is a difficult boy." Nickelson went off to the phone.

The Smiths stood on the steps of the south entrance and watched Doris Vickery join other members of the family at the limousine.

"Free for lunch?" Annabel asked.

"Lunch? At a time like this?"

"It's not the food, Mac. I want some time to sit down with you so you can tell me what's gone on here this morning."

"Of course I will, but let me find out a little more before we do that. Why don't you go home. I'm going back in to talk with the bishop and Terry Finnerty. I'll meet you there in an hour or so." She was disappointed at being excluded, but he said that he felt it better, at least at the moment, to pursue this alone.

"I'll stop by the gallery," she said. He kissed her lightly on the lips.

"Mac," she added, "don't get roped in."

He knew she was referring to his involvement with the case of the Kennedy Center murder the past year. He'd pledged to her—more to himself—that despite his excitement and commitment when getting involved, he would remain forever ensconced happily in academia as professor of law at George Washington University.

"Mac." She didn't need to say more.

"I know, I know, but I do owe the bishop a little more of my time, considering that he brought me into this thing this morning—and that the man who was murdered married us. Go home. I'll join you soon."

Her look said it all.

It was always easy getting into something, a lot harder getting out.

Of anything, including debt, affairs, marriage, murder . . . *especially* murder.

7

That Afternoon—Mostly Overcast Now

SMITH NEVER DID make it home for lunch with Annabel, and she would not be pleased. He called twice from the cathedral to say he was still involved in sessions with the bishop but would return as quickly as possible. She responded to his first call with understanding and kindness. His second call was met with the start of the Irish iciness of which Annabel was capable, although she seldom displayed it, making its infrequent use that much colder.

Eventually— it was sometime after three—he walked into their Foggy Bottom home. "Sorry," he said cheerfully. "I didn't expect to be there so long."

"Evidently," she said.

"Don't be angry, Annabel. I couldn't simply walk away from George and this situation he's in. He's very distraught, as you can imagine. He needed a sympathetic ear."

Annabel looked at him for a moment, then said, "And what do you need?" before walking into the kitchen. Smith followed, came up from behind, placed his hands on her shoulders, and said gently, "I don't understand your anger, Annabel. Most of all, I don't understand your not understanding." He almost added that his immediate concern was that the cynical adage about good relationships being ruined by marriage might be about to take place in his own life. Now that he was a *husband,* did that change the rules? Was he now involved in greater accountability to Annabel than had been the case when they were simply going together? They had never lived together because, for both of them, that would have represented a tactical mistake if nothing else. Did she have to approve his every act?

He didn't have to ask. She turned and said in a steady, well-modulated voice, "Mac, has marriage changed us already?"

Her taking the words out of his mouth left him without words. For a moment. "Of course not," he said. "Why would you think such a thing?"

"Because you're acting different. Before . . . before we became man and wife, you involved me completely in everything you did. When you got suckered into the mess at the Kennedy Center, you wanted me at your side. You even dispatched me to New York to talk to that slimy lawyer, and I was with you every step of the way. Now a friend of ours is murdered; another friend—who also happens to be bishop of the National Cathedral—asks for help, and you send me home to make a tuna-fish sandwich for my man when he returns from the wars!"

He coughed, stepped back, and frowned the way he usually did when a student in his advanced criminal-procedure class asked a question he was not prepared to answer. "You know, Annabel," he said, "one of the things that attracted me to you was your independence. After all, you are the owner of a flourishing gallery. Murder . . . law is really my domain." It was a mistake, and he knew it the minute he said it. Annabel Reed had been a successful matrimonial attorney in Washington before chucking it for her primary passion in life—aside from Mac Smith, of course—her gallery of pre-Columbian art in fashionable Georgetown.

She said nothing, but a hint of a smile indicated what she thought of his comment.

"Yes, I know," he said, "you are an attorney. But you didn't deal with criminal matters. George is seeking my counsel because the ramifications of Paul Singletary's murder are substantial. George is primarily concerned that someone from the cathedral staff might have killed him, not a drifter or drug addict, as most people are speculating. I understand his concern, and want to be helpful. I'd think you would expect that of me. Both of us have been involved, at least to some extent, with the cathedral."

She sighed. "Of course I want you to help. I just don't want you to get in too deep. I just . . . I just don't want . . ."

He stepped close to her again and placed his strong hands on her shoulders. "You just don't want *what*?"

A mist formed in her large green eyes. "I just don't want to be treated like a disposable wife, or see you throw away your own new life."

He couldn't help but laugh. "But you *are* my wife. As for my new life: in no way disposable. How would you prefer I treat you?"

"I meant the law school, and I mean the way you used to treat me, like an object of your affection, your mistress, your concubine, your *fille de joie*."

He listened patiently. "You didn't mention 'partner,' " he said.

"I don't want to be your partner, not exactly."

"But you said you wanted to be involved in Paul's case. That makes you a partner."

"A limited partner."

"Meaning what?"

"Meaning that I don't want to spend my day dealing with murder, but I would like to spend *part* of my day being at your side, being useful. Besides, I make lousy tuna-fish sandwiches, and you know it."

"Done!" He cocked his head, narrowed his eyes. "To be honest with you, Annabel, it's easy for me to give in. Now that I've spent time with George and others at the cathedral, I really don't see much need for me. Okay, I am once again a college professor, and you are my obscenely beautiful, talented, brilliant, and successful wi—uh, wanton harlot." He was tempted to turn her toward the bedroom, but there was something unseemly about that idea for the moment. Would he have hesitated before they were married to dismiss the nasty brutish business of murder and then act upon his carnal, lover's instincts? *Had* marriage changed them?

Hell, no, he decided, wishing he were more convinced.

For the rest of the afternoon he graded papers, while Annabel went back to her gallery to pay some bills. She returned at six, and they settled in front of the TV to watch the evening news.

Singletary's murder was the lead story. The police issued a terse statement—the priest had been murdered by an unknown assailant, the method of death a blow to the head. His body had been found in a chapel of the National Cathedral. There were no leads at the moment. The body had been discovered by a woman, identity unknown, whereabouts unknown. The tag line on the newscast: "Former top D.C. attorney Mackensie Smith, now a professor at George Washington University, has been retained by the cathedral in this matter. Stay tuned."

"Damn," Mac said, pouring himself a small glass of Blanton's bourbon over ice.

Annabel was sitting on a couch. She'd changed into a Kelly-green silk robe over nothing else, and was flipping through the latest issue of *Art in America* while watching the news. In her hand was a delicately shaped balloon glass with a small amount of white wine. She looked up. "Have you been retained by the cathedral?"

"Can't they get anything straight? Of course not."

"Have you told George that you would do more?"

"No. Well, I did say that I would do what I could to make his life a little easier . . . give some advice, that's all."

Annabel smiled, the sort of smile Mac could do without and this for the second time that day. "Uh-huh," she said with deliberate sweetness, returning her attention to the magazine.

The phone rang, not an unwelcome interruption for Smith. It was a reporter from *The Washington Post,* who wanted to confirm a rumor that Smith had been retained by the cathedral to defend one of its clergy in the Singletary murder.

"Nonsense!" Smith said.

Other calls came over the next hour, each an attempt to run down a rumor concerning Smith's involvement, or a likely suspect.

"Let's go out for dinner," Smith said after hanging up on yet another caller.

She shook her head. "Put the answering machine on. I'd just as soon bring something in from the American Café."

"All right. What'll you have?"

"Mac."

"Yes?"

"Reality has set in. You are going to be up to your neck in this, aren't you?"

"An overstatement, but yes, I do feel I have to help find the murderer of the man who married us."

She smiled gently and genuinely. "I understand. What will you do first?"

Smith sat down next to her and shrugged. "I told George I'd make some inquiries here and also while we're in London."

"Inquiries about what?"

"About Paul's movements there prior to his returning to Washington. About whatever we can learn here about motives and such."

"The trip to London is our honeymoon. You are aware of that?"

"Of course. And remember that we decided to combine business and pleasure. I have to address that group of barristers, and you wanted to track down leads on those Tlatilco female masks. I'm not suggesting an extensive investigation of what Paul did in London, just some questions. Jeffrey Woodcock should be helpful. I'm eager for you to meet him. He's a nice guy." Woodcock was a highly respected London solicitor, whose firm's clients numbered, among others, the Church of England. He and Smith had been friends for many years, and when Smith and Annabel were planning their honeymoon, Smith had called Woodcock and arranged for them to meet for dinner.

Annabel continued to browse through the magazine. She lowered it to her lap and said, "I've been thinking a great deal about Paul Singletary."

"So have I. Hard not to."

"I've been thinking about his death, of course, but there's more. He was so charming, and so committed to good deeds . . . but that's really all we knew about him."

"What else would you like to know?"

She shrugged.

"We never know everything about anyone. If we did, no one would ever get along, or marry."

She laughed. "How true. Maybe I'm just naturally suspicious . . . no, skeptical, or at least wary, of anyone in the limelight here in Washington. How much do we really know about the whole life of Paul Singletary?"

"Wary? Even of me?" Smith said.

"*Especially* of you."

Smith grunted. "I'll have to ponder that. What's your pleasure?" he asked as he pulled a restaurant takeout menu from a drawer.

She tossed the magazine to the floor and sat up straight, the folds of her robe falling loose and exposing the slope of one lovely white breast. "*You're* my pleasure, Mr. Smith."

"Are you about to make conjugal demands on this aging body?"

"To the contrary. I am abandoning my role as a wife, and reverting to the whorish role that I enjoyed for so long *before* we got married."

"You're sure this is the time for sex, Annabel? There's been a murder in the national place of worship, of all things."

"And nothing will change that. If I am going to lose you so early in my marriage to your need to meddle in murder, I insist upon due compensation."

"What about dinner?"

A tall woman, she stood up and allowed the robe to fall in a soft green pile around her feet. Nude, she looked down at him and said, "Somehow, I don't think we'll be hungry. But if we are, I'll play wife again and whip up a sandwich for my dear husband. I make excellent tuna-fish salad. Or hadn't you heard?"

With a rolled-up magazine, they convinced Rufus to vacate the king-size bed, and for twenty minutes or so—neither was counting—forgot about everything except themselves. Murder would just have to wait.

8

Friday Morning—Sunny, But Rain Forecast

LONG BEFORE THE automatic coffee maker had a chance to trip on, the phone started ringing. Two calls were from press people; the other was from the bishop, who asked if Smith had time to meet with him late that afternoon. Smith said it looked like a full day, with two classes, one a seminar, but that he would find an hour. They settled on four o'clock at St. James's home.

"What should I tell others who call?" Annabel asked sleepily. She stood near the front door in robe and slippers as Smith prepared to leave for the university.

"Tell them I expired," he said, slipping into his raincoat.

"Don't even joke about something like that," Annabel said.

"Tell them there is no sense in calling me, because I have no official connection with the investigation of Paul's murder." He kissed her on the cheek, then changed his mind, found her lips, and pressed hard. "I wish I had time to stay around. You exude a certain heightened sensuality early in the morning."

"Don't feel you've missed anything," she said. "I exude a certain exhaustion but I'll be out of here in a half hour. Lots going on at the gallery today, including a meeting about the fund-raising exhibition we're doing for St. Albans." St. Albans was the Episcopal church on the cathedral grounds that served a local congregation. Annabel had recently taken over a vacant store next to her gallery in Georgetown and promptly committed the new space to St. Albans's mission fund for a showing of artists who had some connection with the church. It would take a month for renovations on the gallery's addition to be completed; the exhibition was scheduled to be hung in six weeks.

Smith took Rufus for a long walk before going to his class. Rufus needed the exercise and Smith needed to think. They wandered Foggy Bottom, an area of Washington defined by Eighteenth Street on the east, Constitution Avenue on the south, the Potomac River and Twenty-sixth Street on the west, and Pennsylvania Avenue on the north. Originally a malarial marsh incorporated as Hamburg but called Funkstown after Jacob Funk, who'd purchased the original land, it eventually became known as Foggy Bottom, an unkind reference to the foul emissions produced by the many industries that once had been settled within its boundaries. Today, it is an attractive neighborhood that is home to the Kennedy Center for the Performing Arts, George Washington University (the second-largest landholder in Washington after the federal government), and the departments of State and Interior. It had been Mac Smith's home ever since his wife and son were killed and he'd left his luxurious Watergate apartment suite and bought the narrow two-story taupe brick house on Twenty-fifth Street, its trim, shutters, and front door painted Federal blue, its rooms devoid of painful memories that had started to suffocate him as a Watergate widower.

He returned Rufus to the house, and after carefully checking his briefcase, which he had checked and repacked the night before (he could not go to sleep without having prepared his briefcase for the following day), and taking his raincoat from the closet, as rain was predicted, headed for Lerner Hall. A reporter from the *Post* was waiting on the front steps, along with two uniformed officers from the MPD.

"Mr. Smith, could I have a word with you?" the reporter asked. One of the officers motioned Smith to approach them. Smith excused himself with a word to the reporter and went to where the officers stood. "Mr. Smith, we tried you at your home, but your wife said you'd left."

"Yes, I took a walk. My dog and I, that is. What can I do for you?"

"Chief Finnerty would like a word with you."

"Now? I have a class to teach."

"He said for us to bring you to him as quickly as possible."

"You'll just have to tell him I won't be available for the next two hours."

"I'll call in," the other officer said. He returned from the squad car and said, "The chief says we should wait for you, Mr. Smith. He says you should teach your class, but that he would like to see you right after it."

Smith looked at his watch. "All right, but you have two hours to kill."

"No problem, Mr. Smith." Of course not, Smith thought. Cops were experts at killing time. They had to be.

Smith headed for the door, but the reporter intercepted him again. "Mr. Smith, I'm Mark Rosner from the *Post*. Give me a few minutes?"

"Sorry, I can't. I'm already running late for my class. Besides, I have nothing to talk about."

"The Singletary murder," Rosner said. "Aren't you serving as counsel to the cathedral?"

"No."

"But it's my understanding that—"

Smith flashed a broad smile. "I think you should find better sources. I'm a college professor who happens to be a personal friend of the bishop of the cathedral. Excuse me, I don't want to be rude, but I'm afraid I'm about to be." He walked away, leaving the reporter with an expression on his face that indicated both annoyance and ambivalence.

When Smith entered the lecture hall, most of his students were in their seats. They were a decent lot for the most part, with a few exceptions. That they were bright went without saying; you didn't get into GW's law school unless you could demonstrate as much. The problem, Smith often thought, was that, as with medical schools, intelligence and grades were virtually the sole determining factor for admission to law schools. But how do you judge a young man or woman's sense of humanity, commitment to decency, to social justice, to using an excellent legal education to give something to the world and not just to take from it? When he dwelt too much upon that subject, as this morning, he became depressed, so he pushed it from his mind, went to the lectern, unloaded his carefully arranged briefcase, and wished the students a good morning.

"Professor Smith," Bob Rogers said, "anything new on the murder of the priest?"

Smith had expected questions about Paul Singletary's murder, and had decided during his walk to dismiss the subject as quickly as possible. He looked at the questioner over half-glasses and asked, "Have you read the newspapers, watched television?"

"Yes, sir."

"Then you know as much as I do."

There was a ripple of sarcastic laughter.

"What's funny? No, sorry, that's not true. Father Paul Singletary was a friend of mine."

Another student, Joyce Clemow, retorted, "Which is why we thought you'd know what was going on."

Before Smith could answer, another aspiring lawyer, Joe Petrella, said, "I heard you're going to defend whoever in the cathedral murdered Father Singletary."

Smith placed his glasses on the lectern and shook his head. "What kind of attorney will you end up being, Joe, if you're content to go with rumor that has no basis in fact?"

Petrella sheepishly lowered his head. Beside him, Smith's best student, April Montgomery, a thin, pale young woman with a facial tic that made it appear that something had lodged temporarily in her nose, said, "Do you believe it was an outsider who killed Father Singletary—say, a homeless person who came into the cathedral early in the morning?"

"I have no idea," Smith said. "The police have just begun their investigation."

"Have they found the woman who discovered the body?"

"Not that I'm aware of," Smith said. Other questions sprouted until he threw up his hands in a gesture of surrender. "Look," he said, "we have a great deal to cover here this morning, but okay, since the only thing on your minds seems to be the Singletary murder, let's take fifteen minutes to discuss it." He leaned on the lectern, thought for a moment, then said, "Here is what I do know. Father Singletary was killed by a blow to the side of his head. It appears upon casual observation of the wound that the object was heavy, and that it had a lip or ridge that caused considerable compression of the skull. MPD's Forensic Unit did a thorough job of analysis of the crime scene, which was the tiny chapel known as Good Shepherd. Singletary was found sitting in a single pew, his body slumped against a wall. There appears to have been little bleeding, which has caused those who were on the scene to raise a question." He paused. They looked at him. "Which is—?"

April Montgomery said, "Whether he might have been killed elsewhere and moved to the chapel."

"That's interesting," Joy Collins said. She was the most exuberant of Smith's students. "They didn't have *that* on TV or in the papers."

"It will be, as soon as enough of the right questions are asked and facts digested. An autopsy is being performed or has been performed on the Reverend Singletary, and perhaps that will determine a number of things, including—what?"

Several raised their hands.

"The approximate time of his death, lividity, the advancement of rigor mortis, body temperature, the level of potassium in the eye fluid, rate of decomposition," said Bob Rogers, who usually had such lists at his command.

"Right. All will be taken into consideration. Many color photographs were shot, and detailed sketches were made. Each of you, of course, is familiar with the techniques used to evaluate a crime scene." He surveyed their faces; he'd become a forensics expert when he was practicing criminal law. It was vitally necessary to understand forensic medicine in order to mount a credible defense for a client. Some of his students didn't seem to be interested in such things, aside from morbid curiosity.

"Any speculation on motive?" April asked.

"No, but there soon will be. That will all be part of the criminal profile that develops once more information has been gathered by the authorities." Smith knew that as scornful as Terry Finnerty (like most local law-enforcement officers) was of the FBI, he would need the help of the bureau's Behavioral Science Unit—now part of the National Center for the Analysis of Violent Crime (NCAVC)—in developing a description of the type of person who might have committed the murder, using both psychological and investigative input. He told them so.

"Maybe it was somebody who hates the church and clergy, somebody who flunked out of a seminary, or who was brought up in a repressive religious household," Petrella offered. Joe Petrella seemed to especially enjoy the drama of law.

"Maybe."

"Was Father Singletary married?"

"No."

"Was he . . . gay?"

"Why would you ask that?" Smith asked.

"Well, you know clergy, they have—"

"Paul Singletary was an Episcopal priest, not a Roman Catholic. Episcopal priests are free to marry and to have children. Why would the fact that he was a priest raise a question of his sexual orientation?"

"Homosexuals are free to be homosexual, or to be heterosexuals, or to be bi-, to marry, and to have children," said April.

She was right, of course, and Smith ignored that line of conversation. He said, "The basic supposition at this moment is that Father Singletary was murdered by someone whom he confronted in the chapel, most likely an outsider. This unknown person would fall under the category of an unorganized murderer. All signs point to a lack of premeditation since no knife, gun, or other formal weapon was used. It is also safe to assume at this juncture that Father Singletary did not know his assailant, and was taken by surprise."

"But if he was murdered elsewhere, as you suggested was a possibility, Professor Smith, and brought to the chapel, that would certainly indicate a more organized murderer," Joyce Clemow said. "If that happened, the murderer didn't just swing something at Father Singletary and run. He thought about it, and spent time with his victim."

"You are correct," said Smith. He looked at his watch. "Our fifteen minutes of diversion are up. I would now like you to turn to the cases assigned on writs of habeas corpus."

* * *

Chief of Homicide Terrence Finnerty sat in his office with six other detectives assigned to a task force to investigate Paul Singletary's murder. Smith waited outside until the detectives left, and Finnerty invited him to come in.

"Sorry to screw up your day, Mac," Finnerty said as he poured himself a cup of black coffee from a battered Thermos. "Want some?"

"No, thank you. The British knew what they were doing when they named cop coffee 'tonsil varnish.' "

"Hey, this ain't bad coffee, Mac. My wife makes it fresh every morning."

"That's different. Thank you anyway."

Seemingly pleased that he'd set *that* record straight, Finnerty leaned back in his chair, put his scuffed black shoes on the edge of his desk, and squinted at some papers in a file folder.

"Any word yet on the autopsy?" Smith asked.

"No," Finnerty answered without looking up. "I'll get a prelim from the M.E. this afternoon. It'll take a while for the blood and urine samples to be run. We're busy in the chop shop." He glanced up at Smith. "Any ideas?"

Smith laughed. "Is that why you had me brought down here, to ask if I have any ideas? Why would I have ideas? Once you and your people took over, I was out of the picture, still am."

"Not in the papers."

"I just know what I read in the newspapers."

"Bull! After the funeral for Vickery you hung around the cathedral a long time, holed up with the bishop for at least a couple hours."

"Who told you that?" Smith asked, knowing the answer. Obviously, Finnerty had had one of his people keep an eye on his movements.

"What did you talk to the bishop about?"

"About having lost a friend," Smith replied.

"Two hours to talk about that? Must have been a hell of an interesting guy."

"He was. You know his reputation. Paul Singletary was probably the most involved and visible clergyman in Washington."

"Yeah, I know, but that's just the public side. Tell me about Singletary, his private side. You knew him pretty good, right?"

Smith thought of Annabel's comments. "Probably not as well as you're assuming. I wouldn't call him a *close* friend."

"You asked him to marry you."

"No, I asked him to officiate at our wedding, which doesn't necessarily indicate closeness. We wanted to be married in the cathedral. Bishop St. James was out of town. We knew Paul, and asked him to conduct the service."

"How come you were the one the bishop called the minute the body was discovered?"

"I keep asking myself the same question. Annabel has been active in church affairs for a number of years, and I've been involved in a few aspects of the cathedral's activities, been called upon to give some legal advice on occasion. I guess the combination of knowing the bishop fairly well and being an attorney was good enough for him to think of me first. I wish he hadn't."

"He like girls?"

"Father Singletary?"

"Yeah."

"One of my students assumed Paul might have been gay because he was a single clergyman. Are you making the same assumption?"

"No, Mac, not at all, but I have a feeling we're going to have to get to know the *real* Father Singletary if we're going to have any chance of solving this case."

Finnerty was right, of course, especially if Singletary's killer turned out not to be a total stranger. In order for an effective profile to be drawn of the murderer, the police and the FBI's Behavioral Science Unit would need knowledge of how Singletary lived, his friends, his hobbies, his haunts, everything about how he lived his intimate life on a daily basis.

"Paul was an attractive and engaging man," Smith said. "He was dedicated to helping the disenfranchised of our society, and worked hard on their behalf, sometimes to the consternation of his peers and colleagues. I know he also found time for some semblance of a social life. Yes, he did like girls. I recall two occasions when he was accompanied at social gatherings by a woman."

"Same woman?"

Smith shook his head. "No, two different women, both very attractive, I might add."

"He was in London just before it happened, right?"

"So I understand." Smith remembered George St. James's mentioning that Singletary had returned from London a day earlier than scheduled. Why? That was one of the things he told the bishop he'd try to find out when he went to London on his honeymoon. Should he bring it up with Finnerty? He decided not to. Probably had no significance, but let Finnerty earn his money.

It dawned on Smith that he was rapidly shifting into the defense-attorney mode—maybe not officially, but certainly psychically. This both interested and dismayed him.

"We got a description from the bishop's wife. Not a very good one, but it was the best she seemed to be able to do. Here." Finnerty handed Smith a typed transcript of what Eileen St. James had given the interviewing officer.

White female—somewhere between 40 and 60—reddish hair that probably was dyed because there were a lot of black roots— short, maybe five feet, maybe a few inches taller—kind of a narrow little face—pale complexion—had a black mole on her cheek (couldn't remember which cheek)—wore a skirt (doesn't remember color)—a black (or dark blue) sweater with buttons— another sweater, color unknown, underneath, maybe a white blouse under that—no recollection of shoes—no distinguishing marks other than the black mole—nervous personality (but Mrs. St. James said that could be because she discovered a body)—high voice (but she was crying all the time, so hard to tell what her voice was really like)—no accent—twisted her hands around each other a lot—used terms like "Dear Jesus" and "Father in Heaven"— maybe had alcohol on her breath but can't be sure.

Smith looked up from the page into the small black pupils of Finnerty's eyes. "I think it's surprisingly detailed, considering the circumstances. The bishop's wife is observant," he said.

"Or the cop asking questions was good."

"Are you asking whether I know this woman?"

Finnerty shrugged. "She doesn't sound like either of the women I saw Paul Singletary with on those social occasions, if that's what you're getting at."

"Not his type, huh?"

"No, not his type."

"You ever get involved with any of his knee-jerk work?"

Smith found the term offensive, but didn't respond to that. He said, "Just once. Father Singletary was having a legal problem running a soup kitchen. Some of the neighbors hired an attorney and brought suit to have the place closed down. Singletary didn't ask me to help. He brought it up at one of those social occasions I mentioned earlier, and I went to bat for him, talked to the neighborhood attorney and got him to understand that he didn't have any legal basis upon which to demand the closing of the kitchen. I don't think I've been involved in any other aspect of Paul's . . . 'knee-jerk' . . . projects."

Finnerty grinned, obviously pleased that he had annoyed Smith, which only annoyed Smith more. "Any truth that you're going to defend whoever murdered Singletary if it turns out he's from the cathedral?"

"No truth whatsoever," Smith said. "Is that it, Terry? If it is, I really would like to get back home. I still have a busy day ahead of me."

"Including spending a little time at the cathedral again?"

"Maybe."

"Careful, Mac, don't get too religious."

"No need to worry about that, Terry. Call me anytime. I'm as anxious as everyone else to see you resolve this. Good luck."

"It's sickening what's happened to this city," the woman standing outside the Georgetown townhouse said to the uniformed policeman guarding the front door. "Animals, nothing but animals," she said. "He was such a good man, and they killed him. They should rot in hell, whoever killed Father Singletary." The officer responded with a series of "Uh-huh"s.

Inside, two of the six detectives assigned to the Singletary case took photographs of the apartment and made notes. Its furnishings and decoration were eclectic, unconcerned Early Bachelor. The sofa and chairs were threadbare. The walls needed painting, and two cheap area rugs were stained and curled at the corners where double-faced tape had dried out and let loose.

"Nice VCR," Joe Johnson, a black detective, said. It was a new model with many advanced features, and was hooked up to a large NEC video monitor. A wall of videotapes framed the equipment.

"No books," Vinnie Basilio said.

"These Bibles," his partner said.

"Whattaya expect a priest to have, porn?"

Johnson laughed. "Could be." He started to tell of a case he'd worked on just after he'd been promoted to detective, a story his partner had heard too many times. He cut him off. "What I don't figure is the security system."

"Say what?"

"The security system on this place. *Every*thing is wired, and this kind of system costs big bucks. What the hell would a priest have that's so important he'd put in such a system?"

Johnson laughed again, a pleasant rumble from deep inside. "A good VCR and TV."

The Italian American shook his head and grimaced. "Nah, this security system had to cost ten times what he was protecting. I don't figure it, a priest doing this."

"Hey, man, he was no ordinary priest, right? I mean, this guy was in the papers every other day, walking the mean streets with the crackheads, feeding bums, stealing teenybopper hookers from their pimps. Maybe *that's* why he's got this system in here, to protect his neck."

"A lot of good it did him."

Detective Johnson responded to a knock. Finnerty stepped into the living room and closed the door behind him. "Anything?" he asked.

They recounted what they'd been discussing. Finnerty did not seem as impressed with the security system as Basilio had been. "Files, letters, anything like that?"

"We didn't look yet," replied Johnson.

"Well, get to it quick," Finnerty said. "We're about to lose the place."

The two detectives looked at him.

"The feds are coming in," Finnerty said, his disgust obvious.

"How come?" Basilio asked.

"Beats me. As far as I'm concerned, it's strictly a D.C. murder, but I got the word that when the feds get here, they run the ball club, so you remember that, too."

"Sure. No skin off my nose. They'll just screw it up like they usually do," Basilio said.

Johnson laughed.

Finnerty and the two detectives quickly started going through a small desk in the bedroom. There was very little in it—a drawer for paid bills, a drawer for unpaid bills, some blank stationery and envelopes, pens and pencils, no personal address or phone book, no photographs except a few of Singletary with dignitaries that hung above the bed.

"You wouldn't figure he'd live here in Georgetown," said Detective Basilio.

"Why?" Finnerty asked.

"Because he's big in the ghetto. How come he doesn't live in the ghetto? What was he, one of those liberals who beats it back at night to where the decent folk live?"

Neither Finnerty nor Johnson had a chance to comment because there was another knock at the door. Finnerty opened it to two young men with short, neat haircuts who wore inexpensive but nicely fitted and neatly pressed suits. One of them, who had a round face with red cheeks, said to Finnerty, "Can I talk to you?"

They went out into the hallway, where the agent showed Finnerty his identification. "We're going to be spending time in the apartment, and we need to be left alone. I'd like you to move your uniformed man up to this floor and have him take a position outside the door. We'd appreciate somebody on that duty twenty-four hours a day."

Finnerty was tempted to tell them to provide their own personnel now that they were coming into it, but he didn't. He'd learned long ago that shooting off his mouth in these situations accomplished nothing. Worse, it often got him in trouble, the kind of trouble he didn't need with two years to the pension. Instead, he returned to the apartment and told his detectives it was time to leave.

The two agents stood in the center of what had been Father Paul Singletary's living room. The one with the round face, who was in charge, removed his suit jacket and carefully draped it over the back of a chair that was beside a small, cheap Formica table. "Might as well get to work," he said to his partner, who had blond hair and a large mouth defined by thick lips. He, too, had removed his suit jacket, exposing beneath his white shirt a body that had pumped a lot of iron. "What's first?" he asked his superior.

"The tapes. Looks like we're in for a long night at the movies."

At three o'clock that afternoon, Bishop George St. James received a visitor to his office in the cathedral's administration building. His name was Jin Tse, and he was a heavyset Korean who wore a suit that said Savile Row.

"Good of you to see me on such short notice," said Tse, settling himself in a comfortable chair facing the desk.

"Frankly, I would have preferred to see no one today," St. James said, "but I do respect your reasons for wanting to meet as quickly as possible, Mr. Tse. If my mind seems to wander at times, please forgive me. The full impact of what has happened here, and to Father Singletary, is just beginning to sink in. It's like being run over by a sixteen-wheeler, if you understand."

"Yes, of course, and I offer you my deepest sympathy. His death has been a terrible shock and loss to us at Word of Peace, too."

"As I can well imagine," said St. James. "Actually, we've been dealt a double blow here. Not only is Father Singletary gone, but Adam Vickery, who performed wonders for us in managing our building assets, also died."

Tse nodded.

"Ironic, isn't it, that two men who supported the cathedral should die so close together? Of course, Adam Vickery's death was natural, part of the order of things. As for Father Singletary . . . well, being murdered is never natural."

Tse cleared his throat before saying, "Bishop St. James, the reason it was necessary to meet with you as quickly as possible was to alleviate the fears many of the leaders of Word of Peace have been feeling since Father Singletary's murder. Our goals depend a great deal upon the continued support of such institutions as this cathedral, and the church it represents. Paul . . . do you mind if I call him Paul?" The bishop shook his head. "Paul was always so proud that his bishop had committed himself and the church with such vigor and determination to Word of Peace." Tse spoke perfect English; to hear him on a telephone would lead a listener to believe that a native-born American who'd studied elocution was speaking. "As you might be aware, our movement has its detractors. With the unfortunate death of such a leader, it gives them what they might perceive as a golden opportunity to increase their attacks upon this crusade. What I need to be able to do is immediately inform my people that Paul's death has not weakened our cause but, in the tragic but time-honored tradition of martyrdom, has actually enhanced our efforts to bring peace to this world."

What St. James had apologized for at the beginning of the meeting was now happening. He was having trouble concentrating on the well-formed words of this Korean gentleman sitting across from him.

St. James had heard of Jin Tse from Paul Singletary, although as he reflected upon the priest's comments, he realized Singletary had offered little information about the man. Paul had told him that Tse was one of the prime organizers of Word of Peace, particularly in the Washington area, where the Korean was engaged in intense lobbying of politicians who might throw their weight behind the movement. The bishop was sorry that he had agreed to meet with him, not because of the crush of cathedral business or out of his deep sense of loss, but because he really didn't like Tse. He couldn't pinpoint why. Tse was pleasant enough, courteous to a fault, and had been respected by Singletary. Yet something bothered St. James about him, and he decided to end the meeting.

"Mr. Tse, it is difficult for me to devote much thought at this moment to Word of Peace, although I do believe in it." (Did he? He'd never been sure. He did believe in its goals, however.) "It's a matter of priorities at this point. We have Father Singletary's funeral coming up as soon as his body is released by the authorities, and there is the continuing need to cooperate with those authorities in bringing to justice the individual who committed this deplorable act of violence. I can tell you, however, that whatever support I offered Father Singletary in his work with your movement has not changed. If that puts your mind and the minds of your people at rest, then I am pleased to be able to express it to you."

Tse realized that the bishop was ending their meeting. He stood, smiled, and extended a hand laden with heavy rings. St. James took it. "Your generosity, Bishop St. James, is exemplary. I could ask for nothing more than to have heard the words you have just said. The spiritual and financial commitment made to Word of Peace by this shrine of national worship will be instrumental in bringing about a just and lasting peace for people all over this globe. You are truly a man of God."

St. James was now even more uncomfortable. He withdrew his hand from the Korean's metal-wrapped fingers and escorted him to the door. "You'll be at Paul's funeral?"

"Of course," said Tse. "Indeed, hundreds of supporters of Word of Peace will be there to pay a final tribute to one of the most gentle and committed men I have ever had the pleasure of knowing."

"Yes, well, thank you for coming here today. Good-bye."

Tse was driven away from the cathedral in a large gray Mercedes sedan that had been parked at the doors of the south transept. The driver turned left onto Wisconsin Avenue, which took them in the direction of Georgetown. A nondescript green Ford Fairlane that had been parked across the street fell in behind them. Two young men with close, neat haircuts were in the second car. The man on the passenger side dialed a number on the vehicle's car phone. A female voice answered, "NIS."

"Samuels."

"One second."

A male voice came on the line.

"Samuels. We're continuing contact with Buddha by vehicle."

The man on the other end, who managed the surveillance unit, said, "Report again when mode of contact changes."

"Right," the young man named Samuels said. He hung up the phone and said to the driver, "Are Marsch and Williamson picking up from us later?"

The driver said, "No, they're over at the priest's apartment. I don't know who's spelling us, and I don't care, as long as I get to go home by eight. If I don't, someone will kill me and you'll have another investigation. Look for my wife. It's our anniversary."

The Mercedes pulled up to the entrance of the Watergate Hotel, and Tse emerged. His driver pulled away. "I'll pick up Buddha," Samuels said, jumping out of the car. As the driver was about to follow the Mercedes, Samuels said through the open window, "If you don't make it home for your anniversary, my couch opens up. See ya."

9

Monday Morning—
Overcast and Chilly; Funeral Weather

THE RIGHT REVEREND George St. James, bishop of Washington, looked out at the thousands of faces of those who'd gathered in the cathedral's nave to mourn the loss of Canon Paul Singletary. His mind wandered for a moment. He peered down the more-than-five-hundred-foot aisle leading from the altar to the west entrance and, distracting himself from the unpleasant task at hand, observed once more with interest that the aisle wasn't straight, that it did a little jig at approximately the halfway point, a deliberate act by the architect to avoid the "narrowing railroad track" visual phenomenon.

He cleared his voice and said from the pulpit, *"They do rest from their labors and their works do follow them."* His words rang out through the cavernous cathedral.

Joining Bishop St. James at the high altar were other members of the cathedral's and St. Albans's clergy, including Jonathon Merle and a young priest from St. Albans, Carolyn Armstrong. Annabel, who'd come to know Reverend Armstrong while planning the forthcoming show in Annabel's gallery, had remarked to Mac after first meeting her that the young woman was striking, and all the more so because of what she represented. She was one of those fortunate women who need no makeup, and the fact that she could present a bare and unadorned face to the world worked perfectly with her calling. An aura of sweet divinity surrounded her. At the same time, she was a woman who could hardly be missed. She was tall and had thick black hair that she rarely wore loose; when attending to her priestly duties she caught it up into a casual chignon. Her skin was flawless, and the contours of an amply endowed body were only partially obscured beneath her vocational garb.

Mac and Annabel held hands as they sat in one of the forward pews. Their thoughts sometimes coincided, other times were far afield. Naturally, visions of their wedding day in the Bethlehem Chapel kept returning, Paul's handsome, smiling face bestowing God's grace upon their union, the implied playfulness in his voice and the twinkle in his eye, his easy banter with them outside the cathedral. As those pleasant thoughts ebbed and flowed, there was also a natural anger. How senseless, how wrong, for this dynamic man to have his life end in such a brutal and wanton fashion.

Smith looked around. Two distant cousins of Singletary's sat together at the far end of a pew. Chief of Homicide Terrence Finnerty was in the crowd along with what Smith assumed were other representatives from the MPD. The Word of Peace contingent numbered in the hundreds. Whole inner-city classes of school-children, mostly black and Hispanic, had been brought to the service by their teachers. The vice president of the United States had made a last-minute decision to attend, which had thrown the security people into turmoil. He sat quietly with his wife and two Cabinet members, a dozen Secret Service agents surrounding their entourage.

Most of the other mourners, Smith decided, were people who probably had had no direct contact with Paul Singletary, people who were saddened and outraged by his murder and who'd come to pay their simple respects to a man they didn't know but whose reputation for good works had touched each of them in some unspoken, intangible way.

The choir was a combination of the cathedral's boys' and men's choirs. They lined both sides of the aisle of the chancel and sanctuary that led to the high altar. From outside came the constant whir of a helicopter hovering above. Barked orders through a bullhorn on occasion added yet another alien sound.

Reverend Armstrong read a section from the Scriptures, its words acclaiming all who carry out the Lord's good work on earth by comforting the sick and ministering to the poor. The message was so fitting that as she reached the end of the verse, her voice broke and it was apparent that she had to fight for control to complete the reading. Her near-breakdown brought sobs from people throughout the congregation.

Jonathon Merle was next. In contrast to Canon Armstrong, he was more patrician and steely than ever. He read from the Gospel in a flat, businesslike tone, his eyes never leaving the printed page, his cadence that of a man getting through a ritual as coolly and perhaps even as quickly as possible.

Bishop St. James sat in the great carved stone Glastonbury Cathedra, "the bishop's chair." When Merle had completed his duties at the pulpit, St. James slowly stood and walked to take his place. Mac Smith noticed the fatigue in his friend's gait. It was confirmed when he started to speak, his voice heavy and weary, a sense of profound sadness clinging to every word.

"Reverend Canon Paul Singletary loved many things in this life, but mostly he loved the God he served so admirably. He was a man whose spirit could be lifted by music, and there were always favorite hymns that he would listen to when in need of personal renewal. One of them speaks eloquently of the blessed rest in our Saviour's hands that he has undoubtedly found. I know he is with us today and will take delight in once again hearing this hymn that meant so much to him."

St. James returned to his stone chair as choirmaster Wilfred Nickelson conducted the combined choirs. The magnificent ringing sound of the accompanying organ seemed to lift the voices up a hundred feet to the gray shadows of the nave's ceiling.

> *"Now the laborer's task is o'er,*
> *Now the battle day is past;*
> *Now upon the farther shore*
> *Lands the voyager at last.*
> *Father, in thy gracious keeping*
> *Leave we now thy servant sleeping."*

Joey Kelsch, who stood at the front of the boys' choir, delivered the final two lines of each verse as a solo. Early in the hymn, the words soared from his lips and throat. Then, as he began the later lines of the last verse, he faltered. People leaned forward. Choirmaster Nickelson looked sternly in his direction. Would he complete the two lines? the congregation silently wondered. Joey looked up from the hymnal he held in both hands. His gaze went from the men's choir across the chancel to the congregation, to Bishop St. James, Father Merle, and Reverend Armstrong, then back to the congregation. His blue eyes were alight with fear. He managed to sing the final words, quickly turned away, and crouched as the suppressed sounds of his vomiting nonetheless reached them and faded with the final notes of the organ.

St. James returned to the pulpit. Should he mention the unfortunate and untimely illness of the choirboy, who was slinking away in shame?

He drew a deep breath and said, "Father Paul Singletary devoted much of his life to serving his fellow man. He did this in the ghettos of this city, in the drug-rehabilitation centers, and in the kitchens where the homeless are nourished. Of course, he also served his country admirably. He was particularly fond of this prayer, often used on shipboard during storms or in times of war." St. James adjusted his glasses and began to read: "O most powerful and glorious Lord God, at whose command the winds blow and lift up the waves of the sea, and who stillest the rage thereof; we, thy creatures, but miserable sinners, do in this our great distress cry unto thee for help. . . ."

When St. James had finished the prayer, and preparations had begun for the closing portions of the service, Annabel whispered to Mac, "That poor boy."

"I know. There's lots of flu going around. Kid must be terribly embarrassed. Say, did you know that Paul was in the military?"

"No."

"I gather from what George said that he might have served in the navy, maybe on board a ship. That's a slice of his life I knew nothing about."

Their attention returned to the altar. "Let us pray" was the call. Mac and Annabel sank to their knees. Their fingers found each other's once again as they prayed along with the bishop for the salvation of Singletary's soul.

Outside, Mac introduced Annabel to Terry Finnerty. He asked the detective, "Anything new?"

Finnerty shook his head.

"Nothing further in the autopsy findings?"

"Nah. Nothing under his nails, no fight."

"Meaning he knew the person who killed him?" Annabel said.

"Maybe, maybe not. Maybe he didn't know the person, but it happened so fast he didn't have a chance to put up a fight."

"The word is getting around, Terry, that the body might have been moved from another place." Smith couldn't be critical of such rumors. He'd helped to spread the word in his own law class. "Are you still leaning in that direction?"

Another shrug from Finnerty. "Yeah, I think it's a good possibility. What I need now is that woman who found the body. We put out a composite on her based on the bishop's wife's description. Maybe we'll get lucky. Nice meeting you, Mrs. Smith. You must be a saint to put up with this guy." He laughed to indicate he was kidding.

"I felt so sorry for Carolyn Armstrong," Annabel said as she and Mac walked toward their car. "I didn't think she'd make it."

"Neither did I," Smith said. "Did she know Paul pretty well?"

"I suppose so. They worked together. Everyone at the cathedral is broken up, except Father Merle, who is so controlled. She had trouble keeping from crying two days ago when we met about the art show. I still can't believe it."

Smith opened the door for Annabel. "As you said, she certainly is beautiful."

As they waited in a line of traffic to turn onto Wisconsin Avenue, Mac said, "I can't get that poor choirboy out of my mind. How embarrassing to throw up in the middle of your solo at the National Cathedral."

"I know. Did you see the look on the child's face just before it happened? He seemed to be searching every corner, every crevice, for something."

"Maybe for a place to hide. Let's change the subject. Did you get the feeling from Finnerty that he was a lot surer that the body had been moved than he was letting on?"

She shook her head. "No. Why do you say that?"

"Oh, I don't know, just something about him. I got to know him fairly well when I was practicing, got to know when he was lying and when he was being straight. If Paul was murdered elsewhere and his body taken to the Good Shepherd Chapel, it adds weight to the possibility that someone who knew the cathedral killed him, not just a drifter Paul stumbled into in the chapel. Good Shepherd, open all day and night, is the most obvious place if the stranger-as-killer theory is at the top of the list."

She nodded. "What I can't fathom, Mac, is why anyone would kill him even if they had met suddenly in that little chapel. Nothing was taken from Paul. The newspapers said his wallet was intact, there was money in his pockets. What could he have come upon that would warrant killing him? Two people passing drugs? I don't think drug dealers would come to a chapel in a cathedral to do business."

"Drug dealers will deal anywhere. Speaking of business, how are preparations coming for our honeymoon?"

"Good. I checked with the travel agent, and all the confirmations are back. I do want to pick up a dress and a blouse or two before we go. Other than that, I'm set. How about you?"

"I'm ready. I still have to work on my speech, and I want to talk with George before looking into Paul's movements in London. I'd say we're in pretty good shape." They were stopped at a light. He leaned over and kissed her on the cheek. "I love you very much, Annabel."

"Why this sudden gush of affection?" she asked.

"Just a spontaneous eruption of understanding of how good life can be. That is, when you're alive and with the right woman."

Later in the day, Bishop St. James held a meeting of cathedral and St. Albans clergy. He used the occasion to assure them that while Paul Singletary's murder had disrupted things, to understate, it was necessary for each of them to get on with the important task of moving forward on many missions vital to the cathedral's future. He was only slightly annoyed when Carolyn Armstrong interrupted to ask who would replace Paul.

"I'm afraid I haven't given that much thought," St. James said, "but I know it has to be addressed. Until it is, we're all going to have to assume some of the burden that Paul carried." He checked Merle's reaction. As dedicated as Merle was to his religion and cathedral, taking on additional workload would not please him. Jonathon always wished for more time (as many of the clergy did) to use in personal meditations and for sermon writing and research. In addition, he was somewhat shy, a condition covered over with bristles, and uncomfortable in face-to-face work with coy people. He *cared,* but never knew how to show it.

"Will you go outside for a replacement?" Armstrong asked.

"I have no idea what steps will be taken to replace Paul. We'll discuss that at another meeting." He took in the rest of the room. "We're so close to seeing this cathedral completed that we can't allow anything to deter us from that goal. I know how difficult it is to focus on our tasks, but Paul, like all of us, lived for the day when the final stone would be placed in the West Tower. He can't be here to rejoice in that moment, but we can deliver it to him."

The bishop left the room for a few minutes to greet a visitor.

"How unfortunate, the Kelsch boy interrupting the service like that," said Jonathon Merle.

"Much worse for him, poor dear," said Carolyn Armstrong.

Choirmaster Nickelson said, "He's a difficult young man. I've been having nothing but trouble with him since the night before the murder."

"Really?" Merle said.

"Yes. He'd been cutting up in rehearsal, and I assigned him a punishment detail in the choir room that night."

"How late was he there?" Merle asked.

"He was supposed to stay until eleven. I assume he did."

Merle grunted and looked at the door as the bishop entered. They spent another twenty minutes together before St. James ended the meeting by leading them in prayer.

Outside in the hallway of the administration building, Carolyn Armstrong said to Nickelson, "Has Joey Kelsch ever said anything about Paul's death?"

"Not to me," Nickelson said.

"He should talk to someone. He may need counseling. I was upset myself during the service, but to become physically ill might represent some deep turmoil he's going through about Paul's murder."

"Maybe. I'm not a shrink. I conduct a choir. Excuse me, Reverend, I have an appointment."

"Well, I *don't* conduct a choir," she said after him, realizing how silly her comment was. *And your mother wears army boots.* She left the building and walked to St. Albans, where she always felt more at home than in the cathedral. St. Albans was *her* church, a small country parish in the imposing shadow of the titanic National Cathedral, a true place of simple faith and worship without the destructive intrusions of power and politics, manipulation and machinations of the cathedral itself.

The meeting of the bishop and his staff had begun at noon. Simultaneously—although five hours later in London—the Reverend Malcolm Apt escorted solicitor Jeffrey Woodcock to one of the doors to Lambeth Palace. They'd been meeting for an hour.

Woodcock, who was short and round and who attempted to cover his bald pate with strands of hair from low down on his right side, energetically shook Apt's hand. "This was a most useful meeting, I do say, most useful."

"Yes, but unfortunate that it needed to take place, Mr. Woodcock. While this whole business is obviously a legal matter, there are potentially damaging ramifications where the image of the church is concerned. I feel confident after this meeting that you are fully aware of that fact, and that you understand the need to proceed cautiously in order to avoid unseemly scandal."

"Of course. I assure you that any legal maneuvering will be done with discretion. Good evening, Reverend Apt."

"Good evening, Mr. Woodcock."

Woodcock had intended to return to his office, but considering the hour decided instead to go directly to his club for a quiet drink and dinner. His family was in the country on a brief holiday, leaving him to fend for himself, something that, despite his brilliant law career, he was remarkably incapable of doing. His wife did everything for him; when she was away, he found the familiar comfort of the club to provide a sense of shelter.

Malcolm Apt, on the other hand, was supremely confident in his ability to handle every aspect of his life without the help of others. He went into Lambeth's kitchen, made himself a simple dinner of steamed vegetables and boiled chicken, and took it to his office.

At nine, he called for a taxi, slipped on his black raincoat and black rain hat, and waited near the entrance. He climbed into the black London taxi that had been dispatched and said, "The Red Lion pub on Waverton in Mayfair."

When the cab pulled up in front of the pub, Apt paid the fare and looked out through the window at a dark blue Ford parked down a narrow street a dozen yards away. He checked his watch; he was precisely on time. He got out of the cab and watched it drive off, its lights reflecting off glistening pavement that had been moistened by a brief shower. He strolled casually in the direction of the Ford, and when he reached it, climbed into the backseat.

Without a word, the driver got out and entered the pub, where he announced that Mr. Leighton's car was waiting. He returned to the car, again saying nothing to Apt.

Ten minutes later Brett Leighton, wearing his customary tweed suit and carrying an umbrella, came to the car and climbed into the back to join Apt. Bob drove slowly and without purpose through Mayfair, its small, exclusive shops closed, only an occasional person walking on the streets. Leighton and Apt spoke in hushed tones. After a half hour, Leighton said to Bob, "Home, please." He turned and said to Apt, "Bob will drive you back to Lambeth."

"No, I prefer not," said Apt. "He can take me to a busy intersection where there will be taxis."

"As you wish," Leighton said.

Leighton, about to exit the car as it stopped in front of his Belgravia home, said to Reverend Apt, "Remember, she is a real problem. We must keep that in mind at every step."

Apt was annoyed at being reminded of what he felt should have been obvious. He gave Leighton a slight, sour smile and watched the long, lean assistant director of MI5's "B" Division stop to admire a large stoneware pot of mums in front of his house before inserting a key in the door and disappearing inside.

"The nearest taxi queue," Apt said curtly. He was dropped off at Sloane Square, where he immediately got into a cab. Bob, who'd been handed an envelope by Leighton, drove to the Lamb and Flag and indulged in a dinner of a T-bone steak served heavily salted and vine-gared in a brown paper bag, and a Directors bitter. His wife had told him that he could take care of his own dinner if he came home late again, which is what he was doing. Better food here than what she was likely to have left for him.

And better conversation, too. Maude always asked too many questions, while he'd made a perfectly good life by asking next to none.

10

The Following Sunday—
Outside Temperature, Minus 68 Degrees

"To us," Mac Smith said, touching the rim of his glass against Annabel's. "Airborne at last."

"To a sublime honeymoon," she said.

The Pan Am 747 had lifted into the air over New York's John F. Kennedy Airport, banked left, and reached its cruising altitude of thirty-seven thousand feet for its flight to London.

"Nice champagne, nice to be here," Smith said. "It's been a mad scramble the last few days."

It had been. Under the unwritten but well-understood law of diminishing time when preparing for a trip, Smith had found himself racing to fit everything in.

First, there had been an emergency meeting of the cathedral chapter to discuss a number of procedural questions, the most pressing of them, in the bishop's view, being what action would be taken should

Singletary's murderer turn out to be connected with the cathedral. Smith had declined Bishop St. James's invitation to attend, but the bishop was relentlessly persuasive. Representatives from the cathedral's law firm were there, too, neither of whom had any experience in criminal law.

"Highly unlikely it was anyone from the cathedral," said the chapter president, "but better to be prepared."

Smith certainly agreed with that thinking. He was asked whether he had learned of any further developments from the MPD. He had; Smith had met that morning with the chief of Homicide. The final autopsy results were in, and Finnerty had given Smith a copy of the medical examiner's notes.

Pressed for details, Mac avoided them, but one nice gray-haired, carefully coiffed and garbed parishioner kept asking to know everything. Smith winced, finally said, "All right," and proceeded to read. ". . . skin and subcutaneous tissue crushed against underlying bone . . . surrounding bruising characterized by rough and uneven edges . . . hairs, tissue and damaged blood vessels, customary in such injury, at base of wound . . . wound crescent-shaped—two and three-quarter inches (weapon not blunt) . . . force of blow substantial . . . fractures to skull depressed and comminuted . . . considerable bone splinters driven into soft tissues . . . heavy hemorrhaging (blood vessels bled into space between skull and brain membrane) . . . internal bleeding collected between dura and inner surface . . . fracture and secondary radiating fissures indicate blow was delivered in a horizontal plane . . . minimal hypostatic staining of skin on lower back and back of neck . . . body temperature eighty-two degrees (subject was clothed and indoors—rate of cooling necessarily slowed by virtue of cause of death) . . . level of rigor not advanced (stiffness confined primarily to face) . . . time of death approximately ten P.M. night prior to discovery of victim . . . analysis of abdominal contents support estimated time of death . . . analysis of clothing and body indicate absence of substances other than belonging to victim . . . clothing clean . . . no bruises on hands or arms to indicate defense taken against weapon . . . death was instantaneous . . ."

Smith looked around the table. The nice gray-haired woman went grayer still, and Smith repressed a small sense of satisfaction. The blunt, unpleasant words of the report had had their predictable effect on others, as well. Some feigned disinterest by looking away. One man's face was drained of blood; Smith wondered if he would be the latest Episcopalian to become ill. "How horrible" . . . "Sad" . . . "Barbaric" . . . "Brutal," said the chapter members.

"Do the police feel that anything in the report is useful to their investigation?" Smith was asked.

"I haven't discussed that with them at length," he replied. "They're being very cooperative with me, particularly Chief Finnerty. He and I go back a long way. He really doesn't have any obligation to share this information, but he seems to view me as having an official capacity. I haven't dissuaded him."

"You will handle the defense if someone from the cathedral is charged?"

"I haven't committed myself to that yet," Smith said. "I suppose, like all of us, in a way, I'm hoping that it will turn out to be a stranger, or at least someone not close to the cathedral. I have promised the bishop, however, that I will be as helpful as possible. That is still my intention." Bishop St. James's smile spilled over with appreciation.

Smith and the bishop met privately following the chapter meeting. St. James handed Smith a letter of introduction to the archbishop of Canterbury as Smith had requested. "You're likely to see Reverend Malcolm Apt," St. James told Smith. "It may be difficult to see the archbishop in person, but this letter might help. I'll call Apt."

"I was intrigued with something you said during Paul's funeral," Smith said as he slipped the letter into his jacket pocket. "Was Paul ever a chaplain?"

"Yes."

"Navy, I take it."

"Right."

"When?"

"Evidently, soon after he was ordained. He rarely spoke of it. Maybe once, twice, as I recall. He did love that verse, though, and liked to use it when comforting the bereaved."

"How long did he serve?"

"I have no idea, Mac. Why?"

"Just want to know as much as possible about him. Well, I have to go. I'll call when we return."

St. James placed a hand on Smith's shoulder. "You know how grateful I am."

"Yes, I know."

"Have a safe trip, and don't spend all your time on this. Remember, it is your honeymoon."

"Annabel will see to it that I don't forget. Good night, George."

Smith's next meeting was with Tony Buffolino, the former Washington narcotics detective who'd been dismissed from the force for taking money from a South American drug dealer. A highly decorated cop, Buffolino had never touched any of the loose and plentiful dirty money available to narcs until a flood of bills for cancer treatment of a son washed him against the wall. As his attorney, Smith managed to quash criminal charges, but couldn't stave off Tony's dishonorable discharge from the MPD. For a time, Buffolino blamed Smith for making that deal. He'd loved being a cop, loved it even more than the freedom Smith had won for him. Then, after years without contact, Smith had called him in to help with the investigation of the murder of the presidential candidate's aide at the Kennedy Center, and found him a job when the investigation was over.

When Smith walked into Tony's Spotlight Room at noon, he found the cop-turned-restaurateur sitting at the bar. The establishment, sandwiched between two topless clubs on lower K Street, was open only at night. A young Hispanic swept beneath tables on which chairs had been stacked. The PA system played Sinatra. A heavy smell of tobacco and perfume hung like the red velvet drapes behind the small bandstand on which a set of drums and several electronic musical instruments stood abandoned like tools of war awaiting the next deafening battle. Illumination came from spotlights covered with red and blue gel. "Las Vegas Comes to D.C." a poster outside read.

"How goes it, Tony?" Smith asked as he joined him at the bar.

"*Mezza-mezza,*" Buffolino said. He looked up from the copy of *Variety* he'd been reading. "How come you never come in here, Mac?"

"Here I am."

"I mean at night when the action's going. You and Annabel come to the gala opening, then I never see you again. I got a dynamite show in here for a couple 'a weeks. The chick singer is a knockout, Mac, and I got a mimic who does the wildest obscure people you ever saw."

"That sounds safe . . . for a mimic," Smith said. "How is Alicia?"

Buffolino looked around before saying in a low voice, "Wonnerful. Loving and kind and drivin' me nuts." He sighed. "Things were good till we got married. You marry 'em, and they change."

"Ah, yes, I've heard that. And you should know, since this is not your first time around. Give her my best."

"I will. Same to Annabel. So, what brings you here? You sing? Always wanted to do stand-up comedy?"

"I was wondering if you were up to a job."

"PI stuff? Nah. Thanks, though. Too busy with the joint."

"Well, that settles that."

"You want a drink?"

"No, thanks."

Buffolino yelled in pidgin Spanish at the cleaning boy to bring them coffee.

"Not for me," Smith said, standing.

"Sit a minute, Mac. Relax. Coffee's not a drink. Good for your nerves. Keeps them hummin'. I kind of miss us talking." He grinned. Buffolino was a handsome man in a coarse, thick-featured way. He had sleepy, heavy-lidded eyes—bedroom eyes, they were once called. His was a fighter's face.

Smith ignored the liqueur Tony was offering but sipped the steaming hot mug of coffee set before him. "Too early in the day for anisette," he said.

"Might keep you awake, uh?"

"Something like that."

"What's the case, the priest?"

"Yes. How did you know?"

"When I'm not too busy, I watch a little TV. Your name came up. Somebody charged?"

"No, but on the assumption that someone will be at some point, I'm lining up what ducks I can."

"What would you want me to do?"

"Check into Father Singletary's background. Everything. Discreetly, though. I have to go out of town and don't want to lose time here. Annabel and I are leaving tomorrow for London on our honeymoon. We'll be back in a week. I have to find someone who can move on it. Need a report ready when I return."

"Yeah, well, Mac, maybe I could do it. Be good to get away from here for a while. Maybe good for Alicia 'n me, too. It's too close bein' together all the time. Yeah, I'll do it. What's a week? Besides, if I have to tell you the truth, and to you I *do* have to tell the truth, I'm not exactly what you'd call busy. Business is lousy."

"Sorry to hear it." Smith stood and clapped Buffolino on the back, then handed him an envelope. "A retainer. And the particulars on what we know so far."

Buffolino looked at the check. "This is a tenth, huh?"

"It's a third."

"Yeah? Okay, but only for you."

"Me and a house of God. Do you good to get out of this place and try another. Thanks. See you in a week."

"*Ciao,* baby."

Smith's last commitment before he and Annabel left for London was at the Sevier Home in Georgetown. He never seemed to find the time to visit his mother as much as he had promised himself he would, which always prompted a nagging feeling of guilt that was uncomfortable—and unnecessary, he reminded himself whenever it set in. For this visit, he had blocked out most of the afternoon.

They spent a good deal of it out in the gardens surrounded by English boxwood and huge azalea bushes, holly, and black walnut trees. Josephine Smith always insisted that her son stop and read a plaque in the ground along Azalea Walk:

> *The kiss of the sun for pardon,*
> *the song of the birds for mirth,*
> *one is nearer God's heart in a garden*
> *than anywhere else on earth.*

These times with his mother were always peaceful. They could also be inspirational or amusing when he was depressed. His mother was an unfailingly optimistic person. Her standard response to "How are you?" was "Wonderful. I got up this morning, took a breath, and it worked. What more could I ask for?"

They finished their visit by sitting on the expansive porch that overlooked the gardens. They were alone; another resident of the home played the piano—badly—on the other side of the window behind them. "Well, how does it feel to be a married man again?"

"Good," Smith said, taking his mother's hand in his. "I'm a very lucky man to have someone like Annabel."

"I wondered how long it would take you to come to that conclusion," said his mother. "You certainly dragged your feet."

He laughed. "Mother, you and Dad sent me to law school so that I would learn to weigh all the facts and not make snap judgments."

"No matter, it makes me feel good and proud that you and Annabel are now married. I never did like the arrangement you had."

"Why not? It worked very nicely."

"I like things tidied up, Mac. And the law to go with love. Marriage does that."

"Yes, it certainly does. I really have to be going. I still have things to do before we leave."

"London," she said wistfully. "It's been a long time since I've been there."

"We'll go soon, the three of us, maybe in the spring. The weather is better then."

Each knew what the other was thinking. As healthy and vivacious as Josephine Smith was, the reality that she was in the final phase of her life could not be denied. Would she be alive to take to London in the spring? Mac mused. He dearly hoped so. Although he didn't spend nearly enough time with her, he liked the fact that she was there, alive, that her first breath in the morning continued to "work," and that she was available to him. He didn't look forward to the day when she wouldn't be.

After Mac and Annabel's plane had passed Cape Cod and they had been served caviar and smoked salmon, Mac showed her the written autopsy report. When she was finished reading, she said, "Charming prose style. Anything in here strike you as unusual?"

"Yes."

"What?"

"The item about the weapon having been swung on a horizontal plane."

"Yes?"

"Paul was sitting in the pew when he was found. It seems to me that if you're going to hit a man while he's sitting, the blow would tend to come from over his head. You'd hit him more toward the top of the head, not the side."

"Uh-huh."

"So, it also seems to me that unless the murderer was crouching, it's unlikely that Paul was seated when he was killed, as the position of the body suggested."

Annabel thought for a moment. "Or he was hit by a short person.

Then again, it's possible that Paul was struck while standing and fell into the pew."

Smith shook his head. "No, he was sitting there, neat and proper. Sure, he was leaning against the wall, but his body was not in a position that would have resulted from falling there."

"What conclusion do you come to?" she asked.

"I have to assume that because the blow was delivered in a horizontal plane and not from above, you are right, that he was probably standing when he was hit. Then it doesn't make any sense that if he came upon an intruder, was hit, and fell to the floor, the intruder would take the time to prop him up in the pew. Hit-and-run assailants don't rearrange bodies, they just hit and run. It could have been someone he knew, but it was almost surely someone who knew the cathedral. When you add to this the lack of blood, it points to his being murdered somewhere other than in that small chapel and brought there."

"Even so, who would bother to do that? Why would someone do that? Wouldn't there be blood where he was killed?"

"Yes, there would be, unless the murderer did a hell of a good job of mopping up. MPD's been scouring the cathedral, but that's a lot of ground to cover and a lot of dark corners."

"Chances are it didn't happen far from that chapel. Paul was not heavy, but he certainly wasn't a wisp of a man. Maybe the garden outside Good Shepherd."

"Maybe, although the M.E.'s report said his clothes were clean, no grass stains or dirt."

"That doesn't mean they weren't there. I remember you delivering a lecture to one of your classes about how often routine things like that are missed during autopsies and clothing analysis."

"I know, I know, and you're probably right. It's not likely to have happened far from the chapel."

She put caviar, chopped egg and onion on a crustless toast wedge and savored it. Smith disliked caviar and had given his small jar of beluga to her, a ritual they always went through when flying first class. "Did Terry Finnerty raise this when you talked to him?"

"No. He simply handed me the report. No, that's not true. He handed me the report and asked me a lot of questions. I get the feeling he's being nice to me, is cooperating because he sees me as a conduit into the cathedral. He's going to be very disappointed."

As the shiny, immaculate black Austin taxi took them from Heathrow Airport to Duke's Hotel in the heart of London, Annabel snuggled close to her husband. "I've never been on a honeymoon," she said.

"Nor will you ever be on another one," he said.

They fell silent; she knew what he was thinking, that he'd spent his honeymoon with his first wife in London many years ago. They'd stayed at the Savoy, a favorite hotel of Smith's. He'd considered suggesting the

Savoy for Annabel, too, but thought better of it. Too much like bringing a new wife into the home of a former one. He and Annabel had stayed at Duke's on their last trip to London, and decided the little jewel tucked away in the middle of the St. James's district suited them perfectly, with its elegantly furnished suites, attentive staff, and convenient location.

The driver pulled into the tiny courtyard in front of Duke's and, as London taxis are designed to do, turned around, if not on a dime, certainly on a ha'penny. They were greeted with reserved but real enthusiasm at Reception. On previous visits, Mac had always signed them in as Mr. and Mrs. Mackensie Smith. This time he did it with quiet, proud conviction, and legitimately.

It was ten o'clock at night London time, but five hours earlier by their body clocks. The hall porter took their luggage to what would be their honeymoon suite, number 25 on the fourth floor, and Mac and Annabel walked into the small, cozy lounge. Gilberto, the barman, came around from behind the bar and shook Mac's hand, kissed Annabel on the cheek.

"Meet Mrs. Smith," Mac said.

Gilberto, who'd been smiling broadly, frowned. "I have met Mrs. Smith before," he said in his Italian accent.

"No you haven't," Mac said. "We've only been married two months."

The smile returned to Gilberto's face. "Ah, I understand. That deserves a celebration." He went behind the bar, and Mac and Annabel took the two barstools. There were three other couples at tables in the small room, and one pair had overheard the conversation. "Congratulations," the man offered.

Mac and Annabel turned and smiled. "Thank you," they said.

"Let me buy you a drink," the man said.

Gilberto placed his hands on the bar and said to the other customer, *"Grazie,* but this is my treat."

The bar in Duke's Hotel was known to many Londoners and American guests not only because of the professional charm of its barmen, Gilberto and Salvatore, but because they were supported by the hotel in an ongoing search for the rarest ports, cognacs, and Armagnacs. A dozen bottles stood on a special shelf behind the bar. There was an 1802 Napoleon cognac, an 1894 B. Gelas et Fils Armagnac, and a 1908 Ware's port. Only the port was unopened; it was on sale for £500, approximately $750. A one-third gill of the Napoleon cognac, barely enough to cover the bottom of a large snifter, cost £150, or about $225.

Gilberto took a half-empty bottle of Grahams 1945 port that sold for £40 per glass and carefully filled two small, elegantly etched aperitif glasses. He placed them in front of Mac and Annabel and said, *"Salute!* To love and marriage and to my good American friends."

Mac and Annabel held the glasses up to each other, then tasted. "Superb!" Smith said. They placed the glasses on the bar and continued to look at each other. Gilberto put the glasses on a small silver tray. "What suite?" he asked.

"Twenty-five," Smith said.

"I will take these to your room. You may prefer to be there."

Smith knew that Jeffrey Woodcock would insist upon dinner at Wilton's, a popular restaurant on Jermyn Street that served up traditional food in traditional ways in an atmosphere that was a little too stuffy and clubby for Smith's taste. Wilton's, he thought, was the sort of place that perpetuated the stereotype of British cooking as being bland, boiled, and without verve. It was precisely those qualities that attracted Woodcock to it, however. He was as clubby as the restaurant—a perfect match. There was one advantage to Wilton's for Mac and Annabel. It was within a few blocks of Duke's Hotel.

Judith Woodcock, whom Mac had met only once, was an animated woman with gray hair who doted on her husband, which he seemed to relish, and like him was given to repeating. She reminded Mac a little of his own mother, a younger version, of course—he knew Woodcock was sixty-two; Judith was probably within a year or two of that.

After a dinner that surprised Mac with its excellence, the four of them walked back to Duke's and settled at a corner table in the bar. The conversation eventually came around to what Mac called the subsidiary purpose of their visit to London—aside from honeymooning, of course.

"That's shocking, absolutely shocking," Woodcock said when Mac told him that Paul Singletary was the priest who'd married them. "Had no idea," Woodcock said. "I met the poor chap twice when he was over here discussing this Word of Peace project. Charming young man . . . well, perhaps not so young, but certainly charming. Yes, perfectly charming."

Smith pressed his knee against Annabel's beneath the table. She was in a discussion with Judith Woodcock, but Mac knew she was tuned in to both conversations with equally clear reception, something at which she was expert.

"How did you have occasion to meet him?" Smith asked.

"As I said, this peace project he was involved with. The church was reluctant to enter into any sort of supportive posture without consulting the firm for a legal opinion. We saw nothing wrong with it, although I must say there were some individuals involved who are not the sort of chaps I would invite to the club." Woodcock laughed; Mac smiled. "No, not to the club, or to Wilton's, for that matter. Still, nothing wrong with the movement. One can't very well be critical of efforts to bring peace to the world, can one?"

Smith shook his head. "No, one can't." Now I'm repeating, he thought.

"Do your police chaps have any leads?" Woodcock asked.

"Not yet," Smith replied. "One of the things I've promised the bishop of the National Cathedral I'd do while we're in London is to attempt to trace Paul's tracks during his last visit. He evidently returned to Washington a day earlier than he'd planned."

"That so? Why?"

"I don't know. I have a letter of introduction to the archbishop of Canterbury from Bishop St. James in Washington. I was hoping to learn something from him about Paul's visit."

"I can certainly pave the way for you over at Lambeth," Woodcock said. "I was there just the other day."

"You were?" Smith said. "Do you meet often with your clerical clients?"

Woodcock laughed; it had a certain forced ring to it. "No, just on occasion. When something comes up that needs discussion."

"Any talk of Paul Singletary's murder the last time you were there?"

"No, absolutely none." He didn't repeat "None." Smith knew his friend was not being honest.

"Word of Peace?" Smith asked.

"Pardon?"

"Word of Peace. Is that what you were meeting at Lambeth about?"

"No . . . well, yes, that is a continuing topic of discussion."

"The church . . . the archbishop, that is, has been supportive of the movement, I gather."

"Yes, quite."

"Do you deal with the archbishop himself?"

"No, almost never. Frankly, Mac, I'll be surprised if your letter gains you an audience with him. He sees very few people. Rumor has it he's not been well, but I can't confirm that. No, I deal with Reverend Malcolm Apt."

"I know the name. Our bishop mentioned him to me, indicated he's sort of an information officer for the church."

"Yes, that and many other things. He seems to be directly involved in almost every aspect of Lambeth, almost all aspects, a right-hand man-of-all-seasons for the archbishop."

"I intend to call him in the morning," said Smith, "see if I can arrange an interview with the archbishop."

"Well, as I said, don't count on it. Chances are you'll meet with Reverend Apt."

Annabel turned to Jeffrey Woodcock and said, as though she'd been part of the conversation, "You can see that this husband of mine plans a busy honeymoon."

Both the Woodcocks laughed. "Very clever of you, Mac," Jeffrey Woodcock said, "working in enough business to satisfy your Internal Revenue chaps back home. Write off your honeymoon. Damned clever, I'd say."

Smith didn't bother explaining that he hadn't even thought of that until Woodcock brought it up. They finished their drinks and walked the Woodcocks to where they'd parked their Jaguar on Jermyn Street. During the short walk, Smith had the feeling that Woodcock had something to tell him, perhaps a favor to ask, but was not sure whether he should. Smith's feeling was confirmed after Mrs. Woodcock was inside the Jag and Annabel was bidding a final good night to her through the open window. Smith and Woodcock stood next to the driver's door. "Mac," Woodcock said, "I was wondering if I could impose upon you while you're here for a bit of legal consultation. Frankly, I could use the American view of things."

"Go ahead," Smith said.

"Not here, not now. Would you be able to find some time tomorrow?"

Smith glanced over the roof of the automobile at Annabel, who didn't seem to be hearing the conversation. Did he dare build another business meeting into the honeymoon? He decided to take the chance, provided it didn't take more than a little conversation with Woodcock. They agreed to meet the following day at eleven at Woodcock's office.

Back in Suite 25, and bundled up in fluffy terry-cloth robes provided by the hotel, Smith asked Annabel what she thought of the Woodcocks.

"Very nice people. Very nice. Very nice." He laughed. She asked, "What are you meeting him for tomorrow?"

"You . . . ?" Yes, she did have a remarkable ability to tune in on two conversations at once, even across the roof of a car. "I don't know. He said he needed my counsel on something, a legal matter. I really couldn't say no. He did pick up dinner."

"No such thing as a free lunch," she said.

"No, there isn't." He looked at his watch. "I suddenly am very tired. How about settling in for a good sleep?"

"Sounds lovely. Will I see you at all tomorrow?"

"Of course. We'll meet for lunch. We have theater tickets and . . ."

"Sorry, Mac, can't make lunch. Business. I forgot to tell you that I called that collector, Pierre Quarle, and made a date with him for lunch tomorrow."

"You did. What's he like?"

"We've never met, but he sounds absolutely charming, a very cultivated French accent, almost kissing my hand over the phone."

They climbed into the king-size bed and pulled the covers up over them. "Will I see you after lunch?" Smith asked.

"Probably. Why don't we leave messages at Reception, and we'll coordinate, maybe have tea together."

"Sounds fine." He kissed her forehead and turned over.

She started to laugh.

He faced her. "What's funny?"

"Us. We are funny, funny that is, and I think we should enjoy every minute of it. Good night, Mr. Smith."

"Good night, Mrs. Smith." He rolled over again. After a moment of silence, he sat up, lifted her right hand from beneath the covers, kissed it, and said, *"Bonne nuit, ma minette en susucre."*

"What does that mean?"

"Good night, sugarpuss. And if the Frenchman kisses your hand, I'll send Tony over to break his knees."

As Smith and Annabel fell asleep at eleven o'clock London time, Joey Kelsch walked into St. Albans in Washington for his 6:00 P.M. meeting with Reverend Carolyn Armstrong. She hadn't explained why she wanted to see him and he'd tried to make an excuse, but she'd insisted. "It will only take a few minutes, Joey," she'd said. He hoped so.

They sat in the front pew of the small church. They were alone. Reverend Armstrong, who wore a stylishly tailored powder-blue suit over a starched white blouse, smiled warmly at the young boy. He returned the smile tentatively but avoided eye contact.

"Joey, I've been worried about you lately," she said. She placed her fingertips on his hand. "Are you all right?"

"Yes, sure. I'm fine."

"I was so upset for you when you became ill during Reverend Singletary's funeral."

"I'm sorry about that."

"No need to be sorry. It could happen to any of us. I was quite upset myself. Was it the flu?"

"Yes, ma'am."

"You look fine today."

"It was . . . just a stomach sickness. I think I ate something."

"Of course. Joey, I understand that you were working in the choir room the night Reverend Singletary was killed."

"No, I . . . only for a little while."

"Really? Reverend Nickelson said he'd assigned you a punishment until eleven that night."

"No . . . Well, he did, but I . . . I left."

"How early?"

"I . . . I knew Reverend Nickelson was gone that night, so I snuck out. I came in for a couple of minutes. Then I left. Honest."

"I believe you. Well, I was just wondering. You didn't hear anything or see anything that might have to do with what happened to Reverend Singletary that could be useful to the investigation?"

"No, ma'am. I wasn't there long. I left."

She sat back and smiled. "I was thinking how exciting it would be if you'd seen something that could help the police find out who killed Reverend Singletary. Wouldn't that be exciting for you?"

"No, ma'am. I didn't see anything. I swear."

"Fine. Okay, now I want you to promise that if you remember anything, or want to talk about anything . . . *anything* . . . that you'll come to me . . . first. Okay? Promise?"

"Yes, I promise."

"Good, Joey. Thank you for coming."

"Yes, ma'am."

He fairly ran down the aisle and out the door.

11

London, Monday Morning—
A.M. Precip; P.M. Partly Cloudy

AFTER A LEISURELY breakfast in a tea shop around the corner from Duke's, Mac flagged a taxi for Annabel and told her he'd call for messages at three. He returned to the suite, called Lambeth Palace, and asked for the archbishop. A minute later Malcolm Apt came on the line. Apt was cordial. He'd spoken with Bishop St. James about the possibility that Smith might call, and would be happy to meet at Smith's convenience. They settled on two that afternoon.

"I'll have a car pick you up at your hotel at one-thirty," said Apt.

"That isn't necessary. I'll be happy to—"

"Please, I insist. The driver will fetch you at the hotel."

"That's very kind, Reverend Apt. Thank you."

Smith took a brisk walk along Piccadilly, stopping to browse among the books in Hatchard's and the beautifully presented fancy foods in Fortnum and Mason, and ordered something he'd been promising himself for years, a pure silk umbrella custom-crafted for his height from Swaine Adeney, Brigg & Sons. He felt superb; he always did when he was in London (or maybe just because he was away from Washington). As always, he hoped that he could carry a slice of the good feeling back home.

Jeffrey Woodcock's law firm was on Old Bailey Street, two blocks from the Central Criminal Court. His office befitted a prestigious London barrister. Other than one that housed books from floor to ceiling, the walls were paneled in wood almost black in color. The furniture, including Woodcock's massive leather-inlaid desk, were antiques. The only thing that seemed out of place with the serene, time-warp image was Woodcock's personal secretary, Miss Amill, who was decidedly modern. She offered coffee or tea. Smith opted for coffee; Woodcock took the tea.

"Had enough tea since you've been here, Mac?" Woodcock asked.

"Not really, but I suppose I will by the time we leave."

"You'll have to drink three-point-six-two cups a day to keep up with us."

"Interesting statistic," Smith said. "Where did you come up with that number?"

"Read it in *The Times* this morning. Silly. Some study commissioned by a tea company, no doubt. Silly."

"Or a coffee company about to release its next study that more than two cups of tea a day is bad for your health."

Woodcock laughed softly and lifted the cup and saucer to just below his lips. He placed his cup and saucer on the table without drinking and said with furrowed brow, "Mac, you've had a great deal of experience in criminal matters."

"I used to. I teach it now. There's a difference."

"Yes, quite, but it isn't as though you've abandoned crime to teach biology or the decline of the British empire."

"Never practiced crime, Jeffrey. I just teach how to help criminals get away with it. Do you have a criminal case you need some advice on?"

"Potentially." Woodcock carefully formulated his next words. "This is a highly delicate matter, Mac, and despite the fact that we are colleagues, I would not have brought this up with you if you had not already become involved with the church over this tragic Singletary affair."

"I'm listening."

"I indicated last night—splendid evening, by the way . . . your new wife is a ravishing creature and so intelligent, too—I mentioned that I had met Father Singletary on two occasions, both having to do with the Word of Peace movement. That was true."

"And?"

"And . . . and the second meeting—the third, actually—had absolutely nothing to do with law or the church. Mrs. Woodcock and I took a long weekend in the Cotswolds the day after my second meeting with Father Singletary. We have a favorite place in Broadway . . . Buckland, actually, but Buckland really isn't much to talk about. At any rate, we particularly enjoy a hotel there called the Buckland Manor. Lovely spot, lovely."

"Was Paul Singletary there?" Smith asked, assuming it was the connection Woodcock was getting to.

"Yes, he was. You can imagine how surprised I was to drive two hours out of London and see him again after having been with him only a day earlier."

"He was staying at Buckland Manor?"

"Yes."

"Did you find some additional time to talk about Word of Peace?"

"No, we didn't. In fact, after we bumped into him as we were coming into the hotel, Father Singletary seemed to make a point of avoiding us."

"Why would he do that?"

"I suppose because he considered his circumstances to be somewhat awkward. That's speculation on my part, of course."

"What circumstances?"

"He was spending the weekend there with an extremely attractive woman."

Smith silently wished the sexual cynics in his class were there with him to hear this.

Woodcock cleared his throat. "Of course, Mac, Mrs. Woodcock was slightly taken aback once I told her who he was. It meant nothing to me, of course. I really don't concern myself with such things."

"No, of course not."

At this point Smith was wondering why he'd been called to meet with Woodcock. Bumping into an Episcopal priest with a beautiful woman on his arm in a hotel was mildly titillating but hardly grist for the collective legal brains sitting in Woodcock's office.

"I never would have given this a second thought, Mac, until three days ago."

"What happened three days ago?"

"I received a call from Reverend Apt at Lambeth."

"I spoke with him this morning. We're meeting at two."

"Good. Father Apt's call to me sounded quite urgent. He was upset. You couldn't miss that on the phone. I went to Lambeth, and we spent an hour discussing the situation. It seems that Malcolm Apt had been visited earlier in the day by a young woman who brought him disturbing news."

Mac's mind was now drawing intriguing scenarios. Was it the same woman Woodcock had seen with Singletary at Buckland Manor? Every time he speculated on what Woodcock was about to say next, he was right. It made him feel good. If only it didn't take so much time.

"Switch to tea, Mac?" Woodcock asked.

"No, Jeffrey, thank you. I want to save my three-point-six-two cups for Annabel."

Woodcock laughed. "Jolly good, Mac. Well, this young woman's name is Clarissa Morgan."

"The same woman you saw with Father Singletary in Broadway, I take it."

Woodcock slapped his hands on his knees and leaned forward. "Exactly! Exactly!"

"How can you be sure?" Smith asked. "You only saw her once at Buckland Manor. Was she introduced to you as Clarissa Morgan?"

"No, but he did mumble her first name, which I seem to recall was Clarissa. Can't be two different women."

Smith stifled the temptation to point out that despite his friend's preeminent position in British law circles, his logic tended on occasion to be shaky. Instead, Smith asked, "Did she indicate to Reverend Apt what this so-called disturbing news was?"

"No. She told him that she'd been Paul Singletary's lover right up until his death. In fact, she claimed that she'd been with Father Singletary the night before he died, that they'd slept together at her flat."

"Hardly the stuff blackmail is made of. Unless she's married. She's looking for money?"

"Yes. She told Reverend Apt that Singletary owed her a large sum, and that she was not looking for anything more than what had been promised her. She also hinted that if she revealed her past—and present—she could uncover much unpleasant news about Singletary's involvement with her and with other causes and institutions, yes, that's what she said: causes and institutions."

" 'What had been promised her'? In return for what?"

"She wouldn't be specific with Apt. She suggested that he call her in a few days. He's naturally reluctant to do that, which is why he contacted me. He wants *me* to call her."

"I suppose you'll know a great deal more after that call. How can I help?"

"I thought perhaps *you* might make that call."

"Why me?"

"To be candid with you, Mac, the major concern here is to keep our client, the Church of England, as far away from scandal as possible. Far away. The fact that this firm and I have been closely linked for many years with the church makes me a part of this institution, too, makes it a bit sticky, if you catch my drift. Also, I thought direct contact might be useful to you in your investigation."

Smith rubbed his eyes. On the one hand, he was not interested in trying to resolve an apparent blackmail attempt by Miss Clarissa Morgan. He had other things to do, including enjoying his honeymoon. On the other hand, if she had been as close to Paul Singletary as she claimed, she could be a valuable source of information, one he didn't want to walk away from.

"It's an odd request but all right, Jeffrey, I'll call her."

Woodcock gave Smith notes he'd made during his meeting with Reverend Apt. Written on the bottom were Clarissa Morgan's name and telephone number.

"You will let me know what comes out of the conversation," Woodcock said as he helped Smith put on his raincoat.

"Of course. I'm not sure I'll call her today, but certainly by tomorrow. You'll hear from me."

The maroon Ford dispatched by Lambeth Palace to pick up Smith was too big to navigate Duke's tiny courtyard. The driver left the car on narrow St. James's Street, the tires on its right side up on the sidewalk, and walked Smith to it from the hotel. "Having a good stay, sir?" he asked as he opened the door.

"Yes, very. I always do when I'm in your great city."

They crossed Lambeth Bridge and pulled up in front of the main entrance to the palace.

"Will you be waiting for me?" Smith asked.

"Yes, sir, I was told to wait."

Smith was greeted at the door by a woman who introduced herself as the bursar. She led him to a small, comfortably furnished study, where the Reverend Malcolm Apt was waiting.

"Welcome to Lambeth Palace, Mr. Smith," Apt said.

"Thank you for seeing me," replied Smith. "And thank you for providing a car. It really wasn't necessary."

"Our pleasure. I hope you don't think we have a fleet of automobiles at our disposal. We don't own the autos, but we have a rather good arrangement with a local car hire."

"It was a very comfortable ride, although I think a large Ford is a little inappropriate for London's narrow streets."

"I've told the car-hire company that very thing. I suppose their attitude is that when driving a dignitary, a large vehicle is in order. Please, sit down." He pointed to a cream-colored couch in the center of the room. A two-shelf bookcase ran along part of the wall opposite where Smith sat. Above it was a window that faced the chapel. Walls and ceiling were covered in oak paneling; a set of gold drapes covered another wall, in front of which was a chair that matched the sofa. Apt sat in it.

"This is called the Old Paneled Room," Apt said. "It was originally Archbishop Cranmer's study, but that goes back a few hundred years."

Smith laughed. "Everything in England goes back a few hundred years. When was Archbishop Cranmer in residence?"

"Fifteen thirty-three. He stayed around quite a while, more than twenty years. He presided over the special commission in 1543. That was when the London clergy took the Oath of Supremacy."

"There was some controversy surrounding it, wasn't there? Something to do with Sir Thomas More?"

"You have an excellent memory for history, Mr. Smith. Sir Thomas More was the only layman invited to the commission. He refused to take the oath giving the king powers over the church. So did the bishop of Rochester. They walked out, and paid dearly for their decision. But, Mr. Smith, as much as I enjoy talking history with you, I'm certain your schedule doesn't allow it."

"Unfortunately, it doesn't." Smith pulled from his jacket the letter of introduction to the archbishop of Canterbury from Bishop St. James and handed it to Apt. Apt placed half-glasses on his nose, read the letter, removed the glasses, and said, "I'm afraid it is quite impossible to meet personally with the archbishop. I assure you, however, that every aspect of our conversation will be transmitted to him, and I will relay to you his responses."

As cordial as Apt was being, Smith didn't like him. He reminded Smith of miscellaneous middle-level managers in corporations who reflect the power of their bosses, or secretaries to physicians who bask in their employers' inflated sense of lofty calling. He also had the feeling that Apt had the ability to talk for an hour about things that had no bearing upon the purpose of any meeting—like Jeffrey Woodcock. British genes, or public-school training?

Smith got to the point. "I've come to London for two reasons, Reverend Apt. The first, at least the one that prompted the trip, was to take my wife of a few months on a honeymoon."

Apt smiled weakly. He did not offer congratulations.

"The second reason has to do with the murder of Reverend Paul Singletary."

"What tragic news that was. It saddened all of us, including the archbishop."

"It's my understanding that Paul Singletary had a meeting with you the day before he died. Is that correct?"

Apt adopted a thoughtful expression. He rolled his fingertips over his thumb and narrowed his eyes. "Yes, I suppose it was. I'm trying to fix the time of Reverend Singletary's death. Yes, we met the day before."

"It is my assumption that the purpose of the meeting was to discuss Word of Peace."

"Among other things."

"Did Reverend Singletary get to speak with the archbishop?"

"No, he did not."

"Why did Reverend Singletary feel it necessary to speak with the archbishop? Was he disappointed when he couldn't?"

"Yes. I was not especially pleased to be the one to tell him that the archbishop's enthusiasm for Word of Peace had diminished in recent months."

"None of us likes to be the bearer of bad news. Why has the archbishop's enthusiasm diminished?"

"A number of reasons. Some of the movement's leaders are not to the archbishop's liking. Then, too, there is the matter of money."

"Money given to Word of Peace?"

"Yes." Apt sighed. "We may be a religious institution, Mr. Smith, but finances do play an important role in how we conduct and manage our faith. We, too, must deal with a bottom line."

Smith thought of George St. James, who seemed always to be in the pursuit of funds. He also wondered whether Apt was hinting at some possible financial indiscretion. He decided to be direct: "Was Paul Singletary under suspicion by you or the archbishop concerning use of Word of Peace funds?"

Apt answered quickly. "No, although Reverend Singletary, for a man caught up in questions of poverty—among other things—was not what you'd call the most frugal of men." Apt's expression said clearly to Smith that this phase of the conversation was over.

"It's my understanding that Reverend Singletary had intended to return to Washington two days after his meeting with you," Smith said.

"Obviously, he returned a day earlier than planned. Do you have any idea why?"

Apt formed a tent with his fingertips and said over it, "No idea whatsoever. In fact, I asked how long he was staying, and he told me he was visiting the countryside. Yes, what he said exactly was 'your limpid countryside.' I remember it well. I hadn't heard anyone describe our countryside as limpid before."

"I'd say it's an apt description." Smith decided not to add the usual "no pun intended." "Do you know where in the country he intended to visit?"

"No, I really don't."

Smith didn't believe him. "I remember from conversations with Reverend Singletary that he was especially fond of the Cotswolds. Did he ever talk about his love of that area with you?"

Apt shook his head.

"Did Reverend Singletary say anything to you that would give me an idea of what he might have done after his meeting with you, whom he might have seen, had dinner or tea with, perhaps gone to the theater with?"

Another flat negative.

Smith leaned back on the couch and shook his head. "I'm afraid this may have been a wasted meeting, Reverend Apt. Of course, I enjoyed meeting you, but I was hoping to gain some insight into Reverend Singletary's movements while he was here. I'm sure you can understand how that could be helpful in solving his murder."

"You are an investigator, Mr. Smith?"

"As Bishop St. James's letter indicates, I am a professor of law at George Washington University. My wife and I have been attending services at the National Cathedral for some time, and I am a personal friend of Bishop St. James, and was a friendly acquaintance of Paul Singletary. In fact, Reverend Singletary officiated at my wedding." Smith stood. "You've been very gracious with your time, Reverend Apt. I appreciate that."

"Please call on me at any time, Mr. Smith. Would you like a tour of the palace? I could arrange to have someone take you right now."

"Tempting, but I have other commitments. Thank you for offering."

Smith's driver returned him to the hotel. As he got out, he said, "Thank you very much. By the way, my name is Mackensie Smith." He extended his hand through the open driver's window.

The driver smiled and shook Smith's hand. "Pleasure to serve you, Mr. Smith. Name's Bob."

There was a message at Reception from Annabel: *Taking tea with Mr. Quarle at the Ritz at four. Please join us if you can. Love, Annabel.*

Smith went to the suite and called the Buckland Manor in Broadway. "My name is Mackensie Smith. My wife and I are staying in London but thought it would be nice to go to the Cotswolds for a few days.

Jeffrey Woodcock, a law associate, recommended you highly. Would you have a room for two nights beginning tomorrow?"

"Yes, sir, we do."

"Look, this is sort of a honeymoon for us. I'd appreciate the best room you have."

"The Vaulted Room is available. It's our finest."

"Sounds perfect." He gave his credit-card number and hung up.

His next call was to the number for Clarissa Morgan given him by Jeffrey Woodcock. "Miss Morgan, my name is Mackensie Smith. I'm an American attorney representing the National Cathedral in Washington, D.C. I was also a friend of Reverend Paul Singletary."

"Yes?"

"I've been asked to call regarding certain claims made by you to Reverend Malcolm Apt at Lambeth Palace."

There was a pause. "Why would you call me about this?"

"Because of my close involvement with the Washington Cathedral and Reverend Singletary. One of my purposes in London is to try to trace his movements just prior to his return to Washington and his murder. I understand you were with him the night before."

"Mr. Smith, I find this most distressing. I don't know who the hell you are. You make certain claims, but as far as I know, you're nothing more than a very glib obscene caller."

Smith had to laugh. "Miss Morgan, I may be many things, but certainly not that. Would you be willing to spend half an hour with me? I think this might work a lot better in person."

She sighed.

"I assure you I am what I represent myself to be, and that I might be able to resolve your claim. But only if we talk."

"I'm busy tonight."

"Fine." He thought to try softening her up. And maybe open her up. "My wife and I are going to the country tomorrow, to the Cotswolds. Are you familiar with a hotel there called Buckland Manor?"

"No."

"It was highly recommended to us by a mutual friend. If you're available tomorrow, however, I'll be glad to postpone our trip."

Another sigh. "I am engaged for the next two days."

I'll bet you are. "Then our schedules coincide nicely. Can we arrange a time to meet the day after I'm back?"

"Why don't you call me then."

"All right. I look forward to seeing you."

Smith shaved before walking the few blocks to the Ritz. As he entered the lavish lobby, London's most famous gathering place for tea, he had two thoughts. One was that he would have to finesse Annabel into accepting his sudden decision to leave the city for two days in the country. He hoped she hadn't made too many unbreakable plans in London.

His second thought was that he wouldn't bother waiting for Tony if this Pierre Quarle character kissed *his* hand. He'd take care of the Frenchman's knees himself.

12

The Next Day, Tuesday—
Warm Sunshine. Perfect Weather for a Drive on the "Wrong" Side

"I DON'T KNOW the man I married," Annabel said as Smith deftly navigated a series of roundabouts outside Oxford and found the road marked RING ROAD WEST.

"Why do you say that?"

"Because if I had to come up with a list of adjectives to describe Mackensie Smith, 'impetuous' would not be on it. I can't believe you simply decided to spend a few days in the Cotswolds, picked up the phone, and did it."

"I thought it would be a nice change for us on our honeymoon. After all, there is more to the United Kingdom than London, and this Buckland Manor is supposed to be superb."

She sighed contentedly and watched the rolling emerald-green hills, hills dotted with picturesquely placed sheep, slide by. She knew this was more than an impulsive fling in the country. Mac had told her of his conversations with Jeffrey Woodcock, Malcolm Apt, and Clarissa Morgan, and that he wanted to poke around a little at Buckland Manor about Paul Singletary's weekend there, apparently with Clarissa Morgan, no matter how much Miss Morgan might deny knowing the place. He had promised Annabel, however, that his poking would consume a minimal amount of their time. The fact was—something Annabel hadn't told him—she'd begun to enjoy the "business" aspect of their trip. It added a certain element of extra excitement and purpose.

She looked at her husband. His expression was intense—no, concentrated was more like it—as he shifted gears with his left hand and met the challenge of driving on the left. There had been a few harrowing moments in London as they tried to find the A40 out of the city, but she'd read the map well, leaving him free to deal with the mechanics of avoiding double-decker buses and other city traffic, all having wandered into the wrong lane.

They stopped in the quaint village of Broadway and strolled its main shopping street. Annabel went into a woolen-goods outlet while Mac stood outside and watched people pass by. He leaned against the building, turned his face to the sun, and closed his eyes. Annabel interrupted his reverie. "I can't make up my mind between two sweaters," she said. "Come help me choose."

Her purchases in the trunk of their rented automobile—he'd recommended both sweaters—they left Broadway on the road Mac had been instructed to take when he'd made the reservation. Ten minutes later they were on a long, graceful access road leading to the magnificent thirteenth-century manor house called Buckland Manor. Before they could open the car doors, a young man and woman came down the steps. "We've been on the lookout for you," said Nigel, the hotel's manager.

"Your directions were excellent," Smith said. "This is Mrs. Smith."

"Welcome to Buckland Manor, Mrs. Smith," said Nigel's pretty assistant, Tracy. "Someone will be out to take your bags. Please, come inside."

Annabel started up the steps but paused. "How beautiful," she said, referring to a stone church next to the hotel. Its rectory was part of the main building.

"Yes, a splendid example of twelfth-century Norman architecture," Tracy said proudly. "You must visit it while you're here."

They were escorted to the Vaulted Room, accurately named because of the way the white ceiling arched up high above. When they were alone, Annabel said, "Mac, it's absolutely magnificent." She hugged him. "I'm so glad you did this." She explored the expansive, tastefully decorated room. The walls were covered in a pale blue paper with a tiny white design. Curtains defining a series of bay windows were the color of cream; a pattern of small roses gave them a nice touch of blush. The large four-poster bed was covered in the same cream-and-rose fabric, as were skirt tables on either side of it. On a table in front of a love seat was a vase of pink gloxinia, a large basket of fruit, and two bottles of Cotswold spring water.

"You make me a very happy bride," Annabel said as they stood at a window and looked out over pastures belonging to the hotel. Rare Jacob sheep stood like clusters of mushrooms in one; two huge Highland steer leaned against each other in another. "I'm happy we came here," she said. "I knew you were smart, but this was a stroke of brilliance."

"Shucks," Smith said, executing a perfect toe-in-sand. "Thank Jeffrey. Jeffrey, that is."

After unpacking, they sat on the love seat and discussed what they would do during their stay.

"I just want to hang around," Mac said. "I want to ask people in the hotel and the village about Paul."

"Why do you think anyone would remember him?" she asked. "As far as you know, he was only here once, the weekend Woodcock and his wife bumped into him."

"Yes, I know, but I have this feeling that he had more of a connection to this place than that. It's my understanding that he always incorporated a trip to the country when he was in London on business. He'd told Reverend Apt that he intended to spend the next day in, as Apt recalls, the 'limpid countryside.' And then there's Clarissa Morgan denying she knows of this hotel. Of course, that could just be embarrassment at having spent a clandestine weekend with a priest. I don't know, Annabel, I just wouldn't feel right not following up on it."

"Well, I am very glad you feel that way, because I am beginning to feel utterly relaxed for the first time in ages."

"Good. If there's one thing a honeymoon should provide it's relaxation." He smiled. "Part of the time anyway."

Nigel, the manager, joined them briefly at dinner that night in the hotel's dining room. Smith asked him about the adjoining St. Michael's Church and was told that it served the villages of Buckland and Laverton. Services were conducted by a traveling Anglican priest. "A nice enough chap with an appropriate name."

"What is it?" Smith asked.

"The Reverend Robert Priestly."

Smith smiled. "A classic case of preordination."

"Yes, quite," Nigel said.

"We have a friend back in Washington who's also an Anglican priest," Annabel said. "He's been a guest here."

"What's his name?" Nigel asked.

"Paul Singletary," Smith said.

Nigel smiled. "Of course. Reverend Singletary has been here on more than one occasion. He and Reverend Priestly are chums."

"I see," Smith said. "I hope we get a chance to meet Reverend Priestly."

"You undoubtedly will," Nigel said. He asked about their plans for the next day.

"I've been reading the guidebooks," Annabel said. "I know there's wonderful shopping, but I hate to waste the precious two days we have doing that. I'm a bit of an amateur bird-watcher. I brought my binoculars and a new camera, and picked up a guide to birds of the United Kingdom. Maybe I'll just spend tomorrow walking and looking."

"Sounds like a splendid idea," said Nigel. "We have a special map for walkers. I'll see that you have it straight away."

"Wonderful!" Annabel looked at Smith. "Feel like joining me, Mac?"

"Do you mind if I don't?"

"Not at all. You do your snooping around, and I'll spend the day with nature."

It was over dessert that Mac mentioned a man eating alone at a table at the opposite end of the room. "He checked in right after us," he said.

"Are you especially interested in him?"

"Not at all, although we probably should introduce ourselves. It's like we made the trip from London together. His car followed us pretty much all the way, and he stopped in Broadway when we did."

"Unusual to see a single man in a hotel like this."

"A salesman, maybe, or waiting for someone. Maybe waiting for us."

"Let's invite him to join us for dinner tomorrow night," Annabel said.

"Let's not. This is our honeymoon. The two of us are the right company. Oh, I get it—you jest."

The next morning they enjoyed a sumptuous full English breakfast. Annabel wore a navy-blue sweat suit and sneakers, and carried a warm jacket. It had turned colder overnight, and fog now veiled the verdant countryside.

"Sure you want to walk in this soup?" Smith asked.

"It enhances the charm," she said. "Besides, it will add drama to the pictures I take." The small automatic camera Smith had bought her for her last birthday joined the binoculars around her neck. In her hand was the simple map provided by Nigel, and the bird book.

"Sure you know where you're going?" Smith asked.

Annabel opened the folded map, and they looked at it together. According to Nigel, much of the route was marked with small yellow arrows posted on trees, although it wouldn't be necessary to look for them until she reached Laverton by paved road. From there, it would be mostly open fields on her way to Stanton Village and up to the old quarry on Cotswold Ridge. It would be downhill from there, Nigel had assured her. He'd also discreetly pointed out that the only public house she would pass on the hike was called the Mount Inn, just outside Stanton. His final suggestion was that since she'd be walking through many pastures, it would be wise to look before she stepped.

Smith looked up at the somber, leaden sky. A gentle breeze swirled the fog around them like steam. They couldn't see the road from the front steps of the hotel. "Why don't you wait until tomorrow for your walk?" he suggested.

"No, this weather really inspires me, Mac. Please don't worry. I'll be fine. Have you ever seen a more tranquil place in your life? The fog even adds a sense of comfort, like being wrapped in a blanket."

Smith grunted. Her romantic interpretation of the day's weather didn't jibe with his. "Well," he said, "if you're not back in the two hours Nigel says it takes for the walk, I'm sending out the Mounties."

"How exciting. But wrong country. I'll be sure to take my time."

Charlie, Buckland Manor's resident bearded collie, came bounding up to them. "Go inside," Annabel said. "You can't come with me." A note in each room asked guests not to take Charlie for a walk without a leash. Some local sheep farmers didn't appreciate Charlie's penchant for chasing their flocks and had threatened to shoot him if he came on their property again. Annabel opened the front door and the dog slunk inside.

Mac and Annabel kissed lightly, and she started up the long drive leading to the road, turning twice to wave. Smith missed the second one because the fog had obliterated her from view.

He went back inside and warmed his hands in front of one of three fires kept going day and night in the public rooms.

"Tea, Mr. Smith?" Tracy asked.

"Yes, I'd love some." When he was served, he asked her, "How can I make contact with Reverend Priestly today?"

"I really don't know, but I'll find out."

She returned a few minutes later. "I called the cathedral in Gloucester," she said. "You are in luck. Father Priestly is scheduled to be here today for a parish meeting. He's due to arrive about eleven."

It was eight-thirty. "Good," Smith said. "I think I'll take a ride to some of the neighboring villages. I'll be back by eleven. If you happen to see Father Priestly, please mention I'd like a word with him."

"Certainly. Enjoy your tea and sightseeing, Mr. Smith, but drive carefully. This fog is the worst I've seen in a long time, and I've seen plenty of it."

Annabel walked slowly along the narrow paved road into Laverton. The ancient row houses lining the road were all constructed of the yellow brick characteristic of the Cotswolds. She reached a red telephone booth that was indicated on the map, crossed the road, and climbed over a low gate, using a crude wooden step that had been provided for walkers. A yellow arrow on the fence post pointed in a direction that would take her across a large grazing wold. The fog seemed to have thickened, if that were possible; she could see vague forms of animals in the distance. Sheep, small cattle? It was hard to determine most of the time. The silence and tranquillity were palpable as she hugged the side of a low stone wall that bordered the field. She heard the call of a bird, stopped, and trained her binoculars on trees immediately to her right. A swallow of some kind. She considered looking it up in her book, but decided not to bother. If she did that every time she spotted a bird, she'd get back to the hotel at midnight.

She continued her walk until reaching Stanton, where she stood in the middle of the deserted main road and took in her surroundings. She saw few birds, but one house was more beautiful than the next, and she snapped some pictures. Where are the people? she wondered.

A church, St. Michael and All Angels', stood in the V where two roads intersected. She meandered through the graveyard studded with ancient stones and approached the door. The sound of a car caused her to stop and to turn. A tan Ford Escort driven by a man moved slowly past the church and disappeared around the corner. All was silent again.

Annabel stood in the middle of the damp, musty church and pondered what it must have been like centuries ago when the faithful came to worship on Sunday mornings. How many hands had shaped the stone and fashioned the stained-glass windows? The ends of some of the wooden pews had been deeply gouged by chains that secured sheepdogs accompanying their masters to church. She looked up at the Gothic pulpit and imagined the words spoken from it to the poor, hardworking members of the congregation.

She looked down; she was standing on a large slab of stone with a skull and crossbones etched into it. She crouched and rubbed her hand over the writing. A man named John Ingles had been buried there in 1705. Below his name was written: JUST IN HIS ACCOUNTS; FAITHFUL TO HIS FRIENDS; MILD IN HIS TEMPER; CONSTANT TO THE END.

How nice to be remembered that way, Annabel thought as she retraced her steps to the front entrance, pausing to drop coins into a poor box.

She walked up a short road leading to the Mount Inn. The agreeable, pungent smell of smoke from the inn's chimney almost physically pulled her up the steep incline and into the cozy interior where a few locals drank and shared stories. One man read the local newspaper, the *Village Voice*, which bore no resemblance to its namesake in New York. Annabel sat at a small table across from the fireplace, where logs arranged vertically crackled, sending orange flames dancing up into the flue. An old woman behind the bar asked if she wanted something. It was too early for anything alcoholic, at least for Annabel, so she asked for a cup of tea. Soon she was sipping the steaming, strong brew and felt herself sinking deeper into the chair as she reached a state of mental and physical détente with herself and her surroundings. Everything was so perfect now. She was married to a man she loved deeply, she was able to indulge her love of pre-Columbian art with her gallery, and she was on her honeymoon in this beautiful place. Sometimes things could be perfect in one's life, not often and never for long, but sometimes. This was a moment she would cherish.

She paid for the tea and continued her walk, taking snapshots as she went. Soon, she'd run out of road again and was moving across vast fields, their green grass rendered even more vivid in the unnatural light created by the fog. Everywhere she looked were shapes, shadows, blurred images of livestock, and the economic backbone of the Cotswolds, its sheep. They would suddenly be there, then disappear just as quickly as the fog made them invisible to her.

The walk to the quarry was now uphill, and Annabel felt it in her legs. "You're out of shape, Annie," she muttered, her breath coming fast, her stride becoming more purposeful as she sought the Cotswold Ridge. From there, Nigel had promised, it would all be downhill.

When she reached the quarry, she sat for twenty minutes on a stone wall. Revived, she tried to follow the crude arrows on the hand-drawn map provided by Nigel. A half hour later she knew she was lost in a sea of washed green and surrounded by an opaque fog.

In the distance to her right was a line of black stick shapes. Trees. The ground sloped slightly to her left. Which way back to Laverton? she wondered. She'd never been very good at directions. But she had to make a decision. She decided to go in the downhill direction, away from the trees. Eventually, she reasoned, she'd have to reach something, someone. After ten minutes she paused and looked back at the row of trees. Something was moving up there. What was it? She squinted in an attempt to pierce the fog. *It* was heading her way. Now she could see that it was . . . someone on horseback. "Wonderful," she said aloud and laughed, suddenly thinking of Mac's promise to send "the Mounties." She'd stop the rider and ask directions back into Laverton. But first, she'd take a picture of this scene that was so eerily beautiful. She pressed off a couple of frames as the figure on horseback, shrouded in the wet fog, headed for her.

The figure was now close enough to be distinguishable. It looked to Annabel to be a woman on the horse, a woman dressed in full riding regalia. The horse was huge and powerful. When it was a hundred yards from Annabel, it suddenly broke out of its slow canter and bore down upon her. It took Annabel a second to react, to realize that she was about to be trampled. She flung herself to one side just as the horse reached her, its powerful hooves thundering close to her head, and kicking up mud and dung as they struck the earth in passing.

Annabel had fallen sharply on her left shoulder and the side of her face. She touched her cheek. There was blood on her fingertips. When she sat up, she looked in the direction the horse and rider had gone. She couldn't see me, she thought: the fog. "Idiot! You damn near killed me." She pulled herself to her feet. Her entire left side was covered with mud. She was trying to remove some of it when she heard . . . hoofbeats. The shapes reappeared, the horse and rider heading for her again. This time she had more time to react. She ran in the direction of a stone wall, slipping, sliding, stumbling, grasping at the fog as though it could be used for support. She looked back once and saw that the rider had directed the horse to turn after her. Gasping for breath, her lungs and heart throbbing with pain, she reached the wall and threw herself over it. The hoofbeats stopped. A moment's silence. Annabel was afraid to look over the wall, but knew she had to. As she began to raise her head, the horse and rider turned and vanished into the fog.

Annabel wasn't sure what to do next. She needed time to pull herself together before continuing, but was reluctant to stay there. When would the rider return? One thing she knew for certain; she couldn't cross any open fields, would have to stick close to fences and walls.

An hour later she sloshed through the deep mud of a Laverton farmer's pigpen, climbed the fence, and reached the center of town. There wasn't a soul on the street. She was still shaking and knew she was wambling as she headed for the marked pathways that would take her back to the hotel. She was almost out of the village when she froze. A large black Labrador, its fangs bared and threatening growls coming from its throat, appeared from behind one of the stone cottages. "Get away, get away!" Annabel shouted. The dog stopped a few feet from her and continued to growl. "No! Get away, I said!" Annabel yelled.

A window in the cottage opened, and a woman stuck her head out. "Don't be yelling at him. He won't hurt you. He doesn't bite."

"Well, you're sure not going to prove that by me," Annabel snapped. "Get him away from me."

The woman called the dog's name. The animal backed off, still growling, and returned to the back of the cottage.

Annabel's legs were jelly, and she had trouble catching her breath, neither condition abating by the time she reached Buckland Manor. She entered the small foyer and collapsed on a bench, starting to sob. Nigel and Tracy ran from the office. "What's the matter?" he asked. "You look a fright."

Annabel looked up at them. "I've had a terrible experience."

"Your face is bruised," Tracy said.

"I know." Annabel looked down at the legs of her sweat suit, which were covered with mud and sheep dung. She trembled, deeply chilled. "Please, I just want to get to my room and take a hot bath. Is my husband here?"

Tracy looked at a clock on the wall. "He took a drive but said he'd be back at eleven to see Reverend Priestly." It was twenty to eleven.

"Come," Nigel said. "We'll help you upstairs."

They brought her tea and a bottle of port. Once she assured them that she was all right, they left her alone. She soaked in the tub, but as soothing as its warmth was, she could not stop the internal shaking.

Wrapped in the hotel bathrobe, she poured herself some port and gulped it down, then did it again. She also had tea. Soon, the trembling began to subside, and she was able to focus more clearly on what had happened.

There was a knock on the door. "Come in," she said. "No, wait—who is it?"

"Nigel." He came into the room. "Just checking on you, Mrs. Smith. Feeling better?"

"Yes, much, thank you. Is my husband back?"

"No, but we're keeping an eye out for him. He'll have been slowed up in the fog. We'll send him up the moment he arrives."

"Thank you. You're all very kind."

"Anything to be of help. We feel distressed that we sent you out like this, and it turned out to be such an awful morning. What did happen to you, Mrs. Smith?"

Annabel leaned her head back against the love seat. "I'm really not sure," she said, "but I'll be happy to share it with you once I've figured it out myself."

"As you wish." Nigel lighted the gas fireplacc and said he would be available for anything she needed.

Mac Smith parked on the street side of St. Michael's opposite the hotel and near the church's main entrance. He assumed that Priestly would be in the church holding his parish meeting. Smith was a few minutes late. If Priestly was not there, he'd look for him in the hotel.

The church was empty. And cold. Dank. Smith peered up at the high ceiling created of wainscoting that had been intricately decorated. The unworldly, fog-filtered light from outside passed without purposeful effect through large stained-glass windows depicting Baptism, Marriage, and Extreme Unction.

Might as well check at the hotel, Smith thought as he walked toward the rear door. He would not have stopped, would not have seen anything more, if the interesting ornate carvings on the high backs of some of the pews hadn't caught his eye. He stopped and ran his fingers over the carvings, and glanced down and saw a shoe—a man's black shoe. Smith bent over. His eyes traveled up the length of a man's black trousers, then to the torso and its clerical collar, and finally to the head. His mouth and eyes were open. The man was, Smith judged, in his midforties, certainly no older than fifty. His gray hair was short, a crew cut, actually. Just above the ear on the side of the head that faced up was a long, oozing wound that had intruded deeply into the skull. A bloodied instrument of death lay on the pew's bench. Smith sensed that he hadn't been dead long, maybe only minutes.

Smith left the church and found Nigel in his office.

"Mr. Smith, your wife is upstairs. She's quite all right, but she evidently had a harrowing experience on her walk this morning."

"Is she hurt?" Smith asked, starting for the stairs.

"No, no, but shaken. She asked that I send you up the moment you arrived."

"Thank you."

"Did you meet up with Reverend Priestly? Has he been very delayed?" Tracy called after him.

Hearing that Annabel had suffered some mishap had caused Smith to forget for the moment what he'd just discovered in the adjacent church. He paused at the foot of the stairs and said, "Yes, I think I did. He's in the church now. And he's very dead."

13

"CALM DOWN, Mrs. Waters," MPD Homicide chief Terrence Finnerty said. Present in an interrogation room were a department stenographer, another detective from the Singletary murder task force, and Mrs. Waters's son, Brian.

Evelyn Waters had been crying and praying ever since detectives had picked her up at her house an hour earlier. She looked surprisingly the way Eileen St. James had described her. Finnerty was impressed; usually, they never looked the way witnesses said they did.

"Mrs. Waters, there is nothing to be this upset about," Finnerty said. "If you don't calm down, we'll be here all day."

Her son, Brian, said, "My mother is a very religious person, Captain Finnerty. She's also very fragile, as you can see."

"Yeah, I know all that, but if we can't talk to her, we'll get nowhere."

Brian sat on the edge of the table next to his mother and placed his hands on her shoulders. "Mom, please, try to pull yourself together. You aren't in any trouble. They just want to ask you some questions to help find whoever killed the priest."

She took a rapid series of deep breaths and vigorously shook her head. "How could you do this to your own mother?"

"Mom, I couldn't see you living the way you've been ever since you discovered that body. I did it because I love you. These people aren't out to hurt you. They just want you to help them." He said to Finnerty, "She's been a wreck ever since that morning. I didn't know what else to do but call you."

"You did the right thing, Mr. Waters. Try to convince her she's doing the right thing."

No matter how upset someone is, there is just so much energy of despair, just so many tears in the tank. Eventually—it was only minutes but seemed like hours to Finnerty—Evelyn Waters gained enough composure to apologize, and to indicate that she would try to answer his questions.

"What I'd like you to do, Mrs. Waters, is to remember exactly what happened that morning from the time you entered the chapel to when you discovered the body, went up to the bishop's dressing room with the bishop's wife, and then left. Take your time, and don't worry if you forget things. We'll help you."

She looked up into her son's eyes. He was a nice guy, Finnerty decided, a little wimpy maybe but okay. Brian Waters touched his mother's shoulder again and gave her a reassuring smile. Finnerty pegged him to be in his late twenties. They'd had a chance to talk a little before bringing his mother into the room. He'd dropped out of college and was working as a salesman in an auto dealership on Wisconsin Avenue, not far from the cathedral. He lived with his mother; she had been widowed for eight years. According to the son, his father's death sent his mother into religious immersion. She attended six o'clock mass almost every morning at the cathedral, made most noontime masses in the War Memorial Chapel, and spent her time away from church reading the Bible and listening to religious broadcasts. "Did she often go to that little chapel by herself at odd hours?" Finnerty had asked. "When she was especially upset," the son had replied.

"Okay, Mrs. Waters, let's begin," Finnerty said. "I assume you went to the chapel because you were upset about something. Is that correct?"

Mrs. Waters bit her lip against another torrent of tears. She tried to reply verbally, but ended up simply nodding.

"What were you particularly upset about that morning?"

"I . . . it all seemed so hopeless."

"What did?"

"Life . . . my life . . . everything happening in the world. He has to come and stop it."

"Who has to come and stop it?"

"Jesus, the son of God. He's our only hope for salvation. I'd been up all night and . . ."

When she didn't continue, Finnerty asked her why she'd been up all night.

"I couldn't sleep. I had on my movies."

"Movies?"

Her son spoke for her. "She buys videotapes from religious organizations, from radio and TV evangelists. She watches them when she can't sleep."

"I see," said Finnerty. "Go on, Mrs. Waters. Did something on one of the tapes especially upset you?"

She shook her head.

"Then why did you come to the chapel? What time did you come to the chapel?"

She looked up at her son.

"Go ahead, Mom," he said. "You didn't do anything wrong."

She raised her hands as though to indicate the futility of trying to remember the precise time. "Seven, yes, maybe seven-thirty."

"In the morning."

"Yes."

"Did you drive there?"

"No. I walked."

Her son answered. "She doesn't drive, and when we looked for a new apartment in the neighborhood a few years ago after my dad's death, it made sense to be within walking distance of the place where she spends so much of her time. It's also near my job."

"Okay," Finnerty said. "How many times a week do you end up in that small chapel, the Good Shepherd one?"

Another fluttering of the hands in frustration with the question.

"Had you been there earlier in the week, the day before you found the body, two days before?"

"No. Yes, two days before. I went there at night."

"What time at night?"

"Eleven."

Finnerty knew she'd guessed at that time, and renounced trying to pin her down. It really wasn't important. He said, "Okay, Mrs. Waters, you walked into the chapel. First, you had to enter the cathedral. Did you come through those doors just outside the chapel?"

"Doors? What doors?"

"There are doors that separate the inside from the outside. Just inside those doors is the chapel."

For the first time she exhibited an emotion other than despair. "Yes, of course I came through the doors. How could I get to the chapel if I didn't?"

Finnerty was pleased that she'd snapped at him. Could be a sign she would get through the rest of the interview without more sobbing and invoking the name of God. "I came in to pray," she said softly.

"Did you see the body right away?"

Oh, God, Finnerty thought, my mention of "body" has turned on her faucet again.

"Please, Mrs. Waters, I'm trying to be gentle and to use the right words, but you must—"

Her son now demonstrated a sternness that hadn't been there before. He said with grit in his voice, "Mother, *stop* it and answer the questions."

She looked at him as though he'd physically assaulted her, but his tone had its effect. She looked at Finnerty and said, "No, I did not see the body right away. When I go to that chapel, I sit in the back pew."

"The one immediately opposite the door?"

"Yes."

"And so you walked into the chapel and sat in that back pew. Was there anyone else in the chapel?"

"No, only . . ."

"Only what?"

"Only . . . him." She found the strength to say, "The body!"

"Did you notice the body as soon as you sat in that pew?"

"No. I prayed . . . for a long time. Then I went to the altar."

"To do what?"

"To be near it."

"I see. Go on."

"Then . . . then I happened to look at the little pew against the wall, and I saw him."

"Mr. Singletary."

"Somebody. Yes, Father Singletary."

"What did you do then?"

"I was shocked. I thought he was alive. I said something to him."

"What did you say to him?"

"I said . . . 'Excuse me,' I think I said. Then I saw his head, and I started to scream."

"That was when Bishop St. James came in?"

"Yes."

"Did you stay in the chapel long with the bishop?"

She shook her head. "No. He took me away."

"Upstairs, to his room?"

"Yes." As the memories of that moment in Good Shepherd Chapel flooded her, she began once again to cry, softly this time, childlike.

Finnerty raised his eyebrows at the stenographer. She nodded that she'd got everything. He said to Mrs. Waters, "I know this has been tough for you, but I appreciate your coming here." To her son he said, "Thanks."

"I thought it was best for her," Brian Waters said.

"Why don't you take your mother home. We'll want to speak to both of you again, so don't go anywhere."

"Fine." Brian took his mother's elbow and helped her from the room.

"Captain, there's a long-distance call for you," Finnerty's secretary said through the open door.

"Long distance? Who's calling?"

"Mackensie Smith. He's calling from England."

"I'll take it in my office."

"Bored with your honeymoon, Mac?" Finnerty said upon picking up the receiver.

"Hardly," Smith said. "I'm calling because there's been a murder here that I think could have bearing on the Singletary case."

"How so?"

"A parish priest in Buckland has been murdered in the small church next to our hotel. His name was Robert Priestly. I found his body about an hour ago."

"How do you figure it means anything to the Singletary case?"

"A couple of things. First, Singletary and Priestly were friendly.

Second, Singletary probably came out here to see him. Third, he was killed by a blow to the head. This time the murder weapon was on the scene."

"Yeah? What was it?"

"A candlestick."

"Come on, Mac. What do you think happened, the person who killed Singletary here in Washington flies over to England and kills this priest in this town of . . . what was the name?"

"Buckland."

"Don't make sense to me," Finnerty said.

"Murder seldom makes sense, but suit yourself, Terry. I thought it was worth calling you about. Remind me not to bother in the future."

"Okay, Mac, hold on. I appreciate you making a long-distance call and all that. By the way, I just got finished interrogating Evelyn Waters. She's the lady who found Singletary's body."

"Did she shed any light on what happened?" Smith asked.

"Not yet, but it's good to know who she is. When are you coming back?"

"Soon. Who is she?"

"Just Mrs. Waters. Nice lady, kind of pathetic, a religious nut."

"Well, I'm glad one piece of the puzzle is in place. I'll check in with you when we return."

"Hey, Mac, you say *you* found this priest's body? I thought you were on your honeymoon. What are you doing over there, playing cop?"

"No, just happened to be in the wrong place at the wrong time. I'll talk to you when the call is cheaper."

14

London, Friday Afternoon—
The Fog Persists

SMITH AND ANNABEL sat at their table in the small bar at Duke's. Gilberto had served them Grahams 1945 port as a farewell gesture; their flight back to the States would leave in four hours.

"She's disappeared," Mac said. "After calling her number all day yesterday, I got hold of Jeffrey Woodcock. This morning we went to her apartment—flat, I guess it's called here—and it was empty. The land-lord let us in. The place was bare, not a trace."

"That sends a message, doesn't it?" Annabel said.

"It sure does. This Clarissa Morgan puts the arm on church officials at Lambeth Palace. She claims she's owed money because of Paul Singletary. The church contacts Woodcock, and Woodcock has me call her. She's hardly what you'd consider friendly on the phone, but she does promise to get together when we get back. She obviously can't pursue her claim—call it blackmail—if she can't be found."

They'd driven back to London two nights before, after having been interrogated in Buckland by local authorities, and after spending another two hours in the sheep meadows where Annabel almost lost her life.

Their decision to return to the scene was made an hour after Smith had gone to the room to comfort his wife, and to find out from her what had actually happened. She gave him a full account, but his lawyer's instincts and training caused him to follow up on her answers, sometimes to the point of angering her.

"I'm not on a witness stand," she'd snapped twice. Both times he apologized but pressed forward, attempting to wring every bit of information from her. Once, when she balked at his questioning, he said, "Annabel, there is a murdered priest in the church next to this hotel, and someone apparently tried to murder you. Come on, now, go over it again while it's still fresh in your mind."

"It will always be fresh in my mind," she said.

"I know, but humor me. You were relieved when you saw this person on horseback coming out of the trees in the distance. Did you yell?"

"No. The rider seemed to be heading in my direction. I figured I'd wait until whoever it was came close enough for me to ask directions. I snapped a couple of pictures and—"

"You snapped 'a couple of pictures'? Of the rider?"

"Yes. Damn, I forgot about that. Worse, I don't have the camera."

"Where is it?"

"I think I tossed it as I tried to get out of the horse's way."

Smith glanced to a table on which her binoculars rested. "You have your binoculars."

"Yes, they were around my neck. I'd shoved the camera in the pocket of my jacket and took it out to take the pictures. It was such a beautiful scene. I thought the fog would add something special to it."

Ten minutes later, after Annabel had exhausted her memories of the event, Mac said, "We have to go back and get that camera."

Annabel nodded. "I know. I was waiting for you to say that. I hate to."

"You don't have to come. I'll round up some people and—"

"Don't be silly, Mac. I'm the only one who knows where I was." She smiled. "I *think* I know where I was. At any rate, I'll do my best. I just hope the woman on that horse didn't come back and grab it."

Mac and Annabel huddled with Nigel and Tracy over the walking map Annabel had used, and identified an area where the near-miss might have taken place. Nigel assigned as many members of the hotel staff as he could spare. Some had cars, and they drove in a caravan to a point that precluded having to retrace Annabel's long trek on foot. The fog hadn't lifted, but as Annabel stood in the center of one of the fields, she said, "Yes, it was right about here." She pointed to the wall she'd thrown herself over, and indicated the trees from which the rider had emerged. Smith, Annabel, and the hotel workers fanned out. Within minutes, a kitchen worker held up the camera, a wide grin on his boyish face.

They returned to the hotel and sat in one of its public rooms with local police. Mac replayed the circumstances surrounding his discovery of Reverend Priestly's body, and when that subject had been exhausted, it was Annabel's turn to describe what had happened to her in the sheep pasture.

"I understand you took some snapshots of the wayward equestrian," the investigating officer said pleasantly.

Annabel looked at Mac. "Yes, that's true."

"I also understand you returned and found the camera, Mrs. Smith."

"Yes, we were very fortunate."

"I'm afraid you'll have to leave the roll of film with me."

"Inspector," Mac said, "I understand why you want it, but it has significance for us, too. Do you have photo-processing facilities at your headquarters?"

The inspector shook his head. "Afraid not. We send it all up to London."

"Fine," Smith said. "Can we arrange to have two sets of prints made in London, one for you, one for us?" He smiled. "It would be nice to have something to remember this lovely day in the Cotswolds."

"Fair enough," said the officer.

Mac rewound the film and removed it from the camera, then handed it to the officer, who, in turn, gave it to one of his men with instructions to have it driven to London immediately. Mac gave the officer their Washington address and was assured a set of prints would be sent there by courier.

"Hate to say it," Annabel murmured, "but the pictures probably won't amount to much with all that fog. I did have fast film, though."

After the authorities had left, Mac and Annabel sat with Nigel and Tracy. Mac brought up Paul Singletary again. "What did he do when he was here?" Smith asked Nigel.

"Relaxed, I suppose," Nigel said. "He had a favorite room, one facing the gardens behind the hotel."

"He was here one weekend with an attractive woman named Morgan. Do you recall that?"

"Yes, I do."

"Did they share the same room?"

Nigel grimaced. "I don't think it is appropriate for someone in my position to reveal such information."

"And I respect your discretion," Smith said, "but we're talking about two murders here, first Reverend Singletary's, and now your local parish priest's. Mrs. Smith and I are here in the United Kingdom on our honeymoon, but there is another purpose for this trip. I am serving as legal counsel to the National Cathedral of Washington. Father Singletary, who was murdered there, was a friend. He officiated at our wedding in August. Bishop St. James of the National Cathedral asked me to look into Reverend Singletary's movements while he was here in England. He was in London the day before he was murdered, but told people he would be spending the next day in the country, presumably here, before returning to Washington. That obviously didn't happen, because he was murdered the next night."

"I see," Nigel said.

"Was that the only time he came here with a woman?" Annabel asked.

Tracy said, "Yes, I think it was."

"Did they see anyone else while they were here?" Smith asked.

"No, they kept very much to themselves, which would be expected," Nigel said. "Except, of course, for Reverend Priestly. As I told you, they were chums."

"Because they were fellow priests?"

"More than that. I overheard them talking one day in the library," Nigel said. "They evidently went back a long way, perhaps to university."

"Anything else you remember about the conversation you overheard?"

"Not really."

"Did Reverend Singletary and Reverend Priestly get together the weekend Singletary was here with Miss Morgan?" Annabel asked.

Nigel and Tracy shrugged. "I don't recall," Nigel said.

"Well, you've been very generous with your time and information," Smith said. "I think we'd better head back to London."

"Mr. and Mrs. Smith, I can't tell you how upset we are that your initial visit to Buckland Manor involved such horrible experiences. Being the one to find the body of Reverend Priestly must've been a ghastly occurrence. And you, Mrs. Smith, almost being killed by an irresponsible equestrian is appalling. We've never had anything like that happen before. Please accept our apologies for the two days you've had to endure. And come and stay with us again as our guests—on the house, I think you say."

Smith smiled and shook the young manager's hand. "It's a wonderful house. Aside from priests being murdered and my wife almost being run over by a horse, we enjoyed our stay very much. Ideally, we'll come back one day and have the sort of tranquil vacation you're used to providing."

*   *   *

Mac and Annabel were early for their flight and settled into the Clipper Club at the airport. Mac called Jeffrey Woodcock and asked, "Anything new on Miss Morgan?"

"No, Mac. Most unusual, most distressing."

"Do me a favor, Jeffrey. See if you can find out if Reverend Priestly was involved with the Word of Peace movement."

"Shall do, Mac. Again, horrible what happened to Annabel. Please give her our warmest regards."

"Could have been worse. A hell of a lot worse. She might have ended up permanently planted in that field in the Cotswolds."

15

Washington, D.C.,
That Evening—Chilly

THEY ARRIVED at Foggy Bottom too late to spring Rufus from the kennel. The grating electronic voice on the answering machine informed them that there were eleven messages. Mac noted the names and numbers on a yellow legal pad. Some could wait; calls from Bishop St. James, Terry Finnerty, and Tony Buffolino would be answered immediately. He called the bishop first.

"Welcome back, Mac. Good trip?"

"Depends upon how you look at it, George. Annabel and I had some fine moments, although the whole thing was not what you'd call without incident." He told the bishop of Annabel's strange experience while walking in the fields, and of the murder of the parish priest, Robert Priestly.

"That's horrible!" St. James said. "You say he was killed in the same manner as Paul?"

"A blow to the head, only this time the weapon, a candlestick, was left at the scene."

"I see. Was there any connection between Paul and this Reverend Priestly?"

"You didn't know about him?"

"No."

"There was a specific link between them. They evidently knew each other pretty well, and often spent time together when Paul was in England. I'll fill you in on this tomorrow. I have a class in the morning but thought I'd come by the cathedral after that. I should be there about noon."

"They have you working on Saturday."

"A makeup class. The price you pay for a honeymoon. See you tomorrow."

Smith failed to connect with Finnerty, but reached Tony Buffolino at the Spotlight Room. "You called while I was away?" Smith said.

"Yeah. When did you get back?"

"A little while ago. What did you get on Reverend Singletary?"

"Mac, I spent a pretty good hunk of time on it."

Smith asked when they could get together.

"How about tonight?"

"No, Tony, we're beat." It was eight o'clock in Washington, one in the morning London time. "How about tomorrow afternoon?"

"Can't do it, Mac."

Smith put his hand over the mouthpiece and said to Annabel, "Feel like a little nightclubbing?"

Her expression was what Smith would have expected if he'd suggested a walk in a foggy Cotswold sheep pasture. "Just for an hour," he said.

She shook her head, and Smith knew she meant it. He said to Buffolino, "Annabel is exhausted, but I'll be there in a half hour."

"Great."

"Is there a place we can talk quietly? I really don't feel like hearing what you've learned while your impressionist does obscure personalities."

"I got an office in the back. Lousy view of the stage. See ya."

"You don't mind, do you?" Smith asked Annabel after hanging up on Buffolino.

"Absolutely not," she said. "I'm going to take a hot bath and unpack. Frankly, I think you're crazy, but I'm beginning to wonder why that would surprise me." She came to him, wrapped her arms around his neck, and kissed him. "Don't be long, Mac. You have your class first thing in the morning, and I have to get cracking, too. Let's cuddle up for a good night's sleep."

"With even half of that invitation, I'll be back quicker than I planned."

There weren't many customers in Tony's place, and the show hadn't started, for which Smith was grateful. Three bored musicians played slow music with a backbeat. A couple danced.

"A table, or do you prefer the bar?" a sunken-cheeked young woman wearing minimal clothing asked.

"I have an appointment with Mr. Buffolino."

"You do? I'll tell him you're here. What's your name?"

"Smith, Mackensie Smith."

Alicia Buffolino appeared from the rear of the club. For a second, Smith wasn't sure it was Alicia. She had always worn her auburn hair long, and was fond of tight shiny toreador pants, and tight shirts scooped low at the neck. Now she'd had her hair cut into a trendy bob, had applied a considerably lighter hand to her makeup, and wore a nicely tailored rust-colored suit and white blouse with a bow at the neck. "Good to see you, Mac," she said, kissing him on the cheek.

"Nice to see you, too, Alicia. Forgive me if I make no sense. We just got back from London, and I'm still operating on their time. Is Tony here?"

"He's in the office going over bills. We have more bills than customers. Come on back."

If Alicia and Tony hadn't called it an office, Smith would have assumed they were in a storeroom. Except for a small, genuinely distressed desk, a chair that had suffered too many heavy sitters (and maybe a hand-grenade attack), and a leaning tower of battered black file cabinets, the rest of the room was piled with boxes. Buffolino sat at the desk going through a swirl of papers. The minute Alicia opened the door he stood up and said, "Hey, Mac, good to see you again." To Alicia: "Get a chair for Mac, would you?"

She returned with a folding metal chair that she noisily snapped open. "Anything else, Your Majesty?" she asked before slamming the door behind her.

Buffolino shook his head. "Man, she gets more difficult every day."

Not long before she's former wife number three, Smith thought. "So, Tony," he said, sinking into the chair, "tell me what you've found out about Paul Singletary."

Buffolino reached into the bottom drawer of the desk and pulled out a folder. Written on the cover was MAC SMITH. He slid the top piece of paper across the desk to Smith, who put on half-glasses and read it.

"Whattaya think?" Buffolino asked.

"Pretty thorough," Smith said. "A lot of it I know, but there are some interesting items in here. This reference to his military service. Where did you get that?"

"I got a friend in military records in St. Louis. She gave it to me over the phone."

"I'm not sure I understand this joint commission Reverend Singletary was assigned to. It says here he served aboard a destroyer that had been outfitted with sensitive, classified gear, and that the crew was made up of American, British, and French naval personnel. What else do you know about that?"

"What you see is what you get, Mac. What caught my eye was how short a time he served, less than a year. I guess clergy don't get put on extended assignments."

"I'm not sure that's true, but it's worth checking into. There's no reference here to the type of discharge he was given."

"I asked my friend in St. Louis about that. She said the only notation in his file was 'Discharge: Official.' "

"I've never heard of that designation before, but I suppose all discharges are 'official,'" Smith said.

"I'll check it out," Buffolino said, scribbling a note on the folder. The other papers in the file were not as neatly organized as the first, and Buffolino read from them. Smith stopped him when he got to Singletary's travel itinerary back to Washington the day of his murder. "You say he arrived at two-thirty in the afternoon at Kennedy Airport in New York, and took a shuttle to Washington from LaGuardia. That would place him back here at approximately five o'clock."

"Right."

"Anything else about his trip home?"

Buffolino smiled. "Yeah, there is. Seems he was accompanied by a foxy lady."

"Really? Another friend in strange places tell you that?"

"As a matter'a fact, yeah. I got this gal I used to see once in a while . . . between marriages, of course . . . and she works in crew scheduling. I told her I needed the names of the stewardesses who worked the flight from London to JFK that Singletary was on, and she gave them to me."

"They're not called stewardesses anymore, Tony, they're called flight attendants."

"They're all 'Coffee, Tea, or Me' to me. I called some of these stews —attendants, and told them straight out that I was an investigator looking into the murder of Reverend Paul Singletary, which happened at the National Cathedral. I told them that it was very important that if they remembered anything about a priest on that flight that they share it with me. It took me five calls before I connect with this—" He glanced down at a note on the paper. "Her name is Anne Padula. She tells me she remembers him very well."

"Why?"

"Why what?"

"Why would she remember him? How many passengers are on those flights, two hundred, three hundred?"

"Yeah, probably, only this Anne Padula got to talking to the reverend. She told me she spotted him the minute he walked in because he was a very handsome guy, especially for a guy in a collar. She told me she wasn't the only female on that flight who gave him a look more than once, including the lady sitting next to him."

"Sitting next to him? I thought he traveled with a woman."

"Well, this stewardess didn't know that right away. What interested her was that they seemed to strike up a friendship pretty fast for a couple'a people who just happened to sit next to each other on a jumbo jet. Then she gets talking to both of them and she gets a sense that even though they came on the plane separate, they knew each other from before. You know, women like this Padula have pretty good instincts, especially working with the public all the time. Anyway, she tells me that she becomes convinced that they came on board separately for deliberate reasons."

"Did she describe this woman to you?"

"Yeah, she did, only she really didn't remember what she looked like as much as she did the reverend. She says this woman was kind of cool-looking, black hair, very fair skin, maybe talked with a British accent. Had big shoulders, she says."

Smith grunted. "She couldn't be sure about the accent? Not hard to recognize a British accent."

"Yeah, except the lady didn't say much. In fact, the lady seemed annoyed that a pretty stew was talking to the reverend."

"Interesting," Smith said. "Did you find out anything else from this flight attendant?"

"That's about it, Mac."

"Did you learn anything about Singletary's movements between the time he arrived in Washington on the shuttle and when he was murdered in the cathedral that night?"

Buffolino shook his head.

"Did your flight-attendant friend notice how Singletary and this woman left the plane? Did they leave together? Did she happen to see them in the terminal, maybe out at a cab stand while she was waiting for a crew bus?"

"Nope. That's all she could tell me, only I figured it was pretty impressive. How many times do you find anybody who actually remembers somebody?"

"Not often," Smith agreed. "What else do you have?"

"Let's see." Buffolino looked at his notes. "Nothing except—there's an interesting turf war goin' on with this case."

"How so?"

"MPD . . . Finnerty . . . you know him pretty good . . . Finnerty and the MPD start out investigating the murder. It's being handled like any D.C. homicide."

"Where is the jurisdictional dispute?"

"Well, here's where it gets interesting. MPD sent guys to Singletary's apartment. Routine, right?" Smith nodded. "But I hear from some friends I got in the department that anything having to do with Singletary's apartment, personal life, clothes—all of it has been put under wraps by another agency."

"Which agency? The FBI?"

Buffolino shook his head and smiled again. "The navy." Buffolino glanced down at his notes again. "Naval Investigative Services, to be exact."

"Because of the time he spent in the navy, short as it was?" Smith was almost talking to himself.

Buffolino shrugged. "Beats me, but that's the word I get. And these." He pulled a sheaf of clippings from the file folder and slid them to

Smith. "I figured you'd want to keep up on what the press has been saying while you were gone."

"Much obliged, Tony. Good thinking."

"Yeah, sometimes I think pretty clear . . ." His brow furrowed, and he looked toward the door. "And sometimes I don't."

There was a loud knock on the door. "Yeah?" Buffolino yelled.

Alicia poked her head in. "It's time for the show, Tony."

Buffolino looked up at a black-and-white kitchen clock hanging precariously from a nail. "Excuse me, Mac, I always introduce the show."

"You don't have to," Alicia said. "I can do it."

Buffolino stood and waved the notion away. "Nah, people in a joint like this want to see a guy be the MC. Right, Mac?"

Smith wisely said nothing.

Through the closed door came the ragged roll of a snare drum and the crash of a cymbal. Then a cranked-up amplification system blared Buffolino's welcome to Tony's Spotlight Room. He told a few bad jokes before introducing a singer who'd come "direct from Las Vegas," and who was "destined to be one of America's great singing stars."

The trio vamped her on, and she launched into a frenetic version of "Everything's Coming Up Roses." Smith grimaced; he was glad Annabel was home soaking in a tub. He wished he were.

Buffolino returned to the office. "Anything else for me?" Smith asked.

"That's about it. Want me to keep going?"

"Yes, I do. I want you to find out whether a woman named Clarissa Morgan was in Washington the day of Paul Singletary's murder. It's likely that she was the woman with him on the flight from London. I also want you to start running some background checks on various cathedral personnel, as you get time. Start with a Canon Nickelson, the music director, and do a couple of the clergy, Reverend Jonathon Merle and Reverend Carolyn Armstrong, maybe a few other names I'll give you later."

"Carolyn? That's a *priest*?"

"A beautiful one, as it happens. We're talking Episcopal here, Tony, not Catholic. I also want you to see what you can find out about this naval-intelligence interest in the case. While you're at it, see if there is anything going on at MPD that hasn't been publicly announced. In other words, keep digging on all fronts, and keep me informed."

Buffolino had a way of asking for money without having to say it. Smith had brought a check with him; he handed it to his oddball investigator.

"Thanks, Mac. You in town the next couple of days?"

"Absolutely."

"Good. I'll be in touch. How's your pretty wife?"

"Annabel is splendid, thank you. Tired from the trip, but good. How's that boy of yours?"

"Billy? He's doin' real good. Looks like the cancer is in remission. I keep my fingers crossed, though."

Smith stood. "Good, good. I have to leave, Tony. I'm teaching a class at eight tomorrow morning." They shook hands. "Nice work. Keep it up."

When they reached the door to the club, Buffolino asked whether Mac wanted to stay for the rest of the show—complimentary, of course. Smith looked back at the singer, who was doing a version of Judy Garland with "Over the Rainbow." Some men at the bar leered at her. Two couples danced—moved together was more accurate. Light reflected from a revolving mirrored ball danced off them like photokinetic confetti. "I'd love to, Tony, but the trip took a lot out of me. Give me a call tomorrow." He stepped out onto K Street, lowered his head, and walked quickly to his car.

16

Washington, The Next Day—
Horizontal Rain

"HOW WAS YOUR honeymoon, Professor Smith?" Joe Petrella asked.

"Busy but pleasant," Smith replied. The class laughed. He hadn't realized what he was saying, or what they were inferring, and he was tired and out-of-sorts. Not having had time to adequately prepare for class added to his grumpiness.

"The woman who found Reverend Singletary's body came forward while you were gone," Joy Collins said, excited.

"Yes, I heard."

April Montgomery, his thin, pale, exceptionally bright student, asked, "Did you spend part of your honeymoon in London investigating what Reverend Singletary did there the day before he died?"

Smith removed his glasses and leaned his elbows on the lectern. "What would lead you to that conclusion, Ms. Montgomery?"

She wiggled her nose and said, "I read that Reverend Singletary had been in London the day before he died, and it struck me as an interesting coincidence that you chose to take your honeymoon in London at this time."

Smith couldn't help but smile. "Did it?" he said. "All right, let's take another fifteen minutes to discuss the murder of Reverend Paul Single-tary." He was less annoyed at this intrusion than he'd been last time. It would consume some of the time he'd have trouble filling with course materials. And the kids might even help him reason things through.

"I said my honeymoon in London was busy but pleasant. Half was untrue." He told the class about Annabel's coming close to being trampled to death in the field, and about discovering the body of Reverend Robert Priestly.

"Wow!" Joy Collins said. "Some honeymoon."

Smith laughed gently. "Yes, it was not run-of-the-mill. Now, let's harness the considerable intelligence in this room and come up with any possible connection between the murder of a Reverend Paul Singletary in Washington and the murder of a Reverend Robert Priestly in England, both in church, and, not by the way, Priestly was also killed by a blow to the head. The only difference is that the murder weapon was left behind in Reverend Priestly's case. It was a heavy brass candlestick that was covered with blood—Reverend Priestly's blood, of course —and had been left on a pew next to the body."

Smith studied his students' faces as they sought to forge a defensible link between the two murders. Ms. Montgomery was the first to offer an opinion. "It could have been sheer coincidence," she said.

"Yes, that is a distinct possibility," Smith said. "Oh—sorry. I should add, too, that Reverend Singletary and Reverend Priestly were friends. Not only had they followed the same professional calling, they evidently went back quite a way, perhaps to their college years."

"It's unlikely that the same person committed the two murders," another student said. "I can't conceive of the spontaneous murderer of Reverend Singletary flying all the way to England to kill his friend. Doesn't make sense to me."

"Somebody else said that, also. Doesn't make sense to me, either, but would the murders have had to be done by the same person? And remember, Paul Singletary was part of two worldwide organizations, with members on many continents," said Smith.

"Two?" said Joe.

"The Anglican-Episcopal-Protestant church," Joy Collins said, calmer and more reflective now.

"And . . . ?" Mac asked.

"Word of Peace," April Montgomery put in.

"A conspiracy."

"Possibly," Smith said. "But what would be behind a conspiracy to murder two priests?"

"Hatred for the clergy," said Joe Petrella, the student who had voiced a similar observation during the previous discussion.

"Could be," Smith said, "but that's too lurid, too tabloidish for me. At least for the moment."

Smith was asked, "Do you think it was the same murder weapon? I mean, the weapon that was used to kill Reverend Singletary was never found, from what I've been reading."

"That possibility has been raised with the British authorities. Naturally, they're doing a thorough analysis of the weapon, although chances of finding any physical evidence that would link it to Reverend Singletary's murder are remote."

"Has anyone checked to see whether a candlestick is missing from the National Cathedral?"

Smith said, "MPD has been looking for every candlestick on the premises. The shape and nature of the wound to Reverend Singletary's head could certainly have been made by such an object."

"You said your wife was almost killed in a field, and that it appeared to be deliberate because the horse and rider returned and went after her again. What connection does that have with the priest's murder?"

"That is a puzzling aspect. We have to be open to the possibility, as April is, that there was no connection—though murderous intent was in the air."

"Maybe the same person who tried to run down your wife killed the priest, although I can't imagine what they would have had against her, either," Bob Rogers said.

"Maybe," said April Montgomery, "the person had something against *you*, Professor Smith."

A Boeing 707 with U.S. NAVY painted on its tail banked over Annapolis and picked up a compass heading of 225 degrees until entering the airspace of Andrews Air Force Base. The navy lieutenant commander at the controls received permission to land, and soon the four-engine aircraft taxied up to a long gray limousine with tinted windows. A boarding ramp was rolled to the side of the plane. The door opened, and two uniformed military personnel came down the steps, followed by a gray-haired man wearing a tweed suit and carrying a tan raincoat over his arm who seemed to lean slightly to his left as he walked. A naval officer who'd been in the limousine approached the visitor when he reached the bottom of the steps and extended his hand. "Captain Ely, U.S. Navy, Mr. Leighton. Hope your flight was smooth."

"Yes, quite," Leighton said. "Damned foggy in London. Wondered if we'd get off."

Captain Ely escorted the assistant director of MI5's "B" Division to the limousine, and climbed into the backseat with him. The driver had received his instructions before the plane's arrival and immediately drove off, taking Maryland Highway 4, also called Pennsylvania Avenue S.E. He stayed on the road after crossing the District of Columbia line until they reached the historic Washington Navy Yard on the Anacostia River, a seventy-five-acre spread known for much of its history as the Naval Gun Factory; it dated back to President John Adams's purchase of the site in 1799. They drove along narrow roads defined by old gray stone buildings, past the Navy Memorial Museum, one of the longest buildings in the world, and past the Marine Corps Museum and Submarine Museum before pulling up in front of an administration building. Their credentials were checked at a desk inside the door, and a phone call was made. "You can go up now," Leighton and Ely were told. A few minutes later they entered the office of Rear Admiral Stuart Zachary, chief of operations for Naval Investigative Services. With him were Rudolph Kapit of the FBI's counterespionage division, CIA representative Robert Wilson, and Louis Malvese of the State Department's European Section.

"Good of you to send a plane for me," Leighton said after Ely had left and the others had settled around a large circular table in a corner of the spacious office.

"We appreciate your agreeing to come on such short notice, Mr. Leighton," Admiral Zachary said. "We thought it was important enough to do whatever we could to expedite this meeting, especially in light of the death of Reverend Priestly in Buckland."

"Yes. Tragic affair," Leighton said. "The local authorities have been most cooperative. We're receiving daily reports on the progress of their investigation."

"That's good," Zachary said.

"How long can you stay in Washington, Mr. Leighton?" the FBI's Kapit asked.

"That depends entirely upon you," Leighton responded. "I'm here at your request."

Malvese, of State, a short, square man with a pugnacious face, said, "I don't think this meeting would have been necessary if recent events hadn't occurred. There seem to be a lot of loose ends—too many of them, for my taste, to let them slide. These operations always make such simple sense when they're conceived, but then they take on their own damn life. I promised my boss I would come back from this meeting with a clear view of where we are and where we're going." He looked at the others. "I hope I won't disappoint him."

"The report the agency received last night was confusing, Brett," Wilson said. He knew Leighton well; they'd cooperated on a number of projects over the years. They bore a striking resemblance and might have been mistaken for brothers except for their accents, which they'd once explained away to someone by claiming that their parents divorced shortly after their births and had raised one of them in the United States, the other in Great Britain. The woman who'd noted their resemblance believed the story, which provided the two men with a good laugh after the party.

"Frankly, I'm not especially interested in your reports," Malvese said in a voice that matched his bellicose face. "This whole affair has greater diplomatic implications than your reports consider."

Admiral Zachary said to Wilson and Kapit, "Let's bear in mind, gentlemen, that this is still an NIS operation. We appreciate what help the CIA and the FBI have given us, but it remains our ultimate responsibility."

Leighton smiled to himself at the tension among the four men. How typically American, he thought, to spend so much time defending their positions, justifying their existence, and never fully cooperating to get the job done. True, enough of that went on in British intelligence, but those incidents somehow seemed to be resolved earlier in the game, had less impact upon final solutions. He took out a long, thin brown cigarillo. "Mind if I smoke?"

They did, but all shook their heads no.

Leighton lighted the cigar with an elegant flourish and savored its taste. "Well," he said pleasantly, a smile on his lined, ruddy face, "where do we begin?"

Admiral Zachary answered the question. "Let's start with Clarissa Morgan. What is her condition?"

"Splendid," Leighton said. "Miss Morgan is quite well, I assure you."

"I'm not particularly interested in her health," said Zachary.

"No, I expect not," Leighton said.

"What went wrong?" Kapit asked.

Leighton arched his sizable eyebrows. "What went wrong?" He said to Wilson, his CIA friend, "I think I covered that subject in my conversation with you last night."

"Which doesn't answer the question," Zachary said, making no attempt to hide his annoyance.

"Let me assure you that Miss Morgan is quite secure, and will no longer play an active role in this matter."

"Not good enough," Malvese said.

Bob Wilson stepped in. "Brett, let me try to summarize the concerns of the others. Reverend Singletary was murdered here in Washington at the National Cathedral. Your Clarissa Morgan accompanied him from London the day he was killed. Your people have acknowledged that. Now, it is our understanding that she returned to London and attempted to blackmail the Church of England. That seems to be highly irregular behavior for someone in your employ."

Leighton laughed softly and drew on his cigarillo. "As I said moments ago, Miss Morgan is secure. No longer in our employ but in our care."

"Meaning what?" Kapit asked.

"Meaning that we are in the process of resolving her indiscretions and making sure that her impetuous and unprofessional, to say nothing of greedy, behavior will not be repeated. We view her as purely a local personnel problem. No concern of yours."

Malvese's laugh was not born of merriment. "No concern of ours, you say? Infiltrating Word of Peace was a joint project, as I understand it. We gave our okay at State because it was presented as a—how was it put?—a 'benign' covert exercise designed only to gather information. There are now two dead priests, and a woman operative from British intelligence holding up the Church of England for money. Benign? Damned malignant if you ask me."

Leighton was tempted to say he *hadn't* asked the combative little representative from the State Department. He allowed the urge to pass and asked Admiral Zachary, "Did your examination of Reverend Singletary's videotapes provide you with what we hoped it would?"

"No."

"Pity. I had the utmost faith in our source of information regarding this matter."

"Miss Morgan?" Zachary asked.

"Among others. We know that certain tapes, which looked like ordinary commercially recorded cassettes, were given to Reverend Singletary by his friend Reverend Priestly, late of the British Navy. Late of everything, I suppose. Now I get the impression that either they've disappeared or you've found them and nothing incriminating was on them."

"How do you get that impression?"

"By the look on your faces and by what is not being said." His voice took on a sudden lilt, and he smiled at Admiral Zachary.

"No offense, Mr. Leighton," Kapit said, "but your information may be as unreliable as your agent. We know that Singletary and Priestly exchanged sensitive information when they were together in that joint naval exercise, and we also know that the contact continued for a period of time after that. We do not, however, have any hard evidence that it was a sustained involvement over the course of years. We've exhausted every resource we have to trace the videotapes you claim were in Reverend Singletary's possession. He had many—but not the ones for which we were looking."

"Which doesn't necessarily mean, Mr. Kapit, that they weren't in his possession. Perhaps there is something you've overlooked."

The admiral shook his head. "No, Mr. Leighton, I have to go along with Kapit."

Leighton sighed and sat back, crossed one long tweed-clad leg over the other. He didn't buy what they were telling him, not in the least, but if he was annoyed, it was more a matter of their transparent denials than of the tapes themselves. "Well," he said, "the reality seems to be that the videotapes passed by Reverend Priestly to his cause-driven friend, the Reverend Singletary, have been lost, have disappeared, have perhaps been recorded over with some of your American . . . sitcoms. Singletary was to have used them to thwart American military plans, perhaps, since the cause of peace, or the poor, or the environment always seems to go with an antimilitary stance. And they were to be transmitted to others in the Word of Peace organization. Does that really matter? The technology represented on those tapes has little relevance to today's sophisticated weaponry. Antiquated equipment, already compromised, already replaced, videotaped by amateurs like

Priestly. That's all that was on those tapes. Of course, we thought it worthwhile to recover them once Reverend Singletary died, but they are no longer important to us—or to you, I might add. Just a matter of tidying up loose ends."

Leighton's CIA friend smiled. The Englishman had a way of politely speaking down to whomever he was with, regardless of their rank or position. Most impressive was that those same people listened.

Leighton surveyed the faces at the table before continuing, "It would have been nice to have the tapes, but they would have had considerably more value when Reverend Singletary was alive, helped to keep him in line. The question now is how his death compromises our effectiveness within this bloody so-called peace movement."

"It seems the loss of Priestly would pose a bigger problem in that regard," Kapit said.

"Not really. Priestly was a decent chap who served his purpose in a peripheral way. He did, after all, introduce Miss Morgan to Reverend Singletary as instructed. A regular Cupid. He was, you see, our man." Leighton stubbed out his cigarillo.

"And strictly another personnel problem you resolved locally," Kapit said.

Leighton didn't respond. Immediately. Then he said, "We did not."

"Where is this going?" State's Louis Malvese asked. "That's what I need to know."

Leighton shrugged. "I thought you might answer that," he said.

When no one did, he added, "Tell me about this Mackensie Smith."

"What about him?" Wilson asked.

"He seems quite in the midst of the muck, wouldn't you say?"

Kapit said, "Mackensie Smith is a former criminal attorney who chucked his practice after his wife and son were killed in an auto accident. He later joined the faculty of George Washington University's law school."

"He certainly doesn't act as I would expect a professor to act. He found Priestly's body. He was at the hotel in the Cotswolds checking on Singletary's every move. He's friendly with a solicitor in London named Jeffrey Woodcock, who numbers among his clients the Church of England. Woodcock gave this Smith Clarissa Morgan's number and asked him to call her, which he did. Why?"

No one had an answer.

"She called us immediately, and we followed up. Seems Smith claimed to be on his honeymoon. Not a bad cover."

"He was married in August at the National Cathedral by Reverend Singletary," Kapit said. "They were friendly."

"Did he meet with the Morgan woman?" Wilson asked.

"No. He was on his way into the country for a few days. She told him they'd meet when he returned."

"But they didn't."

"Of course not. By the time he returned to London with his bride, Miss Morgan had vacated her premises."

"And gone where?"

"To a secure place."

"The Cotswolds?" Kapit asked.

Leighton's only reply was a tiny smile.

There was a period of silence at the table, broken when Louis Malvese said, "I must have one direct answer, Mr. Leighton."

"Yes?"

"It seems we are not to meddle in your local personnel problems."

"That view is certainly appreciated, Mr. Malvese."

"But what about *our* local personnel problems?"

"Specifically?"

"Reverend Paul Singletary."

"Your question?"

"Did you, or anyone in MI5, have anything to do with his death?"

Leighton lighted another long, thin brown cigarillo. He used the smoke as though it had some medicinal power to clear his thoughts and to help formulate an answer. He looked across the table at Malvese and said through the blue haze rising from the cigarillo's end, "We all had something to do with the demise of Reverend Paul Singletary, at least spiritually. Did we terminate the reverend? No. Did someone from his precious Word of Peace organization? We rather think so."

"Clarissa Morgan?" Bob Wilson asked.

"No," said Leighton. "She wasn't involved in the peace movement aside from keeping us abreast of its activities through Singletary."

"She accompanied him to Washington, was here when he was killed."

"So were you, I assume."

"But I didn't kill him," Wilson said.

"Did your agency?" Leighton asked.

"The CIA? Brett, come on."

Leighton's amused expression caused Wilson to sit back and smile. Nothing absurd about termination on either side of the Atlantic.

A half hour later, Admiral Zachary asked, "Ready for lunch?"

"Famished," said Leighton.

"Good. Please follow me. We've arranged for a nice spread."

She sat in a small, sparsely furnished room in a row house near Battersea Park—fittingly, some would have said, the site of the world's most ambitious and successful home for stray animals. Across the Thames was the Royal Hospital.

"Time to go," said the young man. He had been assigned to her when she was brought there the previous night. "The call came."

"What if I won't go?" she asked, a defiant smile on her lips.

"I don't think that would be wise, Miss Morgan."

"Wise? What do you know of wisdom?"

"Please, just come with us. Don't cause trouble."

"I wouldn't think of it," she said. "Got a fag?"

"Later. Come on. My patience is running thin."

"Do you have a girlfriend?" she asked him.

"I do."

"Are you in love with her?"

"Come on. Let's go."

"I loved him very much. Can you understand that?"

"Who?"

"Reverend Singletary."

"Reverend?"

"Yes. He was handsome and intelligent and good. I loved him. He's dead."

"Oh. Sorry. Please."

"Your Mr. Leighton with all his proper reserve and sense of duty doesn't understand that."

He said nothing, just stood and waited for her to rise from the cot.

"I was supposed to betray him. Then I fell in love. A nasty complication for your Mr. Leighton and his kind. Are you his kind?"

He reached for her.

"Don't touch me," she said, her voice more of a snarl, sufficiently threatening to cause him to withdraw his hand.

He tried a more ingratiating approach. "No great reason to complain, you know. The islands are very beautiful. I plan to go there on my honeymoon."

"Do you? How sweet. I detest heat. My skin is sensitive. I break out in a rash whenever it is hot."

"Miss Morgan, you're causing *me* to break out in a rash. . . ."

"What if I won't go? What if I tell you and your Mr. Leighton to go straight to hell?"

"Miss Morgan, I—"

"Will I be done away with? Will I be 'terminated' like poor Reverend Priestly?" Her laugh was blatantly bitter. "How lies multiply, like stray cats. Will you beat my head in with a candlestick holder to make it appear that there truly is a madman roaming the globe in search of skulls to crush? What fools we've turned out to be." Now she smiled sweetly at him. "Do you enjoy being involved with fools? Did you join up, as I did, thinking you were about to be initiated into a brain trust out to save the British Empire? Poor thing, and so young."

He'd had enough. He left the room and returned with two other men.

Clarissa laughed. "Need help, do you? Well, no need. I shall retire to the British Virgin Islands with grace and a sense of relief. I shall consult the best dermatologist I can find there and ask him for a proper cream for my rash." She stood, straightened the folds of her skirt. "I hope you and your bride suffer a terminal case of heat rash on your honeymoon."

A car was parked in front of the house. As her young guardian of the past few hours opened the door for her, she said, "And please tell your Mr. Brett Leighton and his MI5 that I think he and it are bloody bastards, and I hope they all rot in hell."

17

Forecast: Rain through the Weekend—Of Course

SMITH WAS EARLY for his noontime meeting with Bishop St. James, and used the time to wander in the cathedral. There were a number of tour groups being led by Visitors' Services volunteers. Smith couldn't help but smile at the wonderment on the faces of the children being guided through the massive, imposing cathedral. Then he was sobered. Were they aware of the murder that had taken place there? He hoped not. He'd read in a sidebar story that ran with the continuing coverage of the Singletary murder that requests for cathedral tours had increased since the killing. How unfortunate, yet how human, was the tendency of people to be drawn to violence and sorrow. And scandal. Ford's Theater. Chappaquiddick Bridge. Maybe it wasn't the enjoyment of bad things. Maybe it was more a matter of affirming that things were still okay for those who hadn't suffered. Probably not, was the conclusion Smith invariably came to, but it always made him feel better to rationalize away the alternatives.

He stopped at the Good Shepherd Chapel and stood alone in the center of the small room, looking through the window at the gently flowing Garth Fountain. That the peace of such a sanctuary should be violated by murder was deplorable. There were places where violence was not only commonplace, it was expected. To walk through Washington's inner city was to be constantly on guard. But for violence to happen here, in a space reserved for contemplation and prayer?

He looked at the altar. There was nothing on it except a tiny vase of wilting yellow flowers. His thoughts returned to the small church in Buckland where he'd discovered the body of Reverend Priestly. He saw again, in his mind, the candlestick that had been used to murder Priestly. Such an obvious instrument of death in a church setting. But no weapon had been conveniently left behind here. The Washington police, according to their statements, had examined every cross, chalice, and candlestick in the cathedral. None showed any signs of having been used to end Singletary's life. Could they have missed anything? The cathedral was so large and contained so many "hiding places"—for objects *or* for people. To focus, as Smith was, on finding a churchly weapon not only represented seeking the proverbial needle in a haystack, it was uncalled for. Would he be dwelling upon it if there had not been the coincidence of an Anglican priest's being murdered in a church thousands of miles away? Of course not.

Smith left the chapel and descended the greenish stone stairs leading to the crypt floor.

A sign for visitors pointed the way to the Bethlehem Chapel. Smith stopped every few feet to take in his surroundings. There was another flight of steps to his left. He moved on; a men's room was on his left, then an oak-paneled wall that went up six or seven feet. Above the paneling was a clock visible from the hallway. Just before the wall began was a door with a sign: WASHINGTON CATHEDRAL ACOLYTES. A series of glass display cases came next. They contained antique crosses and other gifts from churches around the world.

As he progressed toward the Bethlehem Chapel, Smith passed a door labeled BISHOP'S GUESTS, then the door to the choir room. Immediately across from it was the entrance to the chapel.

Smith looked back up the hall before entering the chapel. How far was it from Good Shepherd to the Bethlehem Chapel? One hundred and eighty feet, maybe two hundred. A reasonable distance to drag a body, although there was that flight of steps to contend with. Not many of them, though. Certainly not out of the question for the murder to have taken place in any of the cathedral's quiet, secluded corners.

But why? he asked himself. In the first place, why speculate that the body had been moved? The police seemed convinced of it because of the lack of blood in Good Shepherd. A reasonable deduction, certainly, but the lack of blood only suggested that the murder might have happened elsewhere. The much larger question for Smith was: Why move the body? To create the impression that anyone, from anywhere, might have done the deed, since the chapel was open twenty-four hours a day? Why else? Then again, why bother?

As he stepped into the chapel, his eyes went immediately to the Indiana limestone altar. A woman carrying a vase of flowers came from behind it. She approached the communion rail, genuflected, and stepped up to the altar, where she gently placed the flowers between two tall, graceful brass candlesticks, each holding a long, slender white candle. She took great care to be sure that the vase was precisely centered between the candles. Content that it was, she returned to the communion rail, faced the altar, and genuflected again, then started to leave through the door through which Smith had entered.

"Excuse me," Smith said. The loudness of his voice surprised him; they were in a stone boom box.

The woman turned and smiled. "May I help you?" she asked.

"Yes, perhaps you can," said Smith, approaching her. "My name is Mackensie Smith. I'm about to have lunch with Bishop St. James."

"Yes, Mr. Smith, I know who you are."

"I was interested in the routine of dressing an altar," said Smith, "particularly in this chapel. Are you a member of the Altar Guild?"

"Yes, I am."

"Is it the guild's responsibility to take care of the items on the altar— the flowers, the candles, things like that?"

"Yes, we take care of those things."

Smith looked at the altar again and smiled. "It looks beautiful. The flowers are lovely. So are the candles."

"Yes, they are."

"Is the Altar Guild responsible for keeping the candlesticks shined?"

"In a sense, yes. Sometimes we polish them ourselves, although that's generally left to the maintenance staff. We keep an eye on them, though, and when we see one that needs attention, we point it out to them."

"Do the same candlesticks always remain on the same altar? Are those holders up there designated for the Bethlehem Chapel?"

"Oh, no, it would depend upon the service to be celebrated."

"Of course it would. Do you happen to know whether that set of candlesticks has been on this altar for a while?"

"No," she said pleasantly. "They were put there just this morning."

"What about the ones that were there before?" Smith asked.

"They're in the back of the altar. It's a big area, and some things are left there, but never for long. I put the candlesticks that were on the altar back there myself." She laughed. "You certainly have a deep interest in candlesticks, Mr. Smith."

Smith joined in her laughter. "Well, candles always add so much to the visual beauty of a service. I sometimes think of earlier times when candles were the only source of illumination."

"I think about that, too. Of course, they do have even greater symbolism. Some think that two candles represent the divine and human natures of God, but I prefer to think that lights on the altar signify the joy we receive from the light of Christ's Gospel."

"That's nice," Smith said. "Would it be permissible for me to go behind the altar?"

"Of course. I'll turn on the lights."

They stepped behind the altar, and Smith looked at the vault to his left. The woman explained that the first bishop of Washington, Bishop Satterlee, and his wife were interred there.

Smith's attention next went to a pair of candlesticks on a table. "Excuse me," he said, picking up one of them and lightly running his fingertips over the entire rim of the base, then doing the same with the other. He had a feeling the woman was looking at him strangely. He said pleasantly, "Yes, I do have a deep interest in these things. I'm a collector of sorts. My wife has a gallery." He knew it wasn't necessary to explain his actions, but he did anyway. He checked his watch. "Time to meet with the bishop. You've been very kind. Thank you."

"Any time, Mr. Smith." She hesitated, and he leaned forward to encourage her to say what she was holding back. "Mr. Smith, I know you were a friend of Reverend Singletary's, and that you are helping the cathedral in this matter. Is there anything new? Will they ever find the person who killed him?"

"I don't know," Smith said. "All we can do is hope and pray like everyone else that his killer will be brought to justice. Thank you again. I am late."

When Smith walked into the bishop's study, it was immediately apparent to him that St. James was agitated. No, distraught and angry more aptly described his mood. Smith mentioned it to him as they sat down for a lunch of onion soup, egg salad, and popovers, served by a member of the kitchen staff.

St. James locked eyes with Smith. "It's probably not for a bishop to say, but it's been one hell of a morning," he said. "I can do without such mornings."

"Care to share it with your rabbi here?" Smith asked.

"I have to share it with somebody. I've spent most of this morning with two of my canons, Merle and Armstrong."

"They must have said something out of the ordinary to upset you so."

"They certainly did. You know, Mac, from the moment of the initial shock of Paul's murder, my concern has been to protect this cathedral from any scandal that might result. You know that, don't you? You understand how important that is to me."

Smith nodded.

"I sometimes wonder if I would do anything to protect and preserve the cathedral's image, perhaps to a fault."

"That's always possible, George. Have you—done it 'to a fault'?"

St. James sat back and pushed his plate away. He sighed and chewed his cheek as he formulated what he would say next. Smith decided to help him along. "Tell me about the conversation you had this morning with Merle and Carolyn Armstrong."

St. James took Smith's lead. "How do I begin? At the beginning, of course. As you know, the police questioned everyone who was in the cathedral the night of Paul's murder. There doesn't seem to be any doubt, does there, that he was killed the night before the body was found?"

"That seems to be firmly established."

"Reverend Merle told the police that he was not in the cathedral that night."

"And?"

"And he has been contradicted."

"Who contradicted him?"

"Reverend Armstrong. You know her, I believe."

"Not well, but Annabel and she have become friendly over the past few months. They've been working together on the mission fund-raiser that's being held at Annabel's gallery. Why would Reverend Merle have lied about being in the cathedral? He'd have every right to be here."

"I don't know, but he continues to maintain that he was not here. He says Reverend Armstrong is mistaken. I think the police tend to believe her, Mac. They've been back twice to speak with Merle."

"You can't blame them for that, considering the conflicting testimony. What do *you* think, George? Was Merle in the cathedral and is he lying, or is Reverend Armstrong lying, or mistaken?"

"I have no idea. Jonathon assures me that he was not here that night, and I have no reason to disbelieve him. On the other hand, I have no reason to question the honesty of Reverend Armstrong." His smile was pained, and he slowly shook his head. "It almost doesn't matter who is telling the truth. The result is that instead of my clergy pulling together and closing ranks in the interest of protecting this cathedral, they are now squabbling. It would be bad enough if they did it privately, but Carolyn Armstrong has made it plain to the police that she is certain Jonathon was in the cathedral that night. Their behavior is so destructive."

"Yes, but there isn't much you can do about it."

"I'm well aware of that." St. James hadn't meant to snap at Smith. He apologized.

"No apologies needed, George. You've been under the gun ever since this happened. This kind of pressure takes its toll. What concerns me is why either of them might lie. Does Merle think that if he denies that he was in the cathedral, no one will consider him a suspect? Or, is he lying because . . . ?"

"Exactly what I was thinking, Mac. Is he lying because he has something to cover up?"

Smith put his finger in the air. "Or is there a reason for Armstrong to lie about Merle? Could this be an attempt to get some kind of shot at him?"

"I almost don't want to know. Eat something, Mac."

Smith laughed. "Before it gets cold? It's already cold, which is what egg salad is supposed to be." He ate some of the salad and half a popover.

St. James appeared to be having difficulty finding a comfortable position in his chair. There was more going on in the bishop's mind than this conflict between his two canons, Smith knew. St. James eventually got up and went to a window overlooking the cathedral close. He stood erect, his hands locked behind his back, his upper body moving with each deep breath, the body language of a man summoning up the fortitude to face a further unpleasant reality.

"The egg salad is good, George, but I prefer conversation," said Smith.

The bishop gave Smith a strong, definitive nod of his head. "You read people pretty well, don't you, Mac?"

"Sometimes. I think this might be one of them. Come, sit down."

After St. James returned to his chair, Smith said, "All right, you have a potential problem because of the conflicting stories of two of your canons. What else happened this morning that has you so uptight?"

St. James let out a baleful sigh. "Just about everything has me upset, Mac, all having to do with Paul's murder. Reverend Armstrong's accusation about Merle being in the cathedral that night wasn't the only thing she brought up this morning. I'm meeting this afternoon with a Korean gentleman named Jin Tse. I met with him immediately after Paul's death. Mr. Tse was anxious . . . I suppose I can't blame him . . . that the cathedral's support of the Word of Peace movement not diminish because of Paul's passing. I assured him it wouldn't, although I must admit I was not acting out of deep conviction. Frankly, I don't like Mr. Tse, and although I can't quarrel with the stated purpose of Word of Peace, I have had many uneasy moments about it. These movements sweep up people with all sorts of motives, and Word of Peace seems better supplied with self-seekers than peace-seekers. It occurred to me when you mentioned the murder of Reverend Priestly in England to ask whether he had any connection with the movement."

"Not that I know of, unless his friendship with Paul is an indication. Why do you ask?"

"Do you think it's possible . . . ?"

Smith waited for the bishop to complete his thought.

"Do you think it's remotely possible that whoever murdered Paul had some connection with Word of Peace?"

"Of course it's possible, George, and I've pondered that. It's also just as plausible that Paul was murdered by someone not *from* Word of Peace, but who was an enemy of the group." Smith narrowed his eyes. "You obviously are doing more than speculating here. What triggered this question?"

"I believe the purpose of the meeting this afternoon is to encourage me to delegate someone to take Paul's place in the movement."

"Who gets the nod?" Smith asked.

"I could be cruel to both parties and assign Reverend Merle."

Smith laughed. "Merle? He doesn't strike me as the type to get involved in liberal causes."

"Exactly. That's where the cruelty comes in. It certainly wouldn't be fair to Word of Peace, either. The obvious choice is Reverend Armstrong. She was very much in sympathy with the movement and Paul's connection with it." He lowered his eyes. "At least I thought she was until this morning."

"What did she say to change your mind?"

"She told me that she'd warned Paul only a few days before his death to be careful of the people from Word of Peace. She told him—at least she claims to have told him—that some of the people were evil zealots who would not allow anything or anybody to stand in their way."

Smith shrugged. "She's right, of course. Extremists on any side of an issue tend to be myopic. Did she name anybody in particular?"

"No. Unfortunately, I had to leave the room at that moment to take a long-distance call from my son, who was on the phone with his mother. When I returned, she was pacing the room and anxious to leave. I asked her to elaborate, but she said she was too upset."

"Did you believe her, George? Do you think she actually did warn Paul?"

"I certainly believed her then, or at least took it as a simple statement of fact. Sitting with you always changes my view of such things. I must admit that you create in me a certain cynicism, or at least skepticism, when it comes to believing people. Not very healthy for a bishop."

Smith pushed back his chair and stood. "Maybe healthier than you think. Jesus had plenty of reason to be cynical and skeptical about some of his so-called friends. Look, George, I'd like to have a few words with Reverend Armstrong. Is that okay with you?"

"I suppose it is, although I wouldn't want her to think I divulged information from our private conversation."

"Don't worry about that."

"I just realized sitting here how selfish I've been during this lunch. You went through some horrendous experiences in England, and I haven't even mentioned them. How dreadful to have discovered that priest's body, and to have had Annabel almost killed."

"It was upsetting at the time, but I suppose we can dine out on the stories for a while. Funny, before I arrived here I spent some time dwelling on the possibility that a candlestick was used to kill Paul. I suppose I wouldn't have become this fixated on it if Reverend Priestly hadn't been killed by one. I just can't get it out of my mind."

"Because both were priests and were murdered in a church?"

"That probably has something to do with it, although I won't try to defend the notion. It's like the shrinks say. Tell someone not to think of a pink elephant, and that's all you can think of. Are you sure the police had access to every candlestick in the cathedral?"

St. James extended his hands in a gesture of helplessness. "How could I possibly know? I have many duties, but the candlestick inventory isn't one of them."

"I would hope not. I just thought you might be aware of another place within the cathedral that the police might have overlooked."

St. James shook his head. "No. I have to assume they were thorough. Besides, any object could have been used to kill Paul. Any object."

Smith thought of Jeffrey Woodcock's tendency to repeat, and the fact that George St. James never did. But he had now. For emphasis, obviously. "Well," Smith said, "if you think of something or someplace that might have been passed over in the investigation, let me know. In the meantime, I have some things to attend to, including a wife who would probably like to see a little of me this weekend. I plan a Sunday with the phone off the hook and my shoes never leaving the closet. Thanks for lunch, George. Tasty."

Smith returned to the cathedral's nave and wandered its imposing dimensions, stopping to reflect upon the seven-feet-six-inch-tall white Vermont marble statue of George Washington. He paused in the St. Paul tower porch, dedicated to the memory of Winston Churchill; in Glover Bay, which celebrates the first meeting of those interested in building a national cathedral in Washington, held at the home of Charles Carroll Glover in December, 1891; in Wilson Bay, which contains the body of former president Woodrow Wilson, the only American president to be buried in the District of Columbia. Then Smith looked up for a long time at the Space Window, a stained-glass jewel high above the south aisle. The plaque said it had been created by Rodney Winfield, and was designed around a piece of lunar rock presented to the cathedral by the *Apollo XI* astronauts. No matter how many times he visited the National Cathedral, there was always something else to observe, to learn from, to wonder at.

He started to leave by the south transept, but couldn't resist the urge to visit the Good Shepherd Chapel once again. He stood outside—a young couple was praying in one of the pews. Smith backed away and retraced his steps to the Bethlehem Chapel. As he looked in at the altar, he heard a noise behind him. He turned and saw that the door to the choir room was slightly open. It suddenly closed.

Smith knocked on the door. No one responded, although he could hear a piece of furniture being bumped, then heard a door open and close. He turned the handle on the door, and it opened. He stepped into the choir room and looked around. It was empty. He quickly walked to the only other door, which led to the outside. He looked through the glass in the door, and saw a young boy running in the direction of the St. Albans school. Smith couldn't be sure, but it looked like the young choirboy who'd sung so beautifully at his wedding, and who'd become ill during Paul Singletary's funeral. Why does he seem so frightened? Smith wondered.

He returned to the door through which he'd entered and opened it a crack. He could see directly across into the front of the Bethlehem Chapel. He opened the door farther and put his head out, looking to his right down the hallway leading to the set of stairs that went up to the Good Shepherd Chapel. The stairs were empty; nothing seemed amiss.

He wasn't even aware of the drive home. His mind was too filled with questions.

18

AT 6:00 A.M. Monday morning, Smith sat in the small study in his house in Foggy Bottom and peered at a pile of briefs his students had written. He'd just got up, was in his robe and pajamas. He'd decided to block out as much of the day as needed to read the briefs, and then to visit his mother at the Sevier home. He looked forward to spending time with her; he didn't look forward to the briefs, but they went with the territory.

Rufus paced the room in his customary manner of communicating his needs to his master.

"In a minute," Smith said as he turned on a small, powerful battery-operated shortwave radio that was tuned to the BBC. He often did this, if only to be able to offer a different analysis of world news at lunch. Could seem pretentious, but he liked the calm and reach of the British Broadcasting Corporation. He listened to the comforting, careful, assured voice of the British newscaster's report on events in the United Kingdom, and was disappointed there was no mention of the Priestly murder. Then, again, he reasoned, why should there be? Priestly was nothing more than a local parish priest in the Cotswolds, hardly the sort of crime victim who would interest broadcasters in the major cities.

He opened his telephone book, found Jeffrey Woodcock's number, and dialed it. It would be approximately eleven o'clock in London. Miss Amill put him through.

"Mac, good to hear from you. Have you settled back in to your Washington routine?"

"No, but I'm in the process. Jeffrey, heard any more from Clarissa Morgan?"

"No, although I understand she has left London. Good riddance, I say."

"How did you find that out?"

"Reverend Apt at Lambeth called me, said he'd received a call from her. She's no longer pursuing her claim, and was leaving London. I think she said she was leaving the country, as a matter of fact."

"Apt told you that?"

"Yes. Meant to call you. I was delighted, relieved, as I'm sure he was. Bloody nuisance, that kind of conniving woman. I'm sure her claim had no merit, but these people can make problems for others, wouldn't you say?"

"Yes, they certainly can. Have you heard anything new about the murder of the priest in Buckland?"

"Just smatterings. Dreadful that you had to discover the body. Dreadful. Hardly British hospitality at its finest. No, I think the last report I heard was that the local authorities had no leads. Probably have dropped the case by now. Obviously, some demented person, some lob who happened upon Priestly and killed him for whatever he had in his pockets, poor fellow."

"Had he been robbed?" Smith asked.

"I don't know. I just assume he was. Would you like me to check? I'd be happy to check."

"Yes, I'd appreciate that." Smith gave Woodcock the name of the lead investigator in Buckland who'd questioned him and Annabel. "By the way, Jeffrey, did you have an opportunity to find out whether Father Priestly had been involved with Word of Peace?"

"Glad you reminded me. Yes, as a matter of fact I did. Seems he was, at least according to one of the chaps from the organization here in London. Not heavily involved, though. Attended a meeting or two. About it."

"Appreciate the effort, Jeffrey."

"No bother, no bother. Terribly early for you to be up and around, isn't it?"

"I'm an early riser, although this is a little early even for me. Couldn't sleep. Lots on my mind, Jeffrey. Besides, I have a ton of work to do today, and thought I'd get a jump on it. Best to Judith. I'll call again in a few days."

Smith sat back in his leather swivel chair and pondered the conversation. How remarkably similar both murders were. Each priest was hit on the side of the head with what seemed to be an object of roughly the same dimensions. Both were alone in a religious facility, and in both cases it was assumed that the murderer was nothing more than a demented drifter, a derelict, a total stranger who happened upon them. "Can't be," Smith grunted.

Rufus had given up subtle communication. The Dane placed his large head on Smith's leg and growled, wagging his tail at the same time to make sure Smith knew it was not an act of aggression. Smith looked down into the beast's eyes and smiled, roughed up the hair on its head. "Okay, I wouldn't appreciate it if you kept me from heeding nature's call. Come on, we'll go out in the back."

Minutes later, mission accomplished, and Rufus's food disappearing from a large stainless-steel bowl on the kitchen floor, Smith poked his head into the bedroom. Annabel was still asleep. "Hey, I thought you had a busy day, too."

A tousled mane of red hair came up off the white pillow, and a sleepy voice said, "I do, but not *that* busy. What are you up so early for?"

"I always get up early. You know that. I walked Rufus and fed him, and talked to Jeffrey Woodcock in London."

"About what?"

"About whether there'd been any further news on Priestly's murder. I listened to the BBC, but they didn't cover it. I'm getting in the shower. What does your day look like?"

Annabel sat up in bed and shook the sleep from her head. "The accountants are coming in this morning, and that fellow I hired starts today. Let's see, I really have to start getting ready for inventory . . . oh, and I'm meeting with Reverend Armstrong at four o'clock."

"You are? I had an interesting conversation with George St. James about her."

"Concerning what?"

"Concerning the fact that a few days before Paul was murdered, she expressed her concern to him not only for the image of the cathedral because of its backing of Word of Peace, but because she was concerned for Paul's safety as a result of his involvement."

Annabel swung her legs off the bed and stood. All sleep was now gone. "She told that to George?"

"Yes. I told him I wanted to have a conversation with Reverend Armstrong. Maybe you could do it better and easier."

Annabel slipped on her robe and slippers and went into the kitchen to pour a cup of coffee. Smith followed. "What do you want me to ask her?"

"I don't know, but be subtle about it. George is concerned that Armstrong not think their private conversations are being spread to other people. Maybe just getting into a talk about Paul and Word of Peace will cause her to bring it up."

"I'll try," she said.

It was busier at the gallery than Annabel had expected. The carpenters working on the renovation of the additional space were noticeably behind schedule, which upset her. She didn't show it; instead, she was cordial and urged them to work a little faster—applying honey instead of vinegar, an approach she usually found more effective than complaining.

The new person she'd hired for the gallery, a young man just out of American University's fine-arts program, seemed more interested in demonstrating his academic knowledge of pre-Columbian art than in listening to what Annabel had to say. That, too, annoyed her, but she kept her feelings in check and suggested he find a quiet corner to read the catalog of pieces currently on display in the gallery.

In the midst of this, she had to sit down with her accountants, who were critical of her handling of the new bookkeeping system they'd implemented. And no wonder.

By the time four o'clock rolled around, she was happy to see everyone leave, and to welcome Carolyn Armstrong to the gallery.

"It's been a crazy day here," Annabel said. "I haven't even had a chance for lunch and was about to order something in. Join me?"

"No, thank you, I had lunch."

Annabel ordered a salad for herself, and two cups of tea. The women settled in her office and, once again, Annabel was quietly taken with Carolyn Armstrong's natural beauty. One thing was different this time, however. The priest was visibly nervous, something Annabel hadn't seen in her before, but it was there, unmistakable and disconcerting. Armstrong's serenity had always added an extra dimension to her appeal.

"First of all," Annabel said, "the good news. They're running behind on the renovations next door. They assured me today that they would finish in time for your exhibition and I have every reason to expect they will, but it's going to be close."

"Why is that good news?"

"Because everything else is worse. But you don't want to hear about my bookkeeping problems."

"I'm sure it will all work out," Armstrong said. "I have two more artists for the show." She handed Annabel biographies of two Washington artists whose work she felt was worthy of being included.

"Yes, I know this person," Annabel said. "She's *very* good. She'll be a real addition to the show. I'm not familiar with this other name."

Armstrong filled in the man's background, and Annabel was reasonably pleased with this second choice. Not absolutely original, but okay.

There were myriad details to go over concerning the upcoming exhibition, and they worked steadily to resolve them over the next hour. It was now dark outside; the pinspots Annabel had softened with dimmers gave the gallery a warm, inviting glow. She was locking the front door and turning a small sign to indicate the gallery was closed when Armstrong came from the office and examined the valuable works of art on display. "So beautiful," she said.

"Yes, I love coming here," Annabel said. "I find a lovely sense of quiet and solace when I'm here . . . and when contractors aren't."

Armstrong, whose attention was focused upon a black basalt feathered serpent on a Lucite pedestal, said without turning, "I've been looking for quiet and solace ever since Paul's death." She faced Annabel. "I always found those things in my faith, in being able to use the quiet sanctuary of a church to ask for them from God." A rueful smile came to her face. "It hasn't been working lately."

"Yes, I think I can understand," Annabel said. "Something that senseless and tragic is a pretty powerful force to overcome. I have many moments during the day when I think of Paul, of my wedding day. Of course, I didn't know him nearly as well as you did."

Armstrong looked back at the black serpent. Annabel came up behind her and stood silently, then asked, "Would you enjoy an early dinner together, or a drink?" The other woman had begun to cry. Annabel couldn't see her face, nor was there any sound, but the telltale movement in her back and neck revealed her sobs. Annabel tentatively placed her hand on the priest's shoulder. "Come on," she said, "let's go and have a bite. I just ate, but it was only a little salad. For some reason I'm hungry again."

Armstrong turned and pressed her eyes shut, opened them, and managed a small smile. "Yes, I think I would like that. I'm not due back at St. Albans until eight. Are you sure you have the time?"

"Of course. I just have to call my husband." It sounded good to say that.

Smith had just returned from visiting his mother at Sevier House. Annabel told him of her plan to have a quick dinner with Carolyn Armstrong.

"Fine," he said.

"How was your mother?"

"Good, although she got a call from a British journalist in Buckland who's doing a story about the Priestly murder."

"Why would he call *her*?"

"About me. The English tabloid press will try to track anybody down, anywhere—at least by phone. He asked for an interview, and she told him she didn't give interviews. Or read them." Smith laughed.

"Did you finish reading all those briefs?"

"Yes. Some were pretty good, one was excellent, most of the rest were ho-hum, one or two positively illegal. Have you had a chance to talk to Carolyn Armstrong about Paul?"

"No, but I suspect that will come up. She has to be back at St. Albans by eight. I should be home around then. There's leftover chicken in the refrigerator, and some frozen dinners."

"I'll manage just fine," Smith said. "Desolate, but fine. Enjoy your dinner. Love you, Mrs. Smith."

"Me, too, Mr. Smith."

Annabel Smith and Carolyn Armstrong left the Georgetown Bar & Grill at seven-thirty and said good night on the sidewalk. Annabel was happy to see that Carolyn's spirits were elevated. She'd become animated, even verbose, during dinner, and seemed anxious—no, "desperate" was a more accurate description—to talk to Annabel about anything and everything, including Paul's murder.

Annabel was eager to get home to share the conversation with Mac, but the minute she walked through the front door, she knew he wasn't there. She went to the study and read the note he'd left on the desk: *Have gone to MPD—Reverend Merle has been taken in for questioning—*

George called and asked if I would go—hope dinner was pleasant and productive—back as soon as possible.

He called a half hour later and said he expected to finish up shortly and would head straight home.

"Have they arrested Merle?" Annabel asked.

"No, just brought him in for questioning. He came willingly, but it's good I was here. I'll fill you in."

Annabel sat at the desk and made notes of what she remembered from dinner. She turned on CNN, but when there was nothing of local interest—aside from national and international politics, subjects which, in Washington, were considered local news by many—turned to a local newscast. There was a brief item about Jonathon Merle's having been taken in for questioning, although the wording of the report made it sound as if he'd been arrested.

She kept looking at the clock; Mac was a lot later than he'd indicated he would be. Finally, at almost eleven, he came through the door and received his customary exuberant, face-washing, stand-up greeting from Rufus.

"Where have you been?" Annabel asked.

"Tell you all about it as soon as I've taken the beast out. You didn't, did you?"

"No, I did not." She loved Rufus, but never enjoyed being dragged through the streets of Foggy Bottom by this powerful, albeit magnificent, four-legged animal.

Upon his return, Smith poured himself a brandy, a Nocello for Annabel, and joined her in the den. "Who goes first?" he asked.

"You," she said. "You show me yours, and I'll show you mine."

They both laughed. Smith then recounted for her what had occurred at MPD. Merle had been asked late in the afternoon to make himself available for questioning. Initially, he'd balked, but changed his mind after conferring with Bishop St. James and went with two detectives to MPD headquarters on Indiana Avenue. The questioning focused on two things: First, the inconsistency in his story about being in the cathedral the night of Singletary's murder. He stuck to it, claimed he'd retired to his apartment across the street in the Satterlee Apartment Building, where he spent the evening preparing a sermon he was to give the following Sunday. He had no one to verify that, nor could he explain why Reverend Armstrong would claim to have seen him in the cathedral that night. She was mistaken, Merle said, although Smith commented that the way Merle put it left little doubt in anyone's mind that he felt she was deliberately lying.

The other line of questioning had to do with rumors that Merle's personal dislike of Paul Singletary was intense. Merle did not deny that, although he repeatedly said that his feelings about Singletary—about any other human being, for that matter—could never be strong enough to wish him bodily harm.

"How did the police accept his answers?" Annabel asked.

"In their usual delicate way, with lots of sighs, raised eyes, grunts, and moans. I don't think they seriously consider him a suspect, but you never know. I'm just glad I was there as his counsel."

"That was your official role?"

"Yes."

"Then you're in all the way."

"I now have a client named Reverend Jonathon Merle, if that's what you mean."

"Damn!" she said.

"We'll see what develops next. Enough of this. Tell me about your dinner with Carolyn Armstrong."

"Well, let's see. We had dinner at the Georgetown Bar & Grill. I had a club sandwich, she had a salad with smoked chicken."

"I wasn't looking for the menu," Smith said. "Did you have a chance to get into the conversation she'd had with George the day before Paul's murder?"

"It came up. She said that she'd warned Paul early on about his involvement in Word of Peace. She said she asked him to get out, but he sort of laughed it off."

"Was she specific about any of the people in Word of Peace who might have been a threat to his life?"

"No, although I had a feeling that there could be a person or two whom she knew more about than she was willing to share with me. Nothing more than that, Mac—a feeling. Anyway, I asked plainly whether she thought someone from Word of Peace had murdered Paul. She said she thought it was a possibility, but then she focused more on Merle."

"I don't wonder," Smith said, "the way she was quick to tell the police that Merle was in the cathedral. What did she base her feelings on?"

"Mutual dislike. It wasn't easy for her to be this critical of a fellow priest, but she was candid. She told me that Merle was a warped and evil man, paranoid, jealous of Paul, and a man she felt was sufficiently unbalanced to have done such an act."

"You might say that Merle has a real enemy there."

"He sure does. What do you think?"

"About Merle, or about Word of Peace? I suppose they're all players in the game, not to be summarily dismissed, but I don't know. I wish I did."

They changed and climbed into bed. Annabel browsed through a lovely book Smith had bought for her, *The Artist in His Studio,* while Mac picked up where he'd left off with material for his next class at GW. Just before they turned off the lights, Annabel said, "There's one more thing I should mention about my dinner with Carolyn."

"What's that?"

"She was madly in love with Paul, and I think it even went beyond that. I think they were in the midst of an affair, a very serious one, when he was killed."

"She said that?"

"She didn't have to. Trust me. Good night, Mac. Sleep tight."

19

The National Cathedral,
5:00 A.M. the Following Morning—
Frost on Everything

HIS EYES WERE fixed upon the sword embedded in the heart of the Blessed Mother, rendered in tempera over gold leaf. The profound sorrow on the face of Mary Magdalene, who knelt at the feet of the Blessed Mother, radiated out into the Chapel of St. Joseph of Arimathea.

He lowered his eyes and leaned farther forward, his long, angular frame hunched over the wooden communion rail. Lips moved in silent prayer. It was cold in the chapel, perhaps because of the symbolism of Christ's death as well as the natural early-morning chill contained by the stone walls.

He looked up again, and his lips stopped moving. St. Joseph of Arimathea, he thought, the Jew who took Christ's brutalized body into his sepulcher because there was room there, and because there was room in his heart, too, for the crucified martyr.

Opaque, sunken eyes moved to other depictions on the mural behind the altar. Dominating the center was the Christ of Good Friday who had given His life so that others—so that we could enjoy an everlasting life through His grace.

"Forgive me, Father, for I have sinned," he said, embracing the richly polished wood of the rail as though to squeeze understanding and compassion from it. "Forgive me, Father, for I have sinned."

A cough. He looked over his right shoulder at one of two sets of carpeted stairs. No one. The maintenance man who'd cleared his throat as he started to enter the chapel had seen the figure at the communion rail and quickly backed out. You learned certain rules when working in the National Cathedral, among them that prayer was more important than polishing and was not to be interrupted. Maintenance chores could always wait.

Reverend Jonathon Merle made the sign of the cross and slowly stood, using the rail for leverage. Although he was no longer in a sub-missive prayer position, his concentration was as total as it had been when he was on his knees. He searched the faces on the mural. For what? Did they understand? he asked himself. Were they more than inanimate figures of garish paint and gold leaf? Could they hear his pleas for help? Did those beautiful figures function as conduits to *Him,* or was there a more direct communication?

Merle jerked his head left and right, looked up at the arched ma-sonry ceiling thirty-nine feet above, supported by the substantial stone pillars more than twenty-seven feet in diameter. This was a chapel he avoided when possible, so depressing was its theme. The other chapels rang out with the joy of salvation: the Bethlehem Chapel dedicated to the birth of Christ; the Resurrection Chapel a triumphant proclamation of Christ's having risen in victory. But this chapel was different, with its Norman altar, its green-and-brown stone floor like that of a Roman amphitheater, the attempts by the muralist, Jan Henrik DeRosen, to mitigate the horrible theme of crucifixion through the use of colors so vivid that they only masked what any true believer felt.

Merle went to the center of the chapel and stood on the stone floor. Now he was shaking with anger; it was as if he were there in the scene depicted in the mural, had been there on that infamous day. How dare they, he thought, and his shaking intensified. His fists were clenched at his sides, and his head slowly moved back and forth. There was no cough this time, but Merle sensed that someone was looking down upon him from the top of the stairs. He looked in that direction and saw the maintenance man quickly walk out of view.

"Don't let this happen to me," Merle said to Him. Merle cried in-wardly, but his eyes remained dry.

Then he stood ramrod straight, and his mouth pressed into a tight line. He walked up the stairs at the opposite side of the chapel, left the cathedral through the south transept, and sat on a bench in the Hortu-lus, the "Little Garden," centered on a ninth-century French baptismal font. He sat there until the sun had risen and Bishop St. James would be in his study.

"Yes, Jonathon?" St. James said after Merle had knocked and had been invited to enter.

Merle sat in a chair across the desk from the bishop and stared at him.

"Jonathon, is something wrong?" St. James asked. "You look deeply troubled."

"I . . ." Merle started to say, then fell silent.

St. James got up and came around to the priest. He knew it had been an ordeal for his canon to be interrogated by the police. He leaned back against the edge of his desk, folded his arms across his chest, and tried a little humor. "Are you upset because I never followed through on my offer of a Chinese dinner?" He instantly realized it was inappropriate, and certainly not effective. Merle looked ready to cry at any minute, but there was such an aridness to him that it seemed inconceivable that there could be moisture within.

"Does this have something to do with Paul's death?" St. James asked.

Merle sat perfectly still for what seemed an eternity. Then, with an almost indiscernible movement of his head, he nodded that it did.

St. James drew a deep breath and allowed his body to slump. Was he about to hear that Merle had murdered Paul? He silently said a quick prayer: Dear God, please do not let it be that. But he also had to honestly admit to himself that he had wondered from the start whether Jonathon Merle had killed Singletary. The animosity between them was overt. Devout as St. James knew Merle to be, and yes, good and decent, the bishop also recognized an enigmatic force within the priest, the sort of force that seemed endemic to social misfits, to those seemingly decent and good people who do dreadful things, who gun down fellow workers at a plant, or who follow their inner demons to cleanse the world by murdering prostitutes.

"Jonathon, you know you can trust me. Whatever is weighing so heavily on you can be handled more easily if it's shared."

Merle had been looking down at his hands, clasped in his lap. He raised his head and peered into the bishop's eyes with an intensity that could be interpreted as seeking understanding or revealing his distrust.

"Tell me, Jonathon," St. James said, forcing a smile and placing both hands on Merle's bony shoulders. "Tell me."

Merle spoke in a monotone. "I was treated like a common criminal. I sat in a room where the dregs of society sit, and was subjected to the same scorn. The only difference is that they deserve it. I do not." He leaned forward. "You should have seen what happened. You should have seen their expressions when I honestly answered their questions. They looked at me as the Blessed Mother looked at the Romans who put Him on the Cross. They saw nothing but guilt, nothing but degradation. It was humiliating."

"Yes, it must have been," St. James said. "Sorry I wasn't here when you returned. I was glad that Mac Smith was with you."

"Not all the time. He came later."

"Yes, of course he did. He didn't know you had gone to be questioned at first. Wasn't he a help once he got there?"

"A help? He is one of them. He does not understand that a man like me, a man like you, answers to someone above their worldly views."

"Mac Smith is a good man, Jonathon."

Merle sighed, and his head fell forward.

St. James returned to the chair behind his desk. "Jonathon, I understand the pain you're feeling, and I have considerable sympathy for it, but is that all that has brought you here this morning? Is it simply the pain, the humiliation, of having been questioned at police headquarters?"

Merle's head came up. "No, there is a much heavier burden upon me."

"And what is that burden?"

"That . . . I have been forced to suffer such debasement and degradation while the one who should bear it walks free."

St. James sat up straight. "What do you mean? Are you saying that you know who killed Paul?"

Merle's face opened up, blossomed as though he had awakened from a deep sleep. "Yes," he said.

Again, Bishop St. James had hoped it would not come to this. Did the priest sitting across from him really know? If so, was he about to point his finger at someone within the cathedral, someone who, if guilty, would bring disgrace to the institution he loved so much? He didn't ask for a name.

"She is a slut," Merle said.

"She is a . . . a slut? Jonathon, to whom are you referring?"

"Reverend Armstrong."

"Oh, my God," St. James said, bringing his hand to his face and rubbing his eyes.

Merle was now more animated. "Don't you see? She shared his bed. She slept with him, fed his carnal instincts."

St. James flapped his hands in the air as though to obliterate everything that was happening at the moment. "Jonathon, you are saying that Reverend Armstrong and Reverend Singletary . . . had an affair?"

The smile that crossed Merle's face was the first that morning. "Of course," he said. "Everyone was aware of it. I knew about it long ago. Didn't you?"

"No, I did not, and I am not sure I believe it now. How can you make such an accusation? Do you have proof of this?"

Merle's smile widened. "Oh, my dear friend and bishop, it has been going on under your nose for so very long."

St. James abruptly went to the window and looked out over the close. "Are you saying that not only did Reverend Armstrong and Reverend Singletary have an affair, but that she murdered him as a result of it?" His hand gripped drapes that had been parted to allow the morning sun to enter the study. His eyes were closed tight: Please don't say yes, he prayed.

But Merle affirmed in a voice that had gained volume, "Yes, that is what happened."

Bishop St. James released his grip on the drapes and turned to face his priest. "I pray that you are wrong, Jonathon."

"I have been offering that same prayer ever since it happened," Merle said. "Unfortunately, my prayer has not been answered."

The aloofness behind Merle's statement angered the bishop. He gave Merle a hard look and said, "If you have any evidence to support what you are saying, Jonathon, you must come forward with it to the proper authorities. I'll stand with you, but you must have evidence, must have proof, before you make such accusations."

Naturally, it had occurred to the bishop that Merle's statements might represent nothing more than giving tit for tat. Carolyn Armstrong had implicated Merle in the Singletary case, at least to the extent that she claimed he was lying about his whereabouts the night of the murder. Was this a misguided attempt to get even? More disconcerting was the question of whether this was a way of turning the spotlight from himself to Armstrong because . . . because perhaps he *had* been in the cathedral that night, and . . . and *had* murdered Singletary.

No. That contemplation was too painful. The bishop said, "Mackensie Smith has been extremely helpful in every aspect of this unfortunate situation. He functioned as your attorney during most of the questioning at police headquarters. He is a friend of mine and of this cathedral. I would like you to tell him what you've told me. I trust his judgment. Will you do that, Jonathon?"

"Yes."

"Good. I'll call him now."

Merle stood and started for the door.

"Please stay until I've reached Smith and have arranged for you to get together."

"I have work to do, Bishop. You know where to reach me. Thank you for your time."

After Merle had left and closed the door, St. James sat in his chair and tried to sort out what had happened. There was such anger in the man; his parting words had been uttered with a wind-chill factor of minus sixty. Was there any truth to what he'd said? St. James tried to pray but was incapable of it. What would he ask for, what sins would he confess? Instead, he picked up the phone and dialed Smith's home.

20

Later that Morning—
The Frost Has Melted, But It's Still Chilly

CHOIRBOY JOEY KELSCH and his mother sat with other mothers and children in the waiting room of his pediatrician, Dr. Gabe Griffith. Joey had been cared for since birth by Dr. Abraham Goldin, who'd retired six years ago and sold his practice to the young Dr. Griffith and two associates. They'd built it into one of Washington's thriving pediatric partnerships. Some mothers of children who had been Dr. Goldin's patients weren't sure they liked the new, younger, and decidedly trendy pediatricians, but few had abandoned ship. The long waits that were never the case with Dr. Goldin were balanced by not having to seek out a new physician in another part of town, arrange for records to be transferred, and all the other inconveniences inherent in a change of doctors. Besides, this new group of Young Turks were local celebrities of sorts. Dr. Griffith wrote a column for a weekly newspaper, and conducted a talk show on one of the cable channels. Claiming Dr. Gabe Griffith & Associates as your pediatric group conferred panache akin to that of having the Gene Donati Orchestra play your wedding or François Dionot cater your bar mitzvah.

Joey and his mother waited almost an hour. Finally, a nurse said with studied pleasantness, "Joey, Mrs. Kelsch."

When Dr. Griffith finished examining Joey, he said, "Looks in great shape to me. A fine, healthy young man." Mrs. Kelsch's expression told the doctor his evaluation had not appeased her.

"Tell you what, Joey, how about going back into the waiting room while I chat with your mom for a few minutes?" Griffith said.

Joey didn't hesitate. He was gone within seconds.

"You said he's been acting strange lately," the doctor said. "In what way?"

"I don't know, Doctor, it's hard to pin down. Joey has always been high-strung and hyperactive, but ever since—" She looked up at the ceiling as though wanting to affirm that what she was about to say had validity. Evidently, she decided it did, because she continued, "Ever since Reverend Singletary was murdered at the cathedral, Joey has been a different boy. He sulks a great deal, and sometimes is downright arrogant and nasty."

"Well, you're right, it could have something to do with that event. Was he close to Reverend Singletary?"

"Not that I'm aware of. He certainly knew him because of going to school there and being active in the choir, but he never talked about Father Singletary to my husband or me. It's as though that event changed him." She told the doctor how Joey had vomited while singing a solo during the funeral.

Griffith, who was sitting behind his desk, ran his fingertips through a carefully arranged set of gray-black curls and shook his head. "I wouldn't worry about this, Mrs. Kelsch. Joey is a sensitive boy and has probably taken a great deal of this to heart. He also has the demands of school, peer pressure, and all the other things that work on a youngster of his age. No, I wouldn't concern myself about it."

"But you aren't living with it, Doctor," Mrs. Kelsch said.

Griffith smiled. "That, of course, is very true. Tell you what, Mrs. Kelsch. If you think it's sufficiently serious, maybe Joey should see a psychiatrist, talk it out, deal with whatever it is he's feeling about Reverend Singletary's murder. I can refer you to some excellent ones."

"A shrink for Joey? No, I think that would be more destructive than helpful."

"Well, that's the only advice I can offer. I'm a pediatrician, not a psychiatrist. Think about it. If you decide to give it a try—and some of the people we work with are top-notch—I can arrange an appointment. By the way, anything new on the reverend's murder?"

"I have no idea, Dr. Griffith," she answered. "My husband and I discussed taking Joey out of the cathedral school, maybe placing him in another private school just to get him away from there."

"That's a decision only you and your husband can make, but I wouldn't be too hasty about it. Keep an eye on him, and talk to your husband about getting Joey some professional counseling. Have a good day, Mrs. Kelsch."

Joey's mother tried to make light conversation as they drove home in their new red Volvo wagon, but Joey would have none of it. He sat in a defiant shell against the passenger door and would not respond to his mother's questions and comments. His withdrawal made her increasingly angry, and by the time they walked through the door of their home, she was screaming at him. He immediately went upstairs and slammed his bedroom door.

Maybe Dr. Griffith was right, she thought as she fixed herself a cup of herbal tea in the kitchen. Maybe he does need counseling, some sort of professional intervention. Lord knows, she and her husband had been unable to reach him. That's what shrinks were for, to reach people.

She carried her tea upstairs after having decided to suggest to Joey that they see a counselor. She knocked on his door; there was no answer.

"Joey, it's your mother."

When there still was no response, she tried the door, but he'd locked it from the inside. She banged on it with her fists. "Joey, open this door immediately! This is ridiculous, and I will not stand for it." She beat on the door again even harder, and the teacup and saucer in her left hand fell to the floor, the tea creating an instant brown stain in the thick white carpet.

She heard the lock turn and the door opened. Staring up at her was her only son. She had seen anger before on his face, but nothing to equal this. His eyes filled, and he screamed, "Leave me alone! You don't understand!" He pushed by her with enough force to propel her against the wall and bounded down the stairs. She heard the front door open and slam shut.

"My God," she muttered as she picked up the cup and saucer. What should she do?

She walked into his room and looked around. Was he using drugs? The thought sent chills through her. No, of course not. But people said that parents who assumed their children would *never* use drugs were often the most disappointed ones. She should have raised that possibility with Dr. Griffith. But Joey? At the age of ten? Ridiculous.

Still, she opened each of his dresser drawers and searched beneath what clothing was in them. Most of his clothes were in his room at the cathedral school. She reached up in his closet and ran her hands over the shelf, looked under the bed, riffled through books and papers and magazines. Then she glanced up at the wall above his bed, where a National Cathedral calendar had always hung. It wasn't there; it had been torn to shreds, the pieces strewn over his pillow.

She returned to the kitchen and sat at the table. Dr. Griffith had said that academic pressure might be contributing to her son's erratic and unacceptable behavior. Was that what the torn calendar meant, that he no longer wished to attend the cathedral school? Maybe it *was* time to change schools. She'd talk to her husband about that as soon as he returned from his business trip to Denver. Why wasn't he here now? She'd call him that night in his hotel and bring it up, even though he hated those kinds of discussions when he was away. He'd have to listen now. This was serious. This was their only son.

Canon Wilfred Nickelson, the National Cathedral's musical director, seldom came home for lunch. Although he, his wife, Jennifer, and their three daughters lived in a rented house only a few minutes' drive from the cathedral, Nickelson preferred to take lunch in local restaurants. Jennifer often commented that they would save a considerable amount of money if he ate lunch at home, but he never did. The fact was that Nickelson and his wife did not get along especially well; the less time spent with her the better, although he was a relatively devoted father who found time to spend with his family on weekends and in the evenings.

This day, however, he walked through the door precisely at noon.

"Willie?" Jennifer shouted from the kitchen in the rear of the small house.

"Yes, it's me."

She'd been kneading dough for bread; she often baked her own. Jennifer Nickelson was proud of her baking prowess, and had won some area bake-offs. Her hands were caked with flour, and an apron covered her from neck to knee. "What are you doing home?" she asked.

"I have something on my mind, Jen, and I think we ought to discuss it now."

Her eyes widened. "Sounds heavy. Are you sure I want to hear this?"

"It doesn't matter whether you want to or not. You're about to."

She muffled an angry comment and returned to the kitchen. He followed and sat at a small table. "Sit down," he said.

"In a minute, as soon as I finish this."

"Jen, sit down now."

Her husband would never be characterized as easygoing. She'd learned to live with his temperament over the years of their marriage, although some of her family had rebelled by finding excuses for not spending time with Wilfred Nickelson. Jennifer wiped her hands on her apron, filled a pan with warm water, and put her bowl of bread dough on a rack over the pan. Then she took a chair across the table. "What's going on, Willie? You sound as though you're about to announce the outbreak of World War Three."

He managed a smile, which she knew did not come easily. She looked into his eyes and saw something quite different from any expression that had ever been there over the course of their marriage. Usually there was blankness, anger, or cold control. This day, however, she discerned fear, or at least deep concern, in his eyes. She placed her hands on his on the table and asked, "Willie, what's wrong?"

If his smile was forced, his laugh took even more effort. "Wrong?" he said. "Absolutely nothing. In fact, everything is right. How would you like to move to San Francisco?"

"How would I like to *move* to San Francisco? I like San Francisco. I loved that trip we took there a few years ago. How would I like to move there? I wouldn't."

"Why not?"

"Because I like it here. The girls go to school here. We have friends here. Besides, I'm not a fan of earthquakes." She, too, forced a laugh to lighten things.

"Well, Jen, earthquakes or not, we are about to move to San Francisco."

She slumped back in her chair and looked at him as though he were an alien who'd dropped in from another planet. "Willie, what do you mean we're about to move to San Francisco? We live here. You work here."

"Not for long. I've been offered a job as music director at St. Paul's in San Francisco. I took it. We're moving there in a week."

She tried to respond but was incapable of words. Instead, she went to the counter and peered at the bread dough that had begun to rise in the bowl.

"Jen, did you hear me?" Nickelson asked.

"Yes, I heard you," she said in a flighty voice, a voice she often lapsed into when confronted with a confounding situation.

"Jen, sit down again and listen to me. I mean business."

"Yes. That's the problem: I know you do. I just want to make sure—"

The sound of his fist making contact with the table jolted her.

"Damn it, sit down."

She did as she was told, although she did not look at him. He said, "Jen, I hate my job at the cathedral. I've been wanting something else for a long time, and now I have it." He took her hands this time as he said, "What a wonderful opportunity! How many times have you said you don't like Washington, hate the heat in the summer? Think about it, Jen. I'll have a whole new situation that I can be enthusiastic about, and you and the kids can enjoy that beautiful weather out there, enjoy the Bay Area. We need a change, Jen. We desperately need a change."

It took a moment for her to summon up the courage to express what was on her mind. "Willie, I could understand if you had wanted to find another position and we'd talked about it. I think it's wonderful that you've found something that pleases you more, but why so suddenly? You said they offered you the job. That means you must have asked for it."

"Yes, of course I did. I learned of the opening through another music director here in Washington, called, put together a résumé and sent it out, and they want me. Isn't that wonderful?"

"And you never included me in any of this?" Hurt filled her voice.

"I'm submitting my resignation to Bishop St. James this afternoon. I'm supposed to be out in San Francisco in a week. I promised them that. That means you and the girls have a fast job of packing to do. Call a mover this afternoon. They're paying for the move, so don't worry about cost. Just get it done so that we can be out of here no later than a week from now."

"Willie, what will the Bishop say about giving him such short notice? That isn't right."

"Don't worry about that. He'll understand. He'll *have* to understand. Now, I have to get back." He went to the refrigerator and pulled out a plastic container of tuna-fish salad Jennifer had made the day before for the kids. He smeared salad on two pieces of bread, wrapped it in foil, and took it with him to the foyer, where he shoved the sandwich into his raincoat pocket. Jennifer stood in the kitchen doorway.

"No turning back, Jen," he said, pointing his finger at her. "I expect movement on this when I get home tonight." Then, as though he realized he was being unnecessarily belligerent, which would be counterproductive, he smiled, came to her, kissed her on the cheek, and said, "We'll have a wonderful life together in San Francisco."

21

The Next Morning, Wednesday—
Indian Summer

BISHOP ST. JAMES'S call to Mac Smith the previous morning had reached only Annabel's voice on their answering machine. It wasn't until late in the afternoon that Smith returned the call and heard about the bishop's conversation with Jonathon Merle, and that Merle was willing to repeat and elaborate it to Smith. They made an appointment for nine the next morning.

Smith was precisely on time, as was his habit, and sat in the bishop's study with St. James and Merle. Merle told Smith what he'd told the bishop.

"Reverend Merle, what you say is interesting, of course," said Smith, "but as an attorney, I have to question the validity of it." Merle started to respond, but Smith quickly added, "I'm not questioning your truthfulness. I understand that what you say comes out of conviction, but you've told me nothing that would stand up as tangible evidence. Was Reverend Armstrong in the cathedral the night of Reverend Singletary's murder?"

"Yes, she was."

"How would you know that?" Smith asked. "You said you weren't here that night."

If Smith had thought to catch Merle in an inconsistency, he failed. The priest said calmly, "That evening she was scheduled to counsel a group of young couples who are planning to marry, and to prepare a slide presentation in the auditorium upstairs, off the conference center."

"Reverend Armstrong freely admits she was here the night of the murder," said St. James. "She told the police that."

Smith said to Merle, "Why would Reverend Armstrong counsel

young couples here in the cathedral? She's assigned to St. Albans. Are they all planning to be married in the cathedral?"

Bishop St. James again answered the question. "Yes, they are, but there's no need to wonder why clergy from St. Albans perform tasks in the cathedral. All clergy assigned to St. Albans also conduct a great deal of their business here. We have separate buildings and what are basically separate congregations, but there is a great deal of inter-change between the two."

"I see," Smith said. He turned back to Merle. "Do you know how late Reverend Armstrong stayed in the cathedral?"

"You mean the night of Singletary's murder?"

"Yes."

"Why don't you ask her?"

"I intend to, of course, but since you seem to know a great deal about her movements that night, I thought you might save me some time."

"I don't know exactly how late, but it had to be at least ten."

"Why?"

"Because . . . because the slide presentation was extensive."

"You've seen it?"

"No, but I've been told about it." Merle was not quite as composed as when the conversation started. Earlier, he'd stared blankly at Smith as he answered questions. Now his eyes were in motion, and he picked at the skin on the palm of one of his hands. Rather sharply, he said, "Why are you asking me questions like this? I thought you were my attorney. You sound the way the police did, accusing, distrustful."

"Not at all, Reverend Merle, but I promised Bishop St. James that I would help if anyone from this institution were to be accused of Paul Singletary's murder. You're pointing a finger at Reverend Armstrong. All I want to do is to ascertain what tangible facts you have to back up *your* accusations. The police will be much tougher."

Merle leaned forward. His lip curled in anger, and he pointed a long, bony finger at Smith. "You want tangible evidence?" His mouth un-furled in a victorious smile. "Here's one piece of it. A week before Singletary died, I was privy to a conversation between him and Carolyn Armstrong. They didn't know I was listening. I suppose they assumed no one was able to overhear them. They were wrong."

"Where did this conversation take place?" Smith asked.

"By the Garth Fountain outside of Good Shepherd."

"Where were you that you could hear this conversation?"

"In Good Shepherd. I'd gone there to pray. The window was open, and I heard them. At first, I ignored them, but when I heard voices rise in anger, I went to the window and looked out. They were standing next to the fountain."

"Hard to hear conversations out there with the water running," Smith said.

"It wasn't running. The fountain was down for repairs."

"What did you hear, Jonathon?" St. James asked.

"I heard her accuse him of betraying her, of being unfaithful to her."

Smith glanced at the bishop before asking his next question. "You say she accused him of being unfaithful to her. Did she get more specific?"

"Yes, as a matter of fact, she did. She accused him of having an affair with another woman—she didn't say who that was, nor did I wish to know, but she was very clear about it."

"And you understood from the conversation that Reverend Singletary was intimately involved with Reverend Armstrong at that point."

Merle's laugh was sardonic. "What would *you* deduce from that, Mr. Smith?"

Smith nodded, conceding the point. "Did Reverend Singletary say anything in his own defense?"

"He told her to stop being childish, told her that she did not own him and that he was free to do what he wished."

Smith sighed. "Again, Reverend Merle, interesting but hardly reason in itself to accuse Reverend Armstrong of Reverend Singletary's murder."

"They ended their conversation this way, Mr. Smith. Armstrong told him that if she couldn't have him, no other woman ever would."

Smith said, "I appreciate your telling me this, Reverend Merle. Was there anything else said, or done, during that conversation that would lend credence to the notion that she is Reverend Singletary's killer?"

A look of exasperation came over Merle. His voice matched it. "Even if there were, is anything else needed, Mr. Smith? Just remember. Reverend Armstrong is a pathological liar. Just remember that. She and I could never work together as . . . closely as she did with Singletary."

Smith was about to tell him that from a legal perspective a great deal more was needed, but he decided he wasn't there to give a lecture on jurisprudence. That was for his class at GW. He thanked the priest again and watched him leave the room.

"What do you think, Mac?" St. James asked.

"He may know more. But I think that a *motive* has been established for Carolyn Armstrong to be a suspect, nothing more. Merle was certainly known to have disliked Singletary, which gives him a motive, too. I told you I intended to speak with Reverend Armstrong. I didn't do that, but Annabel did. They had dinner together."

"What came out of that dinner?"

"Nothing substantive, although Annabel left it convinced that Reverend Armstrong certainly had been intimate with Paul. Madly in love is more like it. Let me ask you this, George. Since we're discussing motive here, is there anyone else in the cathedral who would have had a motive, no matter how minor, for killing Paul?"

St. James pondered the question before saying, "I don't think so. Of course, none of us go through life without run-ins with other individuals. Paul had his share. I recall him berating one of our maintenance people once. I forget what it was about."

"How long ago was that?"

"Months."

"Is that individual still employed by the cathedral?"

"Yes, but don't read more into this than it deserves. I'm talking about an isolated incident."

"Did you mention this to the police?"

"No, I don't think so. I never thought about it until now."

"Somehow I can't imagine Paul berating anyone," Smith said. "I'd better have a word with this maintenance man." The bishop gave Smith his name. "While we're coming up with suspects, is there anybody else to add to the list?"

"If having a minor squabble qualifies you for the list, I suppose there would be dozens of people. A harsh word here or there, a momentary fit of pique. Canon Nickelson certainly was not personally fond of Paul."

"That so? Why?"

"I could never really put my finger on it, Mac. Something to do with Nickelson's wife. There had been rumors, briefly, that Paul had become involved with Jennifer Nickelson. I confronted Paul about it. I remember it clearly. He laughed and assured me that there was absolutely no truth to the rumors, that he liked Mrs. Nickelson as a person but that they had never done anything more than shake hands. I believed him, of course. Still, the rumor persisted, and I was told that Canon Nickelson was furious about it."

"Did you ask Nickelson about it?" Smith asked.

"No. I felt that would be in bad taste. Frankly, Mac, I've always been aware of Paul's reputation as a bit of a womanizer, but there isn't the slightest doubt in my mind that he had nothing to do with Jennifer Nickelson. Besides, it's all about to become academic."

"Why?"

"Nickelson resigned today."

"Really? From what I've seen—and heard—he does an excellent job."

"Yes, he's a talented musician. He'll be difficult to replace, although what really upset me was that he gave only a week's notice—six days, actually. It puts us in quite a bind."

"It must. Did he give any reason for such a hasty departure?"

"Something to do with a sick family member in San Francisco. But that's not the reason. He's taken a job out there as musical director for St. Paul's."

"Just like that?"

"Just like that."

"Aside from the situation with Paul, how did Nickelson get along with others here at the cathedral?"

St. James sighed. "He wasn't particularly liked. Strange when you think about it. Here's a man who is able to draw the finest musical performances from everyone, yet is unable to draw friendship or affection from those same people. No, he did not make many friends while here." He laughed. "Our students refer to him as Willy Nickel. They occasionally complain to me about him, but children often do that when having to deal with someone like Nickelson who demands the best of them."

Smith stood and stretched. "Give me a bit more of your evaluation of Jonathon Merle. I know you don't particularly like him, but is he what you would term a balanced, rational person?"

St. James's face clearly said he wished that question had not been asked. He answered it this way: "We all enter into this calling, this vocation, because we have been touched by something that cannot be explained by scientific methodology. We become priests and nuns because we believe deeply in something that no one can prove even exists. There is, of course, the Ayn Rand theory of self, which says that a nun becomes a nun because she is uncomfortable with the secular life, and satisfies her selfish needs while, at the same time, doing good. She's happier, and the lepers are treated. It's a nice theory, but with all due respect, Ms. Rand's view does not satisfy me. Maybe it holds water in some cases, but not all.

"The problem is that because this work, this calling, draws people who are bound up in some degree of mysticism, it often appeals to certain individuals who are not especially rational or grounded in a sense of reality." He raised his eyes and shook his head. "I wish I weren't saying this, because it is blatantly unfair to Jonathon. He's a good man and a fine priest. He believes fervently in his calling and his faith . . . but perhaps, on occasion, he believes a little too strongly and is intolerant of any deviation from it. He can be zealous about that to the same extent that Paul was about his work with social programs. And he has his own problems, which keep him from the perfection he seeks in himself. And others."

"Yes, I understand," Smith said. "I have to go. Thanks for your time, George. I'll be in touch."

After Smith left his meeting with the bishop and Merle, he went home to wait for Tony Buffolino to arrive. Buffolino had called the night before, saying he had some interesting information. He arrived, showing signs of his old excitement.

"First of all, Mac, you told me to check into the backgrounds of the two Reverends Merle and Armstrong. What I came up with ain't exactly a moon landing, but I think it's worth passing on."

"I'm all ears," Smith said.

They sat at Smith's kitchen table. Smith had made coffee and placed a plate of jelly doughnuts between them. In a moment or so, Buffolino was on his second. "First of all, this Merle is a pretty dull character."

Smith laughed. "I suppose you could call him that. Uptight, upright, but not a barrel of laughs. Is that all you've found out about him?"

"Yeah, except for one interesting period in his life that wasn't so dull."

"What period was that?"

"The two years he spent in a loony bin."

Tony's tendency to use the cruel vernacular often riled Smith, but he knew that if he raised an objection he would only prompt a debate over calling a spade a spade, as Buffolino called it, or telling it like it is.

"Go on," Smith said.

Now Buffolino referred to notes, and gave Smith the dates of Merle's confinement to a mental institution in Ohio. It had taken place fourteen years ago, and the official reason for his confinement was "schizothymic personality." He fumbled the first word.

"Technical term for schizoid," Smith said. "Any information on how his treatment went, and the prognosis?"

Buffolino shook his head and helped himself to another doughnut. "These are pretty good, but I'm not too hungry. No prognosis, but he put in a good two years, that's for sure."

"Okay, Tony, next."

"Next, this beautiful Reverend Carolyn Armstrong. A nice lady, it seems to me."

"Why do you say that?"

"Well, she came out of a tough life. She looks like class, but she's been over some bumps. I mean, she was born illegitimate and dumped by her mother. Grew up in a series of foster homes down in Newport News, and even spent time in orphanages. I didn't think they had them anymore."

"I suppose they do. Hmmm. Not an easy beginning for a young woman. But she certainly seems to have pulled her life together."

"Yeah, she sure has. She started pretty young trying to get it together."

"What do you mean?"

"She was in a beauty contest when she was sixteen."

"Beauty contest? Did she win?"

"Sure did, Miss Newport News."

"Did she go on in the beauty-contest business? Did she win other titles? Was she Miss America?"

Buffolino shook his head. "Nah. She's good-lookin', but no Elizabeth Taylor."

"Anything else about her?"

"A lot of boilerplate, nothing that matters where this case is concerned. I do have one thing on another front, though."

"Please."

"The police have what they consider a pretty good suspect."

Smith's eyes widened.

"You know that woman who found the body, that Mrs. Waters?"

"Sure."

"Well, she's got a son named Brian."

"So I gather."

"It seems this Brian Waters used to live in Newport News, too."

"Which means what?"

"Which means I have no idea whether he ever knew Reverend Armstrong, but I do know he was arrested twice for assault. No convictions."

"MPD likes him as a suspect?"

"Yep."

"Then why would he have come in with his mother—walked right into the police's hands?"

"Because," Tony said, "—maybe I'll just finish this last one—he knew they'd find his mother somehow. She was hysterical and would have eventually turned herself in or gone back to Mrs. Bishop, and the guy figured better the heat should be on his mother, with him the good guy, than on him. Besides, one of those assault charges in Newport News had to do with him knocking around a priest down there."

Smith poured himself more coffee and drew a deep breath. "How hard are they working him, Tony?"

"Hard enough to have brought him in twice for questioning. My friend told me they consider this guy a head case. But he comes off like a very nice and normal human being."

"So why did they turn to him? Oh, I guess I know."

"Why?" Tony said, surprised.

"Because he's a car salesman. They check on anybody in certain occupations."

"Just like on Italians or guys with beards. Car salesman—so he knows how to make nice to people. But my friend tells me that the elevator doesn't always reach the top floor with Brian Waters. Want to know something else about him?"

"I want to know anything you know."

"This guy is right of John Birch. He belonged to one of those neo-Nazi groups in Newport News, one of those hate organizations."

"Does he have any affiliation like that here in Washington?"

Buffolino shrugged. "Beats me. Haven't finished checking yet. But this is a guy who ain't destined to love a guy like Singletary who's talkin' all the time about the rights of the blacks and Hispanics and the poor, not a character who has already punched out one priest. You get my drift?"

"Yes. What's your friend's line on Brian Waters? Do they think they have enough to arrest him?"

"Not yet, but they're digging. I mean, the guy lives with his mother a couple of blocks from the cathedral. She's a religious fanatic, he's a fanatic in another way. Hey, I could come up with worse scenarios."

"Yes, Tony," Smith said, "you could."

Later that afternoon, he attended a faculty meeting at the university. Smith considered such meetings to be necessary evils or, at best, ritualistic necessities that had to be indulged. Everyone, sociologists said, needed a hangout at which to spend time in friendly surroundings and with people who shared a common purpose and background. Meetings were like that, Smith had decided years ago: they represented a need to gather together and affirm that everyone was involved in the same pursuit, more or less, and actually could get along, at least within the conference room.

The meeting lasted a lot longer than he'd anticipated or needed; this nothing new, it never seemed to fail. He left just in time to make a date he'd arranged earlier in the day with an old friend, Cameron Bowes, who'd been Voice of America's CIA liaison for the past ten years, and with whom Smith kept in touch. Smith had few close friends in government agencies, but Bowes certainly headed the short list.

They met in the lobby of the Four Seasons Hotel in Georgetown, where a pianist in a tuxedo played show tunes as background for Washington's movers and shakers in their comfortable little corners, large ferns providing "cover" as they talked about big things. Cameron Bowes was a slender, almost diminutive man, with silver hair, a face filled with lines, and interesting angles, and who wore expensive clothing like a model. He was also an unfailingly interesting companion over a drink, erudite and well-read, a man whose interests transcended the day-to-day demands of his VOA position.

After they'd been served drinks by a young woman in a floor-length green-and-yellow jungle-pattern gown, Bowes said, "A toast to the end of summer in Washington and to the Redskins. Your evaluation, Mr. Smith, of our favorite team."

"I haven't given much thought to it, Cam. I suppose I'll get into the season when it's almost over, provided they make the play-offs."

"Spoken like a true sports fan, although I think you're going to be very disappointed if you're waiting for that. Tell me, Mackensie, what's new on your plate aside from having committed your considerable legal talents to an entire institution of higher religion?"

Smith laughed and sipped his bourbon. "What do *you* hear about murder most foul in the National Cathedral?"

"Spooky places, cathedrals. I've toured all the biggies around the world. Not that I consider myself an aficionado of temples of worship, but my wife seems to think that a trip *anywhere* is wasted without spending at least some time in them. This Singletary was a controversial guy."

"Yes, he was, although a lot of the controversy may have been unjustified. Hell, wanting to improve the lot of his fellow man and wanting world peace shouldn't spur controversy. Agree?"

"Sure, but there are lots of people who don't. They prefer to see the situation remain exactly as it is, a growing number of rich people worrying about their capital gains, and a growing number of poor people trying to find money to feed their kids breakfast before they go to school so that they can learn what a capital gain is. Or capital. Anything new in the investigation?"

Smith shook his head and looked around the room. There were a number of familiar faces, faces that ended up in the newspaper now and then. He suffered one of those assaults of ambivalent feelings that sitting in such a place sometimes triggered. On the one hand, he liked being there, was at home in places of power. On the other hand, he knew so much of it was a sham, more a play than a reflection of real life. We're all players, the bard had said. Sometimes Smith enjoyed his role of the moment; it was after he'd got offstage and was home with time to reflect that he knew he really didn't like playacting very much. Not for himself.

Bowes seemed to have drifted into his own private thoughts, too. He said absently, "How deeply involved have you gotten in Word of Peace?"

Smith heard him but didn't react immediately. He was still analyzing his feelings about being there. He turned and raised his eyebrows, shrugged. "Not involved at all, although it keeps looming as a consideration where Singletary's murder is concerned. Why do you ask?"

"Well, Mac, Word of Peace has not gone without the Company's attention. Interesting assembly of characters in Word of Peace, lots of fine people with unassailable motives, a few others whose motives don't stand up to scrutiny."

"Is that so?" Smith said.

"How close are you to the bishop, Mac?"

"We've been friends for a long time."

"Then you have his ear."

"Yes, I think so."

"Why don't you give your friend the bishop some good advice. Why don't you tell your friend that he should disassociate himself as quickly as possible from anything having to do with Word of Peace."

Smith smiled. Among many things he liked about Cameron Bowes was that after an opening of amiable indirection, directness became part of the package. "Tell me more, Cameron. Tell me why I should advise him to do that."

"To avoid scandal, to avoid more controversy, to avoid further involvement in a mixed bag of good news–bad news people." Bowes looked around the large, lavishly furnished lobby before leaning close to Smith and murmuring, "Word of Peace has been infiltrated by damn near every intelligence organization in the world. When the movement started, it was pure, if you can call any movement pure. But it immediately attracted all sorts of global hustlers who use movements like this the way Wall Street rainmakers smell a takeover and jump in with junk bonds, et cetera. It's a classic case of cause and effect—or, start a cause and get several effects. The good guys come first, then the bad guys, then the good guys working undercover."

"I can't believe I'm hearing this from you."

"What's so difficult to believe?"

"That you would assign black hats and white hats so easily.

Intelligence organizations aren't always, to use your simple phraseology, 'good guys.' Anyhow, who are our major players?"

"The CIA, among others. The navy's in. The British have an even greater presence."

"Any special reason?"

"The Church of England." Bowes finished his drink. "They got suckered in like the National Cathedral did because of the passion and commitment of people like Paul Singletary."

Smith asked, "Should I be looking at Word of Peace as the place to find a murderer?"

"They're as good a place to look as any. Don't tell me you haven't thought about that."

"Of course I have. Any aspect of Paul Singletary's life has to be looked at, and I'm sure everyone with some official connection to this case is doing just that. But I've been looking into narrower possibilities. Somehow, Cam, even though Paul was deeply involved in the movement, I can't conceive of his being killed because of it."

As another round was served, Bowes stopped talking. When the waitress had gone, he said, "Ever hear of a Korean named Jin Tse?"

"Yes. Bishop St. James mentioned him to me. Jin Tse seems to be the point man for Word of Peace here in Washington. Singletary told the bishop about him, and after the murder, Jin Tse sought out the bishop to be sure of the cathedral's continuing support."

"Mac."

"What?"

"Jin Tse is not good news. Jin Tse works directly for Korean intelligence. He's also a known assassin." Bowes mentioned two political assassinations that had taken place over the years.

"Jin Tse did those?"

"That's our best information."

"Maybe he 'assassinated' Paul Singletary," Smith said.

"Maybe. Rest assured that possibility is being given very careful consideration."

"This has all been very illuminating, Cameron."

"What are friends for, if they can't illuminate their favorite people? Want to know what I think?"

"Only if you'll be honest with me about your source of thinking."

"What do you mean by that?"

"I mean that I would like you to differentiate between what you've read in the papers like any other citizen, from what you're telling me man-to-man, as a friend, and what you're telling me because of the Company's interest in this case. By the way, I assume the CIA's file on this has gotten pretty thick."

"Yes, and it includes material on Reverend Singletary's murder. I happen to know that by now a portion of it also has to do with Mackensie Smith."

Smith started to say something, but Bowes continued, "Every move you've made since you became involved is known to those charged with following this case. Quite an interesting honeymoon you had in London."

"That, too, huh?"

"Uh-huh. I don't want to belabor this, Mac, but we're talking big stakes here. If Word of Peace was involved in any way in Reverend Singletary's murder, it shouldn't take a genius to figure out that they will stop at nothing to achieve their goals, whatever they are, and that includes demonstrating an absolute lack of reverence for a law professor at George Washington University and his pretty wife. Be careful, Mac. There's a war going on. Singletary was only a skirmish."

22

The Next Morning, Thursday—
Still Pleasantly Warm

IF THE FBI had not decided to arrest overnight a number of people in Washington involved with Word of Peace, the small story in the morning paper about the cathedral case would have been given a more prominent position on page 1, perhaps at the top, run in 24-point Helvetica bold. Instead, it was relegated to the bottom, its headline in 14-point Geneva, and in italics.

The lead story was the FBI's sweep of Word of Peace leaders, including Jin Tse and some of his associates. Others caught in the net included a breakaway Catholic priest, the black leader of one of D.C.'s urban coalitions for the poor, a West German businessman, a South American embassy official, and a faith healer from Oklahoma who had somehow established a mission in Washington under the auspices of Word of Peace. Charges ranged from fraud to extortion, spying to conspiracy.

"Read this," Mac said, handing the paper to Annabel. She sat on the edge of the bed, and the widening of her eyes mirrored her reaction to what she was reading. "Wow!" she said, tossing the paper on the bed.

Smith had given Annabel a reasonable account of his conversation with Cameron Bowes at the Four Seasons, but had deliberately skipped the warning Bowes had issued. As he reflected upon it after parting from Bowes, he became increasingly concerned. Bowes was a straight shooter, not a bigmouth; he played it as close to the vest as any employee of a sensitive agency was expected to do. That he'd brought the subject up at all gave it, at least in Smith's eyes, considerable weight. He hadn't mentioned it to Annabel because he didn't want to concern her, although he would continue to be concerned about her, but he knew she wouldn't buy that decision. She'd want to know about any danger to him. She wanted to be a "partner," but only a limited partner, she'd told him. That didn't mean unduly upsetting your partner. Did it?

"How do you think this relates to Paul's murder?" Annabel asked. The story had ended with a note that Paul Singletary, the murdered Episcopal priest, had been actively involved with Word of Peace. The final line of the article directed readers to a parallel story about new developments in the Singletary case at the bottom of the page.

The headline on the smaller story read MURDER WEAPON FOUND? According to Chief of Homicide Terrence Finnerty, an anonymous caller to the police late the night before had directed them to the National Cathedral's Children's Chapel, where, according to the caller, the instrument used to kill Reverend Paul Singletary would be found. The police responded to the tip, removed two candlesticks from the altar, and, according to Finnerty, discovered that the base of one was dented in a pattern consistent with Singletary's head wound. Laboratory analysis revealed that a fragment of hair matching the deceased's was found, and that a miniscule residue of human blood of the same type as Reverend Singletary's was on the holder. There were no fingerprints. Examination of the holder involved the use of a mass spectrometer and other sophisticated forensic devices. The police had no knowledge at the time of the identity of the anonymous caller, except that it was a male.

When Annabel finished reading that story, she asked Mac, who'd slipped into sweats in preparation for a brisk morning walk, what he thought of it.

"Hard to tell at this juncture," he said, "but I have this nagging feeling about one thing."

"What's that?"

"That whoever put the holder on that altar and called the police is intimately connected with the cathedral, really knows it."

"You mean the murderer? No, it wouldn't have been the murderer who put the holder in that chapel and then called the police."

"I wouldn't think so. Why would a murderer successfully hide the weapon for this amount of time, then put it out in the open for the police to find?"

"Unless it served the person's purpose. If Paul's murder was not connected with the cathedral but the killer wants to have the investigation focus more intensely on cathedral people, it isn't a bad move."

Smith immediately thought of Brian Waters, the son of the woman who'd discovered Singletary's body, and who, according to Tony Buffolino, had become a prime suspect. He'd told Annabel about his conversation with Buffolino.

"Could be Waters," she said, as if reading his mind.

"Could be a lot of people, Annabel. I'll call Finnerty later and see if I can learn anything else. In the meantime, I'm ready for some air. I'll be back in forty-five minutes. Will you be here?"

"Probably. I'm not opening until ten."

They kissed, and Smith started for the kitchen, where Rufus's leash hung by the back door. He stopped in the doorway and turned to look upon this beautiful female creature who was his wife. He'd shared almost everything with her—should he tell her about Bowes's warning? He had to. "Annabel, I filled you in on what Cameron Bowes had to say last night, but I left something out."

She raised an eyebrow questioningly.

"Cam said he thought Word of Peace was a dangerous organization. He told me it's been infiltrated by many intelligence organizations, including people like Jin Tse, who, according to Cam, is not only linked to Korean intelligence, but is a political assassin. He also told me that the CIA has built quite a file on Word of Peace, and that you and I have prominent space in it. Even our honeymoon was tracked."

"That's horrible," she said. "What the hell did they do, put cameras in our hotel suites?"

"Probably not, but they certainly knew our movements in London. The reason I'm telling you this is that if there is some threat to us by virtue of my being involved with the cathedral and Paul's murder, I want to keep you as far away from it as possible." As he said it, he thought of his mother in Sevier House. Could she also be in danger because of him? No rational person would think so, but a reporter had tracked her down—or was it a reporter?—and there was a well-documented lack of rationality when it came to zealots and cause groups, to say nothing of intelligence organizations, including the CIA and MI5— and not forgetting Cosa Nostra and Colombian drug czars. None of them played by the same rules as the rest of the mostly rational folks. When groups like those decided the chips were down and the stakes were high enough, it was women and children first—forget about lifeboats.

Smith shoved his hands in the pockets of his blue nylon windbreaker. "I don't know how much credence to give what Cameron said, but he's always played it straight with me. I think he told me those things because he truly considers me a friend, and I can't ignore what he said."

"How much danger are we in?" she asked.

"I have no idea, Annabel, but we do know someone tried to run you down, trample you to death, in that sheep field. I know we've been watched. And now this bunch from Word of Peace has been arrested and charged with a laundry list including subversive activities, misuse of funds, money laundering, and God knows what else. Maybe you ought to go away for a while."

Annabel laughed. "Mac, that's grade-B black-and-white-movie stuff.

We're not on late-night TV. Go away? Where would I go? *Why* would I go?"

Her response nettled him, and he responded angrily, "Sorry if I come off as grade-B material, Annabel. I suggested it because I love you."

Oooops, she thought. She crossed the room, wrapped her arms around him, and gave him a long and intense hug. "Mac," she said into his ear, "you are anything but grade B. To me, you are the all-time leading man. I didn't mean anything by it. Still, I'm not leaving you."

"Please," he said, "don't ever leave me."

"Have a good walk. I love you."

"And I love you, Annabel Smith." He turned to Rufus, who was sitting at attention. "Come on, beast, let's go sniff up the neighborhood." He looked back at Annabel. "One thing's for sure, Annabel, nobody would mess with us with Rufus around."

"Sure," Annabel answered. "Any stranger with a gun and a dog biscuit wins. Go."

Smith's brisk walk with Rufus always gave him time to think, something he did better with legs moving and fresh air pumping into his lungs and circulating to his brain.

The first fifteen minutes were characterized by exuberance for dog and master. The middle quarter-hour found dog still charging ahead while master grappled with a damnable set of conflicting thoughts— questions, really—about recent weeks in his life. By the time the two were on the last leg of their morning circuit of Foggy Bottom, dog had slowed down and was panting, and master had come to the conclusion that everything, including the walk, had gone on long enough. His only commitment to Bishop St. James had been to give his friend unofficial legal advice, and to perhaps serve as counsel should the accused murderer come out of cathedral ranks. That should have been it. Instead, he'd found himself playing investigator again, discovering the body of a priest in the idyllic Cotswolds, almost losing his bride in a sheep pasture, and now being warned by a friend who was up on things in the nation's leading spookery that his involvement might cause harm to him and to those he loved. "For what?" he asked himself aloud as he opened the front door. "Enough!"

"Enough what?" Annabel yelled from the living room.

"Enough of this life. I'm a college professor, damn it, not a gumshoe! Let the police find out who killed Paul, and if it's somebody I care to represent, I will."

She appeared in the doorway. "What brought this on?"

"A walk with the beast and time to think. I'm sorry about all this, Annie. It's my fault, getting us into something like murder. You and I are esteemed members of the academic and artistic communities of Washington." He proclaimed it with exaggerated pomp, his hand on his heart. She started to giggle. "Therefore, the dirty business of murder and murderers shall henceforth be left to those of lesser stature and baser instincts."

"Bravo!" She applauded. "But what about Reverend Merle?"

"I did him a favor. He's not my client." He bowed. "Time for this sage to shower, which I understand places me closer to God, and to bestow my infinite wisdom upon my class of misguided achievers. Gimme a hug and a kiss, baby." He wrestled her into the living room and fell on top of her on the couch.

"You've gone mad," she said, gasping.

"I have, and I love every minute of it."

She rammed the heels of her hands against his chest and slid out from under. "Do you think you can sustain this burst of affection until tonight?"

"Do I have to?"

"Yes, and I look forward to the evening." She stood. "Now, learned professor, go get clean and teach. We need the money."

Smith didn't wait for his students to raise questions about what they'd read in the papers and seen on television. He announced, the minute he stepped to the podium, "Let us take what has become our daily fifteen minutes to discuss murder at the National Cathedral. You know what I know via the free press. Any comments? Any suggestions? Brilliant insights?"

Everyone in the room offered at least two of the above in the next ten minutes or so, but none of their speculations caused Smith's mind to turn down a new alley with a light of revelation at its end. He shared with them one small bit of information he'd received as he was leaving the house. Jeffrey Woodcock called from London to say that the slain priest, Robert Priestly, had indeed been robbed. His wallet had been taken, and it had been found in a public trash can in the picturesque village of Chipping Campden. Whatever cash had been in it was missing; everything else seemed to be intact.

"So?" April Montgomery asked.

"So, it means that the murder of Priestly now differs in two ways from the murder of Singletary. Not only was the same type of murder weapon, which could have been coincidental, left at the scene in Priestly's case, and not in Singletary's, but robbery might have been the motive. It certainly wasn't where Reverend Singletary was concerned. His wallet hadn't been touched."

"Meaning that two different killers were involved," Joy Collins offered.

"Meaning only that such a possibility exists." Smith asked what their reaction was to MPD's announcement the night before that the possible murder weapon in the Singletary case had been found. Their collective reaction pretty much paralleled his and Annabel's—namely, that the circumstances under which the weapon had been found were more interesting than the weapon itself. Bob Rogers, who tended to be the most reticent of Smith's students, suggested that whoever placed the candlestick in the Children's Chapel and called the police obviously knew who the murderer was and had been hiding the weapon in order to protect his or her accomplice.

"Then why would this person come forward now and lead the police to the weapon?" Smith asked.

"Maybe they had a falling-out," Joe Petrella said.

"Possibly, but why just lead the police to the weapon? Why not place an anonymous call and inform the police of the murderer's identity?"

"Maybe they didn't have that much of a falling-out," April Montgomery said, the hint of a rare laugh in her voice.

Smith smiled and changed the subject to the FBI sweep of Word of Peace.

April said, "I knew you'd bring that up. If you hadn't, Professor Smith, I would have. Reverend Singletary was involved with that organization. It seems to me that any one of those lowlifes arrested last night could have killed him."

Smith raised his hands into the air. "Wait a minute," he said sternly. "Simply because a movement dedicated to something worthwhile is tainted by certain individuals is not cause to paint that organization with a broad black brush."

"I agree," said Joyce Clemow. "But do you think Reverend Singletary might have been doing something . . . well, dishonest, or destructive, or even disloyal?"

"No, I do not think that is much of a possibility. I think Reverend Paul Singletary was a good man whose goodness led him, at times, into situations he would have been better served by avoiding." Smith looked at his watch. "All right, on now to the subject of effective plea bargaining."

As Smith was about to leave the building, Dean Jaffe's secretary handed him a three-page fax that had arrived from Jeffrey Woodcock in London. It was a column in a British tabloid. Woodcock had scribbled on top of the first page, *"Thought you'd be interested in this, Mac."*
The article began:

The brutal, grisly, bloody murder almost two weeks ago of an Anglican parish priest named Priestly in the peaceful Cotswolds raised little interest outside of local authorities there. But this reporter and this newspaper have recently learned that the deadly blow to Priestly's head might not have come from some lob looking to empty the priest's pockets of his meagre belongings, despite the fact that the slain clergyman's wallet was found days later in a neighbouring village. To the contrary, the wielder of the life-taking candlestick could well have represented an intelligence organization, even our own esteemed MI5, whose service to the Crown has not been without incidents of snuffing out life for the "greater good."

Highly-placed sources who have agreed to speak with this reporter only on the condition that their names not be revealed claim that the Reverend Priestly lived a life far more exciting than administering last rites to dying sheep farmers. In fact, according to these highly-placed sources, Reverend Priestly had been asked to leave the military service under questionable circumstances early in his career. A copy of Priestly's military discharge papers obtained by this reporter lists the reason for his severance from the service as "official," a term often used by military authorities to get rid of a troublesome person without saying anything good or bad about him.

Seems Priestly's dirty deed had to do with a joint naval exercise between British and U.S. troops. According to our highly-placed sources, the Reverend Priestly, a decidedly left-of-center chap, walked away with some extremely sensitive videotapes on which the latest military technology was demonstrated in living colour. Our sources tell us that he passed those tapes on to a friend who shared his bleeding-heart tendencies. The identity of that friend is unknown, although this reporter is in the process of tracking him down.

The article went on to outline in sketchy terms more of Priestly's background. Then it got to Word of Peace.

The Reverend Priestly was involved in a number of causes, local and international, most notably Word of Peace, a group whose professed purpose is to bring about peace on earth, but whose members evidently had less spiritual things on their agenda. A number of leaders of the movement were recently arrested in Washington, D.C., and charged not only with using funds raised for peace to line their own pockets, but with harboring a sizable nest of political operations. An Anglican priest named Paul Singletary, who was murdered in Washington's National Cathedral, was a leading voice in the organization. Whether he would have been arrested, too, must remain conjecture, but our highly-placed sources assure us that he was a close friend of the slain Cotswolds priest, and we have further learned that he served with Reverend Priestly during that joint naval exercise. Whether Singletary was, indeed, the friend to whom Priestly passed the classified videotapes is unknown at this time. It is known, however, that Priestly had recently indicated to a close friend—perhaps Singletary, who visited with him in the Cotswolds only days before his own murder —that he was about to make public what he knew about the flim-flam going on within Word of Peace. That, of course, would be sufficient reason for that organization, or at least someone from it, to silence him forever.

But there is more. Other highly-placed sources have informed this reporter that Reverend Priestly had been recruited by our own intelligence organization, MI5, and that he did its bidding to avoid having his unsavoury military indiscretions exposed. Was the Reverend Priestly about to blow the proverbial whistle on MI5?

Stay tuned.

Smith finished reading the fax, shoved it into his briefcase, and headed home. He and Annabel had discussed how little they really knew about Paul Singletary. But if there were even a modicum of truth to the suggestion that he'd passed classified tapes, he'd been a total stranger.

Clarissa Morgan watered plants in the villa on Virgin Gorda that had been rented for her. She then left the low white house carrying a small yellow carry-on bag, which she placed on the passenger seat of a white Toyota Corolla that had been leased for her. She opened the driver's door, paused to look out over the shimmering azure waters that surrounded the British Virgin Islands, got into the car, and drove slowly around the island until arriving at Beef Island Airport, where she parked and entered the terminal. She knew she'd been followed by the same man in the Toyota minivan who'd been her shadow since her arrival in the BVI. She didn't care, had never bothered to find out who he was. It didn't matter. She knew *why* he followed her, and *who* had told him to. That was enough. It was all enough. "Enough!" she'd said to herself two days ago after returning home from dinner at a local restaurant. "Enough!"

"Your flight is delayed, Miss Morgan," the petite, pretty native ticket agent said.

"How long a delay?"

The agent looked at her computer terminal. "Probably only a half hour."

"Not so bad," Morgan said, thinking that for Air BVI it represented being ahead of schedule. "Thank you. I think I'll have some tea."

The ticket agent watched the woman cross the small lobby and thought, Nice to deal with a visitor who doesn't take a delay as a personal affront.

The man who'd been standing near the door approached the agent. "I overheard you telling that woman that her flight was delayed. Is that the flight to New York?"

"No, it's to San Juan."

"But it connects to flights to New York."

"It can. It connects with many flights."

"Thank you."

The man, whose cheeks bore the spidery red lines of a heavy drinker, looked around the lobby as though in a state of confusion.

"Is there something else I can help you with, sir?" the agent asked.

He was startled at her voice. "No, no, thank you very much." He walked in the direction of the small concession stand that sold coffee, tea, and sweets. He stopped a dozen feet away and watched Clarissa Morgan as she was handed a Styrofoam cup, paid the attendant, and went to a bench against the wall. Once seated, she looked at him and smiled. He turned away, glanced back, then went outside.

A half hour later Clarissa Morgan gave her boarding pass to the attendant, climbed the drop-down stairs, and disappeared through a door. The man went to a public phone. He pulled a dozen scraps of paper from the pocket of his soiled safari jacket, cursed, dropped several others to the ground, picked them up, cursed again, and found what he was looking for. He put on glasses, leaned close to the phone's dial pad, and slowly, tentatively, punched in numbers. The operator came on the line, and the man gave her a long series of numbers. "Collect," he said. "Make it collect. Tell them this is Dedgeby from the BVI." His accent was Cockney. He waited for several seconds, and then heard the sound of a phone ringing. After four rings a crisp voice said, "Yes."

"A collect call from Mr. Dedgeby in the British Virgin Islands."

"Hold on." After a minute of static and crackling, the person said, "Go ahead."

"Give me Control."

"Hold on," the man on the other end said. Seconds later another voice came on the line. "Mr. Dedgeby. What do you have?"

"The Morgan woman. She's getting on a plane for Puerto Rico."

"Is that so? Perhaps she has friends there."

"I don't know anything about that," Dedgeby said, wiping perspiration from his brow. He didn't like making a living watching other people. It was too demanding. But it paid well. Besides, it was that or jail. He preferred spending his days and nights in one of the local places, drinking rum. You couldn't do that when you were told to watch somebody, had to be on tap all the time, waiting for them, spying on them, taking away time better spent with friends over some Pussers.

"Mr. Dedgeby."

"Yes, I'm here."

"You say she's boarding a flight to Puerto Rico. Has it left yet?"

"No, it's bloody well still here. These people don't know how to run an airline. Probably sit out there in the heat for another hour."

The man on the other end said, "Thank you for the information, Dedgeby." A loud click broke the connection.

Dedgeby got into his battered minivan. It threatened not to start, but it eventually did, and he drove off, talking to himself, a smile on his face. "Bloody glad she's gone. Hope she never comes back."

* * *

"Leighton here," Brett Leighton said into the phone.

"Sir, we received a call from Dedgeby in the BVI."

"Yes? What did he have to say?"

"Miss Morgan has boarded a flight for San Juan, Puerto Rico."

"I see. Is that her final destination?"

"Dedgeby didn't know, sir."

"Yes. Well, thank you for calling." He hung up.

Two hours later Brett Leighton, wearing a new tweed suit tailored for him at P. A. Crowe in a way that accommodated his slightly leftward leaning posture, boarded a Concorde flight to New York. Once settled, he removed a piece of paper from his inside jacket pocket on which was written a flight itinerary, commencing in the British Virgin Islands and terminating in New York, with a two-hour layover in Puerto Rico.

"Foolish woman," he said quietly.

The man seated next to him turned. "Pardon?"

Leighton smiled. "Nothing, sorry to disturb you. Nasty habit I have of talking to myself at times. Shan't do it again."

His seat companion smiled, too, and went back to his magazine.

Foolish woman, Leighton thought, silently this time. Involving women in such projects was always a mistake, in his judgment, and he'd expressed that view to his superiors on more than one occasion. Too emotional, too impetuous. Too likely to fall in love with the one person they shouldn't. Here she was, promised a chance to stay alive if she'd just stay put. Well, he could have put someone on her in San Juan, but he believed that he knew where she was heading.

"Cocktail, sir?" a flight attendant asked.

"Yes, I think that is much needed. I've taken to talking to myself," Leighton replied pleasantly. "Gin, a double, and please withhold the ice."

23

That Afternoon—
Indian Summer Fading Fast

UPON RETURNING home from class, Smith placed a couple of calls to Terry Finnerty at MPD. He was informed on the first one that Finnerty was away from his office but would return shortly. Smith left his number, but decided not to wait for Finnerty to return his call. He tried again twenty minutes later. This time Finnerty was there.

"Congratulations, Terry," Smith said, "on picking up the murder weapon."

"Sometimes you get lucky."

"I read that you got a tip from an anonymous caller."

Finnerty chuckled. "Nothing but good citizens out there."

Smith ignored the cynicism. "It was a man who called?"

"Yeah."

"What did he say exactly?" Smith asked.

"I'll read it to you. 'You'll find the weapon used to kill Reverend Singletary on the altar in the Children's Chapel in the National Cathedral.'"

"Couldn't have been plainer than that," Smith said. "As I recall, the person who reported Singletary's body was a woman."

"That's right."

"Any doubts about the candlestick?"

"Whether it's really the weapon? Nah. No question at all."

"Thanks for your time, Terry. Just wanted to keep in touch."

"That's what a good lawyer is supposed to do, keep in touch for his client."

"I don't have a client, or have you decided to charge Merle with the murder?"

"No comment."

"What about Brian Waters?"

"What about him?" Finnerty's voice suddenly changed. He'd been relaxed, almost jovial, with Smith. Now, at the mention of Waters's name, he tightened. "What about him?"

"I got an idea you might be more than casually interested."

"Butt out of this, Mac."

"I didn't mean to upset you, Terry. I heard a rumor that—."

"Yeah, yeah, you heard a rumor. What you heard was garbage from that wacko you got working for you, Buffolino."

"I wouldn't call Tony a wacko."

"You call him what you want. I say nobody's home there."

Smith wasn't in the mood to argue Buffolino's relative sanity. "I just thought in light of the anonymous tip about the candlestick that it could have been someone like Brian Waters."

"Brilliant deduction, Sherlock. Great minds think alike. I have to go. Nice talking to you, Mac." He hung up with enough force to make the point that the conversation had, indeed, ended.

After walking Rufus, Smith left just as Annabel was arriving. "Where are you going?" she asked.

"The cathedral. I want to check on something. How come you're home?"

"I left some papers in the den. What are you checking on?"

"Something that's been nagging at me since the last time I met with George. I won't be long. You?"

"I'll be home for dinner. You?"

"Not only will I be home for dinner, I intend to cook it."

"How wonderful. I married the Legal Gourmet. What's on the menu?"

"A big surprise. See you tonight."

When he arrived at the cathedral, two MPD patrol cars were parked immediately outside the south entrance. There was also a van marked METROPOLITAN POLICE DEPARTMENT—FORENSIC UNIT.

Smith entered the cathedral and looked around. The usual tour groups were being led through the massive church by volunteers. Smith went into the War Memorial Chapel, where a member of the Altar Guild was dressing the altar. He looked into the Children's Chapel over yellow MPD crime-scene tape. It was empty. Two new candlesticks rested upon the small altar. He closed his eyes and tried to imagine what had occurred that fateful night. Had the murderer actually killed Paul in the Children's Chapel and dragged the body all the way to Good Shepherd? Probably not, but the idea was not out of the question, either. The entire cathedral was a potential scene of the killing. Distance could not be used to rule out any possibility.

Or had the murder actually taken place in Good Shepherd, the assailant bringing the murder weapon all the way to the Children's Chapel? Why would anyone do that? Then again, why would the person who'd called the police choose the Children's Chapel in which to place the murder weapon? Did that location have relevance, or was it simply the most convenient place? Most important, where had the dented candlestick bearing traces of Singletary's hair and blood been stashed all this time? And why?

Smith crossed the nave and went down the stairs leading to the lower level, where the Bethlehem, Resurrection, and St. Joseph chapels were located. He went to the Bethlehem's door. Another yellow crime-scene ribbon blocked access. Inside, a Forensic team was going over the floor of the chapel with some sort of electronic gear. The man operating the unit was dressed in a white lab coat. His eyes were glued to a screen on which eerie green lines were in constant motion. "Terry Finnerty here?" Smith asked over the yellow tape.

One of the Forensic men looked up. "He's upstairs with the bishop, I think."

"Thanks."

Smith knocked on the door to St. James's study. "Come in," the bishop said.

St. James was seated with Finnerty and two members of the cathedral chapter, and Smith joined them in a semicircle of chairs around the bishop's desk.

"Didn't think I'd see you," Finnerty said. "I was just telling the bishop why we've sent in a Forensic team to go over other areas. We figure that whoever murdered Singletary did it outside the little chapel where he was found, but not *too* far away. Make sense to you?"

"I've been thinking that for a while." Smith hadn't meant to upstage Finnerty, but the sour look on the detective's face indicated he had. Smith decided not to mollify him; he'd thought of it before the detective assigned to solve the murder had, so let it be.

St. James managed a weak smile, sighed deeply, and shook his head. "When will this be over?" he asked.

Smith nodded at Finnerty. The wiry little detective said, "That's what the politicos have been asking us. That's why we're back here extending the investigation, you might say. They're putting the arm on my boss, so he puts it on me. Chain of command. Anyway, Bishop, I know you don't like having us around, but it's the only choice we have. They want action. Besides, they invested megabucks in new equipment and like to use it."

One of the chapter members told Smith that an emergency meeting had been called for six that evening. "We hope you'll be there, Mac."

"I don't know, I think I—"

"We know you're busy, and that this is not your 'job,' if I may call it that, but your presence is comforting to all of us," said another chapter member.

"I'll see what I can do about shifting a dinner appointment I made for this evening." That shift wouldn't be easy.

Finnerty and the chapter members soon left, leaving Smith and St. James alone.

"I'm surprised to see you, Mac," the bishop said.

"I didn't mean to barge in, but—"

St. James shook his head. "Here I am being dishonest again. The fact is, I did expect to see you, if not today, certainly within the next few days. You know, don't you?"

"About the candlestick? About the call to MPD telling them it was in the Children's Chapel? Yes. I didn't know as fact, but I had a pretty strong feeling. Your language was too specific to be that of a layman. The only question I have is, why?"

"Yes, that would be the logical question. First, let me tell you how I learned of it. I was passing the Children's Chapel two days after the murder when a member of the Altar Guild, who was rearranging things there, stopped me. She said she had discovered something she thought I would want to know about."

"She'd found the candlestick."

"Exactly, although she didn't know the significance of it. She pointed it out to me because its base was damaged, and thought I might want to have it replaced. I remember laughing, saying something about how the bishop of the National Cathedral has to keep his finger on everything. She is a good woman, and she was embarrassed. I realized I had said the wrong thing. She'd only stopped me because I happened to be there. At any rate, Mac, I went to the altar and looked at the candlestick. I knew somehow the moment I touched it that it was the weapon used to kill Paul. My next thought was that if I was correct, it might somehow give weight to the possibility that he'd been murdered by someone from the cathedral staff.

"Having handy, immediate access to it suggested someone standing near the altar, where laypeople almost never go. Knowing that in the cathedral there are hundreds of candlesticks, I saw no need to get rid of it. The dent was small. A whole lot of things came to my confused mind, but, as always, I guess I wanted no further damage done to the cathedral and its people or to the work of God we're trying to do here. So, foolishly, I hid it, replaced it, and went back to breathing again. Full of guilt, of course."

"I understand your motivation, George, but why didn't you just get rid of it if that was the way you felt?"

"I replaced it on the altar and hid it in my house, but after talking to you about the murder of that priest in England, I knew I might at some time have to make it available to the authorities . . . no matter what the consequences. I suppose I wanted to hedge my bets, as they say." He saw the puzzled look on Smith's face and added, "With Him. I mean, it was bad enough that I didn't report it, but to physically destroy evidence would have gone beyond even my limits of wrongdoing."

Smith sighed and gave his friend a reassuring grin. "Yes, George, destroying it would have been a more serious act. Not that this isn't. By the way. Did the woman who pointed out the damaged holder see you remove it from the altar, make the swap?"

St. James almost laughed. "I certainly hope not. I mean, I assume she didn't. She walked away. As I said, she was embarrassed."

"Is it possible that someone else might have seen you?"

"Unlikely. There were people in the cathedral, but I think I was quick and careful. I was startled for a moment, though, as I was leaving the chapel."

"What startled you?"

"One of our maintenance men was standing just outside."

"Just outside the chapel?"

"Yes. He's a disagreeable sort, always slinking around someplace or other. Some of the staff have complained about him, but no one can find cause to dismiss him. He does his work."

"Is he the same one I talked to after you told me he'd had an altercation with Paul?"

"Yes," St. James said quickly.

"I didn't like him much, either," Smith said. "He told me Paul was always 'on his back,' always being critical. I don't believe that."

"Nor do I. At any rate, he was loitering about the chapel when I took the candlestick, but I'm almost positive he wasn't looking in when I did it."

"Let's hope so. I may talk to him again. I'm glad you called the police, George. As far as I'm concerned, we may be able to think that it never happened."

"Thank you, Mac, but I'm not sure your forgiveness is enough. I've let this entire cathedral down with my foolish, irresponsible thinking."

Smith shrugged. "Don't be too hard on yourself, George. Yes, you made a mistake. You were risking prosecution to serve other purposes. What it says to me is that you're human."

St. James managed a smile. "Yes, I suppose we all are. Flawed. Misguided. Meaning well and doing foolish things. But that was the idea, wasn't it, when He created us?"

"The biggest flaw is in people who don't recognize that they're flawed. You'll work this out with yourself—and with Him, who risked prosecution, too. In the meantime, I'd like to bring up something that's been on *my* mind."

"Are you about to confess something, too? I am in that business, after all."

Both men laughed quietly. Smith said, "I came to a conclusion this morning that I really have to bow out of this case."

"I'm sorry to hear that," said St. James, "but I'm not surprised. This has been a considerable imposition on your time and talents, and everything you have done to this date will always elicit gratitude from me and everyone else at the National Cathedral. I mentioned to the chapter members who were here earlier that I thought we should find money in the budget to pay you."

Smith shook his head and waved his hands. "No, money has nothing to do with my decision, George. I've spent a little for a private investigator, but no matter. I've done this out of . . ." He smiled. "Well, out of my respect for you and our friendship, out of an abiding belief in this cathedral, and a regard for Paul, and . . . and out of my own sense of guilt, I suppose. You mention money for my services. I'm sure you're aware that I only show up here at weddings, funerals, Easter, and

Christmas, and I don't always make the latter two. Let's just consider anything I've done to be a down payment on delinquent tithing."

"As you wish, but don't be so hard on yourself. You spend more time here than simply on those occasions."

"Strictly because of a pragmatic interest in certain events. I don't get down on my knees very much."

"From what I've always heard, you never did, to anyone."

They shook hands, and Smith said he would try to return for the six o'clock meeting.

"No, Mac, no need. I'll explain to the chapter why you are no longer able to be involved."

"Thanks for the offer, George, but I'd rather tell them myself." What he didn't add was that he wasn't sure he would follow through on his decision. In fact, he knew he probably wouldn't, but it had felt good saying it. At least he could tell Annabel he'd tried. And suggest that late dinners were more romantic.

He worked out at the Yale Field House and arrived home at four-thirty. There was the usual variety of messages on the machine, but the last one was less usual. It stopped him cold: "Mr. Smith, this is Clarissa Morgan. I trust you remember me from our brief telephone conversation in London. Sorry to have broken our date, but circumstances seemed to dictate it. I would appreciate a chance to meet with you as quickly as possible. No need to fly to London. I'm here in Washington. I'm reluctant to tell you where I'm staying and have it recorded, but I will make an attempt to contact you again, possibly this evening. Thank you."

"Ah, yes," Smith said as he slumped in the leather chair behind his desk. Rufus put his head on Smith's leg. Smith rubbed his ears, then looked into his friend's large, watery eyes. "Looks like things are about to get interesting, buddy."

24

Later in the Day—
Stormy Weather Ahead

IT WAS THE sort of domestic screaming match the neighbors had got used to since Nickelson and his family rented the small house in the subdued lower-middle-class neighborhood. It was worse in summer; then the windows were open and the sound carried farther and was louder. But even with the windows closed, the force of Nickelson's voice respected no barrier as simple as windowpane or door. You heard it, and sometimes it seemed so intense, so steaming with anger, that you considered calling the police. In fact, you did on a few occasions, and they came and calmed another domestic dispute. No need to haul the husband away, especially not the musical director of the National Cathedral. No blows had been struck, just angry words exchanged between a husband and wife. Nothing new to the D.C. police, or to police in any other city, for that matter.

It was business as usual this late afternoon for the Nickelsons' next-door neighbor. She'd been breading chicken for her family's dinner when the first salvo was fired.

In the other house, Nickelson shouted again, "I told you we were leaving in a week, Jennifer. Nothing has been done! Absolutely nothing!"

"We are not going to San Francisco," she said.

"Damn it!" He sent a row of books from a low bookcase flying to the floor. "You will do what I say." Each word was punctuated with a stab of his index finger.

Jennifer Nickelson turned on her heel and stomped into the kitchen. Their daughters were upstairs trying to do homework. Now they pressed their ears to the bedroom door. Sometimes they fell on their beds and squeezed pillows tightly about their heads.

Downstairs, Nickelson followed his wife into the kitchen. "You have an obligation to me, and don't you forget it," he said.

She wouldn't face him because she didn't want him to see the tears silently rolling down her cheeks. She tried to control her voice—and her trembling—as she said, "You have no right to put us through this." She slowly turned and extended her hands in a gesture of pleading.

"Will, are you so insensitive that you don't see what you're doing to us? Asking us to pick up and leave so quickly is unfair. Please try to understand how disruptive this is to the children, to me."

"I don't *care*," he exploded. "I said we were leaving, and we will leave when I say." His face was flushed with anger, and Jennifer backed away. While he'd never struck her, she always felt he was capable of it, sensed that if the rage boiled to a certain level it would spill over the rim and obliterate any sense of reason, cause him to do things he would not ordinarily, naturally do.

He was capable of exhibiting violence against inanimate things. How many times had those books flown off that shelf, or the table been slammed against a wall, a fist rammed through Sheetrock? They'd patched holes in the wall in every house in which they'd lived. Once, Jennifer had laughed when their oldest daughter baby-sat for a family that was considered a bastion of domestic bliss, a perfect couple. The daughter came home and reported that there was a hole in the bathroom wall where the husband had punched his fist through it. "I suppose there's a hole in the wall of every family in America," Jennifer had said lightly to one of her friends at lunch. "Better the wall than the wife," her friend had replied.

Early in their marriage, the thing that was most difficult for Jennifer to reconcile with her husband's irrational anger was his profession. He was, after all, the Reverend Canon Wilfred Nickelson, an ordained minister. A priest. Jennifer had been brought up in a religious household, her experience with clergy confined to the local Presbyterian minister, a gentle, ineffectual soul who never raised his voice, and who devoted most of his sermons to the forgiving, loving nature of God. Jennifer responded positively to him; her father was an alcoholic subject to fits of rage that included physical attacks upon her mother, and occasionally upon Jennifer and her younger brother. When she met Wilfred Nickelson, she saw in him the same passive kindness that her minister possessed.

Besides, Wilfred was very good-looking and loved music, which Jennifer did, too.

It seemed like only minutes after they were married that his volatile side emerged—about what, she could not remember; few of the issues that sent him into fits of screaming and table-pounding were remembered.

Now, fourteen years later, she faced him in the kitchen with a determination that she hadn't felt before. She would not pack up her family within a week and move to San Francisco. That was asking too much. Any rational person would agree with her. Her mother had agreed when she told her about it, and so did her brother. "Let him go by himself, and you follow later" was their advice.

"Will, we cannot leave here that quickly. It is unfair to the girls. If we must move, why don't you go to San Francisco and get settled, find us a place to live, and we'll follow when it's more convenient."

She thought she'd presented this idea nicely, but all it did was set him off again. He accused her of betrayal, of standing in his way, of threatening to break up the family and keep his daughters from him. She felt sorry for him at that point, so misguided were his reactions. She took a few steps toward him and extended her hands. "Will, I love you. We all love you, but . . ."

His anger had not abated, but he lowered his voice and thrust his face at her. In a way, the lowered, almost whispered voice projected even greater menace. "What is it, Jen, can't you leave him?"

She dropped her arms and stared at him blankly. "Leave who?"

"Him. Your precious Paul."

She tried to say something, but all that would come from her lips was incredulous laughter. "Will, how can you still . . . ?"

He grabbed her by the arm and squeezed, his face now inches away. "Stop it, you're hurting me. The girls will hear. Stop it, let me go!"

He propelled her against the sink. "Can't leave his ghost?" His voice was a snarl.

She started to cry, turned her head away from him. He strengthened his grip on her arm and shook her; now his voice peaked. "He's dead! You can't have him anymore." He grabbed her other arm and shook her violently, her head snapping back and forth as he repeated over and over, "He's dead! He's dead!" And then he hit her, the first time ever, the back of his hand against her eye, his knuckles breaking skin above it.

Upstairs, the Nickelson girls lay on their beds in the fetal position, pillows pressed tightly against their ears.

Nickelson released the grip on his wife and put on his coat. "I will never forgive you for this," he said. The front door slammed shut.

She walked on quivering legs to the kitchen table and fell heavily into a chair. Her first thought was to go upstairs and comfort the girls, but at this moment she wasn't physically capable of it. Besides, they'd see her and only become more upset. She touched the bone above her eye; blood returned with her fingertips.

There it was again, the accusation.

It had been that way from the first week of their marriage. He would erupt over many things, insignificant lapses in the housekeeping, or comments from her that he took in the wrong way, but the worst trigger was always his belief that she flirted with other men, was unfaithful to him. He should have known it wasn't true. What was she, someone who used heavy makeup and batted her eyes at passing males? Of course not. He would interpret her natural openness to another man as a come-on, encouraging attention. She'd never meant it that way, and soon found herself going into a shell socially, barely smiling at men to whom she was introduced and avoiding animated conversations. Couldn't he see that she was a devoted wife who enjoyed being a homemaker, a wife who baked her own bread and dressed her children nicely and tried to create a home filled with warmth and happiness for him?

He couldn't. It was a character flaw, her brother told her one night when she called in a fit of panic. "He should seek help. Find a good shrink. You shouldn't have to live this way, Jen. He might be dangerous, fly off the handle some night, become violent."

Of course, she did not heed her brother's warnings. Will never struck her or the children, aside from an occasional smack on the girls' rear ends when they'd been naughty. But she also knew her brother was right. Inside her husband was the capability to lash out one day over some innocuous provocation; he could hurt someone—most likely her.

The confrontations between them over Paul Singletary began the week Wilfred took up his duties as musical director of the National Cathedral. A welcoming party for them was held. Jennifer was excited about her husband's new assignment. To be tapped for the National Cathedral was a distinct honor. As far as Jennifer was concerned, he'd both earned and deserved the position, and she basked in it—quietly, and without overt display. She was proud to accompany him to his welcoming party. She bought a new dress and spent more time than was her custom preening in front of the mirror.

Will was in good spirits that night. They left the girls with a cheerful baby-sitter and went to meet all the wonderful people who would be part of their new lives in Washington, D.C.

Jennifer's first reaction upon meeting Reverend Singletary was that he was a very handsome man, and very nice. He took special pains to make her feel comfortable in the crowd of strangers. He brought her a glass of punch while her husband was chatting in a corner with a fellow clergyman, and immediately she knew Wilfred was aware of that simple act of graciousness. He kept looking over at her as she chatted with Singletary. Soon, he was at her side.

"You have a lovely wife," Singletary said to Nickelson.

"Yes, thank you." He took her arm and guided her away from the handsome young priest to a knot of people, mostly women.

That night, after they'd got into their robes and were sitting in front of the television, she said, "This is all so exciting, Will. Everyone seemed so nice."

"Too nice," he said, his eyes fixed upon the flickering screen.

"What do you mean? Was there someone you didn't like?"

He glared at her as he said, "Jen, I wish you would become a little more worldly. Just because some of them wear a collar doesn't mean they're all goodness and light."

She laughed nervously. "I know that. It's just that on the surface, they all seemed very pleasant and—"

"Stay away from Singletary."

"What do you mean?"

"Just what I said. Stay away from him. He has a reputation as a womanizer."

"I didn't . . . I didn't know that. I was just being friendly. He brought me some punch and—"

"Enough said, Jen. Quiet. I want to hear the news."

It was only the first of a number of scenes between them over Singletary, each displaying more of Nickelson's wrath. Jennifer tried to avoid Singletary whenever they were together at a cathedral function, but found it impossible to be rude to him. It didn't take much; all she had to do was smile and say hello, and her husband's eyes would be on her throughout the evening. Then, once they were home, there would be the inevitable blowup.

When Singletary was murdered, Jennifer was devastated. Her husband's admonitions had created a curious closeness of sorts between Singletary and herself, at least psychically. It was as though they were secret lovers. She'd come to the conclusion that Singletary knew what the situation was and was willing to play along with it, casting glances at her, his smile playful, a twinkle in his eye. A game. It had become a game, and he was an important figure in her life even though they barely said hello to each other.

All of this went through her mind as she sat at the kitchen table. Eventually she calmed down sufficiently to tend to her injury and go up to her daughters, who had resumed their homework. Jennifer forced a smile. "Hi, girls, how's it going?"

Her daughters turned to her with red-rimmed eyes. "Do we have to go to San Francisco?" the younger asked.

Jennifer stood silent, her eyes trained out the window. She responded in a calm and firm voice, "No, at least not right away." Then she hugged each of them and returned to the kitchen, where she filled the house with the sweet smell of baking cookies.

"Glad you could make it, Mac," a chapter member said as Smith entered the meeting room at six o'clock. He'd considered skipping the meeting and staying home in case Clarissa Morgan called again, but decided to take his chances. The meeting could be important, and he'd get back home as soon as it ended.

"Not much of a chore. It was a dinner date I could easily put off." Which wasn't true. He'd suggested to Annabel that they have a late dinner when he returned from the meeting. Her response was to announce that she was returning to the gallery, where she would try to reconcile those ridiculous spreadsheets and bank statements for those ridiculous accountants, and would take care of her own dinner needs, thank you very much.

Smith joined the others at the conference table and waited for St. James to arrive. When the bishop came through the door, his face was drawn and the corners of his mouth sagged. He said nothing, simply took his seat at the head of the table and stared at the tabletop, his hands flat on it, his fingers spread. He eventually looked up. "There is an urgent matter we should discuss immediately," he said wearily. "I just had a call from Mrs. Kelsch. As some of you know, she's the mother of Joseph Kelsch, one of our students and the most gifted singer in the boys' choir."

The bishop paused and said nothing for a moment.

"He sang at our wedding," Smith said into the silence. "He does have a beautiful voice. He was—"

"He's disappeared," said St. James.

There were muffled responses from the chapter members.

"He was supposed to come home after school, but didn't show up. Mrs. Kelsch became concerned and called the school."

"Why assume he's disappeared?" a chapter member asked. "Maybe he went off with a friend for the afternoon. You know how kids are."

"His room was searched. He'd evidently taken some items of clothing and a small suitcase he always kept in his closet. There is also the possibility that some harm has befallen him. Mrs. Kelsch told me he's been extremely upset lately, so much so that she sought the advice of the boy's pediatrician."

St. James looked at Smith, who said, "It probably is too early to assume the worst. But not too early to find him. The police have been called? Do we know who his closest friends are? Would Joey go to a grandparent?"

"Yes. The police have been alerted. One problem seems to follow another these days," St. James said. "Trouble comes in threes. Isn't that the saying?"

"Yes, and without much substance to back it up," said one of the chapter members, though smiling. The man was one of the more cautious members. "At what point do we worry about this in an official sense, Mac? Is there something we should do to protect ourselves legally?"

Smith didn't appreciate the pragmatic question, but ignored that aspect of it. "I suggest we conclude this meeting as quickly as possible and do what we can to help." He surveyed the faces at the table. "I understand this meeting has been called to deal with another aspect of the Singletary case. Has something new developed on that front?"

St. James answered. "Yes. The police have determined that the murder took place behind the altar in the Bethlehem Chapel."

Smith sat back, and nasty visions filled his thoughts. He could see Singletary sprawled on the stone floor behind that altar, and his mind immediately traced what happened after that—candlestick carefully wiped, blood mopped up from the floor, the body dragged down the hallway past the choir room and up that short flight of stone steps to Good Shepherd. Then, or maybe in reverse order, the murderer sought a place in which to discard the murder weapon. Who could it have been? *Damn it, who did this? Let it be over.* He glanced at St. James, who seemed to be waiting for him to say something. "Sorry, my mind was wandering. I'm glad they've nailed down where the murder took place."

"There's another issue to be raised here this evening," said St. James.

"This recent development seems to indicate more strongly, at least to me, that Reverend Singletary was murdered by someone with a connection to this cathedral, not by a stranger. If so, I want to allocate funds for the defense of that person, whoever it might be." He looked at the members of the chapter. "Mac told me earlier today that he could no longer continue in this role. I know he wanted to tell you himself, but—"

Smith interrupted. "Bishop St. James is right. I did make a decision to disassociate myself from this case. A simple matter of time, or lack of it. But I've reconsidered." Smith realized that his change-of-heart announcement came on the heels of the bishop's mention of funds being available to defend the murderer. Bad timing, he told himself. It would sound like money was behind his decision to back off. He said, "If you intend to finance the defense of Paul Singletary's murderer, that's admirable. But not related to my decision. I'll want only expenses. However, if you think that by creating a defense fund you will, in some way, cleanse the image of the cathedral, you're misguided. The cathedral didn't kill Paul. Eventually, people will come to see that."

"Oh, no, Mac," said a chapter member. "It is much more a matter of responsibility. I suppose you could term it taking care of our own."

"If that's the case, I applaud your generosity and sensitivity. Look, I'm not in this as defense attorney. I don't try cases, nor do I want to. My role is advisory. I will find you an attorney, should that need arise, and will do what I can to help that attorney do the job. Whatever money you come up with goes to that attorney, not to me." He finished with "Enough said. Is there any other reason for me to stay?"

"No, we just have some routine matters to take up," said the chapter president.

Smith stood and said to St. James, "Could we speak privately, George?"

"Of course."

Once in the hall, Smith said, "I got a call on my answering machine from Clarissa Morgan. I told you about her, the British woman who'd had an affair with Paul."

"Yes. You said she'd disappeared from London, never kept her appointment with you."

"Exactly. She says she's in Washington and wants to meet with me. I have no idea what it involves, but I'll follow through. I just thought you should be aware of it."

"Mac, let me ask a pointed question you asked me. Have you called the police?"

"Not yet. I don't want them to get to her before I do. Obstructing justice is getting to be an epidemic around here. But I have a hunch she'll open up to me more readily than to Terry Finnerty. And I think she represents the bigger picture, bigger than our police, bigger even than the cathedral."

"Do you think . . . ?"

"George, I don't think anything at this point, beyond that. She sounded anxious, said she didn't want to leave on my machine the location of where she was staying, and that she would call me again. I've got to get back to the house and be there when she does. If she does."

"Of course. Thank you for coming tonight, Mac."

Smith touched the bishop on the arm. "Getting complicated, isn't it?"

"Too complicated."

"Let a few hours pass where the Kelsch boy is concerned, let his folks and the police look for him. Chances are he'll arrive home full of apologies and excuses. If he doesn't show up soon, call me. I'll be home all evening."

St. James sighed. "Again, what can I say but thank you?"

"Try a couple of prayers for all of us, including yourself, and get a good night's sleep. Forgive my choice of words, George, but for a bishop, you look like hell."

25

A Pelting Rain
In Time for Rush Hour

WHEN SMITH RETURNED home, he discovered a note pinned to the front door informing him that his neighbor had signed for a delivery. He went next door, where Mrs. Sinclair handed him an overseas courier envelope. The return address was Scotland Yard. "Thanks very much, Valerie," Smith said to her.

He returned to his house and opened the envelope. The photos Annabel had taken of the figure on horseback had been blown up into eight-by-ten-inch prints. Smith scrutinized the pictures. The fog, and the distance from which Annabel had taken the pictures, precluded a clear view of the rider's face. What could be discerned, however, was that the rider was fairly big and broad-shouldered yet somehow plainly a woman, although her full British riding getup was almost unisex.

Smith left the photos on the kitchen table and was about to change into more casual clothing when the phone rang. It was Tony Buffolino.

"Hey, Mac, what's happening?"

"What do you mean?"

"I haven't heard beans from you. I mean, I been off the case a little bit, but I'd like to get back on." He spoke in a stage whisper. "Man, this place is drivin' me crazy. I got to get away. Come on, you must have something else for me to do."

"Yes, I might. How are you at finding little boys?"

"Little boys? What do you think I am?"

"Tony, hold the comments and listen to me. Where are you now?"

"At the club, where else? I spend my whole damn life here. That's the problem. Mac, between you and me, I got problems here, and not just with Alicia. Things ain't goin' so good, financially, I mean. I don't know, maybe I should turn this place into another topless joint like the ones on either side. Guys comin' in and out all night, and all the owner's got to do is pay a couple 'a girls. These acts I got here come high. They're all direct from Vegas."

"Vegas, Illinois," Mac said, "and lounge acts from East St. Louis."

Tony laughed. "Come on, Mac, turn me into an honest man again."

"Stay there, Tony. And stay as you are. Don't go topless. I'll get back to you in a couple of hours."

"You want to come down, have a meal on the house?"

"Thanks anyway."

Smith went into the kitchen to make himself spaghetti. Anything was preferable to the "chef" at Tony's Spotlight Room, another assassin. Annabel had left a message on the machine that she was taking her new assistant out for a lifesaving, or life-threatening, dinner: "To tell him he either starts earning his money my way, or he can find another job." Good: she was taking it out on the arrogant assistant.

He filled a large pot with water and put it on the stove, poured mushroom sauce in a saucepan, grated a chunk of Parmesan cheese, and cut a lettuce wedge.

The phone rang; he moved more quickly than he ordinarily would have. Clarissa Morgan was on his mind. That was the call he wanted.

It wasn't she. The dean, Daniel Jaffe, was inviting Mac and Annabel to a party at his house a week from Saturday. Smith's mind wasn't exactly on university party-going. He told his boss it sounded fine to him, that he would check with Annabel, and got off the line.

The water was boiling, and, adding a teaspoon of vegetable oil to keep the spaghetti from sticking, he snapped strands in half and placed them into the water, adding a pinch of salt. He turned the flame low under the saucepan and dashed oil and vinegar on the lettuce. All of this was observed with keen interest by Rufus, who could usually count on Smith to share. This was not always true with Annabel, however. It was a matter of philosophy, of dog rearing. "Of course he begs at the table," she often told Mac. "He begs because you give him something."

"Yes, but now that he's gotten into that habit, it seems a shame to disappoint him."

It was never a serious debate, and the dog knew it, like a child playing one parent against the other. He was better at it than most kids.

Smith watched the TV news in the kitchen while he ate. The discovery of small but electronically discernible traces of blood on the floor of the Bethlehem Chapel had been announced by the police. While that represented a significant finding, it did not move the investigation closer to identifying the murderer.

He fed a few strands of spaghetti to Rufus by holding them above the dog's head and watching him snap them off inch by inch. It wasn't a terribly humane way to reward the animal's patience, but Smith could never resist it when spaghetti was involved. Then he gave Rufus a real serving in his dish.

He put the dishes in the dishwasher and looked at the clock. Annabel should be home soon, unless her career-counseling conversation had been more complicated than she'd anticipated.

Smith was much on edge, and he knew it. Ordinarily, he was able to settle into his recliner and read on evenings like this when he was alone. Not this night. He found himself pacing the house, stopping only to look at the telephone as though it had a life of its own, or should. He tried reading the newspaper but found it lacking. Television didn't appeal, nor did preparing for his next class.

Then, with a ring that jolted his nervous system and threatened to alert all of Washington, the phone went off.

"Hello," Smith said loudly into the receiver.

"Mr. Smith?"

"Yes. Miss Morgan. I've been waiting for your call."

"I'm sorry to be so elusive, Mr. Smith, but I think it prudent. When might we meet?"

"Any time that's good for you. Do you want to tell me a little about why we're meeting?"

"No, not on the phone. I thought . . ." There was much pain in her laugh. "I thought it might be appropriate for us to meet at the cathedral." Smith glanced up at a clock. It was almost eight. "At the cathedral? At this hour?"

"I know it sounds an unlikely place, but it would suit me. Will you?"

Smith thought for a moment. The cathedral could do without new late-night visitors. But he mustn't lose the contact. "I suppose so. When?"

"Would an hour from now be rushing you?"

Smith's concern was that he would not be home when Annabel returned. He'd leave a note. "Yes, I'll meet you at the cathedral in an hour, Miss Morgan. How about the Good Shepherd Chapel—it's open at all hours."

There was silence on the other end, and the thought process she was going through was almost audible. "I'll call you back."

"Miss Morgan, is anything wrong? Can you confirm? Are you—"

A sharp click announced that the conversation was over.

Smith hung up and thought about what had just taken place. There'd been background noise—traffic, some voices. She'd obviously been calling from a phone booth.

He resumed pacing, but was interrupted by a call from George St. James. "Mac, I just received a call from Joseph Kelsch's mother. The police haven't come up with a trace yet."

Smith glanced at his watch. "I have a private investigator who's done work for me. I'm putting him on this. He's . . . he's between assignments and anxious to start a new one."

"How could he help? I mean, if the police haven't been able to find the boy . . ."

"Yes, I agree, except that he is a former Washington cop. He has resources of his own."

"All right, Mac. Maybe I should call Mrs. Kelsch and inform her."

"Sure, but I don't think it's really necessary. My investigator will be checking quietly. I'll keep you informed."

"Good. Have you heard from Miss Morgan?"

"Yes, twenty-one minutes ago. We were in the process of arranging a place and time to meet when she hung up. I think she was calling from a booth. Maybe ran out of coins. Or courage. She suggested meeting at the cathedral, of all places, but I think she might reconsider. How late will you be up?"

"Late. I'll be here in my office at the cathedral probably until midnight. Carolyn and Jonathon are somehow producing drafts of their report, even though they've accused each other of murder. And I have reports to get out. The world is made of paperwork."

"We'll all end up drowning in it one day," Smith said. "Listen, I want to clear this line. I'll be up late, too, and I'll be here unless I run out to meet Lady Morgan. I'll call you."

Buffolino took Smith's call in his tiny office at the rear of the club. "I only have a minute," Smith said. "About the missing boy. His name is Joseph Kelsch, Joey." Smith filled Buffolino in on the circumstances surrounding Joey's disappearance, his address, school, parents. Buffolino knew several places where runaway kids tended to go, and he promised to go out looking. "I'll be up late, Tony. Call anytime."

Smith checked the news again. His friend Rhonda Harrison was anchoring that night, and had just begun an update on the FBI's arrests. She said that a statement had been issued by the director of the FBI that the sweep was the result of an ongoing and long-term investigation of Word of Peace. According to the director, the Bureau had worked in concert with law-enforcement agencies from other countries.

The investigation was focusing on two aspects of the organization's activities. One had to do with the diversion of funds to the personal bank accounts of some of those arrested. The other dealt with subversive activities. Word of Peace concealed, according to the FBI's statement, a network of espionage activity, with the organization used as a cover. Sufficient evidence had been gathered to make a strong case against certain individuals within Word of Peace for the passing of sensitive and classified information to their respective countries or to stateless groups.

According to the FBI, those arrested had established an elaborate web of informants who reported on the activities of a wide range of people involved with Word of Peace. Secretaries, postal workers, custodians, and bank clerks received regular payments in return for passing on information considered useful to some of the group's leaders. Meticulous records had been kept and have been secured, and the individuals named in them will be part of the continuing investigation.

Rhonda concluded, "The director took pains to point out, however, that while many individuals have been accused of wrongdoing, the indictment is not directed at Word of Peace itself as a charitable and well-intentioned movement. Many outstanding individuals and institutions have given considerable support to Word of Peace, according to the director's statement, and it was his feeling that a worthwhile organization had been misused by these named in the indictment."

As Smith watched television, Brett Leighton walked into the lobby of the small and popular River Inn on Twenty-fifth Street N.W., a few blocks from Smith's Foggy Bottom home. He said to the nicely tailored young woman behind the desk, "I'm here to meet Miss Morgan. Clarissa Morgan. She's a guest."

The receptionist checked. "Yes, Miss Morgan is in room twenty. The house phone is over there." She pointed across the lobby.

"Thank you," Leighton said, smiling. He walked slowly toward the phone, glanced over his shoulder, saw that she'd turned her attention to a computer printer running off a reservation, and he quickly stepped into a waiting elevator. Room 20, he thought. He pushed the button for the second floor, stepped out into the carpeted hallway, and went to the door with *20* on it. He rapped lightly. No response. He knocked again, a little louder this time. Still no sound. "Too bad," he muttered, retracing his steps to the lobby and going out to the street. He turned deliberately and walked north, although unsure of which direction to try.

Had he gone south on Twenty-fifth, he would have come within minutes to a public telephone across from the Kennedy Center for the Performing Arts and seen Clarissa Morgan standing a few feet from it.

After abruptly hanging up on Smith—she'd had the feeling that someone was watching her—she'd gone inside the Kennedy Center and wandered around its massive red-carpeted and white, marble foyer; it was like a cathedral of another sort and purpose, she thought. She was tempted to use one of the public phones in the center, but there were too many people and too much noise to make the call. Eventually, she left the building and returned to the booth from which she'd originally called Smith. Now she was caught in a bout of indecision. She knew Smith lived in the neighborhood; maybe it would be better to simply drop in on him. No, she didn't like that idea. It would have to be another phone call. Where should she suggest they meet? He hadn't seemed to like the idea of the cathedral at first. She couldn't suggest her hotel because she knew *they* would probably know she was staying there. They knew everything. Not that she cared, at least she hadn't up until this point. The hell with them. Damn them all. But it wouldn't be fair to Mackensie Smith to bring him into the midst of something even nastier than he'd already experienced—to say nothing of his bird-watching wife.

The cathedral.

It had to be the cathedral. He'd show up. She didn't know it well, but had been there, had a sense of it. It was so large, there would be many places, like that chapel, where she could meet him, tell him everything. For it was time.

She stepped into the booth and reached in her purse. She had a few shillings, but she was out of American change. She swore softly, returned to the Kennedy Center, and went to a gift shop, where she bought a key ring with a ballet dancer dangling from it. She used a traveler's check and asked to be given a portion of her change in silver. This time she ignored all the well-dressed people milling about. There was safety in numbers. She stepped up to one of the public phones and dialed.

26

Now Raining Cats and Rufus-size Dogs

JOEY KELSCH SAT in darkness behind the Jerusalem altar, at the east end of the nave. It was deathly quiet; he wondered whether the sound of his own breathing, which he tried to control, could be heard everywhere, by anyone in the building. Next to him was the small suitcase packed with underwear, jeans, two sweaters, socks, and his favorite Ping-Pong paddle.

He sat on a brilliant blue needlepoint kneeling cushion decorated with sprays of wheat, grape clusters, a spear, and a crown of thorns, symbolic of Holy Communion and the Passion and the crucifixion of Good Friday. He'd taken the cushion from in front of the elaborately carved wooden communion rail that separated the sanctuary from the chancel.

Joey heard movement in the nave and slowly, carefully peered out
over the altar; he saw nothing and glanced up. Looking down on him,
or so it seemed, was a large carved figure of Christ set in one of three
reredos. Quotations from Saint Matthew's Gospel were written on another:

For I was an hungered and you gave me meat; I was thirsty and ye
gave me drink; I was a stranger and ye took me in; naked, and ye
clothed me; I was sick and ye visited me; I was in prison and ye
came unto me.

Farther up was the *trompette en chamade,* Willy Nickel always called
them, the imposing pipes of the great cathedral organ.

He looked over the altar again at the nave's vast emptiness. At the
far end, more than four hundred feet away, was the west rose window, a
soaring circle and an acclaimed tribute to the art of stained glass.

If there *had* been a noise, the source of it was not visible. Joey sank
down onto the kneeling pad again, drew his knees up to his chin, and
wrapped his arms about them. He was cold and frightened, and had no
idea what to do next. He'd entered the cathedral after having decided
he could no longer stay at school. Nor did he want to go home and face
the questions, the scolding that were sure to ensue. There was too
much on his mind, too many things to sort out, too many decisions to
be made. *Damn* Willy Nickel, he thought. If Nickelson hadn't given him
that stupid punishment of sorting music in the choir room, none of this
would have happened. He would have played in the Ping-Pong tournament and probably won. Instead, he was forced to witness the most
horrible thing he could imagine—yet could do nothing about it. There
was no one he could trust or turn to and tell what he saw, what he
knew. It hadn't been easy calling the police that next morning to tell
them a murder had been committed in the National Cathedral. He'd
blurted it out fast to the officer who'd answered the phone, and hung
up immediately. The policeman thought he was a woman. That's what
the newspapers and television said. Joey was glad. After making the
call, he had visions of some special machine attached to the phone at
police headquarters that could immediately identify boys and where the
call was placed and the school of whoever placed it—some supercom-
puter. He'd heard about voiceprints, and how each person's voice was
unique and individual. Yes, he was very relieved when he read they
thought a woman had called. But it was a fleeting and minor relief.
Because he still knew, still had been a witness to the event.

He began to cry silently. Maybe he would just die there. That would
be the end of it. Maybe he would just die and be found behind the high
altar the next morning the way Father Singletary had been found in
Good Shepherd. He prayed without sounding the words, ending his
prayer with "Please tell me what to do."

He didn't know that the police were outside searching the close for him, or that a man named Tony Buffolino was checking the bus station, or that his parents were at home, his mother hysterical, his father trying to calm her but quietly fearing the worst for their only son. Nor did he know that upstairs in the bishop's study, a meeting was in progress at which Bishop St. James and members of his staff worked on a financial report that was expected in two days at the church's executive council in New York City. With the bishop were Reverends Merle and Armstrong and three lay members of the cathedral chapter.

Damn that Willy Nickel, Joey thought again, clenching his fists. More tears ran down his already stained cheeks.

Mac Smith took Rufus for a short walk in the rain, returned to the house, checked the answering machine, and heard Morgan's voice confirming she'd meet him at the Good Shepherd Chapel. He wrote Annabel a note: *Gone to meet Clarissa Morgan at the cathedral. Don't ask why there. It just happened that way. Maybe we'll finally get to the bottom of this. Wanted to see you but will return ASAP. I love you. Don't worry. Mac.*

He checked his watch: time to go. He'd changed into tan corduroy slacks, and slipped a brown cable-knit sweater over the blue button-down shirt he'd worn that day. He'd also changed from black wing-tip shoes to his favorite pair of tan desert boots. He put on his raincoat, gave Rufus a reassuring pat on the head, and headed for the front door. The ringing phone stopped him.

"Mr. Smith?" a woman asked.

"Yes."

"This is Helen Morrison at Sevier House."

Smith's heartbeat accelerated. "Yes, Miss Morrison. Is my mother all right?"

"No, Mr. Smith, that's why I'm calling. She's taken a bad fall, and we think she's broken her hip. She hit her head pretty hard, too."

Oh, God. "Where is she?"

"The ambulance has just arrived to take her to the hospital. We've made her as comfortable as possible. I wanted to let you know as soon as possible."

"Yes, thank you. What hospital is she being taken to?"

"Georgetown University."

"I'll be there as quickly as I can."

It was nine-thirty. There was no debate in his mind about which obligation to meet. Maybe I can swing by the hospital, make sure Mother is being properly cared for, and then find Morgan, he thought. He'd be late at the cathedral, but so be it.

He half-ran down the street to the garage they rented. Three minutes after he'd driven off, Annabel arrived, noticed that Mac's car was gone, and went to the house.

She opened the door, hung up her coat, and went to the kitchen.

Mac's half-consumed cup of coffee was on the table and still steaming. Next to it was the pile of photographs from London. She looked at them carefully; a chill went through her as the memory returned of that day in the sheep meadow.

Usually when she came home to an empty house, her initial response was to go to the study in search of a note Mac might have left her. This night, however, she first went to the bedroom and changed into silk pajamas, a robe, and slippers. She made herself a cup of tea and then strolled into the study . . . saw and read the note.

"Not without me, you're not," she said.

Minutes later she was dressed again and pulling her still-damp raincoat from the closet. She shoved the photos in her oversized handbag and headed for the front door. Instead, she went to the answering machine and changed the outgoing message. "This is your partner, Mac. I'm on my way to the cathedral to be with you. If this is somebody else, leave a message after the beep."

It was raining harder now as she sprinted in the direction of their garage. By the time she reached it and opened the door, her shoes were soaked from puddles she hadn't bothered to avoid. She turned the ignition key. Nothing. Can't be, she thought. It started fine all day. "Come on," she said, jamming her foot down on the accelerator. No sense trying to talk it into action. She stood on the sidewalk, looked up and down the street. No chance of getting a cruising cab at this hour, in this neighborhood, in this rain. She walked to the Kennedy Center, where a performance in the Opera House was letting out, and was able to grab one of many waiting taxis before the throng of theatergoers poured through the doors in search of those elusive vehicles. "The National Cathedral, please," she told the coal-black driver whose name on the posted license read like that of an African king. As he pulled away, she wiped condensation from the inside of the window and looked out. "Stupid," she mumbled. "You may be a brilliant professor, Mackensie Smith, but sometimes you are just plain stupid. Going to meet that woman alone, late at night."

Then she thought, stupid? Who's stupid? She had just left a message on the answering machine that was crazy. No one should use their machine to tell callers that they're out. No woman should announce where she is going, alone and late at night. Especially not a woman whose life has been threatened.

Well, they were partners—and they could share the stupidity prize— if they lived.

Mac Smith stood at the side of a bed in Georgetown University's emergency room. His mother, whose grip on his fingers was pincerlike, smiled up at him and said, "Don't worry, Mac, I'll be fine."

"Yes, Mother, I know you will. Are you in much pain?"

She closed her eyes and shook her head.

"The shot helped," he said.

Eyes still closed, she nodded.

The orthopedic surgeon on call that night entered the room carrying X rays that had been taken of Josephine Smith's hip and head. "A clean break," he said, slapping the still-wet plates up under metal clips and flipping on the back light. His finger traced a dark line on her left hip. "I've seen worse."

"What about the blow to her head?" Smith asked.

"I see nothing on the X ray that would indicate any sort of injury." He leaned over Mrs. Smith and said, "You're going to be just fine."

She smiled. "I know," she said. "I was just telling my son that. You shouldn't have bothered taking an X ray of my head, not this hard-headed old lady. I take after him."

Smith grinned and massaged her hand.

"We'll make sure you have a comfortable night," said the doctor. "Afraid we'll have to do a little surgery on you, however."

"I suppose you do," she said. "Where do I sign?"

The doctor looked at Smith and laughed.

"Be careful what you give me to sign," she said, wagging a finger at him. "This man is a lawyer, and a very good one."

Ten minutes later a hospital administrator came in with a surgical consent form, which Josephine Smith signed with a weak but deliberate flourish.

"How's Annabel?" she asked Mac when the administrator left the room.

"Fine, although she wasn't home when I left. She was having dinner with an employee. I'd better give her a call."

"Tell her not to be concerned about me."

"I'll tell her, Mother, but don't count on it. You do know she loves you very much."

"Which makes me a fortunate old lady. Go on, now, get home to her. I'll be fine. I'm getting drowsy."

Smith looked up at a white clock with black hands. Ten past ten. How long would Clarissa Morgan wait? He kissed his mother on the forehead and said, "I'll stay until you're asleep. Then I'll go home, but I'll be back first thing in the morning."

He went out to the nurses' station, where the doctor was making notations on a chart that had been created for Smith's mother. "You'll operate tomorrow?" Smith asked.

"Yes. I've already scheduled the O.R. for eight o'clock."

"How long does this kind of surgery take?"

"A couple of hours. I think we can fix your mother up just fine, although she will have a long period of convalescence."

"Yes, I'm sure. Thank you very much, Doctor. I know she's in good hands. I'll stay with her for a while."

When he finally did leave, Smith's focus was on getting to his meeting with Clarissa Morgan, and he forgot about his intention to call home.

He went directly to his car, sat back, and had a sudden urge for a cigarette he hadn't had in fifteen years, told himself what happened to his mother could have been worse, and drove from the emergency-room parking lot in the direction of the National Cathedral.

While it had made sense in the beginning to seek refuge in the cathedral, and to choose the Jerusalem altar because it was the least likely place anyone would come at night, it now occurred to Joey Kelsch that he couldn't just sit there for the rest of the night—for the rest of his life. He'd heard voices, some of them outside and amplified. They sounded like the police. Were they searching for him? That thought caused him to shudder. If they really searched for him, they would certainly find him, even if it took a day or two, and they would ask him lots of questions. They'd hear his voice and maybe remember the voice of the person who'd called to report Reverend Singletary's murder.

He had to find someone, tell someone.

Bishop St. James. He was a nice man who would listen, and would protect him.

Joey stood and peeked over the altar. Outside, powerful lights came and went, piercing stained glass and throwing bizarre, grotesque patterns of color over the nave's stone grayness. Joey decided to leave his suitcase where it was, but he did pick up the kneeling pad and slowly came around from behind the altar with it. He paused, went to the communion rail, and laid the pad from where he'd taken it, in front of a plain block of wood that represented Judas; the rail was made up of eleven other carved blocks, each bearing the figure of a saint.

He tiptoed away from the rail and down the long center aisle, passed the elaborately carved oak choir stalls, and reached the crossing—the cathedral's center—its four gigantic sustaining piers rising up almost a hundred feet, though it seemed to Joey they went to heaven. He had always been impressed with how big the cathedral was, but at this moment it seemed to have grown tenfold, as if it had suddenly been filled with helium gas and expanded like a ponderous gray balloon. He'd never felt so tiny before, a speck upon the floor. He looked down; he was standing on the Crusader's Cross, the cathedral's special symbol.

He seemed so small and alone. Then, somehow, it was as if he felt a presence, but not a scary one, just a kind of all-encompassing and powerful one. He couldn't see a face, but he knew it was there, gentle, smiling, sort of saying, "Everything will be all right, Joey. Go now and do what you must."

He walked to the south transept and down a set of steps to the gift shop and information center, where he knew there was a pay phone. He pulled a small notepad from his rear pocket and opened it to where pieces of paper were inserted. One of them was a list of cathedral clergy and their office and home numbers. They were all there, including the bishop. His heart raced as he found a quarter in his pocket, lifted the handset, and inserted the coin. When he heard the dial tone, he squinted at the touchtone pad and carefully punched in the bishop's home number, hoping not to make a mistake. It was his only quarter.

"Hello," Mrs. St. James said.

Joey gulped.

"Hello, who is this?"

"Ma'am, is Bishop St. James at home?"

"No, he's not. Who's calling?"

"Ma'am, this is Joseph Kelsch. I go to school here."

Had Eileen St. James been visible to him, Joey would have seen her stiffen at the mention of his name. She said, "Yes, Joseph, how nice of you to call. Where are you?"

"I'm . . . I really need to see the bishop right away. It's very important."

"I'm sure it is. Are you near the cathedral?"

"No, ma'am, I'm—" A searchlight swung past the window, its beam bathing the small black alcove in harsh light. Joey's grip on the handset tightened, and he stopped breathing.

"Joseph, please tell me where you are. I'll have the bishop come to you right away."

"I don't know. . . . Could you tell me where he is, please, and I'll go to him."

Mrs. St. James realized she was going to lose contact, and decided to give him what he wanted. "The bishop is in his study in the cathedral, Joseph. He has a meeting, and he's going to work very late. You could go see him there."

"Thank you, ma'am."

There was a pause.

"Deposit fifteen cents for an additional three minutes."

Joey hung up and flattened against the wall as the light once again intruded upon his safe place. He'd never been to the bishop's study, but he knew where it was. He started to leave the alcove but the light came back again and illuminated everything. He crouched below the small booth that housed the telephone and tried to decide what to do next. Was he doing the right thing by going to see the bishop? Maybe he should just go home and forget about it—*try* to forget about it. And so he remained there, huddled and tense, and thought about it.

Clarissa Morgan's message on the machine had confirmed the time and place for them to meet. "The Good Shepherd Chapel," he had said, reasoning that it was sure to be open—the murder had not changed cathedral policy in that regard—and was indoors. No sense having either of them waiting outside in the drenching cold rain pouring over Washington. He was aware of the macabre aspect of meeting there, but it still struck him as a logical place. Also, he wanted to detect any sign of resistance.

Clarissa had agreed.

Now, as she sat alone in the chapel, her mind was filled with conflicting thoughts. She was growing angry at Smith for not being there. It was getting late. Was this some nasty way of getting even with her for skipping out of London on him? No, he wouldn't be that childish. He was a grown man, and a respected attorney and professor. Something must have happened. She'd wait, but not more than another fifteen minutes.

Simultaneously, she thought of Paul. Whenever she did, her emotions shifted between sadness and anger. He was so prone to becoming involved with the wrong people—always the wrong people. She'd pointed that out to him repeatedly, but he never listened. Oh, he placated her from time to time, told her that he was seriously considering disengaging, but he never did, and she'd reached the point where only ultimatums were left. How many of those she had issued him, the most recent when they'd flown together to Washington from London.

His announcement came as a total surprise to her the morning after his disappointing meeting at Lambeth Palace. She'd gone out early to the greengrocer's, leaving him sleeping in her bed. When she returned, he had showered and dressed.

"I have to go back to Washington immediately, Clarissa," he'd said.

"I thought you were going to the country today."

"My plans have changed."

She asked why, but he was evasive. Because she was a neat and orderly person, it was not difficult to ascertain when something in the flat was out of place. He'd obviously used the telephone while she was out. It must have been a call that prompted his sudden change in plans.

"I'll go with you," she said.

"I prefer that you don't."

They fought about it, and eventually he gave in, albeit without enthusiasm, and made two reservations. He'd remained angry until they'd settled in their seats and the flight was over the Atlantic. Then he became more agreeable once again. Clarissa recalled that his change in attitude coincided with the pretty little flight attendant's flirting with him. Her lips tightened. He was such a fool for a pretty face and trim figure, so easily seduced by red lips and pert breasts. She knew; she hadn't had any problem seducing him. Then, of course, it had been a deliberate act that had nothing to do with being attracted to him, nothing to do with wanting to establish a real intimacy with this surprisingly handsome man of the cloth. But it had progressed, as those things sometimes do, until she was in love with him, madly, desperately, insanely in love with him.

The tightness of her mouth softened almost into a smile as she thought of Brett Leighton's warning to her about that very thing. "Remember, Clarissa," he'd said, "we simply want to know everything he's doing in Word of Peace. We simply want to know who he's involved with and what they're doing. Keep it at that, Clarissa. It's a job, one you might even find pleasant, but nothing more than a job."

She'd laughed at Leighton that day, which made him angry. By then, she'd done his bidding before and had seduced those men he wanted seduced so that secrets and information might be transmitted over pillows damp with love. She'd already become jaded and wanted out when she took on the "Singletary assignment" as one last job. After love transcended simple lust, she wanted Paul to take her out of the game that had become distasteful, wanted him to love her, too, to commit himself to her. Which he said he would do, but he had not lived long enough to carry it off.

And so what was left?

Very little.

It was getting later.

27

Wetter Yet

GEORGE ST. JAMES ended his phone conversation with his wife and said to those with whom he was meeting, "Thank God. That was Eileen. She received a call from Joey Kelsch a few minutes ago."

"Wonderful," said one of the chapter members. "Where is he?"

"The boy wouldn't tell her. He insists upon seeing me. She told him I was working here late. I suspect he'll be by soon."

Canon Wilfred Nickelson, who'd been packing personal belongings in the choir room, had stopped off to leave a forwarding address with the bishop and clear up a few other details, and heard St. James make his announcement. "You say he'll be here soon?" Nickelson asked.

"Unless he decides not to come."

"Excuse me," Nickelson said. "Sorry to have interrupted."

"You know, Wilfred, we will miss you," St. James said. Nickelson's announcement of his hasty departure had only added to St. James's generally depressed mood of late. It had been suggested that a big going-away party be held for Nickelson, but a thunderous lack of interest on the part of the cathedral staff caused St. James to offer a modest one, which Nickelson had declined. But the call from Eileen had lifted his spirits. At least the problem of a missing student would soon be over. He suddenly found it easier to forgive his choirmaster.

Nickelson appeared to be flustered by the kind words. He was well aware that his short notice had not sat well with St. James or with others in the cathedral. He said, "Thank you, Bishop. I'll miss you, too."

As Nickelson left the study, Annabel's African king turned off Wisconsin and drove into the cathedral close. She had expected to arrive at a virtually deserted cathedral at this hour. Instead, there were MPD cars everywhere, and lights played over plantings on the grounds.

Annabel paid the driver and stood on the steps of the south transept, wondering where Mac would have arranged to meet Morgan. The time would have helped determine that. The cathedral was locked after dark unless a special religious event was taking place. He might have opted for an outside rendezvous. No, not in this weather. She pulled her raincoat collar up around her neck and wished she'd had the good sense to bring a hat and umbrella.

Mac would probably—and she knew she was trying to project herself into his mind—would probably have suggested meeting in the Good Shepherd Chapel because of the easy, twenty-four-hour access to it. It dawned on her that she would not have to circumvent the cathedral to reach the outside door off the garth. Because of all the activity, every door to the cathedral was open. She could take an interior route.

As she was about to go through the south entrance, she spotted Chief of Homicide Finnerty coming out of the Herb Cottage, a gift shop selling herbs harvested from the cathedral gardens. "Chief," she shouted, coming down the stairs.

"Mrs. Smith. What are you doing here?"

"Looking for my husband. What's going on?"

"Searching for a missing boy."

"What missing boy?"

"Joseph Kelsch. Mac didn't tell you?"

"No. I haven't seen him."

A uniformed officer came out of his squad car and ran up to them. "Chief, the kid is okay. Headquarters just got a call. The kid called the bishop's house and has arranged to meet him tonight."

"Jesus," Finnerty said. "We spend the night getting soaked out here and the kid calls up? Terrific."

Annabel looked at him incredulously. "Isn't it wonderful he's been found?" she said.

"Yeah, usual runaway stuff and I've got a whole squad out here catching pneumonia."

"By the way, why are *you* here?" Annabel said. "I thought you were in charge of Homicide."

Finnerty put his hands on his hips and looked at her as though she'd mispronounced a simple word. "Mrs. Smith, because of the reverend getting it, I've picked up this cathedral as permanent duty. Anything happens here, they call me no matter what—murder, a kid sneaking off to a dirty movie without telling his parents, a pickpocket working communion, I get it, and I'll be glad when I don't. Excuse me, I want to pull my men off and go see the bishop."

Annabel watched the little detective swagger away, barking orders as he walked. She went up the stairs, entered the cathedral, and tried to get her bearings. She knew where the Good Shepherd Chapel was, but was confused for the moment about how to get there. She considered returning to the outside, but the incessant sound of rain changed her mind. She started across the dimly lighted nave, the squishing sound of water being squeezed out of the crepe soles of her shoes coming back at her loudly, as though tiny microphones in the laces were picking it up and amplifying it through speakers in her ears.

She paused at the crossing and looked down at the large Crusader's Cross. To her right was the high altar; she could not know that Joey Kelsch had returned there and was sitting on his suitcase, pondering whether to fulfill his promise to the bishop's wife. She looked left and squinted to better see across the vast expanse of nave that reached to the west rose window.

Would Mac and Clarissa Morgan be in Good Shepherd? It was only an assumption on her part, of course, but why assume anything? There was a way to find out, and she set off again, her pace faster. She reached the steps and descended.

A single candelabrum on the hallway wall spilled a drop of light through the chapel's open door. Annabel approached, wishing the sound from her wet shoes could be muffled. She stood outside and listened. No voices came from within, but there was movement. Annabel thought of Paul Singletary slumped dead just beyond the door.

She could see only one pew; faint, mottled light from the window illuminated its emptiness. A sound of slight movement came from the high-altar end of the chapel that was out of Annabel's line of vision. She drew a deep breath and stepped through the door.

Standing with her back pressed against the altar in the chapel was a tall, broad-shouldered figure. The silhouette was oddly familiar. Light through the window shone on the left side of her face; the right side was in shadows, a theatrical mask of good and evil. The woman was tense; her right hand was jammed into her raincoat pocket, and her eyes were wide.

"Miss Morgan?" Annabel asked.

The other figure's deep sigh filled the small space. Her body then physically and visually lost its tautness, and she half-smiled. "Mrs. Smith. Yes, I am Clarissa Morgan."

"Sure you don't want me to keep a couple of officers around?" Finnerty asked Bishop St. James. He'd found him in his study, where the meeting was still in progress, and called him into the hallway.

"No, thank you," St. James replied. "They might scare the boy off."

"You don't know where he called from?"

St. James shook his head. "My wife said it was definitely a phone booth. Could have been any one, a mile away or here, for all I know.

Anyhow, I think he'll show up. My wife said he sounded committed to seeing me."

"Okay, your call, Bishop. We'll keep an eye out for him. If we spot him we'll—"

"If he doesn't show up here in a reasonable amount of time, I'll let you know. In the meantime, all I can do is thank you for your quick and professional response."

"Thanks," Finnerty said. "That's our job." He didn't consider searching for lost kids *his* job, but it seemed the thing to say. "Hey Bishop," Finnerty said suddenly, pointing to a high open window at the end of the hall through which rain was streaming, "you got a ladder or chair? I'll get one of my men to close up that window before we go."

"Oh, for Pete's sake," the bishop grumbled, "the custodian should have been around hours ago, when the rain started, to close any open windows. No, don't bother one of your men. I'm sure he'll be around soon to close that window—and to mop up that puddle."

"Well, okay," Finnerty said. They shook hands, and Finnerty left and headed for his car.

St. James returned to his study, where the two lay chapter members were preparing to leave. The work had gone more smoothly and quickly than St. James had anticipated. The report needed only finishing touches, which Merle and Armstrong were working on, civilly but with a distinct distance.

Once the chapter members were gone, St. James yawned, then said to his two clergy, "I'd call it a night, too, but I have to be here for Joey. If he shows up."

Merle said, "No need to do that, Bishop. You never can tell when that might be. Reverend Armstrong and I will be here for a while, to complete this document. If you have something else to do, go ahead and do it. Catch a few winks. We'll get in touch with you the minute he shows up."

St. James sat behind his desk and considered the offer. Merle had his kinder moments. The bishop was fatigued; it had been a long day and night, and he sensed he was coming down with a cold, maybe even the flu, which he'd heard was taking on the proportions of an epidemic in the Washington area. He'd tripled his intake of vitamin C that day in the hope of fighting off whatever was brewing inside. He'd got soaked late in the afternoon, and there was still a dampness to his clothing that passed through his skin and assaulted his bones. Besides, despite their recent differences, Merle and Armstrong seemed to be reasonably cooperative with each other, and with him. He said, "I really want to be here when Joseph arrives, but I could use a little time at home, maybe a hot bath and a cup of Eileen's tea. How long will you stay?"

"Probably another hour," Carolyn Armstrong said, looking up and smiling. "Go take that bath and enjoy the tea."

St. James stood and stretched. His muscles ached, and the prospect of sinking into a hot tub became almost overwhelming. "I think I will, but I'll be back in less than an hour. If he shows up, please call immediately."

As St. James prepared to leave the cathedral, he had a spasm of second-guessing. Joey Kelsch had specifically told Eileen he wanted to see the bishop. Would the boy bolt when he arrived at the study and found only Reverends Merle and Armstrong there? St. James reasoned Joey wouldn't—rationalized it, actually. Both canons were well known to all the students in the school. There shouldn't be any problem. Besides, they would call him, and he would return as quickly as possible, even if it meant cutting short his soak. He buttoned up his raincoat and went out into a blowing rain, forecast to be "occasional," that had become a District of Columbia monsoon.

Tony and Alicia Buffolino sat in their storeroom-cum-office at the rear of Tony's Spotlight Room. Outside, the band, now reduced to a piano player and drummer, labored through their repertoire of songs that all sounded alike for the entertainment of a half-dozen customers who all looked alike. On the desk was a tall pile of bills and a spreadsheet Alicia had worked up earlier in the day.

"It's no use, Tony," she said. "We can't pay these bills—we can't even pay the entertainers anymore." The piano player and drummer were the sole source of entertainment that night.

"Yeah, yeah, I know. Maybe we could do some kind of special promotion. Or, if you'd let me bring in a couple 'a strippers, say, it would be different."

"Absolutely not," Alicia said. "I will not have women taking off their clothes in my club."

"*Your* club?" Tony guffawed. "This joint was my idea, and all you do is get in the way with No this, No that."

"That isn't fair, Tony."

"Yeah, well maybe I'm not fair, but this place ain't fair, either. We gotta have a gimmick, like the song says, or find some way to get people in here and keep them alive and around before they go out or pass out. We could go topless, maybe."

"*You* could go topless. All you seem to be interested in is what you've always been interested in. This place is turning you into some kind of lowlife. I thought you were better than that."

"Yeah, I thought I was better, too. But those bills are telling me somethin', that nothin's getting better." He thought, yes, he had been better somehow, when they first met. He had been working for Mac Smith and life had started over. Now it was turning over, headed for the bottom. He flared up at her: "Well, I thought you were better, too. Whatta you know about this business, a waitress."

She clenched her fists and said, in a burst of sheer frustration, "All you were was a cop, Tony Buffolino, and that didn't work out, either."

Her look of disgust and despair hit him like a blow before she slammed the door on her way out.

He slumped in his chair and shook his head. What had he got himself into this time? Another marriage, and a business partner who didn't understand how things worked. He could make something of the club if he didn't have to listen to her. But he also knew—and had trouble admitting even to himself—that maybe he wasn't being square with her. Maybe she was right; he was an ex-cop who'd been bounced off the force and who decided to become a big-shot club owner—and couldn't even meet the payroll. Some big shot.

He needed to talk to someone who understood him, who'd support him. During a previous conversation with Mac Smith, Tony had lapsed into a round of complaints about Alicia and the state of their marriage. Smith had suggested they see a marriage counselor.

"A shrink?" Tony had said. "What's a shrink gonna do, put us on a couch together?" He laughed. "Hey, maybe that would help."

"Don't be so cynical about counseling, Tony," his professor friend had said. "Alicia seems like a nice person. She's obviously crazy about you, which I suppose casts suspicion on her judgment, but I don't think you want to lose her. Remember, she's Number Three."

Buffolino had told Smith he'd think about it, which he did. He'd suggested to Alicia that night that maybe he'd be willing to go to a counselor, and she'd responded enthusiastically. But they hadn't gone any further because, as Tony had to admit to himself, he couldn't bring himself to make the call, and wasn't about to let Alicia choose the person who would attempt to help pull their marriage together. If they saw a shrink, it would be his guy.

Dumb, he thought as he sat dejectedly in the battered office chair. Smith had been right; he didn't want to lose her. Tomorrow, he'd suggest she pick a counselor and make an appointment. Tomorrow. Couldn't make the call this time of night unless it was to cops, the hospital, or the local funny farm. Sometimes they all seemed to be one place.

He picked up the phone and held it in front of him. Who should he call? He had to call somebody, get out of here, at least for the evening. There was no show to introduce, so he wasn't needed. He considered calling one of his ex-wives, but they were both a source of pain out of the past. Right. Mackensie Smith. He'd call Mac and schmooze with him awhile. But the machine said:

"This is your partner, Mac. I'm on my way to the cathedral to be with you. If this is somebody else, leave a message after the beep."

"Huh?" He'd never heard that kind of message from Smith's machine before. He dialed the number again, got a busy signal, waited, then once again tried the number and got the same message from Annabel.

He hung up and frowned. What was Smith doing at the cathedral at this hour, in this weather, and why was Annabel going to meet him there? What had she called herself? His "partner"? Partner in what?

Buffolino had canvassed a number of places where runaways tended to go. He'd come up empty. All he'd learned was that the boy had been reported as missing to the police, and that Terry Finnerty was leading a squad on a search of the cathedral grounds. Why Finnerty? He was Homicide. Did this kid have something to do with Singletary's murder?

It was all too much for Tony to ignore, particularly in light of his desperate need to get away from the club, the bills. He put on his old raincoat and slouch hat and walked into the club, where Alicia was berating the piano player for having taken his break too soon. "Forty on, twenty off," she said.

"We played forty-five last set," the pianist said, downing a glass half-filled with amber liquid.

"I'm leaving," Tony said.

"Where are you going?" Alicia said.

"I got somethin' else to do."

A blast of rain hit his face as he went outside. He ducked quickly into one of the two topless clubs that flanked Tony's Spotlight Room and looked around. The room was packed with men who ogled a tall, lithe young woman wearing gloves, high heels, a bored look, and absolutely nothing else.

"Hello, Tony," the club's owner said. "Want a seat?"

"Nah, just checkin' out the competition."

The owner laughed. "Doin' pretty good, huh?"

"Yeah, congratulations, I got to go." To kidnap some customers, he thought, pulling his coat together.

"I can't understand what happened to my husband," said Annabel, who sat with Clarissa Morgan in the two-person pew at the front of Good Shepherd Chapel. "I hope he hasn't had an accident. The weather is dreadful."

"It can be even worse in England, in London or, say, in the Cotswolds," Morgan said.

"Yes, I suppose it can be. The last time we were there, I had an experience I'll never forget." Annabel looked at Morgan. She pulled the photographs from her purse and handed them to the other woman. Morgan's expression said many things, including a silent statement that she didn't need photographs to know about Annabel's nearly being trampled to death. She glanced at the pictures, then gave them back to her.

"That's you on that horse, isn't it?" Annabel said.

"Yes. I owe you an apology for that, Mrs. Smith."

Annabel shifted so that she more squarely faced the beautiful British woman at her side. "Why? I didn't even know you."

"That's correct," Morgan said, clasping her hands on her lap and looking down at them. "I was told to do it by my employer."

"Your employer? What employer would tell you to kill somebody you didn't even know?"

Morgan denied Annabel's assertion. "I didn't intend to kill you, Mrs. Smith. I was told to frighten you, rough you up, make you and your husband decide you had better things to do than snoop around sheep pastures and churches. We couldn't get to him, frighten him off, but if you were threatened, he'd be more likely to pull out."

Annabel leaned against the back of the pew and looked at the depiction, above the altar, of the Good Shepherd cradling the lamb. "I'm sorry. I don't understand violence."

"Better you don't, Mrs. Smith, better you don't understand many things surrounding Paul's death."

"Maybe you're right, but I'll reserve judgment about that. Who were you working for? Who told you to scare us off?"

"I'd rather not say. The organization represents interests far larger than you and me." She sighed and said with a sense of relief, "I no longer work for them. That's why I'm here, to see that no one else is hurt." Annabel's next questions received only evasive, noncommittal answers. She thought about Mac. Where *was* he? Did the organization to whom Clarissa referred intend to do harm to Mac, to her? she asked.

"They do what they feel they must," Clarissa said. "We don't count for very much."

"Did *they* . . . did they kill Paul Singletary?"

Clarissa raised her head, the long, perfect line of her jaw, nose, and forehead turned into a lovely silhouetted cameo in the light from the garth. "In a sense," she said.

"Did you kill him?" Annabel asked.

Morgan said nothing.

"You had an affair with him. Did you do that because your employer told you to?"

"Yes."

"How dreadful."

Clarissa turned and stared at her.

"I mean, for Paul," Annabel said. "Did he ever know?"

"No, never. I would never have done that to him. You see, Mrs. Smith, I came to love him very much. It didn't happen at the beginning. At that point it was just another assignment, the sort of assignment I'd become quite expert at. But then something happened that had never happened to me before. I committed the cardinal sin . . ." She laughed bitterly. "What an interesting choice of words. Possibly I should say canon sin. In any case I committed the sin of losing sight of why I was with him, losing myself to him in every way."

"And?"

"And he lost his life because of it, I believe."

Both women tensed as they heard the doors leading to the outside swing open. Mac Smith stood in the chapel doorway. Annabel immediately went to him and wrapped her arms around him, wet raincoat or not. "Thank God you're here," she said. "What happened? I got your note, but—"

"Mother took a fall. Broke her hip."

"How terrible. Is she all right?"

"She's fine. She's at Georgetown University Hospital, resting comfortably. They're doing surgery on her tomorrow." He looked over Annabel's shoulder and saw the woman seated in the pew. She hadn't looked in their direction, as though not wanting to intrude upon their privacy.

Smith said, "Miss Morgan. Sorry I'm late. There was a family emergency and—"

She turned. "I heard. I'm sorry about your mother."

Smith moved to the altar and looked down at her. Annabel remained in the doorway. "I'm sorry we missed each other in London, Miss Morgan," Smith said, "but I'm glad you're here and called me. The question obviously is, why? What brings you to Washington?"

Clarissa Morgan sat deep in thought as Mac and Annabel waited silently. Then the woman looked up at Smith and said, "I came here because I wanted to do something decent for once, Mr. Smith."

"Go on."

"You see, I've caused a great deal of pain and suffering for many people. I'm not that old, but I've spent much of my adult life lying and cheating and not really caring about the results. That happened with Paul. I lied to him. I cheated him. I manipulated him into a situation in which he lost his life. I would like to atone for that." She looked around the chapel. "I suppose this is a fitting place for the atonement of Clarissa Morgan."

"I don't think place matters when someone is trying to unload a heavy conscience," Smith said.

"No, I suppose not."

"Are you talking about your attempt to blackmail the Church of England?" Smith asked.

"Oh, goodness, no. I saw that as my way out. But it was a silly attempt, ridiculous actually, very amateurish. I should have known better. I thought that by accumulating a goodly sum of money quickly, I could take myself away, disappear, but that wasn't to be. They paid me well, but—"

"*Who* paid you well?"

"Your wife and I have gone into that a bit."

"Except I have no idea who it was you were working for," Annabel said.

Mac and Annabel, looking at Clarissa Morgan from their respective vantage points, were surprised to see her begin to cry.

"Can I get you something?" Smith asked.

"No, please, just . . . could you leave me alone for a few minutes?

Paul's death does this to me at the oddest times. I'd just like to be alone here." She touched a handkerchief to her eyes. "I might even pray. I haven't done that since I was a child."

Smith nodded at Annabel. "We won't be far," he said.

They went out into the hallway and shut the door. Annabel grabbed his arm, whispered, "Mac, I think she killed Paul."

"That thought ran through my mind. But . . . did she say anything specific?"

"No, damn it, she has this elusive way of talking around things, but for a moment I was gripped with the belief that she killed Paul. She's a very troubled woman. She seduced him on the order of somebody she calls her 'employer,' whoever that is. She talks like a spy, a regular Mata Hari, entrapping men for this employer or organization. That must be it. She must work for an intelligence organization, and she seduced Paul for some purpose of theirs."

"Cam Bowes was pretty direct about the heavy involvement of intelligence agencies in Word of Peace. What do you think, Annie, that she set Paul up to be killed, or actually did it herself?"

"I don't know, but she is capable of taking physical action—of several kinds. Clarissa Morgan was the person on horseback in the Cotswolds."

Smith grunted. He wasn't surprised. Clarissa Morgan knew when they would be in the Cotswolds, and where they were staying, because Smith had told her. "Look, I'm not happy you're here," he told Annabel, "although I can understand why you are. I'm going back and see if I can get her to tell me what she came all the way to Washington to say."

"What do you want me to do?"

"Find a phone and get George. Tell him you're here and that you need a safe place to park for a while."

"All right," Annabel said. "Please be careful, Mac."

"I will."

"I'm sorry about your mother."

"Happens to people that age. The doctor said it was a clean break and should heal nicely. She'll be fine, I hope. What I want to make sure is that *you* stay fine."

He watched her go up the stairs. She turned, then disappeared from his view.

In the choir room, Canon Wilfred Nickelson placed the final piece of music personally owned by him into a box and put the cover on it. He heard footsteps in the hall and opened the door slightly. Reverend Merle was about to enter the Bethlehem Chapel.

"Finish the report, Jonathon?" Nickelson asked.

"Yes."

Fifteen minutes later, Joey Kelsch tentatively looked around the edge of the high altar. He saw nothing, no one. Suitcase in hand, he left the sanctuary and chancel and made his way along the wall to the stairs leading to the bishop's study. He moved as carefully and quietly as a cat. More than anything, he did not want to meet a single person before reaching the bishop. Once, when he thought he heard footsteps, he stopped and ducked behind a pillar, but he decided he had imagined the noises.

He walked down the short hallway and stopped in front of the study. A typewritten note hung on the door: *Joseph—I'm waiting for you in the Bethlehem Chapel. Please meet me there. Bishop St. James.*

Joey didn't know what to do. He'd assumed—counted on—the bishop's being in his study as his wife had promised. Joey didn't relish the thought of going back down to the crypt level, but didn't see any other choice. The bishop must have had business that took him there, and if Joey didn't show up, he might offend the one person in whom he was putting his faith.

The note was tacked to the door with a yellow pushpin. Joey yanked the note loose and put it in his pants pocket. Nobody else should know he was there. He was frightened, but also relieved. It would soon be over. Then maybe everything would be the way it was before, and he could enjoy his life again.

He'd just passed the entrance to Good Shepherd Chapel when someone loomed large in the doorway. There was a light on behind the person. "Joey," Mac Smith said. The boy froze in his tracks. The voice had been a man's, but all Joey saw was the face of a woman. He bolted from where he'd been anchored to the floor and raced down the stairs, stumbled and sprawled on his belly at the bottom, his suitcase flying across the hall and hitting the wall. He scrambled to his feet and continued down the hall toward the Bethlehem Chapel. He ran so fast he almost went past the door, but stopped by grabbing the frame and pulling himself back. He looked inside; the chapel appeared to be empty. He looked up the hall and saw two people, the woman he'd seen through the doorway of Good Shepherd, and a man. They stopped at the foot of the stairs and watched him.

He stepped inside the chapel and went to the middle of it, next to the communion rail. "Bishop St. James," he said, his words echoing back at him. "It's Joey Kelsch. I got the note."

Smith and Clarissa Morgan went on to the chapel but paused in the hall; they could not be seen from within, but they could hear.

"Bishop, Bishop, it's Joey."

"No need to be afraid, Joey," a voice said. Joey turned in its direction. Someone stepped from behind the altar.

"Where's the bishop?" Joey asked, his voice breaking.

"He'll be here in a minute, Joey. He asked me to talk to you first."

Suddenly, Joey was a caged animal. He turned in a circle, his eyes open wide with a plea for help, his small body starting to shake.

"Come here, Joey. Come to me."

"No . . . I want the bishop." He turned and went for the door through which he'd entered, but another person stood in it. A tight whine came from Joey's throat.

The figure at the altar took several additional steps into the sanctuary and glared at the person standing in the doorway. "What are you doing here?"

"I've come to right a wrong," Clarissa Morgan said.

Mac Smith took a step forward so that he could look through the door. Morgan entered the chapel and stood in direct confrontation with Reverend Carolyn Armstrong.

A male voice sounded from the back of the chapel: "Come here, son, it's all right."

Smith looked in for the source of the voice. Canon Jonathon Merle stood in the middle of the aisle. "You have nothing to fear from me, Joseph. Come." He extended his hand and beckoned with long fingers.

As Joey backed away from Merle, Smith heard footsteps behind him. He turned and saw Canon Wilfred Nickelson coming down the hall with purposeful strides, his face hard. Nickelson stopped when he saw Smith. Smith cocked his head and stepped back, leaving room for Nickelson to pass. Nickelson appeared to have been heading for the chapel, but he turned and went back up the hallway, pausing once to look over his shoulder, then bounded up the stairs toward Good Shepherd.

Smith wheeled to get inside the chapel. Joey had sunk to his knees and was sobbing. Clarissa Morgan went to the boy, looked down at him, then stepped up onto a small rise in front of the communion rail. Directly behind it was Carolyn Armstrong.

"How dare you come here!" Armstrong said.

"How dare *I* come here? I think I have more right here than you do, Reverend." She stressed the last word; her scorn was palpable.

Armstrong took a step forward, her face only a few feet from Morgan's. "How could you set foot in this chapel after what has happened?"

Smith could see that Morgan was smiling, and in contrast to Carolyn Armstrong's overt anger, which caused her to shake, was composed and very much in control of herself. She said, "Paul loved me, and you couldn't bear that, could you?"

Armstrong was mirthless. "Loved you? He detested you, only he didn't know it. You deceived him, used him, and when you couldn't use him anymore, you killed him."

Morgan looked again at Joey Kelsch, who still crouched on the floor, trying to make himself as small as possible. "You seem to have quite an effect on this young boy. He's absolutely petrified of you."

"He's an emotionally disturbed child. Get out of here! The sight of you disgusts me."

The uncharacteristically loud voice of Jonathon Merle now filled the small chapel. He had walked up the aisle until reaching Joey, then said to Carolyn Armstrong, "Who is this woman who violates this chapel?"

Clarissa Morgan said, "Ah, Reverend Merle. Paul told me about you. He described you perfectly. How sad he had to spend so many of his days with hypocrites."

Merle made a move toward her.

She said, "Don't you dare touch me. I don't intend to suffer at your hands or anyone else's, as Paul did."

"I'll call Security," said Merle.

"By all means." Morgan came to the closed communion rail, lifted the hinged portion, and threw it back with such force that it threatened to break. Armstrong, shock on her face, stepped back until she met the edge of the altar. Morgan came through the rail's opening and took one slow, small, deliberate step. "You couldn't bear the thought that he loved another woman," she said. "You have this facade behind which you hide, the uniform of God, your privileged place before altars, yet you couldn't forgive him, or me, that we were in love."

"Love? He didn't love you!" Armstrong screamed. "He hated you. He saw a pretty English face and your . . . experienced sexual favors, but he never loved you!" Her body went into a tremor, and she lowered her head, wrapping her arms about herself. "He never loved you. He loved me, but you wouldn't let him see it."

Tony Buffolino had come through the door leading to Good Shepherd, heard the voices downstairs, and found his way to the chapel. He stood with Smith and watched the scene being played out at the altar.

Merle said, "Reverend Armstrong, come with me. This woman is demented."

Morgan said, "You hated Paul. Paul told me so. Why are you defending her?"

Armstrong snorted. "Defending me? How absurd."

"How can you claim to be a messenger of God when you know what you did? You killed him, murdered him in cold blood." Morgan took another step toward Armstrong; they were less than two feet from each other.

"I'll get Security," Merle said, and turned.

The women ignored him. "Paul returned to Washington a day early because of a phone call from you," Morgan said. "He told me on the plane why he was coming back, and he promised to end his relationship with you so that he and I could find a life together."

"That's a lie," Armstrong said, extending her arms behind her and placing them on the altar.

"He told me that you were insanely jealous of us, that you'd threatened to smear him and ruin his reputation as a priest."

"That's not true. I hated the fact that he was involved with a woman like you, a user, a woman who cared nothing for him except what you might get from him. I told him that many times."

"Yes, you did, and he didn't believe it. He also never hesitated to tell you about me, about his feelings for me. I suppose it was cruel of him to do that, but I'm glad he did."

Clarissa Morgan knew that Paul never really loved her, but she also knew that he felt increasingly, desperately trapped by his relationship with Carolyn Armstrong. It was something she did not admire about

Paul, his tendency to talk freely about other women. He'd talked about
Armstrong a great deal on the plane, and Clarissa had begged him to
disassociate himself from her, to give himself a chance to see whether
he did—could—love *her*. He promised her he would give himself that
chance. He wasn't allowed to live long enough to follow through on
that decision.

Hearing movement behind her, Morgan turned. Merle was walking
toward the crouched, shaking Joey Kelsch. The boy looked up into
Merle's eyes, then looked at Morgan as she said loudly, as though
addressing a crowd, "She murdered him!"

Joey shoved his hands against Merle's legs, scrambled to his feet, and
ran toward the rear of the chapel. Merle lost his balance, then started
after the boy.

"Watch out!" Buffolino yelled from the door.

Carolyn Armstrong had lifted a brass candlestick from the altar and
was coming at the other woman with it. Morgan whirled, tensed, and
pulled herself into a defensive shell, hands covering her head, knees
bent.

Smith and Buffolino ran into the chapel. "Get the boy, Tony," Smith
called. He vaulted the altar rail and said to Armstrong, "Why not give
that to me, Reverend." He extended his hand.

"You don't understand how it was," Armstrong said, her body shaking.

"No, I probably don't, but I'm sure you can explain it."

Then, suddenly, Armstrong raised the candlestick again and threw it
at Clarissa Morgan. It missed and ricocheted off the stone floor with a
deafening clang. As the sharp sound of metal hitting stone reverberated
throughout the chapel and faded, Buffolino came from the rear of the
chapel. Joey had tried to hide in a pew, and Buffolino had half-coaxed
him, half-dragged him from it. He held Joey by the arm, firmly but
somehow gently herding Merle, too.

"Tell them how it happened, Jonathon," Armstrong said in a whisper.

Merle looked desperately at Smith and Buffolino. "I don't know
what she's talking about."

"Tell them how after I hit Paul, *you* offered to move his body to Good
Shepherd so that it might seem that an outsider killed him. Tell them,
Jonathon. You are a man of God. For God's sake, tell them the truth!"

There was silence as all eyes turned to Merle. He didn't seem to
know what to do, what to say. He looked from one face to the other,
then finally fixed upon Mac Smith. The taut muscles of his gaunt cheeks
and chin sagged; his thin lips began to tremble. Slowly, he raised his
hands palms-up at Smith in a weak plea for understanding. "I . . . I
didn't want to move him. Oh, God, no, I didn't want to do that. It was
terrible seeing him on the floor, blood running from his head. It made
me sick. I was so sorry—for both of them."

He glanced at Armstrong, then back at Smith. "She didn't mean to
do it, Mr. Smith. I know that. God knows that. Singletary could be cruel

to her. I saw it more than once." He looked at Armstrong before continuing. "She wouldn't have hurt him if he hadn't driven her to it. How much can a person take? I asked her once to give him up and to be my friend. I told her I could help her forget him and make her happy."

Smith looked down at the floor. This sudden tenderness by the stiff-necked Jonathon Merle, whose severe features were the stuff of caricatures, embarrassed Smith.

Merle continued, "I told her I wouldn't do it, but she pleaded with me. She told me that if the police thought Paul had been murdered by an outsider, they wouldn't suspect her. Even so, I still refused. But then she told me that the cathedral would be ruined if it got out that one member of its clergy had killed another. I believed that, Mr. Smith, I really did, and I took Paul's body to Good Shepherd for that reason."

Smith thought of Bishop St. James and his ill-advised attempt to hide the murder weapon because of the same faulty reasoning. How many wrongs are done in misguided attempts to do right?

Smith said to Armstrong, "I believe Reverend Merle. He's telling the truth, isn't he?"

Carolyn Armstrong's face was tight and bitter. But then her body convulsed as she started to sob. Her hands went to her face, and she sank to her knees in front of the altar.

Merle, too, started to cry, but the only visible signs were large tears that ran slowly down his cheeks and found the corners of his mouth. "There was one other reason," he said, with difficulty. "I love her."

Smith went to Jocy Kelsch and put a large hand on the boy's shoulder. "Joey, I know you've been through a lot, but everything is going to be all right."

Joey looked up into Smith's eyes. "I saw him," he said. "I saw him moving Father Singletary the night I was in the choir room."

"Yes, we know," Smith said. "We know now what happened." He spoke to Buffolino. "Make sure neither of them leaves here. I want to make sure this boy gets back to his family. And I want to call Finnerty. On time for once. And he'll be coming back here again tonight."

28

Two Nights Later—
A Lovely Fall Evening
in the Nation's Capital

"SAD, HUH?" Tony Buffolino said.

Tony, Mac, Annabel, and Alicia sat in a banquette along the wall of Tony's Spotlight Room. Alone on the bandstand, a sallow-skinned man with flowing gray hair, wearing a blue tuxedo jacket with sequins, lethargically played a keyboard while an electronic drum machine provided a cha-cha-cha rhythm.

"Well, maybe it was just the wrong idea in the wrong place," Smith said. "Maybe Washington, D.C., just isn't ready for a Las Vegas nightclub. Besides, there's no gambling."

"No gambling? This whole place was a gamble. But you're right, Mac. I had a good idea, but I bet against the house. I was ahead of my time in D.C."

"Exactly," Annabel said.

"Don't be too hard on yourself, Tony," Alicia Buffolino said. She touched his hand and smiled. "It just wasn't meant to be. Besides, I have to take some of the blame here. I wanted you to be more than a private detective following cheating husbands. I wanted you to be a businessman. This was just the wrong business."

Tony grinned at Mac and Annabel. "Ain't she somethin'?" he said.

"Yes, I think she is exactly that, Tony," Annabel said.

"Do you know what the shrink told us this afternoon?" Buffolino asked.

Mac and Annabel raised their eyebrows.

"The shrink—she's a woman, which don't exactly make me happy, but she seems pretty straight—she told me I don't always sound the way I'm thinkin'. She got us into a conversation and taped it on a video-camera. Then she played it back. I got her point. There I was thinking nice things and telling them to Alicia, but when I see myself on the tape I sound mad, like I'm puttin' her down."

Smith smiled, said, "We're all guilty of that at times, Tony. Sounds like you're going to get a lot out of marriage counseling."

Alicia said, "All I want out of it is a good marriage with this knuckle-head."

"Hey, don't call me a knuckle . . . Whatta you . . . ?" He broke into a big smile and embraced her. "Yeah, I guess sometimes I am a knucklehead."

The only other person in the club was a Hispanic busboy who also functioned as bartender for Tony and his guests.

"Did you cook up our meal in the kitchen?" Smith asked.

"Nah," Buffolino said, "I had takeout brought in."

The Chinese food was set out in bowls on the table. A sign on the front door said: PRIVATE PARTY IN PROGRESS—NO ADMITTANCE.

Annabel tasted an eggroll and said, "I really feel sorry for Clarissa Morgan."

"Not Carolyn Armstrong?" Smith asked, spooning beef with snow peas onto his plate.

"Of course I feel sorry for Carolyn, but in a way Clarissa's story touches me even more." She sat back. "I could see myself ending up in that kind of life. I mean, it must have seemed exciting in the beginning, a beautiful young woman being a paid agent for British intelligence, at first merely dating, then later seducing men who have secrets important to the state, living the high life and being paid well on top of it."

"Didn't get her far," Buffolino said through a vast mouthful of shrimp fried rice doused with sweet-and-sour sauce and Chinese hot mustard.

"I know," Annabel said, "and that's my point. She did what she was told to do, and then simply because she fell in love with Paul, they cut her loose."

"Not quite as cruelly as Reverend Priestly was cut down in Buck-land," Smith said.

"Why did British intelligence kill Priestly, Mac?" Annabel asked. "I'd have put my money on the murder being the work of someone from Word of Peace."

"Then you'd have won your wager. Maybe you should put in gambling here, Tony. The problem was that Priestly, who once was a Young Turk allied with Paul Singletary, had gone over to MI5. He was no longer trying to pass along useful data and weapons information and such to help Word of Peace; he'd become suspicious of certain charac-ters high up in it and went over to become an agent for the Brits, who fed him bits of this and that. His role now was to get the goods on the bad apples in the peace movement. Problem was that the heavy hitters in Word of Peace got wind of it—twigged to it, as the English say—and wanted to eliminate this source who had become a danger to them. Once Paul was killed here, in such a distinctive fashion, Mr. Jin Tse, who was not only a mover and shaker in Word of Peace but an acknowl-edged terrorist and assassin to boot, flew to England and hit Priestly in a manner calculated to make it seem that the murders were parallel—

to divert attention, obviously, from his organization—since he knew that they *hadn't* killed Paul Singletary.

"But wait a minute, Mac," Annabel interrupted, "how could Jin have known to kill Priestly with a candlestick? At that time nobody but Armstrong, Merle, and, I guess, St. James, knew what the murder weapon used on Paul was."

"I think one other person knew," Mac said, "and George confirmed my suspicion yesterday when he told me that one of the cathedral custodians skipped town the night of the storm, the night the evening news carried the story about the FBI sweep of Word of Peace's petty spies. My hunch, and this is all based on circumstantial evidence until the police can find him for questioning, is that the maintenance man at the cathedral saw St. James switch candlesticks, and make a nervous display of it at that. George is a charming guy and a wonderful bishop, but I assume he's not the smoothest of men when it comes to removing murder weapons. The maintenance guy reported it to Jin Tse, who is smart *and* inscrutable. He saw the opportunity to use a similar weapon in the Cotswolds. As it turned out, he's more inscrutable than smart considering the time he's facing. Of course, Word of Peace might have gotten to killing Paul anyway because of the unwanted attention he'd been attracting with his overactive love life, or at least sex life. Not only that, he was tottering on the edge of being accused of feathering his own nest with their funds. Which he was, in fact. The trips to England to see his mistress; the very expensive security system in his apartment, installed because Paul was beginning to think that his whole life, the whole shaky, secret edifice, could bring him down. Whether he was afraid of MI5 or the CIA or others in the peace organization may never be known—but he wasn't paranoid. Treason is a good reason to be fearful. And he was sincere about almost everything in the movement."

"You mean attempted treason," Tony put it, "don't you? Didn't I hear that the street value of the tapes meant they were not exactly prime stuff?"

"Right. But stealing the wrong stuff and turning it over, or holding it to turn over at the 'right time' to a nation's enemies, is treason whether the tapes were outdated or not. The British only let Priestly get hold of weak material from the start, and he and Singletary held on to it too long. It's like strong narcotics or weak narcotics—it matters to addicts but not to the law. When MI5 confronted Priestly with knowledge of his taping and other acts, stuff he had been feeding to Paul, he had an extra reason to be 'turned,' and to work for them. Also, he was beginning to want out, didn't much like using his friends, made the mistake of letting that show. Jin and company figured that he might tell all he knew about Word of Peace, information he'd gotten from Paul, to buy his way clear."

"What I don't understand," Annabel said, no longer attempting to eat, "is why those two priests should have been engaged in intelligence trafficking, anyhow."

"Oh, sure you do. They met when both were in the military, engaged in joint exercises of the two navies, and became good friends. You can almost hear the conversations between them, young idealists, ministers in the military, bemoaning the money spent on weapons while much of the world is dirt poor, deciding over a few beers late at night that they had to do something to help prevent further escalation or nuclear destruction." He frowned. "The problem with those two was that they were naive, inept. Priestly eventually paid the price, as Paul might have, long after most other young idealists have put on pinstriped suits and taken managerial jobs with defense contractors. Really a shame."

"What a world," Annabel murmured. "Believe in peace and work for it, and get killed because of it."

"You are, as usual, too nice. Paul wasn't killed for his commitments but for a lack of them. Especially toward women." He sipped Chinese tea, now cold. "Well, at least they gave Clarissa Morgan the option of leaving England and settling in the British Virgin Islands, which, I might point out, is not exactly hardship duty."

"She seemed so resigned about going back there. This Mr. Leighton . . . what did she call him, her 'control' . . . seems to call all the shots in her life."

"Your expression is almost too appropriate. I propose to call the shots at this table: a toast." He held his glass of Blantons high over the table. Buffolino picked up his glass of Don Q rum and Coke, and Annabel her white wine. "What are we toasting?" she asked.

"First, George St. James and his return to his relatively normal life as bishop of the National Cathedral. Of course, what he prayed wouldn't happen did happen. One of his own was the murderer. Which proves that even for a bishop, not all prayers can be answered. He's gotten some phone calls. One woman said she would no longer contribute to that 'den of iniquity' posing as a cathedral. But he—and the cathedral will ride it out because they must. We need him, and the cathedral."

"You bet. A great institution, some great people—and an eternally good cause. What's the second thing we're toasting?" Annabel asked.

"The end of a sad, nasty, and upsetting episode in our lives," Smith said. The rims of glasses clinked together. "And," Smith added, "I propose a toast to the National Cathedral getting back to its business at hand, namely setting the spiritual pace for this increasingly hedonistic slice of society."

"Amen," Tony said. "What's that mean?"

"Hedonistic?" Smith said.

"Yeah."

"Caring about your own fanny more than anybody else's."

"Makes sense to me," Buffolino said, raising his glass again.

"What do you think will happen to Jonathon Merle?" Annabel asked.

"Hard to say," Smith replied. "He was an accessory under the law, but I have a feeling they won't go hard on him. He walked in on them right after she'd hit Paul with the candlestick, and bought her rationale that if the body were found in Good Shepherd, it would appear that someone from outside the cathedral had murdered him. He had finally found someone on earth to truly love. Also, Merle is a good soldier. Jonathon believes in the cathedral and what it stands for, and thought he was doing the 'right' thing. He wasn't, of course, but he'll have to answer to a lesser god than he's been used to." Smith shook his head. "Nickelson is a sad case. Because he was convinced his wife was playing around with Paul, he had good reason to think he'd be accused of the murder. Frankly, he's better off in San Francisco, and the cathedral is better off without him."

"His wife would be better off without him, too," Annabel said, "but that's another story."

Buffolino gestured to the bartender. "Another rum and Coke." He also ordered for Mac and Annabel, but they demurred. Buffolino said, "I really feel sorry for that kid, Joey. Man, he must be some mess, running away like that, having seen Merle dragging a body up the hall. Tough on a kid."

"Yes, it is," Smith said. "Interesting that Armstrong was convinced Joey had seen *her* moving the body, not Merle."

"Do you think she would have hurt the boy?" Annabel's concern, even after the fact, was etched in her face.

Smith shook his head. "I don't think so. Killing Paul was not a premeditated act. She was the woman scorned, and she lashed out."

"Whattaya think she'll get?" Buffolino asked.

"I don't know. Susan Kellman is a good attorney, a good choice to defend Armstrong, if I do say so myself. I think they'll probably do well, fairly well. Word of Peace is another matter."

"I'm glad that the cathedral and the Mother Church have disassociated themselves from it," said Annabel.

"I suppose so," Smith said, "but it's kind of a shame, too. We could use more effective peace organizations. Too bad a few factions decided to make use of it for their own purposes."

"More ribs?" Buffolino asked.

"No, thanks. Not those ribs, anyhow," Smith said. He took Annabel's hand and asked, "Dance?"

She giggled. "Here? Now?"

"Yup. Excuse us, Tony."

Buffolino smiled as he watched the Smiths take to the small dance floor.

"What would you like to hear?" the musician asked.

" 'Our Love Is Here to Stay,' " Annabel said.

They danced close, their cheeks touching, Annabel humming the melody along with the pianist, who seemed to have become inspired by two live, moving bodies. Halfway through the song, Mac whispered in her ear.

"No," she said, pulling her head back and laughing.

"Why not?"

"Do you really think he'll know the answer?"

"Bet you a hundred bucks."

"You're on," she said.

Smith guided her close to the bandstand and said, "Excuse me," to the musician.

The musician leaned over the keyboard, his fingers still working the keys. "What?"

"Do you know your fly is open?" Smith asked.

The pianist laughed. "If you can hum it, I can play it."

Tony Buffolino suddenly appeared next to them. "Mind if I cut in?" he asked.

"Not if she doesn't," Smith said.

She didn't. As they danced, Tony leading manfully, half as tall as she, he told her that he was out of the nightclub business for good, that he wanted to turn over a new leaf with Alicia, and that his best days—and nights—were spent working for Mac. She smiled. Even Tony was becoming nicer. But she hoped there would be few occasions for Tony to get assignments from Mac. Still, looking over Tony's head at her husband, she wasn't so sure.

Later that night, while they sat propped up in bed and browsed through the newspaper—Rufus providing a breathing footboard—Smith asked, "Say, did you really find that phony Frenchman Pierre Quarle handsome and charming?"

"Yes. Didn't you?"

"No. He had bad breath."

"I didn't notice."

"You were blinded by the accent, and your nose shut down."

"I was not. Mac, are you jealous of me?"

"At times."

"Don't ever be. I am your woman, and will be for the rest of my life."

"Then I won't be . . . jealous. All the time. Just stay away from Frenchmen with halitosis. And especially from any man without it. If you don't—"

"What will happen if I don't?"

"He becomes a meal for the beast. Right, Rufus?" He cued the dog with his right foot.

The Dane growled and shifted position. Smith and Annabel turned off their reading lights.

"Good night, Professor," she said.

"Good night, Patron of the Arts."

"Never again."

"Never *what* again?" Smith asked.

"Two never-agains. First, never hire an assistant who thinks he's smarter than you are but turns out to be merely impossible. And two, never get involved in murder."

"You can count on that. I'll never get caught up again in any murder in a national cathedral."

"Yes, I'm sure you mean just that. Good night, Mr. Smith."

"Good night, Mrs. Smith."

MURDER
AT THE
KENNEDY
CENTER

For Aimee Elizabeth Daniel
with love
from Gammy

1

MOMENTS AGO, she'd been angry and filled with the bravado such anger generates. She'd threatened, the volume of her voice kept low, the intensity high-pitched.

Now, she saw it. It was a revolver. Not a big one. There was a toylike quality to it.

"Don't be ridiculous," she said, her voice cracking, a tentative laugh behind the words indicating the fear that gripped her body. "No, please, don't do this. We can . . ."

The gun was thrust forward, its short barrel ramming sufficiently hard into the softness of her belly to move her back a step.

"Oh, no."

She saw the finger squeeze the trigger. Her flesh muffled the report. The bullet penetrated her, taking with it muscle and nerve, bone and skin. It tore through her back, slower and wider than when it had entered.

She was driven backward, her beautiful eyes open wide and fixed on the last sight they would ever see, the face of her murderer.

2

"WELL, LESLIE, how does it sound to you?"

The wife of Senator Kenneth Ewald smiled at Ed Farmer, her husband's campaign manager, an aide who seldom smiled himself. "Everything sounds wonderful, Ed. We all think we know about show biz, but I had no idea how much was involved in putting together an event like this. Ken will be delighted."

"That's because it's a one-time event; everything has to be invented or imported for the occasion," Farmer said in his characteristically flat tone. "There are very few genuine experts. It's like a presidential campaign."

The others in the Kennedy Center's George Rogers Clark Room agreed that everything seemed to have been covered; everything and everyone was in place or would be. From above, ceramic birds and animals looked down on them as if holding a meeting of their own, or judging this one.

The Marshall Boehm family had donated the room to the Center, including the collection of ceramic wildlife, and it was a popular tourist stop; there had been more than 85 million visitors to the handsome, sprawling arts complex since its dedication in 1971. The Clark–Boehm Room was seldom used for meetings, but a socialite on the committee who liked little animal and bird sculptures had pulled strings.

"It's a shame that Mac Smith couldn't be at this final meeting," Mrs. Ewald said, "after everything he's done to help us get this started and on track, and keep us legal. But his teaching comes first. It certainly looks as if it'll be worth the time and talent and money of everyone here, and we've certainly stocked the pond with celebrities."

"Boris," Farmer said, "have you any final comments?"

Seated at the opposite end of the table was a menacing man with a shaven head, hooked nose, and absolutely black eyes like moles in his head. Boris Trenka was the Kennedy Center's artistic director.

Trenka, who'd defected to the United States ten years earlier, after many years as artistic director of Russia's Bolshoi, said in a low voice thick with an accent, "This is a *television* production. I know nothing of television."

Farmer sighed. That was all he had heard from Trenka since they began to work on a musical gala to advance the presidential candidacy and the coffers of Ken Ewald, senator from California.

"I don't think we should adjourn until Georges returns," said one of Trenka's aides.

Another aide remarked, "I suppose he's still having trouble working out Sammy's transportation. There was a foul-up."

"I don't think we need to be concerned about the travel arrangements or the lives of the rich and famous," Farmer said. "That's Georges's job."

"I should hope it's not ours," said Trenka haughtily.

Farmer ignored him and looked at an attractive young woman seated to his left. "The stars will get here. Anything we've neglected to cover, Andrea?"

Andrea Feldman had worked with Ewald for a little over a year. Because a great deal of her five feet nine inches was in her legs, she didn't appear to be tall when seated. She had thick black hair that hung loosely to her shoulders, and a face surprisingly fair considering the dusky color of her hair and striking eyes. She wore a smartly tailored gray suit and white blouse with a simple collar, and her makeup was so expertly applied as to be undiscernible. Her nails were without polish, and the only jewelry she wore was a simple gold band on the ring finger of her right hand. She smiled. "No, Ed, I think that covers it. With all the high-priced talent around here, I can't imagine anything going wrong."

The door opened, and Georges Abbatiello entered the room. A veteran director of TV music specials, including the previous year's Grammy Awards, he was a short, slight man with thinning hair, a perpetual look of harassment, and hands in constant flight, small birds hovering around a feeder—or a meeting. "Sorry I'm late," he said, "but there's been a misunderstanding with Sammy's people." He plopped in a chair next to Trenka and said, "Sammy is marvelous, just dances through these problems, you know, the old soft shoe." He looked at Trenka. "Have I missed anything?"

Trenka said, "I think not. There is little to miss."

"Oh, there is something else," Andrea Feldman said, holding a finger in the air. "Miss Gateaux's manager wants us to put her on later in the program."

Abbatiello stood, hands moving. "That's ridiculous, impossible."

"Why?" Farmer asked.

"Why?" Abbatiello said in a voice that had risen to fly with his hands. "You don't just arbitrarily change the order of guest appearances. We've choreographed this down to the last second. The final version of the script is being typed at this moment. The orchestra has rehearsed everything in order. No, tell Ms. Gateaux's manager that one thing we don't need now is a diva's temperament." He sat down, elaborately weary.

"Why did you wait until now to bring this up, Andrea?" Farmer asked.

"I talked to her manager just an hour before the meeting and made a note to bring it up, only it got lost in the shuffle. She wasn't demanding it—was very nice, actually."

"I think it's ridiculous to have her on the program anyway," an Ewald media consultant said. "The senator, as everyone knows, is a jazz lover. He knows nothing from opera, so why have an opera singer? Opera doesn't pull in many votes."

"Jazz pulls even fewer. Are we really going to debate this now?" Farmer asked.

"I disagree," said Trenka, the first hint of amusement in his voice all day. "At least we will have some serious music represented."

"This whole conversation is academic," Farmer said, closing the briefcase in front of him to make the point that he was about to leave. "Roseanna Gateaux has been invited to participate, and she will. The senator likes jazz but was especially pleased when she agreed to appear on his behalf, and that's that." Farmer, a slender young man with rimless glasses, a hairline that had started its rapid rise in law school, and a fondness for colorful wide-striped shirts, bow ties, and penny loafers, had been with Ewald since the senator's early days in California as a national political figure.

"What do you think, Mrs. Ewald?" Andrea Feldman asked.

Leslie Ewald smiled. "I think I share Mr. Trenka's appreciation for having opera represented in the musical fare. I happen to particularly enjoy opera, and Ken loves jazz. One doesn't preclude the other. I think it's nice that both will be heard. Maybe we should include some rap music, too." There were a few smiles.

Farmer stood. "And," he said, "let's not go changing performance schedules at this late date. The show is tomorrow, and there's enough for this committee to do to make sure the parties and such go well. Thank you all very much, ladies and gentlemen, for taking yet more time this afternoon." To Andrea, he added, "Call Ms. Gateaux's manager, tell him to convey to her that we love her, that it is too late to make changes, that her part of the show is prime time, before audience fatigue sets in and before we lose part of the TV audience to a very popular network comedy that cuts in before we're finished. She's an artist, she'll understand."

Farmer and Leslie Ewald were the first to leave the room. As they led two Secret Service agents into the upper lobby outside the opera house, Farmer growled, "Stars. Spare me."

"I know, Ed, but it is wonderful that all these artists have agreed to appear on Ken's behalf tomorrow night. The jazz lineup alone reads like a Who's Who, and also having performers like Sammy Davis, Jr., and Joan Baez is really an incredible affirmation of their belief in him."

"More like a belief in having someone in the White House who appreciates them. Some of these performers aren't exactly what you'd call left-wing Democrats. Once they saw Ken pick up a head of steam in the primaries, they seemed to have forgotten the impurity of his ideology." He laughed scornfully. "Like all the other committee frauds."

Ewald had come in fourth in the Iowa caucus in February, third in the New Hampshire primary the same month. There was talk of dropping out. Then he took sixteen of the nineteen states on "Super Tuesday," March 8. That was when Perry, Bradley, Cuomo, Gore, Nunn, and Alexander called it quits, leaving only Ewald and Jody Backus in the remaining pro forma races.

Farmer and Leslie Ewald crossed the sprawling main lobby and passed through the Hall of Nations, the flags of all countries currently maintaining diplomatic relations with the United States lining the soaring white marble-veneer walls above them. Farmer helped Leslie on with her raincoat and opened the door to the outside, where her limousine waited. "Ride?" she asked.

"No, thanks. I'm going over to the office." The senator's private campaign office was across the street in the Watergate Office Building.

Leslie extended her hand. Farmer took it. She said, "It's going to work, isn't it?"

"The show tomorrow night?"

"No, the campaign. He's going to become president."

Farmer released her hand. "Let's just say things are looking good, but you never know. The last primary can't hurt him, and then the convention will be the coronation. As candidate. Unless something happens that throws everything off—which would open up the convention as it hasn't been opened for years."

She stared at him; he was never optimistic, which, she often thought, was unusual for the campaign manager of a man running for the White House. But every time she had those thoughts, she reminded herself that Ed was right, that in the rough-and-tumble, right-and-left, right-or-wrong democracy called the United States, there should be no celebrating until the final ballot had been cast on November 8, and until the Electoral College had pronounced its verdict.

She said, "Thanks for everything, Ed. The gala is going to be wonderful. What a send-off to the convention, what a boost. I may even find it gala and relax and enjoy myself."

"When you think about boosts and lift-offs, remember NASA and the *Challenger* astronauts," Farmer cautioned darkly.

Without another word, Leslie Ewald got into her limousine.

Not far from Kennedy Center, in George Washington University's Lerner Hall, Mackensie Smith peered over his lectern at the students in his crowded class on advanced criminal procedures. He was a craggy, fine-looking man in heavy horn-rimmed glasses.

"I think that does it for today," he said, running his fingers over stubble on his cheeks, which seemed to reappear in minutes no matter how many times he shaved. "Aside from the cases you've been assigned to analyze by the next time we meet, I have an additional assignment for you." He smiled as assorted groans welled up. "I expect you to watch the musical salute to Senator Ewald tomorrow night."

A young man named Crouse said, "Professor Smith, I thought the classroom was not to be used for political purposes." The other students laughed along with him.

"And this classroom isn't," Smith said, closing his portfolio of lecture notes. "All I'm suggesting is that you take an hour out of your busy schedules and enjoy some good music. I expect well-rounded attorneys to graduate from this university."

"Professor Smith," a young woman called.

"Yes, Ms. Riley?"

"When Senator Ewald is elected president, will you be his attorney general?"

Smith sighed; he was tired of the subject. "If Senator Ewald becomes the next president of the United States, he will undoubtedly choose someone for that post who wants it. That rules me out. Watch the show. You'll be quizzed on it."

He went down H Street to Twenty-second, took a left to G, stopped in at DJ's Fast Break for a sandwich to go, and slowed to a leisurely walk in the direction of his home on Twenty-fifth. The sky was overcast, and mist that threatened to degenerate into drizzle gave the air a thick quality. It was early June but felt like April, which, Smith reminded himself, was better than feeling like August in Washington, D.C. He pulled the collar of his raincoat up closer to his neck and thought of that question he'd been asked so many times since Ken Ewald seemed almost assured of his party's nomination.

Mac Smith and Ken Ewald went back a long time together. Their relationship wasn't intensely political. Smith had never been much interested in partisan politics, but certain issues, certain causes, had always been dear to him, and he approved of Ewald's stance on them.

They'd first met when Ewald had begun to push, vigorously and at great political risk, for legislation on gun control, particularly handguns. Smith, at the time, was one of Washington's most respected attorneys, especially in criminal law, and had been asked to testify at hearings held by Ewald's committee. Shortly after Mac Smith's appearance, he received a call from Ewald inviting him to a dinner party at the senator's home. That began a limited friendship that had deepened over the years. It wasn't that they spent much time together; their busy individual lives precluded that. But there were other parties, issues, occasional plane trips together, and Smith found himself not only the senator's friend, but an unofficial legal—and, at times, personal—adviser to Ewald and his family.

Issues beyond gun control drew Smith to Ken Ewald. The current president, Walter Manning, had little interest in the arts, and his administration reflected it. Ewald, on the other hand, was the leading Senate voice in support of all things cultural, and every writer and artist, every musician and theatrical performing-arts group in the country, knew that any slice of the Federal pie designated for them was the direct result of these years of Ewald's unfailing championing of their cause.

From Smith's perspective, Ewald was a well-balanced politician. As a freshman in Congress, he'd vigorously opposed the war, yet was a staunch supporter of maintaining military superiority over the Soviets. He'd called for the return of a WPA in which all able-bodied welfare recipients would work, or undergo training while collecting assistance, except the mentally ill, homeless, and AIDS victims. He had his faults, of course, but Smith had few reservations about supporting the man in his run for the White House, especially after the reign of Walter Manning.

Smith turned the corner at Twenty-fifth and headed for home, his narrow, two-story taupe brick house with trim, shutters, and front door painted Federal blue. Attorney general? he thought. It brought a smile to his face. He had thought of many things he might be interested in doing with the rest of his life, but being directly involved in executive-branch politics was not on the list.

He opened the door and entered the place that had been his home for the past seven years. Rufus greeted him with unwelcome enthusiasm. "Stay down," Smith said, pushing on the blue Great Dane's huge head. When Rufus stood on his hind legs, he looked his master in the eye.

Smith answered the ringing phone in his study, making sure to put his sandwich on top of the refrigerator, out of Rufus's reach.

"Mac, it's Leslie."

"Hello, Leslie, how are you?"

"Tired but happy. I just came from the final meeting on the show and party. It's going to be lovely, Mac. I'm so excited."

"Splendid. I assume Ken shares your enthusiasm."

"I think so, although I haven't seen him enough to find out. I'll be glad when the last of the primaries is over, the convention is behind us, and . . ."

Smith laughed. "And you're choosing drapes for the Oval Office."

"I don't dare say it. Bad luck to say such things. At least that's what gloomy Ed Farmer would say."

"Somehow, Leslie, I don't think luck will have much to do with it."

"I just wanted to tell you how well the meeting went, and to thank you again for your help."

"I didn't do much."

"More than you think. It's always comforting to have the clearheaded wisdom of Mackensie Smith on tap. I've got a last-minute idea Boris and Georges won't like. Have to run, Mac. See you tomorrow. Don't forget to shave and wear a clean shirt."

3

KEN EWALD, senior U.S. senator from California, stood alone in the anteroom behind the president's box in the Kennedy Center's opera house. Chairs upholstered in a white, green, and red floral pattern surrounded a glass-topped coffee table. The carpet was the color of ripe cherries. Small paintings dotted pale green walls.

He walked to where the seal hung next to the door and removed it from its hook. His fingers traced the raised wording: SEAL OF THE PRESIDENT OF THE UNITED STATES. The letters were in blue, the background gold. An eagle dominated the center, its breast a shield of red, white, and blue. The seal was always on the wall, unless the president and his party were attending an event in the opera house. When that happened, it was hung in front of the box for the audience to see. Tickets to the box were part of the president's patronage—to give, if he wished to share them. Otherwise, the box stood empty during performances.

Ewald opened the door and stepped into the box. Below were

twenty-three hundred empty seats. The party to kick off that night's musical gala was in progress onstage. Ewald had been down there moments before. Bored, he'd wandered up to the box. The lead Secret Service agent assigned to him for the night, Robert Jeroldson, remained outside in the foyer on Ewald's instructions.

He looked down at the stage where Leslie, their son, Paul, and daughter-in-law, Janet, stood with some of the celebrities who would perform that night. His physical distance from them at that moment was symbolic; never before had he and Leslie worked so closely together, yet he knew the inherent pressures of seeking the presidency created tremendous and understandable pressures on her, and on their marriage. A politician's wife—she garnered more votes than any platform could.

He surveyed the stage for other familiar faces. They certainly were there, some pleasing, others representing necessary evils. He looked around the empty box and wondered at those who'd occupied the White House in the past. Some had spent considerable time in this presidential box. Others, like the sitting president, Republican Walter Manning, had been openly without interest in the artistic events that gave life to the nation's cultural center.

He looked down at the seal in his hands and was suddenly overwhelmed at the significance of the office it represented. The decision to run for president had not come easily to him. He'd spent countless hours of private debate over whether he was indeed qualified to lead a nation that not only was the most powerful on earth, but meant so much to him. He knew he was up to the task as far as experience and insight into the workings of government went. Years in Congress—first in the House, then in the Senate—had given him a broad and deep understanding of how things worked, how things got done. But was that enough? Did he want it badly enough, was there enough of the proverbial fire in his belly to carry into the job itself?

He thought back to when Eugene McCarthy had sought the presidency. McCarthy had been on a television talk show. The host—Ewald couldn't remember who it was—commented that certain critics of McCarthy claimed he did not want to be president bad enough, to which McCarthy replied, in his urbane manner, "No one should want to be president *that* bad." McCarthy had gone on to say during that interview that he thought every president should take off one day a week to read poetry, or to listen to music. Ewald had smiled at that comment; it represented, to some extent, his own feelings, even though he knew the suggestion was impractical.

He also thought back to Ronald Reagan, the only president who seemed to come out of the White House looking better and almost younger than when he'd entered. Days off to read poetry and listen to music (or to watch old western movies)? Perhaps. It really didn't matter. The fact was, Ken Ewald *did* want to be president of the United States, because he felt the things he believed in were good for the country, would take it from a White House mortgaged to big business, oil, and the furthest right of military interests, and return it to a White House in which people mattered more than machines and money.

He went back to the anteroom and hung the seal on the wall. Critics said that he was naive in some of his plans involving social welfare. There were his own dark moments when he thought they might be right, that the only way to govern America was to be hard-nosed, isolated, ruthless. Maybe. But even in those small hours, he told himself that he was not without his own hard edges, his own recognition that to govern effectively *was* to compromise, to allow pragmatism to take the edge off dreams. He was ready to do that. His dreams would be accommodated in the larger context of being president. First, you had to win. You had to *be* there if any part of any dream was to be realized.

By the time he returned to the stage, the party had gained momentum.

Ewald was delighted to see Paul. His son's successful import-export business had kept him in the Far East for two weeks, and there had been a question whether he would make it back in time for this salute to his father. Ewald had to smile as he thought of the telephone conversation they'd had a few days ago. Paul had called from Hong Kong, and after some talk about how well the campaign was going, he'd concluded with, "Dad, you know I'll be there if I have to rent a Chinese junk and row it all the way back myself." Ewald often told his friends that if you were only going to have one child, you were lucky to have one like Paul.

His daughter-in-law was another story. Small and slender, lips abstemious and poorly defined on a pinched face, Janet was a moody young woman—at least when Ewald was around her, which, he was grateful, wasn't often. What his handsome, successful son saw in her was beyond him, although he'd settled long ago on her superior bosom, surprising for such an otherwise meager frame.

Ed Farmer joined him. Ewald grinned, nodded, and said, "She's a beautiful woman, isn't she?" referring not to Janet but to Roseanna Gateaux, surrounded by a group of admirers off to the side of the sixty-four-feet-deep stage, a stage almost as large as the Metropolitan Opera House at New York's Lincoln Center, or Russia's Bolshoi.

His campaign manager said nothing.

"Just lusting in my heart," Ewald said, his smile expanding at the corners of his mouth. That smile, and the form it took, was part of the boyishness that balanced the crags and lines in his tan face. Soft, curly brown hair helped, too. He was forty-six, one of the youngest presidential candidates since John Kennedy.

Farmer looked meaningfully in the direction of a Washington columnist, stationed nearby behind a glass of champagne. "Keep those lines to yourself until after you're president . . . *Senator,*" Farmer said sharply. "Come on, we need photos."

Ewald watched Roseanna Gateaux move gracefully to where a pianist, bassist, and violinist recruited from the National Symphony played show tunes, their melodies floating harmlessly up into a canyon of lights, pipe battens, grids, fly lines, and counterweight pulleys.

"Let's do some photos," Farmer repeated.

"Now?"

"Yes. How often are all of you together? We'll pose you with some of the stars, then do the family." Farmer gripped Ewald's arm and guided him to where his family stood with a few of the artists who would appear later that night. Ewald extended his hand to the pianist Oscar Peterson. "I've been collecting your records ever since they came out of Canada on ten-inch discs," Ewald said.

Peterson shook Ewald's hand and smiled. "That's nice to hear, Senator Ewald. You're talking about a long time ago."

"Yes, I know," Ewald said. "I was turned on to jazz in my early teens. I remember very well the first two records I ever heard. Really heard, that is. One featured you—it might have been your first recording—the other was a Dixieland album led by Muggsy Spanier."

"That's an eclectic beginning," said Peterson, considered among the greatest pianists in the history of jazz. Leslie Ewald joined them.

Ewald turned next to Sarah Vaughan. "I've been a fan of yours for almost as long, Ms. Vaughan. I still say the record you cut for Emarcy when you were nineteen—the one with Clifford Brown, Herbie Mann, and Jimmy Jones—is the finest jazz vocal album ever recorded. My wife will testify to the fact that it's played loud and often in our house."

She thanked him. "How nice it will be to have a president of the United States who appreciates American music."

Ewald laughed. "More than just appreciates it. Devoted to it is more like it. I plan to have regular jazz concerts at the White House."

"Provided you get the nomination and are elected, Ken," Leslie Ewald said. His smile never broke, but there was a fleeting anger in his eyes as he looked at her.

Peterson graciously excused himself.

Sarah Vaughan turned to Ewald and said, "I understand one of your favorite songs is 'Lover Man.' "

"That's right."

"I'll be singing it tonight just for you."

"Wonderful! I can't wait."

The singer walked away to join trumpeter Ruby Braff, bassist Ron Carter, and drummer Mel Lewis, who were laughing at a joke one of them had told.

Farmer had collared the campaign photographer and set up shots of Ewald and family with some of the jazz musicians. When they were through, Ewald turned to his son. "I'm very happy you could make it back, Paul. This whole thing wouldn't have meant nearly as much without you."

"Well, I have to admit that rowing that junk took something out of me, but here I am." They both laughed. Ewald turned to his daughter-in-law and asked how she was.

"Just fine," Janet replied. To Paul, she said, "Let's go."

"They want a picture of us, son."

Paul looked at his wife. "Two more minutes, Janet. I want my picture taken with the next president of the United States."

Janet tugged Paul's arm. "Please."

"Take the picture," Leslie Ewald said to the photographer. She moved close to her husband; Janet was at Ewald's other side.

"Big, happy smiles on everyone," Farmer said. "This is a gala."

Ewald put his arm around his wife and smiled, exposing a solid set of white teeth. Leslie's smile matched his in intensity and attractiveness. As the photographer tripped the shutter and the strobe went off, Paul turned to look at his father. His expression was one of sincere admiration. Janet Ewald, her delicate clasped hands a fig leaf below her waist, managed to look as though she suffered only minor pain.

After a dozen more shots had been taken of the family, Ken and Leslie posed together, just the two of them. Having their pictures taken obviously caused them no discomfort. Every shot was quick, smooth—candidate and wife at a celebrity cocktail party at the national arts center named after John F. Kennedy, whom Ewald frequently quoted in his speeches. He was a "Kennedy man," part of the cosmetic as well as ideological legacy, cut from the same political cloth, tailored and barbered to heighten the effect, and every bit as handsome and charming. After eight years of a conservative administration, the country seemed ready for a return to Camelot. Ewald felt confident that in the general election in November he could defeat the current vice-president of the United States, Raymond Thornton, the obvious Republican nominee.

For a time, he'd been less confident about the Democratic Convention in July in San Francisco, where he would have to bring in enough delegates to defeat his chief opponent for the nomination, southern senator Joseph "Jody" Backus, the leader of the conservative wing of the Democratic party, preferably by the second ballot, after the favorite sons—and daughters—and such.

Backus had started strong in the early primaries, but had fallen behind. Still, the party had changed dramatically as the nation shifted into a more conservative stance. Liberal Democratic beliefs had been denigrated again. There were still some powerful Democrats who were convinced that a candidate like Ken Ewald, with his well-documented commitment to the sort of social programs that seemed to scream of big government expenditures, was anathema to the majority of the electorate, Republican and Democrat alike. It needn't be that way—not all progress and programs required billions. But Jody Backus, even though the numbers coming out of the primaries had placed him behind Ewald in Democratic voter preference, retained considerable clout within the party. Now, with the latest changes in regulations, you could win the primary battle—and lose the war.

Yes, Ken Ewald was confident he could defeat Raymond Thornton in

November. But first he would have to work down to the wire to ensure his nomination in July. Tonight's televised gala from the Kennedy Center would help.

Gerry Fielding, a congresswoman from northern California and an ally, walked up, smiling. "What are you going to do for an inaugural gala, Ken," she said, "with this big production number tonight for a mere candidacy? Remember, for one event Bush had Sinatra and Baryshnikov and Arnold Schwarzenegger."

Ewald said, "We're doing *The Messiah* and I'm singing the title role."

A white-jacketed waiter carrying leftover hors d'oeuvres passed the Ewalds. The senator picked a *spanakopita* from the silver tray and popped the phyllo pastry filled with spinach and cheese into his mouth. Leslie started talking with other people, freeing him to wander away, Farmer at his side, Agent Jeroldson maintaining his usual watchful but discreet distance behind. Ewald stopped to exchange banalities with friends ("Looks like campaigning agrees with you, Senator"; "Your wife looks as lovely as ever, Ken—and you seem to be holding up, too, ha-ha"), or to be gracious to strangers who wished him well in his pursuit of the nomination ("No, Jody Backus and I work closely together in the Senate. It's just that we see things a little different sometimes").

He left the theater, stood on the landing, and looked out over the red-carpeted grand foyer, longer than two football fields ("You can lay the Washington Monument in it and still have room to spare," the tour guides all said). Eighteen Swedish crystal Orefors chandeliers, each weighing a ton, cast uncertain light over the expanse. Ewald saw through floor-to-ceiling windows that a jet aircraft, its whine snuffed out by the building's impressive soundproofing, was making its approach to National Airport, just across the Potomac.

He started down the stairs when a "Good evening, Senator" stopped him.

Ewald turned to face Mackensie Smith.

"Be back in a minute," Farmer said.

"Hello, Mac." Ewald extended his hand.

"You look bored," Smith said.

Ewald laughed. "I can't be bored at my own party, can I? Even if it's just another excuse for photo opportunities. I think the bash after the show will be a hell of a lot pleasanter. I assume you know, Mac, how much I appreciate your efforts in helping to put this night together."

Smith shrugged. "I always wanted to rub shoulders with the stars. Now, I'm getting my chance."

"And?"

"It was less exciting than my mother told me it would be. You should be in your element tonight, Ken. Lots of good jazz to be heard."

"Yes, I love it. Of course, you'll have your addiction to opera satisfied, too."

"That's true, although as with any addiction, the craving only grows stronger after each 'fix.' How's Leslie?"

"Fine. Under some strain, but still comes up smiling."

Smith was two years Ewald's senior. His body was cubelike, not fat but square, solid; he'd been a star linebacker at the University of West Virginia. Ewald's tall, slender physique was more that of a basketball player; indeed, he'd been enough of a court performer at Stanford to make the Pacific Coast all-star team, second string, with the "second string" usually omitted from biographies prepared by his office.

Smith had shaved just before coming to the party, but a heavy five o'clock shadow said he hadn't. His head was covered with a close crop of salt-and-pepper hair. His eyes were the color of Granny Smith apples. The nose was prominent, his chin jutting and strong. He looked at Secret Service agent Jeroldson and said to Ewald, "I could never get used to that." When Ewald didn't respond, Smith added, "Spending my life being watched."

Ewald had been distracted by a couple who'd carried their drinks to the grand foyer and stood gazing up at the seven-feet-tall, three-thousand-pound bronze Robert Berks bust of President Kennedy. He gave his attention back to Smith. "I agree, Mac. Having these guys sleep with me is the only reason I ever considered not running."

Smith smiled and looked down at his empty glass. "Think I'll get a refill before the show starts."

"That's three hours away. You must be getting desperate. Where's Ann?" Ewald asked. Annabel Reed had been Smith's companion for a number of years.

"Out of town, Ken. The irony of it. Here I am involved with my first and last television extravaganza, and she picks tonight to be away on business. She'll be watching at her hotel. See you later. And—break a leg."

Ed Farmer, the rest of the Ewald family in tow, came to where the candidate stood alone. "Time to go to the hotel, Senator," Farmer said. It was now six o'clock; the performance would begin promptly at nine. They'd taken a suite at the Watergate across the street rather than have to return home to kill time.

"Okay," Ewald said. Then, almost to himself, he added, "I wish he'd change his mind."

"Who?" Farmer and Leslie asked in concert.

"Mac Smith. He'd be a tremendous asset to us."

"He already has been," Leslie said.

"I know, I know," Ewald said as they walked down the stairs to the foyer. "I was surprised he agreed to get involved at all, considering his disdain for vulgar politics. Maybe it will give him a taste of campaign excitement and he'll decide to get more active with us. He'd make a hell of an adviser on drugs and other crimes. And a great attorney general."

4

IN ANOTHER SUITE at the Watergate, Sammy Davis, Jr., was playing Pac-Man. The electronic game traveled with him wherever he went. A quart bottle of strawberry soda with a straw was at his side; half a case of it sat in a corner of the living room.

"I know how last-minute this is, Sammy," Georges Abbatiello said from where he sat on a leather barstool, "but I really would like to accommodate Mrs. Ewald. She's a nice lady. She called me a half hour ago and asked if you and Roseanna Gateaux would do a duet. She remembers seeing you do one at some benefit in Vegas a year or two ago. She said she was reluctant to ask because Roseanna had requested a last-minute change in the schedule and we turned her down, but then she figured nothing ventured, nothing gained. Would you be willing to come on again and do a duet with Roseanna? We'll find time by shortening up on the jam sessions."

"Hey, man, happy to. The lady's a gas." He continued to play the game.

Abbatiello smiled. He knew Davis's reputation was that of easy cooperation, but he didn't expect him to be *this* easy.

Things had begun to fall apart in the last hours leading up to the telecast, and Georges and his staff were in a mad scramble to straighten them out. He was used to dealing with the quibbles of performing artists, but most of the problems were coming from the political side— politicians insisting they be onstage when Ewald and his family made an appearance, security people questioning arrangements they should have thought of days before, big egos clashing with bigger egos and lesser significance. He was glad he'd earned his ulcer in show business rather than the political arena. As he'd said to his wife a few minutes before, this was his first and last contribution to politics—*anybody's* politics.

Davis lost the round. "I'll beat this sucker yet," he said, laughed loudly, and joined Abbatiello at the bar. "You want a soda?"

"No, thanks, Sammy." Abbatiello checked his watch. "Give me a fast rundown of how the duet goes—timing and such. And the sheets. We need the lead sheets for the orchestra." Davis's musical director, who'd been dozing in a large leather chair, came to life and worked with Abbatiello on the changes.

At precisely nine o'clock, with the opera house filled with Ewald supporters and friends of supporters out for a pleasant evening—and maybe to be seen—the curtain rose, the orchestra launched into a spirited, jazz-flavored arrangement of "California, Here I Come," and the musical gala in honor of Senator Kenneth Ewald began.

As it turned out, the impromptu duet between Sammy Davis, Jr., and Roseanna Gateaux was the hit of the evening. They romped through a medley of old and familiar songs like "Baby, It's Cold Outside" and "A Bushel and a Peck," the elegant and beautiful diva the perfect foil for the talented, manic, and considerably shorter Davis. Host David Letterman delighted the largely Democratic audience with barbed one-liners about the current administration, who was manning the Manning, etc., and roasts of the Republican party in general, and Joan Baez quietly transported those old enough to remember the 1960s back to that quaint period.

The finale was to be a jam session featuring all the jazz musicians who'd appeared in smaller groups. Just before Letterman announced that they would play Ellington's "Take the A Train," Ewald and his family were brought onstage. A restriction imposed by the Kennedy Center management was that there would be no overt political speechmaking during the evening. Ewald, who had no intention of violating that, simply said, "The kind of artistic and creative energy displayed here tonight is symbolic of what this great nation has always spawned . . . in its excellence and diversity and community." He turned and looked at his family, smiled broadly, and went on, "And all of us thank each and every person who has made this night so memorable. We are deeply grateful." Then, on cue, he turned to the assembled musicians and said, "Okay, they said I could count this one off." He tapped his foot and counted, "One, two, one, two, three, four." Oscar Peterson began the intro, and the Ewalds were led from the stage to take their seats again in the front row.

The finale was slightly disjointed and cheerful, as such numbers tend to be, but well received. The party preceding the performance had been small, the guest list carefully considered. Now, the larger party began. Had the weather been nasty, the Grand Lobby would have been used. Because the weather had turned nice, it was held on the vast wraparound terrace of the Kennedy Center.

Mac Smith, who'd quickly grown weary of being congratulated for having helped put together the evening, got himself a scotch and soda and found a relatively private spot on the west side of the terrace. People were milling everywhere; a six-piece band played hyper-amplified rock and roll, and hundreds of guests, young and old, gyrated to the rhythms on a large dance floor. Smith was thinking of Annabel Reed and what she might be doing at that moment in New York when the bulky body and round face of Jody Backus circumvented knots of people and headed his way. Ewald had insisted that all his Democratic rivals be invited, and most of them had showed up, including Senator Backus.

Smith had met Backus a number of times at social gatherings. Although the conservative senator represented few political and social ideas shared by Smith, he'd enjoyed those previous meetings, for Backus was a jovial, easy-talking conversationalist, with a bottomless reservoir of anecdotes and a tendency toward blunt truth.

"Hello, Senator," Smith said, extending his hand.

Backus took it in one of his own large hands and shook his head. "Looks like you and my dear colleague from the Senate pulled off quite a coup here tonight, Mac Smith."

"With lots of help," Smith said.

"I'm impressed. Nobody helpin' this ol' boy has come up with anything this good."

Smith laughed. "We had a few moments of inspiration, that's all."

"And tons a' bucks, I'd say. Good thing Ken's daddy made all those millions out in California. All that talent really work for nothin'?"

Smith nodded. "They were the *only* people who worked for nothing. You're right, Senator, it cost quite a few bucks."

Backus and Smith looked out over the crowd. "That's one thing about us Democrats that the Republicans don't have," Backus said.

"What's that, Senator?"

"The ability to have a hell of a good time."

"You ought to make sure that it's written into this year's platform," Smith joked. "A good time will be had by all, and twice in every pot."

Backus thought for a second, then laughed. He shook Smith's hand again and said, "I just want you to know, Mac, that if I don't manage to get me the nomination in July, your man has my support one hundred percent, and he can count on it."

Smith started to say that Ken Ewald was not exactly "his man," but decided to hold off. Backus waved, walked away, and Smith was joined by a plainclothes friend who was part of the Center's security staff. Together, they enjoyed watching the characters and the dancing, some skillful, some merely animated. During the slower numbers, Ed Farmer danced sedately with a gray-haired woman, the wife of the majority leader, but was interrupted after a few minutes, naturally, by a phone call. Ken Ewald and his wife made a comfortable portrait of grace in motion and drew applause. The beat changed and the volume increased. Andrea Feldman, the young woman on Ewald's staff who'd been so helpful in setting up the gala, had captured the attention of others on the dance floor as she expended frenetic and somewhat erotic energy with a tall, handsome young blond man who'd removed his suit jacket, and who wore red, white, and blue striped suspenders over his white shirt. Andrea's purple silk dress closely followed every contour of her splendid figure. Around her waist was a vibrant belt, more a sash, created of multicolored feathers from exotic birds.

"I'd like to see you out there dancing like that, Mac," the security man said.

"I would, except Annie isn't here." He smiled at the image; he had little taste whatsoever for most of today's popular music, and preferred his dancing to be quiet and pleasant, bodies gently touching, a soothing melody and subtle beat in the background.

The band ended the "song" it was playing, and Farmer took the microphone. After congratulating everyone who had played a hand in creating the evening, he asked for a warm round of applause for the "next president of the United States, Ken Ewald."

The applause he wanted was forthcoming, and Ewald bounded up onto the bandstand and took the microphone. As he began, Mac Smith thought, He's an effective speaker in any situation, no doubt about that, and always natural. And in a nation that thought itself suspicious of oratory, what a wonderful—and critical—ability that was for anyone seeking office . . . seeking success in any endeavor, for that matter. This night, Ewald almost threatened to burst with honest enthusiasm, and when he'd finished his brief talk, the applause was twice as loud as when he'd been announced.

Suddenly, a detonation of Vesuvius fountains and Catherine wheels sprayed broad strokes of lacquered, multicolored light greens and reds and yellows—across the black sky, the vividness of the colors dissipating as they trickled down the canvas to the horizon. All eyes turned in the direction of the fireworks; "ooohs" and "aaahs" blended with the snap, crackle, and pop of the display.

The sky show lasted ten minutes. As the last traces of sulfurous smoke wafted toward the party and the applause by a few overzealous souls continued, the band began playing, the dancers flocked to the floor, the portable bars were surrounded once again, and the party moved back into high gear. Washingtonians were often ready to party, Smith thought, for what they did by day was no party. *For* the party, perhaps, but no fiesta.

He waited until he felt it was appropriate for him to leave—a few minutes before midnight on his watch—and sought out those to whom he should say good-bye. He started toward the Ewalds, but they were busy. He thought of Andrea Feldman, but saw that she was in a shadowed area of the terrace talking with a man who looked like Ed Farmer, and although Smith could not hear what they were saying, their faces and body language suggested that theirs was not a pleasant chat. He found a few others he was looking for, then left the Kennedy Center, enjoying the pristine night that had displaced the wet weather of the previous day.

As soon as he entered his Foggy Bottom home ten minutes later, he threw off his raincoat and called Annabel at her New York hotel.

"It was a wonderful show, Mac," she said. "I loved every minute of it."

"Thanks. From a pragmatic point of view, everything worked, everyone seemed to be happy with it, we'll pay the bills, make some money, advance the candidacy, and I'm glad it's over. As little as I had to do with it, it still took too much of my time. How are things with you?"

"Fine. My dinner with the investors went well. Damn, Mac, I am sorry I couldn't be there, but you know that—"

"Annie, when you have serious investors from Europe who tell you the only time they can meet is for dinner one evening, you don't beg off because you have a party to go to. Of course I understand. I'm just glad it went well. When are you coming home?"

"I'm shooting for the noon shuttle. I'll go directly to the gallery."

"I'll call you there."

"Call me every minute. I miss you, Mac."

"I miss you, too, although I have to admit that what I missed most was not being able to do the funky chicken with you."

"Mac, are you . . . ?" She started to laugh, wished him a good night's sleep, and they ended the conversation.

Eleven o'clock was Smith's usual bedtime. This night, however, he found himself wide awake, and picked up where he'd left off reading Edmund Wilson's *The Thirties.* He finished a series of entries on the famous Scribner's editor Max Perkins, and looked at the Regulator clock in his study. It was almost four in the morning. Smith marked his place with a bookmark and said to Rufus, "Come on, it isn't often you get to be walked at this hour."

He put on a George Washington University windbreaker, slipped the choke chain over Rufus's head, and they went out to the street. It was a beautiful night—or morning; Smith breathed deeply, and a smile crossed his face. He was one of those people who was profoundly affected by the weather—hating the hot and humid summers, growling about the icy winters that sent inexperienced D.C. drivers sliding into each other with frightening regularity, and loving times like this, feeling good and doubly alive because of them. "Come on, Rufus, let's move and get some air in our lungs."

There was no such thing as a brisk walk with Rufus. The Dane was too interested in stopping to smell territorial markers left by previous visitors. They meandered, stopping-and-going, in the direction of the Kennedy Center, where only hours earlier there had been so much activity, so much gaiety. Now, everything was still. Lights from the Center shone brightly in the black night.

They had to wait at a corner as a D.C. cab careened past them viciously. "Dumb bastard," Smith snarled as he watched the red taillights disappear around another corner, but decided nothing must spoil his mood. He looked left and right, then set off at a trot across the broad avenue separating the Center from where they'd stood.

The man and the dog slowed to a walk and went up the ramp leading to the Center's front entrance. Smith had never walked Rufus there before, but, then again, he had never been out quite this late with his best friend before.

There was little for the nosy canine to investigate on the ramp. They stopped to look down over the Potomac for a few minutes, then turned and retraced their steps back in the direction of the house, walking this time on the far side of the fountain.

Smith hesitated in front of a massive horizontal relief that was the centerpiece of a small, parklike area, the relief called "War and Peace." A plaque on it read AMERICA 1965–1971—DONATED BY THE GOVERNMENT OF THE FEDERAL REPUBLIC OF GERMANY. Funny, Smith thought, how much of the Kennedy Center had been given by other governments, other nations. The intimate Terrace Theater had been a gift of 'Japan; the huge chandelier in the opera house was from the people of Austria; marble lining the grand halls came from the citizens of Italy; paintings from Peru; meeting rooms through the generosity of Africa and Israel; sculpture from Great Britain—foreign tributes everywhere to the American arts center that had been conceived by President Eisenhower, nurtured by Lyndon Johnson, and eventually designated as the only memorial in the nation's capital to the slain John F. Kennedy. Smith had taken the tour of Kennedy Center more than once, and had been privy to many of its inner dimensions at meetings and social events. No matter how many critics had taken aim at Edward Durell Stone's long, horizontal architectural approach, Smith was glad it was there, and that he lived near it. It was, in effect, the centerpiece of his neighborhood, and he always felt particular pride in what it symbolized.

Funny, too, how a structure so full of life a few hours earlier could be so devoid of it now.

"Come on," he said, yanking at Rufus's leash. Rufus balked; because of his size and strength, when the dog balked, he almost always prevailed. The Dane pulled hard as he tried to go behind the relief to where a small cluster of wooden benches provided seating in the midst of carefully tended shrubs, bushes, and small trees.

"No, come on, Rufus, we don't want to go back there."

Rufus kept up the pressure on his leash; Smith finally gave up and went with him. Once behind the relief, Smith tried to see what the Dane would wet down, or what had captured the dog's attention. A half-moon provided some illumination. The first thing Smith saw was a long, colorful feather on the ground. Rufus sniffed it and continued pressing into the shrubbery. "Hey, Rufus, what are you . . . ?"

Then he saw what the dog was after, a silk-stockinged female foot. A shoe with a medium heel rested close to it. *"Damn,"* Smith muttered as he shortened the leash and moved closer, fearing to interrupt something private. Now, the length of a shapely leg was visible, and then the woman, her skirt hiked up her thighs. Rufus, as though understanding what was at stake, stopped pulling and stood at attention, a low growl coming from his throat.

Smith pushed aside a low branch. He saw what he sensed was the full body, and knew immediately who it was by the exotic feather belt around her waist. "Good God," he whispered as he stepped over her legs. Andrea Feldman's arresting eyes were wide open—but gone to glass. Her mouth was open as well. Blood had oozed from her chest through the fabric of her dress. Her purse was on the ground; it had opened and its contents bled into the dirt, too.

Smith crouched and took her wrist. Then he looked at the debris of her death. Lipstick. A small makeup mirror. A pen. And a key, obviously from a hotel. Smith read the writing on the large red plastic tag attached to it: BUCCANEER MOTEL, ROSSLYN, VIRGINIA. The numeral 6 was also imprinted on the tag.

He led Rufus to the front of the relief, looked for someone, saw no one, and quickly ran, the dog leading the way, to the house, where he burst into the living room, thumbed through his phone book until he found the number he wanted, and dialed.

A deep, sleepy voice answered.

"Joe, Mac Smith. I'm sorry to wake you, but there's been a terrible accident. Maybe a murder."

Joe Riga, chief of detectives of Washington's MPD, was now awake. "Where? Who?"

"A young woman named Andrea Feldman, who worked on Ken Ewald's staff. I was walking my dog near the Kennedy Center and found the body."

"Why didn't you call—?"

"Nine-one-one? Joe, I don't know what this means, but I have to . . . well, there could be ramifications. Considerable ramifications. If you want me to call nine-one-one, I will, but . . ."

"No, Mac, sorry I even suggested it. I understand. Where's the woman, the body? You sure she's dead? Okay, forget that last."

"Behind the large relief across the fountain from the Kennedy Center, in front. She's in the bushes."

"I'm on my way."

"Fine, I'll meet you there—and Joe . . . I would appreciate it if we could keep this quiet for a few hours."

"We can keep it quiet until I see the body and call it in. I can't do more than that. It probably won't keep for long anyhow. You know this town."

"Sure do. And thanks."

"You can make a positive ID on her, Mac?" Riga asked as they stood over the body.

"Yes. Her name is Andrea Feldman."

Riga handed Smith the flashlight he carried, squatted, took the chin between his thumb and index finger, and gently moved her jaw back and forth. "Still slack," he said. He slid his hand down the top of her dress and nestled it in her armpit. "Didn't happen long ago," he said as he removed his hand and stood. "Still some warmth. I'll call it in."

"Joe, maybe you can do one favor, a legal one."

"What?"

"Let me get hold of Ewald and tell him what's happened before the identification is announced. All I need is an hour, or even a few minutes."

"No problem." Riga called in for backup and a forensic unit to come to the scene. "Identity of victim uncertain," he said into his radio.

Smith thanked him and returned home, where he dialed the Ewald house.

A sleepy Leslie answered.

"Leslie, it's Mac Smith. Sorry to be calling at this hour, but this is important. Is Ken there?"

"Yes. Why?"

"Leslie, Andrea Feldman has been murdered."

There was silence on the other end of the line.

"I was walking Rufus and discovered her about an hour ago. Someone shot her outside the Kennedy Center, across from the main entrance."

"Mac, this is dreadful. Who could have done such a thing? Where is her family?"

"I have no idea, but I thought Ken ought to know right away."

"Of course." She turned away from the mouthpiece and murmured. Ewald came on the line. "Mac, could you come here right away?" he asked.

"Of course, but . . ."

"Please, Mac, come now."

"Sure. Anybody there to make some coffee at this hour?"

"Of course. This is unbelievable. She was at the party. She was alive. I'm shocked."

"So was I. Hot, black, and strong. I'm on my way."

5

THE STATELY TWO-STORY redbrick Ewald home was on the upper reaches of Twenty-eighth Street in Georgetown; behind it, Oak Hill Cemetery. The house sat on a rise of land, giving its occupants a view of the Dumbarton Oaks mansion and gardens.

Smith pulled up in his blue Chevy Caprice and told one of two uniformed security guards that he was expected. The guard used an intercom to confirm it, and pushed a button that caused black iron gates to open electronically. Smith pulled into the circular driveway and was about to knock on the front door when Leslie Ewald opened it.

"Hello, Leslie."

"Hello, Mac." She looked past him to the front gate. Smith observed her closely. The flesh around her eyes was spongy, like putty that has been rubbed with a thumb covered with pencil lead. Lines he hadn't noticed earlier in the evening seemed suddenly to have exploded at the corners of her mouth. She bit her lip, realized he was looking at her— realized he was there. "I'm sorry, Mac, please forgive me. I hate having to . . ."

She looked at the gate again. Smith, too, looked.

"We've always had one guard. Now, there are two. Ed Farmer had the extra sent over as soon as we told him about Ms. Feldman. They're going to install an electrified fence around the property—like one of those things that fries bugs." She looked up at the portico roof. "Cameras, too. God, how I hate it all!"

"Beefing up security might be wise," Smith said, "considering Andrea Feldman was a close working member of the staff. The media people and others will be all over you when it comes out."

"Yes, I suppose you're right."

"Let's go inside," Smith said.

She ignored him and pointed to her left. Parked on the road at the corner of the property was a small white car.

"Who's that?" he asked.

"Press. They were at police headquarters. I suppose we'll end up being surrounded."

As she entered the foyer, she started to cry. Smith followed and shut the door behind them. She looked at him with round, moist eyes that were spilling tears down her cheeks. Her body heaved, and she threw herself against him. He wrapped his big arms about her thin shoulders and held her for a time, saying softly, "Easy, easy. It's terrible that Andrea Feldman has died but . . ."

"You don't understand, Mac."

"I assume I will quickly."

"Yes, very quickly." She regained her composure, even forced a smile. "I haven't fallen apart in years." She took his hand. "Come, Ken and Ed Farmer are in the study."

As she opened the door, Farmer came through it, followed closely by Ewald. "Mac, good to see you, thanks for being here," Ewald said, putting his hand on Smith's shoulder. "Back in a minute."

Leslie looked as if she might cry again, so Smith asked if he could have a drink before the coffee. "It's been hours since the party." He really didn't want one, but his strategy worked. She now had something to do. She quickly departed, leaving him alone in the paneled room.

He'd been there before on dozens of occasions, yet for reasons he couldn't identify, it was strangely new to him at this moment.

Two walls were taken up with floor-to-ceiling bookcases. A third wall contained cases with glass doors that housed Ewald's extensive collection of antique guns—a strange hobby, Smith often thought, for someone perpetually at war with the NRA. "They're beautiful to look at, and they have great historic meaning. Shooting them is another matter," Ewald always said when questioned about it. Smith had always found Ewald somewhat enigmatic—predictable in a few unappealing ways, persuasively attractive in others. A human being.

Leslie returned carrying a scotch on the rocks for him, a balloon glass containing a dark liquid for her, partly consumed. "Did I get it right, Mac, scotch?"

"Yes, might as well stay with it. What are you drinking?" To keep her talking.

"Brandy and port. When Ken and I were in Scotland a few years ago, we took a particularly rough boat trip to the Orkney Islands. My stomach was queasy, and I asked the bartender for some blackberry brandy. He insisted a combination of port and brandy was more effective. He was right. I've felt like throwing up ever since we got your phone call, but this settled my stomach right down."

When they were seated on adjoining flowered love seats around a leather-topped coffee table, Smith said, "Okay, tell me about it. Don't mince words, just be direct. I know the death of anyone we know is terribly upsetting, but I'm reading into this something beyond that. Am I right?"

"Yes, you are *very* right."

"What am I right about?"

"I don't know where to begin. I suppose I should just tell you that—"

Ewald and Farmer returned. Ewald pulled a red morocco leather chair on casters up to the table, settled his long, lean body in it, and crossed one leg over the other, the casualness of the pose in stark contrast to the tension-stiffened body of his wife. Farmer stood by a window behind Smith.

"Leslie was just starting to tell me about a particular concern you have with Andrea's death."

Ewald said to his wife, "Go ahead, might as well continue." Smith couldn't decide whether Ewald was angry at Leslie or feeling an anxiety that his outward appearance didn't reflect.

Leslie shook her head and looked down at her drink.

"All right, I'll pick it up from there," Ewald said. "Evidently, Andrea was murdered with a weapon that belongs to me."

The expulsion of air through Smith's lips was involuntary—and necessary. He sat back and listened to Ewald's further explanation.

"I've had a registered handgun in the house for years. Leslie had been expressing concern about the amount of time I'm away, and I thought simply having it on the premises would be comforting to her." He looked at Leslie; she continued to stare down into her port and brandy.

"It was a small stainless-steel Derringer, a three-inch .45 Colt. It's been sitting in a drawer in the bedroom for God knows how long. At any rate, after you called with the news about Andrea, I opened the drawer. Don't ask me why, but I did. The gun is gone."

"Who had access to it besides you and Leslie?" Smith asked.

Ewald looked once again at his wife. "Everyone in the house," she said.

"Family?" Smith asked.

"Yes, family, visitors, household staff, campaign staff. A cast of thousands."

Smith thought for a moment before asking, "Is that what's concerning you so? Or do you think that someone in this household is going to be accused of her murder?"

Ewald didn't reply, but Leslie did, in a low, flat voice. "Yes."

"Someone from your staff, Ken?"

"No," Ewald said, looking at Leslie for the first time as if to receive approval of what he was about to say next. She was without expression. He said, "We feel there is the possibility that Paul will be charged with the murder."

"Why do you say that?" Smith asked.

"Because . . ."

Leslie Ewald finished the sentence. "Because Paul was having an affair with her." Smith started to speak, but Leslie forged on. "Paul was having an affair with Andrea Feldman, and last night he did not return home."

"You're sure?"

"Yes. We talked to Janet."

Smith was processing what she'd said. Both things pointed at Paul Ewald as a suspect, but they were hardly conclusive. Smith added a third element; Paul obviously had access to his father's pistols.

Smith realized Ed Farmer was still standing by the window. He'd forgotten Farmer was in the room. He turned and looked at the campaign manager, then asked Ken and Leslie whether there was any other information.

"Janet knew about Paul's affair with Andrea," Leslie said. "It caused a tremendous rift in the marriage, naturally, and I know Janet had issued an ultimatum to Paul."

Farmer started to leave the room. "Drink, anyone?" he asked.

Smith and Ken Ewald passed, but Leslie asked him to refill her glass. When Farmer was gone, Smith said, "Have you called me here as a family friend, as a lawyer, or for my reaction to this in terms of your campaign?"

"All of that, but especially number two, Mac," Ewald said. "If Paul is charged, we want you to defend him." Leslie sat up straight, closed her eyes tight, and started to cry convulsively.

Ewald moved to her side and put his arm around her. "Take it easy, honey; chances are Paul's not going to be charged with anything. Mac, we just need your advice."

"I think I ought to say something right now," Smith cautioned. They both looked at him. "I've been a quasi–legal adviser to this family on a very informal level, and I *used* to be a practicing attorney. I am now a contented college professor, teaching law at a major university. I'm sorry, but I could not take on Paul's legal defense."

"We know how you feel, Mac, but if we've ever asked a favor of you, this is it. Please, at least consider it."

"Of course I'll consider it. But you have to know where I am. And I just got there in recent years. Look, I want to make a few informal phone calls, maybe pick up some information that will be helpful to you whether or not I have anything more to do with this officially. You know I'll help if I can. I'll get back to you later this morning."

They walked him to the door. As he shook Ken's hand and kissed Leslie on the cheek, he found himself gripped with a sense of pathos and concern. Obviously, the three of them knew that if Paul was charged with the murder, not only would it be a tragic personal experience, it could have a severe impact on Ken Ewald's drive for the White House. And though it seemed unthinkable, a conviction could end that drive. As far as Mac Smith was concerned—despite some reservations about Ewald—that would not be good for the country. He chewed on that thought as he drove back to his home in Foggy Bottom.

6

WHILE MAC SMITH made phone calls from home the next morning, Colonel Gilbert Morales entered the White House through the Diplomatic Reception Room. He was accompanied by an aide. Two members of the Secret Service had escorted them from the gate, and they were all greeted inside by Richard Morse, an undersecretary from State whose area of expertise was Central America. "The president will be with you shortly, Colonel Morales. Please have a seat. Would you like coffee, tea, a soft drink?"

"No, thank you." Morales surveyed a variety of spindly chairs until settling his large body into the one that appeared to be the most substantial. Even at that, he was uncomfortable. His aide, a young man in an ill-fitting brown suit whose face was deeply pitted, walked to the far side of the room and looked closely at the wallpaper.

"President and Mrs. Kennedy brought that paper to the White House," one of the Secret Service agents said. "It was made in France in 1934 by Jean Zuber and Company." He and his partner were often assigned to conducting public tours of the White House, and were well versed in its decor and history. The agent added to his description, filling the time: "The painter had never visited the United States, but he used engravings he'd seen as a model for his work. That's Niagara Falls," he continued, in the voice he used with tourists. "That's Boston Harbor."

The aide said nothing and took a chair next to Morales.

Undersecretary Morse inquired about Mrs. Morales.

"She is fine, thank you," Morales said. "She is very busy with humanitarian efforts for our people."

"Yes, I'm sure she is," Morse replied. "Gathering medical supplies from private sources, and so on."

Colonel Gilbert Morales had been the military leader of Panama and a staunch ally of the United States. Deposed in a coup staged by the current Panamanian leadership, he'd fled with his family, settled in Washington, and immediately launched an intensive lobbying effort on behalf of forces in Panama still loyal to him. He'd found sympathetic ears in President Walter Manning and his administration.

A door opened, and a young man in a blue suit stepped into the room. He said to Morse in a library whisper, "The president is ready." They all went upstairs to the State Dining Room, where President Manning, Vice-President Raymond Thornton, Secretary of State Marlin Budd, and Senate Minority Leader Jesse Chamberlain were seated at the large dining table. The Panamanian was directed to a chair next to Secretary Budd. His aide stood awkwardly to the side. "Mr. Morse," Budd said, "please see that our young visitor is extended every courtesy downstairs."

"Yes, sir." Morse led the aide from the room.

"Well," President Manning said, "here we are again, Colonel Morales. It's getting to be a habit of sorts, isn't it?"

Morales smiled. "Yes, Mr. President, a habit of which I heartily approve. Your concern for my people, and for justice in my country, is very much appreciated, not only by me and Mrs. Morales, but by every freedom-loving Panamanian."

Morales looked at Chamberlain, a heavyset Texan who'd been elected to the Senate for seven consecutive terms and who anchored the Republican conservative caucus. "You, sir, of course, have always shared President Manning's love of freedom. I bring you fond wishes from my wife."

"Thank you, sir."

"And, when you are elected the next president of the United States, Mr. Vice-President, our fight together for justice and democracy will continue."

"I can pledge you that, Colonel," Thornton said. "Your cause is my cause."

"*Sí,* and I am grateful."

Secretary Budd said flatly, "We wanted to meet today, Colonel, to discuss certain realities that might have to be faced in November."

A wide, radiant smile had been on Morales's face from the moment he entered the room; Budd's words caused it to fade.

"I suggest we have lunch," Manning said, "then get down to business. I don't have much time." He touched a button on the side of the table, and three waiters appeared. "We're ready," the president said wearily. He slumped back in his chair and sighed.

After twenty minutes of aimless chat between the Americans and Morales, the waiters cleared the remains of a grilled swordfish and avocado salad, biscuits, and rice pudding, and served coffee. Secretary Budd then leveled with Morales. "To be blunt, Colonel Morales, we in the administration don't see any hope of further aid to you before President Manning's term ends."

Morales lighted a cigarette and drew deeply on it. He looked at Senator Chamberlain, whose cigar added to the rising blue smoke in the room. "There is no possibility of passage of the new aid bill in Congress?"

"Afraid not," Chamberlain said, coughing. "It's dead, absolutely dead. Damn shame."

"Yes, especially for my people, many of whom will be dead as a result. Of course . . ." He looked at Raymond Thornton, who sat ramrod straight. "You will be the next president, Mr. Thornton." The smile returned to Morales's broad face.

Thornton spoke in measured tones. "Colonel, we fully expect victory in November, but, as you know, nothing is certain on Election Day. Promises to be a tight race. We expect Senator Ewald to be the choice the Democrats will make, and—"

The president interrupted. "Senator Ewald has considerable popularity, Colonel Morales. It is my estimation that the next administration will probably be a Democratic one."

"That might be overstating things a bit, Mr. President," Thornton said, his voice less modulated now. "I wouldn't write us off yet."

"I'm too old, Raymond, to indulge in flights of fancy," Manning replied. "The country's ready for a change. It's the cycle." To Morales, he said, "We vote in cycles in this country, Colonel. We've had a long Republican run, and the odds are against it continuing any longer. As I said, you and your people had better be looking for other ways to regain power."

"I see," Morales said. "There is, of course, the private sector that continues to help us."

"Not as much as it did before," Secretary Budd said. "Any further help from individuals is going to have to be given with much more discretion than in the past. The indictments and the media have seen to that."

"The Reverend Kane has pledged his continued support to me,"

Morales said. "He has told me as recently as yesterday that he will continue to fund the missions he has established in my country."

Reverend Garrett Kane presided over the most popular and richest television evangelical ministry in America. Blessed with a voice that one writer had described as sounding like "a one-man gang," and with bright blue eyes that promised each television viewer he was speaking only to him or her, Kane had avoided the pits into which other TV evangelists had sunk in recent years. His ministry's financial house was in meticulous order. The Kanes—his wife's name was Martha, although she was popularly known as Bunny—lived a relatively modest personal life, Buicks rather than Jaguars, expensive but conservative clothing, a house in the hills of California's Orange County that would have been appropriate for the president of any medium-sized high-tech company. As Kane explained it, "Jesus meant for us to live decently, but the man who needs to display his wealth is a man for whom Jesus would have wept in sympathetic contempt."

Garrett Kane had not lined his pockets with the millions that poured into his offices every week. Instead, they were directed to other causes precious to him: "Our artistic endeavors will forever mark us as a civilized and a decent people!" or, "The extent to which we devote our God-given energies and resources to eradicate from this earth the evils of Godless Communism shall determine, in the eyes of the Lord, our eventual place in His everlasting kingdom." His favorite cause was the guerrilla resistance movement in Panama, where for years "freedom fighters" had been engaged on behalf of Colonel Gilbert Morales in an attempt to overthrow the regime in power. According to the Manning administration, Morales, and Garrett Kane, the regime was Communist-directed.

President Manning pushed back in his chair and stood. "Colonel Morales, thank you for joining us for lunch. You, and what you stand for, will always have a place at my table."

Secretary Budd stood, too, and said, "Serving you lunch is one thing, Colonel. Money for your cause is another. The reality is that every sign points to Senator Ewald succeeding this president next January. Ewald, as you are well aware, not only vows to cut off any hope of further aid to your cause, he's been pushing for an investigation into Reverend Kane's financial support of you. Those so-called humanitarian missions Reverend Kane has set up in your country are pretty transparent. I wouldn't bank on Kane's support much longer."

Morales was led downstairs by Undersecretary Morse. Thornton left the White House for a campaign meeting across town, while Secretary of State Budd accompanied the president to the Oval Office.

"I think I'll take a nap," Manning said.

"You have two appointments this afternoon, Mr. President. The Canadian trade delegation is due here in fifteen minutes, and—"

"Why are *they* coming?"

Budd frowned. "To discuss extending the free-trade agreement into other areas. We met on that yesterday, remember?"

The president stood in the middle of the room, confusion on his face. "Sir, I can always . . ."

Manning's tone was suddenly angry. "I'll meet with them. I thought you meant some other group that I hadn't agreed to meet with. Let's be a little clearer around here in our communications."

"Yes, sir."

Gilbert Morales and his aide climbed into the backseat of a very long black limousine. Seated on two jump seats were armed bodyguards. Another sat in the front passenger seat, a sawed-off shotgun on the floor beneath his feet. The driver turned and looked at Morales, whose face reflected his frustration. He shook his head and peered through the window at the White House. He realized the driver was waiting for instructions. "Headquarters," he said.

Fifteen minutes later, Morales and his entourage rode the elevator to the eighth floor of an office building across from the Kennedy Center and entered the Panamanian Maritime Mission. Morales ignored the receptionist's greeting and went into a large office on whose door was a sign: DIRECTOR. He picked up a phone and dialed a number. When a male voice answered, Morales said, "Where is Miguel?"

The person on the other end, who seemed confused at the question, said after a false start, "He is on his way to the airport, Colonel. You instructed us to—"

"Bring him back. We may have need of him again."

Morales hung up the phone and looked at the morning's newspaper on his desk. A portrait of Andrea Feldman dominated the space. A headline accompanying the photo read EWALD CAMPAIGN AIDE SLAIN.

He stared at the paper, then picked up the phone and dialed long distance.

"Kane Ministries," a pleasant female voice answered.

"This is Colonel Gilbert Morales. I must speak with him."

7

SMITH PLACED A number of calls after meeting with Ken and Leslie Ewald. He was unable to reach MPD detective Joe Riga, but did connect with Rhonda Hamilton, a good friend and one of Washington's best-known investigative journalists. They would get together for a quick lunch at the Foggy Bottom Cafe, a few blocks from his house.

He was about to walk Rufus when the phone rang.

"Mac, it's Leslie."

"I was just on my way out. How are things?"

"Horrible. Could we talk again today? I need very much to see you."

"Yes, of course. Has something else happened?"

"It's all so confusing, Mac, and I desperately need a steady hand like yours to help sort it out. I know I'm imposing but . . ."

"No imposition, Leslie. I'm meeting someone for lunch, have a faculty meeting at three, a wasted hour, but I'll be free after that."

"Could you come by the house at five?"

"I'll be there."

"Thank you, Mac."

"Don't be silly. Is there something I should be thinking about before I get there?"

She sighed. "No, I'll explain when I see you."

The phone rang again. It was Annabel Reed.

"Where are you?" Smith asked. "At the airport?"

"No, I caught an earlier shuttle. I just arrived at the gallery."

Annabel's art gallery, located in Georgetown, specialized in pre-Colombian art. Like Mac Smith, she'd given up a lucrative practice, although their reasons for abandoning law were different. For Smith, it had been fatigue and disillusionment. For Annabel, it represented a more positive career change. Art, particularly pre-Columbian, had begun as an interest, then became her passion. As law had once been for her.

She'd graduated with every conceivable honor from George Washington University Law School, and within four years had built a reputation in Washington as an effective, shrewd, and compassionate attorney. Much of her practice was in divorce cases. Unlike some women specializing in that often-distasteful area of law, she was not known solely as a champion of women's rights. She viewed men going through the pain of divorce with equal sympathy and understanding. At least, she tried to. Whatever her approach and philosophy, they worked, and her income reflected it.

Then she'd bought a half-interest in the gallery from an elderly friend who'd retired as curator of the pre-Columbian collection at Dumbarton Oaks, and who'd opened the gallery to fill his retirement days. It was becoming *too* successful, to the chagrin of his wife, who viewed their retirement as a chance to travel. He needed a partner, and offered Annabel the chance. She didn't hesitate, although she was less than completely honest about why she bought in. She rationalized to friends —more important, to herself—that she'd simply made a wise investment. But she knew deep down that going into the gallery would be a first step toward leaving the law and indulging herself in something with which she had greater psychic affinity. When her partner became terminally ill, she bought his half, continued to practice law and to oversee the gallery's growth for a year, then announced she was closing her offices.

"I heard in the cab what happened last night," she said. "How horrible. You knew her?"

"Yes. Some. I worked with Andrea Feldman on the gala committee. Smart as a whip. She'd been on Ken's staff for about a year. It was a shock to everyone."

"I heard Brian Burns on WRC quoting the police as saying they have a lead in the murder."

"Really? They say who?"

"No. I think they said there'd be a press conference tomorrow morning. The cabbie started talking, and I missed the rest."

"There are some upsetting aspects to this where Ken is concerned," Smith said.

"Yes, the cab driver told me the weapon belonged to Ken. Does that mean . . . ?"

"They've traced it to him already? I didn't know that." He mentioned his scheduled five o'clock meeting at Ewald's house.

"I thought we were having dinner."

"We are, after I see Ken and Leslie. Feel like Italian? I thought we'd go to Primi Piatti."

"Too heavy," she said. "I've been wanting to go back to Nicholas."

"Fine with me. See you there at seven?"

"You aren't picking me up?"

"I'm not sure how long I'll be with them." When she didn't say anything, he said, "Seven. At the bar. We'll have a drink. I'll make a dinner reservation for seven-thirty."

"All right."

Rufus roared his desire for a walk as Smith hung up. "In a minute," he said, dialing a number.

"WRC," a woman answered.

"Rhonda Harrison, please. Mac Smith calling."

"Hello, Mac, canceling lunch on me?"

"Of course not. Look, someone just told me that Brian Burns reported a break in the Feldman case."

"Right," she said. "Brian got it from a source at MPD."

"Specifics?"

"No, except having found the weapon. It was registered to Senator Ewald."

"Is there a press conference tomorrow?"

"Supposedly, although we can't confirm it. Another MPD surprise party."

"A surprise press conference?" Smith laughed. "Should produce a hell of a crowd. Can I talk to Brian?"

"He's in the booth. Want him to call you?"

"If he has any hard news. I'll be out for ten minutes. Thanks, Rhonda. See you at lunch."

As he walked Rufus, Smith felt the surge, the charge, and realized that events last night had opened a small valve in his body, releasing a shot of adrenaline. He was ambivalent about the sensation. Before he'd retreated to the life of a college professor—a decision he made shortly after his wife and son were killed by a drunk driver on the Beltway—those valves used to open all at once, sending a rush of energy and excitement through him. He lived for those moments, was sustained by them.

Not anymore. Those valves had been rusted shut for a time, and he'd become used to doing without the juices.

Until now. This moment.

Rufus pulled on his leash in all directions, large nose to the ground bombarded by the scent of leaves, stilted grass, bricks and concrete, iron railings wet-marked as calling cards by previous visitors out for a walk, and discarded fast-food wrappers, several of which Smith picked up and tossed in a neighbor's garbage can. "Slobs," he muttered.

Rhonda Harrison was seated at the Foggy Bottom Cafe's small bar when Smith arrived. The restaurant, located in the River Inn on Twenty-fifth Street N.W., was packed. Groups of people waited in the hotel's lobby for tables to open.

"Hi, Mac," she said as Smith managed to squeeze in behind her.

"Hello, Rhonda. They must be giving away the onion rings."

"Looks like it." She was an attractive woman in her early thirties. Inky hair cropped close made her small cordovan face seem larger than it was, and the overall effect was pleasing. She'd been with WRC for six years, and in that time had established herself as a tough but fair reporter who had the knack for getting a news source to talk, and who could find in a story an angle others missed. Besides broadcasting, she'd also been doing a considerable amount of writing lately, long, substantial investigative pieces for magazines.

"Mr. Smith," the bartender said over the multiple conversations along the bar. "Your usual?"

"Sure." He turned to Rhonda. "Want some onion rings to get started?" She nodded, and he added them to his drink order. Soon a heaping plate of one of the inn's specialties stood next to Harrison's Bloody Mary, and the glass of Tecate beer with coarse salt and lime that had been served Smith. "Health," he said, raising his glass.

She returned the toast.

"What's new?" he asked.

"Personal, professional, family, or the Andrea Feldman murder?"

"Your choice, but if we opt for Feldman, let's take a walk."

"Sure, okay, let's see," she said in a voice that was familiar to her listeners. "I have fallen madly in love with the man who will be my husband as soon as I get up the guts to ask him out. I got a raise yesterday. My agent sold a piece to *Esquire*. My family, what's left of it, is fine. Okay? That's my capsule update."

Smith placed a large hand lightly on her shoulder. "I'll be invited to the wedding, of course."

"Of course." She looked around; no one was paying particular attention to them. She leaned close to Smith's ear and said, "Your friend the senator is in some mess."

He hadn't expected such a direct statement from her, and his hesitant response testified to his surprise. "Tell me about it," he said.

"I was going to ask you the same thing. Rumor has it that you're smack dab in the middle of it."

"Who's putting that out?"

He felt a shrug of her slender shoulders beneath his hand. "MPD, some press sources. Brian told me."

"Time for that walk," he said. He told the bartender they'd be back, and they went outside. He asked what Brian Burns had told her.

"That you've been called in to handle defense in the event someone in the family is charged with her murder."

"That's news to me, Rhonda. Last I heard, nobody's been charged with anything."

"I know that, Mac, but the scuttlebutt is that the MPD is looking very seriously in that direction. What will you do, take a leave of absence from the university?"

"Washington, D.C.," Smith growled, "a city of tightly guarded, widely circulated secrets. Where did they find the weapon?"

"I have no idea."

"They sure traced it fast."

"Not hard. It was registered. At least they can't arrest him for possessing an unregistered handgun. Maybe that's part of his anti–National Rifle Association shtick—own a gun, if it's registered."

"Small victory."

"Any of what I've said so far true?" she asked.

"Bits and pieces. Are you going with the story?"

She nodded. "We're trying to put together something for tomorrow morning. Care to comment?" She reached into an oversized purse and pulled out a tiny tape recorder.

"Nope."

"Denial?"

"Nope."

"You know what, Mac?"

"What?"

"The shocker to me is that you'd get involved."

He knew that if he *did* get involved, Annabel would have the same reaction.

"Mac."

"What?"

"You suggested we meet for lunch, not me. What are you after from me?"

He grinned. "I was going to see what you knew about the Andrea Feldman murder. I didn't have to probe much, did I?"

"Not with me. I'm a fan, always have been since you treated this new kid in town with respect during the Buffolino case. Ever hear from him?"

"No. Last I knew, he was living in Baltimore."

"Mac."

"What?"

"You didn't have to probe me for what I know about Feldman. Do me the same favor."

"You've got it all. I can't add anything."

"Have you met with the Ewalds?"

"Yes."

"Are they concerned that one of them might be charged with Andrea Feldman's murder?"

Smith hated to lie to her, but he had to. "No, nothing like that was discussed."

"What about the weapon? Did Ewald indicate it was missing?"

"Rhonda, I really can't talk any more about this."

"Will you give me first crack at an interview? If a charge is brought?"

"Of course not. *If* I were to become involved, and *if* what you think is true, I'd be one hell of a lousy defense attorney talking to the press about the case, even to such an outstanding and beautiful member of it. And since I am not officially involved, I certainly don't have any news value."

"Can't blame a reporter for asking."

"Blame? You're good. I *will* promise you that if there's anything I can do for you, I will. Come on, let's finish off the onion rings—why do they remind me today of handcuffs?—and order a couple of salads." He squinted at his watch. "I have a meeting to get to."

"A meeting about the Feldman case?" she asked after they'd returned to their seats at the bar.

"No, a meeting about faculty appointments, tenure, and such—deadly, deadly dull."

Harrison picked up a small clump of the crusty onions in her long, slender, brightly tipped fingers and held them to her lips. Her expression as she looked at Smith was half-amused, half-skeptical. "Do you know what my gut instincts tell me, Mackensie Smith?"

"I would be delighted to know."

"My instincts tell me that we are about to have a bombshell dropped on this city and on Ewald's campaign. And they also tell me that I am sharing onion rings with one of the major players."

Smith winked at her. "All I can tell you, Rhonda, is that you are sharing onion rings with a man who gave up the active practice of law a while back and is blissfully happy in his life as college professor."

"Bull!"

"Even if I were tempted to become involved in a case again, I would have to do it under the threat of dismemberment by my significant other, Annabel Reed. You've never met Annie, have you? I really should introduce you two someday. You'd get along."

"Not if she knew I was mad about you."

They had their salads at the bar. As Smith laid bills next to his empty plate, he said to Rhonda, "This was a more productive lunch than I anticipated. Knowing you're 'mad about' me has made my day. And now that I do know it, I think I'll keep you and Annabel far away from each other. She's . . . bigger than both of us. Thanks for joining me, Rhonda. Looks like I'd better tune in WRC in the morning."

Smith had no sooner sat down at the conference table with his faculty colleagues when the Feldman murder was brought up. "What's new with that, Mac?" one of them asked.

"How would I know?"

"Come on, Mac, you found the body, and you're an insider with the Ewald family. They're saying on radio and TV that you've been retained in the event anyone from the family is charged. You're a major—"

"Player, yes, so I hear. Okay, I found the body, much to my dismay. To be more accurate, my dog found the body. I have not been retained by anyone. I am very much an outsider and intend to keep it that way, if I can manage it."

"Did you spend time with the deceased at the gala?" another asked.

"Yes. A little." Smith checked his watch. "Good music, a hell of a show. Could we get on with this? I have other appointments."

After Smith left the meeting, one of the professors said, "Sometimes I find it difficult to deal with his arrogance."

The law school dean, Roger Gerry, replied, "The right to be arrogant is earned. Mac Smith has earned that right. But it's confidence and competence you see, not arrogance. He carries it all rather nicely, I think." Gerry adjourned the meeting, a tiny, satisfied smile on his face.

8

"MAC, JOE RIGA."

"Hello, Joe, thanks for getting back to me. How's it going?"

"Too damn busy. Here I am with a year to retirement, and you and that beast of yours have to find a body in front of the Kennedy Center. What can I do for you?"

"I was just wondering whether you'd come up with any leads. I heard on the radio—"

"You should know after years of being a defense attorney that anything said on the radio about a murder isn't true."

"Not necessarily. I heard on the radio that you found the weapon."

"That's right."

"Where?"

"A couple hundred feet from the body, in the bushes. It's registered to your friend Senator Ewald."

"Yes, I heard that, too. . . . Prints?"

"Clean."

"I understand you're holding a press conference tomorrow morning. I hate to wait that long like ordinary citizens to get all the sordid details."

"What makes you out of the ordinary in this matter, Mac? Is it true that if anybody from your buddy's house is charged, Mackensie Smith is back in action as the crusading defense attorney?"

There was no sense in making flat denials any longer, so Smith said, "Could be. I don't know yet. What are you announcing tomorrow at the press conference?"

"There is no press conference. We canceled."

"Why?"

"A mistake. We thought we had it nailed down, but something didn't pan out. We're working on it. What did you know about the deceased?"

"Very little, just that she was smart, hardworking, good-looking—and very bright, in fact. Funny, but I was thinking this morning that I never heard much about Andrea's life, her background, family, that sort of thing. Then again, I really didn't work with her until we helped put together the gala. She was assigned from Ewald's staff to help coordinate things."

"She have any boyfriends?"

"I'm sure she did."

"You were there at Kennedy Center. You talk to her, see her hanging around with anybody?"

"Nothing in particular. Saw her talking, dancing. She danced a lot. She was a good dancer. Caught everybody's attention."

"Not just for her footwork. Who'd she dance with?"

"A couple of young, nice-looking men. They all looked clean and wore conservative suits."

"And maybe one of them got his hands dirty."

"Maybe. Look, Joe, are you working on the assumption that somebody in the Ewald camp killed her?"

"Mac, I'm working on the assumptions, number one, that somebody killed her, and number two, that the gun used traces to the Ewald house. I'm going out to their house in about an hour."

"Really? I'm due out there myself. Mind if I join you?"

Riga laughed, and Smith could see his face, those large, yellowing teeth with the gap in the front. "Sure, why not. I have to get a formal statement from you anyway, something I neglected to do last night. I'll meet you there."

"Fine."

"Hey, Mac, I keep meaning to ask you every time I talk to you whether you ever hear from Tony."

"Buffolino? No."

"Last I heard, he was working private in Baltimore."

"Yes, I heard that, too. Funny, somebody else asked about him recently, too. Good man, Tony."

"Matter of opinion. Maybe we can catch a drink after we leave Ewald. My treat."

"I'm not sure I'll have time, Joe—I'm meeting Annabel for dinner—but let's play it by ear. You're buying? I like that, and if we don't get to do it tonight, I'll remind you of it on a regular basis."

Smith hung up, stretched out on a couch in his living room, and for the moment thought of Anthony Buffolino, one of his last clients as a practicing criminal attorney.

Tony Buffolino had been a Washington MPD detective, a good one, everybody said. He'd had a clean record for fifteen years, a drawerful of citations of merit, letters from appreciative citizens and local politicians, no hint of being on the take, a good cop. Then, after taking three slugs in his right leg—two in the thigh and one in the knee—in a shootout during a bank robbery, he was told he was being retired on full pay. That wasn't what he had in mind. He fought being pensioned off despite constant jibes from fellow officers who dreamed of such a situation for themselves, and despite the pleas of his second wife, who hated seeing her husband leave home each morning and never knowing whether he'd return. He went through extensive physical rehabilitation, passed the physical, and continued on the force as a detective assigned to a special unit formed to combat Washington's growing drug trade. That was when all the trouble started, personal and professional.

Smith got up after ten minutes on the couch, shaved, and drove to the Ewald house. He wanted to get there before Riga.

He had trouble reaching the front gate because of the number of vehicles parked outside the house. There were mobile vans from local television stations, automobiles belonging to a variety of reporters, and two MPD squad cars, their uniformed occupants seated glumly inside them. He was passed through the gate by a private security guard. As he drove up in front of the house, he noticed that the video surveillance camera was in place up on the portico.

Marcia Mims, the Ewalds' head housekeeper, escorted him to the study. "I'm early, Marcia," Smith said. "Any problem?"

"They're upstairs, Mr. Smith. We've nothin' but problems. But not you. I'll tell them you're here."

A few minutes later, Leslie Ewald came to the study. Her eyes were puffy; she'd been crying.

"I came early, Leslie, because Detective Riga told me he had an appointment with you and Ken this afternoon."

Her response was to press her lips together, cross the room to a desk, and lean heavily on it with both hands. "I can't believe this is happening," she said in a low voice.

Smith came up behind her. "It's a dreadful thing, Leslie, this suspicion, but it's not yet an accusation, and you and Ken will see it through."

She turned and looked into his eyes. "Mac, things are moving so fast."

They sat in facing chairs. "Obviously, Leslie, the police have to talk to everyone who could possibly have knowledge about what happened to Andrea. Even if the weapon weren't involved, the fact that she was on Ken's staff would be sufficient reason to have detectives talk to him. Have you spoken with Paul?"

"Of course. He's upstairs with Ken. They've been arguing all afternoon."

"About what, or is that none of my business?"

"To me, it's very much your business, Mac, and I'm personally deeply grateful that you're here. Janet has disappeared."

"When did you find that out?" Smith asked.

"This morning. Paul said she packed a bag and left."

"I see," Smith said. "Any idea where she might have gone?"

"None whatsoever. Janet is . . . well, to be kind, Janet is not the most rational of women, especially when the pressure is on."

"You mean . . . ?"

"Yes, I mean Paul's affair with Andrea, and the fact that he never came home last night. Lord knows where Janet would go, or what she would do."

Smith pondered it, then said, "The police will want to talk to her eventually."

"I know that. I suppose we'll have to tell them. When Detective Riga called to arrange to see us, he asked that the four of us be present."

Smith forced a smile and slapped his hands on his knees. "Detective Riga could arrive at any moment, Leslie. I would like to talk to the three of you before he gets here. Could you have Ken and Paul come down?"

"Yes, of course." She called Marcia Mims and asked her to get them. "Not only is this an awful tragedy for that poor girl, and for us as a family, it could be a tragedy for the campaign. Ken had to cancel an appearance this afternoon. He's flying to Philadelphia tonight."

"Are you going with him?"

"Yes. You can imagine the questions the press will have for us at every step."

"Let's not worry about the press now, Leslie. I'm more concerned that everyone here is in sync."

Ken and Paul Ewald came in, and Smith launched into a series of questions that he anticipated would be asked by Riga. He realized he was back in his old role as a defense attorney, preparing witnesses, trying to head off surprises: "Where did you keep the weapon that was used to kill Andrea Feldman?" "Who had access to it?" "When did you last see it?" "Where was it?" "Why wasn't it secured?" "Where were each of you at the time she was killed?" "Can anyone verify your actions during that period of time?" "How well did you know the deceased?" "Was your relationship with her cordial, or had there been a recent strain?"

The list went on. When he was done, he realized some of the answers did nothing to divert suspicion, not just from Ken or Paul but from any of them. No one had an alibi, but Paul had the biggest problem. He claimed he'd had a fight with his wife and had taken a drive into Maryland for quiet time to think. Yes, he'd had an affair with Andrea Feldman, and, yes, Janet knew about it and had reacted vehemently and emotionally. No, he had no idea where she was. A suitcase was gone from her closet; her car was gone, too. He was very concerned about her, he said.

"Has she often just disappeared like this, Paul?" Smith asked.

"I wouldn't say often, Mac, but it has happened before. Frankly, I'm worried about what she might do to herself."

"Is she suicidal?"

"There have been threats, although I think they were just that, attention-getting outbursts. Still, I may as well level with you. Janet has some psychological problems." He looked at his father, who said nothing. "She's been under treatment for quite a while with Dr. Collins."

"Geoffrey Collins?" Smith said. "I know Geof."

Paul stood and walked the length of the room, came back halfway, and said, "Look, I'm sorry about all of this. I know there's absolutely nothing I can say to either of you to explain it away, or to make it better. I . . . I had an affair, and she's dead now. I know you don't need this kind of complication running for president, Dad, and I would give anything, including my life, if I could go back and make this not happen."

Smith looked at Ken Ewald. Although the senator gave his son a reassuring smile, he obviously did so with some effort.

When Smith asked the senator what he had done following the gala, his answer was terse: "I went to my office across the street and worked until early in the morning. The gala took too much time out of my campaign schedule."

"And you say this Secret Service agent, Jeroldson, was with you the whole time."

"Yes. I mean, I wasn't sitting with him. I was in my office with the door closed, and he was out in the waiting room, the way it always is."

"Riga will want to confirm that with Jeroldson," Smith said.

"Good. Let him. This whole thing is ridiculous. Obviously, no one in this family, or in this household, killed Andrea Feldman. Someone must have broken in, or entered the house under false pretenses and walked out with the pistol."

Smith sighed and recrossed his legs. "Ken, that is always a possibility, but it is, I'm sure you'll admit, a farfetched one. The fact is that Riga's spotlight may sooner or later shine directly on Paul here. As a family friend and unofficial legal adviser who's had some experience in criminal law, I can tell you the evidence is all circumstantial, but still Paul's defense, if he has to make one, is pretty shaky. He had access to the weapon, was sleeping with the deceased, had a wife who was furious about it, and can't account for his—or her—whereabouts."

"Then let them charge me," said Paul, stalking to the door. "I can't do anything about that."

"Don't leave," Smith said, pointing his finger at him. "Riga expects the three of you to be here. It's bad enough that Janet won't be present. That's going to take some explaining in itself."

"I'll be upstairs," Paul said. He closed the door with considerable force.

Joe Riga was accompanied by two younger detectives. Riga was a tall man with a paunch, who wore his black hair slicked back. He handed his raincoat to Marcia Mims and accepted Leslie Ewald's offer to make himself comfortable. His assistants, still wearing their coats, took chairs outside the circle that had been formed by Riga, the Ewalds, and Smith.

"Sorry to take your time, Senator," Riga said. "I guess running for president must have you on the go."

"Yes," Ewald replied dryly.

"I'll try to make this as quick as possible, Senator," Riga said. He nodded at Leslie and Paul to assure them he had them in mind, too.

He went through a list of questions, all asked by Smith during his briefing. Riga was a good interviewer, knowing when to respond to keep an answer going, but most of the time showing no reaction to what was being said, just a few grunts and "ah-hahs," like a Freudian listening to a five-times-a-week patient on the couch.

He asked Leslie to account for her whereabouts at the time of the murder. She said she'd gone to bed following the gala, and assumed none of the household staff would refute that. Riga asked whether any of them could confirm it, rather than just not refute it, and she had to admit they couldn't. "They don't tuck me in," she said rather curtly.

Riga's next series of questions was directed at Ken Ewald. When Smith had asked him about his actions following the gala, Ewald had summed them up quickly. Now, in response to the same question asked by Joe Riga, Ewald went into great detail about what he'd done in his office that night, right down to the memos he'd dictated, notes he'd made, and telephone calls he'd placed.

"We'll want to see a log of those calls, Senator," Riga said in a tone that was neither threatening nor suspicious.

"Of course," Ewald said. "I'll see that you get it, although some of them are highly sensitive in regard to my campaign. I'm sure you can understand the need for discretion in how they're used."

"Sure," Riga said. "You say this agent's name is Jeroldson?"

"Yes, Bob Jeroldson. He isn't assigned to me exclusively, but I seem to end up with him a great deal." Ewald laughed, and Smith sensed the falseness of it, wondered whether Riga had, too. "Jeroldson is a strange type," Ewald said, "although I suppose all Secret Service agents are a different breed."

"How so?" Riga asked. Smith half smiled to himself; never make a statement unless you're prepared for a follow-up question.

Ewald slid over the question like the good politician he was, saying only that Jeroldson seemed to be a brooding, private person.

"Goes with the job, I think," Riga said, offering his own less-than-spontaneous smile.

"I suppose so."

A half hour later, after Paul Ewald had responded to all the detective's questions, Riga seemed to have had enough. He said he wanted to come back the next day to interview household staff, and would also want to spend time with those members of Senator Ewald's campaign staff who had easy access to the house and, by extension, to the Derringer used to kill Ms. Feldman.

After Marcia Mims had been summoned with Riga's raincoat, he looked at Paul Ewald, who sat with what could only be described as a challenging expression on his handsome face, and said, "You know, Mr. Ewald, I'm going to have to talk to you more."

Paul told him he'd be happy to cooperate in any way.

Smith had suggested before Riga arrived that Janet's absence be handled casually, without resorting to an outright lie. "Just say she isn't here, and you don't know where she is," he said. "No sense giving the press or the police something else to chew on." That's the way Leslie handled it when Riga asked about Janet, and he seemed to accept it for the moment. At least he hadn't pressed it.

But now, as he prepared to leave, Riga said, "Please have your daughter-in-law call me the minute you hear from her." He handed a card to Leslie Ewald. "I figured this was a tight family, that you'd know where everybody is all the time, especially when somebody you know's been murdered."

Ewald laughed. "This is a typical American family, running in different directions and trying to find time to sneak one meal a week together."

"Yeah, I know how it is," Riga said. "Thanks for your time and cooperation. By the way, Senator, how's the campaign going?"

"Fine, until this happened," Ewald said.

"I suppose the best thing for you is to get it cleared up as fast as possible."

"It certainly is, and I appreciate the fact that you recognize it," Ewald said.

After Riga and the others were gone, and Leslie and Paul had left the study, Smith sat alone with the senator.

"I have to tell you, Ken, Riga's got a suspicion; maybe a rumor. There's going to be a lot more focusing on Paul."

"I gather that."

"And I suggest we find Janet as quickly as possible."

"My sentiments exactly, Mac. I've never been particularly fond of her. She's so damn flighty, a very difficult person."

Smith didn't respond to Ewald's characterization of his daughter-in-law.

"Mac, if there is a charge brought against Paul, you will represent him?"

"No, I won't," Smith said, not sure whether he meant it.

"You've been a very close and dear friend, Mac, and the last thing I ever want to do with a friend is to put pressure on him. But if this thing gets messy, or messier, there is no one else I feel we can turn to. Please."

Smith averted his eyes and looked at the gun collection on the wall. He thought of Rhonda Harrison's surprise that he would even consider becoming involved, and knew that if he brought the subject up at dinner that night with Annabel, her response would not only be similar, there would be heat and vehemence behind it. Annie liked the fact that he was a professor, was more comfortable with the genteel and quiet pace of the life it afforded them. She had mentioned his health. He also knew there was a certain panache and synergy and symmetry involved —college professor and gallery owner, very intellectual, very noncommercial. He thought of her symmetry.

"Why me? There are plenty of good defense lawyers in Washington. Or elsewhere. You could have almost anyone you might want."

"Because you and I have worked together. You know me, know my family. That's time-saving—and there isn't much time. It will also seem natural. If I call in some high-powered defense lawyer who's handled all sorts of bad characters with money, Paul may get off, but first I get tarred with his attorney's brush. Also, I can trust you. You're bound to learn even more about this one American family, and I need to have whatever comes out known by a man in whom my confidence is absolute, a man I could trust in my . . . Cabinet."

"That isn't a big temptation, if you're trying to bribe me."

"I'm trying to tell you the truth. And there is one other thing."

"What's that?"

"I think you want to see me elected. If Paul gets charged and if this thing drags on, even if we win, we lose. In the next few days or weeks, I either win the nomination and thus the presidency or I'm the next dead body. I don't mean to sound inhumane. I think you want me to be elected—for all the right reasons."

"I'll think about it, Ken. I promise that."

"I suppose that's all I can ask."

Smith got up to leave.

"Mac, can I tell you something in strict confidence?"

"Yes, of course."

Ewald went through a little stutter step as people always do when they're about to reveal something embarrassing. He shoved his hands in his pockets, cocked his head to one side, and did a toe-in-sand with his foot. "Mac, the fact is, I didn't stay in the office the entire time after the gala."

The comment brought back memories to Smith. He sat down. How many times had defendants held to a story until, suddenly, they felt a need to confide in their attorney? Too many.

"I left the office for about an hour," Ewald said.

"Where did you go?"

"I went to the Watergate Hotel."

"What time?"

"I don't know, maybe two in the morning, maybe a little later."

"Why?"

"I had to see someone."

"That might be helpful," Smith said. "It would be nice to have someone in this family who can verify where they were for a portion of the evening."

"That might be true in a normal situation, Mac, but not in this one. You see . . ."

"Ken, just tell me what it is you want to say."

"I saw someone who would make Leslie very upset."

He waited for Ewald. The story's ending was short. "I've been seeing this woman casually for a while, Mac. I'm not very proud of it, but I suppose that really doesn't matter. If I were a womanizer, somebody who was always on the make, it might be different, but this was one of those things that happens in a man's life now and then. You understand."

Whether Smith understood or not was irrelevant. He said, "Why are you bringing this up to me? Maybe you can ask Riga not to share it with Leslie."

"Well, Jeroldson, the agent, went with me. I tried to talk him out of it, told him I was on a private matter and that I didn't want him with me, but there was no way to shake him. He was doing his job, and if he didn't stay with me, he'd be a former Secret Service agent."

Smith's smile was small. "Must have been a very powerful attraction to agree to take Jeroldson along."

"He didn't know who I met. He never saw her, but when the detective questions him, he'll obviously mention that I went to the Watergate."

"I assume he will. If he doesn't, he's lying in a murder investigation."

"The point is, Mac, that I *can't* allow Leslie to find out about this. There was a similar incident years ago, and although it was all very brief, I'm sure the memory still lingers with her. Obviously, I never dreamed that . . . I mean, how would I know there would be a murder of one of my staff members, and that a weapon I owned would be the murder weapon? Ironic, isn't it?"

Smith looked at him intently. "Ironic doesn't do it. Care to tell me who the woman is?"

Ewald shook his head. "It wouldn't accomplish anything."

"Riga will want to know whom you met with at the Watergate. You can't tell *him* it doesn't matter."

"I know, I know, but for now can't we skip names?" Ewald was angry, chiefly at himself.

Smith shrugged. He had little choice; he couldn't force Ewald to reveal who the woman was. He looked into Ewald's eyes and felt, at once, sympathy and anger. Certainly, adultery was not the greatest sin anyone could commit. He'd come close on more than one occasion during his own marriage, and, he knew, could easily have taken the final step that would have carried him from passing lust to transgression.

What angered him was the possible ramifications to the campaign of the man he believed would make the best president of the United States, the best of the recent lot. Was he looking at another Gary Hart, someone capable of self-destruction at the most crucial time in his life? There were differences, of course. Smith had never viewed Hart as an electable presidential candidate, nor did he see Ken Ewald as a compulsive, promiscuous womanizer. Still, the situation was a lot graver than he would have liked.

What had Henry Adams said years ago? "Morality is a private and costly luxury." Morality, Smith had decided long ago, along with its sister metaphor, religion, had caused the death of too many people to be a dependable criterion for judging others, especially in Washington. The city teemed with ambitious young men and women, many living there only part time, away from home, under tremendous pressure to succeed, and sharing a common love of the excitement of politics and the nation's capital. Whatever their political viewpoint, they came with their dreams and ideals only to learn quickly that politics was a far more pragmatic business, necessity constantly being the mother of compromise. Beliefs usually blew away in the wind like dead leaves when they got in the way of accomplishing goals, political or personal—or, frequently, mixed. Morality? For many, it was every man for himself, and every woman, too.

No, he must not judge this man on the basis of a sexual indiscretion. He would remain angry, however. He was entitled to that.

"Look, Mac, I know this puts you in an awkward position, but try to understand."

"I'm doing my best. Is there much of a possibility that this woman is likely to make your affair with her public?"

Ewald smiled. "Hardly. She's mature and intelligent."

"It may become public no matter how mature and intelligent she is. You realize that. The MPD will end up knowing about it, and that means the press will, too."

Ewald nodded. "Yes, I know you're right. I need a little private time to think, Mac. Maybe you could think about ways to keep this quiet, too."

Smith left the house feeling heavier than when he'd arrived. Don't make judgments, he repeated to himself as he drove to the gate, was allowed to leave, and headed in the direction of the Mayflower Hotel. He didn't notice the sealed pink envelope addressed to *Mac* on the passenger seat until he was halfway there.

He stopped for a traffic light and opened the envelope. Inside was a note on Leslie Ewald's personal stationery:

"Dear Mac, thank you for helping in this time of great need. We shall all be eternally grateful to you. Please accept this as only a token, and rest assured that whatever you need is yours. Fondly, Leslie."

A check made out to him for fifty thousand dollars accompanied the note.

9

NICHOLAS'S PALETTE of soft colors on walls and tables, and soft light from a crystal chandelier above, flattered Annabel. She was a beautiful woman in any setting, but, as with all gems—velvet providing a better background than concrete—some settings rendered her invaluable.

She was born with bright red hair, which had burnished over the years into aged copper. She wore it full, creating a glowing frame for her face, which was creamy and unlined. Her eyes were, of course, green, as if ordained, and large, and her nose, ears, and mouth had been created with a stunning sense of proportion.

They'd chosen house specials: salmon with a bouquet of enoki mushrooms for her, lobster in beurre blanc for him, after sharing a cold foie gras with a garnish of beluga caviar. A Muscadet accompanied the meal, inexpensive and unambitious. Mac Smith had had enough of complexity and ambition for one day.

Now, with coffee in front of them, they sat back in their heavy armchairs and looked at each other.

"I am disappointed, you know," she said.

"Obviously. You've played 'the show must go on' all evening, but the actress keeps showing through the character."

"Again, Mac, I ask you why?"

"And, again, Annie, I tell you I'm not sure *why.*" He smiled and held up his hand against what she was about to say. "Maybe we should make a pro-and-con list, like when you're deciding whether to buy a house. Let's see. . . ."

"*We?* You've made this decision yourself."

"I can be dissuaded. Go along with me. I shouldn't do it because it will disrupt the quiet lives we've settled into. I shouldn't do it because it's bound to end up a nasty, public affair that will smear everyone involved. I shouldn't do it because . . ." He smiled again, leaned forward, and extended his hand to her. Her smile was smaller, but she placed her hand in his. He held its silken softness and felt its strength. "I shouldn't do it because the beautiful woman with whom I am very much in love promises to scratch my eyes out if I do." He made a point of looking at her beautifully lacquered nails.

"Worse, Mac," she said. "You do this and I will act like a cornered honey badger."

"A direct attack on the genitals?"

She didn't answer.

"That's a powerful entry in the negative column."

"I should hope so." She withdrew her hand, picked up her coffee, and sat back, observing him over her cup. He looked tired. The weight of the decision he was about to make pulled down on the flesh of his cheeks and the corners of his eyes. Although he'd shaved before going to Leslie Ewald's house, a shadow had reappeared. "If I could hold a mirror up to you at this moment, Mac Smith," she said, "you'd see why you shouldn't get involved in this."

He looked at her in turn. There was conviction behind her objections. Nothing frivolous about them. He wished there were a way to bring about a grand compromise, to do the right thing as well as to indulge his instinctive needs at the moment while keeping her happy. At the same time, this urge to compromise was edged with a certain anger at her: He told himself that, ultimately, he would make his choice based on what was good for him, even if it conflicted with what she wanted.

Easier said than done. He did love her.

"Cognac?" he asked. That suggestion wouldn't prompt an argument.

"No. Don't do it, Mac."

"Let's go."

"Let's talk."

"Not here. Come on, a nightcap at my place. Rufus needs a walk."

"Know what I think, Mac?"

"What?" He motioned for a waiter to bring the check.

"I think you're more concerned with what Rufus thinks than what I think."

"He does have a certain wisdom," said Smith, standing and coming around the table to help with her chair. "Most of all, he never argues with me."

They sat in Smith's den. He sipped a brandy, she an Irish Cream. They said little. Rufus, the Dane, obscured most of a shag rug on which he'd sprawled.

"Okay, I won't," Smith said into his snifter. He'd removed his jacket, tie, and shoes, and sat in his reclining chair. Annabel had staked out a corner of the couch where she'd tucked her stockinged feet beneath her.

"I'm sorry, Mac. I'm acting like an irrational woman."

Smith smiled as he said, "And damned attractive in the process."

"It's just that . . ."

"I think you're right. I don't need the aggravation."

"Maybe you do. Maybe we both do."

"I don't follow."

"Oh, I don't know, Mac, it's just that we're falling into a pretty staid and proscribed life."

" 'Boring' is my translation."

"Not for me, but I sense a certain restlessness in you, especially lately. Don't misunderstand. I love being in love with a college professor. It has a certain snobbish ring to it." She giggled. "And maybe even good for business. But I was thinking as we drove here that maybe getting back into the thick of things is exactly what you need. To make you realize what a nice life a college professor leads, that is."

He narrowed his eyes as he tried to figure out what she was up to. Did she mean what she'd just said? Or was it the old reverse psychology?

He decided to take her at face value. "What about your threat to turn into Annie Honey Badger?"

"Just the animalistic side of Annie. I take it back. No need to buy a metal cup in the morning."

"Whew!" He wiped imagined sweat from his brow.

"Take me home," she said pleasantly, standing and slipping into her shoes. "It was a great dinner." She pressed closer to him, whispered in his ear, "I love you, Mackensie Smith." She kissed him on the mouth, pleasantly, then passionately.

"Sure you don't want to stay awhile?"

"Can't. You have to think. I want your mind focused on me at certain times. Besides, I have a meeting at eight with a dealer from Rio. Tomorrow night. Stay at my place."

"One of these days, we should make it one place," he said.

"One of these days. Maybe."

In her condo in the Watergate's apartment complex, Annabel poured herself a glass of orange juice, lit her one cigarette of the day, and went to her small terrace, where she hunched over the railing and looked out across the Potomac. No sense denying it, she told herself: She was still angry at what would obviously be Mac's decision to become involved with the Andrea Feldman murder.

But she knew it was more than anger she felt; it was something else, and beyond her comprehension at the moment. The fact that it was without definition made it all the more sinister. Yes, that was it. She wrapped her arms about herself as a distinct, sudden chill caused her to shiver. She was afraid of losing Mackensie Smith, not to another woman, but to *something* else.

In that case, the loss would be final.

She quickly went to bed and invited sleep to blot that dark thought from her consciousness.

10

MAC SMITH HAD always been an early riser, although he was capable of sleeping in provided it had been scheduled in advance. Sleeping late had not been planned for this morning, and he awoke precisely at six o'clock to the smell of coffee brewing in the kitchen. To say that Mackensie Smith was obsessive and compulsive about certain ablutions and details was an understatement. No matter what time he returned home at night, he would have trouble falling asleep until he'd prepared the morning coffee and set the timer. Preparing the coffee was a satisfying, relaxing ritual in itself; three scoops of a commercial decaffeinated coffee, two scoops of a water-decaffeinated amaretto blend, and two scoops of amaretto bursting with caffeine. Enough for ten cups; somehow Thursday might turn out to be a long day.

Rufus, the Dane, his nose a finely tuned instrument to most smells, wasn't stimulated by the aroma of coffee. He looked up from where he was sleeping on the floor and observed his master climb out of bed, stretch, yawn, and head for the kitchen. The minute Smith was gone, Rufus climbed up onto the bed and resumed sleeping.

Smith continued his morning ceremonies in the kitchen. He opened windows, turned on WRC, poured his first cup of coffee, then funneled the rest into a carafe so that it would not continue to percolate. WRC's weatherman was in the midst of forecasting a sunny, pleasant day when Smith turned on the station. A minute later, the weatherman turned things over to the anchor, who said, "To repeat our top stories, Paul Ewald, the son of Democratic presidential hopeful Kenneth Ewald, was arrested just hours ago for the murder of Andrea Feldman, a young attorney who worked on Senator Ewald's staff. We'll bring you more details as we receive them. . . .

"The White House has once again avowed its support of rebel forces in Panama loyal to ousted dictator Gilbert Morales. . . .

"A large shipment of cocaine has been intercepted by DEA agents at Dulles Airport. . . ."

Smith called the Ewalds' home. His call was answered by Marcia Mims, whose voice reflected her distress. "No, Mr. Smith, I haven't heard from either Senator or Mrs. Ewald. This is so terrible, so terrible for this family. Oh, my God, Mr. Smith, please do something to help!"

"I'll do everything I can, Marcia," Smith said. "I'll be at my house for an hour. If I don't hear from someone by then, I'll call again."

His next call was to Paul Ewald's place. There was no answer, which didn't surprise him. Janet Ewald was missing, and Paul was in custody. He was hoping—silly game. But you had to try everything, ring every bell, turn over every lead and leaf.

Call number three was to MPD headquarters. He was told Detective Riga wouldn't be back until nine.

"This is Mackensie Smith," he said, and added, "Paul Ewald's attorney. Where is he being held?"

The desk sergeant told him. Smith thanked him and hung up.

He was about to pick up the phone again when it rang. "Hello?"

"Mac, this is Rhonda."

"I just heard on your station about Paul being arrested," Smith said. He sounded gruff, although he had no reason to be annoyed with her. Somehow, getting the news from a radio station rankled, and he couldn't keep it out of his voice.

"Were you called?" she asked.

"No. I'm about to get dressed to go see him."

"You haven't had any conversation with him yet?"

"No. As I said, Rhonda, I heard the news over your station."

"Mac, you say you're going to see him. You are his attorney?"

"Getting dressed and going to see the son of an old friend does not indicate anything, Rhonda. Let's leave it at that."

"Have you talked to Senator Ewald yet?"

"Rhonda, let's drop this. If I am to be Paul Ewald's attorney, that places me under obvious restrictions where you're concerned."

"I understand that, but it doesn't mean I can't stay in touch with you, keep tabs on things through you. We are friends, aren't we?"

"At parties, yes, but our friendship now has some rules."

She laughed. "Sure, it had a few before. But the rules don't preclude me from calling you, or you from answering the phone. Keep in touch, Mac."

"Sure. Do me the same favor."

Showered and dressed, and with Rufus hurriedly walked and fed, Smith was almost out the door when he remembered: He had an early class to teach at the university. He called Dean Gerry at home. "Roger, I can't make my class this morning. I want to call Art Poly to see if he'll cover it for me."

Gerry laughed. "You can cancel it if you want to, Mac."

"No, Roger, they miss enough even when they're there."

"All right, call Art, but I have a feeling I'll be getting more calls like this from you."

"I think you're right," Smith said.

"Look, Mac, I heard the news this morning about Paul Ewald being arrested. I also assume that you're about to handle his defense."

Smith's laugh was rueful.

"Is it true?"

"Probably. I mean, yes, it is. We'd better get together to talk about how to handle this."

"Anytime, Mac. I'm having a few friends over Saturday evening. Perhaps you and Annabel would join us. We can huddle for whatever time you need."

Smith sighed and thought ahead to Saturday. It seemed years away. "I'll ask Annabel as soon as I talk to her. I don't know what my schedule is going to be once I'm in deep in this. If I can't make it Saturday, maybe we can steal some time at the office. I'll let you know."

"Whatever works for you, Mac. Interesting, that you'd get involved in something like this. How well I remember our discussion when you told me you'd decided to close down your practice and join us here in academia."

"I remember that discussion, too. Thanks for understanding about this morning. I'll try to be there Saturday."

Smith opened the front door to leave and was confronted with a half-dozen reporters and photographers who'd congregated on the sidewalk in front of his house. A television remote truck was parked across the street. Smith wasn't sure what to do. His options were to remain inside, give them a statement, or simply walk past without saying anything. The last option seemed the only sensible course, and that's what he did, waving off their questions, saying only to the most persistent, "No comment."

He decided to leave his car in his garage and to walk until he found a cab. The reporters trailed him, but only one continued to match him stride for stride as he put blocks between him and the house. It was a young man carrying a Marantz portable tape recorder and a microphone with the call letters of a station Smith did not know. The young man eventually stopped asking questions and simply continued walking a few paces behind Smith. They reached an intersection where the light was against them. Smith turned and said as pleasantly as possible, "I don't have any comment at this time."

The young man, whose hair was blushing and whose face sported the predictable accompanying freckles, grinned and said, "All I'm asking, Mr. Smith, is whether you're Paul Ewald's attorney. There shouldn't be any mystery about that."

Smith sighed and nodded. "No, there is no mystery about that. Yes, I am representing Paul Ewald in this matter."

The light changed. They looked at each other. Smith narrowed his eyes and said, "You can follow me to Chesapeake Bay, but you won't hear another word."

"Okay," the young red-haired reporter said. "Thanks for answering at least one question."

A few blocks later, Smith found a taxi and had the driver take him to MPD headquarters at Third and C Streets, where, after navigating a maze of members of the press and squinting against flashes from strobe lights, he reached Detective Joe Riga's office. Riga was seated behind his desk, a telephone wedged between ear and shoulder. He was partly obscured by piles of paper and file folders. He saw Smith at the door, waved him in, and resumed his conversation.

Smith went to a window that desperately needed cleaning and looked down to the street. He heard Riga say, "I don't give a goddamn what he wants, the report isn't leaving this office until I get the word from my authorities. Look, I . . . evidently you don't speak English." He slammed the phone down.

Smith leaned against the windowsill and said, "Good morning, Joe. Still in the State Department? You just flunked diplomacy. You sound angry."

Riga picked up a half-smoked cigar and wedged the soggy end between his teeth. "Yeah, I'm angry at all the wahoos who try to pull rank with me, and I have a feeling you're not here to make me any happier. You're officially Ewald's attorney?"

"Yes."

Riga cackled and put the cigar in the ashtray. "Jesus, Mac, I never figured I'd see you back in the saddle as a criminal attorney." Smith started to say something, but Riga continued. "You know something, you should've stayed at the university. Do you know what you're walking into?"

"Probably not, but that doesn't matter at the moment. You've arrested Paul Ewald. Is he charged with Andrea Feldman's murder?"

"Mac, get your facts straight. We haven't *arrested* Paul Ewald. We brought him in for questioning."

"In the middle of the night."

"Yeah. People tend to be home then."

"You didn't have to detain him to question him, Joe."

"In this case, I figured it might be a good idea." Riga shrugged, grimaced, picked up his cigar again. "His wife cuts out, which makes me a little uneasy, you know? I feel better having him cozied up here."

"I don't give a damn what you feel better with, Joe. You have no right to detain him unless you're ready to charge and indict him."

"Yeah, yeah, I know, but *you* know I've got a little time."

"Damn little. Why wasn't I called immediately?" Smith asked.

"We told him he had a quarter to call his attorney, but he didn't. Maybe he doesn't want you."

"I don't think that's the case, Joe. His rights were read to him, I assume."

Riga laughed. "Yeah, we read him his rights. We read them a couple of times, because of who he is."

"With the video running."

"Yeah. We made sure we shot his best side."

"Did he make any statements?"

"Just that he didn't kill her."

"Anything else?"

"Nothing important. They all sound the same when you pick them up and question them about a murder. They go through their shocked routine, then get angry at the outrage of it all, and then they clam up. He followed the pattern. You wanna see him?"

"Of course. Before I do, though, let me ask you a question."

"Shoot." The phone rang and Riga picked it up, scowled at what he heard, and hung up.

"Joe, doesn't it strike you as a little strange that the son of a prominent senator and presidential candidate sleeps with a member of his father's staff, then chooses to shoot her, of all places, in front of the Kennedy Center and with a weapon that belongs to his father?"

Another shrug from the detective. "Maybe twenty years ago. Nothing surprises me in this looney-tune society."

Smith pushed away from the windowsill and took a chair across the desk. "There still has to be some question in your mind about the probability of all this. Paul Ewald isn't a nut by any stretch of the imagination. He's well educated, has a successful import-export business, and has never been in trouble in his life."

"Come on, Mac, what the hell does that mean? What we've got here is a guy who's been importing and exporting with some chick with a body and brains. He's cheating on his old lady. The broad threatens to bust up his marriage, which, because he happens to be the son of maybe our next president, could screw up his father, too. He tells her to back off. She won't back off. He pulls out the gun and figures that'll get her attention, get her to listen. She doesn't. Boom! Another crime of passion, just like in the good old-fashioned murder mysteries. Nothing new. The strength of a single pubic hair is stronger than ten thousand mules."

Riga laughed at his own joke. "I think Freud said that," he said.

Smith realized he was wasting time trying to get Riga to at least acknowledge some doubt about Paul Ewald's guilt. "Yes," he said, "Willie Freud from Anacostia." The phone rang again, and Riga picked it up. Smith stood and pointedly looked at his watch. Riga put his hand over the mouthpiece and said, "All right, I'll get somebody to take you down." He pushed a button on his intercom: "Send Ormsby in here." Riga went back to his telephone conversation. A sergeant entered the office. Again cupping a hand over the mouthpiece, Riga told him, "This is Mackensie Smith, Paul Ewald's lawyer. Take him down to see his client."

Twenty minutes later, Smith sat with Paul Ewald in a room reserved for lawyer-client meetings. It was furnished in pure postmodern police station: a long wooden table and four wooden chairs without arms. At least all four legs on the chairs were the same length. In the interrogation rooms, a half inch of the front legs was sawed off to keep suspects constantly leaning forward. A bright bulb covered by a green metal shade hung above the table. Heavy wire mesh covered the windows, as well as a small window in the door. A uniformed officer could be seen through the window.

Smith and Ewald shook hands. "Thanks for coming, Mac," Ewald said.

"Sorry you're going through this, Paul. You won't have to much longer." They sat at the table, Smith at the head of it, Ewald to his left.

"Let me say a few things at the outset, Paul. I don't know what evidence the district attorney thinks he has to make a case against you, but I'll be informed of that in short order, if he does decide to proceed with charges. I know that you didn't come home that night after the show at the Kennedy Center. I know that you had access to the weapon that killed Andrea Feldman. And I know that you'd been having an affair with her. If that's all the DA is going on, he won't dare seek an indictment. I can assure you of that."

Ewald drew a deep breath, sat back, and looked up at the ceiling. His eyes were closed, and he pressed his lips tightly together. Smith took the moment to observe him. Paul Ewald was a presentable young man. Smith thought of the actors Van Johnson and Martin Milner. Paul had the same boyish quality as his father, although there was a subtle ruggedness to his father's face that Paul did not possess. In fact, Smith had often thought that there was a softness in Paul Ewald that was almost androgynous, half-effeminate, with a certain vulnerability—call it weakness—that was, at once, appealing yet off-putting. Ewald was wearing socks; his shoes had been removed as a matter of procedure. He had on a white shirt open at the collar and gray trousers. As he opened his eyes and looked at Smith, his fatigue was apparent.

"Paul, did you kill Andrea Feldman?"

"Of course not."

"You were sleeping with her, and she threatened to break up your marriage and ruin your father's chances."

"No. Andrea was demanding, but not to that extent. I'd come to hate her, though." Ewald laughed. "Maybe I should have killed her. I'm ending up in the same position whether I did or not."

"Not true, Paul. They have to *prove* you killed her, and if you didn't, they'll have a tough time with that."

Ewald shook his head. "Pardon me, Mac, if I don't enthusiastically agree with you. Have you ever had nightmares that you'd be accused of something you didn't do, but you'd end up paying for it for the rest of your life?"

"Only after I've read novels in which that happened. It won't happen here."

"I hope you're right."

Smith broke the ensuing silence. "Do you have any idea who might have killed Andrea?"

"No, I don't, although women like Andrea Feldman can get people pretty upset."

Smith thought of Riga's comment about mules, but kept it to himself. He rolled his fingers on the tabletop and chewed on his cheek. "Paul, had you been with her to the Buccaneer Motel, the place she had a key to?"

"Yes."

"The night she was murdered?"

Ewald shook his head. "No, we didn't have sex that night."

"Didn't Andrea have an apartment here in D.C.?"

"Yes, she did, but we never went there. I thought it was strange, but she said we should be more discreet than that, go out of town every time we got together." He banged his fist on the table. "Damn it, I should have known better. If things weren't so . . . rotten at home, maybe I wouldn't have . . . hell, no sense blaming circumstances. No sense blaming Janet. The fact was, *we* did not have the kind of life recently that, among other things, promotes a healthy sexual existence between man and wife."

Smith made a few notes on a pad. He asked, "When did you meet Andrea, Paul—*after* she'd joined your father's campaign staff?"

"No. I met her several years ago at a party in Georgetown, sort of a business gathering at the home of one of my important customers. She was there with a date, but we had one of those locked-eyes reactions to each other all night. Before she left, she slipped me her phone number. I sat on it for a while. Then, one night, I had a fight with Janet, left the house, and called her. She suggested we meet for a drink. We did. One drink led to several, and we ended up driving to Maryland, where we made love for the first time."

"I see," Smith said. "Then what? Did you suggest she join your father's staff?"

"I guess so. She told me how much she believed in my father's cause, and how all the issues he stood for represented how she felt about things in this country. I probably did suggest that she apply for a job on his staff. Yes, exactly, that's the way it happened. I suggested it, and told her I would put in a good word for her. She was hired about a week later."

"What did you know about her background, Paul?"

"Not much, Mac. She was actually a very private person. Maybe that's why I trusted her. Maybe that's why we never went to her apartment. Maybe she didn't want anybody there. Sometimes I wondered whether she had a live-in boyfriend, but it really didn't matter."

"Did you ask her whether she had a boyfriend living with her?"

"No. I didn't want to do anything to jeopardize the relationship. To be honest with you, Mac, I loved every minute we were together. It was sex the way you read about in cheap novels. She was *good.*" He looked at Smith, who said nothing. Ewald shrugged. "What can I say? I'm weak."

"You do know that Janet is still missing?"

"Yes."

"You have no idea where she might have gone?"

"None whatsoever. I called every place I could think of with no luck. Janet hates confrontation."

"It seems she confronted you pretty directly about your relationship with Andrea."

"Sure, but those were hysterical moments, times when she'd fly off the handle. She did that a lot. Janet's kind of a split personality. She either reacts emotionally to something and throws a fit, or goes into a shell, runs away and hides. I guess she's in her shell period now."

Smith was taken by the fact that Paul seemed to have little concern about his wife's disappearance—even whether she was alive or dead—but he chalked it up to the strange relationship between them, and the emotionally unsettling situation Paul Ewald was in at the moment. He said, "Paul, I want you to say nothing to anyone unless I'm present. Do you understand that?"

"Yes, I do."

"Not only do you understand it, Paul, will you follow that advice?"

"I'll do my best, Mac. Have you talked to Mom and Dad?"

"No, they're out of town. I intend to touch base with them the minute I leave here. I'm sure they've heard the news by now. You haven't heard from them?"

"No." His eyes misted. "God, Mac, it's bad enough sitting here with you under these circumstances. I'm not sure I can face them. They won't even let me wear shoes—it's like I was a convicted murderer."

Smith patted Paul's arm and smiled. "You'll be out in a couple of hours, Paul, I promise you that." He stood. "MPD's got its neck way out on this, pulling you in like this."

Paul looked up at him. "I can't believe you're agreeing to help me, Mac. I thought you'd decided to never practice law again."

"Which just goes to show how weak *I* am. I don't see how I can do otherwise, considering my long friendship with the family and caring for the cause, you might call it. By the way, Paul, I assume you'll accept me as your attorney?"

Paul's lower lip trembled. "Accept you? How can I not? You're the best." He was crying. "Just lucky for me, I suppose, that I was born . . . with advantages."

Smith was tempted to wrap his arms around him and give him a bear hug, kind of a manly shoring up of his spirits, but he restrained himself. This was no time for gestures of sentiment. At best, they would be misunderstood. Still, he put his hand on Paul's.

Smith indicated to the guard that he was leaving. The door opened. Smith looked back at Ewald, who stood with his back to the door, his body moving in rhythm to his sobs.

"I'll be back, Paul. In the meantime, remember what you've promised me."

* * *

Smith placed a call from MPD to the office of Leonard Kramer, the District of Columbia's district attorney. He was told that Kramer was out of the office and would not return for an hour. "Please have him call me the minute he comes in," Smith said, not trying to soften the anger in his voice. He identified himself to the secretary, indicated that he was representing Paul Ewald, and reiterated the urgency of his call.

A few reporters from early that morning had continued to wait outside Smith's home. He took the same tack—"No comment, sorry"—and entered the house, where Rufus greeted him in his usual exuberant fashion. "No comment for you, either," Smith said, rubbing the huge animal behind the ears. He poured himself coffee from the carafe and sat at the desk in his study. Twenty minutes later, Leslie Ewald called. They'd just returned to Washington. "This is outrageous, Mac," she said. "How dare they arrest Paul!"

Smith thought of Riga's word games and decided not to play them with Leslie. "My sentiments exactly, Leslie. I just came from visiting Paul. He's all right, shaken naturally by the events, but holding up very nicely. I assured him he'd be out before the day is over. I have a call in now to the district attorney."

"Can they do this legally, abduct him out of his own house in the middle of the night?"

"No . . . well, they shouldn't, but they did, and they'll get away with it unless Paul wants to bring civil charges."

"I'm sure that's the last thing on anyone's mind," Leslie said. "Can we see him? I mean now?"

"I could arrange it, but I recommend against it. Give me until early afternoon. I'll be in touch. For now, let me clear the line for the DA's call. I'll be back to you as soon as I know something."

Kramer called and said in a low, rich voice that always seemed to contain an imminent laugh, "The last thing I thought I'd be doing was calling Mac Smith as defense counsel. How are you, Mac?"

"I'd be a lot better if Paul Ewald were sitting at home right now eating a tuna-fish sandwich. What the hell could have prompted you to haul him in this way?"

"Hold on, Mac. There's a division of labor here. We prosecute, MPD investigates."

"You aren't suggesting that Joe Riga did this of his own volition without an okay from you? I know Joe. Doesn't wash."

"You do realize, Mac, that we aren't dealing here with your run-of-the-mill murder case."

"True, but we are dealing with a run-of-the-mill Constitution under which we function. That make sense to you?"

Kramer was silent a moment, then he said, "It was MPD's opinion that Paul Ewald was a threat to disappear. They acted on that instinct, and I can't say I blame them."

"Are you charging Ewald?"

"Not at the moment. He's considered a prime suspect, and sure as hell is an important material witness. We're operating under the theory that Mr. Ewald, the younger of the two, is damned important to the case."

"Who concocted that theory, Len? I get the feeling you're talking about someone other than yourself."

There was silence. Then Kramer said, "There's been a little pressure."

"Pressure? Who'd put pressure on you, Len? Ken Ewald is a Democrat. You wouldn't be sitting in your chair if you weren't, and your boss, too."

"Look, Mac, let's drop this."

"Happy to, Len, provided Paul Ewald is back at home eating a tunafish sandwich by two o'clock."

"We can arrange that."

"I know you can. The question is will you?"

"You have my word."

"Good. You are, of course, aware of the embarrassment to Paul's father, Senator Ewald."

"I'm not in the business of embarrassing presidential candidates." He was angry.

"That may be true of you, Len, but somebody sure as hell knows what the embarrassment factor is here. Thanks."

"Welcome back to the nasty side of life, Professor."

Smith worked through the lunch hour making notes on a yellow legal pad. The ringing of the phone stopped him. It was Annabel Reed calling from her Georgetown gallery. Smith filled her in on what had happened that morning and asked what was new with her.

"I think I'm going to be able to buy Tlazolteotl."

"Tlazolteotl?"

"You mispronounce it."

"So what? What is it?"

"The ancient Aztec goddess of childbirth. I've been negotiating for it with a dealer in New York for a long time. Dumbarton Oaks wanted it, too, but they already have a superb example. That was the point I kept making. I guess I was effective in making it. It's mine!"

Smith smiled at her enthusiasm. He loved her in all weather and temperaments, but responded with special verve when she was high on having captured a prize for her gallery.

"When do you take possession of Tlazolteotl?"

She laughed. "You mispronounced it again."

"Sorry. I've seen pictures of it. That's the stone rendering of a woman squatting in childbirth, right?"

"Yes, but you don't have to be so crude about it. A celebration is definitely in order. My treat, your choice. I'll even go to one of those macho steak houses you like."

"I have a better idea. Let's celebrate at your place. I'd like to stay away from the public for a while."

"Fine, but if we're celebrating at home, the meal is on you. Cook it, or bring it in."

"I'd love to cook it, but I won't have the time to do justice to the sort of meal the goddess of childbirth deserves. Trust me, as they say in Hollywood. Six o'clock?"

"I'll be waiting."

Smith's phone rang all afternoon, causing him to put the answering machine on so he could screen calls and decide whether or not to take them. He debated returning to MPD headquarters to be present when Paul was released but decided against it. Len Kramer was a man of his word. That was confirmed when the phone rang at 2:15. It was Kramer. "Paul Ewald is on his way home to make a sandwich, Mac."

"Thank you," Smith said, "for letting me know."

He called Leslie Ewald and told her that Paul had been released and should be home shortly. He made a couple of other calls before a wave of fatigue came over him. He took a shower and a short nap. Then, before leaving for Annabel's house, he called the Information operator in Baltimore and said, "Last name is Buffolino, Anthony Buffolino. It might be listed as a residence or as a private detective agency." The operator gave him both.

He hung up and stared at the phone, then lifted the receiver and dialed Tony Buffolino's home number.

". . . and so I called his home and got an answering machine. He sounded angry on his message. He said something like, 'I'm not here, so come on over and rip me off if you want. Otherwise, say what it is you have to say and I'll get back to you sometime.'"

Annabel raised her eyebrows and shook her head. "Lovely dinner you brought in. For you, it's takeout; for me, bringing in. Are you sure you want to get involved with him again, Mac?"

"Yes, I think I do. He's exactly the person I need."

"Why do you need anyone?" she asked. "Paul has been released. Do you think there's a likelihood he'll be charged with the murder?"

"I don't know, but it remains a distinct possibility. Besides, if it isn't Paul, it could be someone else very close to Ken and Leslie. Paul's release doesn't end anything, Annabel. To the contrary, I think it represents the beginning of something long and difficult. Tony was a superb investigator, probably the best MPD had. Yes, I think I could use him . . . *if* he calls back, and *if* he's interested. We didn't part company on the best of terms."

"I could never understand that. You saved him from criminal prosecution. He should have been grateful."

"He didn't see it that way. He was bounced off the force, which, for him, was the ultimate penalty. He loved being a cop, loved it like no one I've ever known. At any rate, I asked him to call me at home. If he does, he'll get my answering machine, which, as you know, takes a more civil tone than his."

Annabel laughed. "Of course I know it. It's my voice. I even tried to come up with a British accent for you."

"And you were good. A Brit wouldn't buy it, but Tony will." He moved to where she was sitting on her living room couch and put his arm around her. "When do you take possession of the woman hunched over in childbirth?"

"So crude."

"Just practicing for Tony Buffolino."

"Two weeks. I pick it up in New York."

"I'll go with you, to guard you and the stone brood mare."

"That would be nice. We can make a weekend of it."

He pressed his face to her long white neck. "You know I love you, Annabel."

"Sometimes." The feel of his hands on the front of her robe was too pleasurable to protest. He continued to stroke her, his fingertips tracing the lines of her body beneath the silk, soon teasing, provoking, causing her to make sounds that to Smith sounded like the "meow" of a contented Siamese. She began to touch him, too, and brushed her lips across his, then stabbed fiercely at his lips, laughing until he parted the sash of her robe and moved his fingers over her skin.

"I am at a large disadvantage . . . ," she said playfully, her voice trailing off like his fingers. "Get naked, Smith."

He hated to break the bond between them, but he did. Moments later, they were both nude and heading for the bedroom.

Her housekeeper had changed the linen that morning. Between the clean, smooth sheets, they easily slid into first a gentle, then a more aggressive, display of their hunger for each other.

After they were spent, she whispered only, "Whew!"

"I hate to bring up a rival," Smith said, getting up from the bed, "but I want to call my machine." He picked up the phone, punched in his code, and listened to messages.

"Did Buffolino call?" she asked when he was finished.

"Yes. He said, 'A blast from the past.' Then he added, 'Smith, I want to tell you to drop dead. But I learned a couple of lives ago never to shut the door to anything. Call me. Any hour. I'm up late. I got this thing for old movies.' "

"A character."

"That and other things. Do you mind if I call him now?"

"Why should I mind? You've already seen to it that I've suffered my delightful 'little death.' . . ." She smiled. " 'Deaths' is more accurate."

"I'll use the phone in the living room."

"No, stay here. I can touch you while you talk."

He dialed. "Tony?"

"Yeah. Smith?"

"Yes. I got your message."

"I got yours, too. Hey, I heard about you finding the body of that chick who got it."

"Yes, I was walking my dog, and . . ." Nobody cared that he was walking his dog. "Tony, I have a case that I thought you might be interested in working on."

"A case?" He snickered. "What'd they do, fire you at the U? What'd you do, put the make on a Betty Co-ed?" A louder laugh this time. "Nice young stuff at the U, huh?"

"Nothing like that, Tony. I'd like to talk to you tomorrow."

"That'll be tough. I'm in the middle of . . . renovations . . . on my office . . . suite. I got a big case going. I may win it. It's called prosperity. You want breakfast? You want to *buy* breakfast? I'll come to D.C., any place you say as long as it's good. No greasy spoons, okay?"

Smith couldn't help but smile as he listened to that voice he'd heard so often when he was defending Buffolino. "Sure," he said, "breakfast, my treat, my pleasure. Seven o'clock at the . . . ?"

"Seven o'clock? What, are you crazy? I work nights, man. Make it nine."

Smith sighed. "All right, nine, Tony. Be on time."

"I'm always on time. You know that. I just like to be realistic. You know the airlines build in their schedules all kinds of time so that they look like they arrive on time? All a fraud. All a fraud. I pick a realistic ETA and I make it. I'll see you at nine."

"One question, Tony."

"What?"

"Are you available to take on a case that could run a while?"

"I'm up to my duff in cases, Mac, but I'll check my calendar. Maybe I can juggle things, *if* I decide to work for you. Know what?"

"What, Tony?"

"It'll be good to see you again."

"I'll enjoy it, too. Nine o'clock at . . . where are we meeting?"

Buffolino said, "The Jockey Club in the Ritz-Carlton. We'll have a . . . whatta they call it . . . a power breakfast."

"Fine. Nine at the Jockey Club."

"You got it, Mac Smith." He paused. "Hey, you okay?"

"Yes."

"You sound different."

"You don't. Good night, Tony."

Smith hung up, and was at once amused and annoyed. Buffolino's bravado and bluff was the stuff of all losers. On the other hand, Tony had attributes, strengths that Smith needed, including candor, know-how, street smarts. Smith had once had a good staff, good people, who'd drifted away into other lives when he closed his practice. The little speech he'd made that day informing them of his decision had been difficult. A few cried, a few swore, one or two shrugged it off and promised to go on to bigger and better things. Each handled it in his or

her own way. Of course. Just another instance of life happening while
other plans are being made.

"Mac," Annabel said, touching him.

"What?" He drew a sharp breath.

"Spend the night."

Even though he was an experienced lawyer, there was no argument
from him.

11

TONY BUFFOLINO SAT at a folding metal kitchen table and applied
polish to black wing-tip shoes. He seldom wore them. They were tight
and pinched his toes, but they went with the blue suit he intended to
wear to his breakfast meeting that morning with Smith.

Abercrombie, the smaller and younger of two black-and-white cats
(the other was Fitch, of course), walked across the table and pushed his
head against Buffolino's hand. "Not now, baby, Daddy's got to get out
a' here and earn some cat food." Abercrombie looked at him as though
understanding and approving, arched his back, and sashayed away.

A squeal of brakes caused Buffolino to turn and look out through a
dirt-crusted, smeared window at the street one flight below. It was an
industrial area of Baltimore. A ready-mix cement company was across
the street, flanked by two automobile body shops, both of which, Buffolino knew, were part straight, part chop shops. The car with the loud
brakes had almost hit a homeless drunk named John who slept in
wrecks behind the shops. The driver leaned out his window and cursed
at John, who answered with a series of jerky arm and finger gestures.

Buffolino shook his head as he stood and stretched, causing his
sleeveless undershirt to pull out of his striped boxer shorts. He pushed
dirty dishes aside in the kitchen sink and used a Brillo pad to scrub the
black polish from his fingers. Taking a bowl from the pile, he filled it
with milk and placed it on the floor next to three other bowls that had
been licked clean.

The bedroom was in the rear of the railroad flat he'd called home for
the past two years. It was large enough for an earthquake of a double
bed, a dresser rejected by the Salvation Army, and a yellow plastic table
that served as a nightstand. A telephone, answering machine, windup
alarm clock, and dog-eared copies of *Penthouse* and *Playboy* covered
the surface. Because there was no closet in the room, he'd suspended a

piece of iron pipe with wire attached to hooks screwed into the ceiling. His blue suit was covered with a dry cleaner's plastic. He slipped on the trousers, which were tight around his waist, and swore softly as he sucked in his stomach and hooked them closed. He rummaged through dresser drawers for the blue silk shirt, unhooked his pants, breathed deeply, tucked in the shirt, and tied a white tie around his neck, the skinny end dangling below the fat end.

In the tiny bathroom, he carefully peeled away a piece of toilet tissue he'd used to stem the flow of blood from a shaving cut, ran a comb through thick, wavy black hair with gray at the temples, and turned his head back and forth as he scrutinized his mirror image. Some people said he looked like Dave Toma, the former cop turned actor and antidrug crusader, although Buffolino thought there was more Paul Newman in his face than that. Victor Mature, his first wife had decided. Peter Falk, said wife number two. But neither of them spoke that way after the first few years. Mussolini, said one; baboon said the other.

He strapped on a shoulder holster, poured himself a cup of coffee, and turned on the radio. The weather would be sunny and warm. Yeah, and maybe Buffolino would earn a few dimes to buy his Billy a thing or two.

He let the phone in the bedroom ring until the machine picked up, and he heard the voice of his second wife, Barbara, through the speaker. He picked up. "Hello, Babs. I was on my way out. I got an important meeting in D.C. at the Jockey Club. That's at the Ritz. I got to step on it."

"Tony, is there any chance of getting some extra money this month? The doctor wants Billy to see a bone specialist, and I don't have it."

"Bone specialist? What for? It's in his bones now?"

"No, Tony, no, but the radiation does things, I guess. I'm not sure, but the doctor says I should take him."

"Goddamn doctors. Bloodsuckers. What do they think, we live in Bethesda? Jesus. How much?"

"I don't know. I just need to know you can help out if it's a big bill."

"Yeah, yeah, I'll help out. I got this meeting this morning about a case. You remember Mac Smith? Yeah, he called me and needs me. How's that, huh? It's a big one. Yeah, sure, you got it, Babs. Is he there?"

"No. My mother has him for a few days."

"How's your mother?"

"Fine. She's a big help."

"Yeah, I know. Well, Babs, I got to go. I don't want to be late, huh? Let me know."

"I will. Thanks, Tony."

"Yeah. Say hello to Billy. Maybe I can get out to see him this weekend."

"Try. He asks about you all the time."

"Yeah. This weekend. I'll be there unless this case sends me out a' town. I'll call ahead. So long."

His car, a faded red 1978 Cadillac with a cracked white landau roof and white leather interior gone grimy with age, was parked in front of a body shop. It wouldn't start. "You should junk this, Tony," the body-shop owner grumbled as he always did when Buffolino persuaded him to give him a jump-start. "I can get you a nice '85, '86 cheap. Maybe even the color you want."

"Yeah, that'd be nice," Buffolino said, looking at his watch.

"You tell me what you want, Tony—year, color, accessories, and I get it for you, a couple days." The car started.

"Thanks, man," Buffolino said. "We'll talk about it."

"Foreign, too—BMW, Mercedes, Jag. Whatever."

"Good, great, thanks, Mickey. I owe you." No thanks, he thought. As much as I need new wheels, no custom-stealing for me.

It was stop-and-go traffic once he reached the D.C. city limits. His engine stopped and went, too, dying multiple deaths but recovering each time with distinct moans of protest. Shame innocent murder victims can't do the same, he thought.

By the time he parked around the corner from the Ritz-Carlton, he was fifteen minutes late. "Damn, man," he muttered as he ran around the corner and sped past the doorman.

Smith was waiting at a table. Buffolino paused in the doorway, drew a deep breath, ran his hand over his hair, and sauntered up to the table. Smith stood, extended his hand. "Hello, Tony, good to see you again."

"Yeah." He sat and looked around. "Nice place."

"I assumed you'd been here before."

"Nah. Always wanted to. My girlfriend comes here."

"Girlfriend? Getting married again?"

"Nah. Three times you're out, huh?" He smiled. "You look good, Mr. Smith. A couple a' pounds more maybe, but good. The U treats you good?"

"Yes." Smith motioned to a waiter for menus. "I suggest we order," he said. "I'm sure we both have commitments to get to."

"Yeah. Up to my neck." Tony's schedule called for him to sit in a small spare office he rented from a real estate broker and wait for the phone to ring, hoping it was not someone selling subscriptions or a recorded voice offering choice bargains in travel, real estate, or jewelry.

After they'd ordered, Buffolino asked, "What's this case you called me about?"

What Smith wanted to accomplish from this initial meeting was a sense that Buffolino was still the person he needed, to become reacquainted with the man he'd defended years ago. He answered the question with, "Tell me about yourself these days, Tony. Fill me in on your business. How are your children?"

"They're good. One's got a medical problem . . . Billy . . . I guess you remember. . . . Yeah, well, sure you do. . . . anyhow, nothing I can't handle." He almost asked about Smith's son, but caught himself.

"You have your own agency now?"

"Yeah. Natural move to make, huh? What's an ex-cop know except being a cop? Working private's good. I can pick and choose the slobs I'll work with. Lot a' slobs out there, Mac. This whole country's la-la land. You find that?"

Smith smiled and sighed. "We do have more than our share of strange ones. Another orange juice?"

"I guess so. Fresh-squeezed. It's better than canned."

They filled the next few minutes with small talk. When their breakfasts were served, Smith said, "This case, if it develops, will be a tricky one, Tony. It involves the son of . . . a prominent politician."

"Somebody ice him?"

"No. *He's* suspected of 'icing' someone."

"Yeah? You say *if* the case develops. You're not . . . we're not a sure thing?"

Buffolino tried to hide his disappointment, but Smith picked up on it. "I'm here this morning, Tony, assuming we're going ahead. Naturally, I have a retainer for you." He pulled an envelope from his jacket. In it was two hundred dollars. "If we go forward, there'll be whatever we agree on."

"The family's rich?"

"Yes."

"A big shot. Who they say he kill, somebody in the family?"

"No, it was his lover."

"Happens," Buffolino said.

"Too often. Tony, can you start now?"

"Start?"

"Yes. I've typed out the details." Smith pulled papers from his breast pocket and handed them across the table. "My client is Paul Ewald."

"The senator's son."

"He's a prime suspect in the murder of a young woman with whom he had an affair. Named Andrea Feldman."

"The broad you found outside the Kennedy Center."

"Yes."

Buffolino whistled. "What every candidate for president needs, a son who bumps off a bimbo."

"Andrea Feldman was no bimbo, Tony. She was an attorney working on Senator Ewald's staff. Look, I have to move on. You stay here and read what I've given you. What I want you to do first is to go out to a motel in Rosslyn called the Buccaneer."

"I know that joint. They change the sheets every hour."

"Yes, I'm sure they do. Feldman had a key in her purse to room six at that motel, and my client indicates he'd been there with her, although not on the night she was murdered. I just have a feeling it ought to be checked out. Paul Ewald's picture's in the papers. Show it to the owner if you can, see if he remembers ever seeing him there. All the details are on the notes I gave you. Also, Paul Ewald's wife, Janet, has disappeared. I want you to see what you can do about finding her. And I want you to do some digging into Andrea's background. I've given you what I have, but it's pretty sketchy."

Buffolino sat back and quickly scanned what Smith had written out. When he was finished, he looked up and said, "You want me to check out a murder scene, find the missing wife of the accused, and dig into the background of the deceased, all for two hundred bucks?"

"I told you that was a retainer, Tony."

"And I told you, Mac, that I got some big cases I'm working on back in Baltimore. If I do this for you, I got to drop some of them, and that takes mucho money out of my pocket."

Smith scrutinized him across the table, and although he knew Buffolino was putting up a front, he also knew that the assignments he'd given him were going to take a lot of his time. He said, "Okay, Tony, I'll write you a check for a thousand. Get moving on this and we'll discuss what the real fee will be. Fair enough?"

"Yeah, I trust you, although I don't know why I should."

Smith ignored the comment and said, "Some rules, Tony. You discuss this with no one unless I tell you you can. Everything is reported directly back to me. Agreed?"

"Sure. The usual routine."

"Fine. Enjoy your breakfast," Smith said. "You have my address there." He pointed to the papers in Buffolino's hand. "Meet me at my house tonight at eight."

"Okay. You'll have a check for me? My kid needs some more medical help."

"Yes, I'll have a check for you. You look good, Tony. It's good to see you again, and I appreciate your taking time out of a busy schedule to help me with this."

Buffolino looked into Smith's eyes and remembered the last time they'd been together. When they'd parted company on that previous occasion, he'd felt betrayed. Would he feel the same way again when this was over? It really didn't matter at the moment. He needed the money. He *desperately* needed the money.

"See you tonight at eight," Smith said.

"Yeah, I'll be there. *Ciao.*"

12

BUFFOLINO TOOK his time finishing breakfast. When he was through, he went to a pay telephone, consulted a pocket address book, and dialed the number of police headquarters in Rosslyn, Virginia, across the Key Bridge from D.C. "Detective Glass, please," he said to the desk sergeant.

"Not here. Who's calling?"

"Buffolino, Tony Buffolino. I'm working private on the Feldman case." The sergeant hesitated, obviously not sure whether to believe him or not. Then the sergeant said, "Aren't you the former D.C. cop who . . . ?"

"One and the same, pal. Look, I got information Glass needs on the case. Where is he?"

"Out on an investigation."

"The Buccaneer Motel?"

"Yes."

"Thanks."

He stopped at a newsstand on the way to his car and bought the latest edition of the newspaper. On the front page was a photograph of Paul Ewald that looked as though it might have been taken from his college yearbook. Buffolino retrieved his car and headed for Rosslyn. The radio in the Caddy was as unreliable as the rest of the vehicle. This morning, however, it was working, and he listened to all-news WRC.

"Here's an update on the arrest and release of Paul Ewald, son of the Democratic candidate for president, Senator Kenneth Ewald. According to sources who have asked to remain anonymous, Paul Ewald and the deceased, Andrea Feldman, left the party at the Kennedy Center in honor of his father and went to a motel in Rosslyn called the Buccaneer. The same source has told us that a positive identification was made of Paul Ewald from a photograph shown the motel's owner by police officials. We've also learned that Paul Ewald's wife, Janet, has been missing since the murder, and her whereabouts are still unknown. Finally, Mackensie Smith, formerly one of Washington's leading criminal attorneys and more recently professor of law at George Washington University, has been retained to represent Paul Ewald in the event he's charged with the Andrea Feldman murder. Stay tuned for further developments in this and other stories we're following closely. A Defense Department spokesman said today that . . ."

Buffolino, who was on M Street, thought, Yeah, and Mac Smith and me are a defense department. He cut a hard right onto Wisconsin Avenue, drove four blocks, pulled into a parking space, and ran into a store whose sign said it sold movie and theatrical memorabilia. He came out ten minutes later, made a U-turn, went right on M again, and crossed the bridge into Rosslyn.

It took him a few wrong turns before he came upon the motel, a one-story cement-block building that was located in an area awaiting gentrification or demolition. Most of its yellow paint was a memory, flaked off years ago. It was flanked by a gas station and a rubble-filled empty lot. A large sign heralded its features—waterbeds, adult movies, and special short-stay rates. The doors had once been red. Red draperies hung precariously over each room's single window.

Neighborhood residents, mostly black and Hispanic, dawdled in small groups in front of it. There were a couple of news vehicles parked across the street, and a Rosslyn MPD patrol car blocked the entrance to the parking lot. A uniformed officer leaned against it.

Buffolino went up to the officer. "Hi, Tony Buffolino, working private on the Feldman murder. I'm looking for Detective Glass."

The officer, whose bored expression testified that he'd been on the force more than six months, nodded toward the only open door in the motel—number 6. "He's in there."

Good timing, Buffolino told himself. He said to the officer, "Could you tell him I'm here? He'll want to see me. Tell him Tony Buffolino is here."

The officer slowly walked to the open door and poked his head inside. A few minutes later, Detective Robert Glass emerged, and squinted against a hazy sun. "Hello, Tony," he said, extending his hand.

"Bobby, good to see you. They threw this one at you, huh? What've you got, a couple years to the pension?"

Glass, who looked more like a man who belonged in a corporate office than a police precinct, laughed. "Afraid so. What brings you here? He said you were working private on this case."

Buffolino had rehearsed the answer to that question on his way to Rosslyn. "I've been doing a lot of work the past couple a' years for Mac Smith, the big-shot attorney in D.C. He's the one who defended me, and he's wired tight into the Ewald family. In fact, he's Paul Ewald's attorney. He asked me to stop down here and see what's happening."

"You probably know as much from TV as I do, Tony. Riga from D.C. found a key to this place in her purse, and asked me to check it out." He looked over his shoulder toward the empty door. "That's the room they had."

"You find anything in there?"

Glass shook his head. "We've already dusted the place. There were prints, but not good ones. Prints don't read on sheets." He laughed.

Buffolino laughed, too. He said, "I heard on the radio that the owner of this dump identified Paul Ewald from a photograph. You show him the photograph?"

"Yes."

"No question about it with him? He ID'd him right away?"

"Well, he's an older man, but he didn't seem to have any doubts."

"What about the girl? You show him a picture of her?"

"No. You want to see the room?"

"Nah. I think I'll just hang out a while, maybe talk to the owner."

"Well, we're out of here. I'm leaving a uniform until Riga clears the joint. You look good, Tony. Things are good for you?"

"Yeah, great. You?"

"Good. You ought to come over sometime just for fun. My wife asks for you. Come for dinner. Bring somebody. You married again?"

"Nah. Two was enough. Three you're out. Hey, Bobby, does this thing play for you?"

"What do you mean?"

"I don't know, it's just that I have trouble with the idea that Ewald's son is having a fling with this chick, leaves a big party in honor of his father at the Kennedy Center and brings the broad to this fleatrap, makes it with her, then drives back to D.C., ends up in the bushes across from the Kennedy Center with her, and does her."

Glass smiled. "People do funny things when they're in love. Have to go, Tony. Good to see you again." He shook his hand.

"Who owns this dump?" Buffolino asked. Glass looked toward the motel office where a wizened little old black man stood with a couple of friends. "Him," Glass said. "Nice old guy. Never have much trouble with him. Runs a decent bang-and-run operation." He laughed. "Take it easy, Tony, and remember the invitation to come to the house."

Buffolino got back into the Caddy, found a diner, had coffee and read the newspaper, tearing out the front page and the inside page on which the story about the murder was continued. He shoved them in his pocket and returned to the motel. The red door to number 6 was closed. A uniformed officer sat in front of it.

The motel owner stood outside his office with friends. "Buffolino, United Press," Tony told him. "Can I ask you a few questions?"

"You-nited Press?" the owner said.

"That goes all over the world," one of his friends said, her voice indicating how impressed she was.

The owner, whose name, he said, was Wilton Morse, shook his head. "I'm not talking to nobody. Leave me alone."

"Hey, man, you already talked to the police. I'm just interested in finding out a little about you and your establishment here, maybe give you some good publicity."

Morse seemed unsure whether to continue the conversation or to bolt to the safety of his office.

"That's right, Wilton," a woman said, laughing. "Might turn this place into some kind of Holiday Inn, maybe even a fancy Hilton Hotel where people stay the night." Others laughed with her.

Buffolino grinned. "Mr. Morse, what kind of car did they arrive in?"

Morse shook his head.

"No plate number? You didn't get the plate number when they registered?"

Someone else answered. "People don't register here. Just cash up front."

"I done all my talking to the police," Morse said.

Buffolino knew he was about to lose the motel owner. He said quickly, "You know something, Mr. Morse, you're quite a hero. I mean, hell, you're the one who identified the picture." Before Morse could say anything, Buffolino opened the flap on the envelope he carried and pulled out an 8 x 10 black-and-white glossy print. He shoved it in Morse's face. "I mean, Mr. Morse, when you looked at this picture and said, 'Yeah, that's the man who brought that poor lady here the other night,' you did everybody one hell of a service."

Morse squinted at the photograph, and pulled back to focus better. Others moved in and looked, too.

"You've got good eyes, Mr. Morse, recognizing him from a picture like this."

Morse said, "I always remember a face."

"And a good thing for the citizens of Rosslyn and D.C.," Buffolino said, replacing the photograph in the envelope. "Well, thanks for your time, Mr. Morse." He looked past him at the motel. "You got a real nice place here."

Buffolino didn't arrive at Mac Smith's house in Foggy Bottom until almost nine that night. "You're late," Smith said.

"I got hung up. You got any coffee?"

"Yes." Smith poured them each a cup, and they sat at the kitchen table.

"Well?" Smith asked.

"Well, I spent some time at the motel, and then I headed over to where Andrea Feldman lived, near Dupont Circle."

"Find anything interesting?"

"Yeah, I think so," Buffolino said. "You heard the owner of the Buccaneer identified Ewald from a photograph, right?"

"Yes, I heard that."

"I had a few words with the gentleman who owns that dump. Name is Wilton Morse. Nice-enough old guy. I showed him a picture of the man who checked in with Andrea." Buffolino reached into the envelope, pulled out the photograph he'd shown Morse, and slid it across the table to Smith.

Smith stared at it. "That's Van Johnson."

"It sure is," Tony said after his second cup of coffee and third doughnut. "And it cost me ten bucks. I'm keeping track of expenses."

"Of course."

"I showed this to Morse, the owner, like it was the picture the cops showed him, and he didn't tell me it wasn't Paul Ewald."

"Did he confirm that this was the person he saw come into the motel with Andrea Feldman?"

"Nope. But he didn't deny it either."

Smith sat back and shook his head. "What made you take this photograph there, Tony?"

"I done it before. I saw Ewald's picture in the paper and he looked a little like Van Johnson to me, so I figured I'd try it. Sometimes it works, sometimes it don't."

"Anything else at the motel?" Smith asked.

"No, except Morse, the owner, needs glasses but don't wear them. I could tell the way he was squinting at the picture."

"Very observant. What about Andrea Feldman's apartment. You got into it?"

"No, but I knew the cop guarding the scene. I asked him about where she lived, and he told me it was kind of strange."

"In what way?"

"Well, he said it looked like nobody lived there, real sparse, no pictures, just a couple a' books, clothes in the closet. You know, you figure a career dame like this wants to live good, have comfortable surroundings, but my friend told me that ain't the way it was."

"You've had a busy day, Tony."

"Yeah, and I'm beat. You got anything to lace this coffee with?"

"Sure." Smith placed a bottle of Nocello on the kitchen table and refilled their cups. "Tony, I'm going to need you for a while. Can you shake your other commitments and work with me?"

"I been thinking about that. You know something, Mac, it's good to be back with you. I know we parted on lousy terms the last time, but you can understand that. Hell, it was my career that went up in smoke." Smith started to say something, but Buffolino continued. "Besides, this Ewald thing fascinates me. Yeah, count me in, but it's going to cost you."

"Meaning?"

"A grand a week, plus a place to stay in D.C. I can't be drivin' back and forth to Baltimore."

"Lots of people do."

"Yeah, nine-to-fivers. I'm on a case twenty-four hours."

Smith frowned. "All right," he said, "that can be arranged. A thousand dollars a week and a place to stay."

"I figure I ought to be close to you here, and close to the Kennedy Center."

"Why?"

"Why what?"

"Why do you want to be close to the Kennedy Center?"

"I don't know, Mac, just a hunch. I mean, that's where she bought it, and our client was at that party there. How about springing for a suite at the Watergate?"

Smith sat up straight. "At the Watergate? A suite? I wouldn't have supposed you'd want that after what happened."

"Well, time goes by, huh?" Buffolino grinned. "Whattaya say? Think of it this way, Mac. We're going to need someplace to work out of, right?"

Smith nodded. He'd been thinking the same thing.

"So, we get a suite at the Watergate, you get an office, I got a place to live that's decent and close to everything, and we all get somethin' out of it."

Smith couldn't help but smile. "Okay, Tony, a suite at the Watergate it is."

"Great. Call 'em in the morning, and I'll get over and pick the room. I got to go back to Baltimore and pack some things, get somebody to take care of my cats."

"Pick the room?"

"Yeah. Anything wrong with that?"

"I suppose not. I'll call and tell them you're coming."

"Good enough, Mac." Buffolino stood and slapped Smith on the arm. "Hey, I think we're gonna make a hell of a team."

Long after Buffolino had left, Smith sat in his study, Rufus at his side. He didn't read, didn't make notes, just sat and thought. He realized his head was beginning to droop, looked at his dog, and said, "There is something very strange going on here, Rufus, very strange indeed."

Rufus raised his head from the floor and looked at Smith as though he understood every word. Smith got up. "Come on," he said. "Time for you to go into the great outer world—or outer john. We'll discuss this further in the morning."

13

"MAY I HELP YOU, sir?" a pretty desk clerk at the Watergate Hotel asked Buffolino.

"Yeah, probably. Mr. Mackensie Smith made arrangements for me to choose a suite, and to stay in it for a while. The name's Buffolino, Anthony Buffolino."

The clerk smiled at him and pulled a computer printout from a file folder. "Yes, sir, I have the reservation here. You'll have suite—"

"As a matter of fact, I have a preference. I'd like suite 1117."

"Suite 1117? Let me see. Yes, it's available for the next four days. We have someone coming in after that."

"You can give them another room."

"I don't think so, Mr. Buffolino."

"Let's not worry about it now, I'm sure Mr. Smith can work it out. In the meantime, I'll just go up."

"Of course." He filled out the registration card. "Luggage?" she asked.

He pointed to a battered steamer trunk and two canvas duffel bags. "I'll have . . . them . . . sent up right away," she said. An incinerator would be more appropriate, she thought.

He was handed the key and rode the elevator to the eleventh floor, opened the door to suite 1117, and stood in the archway, his eyes embracing the suite, his tongue almost tasting it—every wall, corner, every brass-framed picture, lush and large plant, piece of furniture.

He stepped inside and rocked back and forth, his toes and heels sinking into the foyer's thick gold carpeting. Closets were to his right. He looked at himself in a mirror that hung over a marble table. A few steps and he was on the fringe of a huge living room. A seven-foot leather couch, three leather chairs, and a large black lacquered coffee table occupied the right side of the room. In front of him, twenty feet away, was a twenty-five-inch color TV. He took a few more steps and turned left. A heavy white table surrounded by four chairs with cane backs and floral print fabric provided a dining area for a full kitchen hidden behind fanfold doors.

He passed the smaller of two baths as he went to the bedroom, a large and airy space with two queen-sized beds, a TV, desk, and a sitting area formed by white leather chairs and a brass table. A brisk breeze through slightly opened sliding glass doors sent gossamer white curtains fluttering into the room.

Outside, on the Astroturf-carpeted balcony, he looked down over the sprawling Watergate complex, then slowly walked the length of the balcony on the bedroom side until reaching the point where it wrapped to the left, around the corner of the suite. From there, he looked down onto the Potomac. Small boats of all descriptions, including an eight-man racing scull, moved with varying speeds through the brown water. Across the river, spires on old Georgetown University buildings spiked up into heavy gray air that had descended on the city.

For a moment, there had been a small satisfied grin on Buffolino's face during his tour of the suite. Now—and suddenly—he closed his eyes and grimaced against an unseen invasion of sound and image. Day turned to night, and time fell away, taking him with it to a night six years ago outside suite 1117. . . .

He was in the hallway, looking right and left. He knocked. The security chain was slipped from its notch, and the door opened. The man was young, black, and dressed nicely. He scrutinized Tony before allowing him to step into the foyer. The door closed. Tony looked in the direction of the bedroom. A tall roses-and-cream blonde wearing a silk robe loosely secured at the waist smiled at him.

"My man," a male voice said from the living room.

He was on the leather couch, his feet up on the black lacquered coffee table. "Tony, right on time. Come in and sit down." Another woman, brunette and still more luxurious than the blonde, sat in one of the leather chairs. She, too, wore a revealing robe. "This is Joanna, Tony, a friend of mine." He laughed and patted her bare knee.

Buffolino sat in a chair facing her. The man on the couch, who was in his early thirties, was Panamanian, although there was little trace of it in his speech. He wore a red silk shirt open to his stomach. Three thin gold chains nestled in a heavy mat of black chest hair. Thick fingers supported multiple rings. Light from a table lamp revealed skin that was pockmarked and sebaceous. "Why don't you and your friend spend a little time together in the bedroom," he said to Joanna. "Freshen up, get pretty for us. We'll see you later." She touched Buffolino's neck as she passed him. Moments later, he heard the bedroom door close.

"So, Tony, my man, we finally get together. That's nice. That's the way it should be, doing business together instead of being competitors. It's like a merger."

Buffolino didn't respond.

"Hungry, Tony? Help yourself." He nodded at the white table near the kitchen. On it was a cut-glass bowl of caviar, surrounded by thinly sliced and crustless toast, lemon wedges, chopped onions, and cooked egg yolks. "The best, man. I ordered up the best for my new partner. What do you drink?"

"Ah, anything. Scotch, vodka, a beer."

"Take whatever you want, baby. It's all there."

Tony poured himself half a glass of Absolut over ice and returned to the chair. The man on the couch raised a partly consumed glass of orange juice in a toast. "To our merger, Tony. To good times for everybody." Buffolino lifted his glass, but only to his mouth.

"Like this suite, Tony? I do. Somebody said once that living well is the best revenge. I like that. It's true. People like you and me should always live well, high style like. Now that we're partners, you'll be living like this, too, as long as you keep doing what I'm paying you to do."

Buffolino stared at him over his glass.

"You're not a big talker, are you, Tony? That's good. Talkers get in trouble. You're a *silent* partner. I like that."

"I got one question for you, Garcia."

"Hey, you got a right to ask questions."

"What happens if this thing goes sour? I mean, you realize my neck is way out, huh?"

Garcia opened his eyes wide and smiled. "And, Tony, my man, you are being paid plenty of green for stretching your neck a little. Besides, anything goes bad on the deal, you come visit me in Panama I got plenty of room, and plenty of friends who'll take real good care of you."

Buffolino knew Garcia was referring to the strongman Colonel Morales, who not only ran Panama with an iron fist, but who was alleged to run that country's multibillion dollar drug industry, too.

"Look, I got to go, Garcia. Just give me the money and let me get out of here."

"Sure, sure, only I thought we could celebrate a little. You order up anything you want, drink, eat, spend a little time with my friends in there."

"Nah, I got other things to do."

"As you wish. You like to keep things all business, that's fine with me. I like that. All business. So, you do understand what our deal is?"

"Yeah."

"Instead of busting my chops like you've been doing, you leave me alone here in D.C., like happens in other cities where I have partners. You keep me out of trouble, let me know when trouble's brewing, make sure your cop buddies don't bust my chops. Right?"

"Right. I don't need a lesson in how this goes down. Come on, Garcia, give me the money before I change my mind."

Garcia crossed the expansive room and returned with a black leather Gucci briefcase, placing it on the table in front of Buffolino. "There it is, Tony. You even get the briefcase as a bonus." He laughed. "I don't mess around. I go first class all the way, like you'll be doing from now on. Every month, you get the same. Oh, but not a new briefcase." Another laugh. "The same bread, twenty-five grand, and all you have to do to earn it is do n-o-o-o-th-i-i-i-n-g." He dragged out the word.

Buffolino took the briefcase and started to get up.

"Come on," Garcia said, "relax. You got the money, right? One more drink between partners." He didn't allow Tony to respond, simply went to the table near the kitchen and refilled his glass. "How's it feel to have twenty-five grand in your hands?"

Buffolino looked at the briefcase, and a wave of disgust came over him, so strong that he wondered if he might become ill. "Listen, I . . ." Garcia rejoined him. "What's the matter?" he asked. "Feel like dirty money because it's drug money? You'll forget about that once you start spending it. It spends the same as clean money, only it's easier to come by. You see that. All you have to do is leave my operation alone, give me a word or two now and then, and get rich, with nobody knowing the difference."

Buffolino took a long swig of his drink. As he was placing it on the table to leave, the first sounds and sights erupted. The whirling blades of a helicopter suddenly loomed up outside, a brilliant light from it pouring through the glass doors and painting everything in the room in harsh whiteness.

"What the . . . ?" Buffolino bolted from the chair and headed for the door. It opened before his hand could reach the knob. Standing in the hall were four men, their guns drawn.

"Cool out, Tony," one of them said. Officers from Internal Affairs. "Nothing stupid."

Buffolino turned and looked at Garcia, who was leaning casually on the television, a smug grin on his face.

"Cuff him," a cop said as another removed Tony's service revolver from where it sat beneath his jacket.

There were so many things Buffolino wanted to tell them instantly, how he never took from anybody before, how his youngest child was sick with cancer and needed expensive medical treatment beyond what his benefits as a cop would cover, how backwards it was to use a notorious drug kingpin like Garcia to trap a cop who'd always been honest, to make a deal with that scum. He said nothing, and was led to a waiting car downstairs.

Tony Buffolino opened his eyes and blinked. That scene had played in his mind thousands of times since it happened. Early—during the hearings, and shortly after his dismissal from the force—he wished he'd run from the suite to the balcony and gone over. Then, as the banal realities of every day prevailed, that thought dimmed. Not the scene itself, not the disgrace, the second divorce, being shunned by friends in MPD, the hatred he felt for those who'd set him up, wired Garcia, caused him to lose what had always meant most to him. That Mackensie Smith had successfully prevented a criminal action being brought against him meant nothing. Anthony Buffolino died that night in suite 1117.

But as he went inside from the balcony and again surveyed the living room, he felt an unmistakable twinge of life. He'd felt it the morning he'd met Smith for breakfast, a sense of having something important to do that day, a meeting, a case, a reason for shining shoes that went unpolished month after month. Something positive to report to Barbara and Julie. Although they were no longer his wives, they meant a great deal to him. Money. Clean money. A sense he was doing something worthwhile for Billy without the accompanying sense of constant deprivation.

"Damn," he said aloud, smacking a fist into a hand. He rode the elevator down and walked into the elegant Jean Louis restaurant.

"We're open at lunch only to club members and hotel guests. Are you a guest of the hotel, sir?"

"I certainly am. Suite 1117."

"Will you be dining alone?"

"Today, yes. I'll have guests other days. I'll be here a while."

"Good, sir. This way, please."

After a quick study of the menu, he said to the waiter, "I'll start with this terrine of fresh and smoked salmon with caviar. Let's see, how about some Maryland crab cakes for a second course, this here—how do you pronounce it?—mousseline of lobster filled with lobster sauce for the third, and the venison stuffed with mushrooms. No, no dessert. I got to stay in shape."

To the wine steward, he said, "Latour? Whatever you say. I'm in suite 1117. I'll be here a while. Remember me, okay?" He handed him a twenty-dollar bill.

14

As Buffolino finished up his several lunches that day at Jean Louis, Leslie Ewald was finishing up a speech to the Democratic Woman's Association at their luncheon in the Mayflower Hotel's main ballroom.

"I suppose the best way to describe Ken's vision of America is to say that he believes with all his heart that every American must have the right to be treated as he wishes to be treated, and would want his own children to be treated. This is not the case in today's America. My husband, when he is president, will work hard to bring this about, and to return us to a nation with a keen sense of justice, equality, and fairness for every man, woman, and child."

Two hundred women stood and applauded. Once the applause had subsided, the press representatives, who sat in a cordoned-off area in the front of the room, tossed a barrage of questions at Leslie. She held up her hands and smiled. "Please, I do have another commitment I must get to, but I will be happy to take a few questions. Before I do, let me say that Ken and I are naturally delighted that our son has been released, and we stand firm in our love and support of him. We feel totally vindicated, as I know he does, but please, it would be inappropriate for us to discuss any aspect of that."

She recognized a reporter, who asked, "Mrs. Ewald, a poll released earlier this morning indicates that your husband's standing has slipped. Do you think this unfortunate affair, even if it's resolved to your satisfaction, has seriously damaged his chances for the Democratic nomination in July?"

Leslie shook her head and said with strength, "Absolutely not. The American people . . . every family in this wonderful country . . . has had to face problems, and they understand the problems we're facing *as a family*. It is distinct and apart from the leadership qualities that Ken will bring to the White House, and I am confident that the American people will sympathize with our pain, and will focus on the issues that are really important to them."

Another questioner asked, "Not only is your son a prime suspect in Andrea Feldman's murder, Mrs. Ewald, but his wife . . . your daughter-in-law . . . has been missing for a few days now. Would you comment on that?"

"No, I won't. Janet, whom we love very much, has undoubtedly gone off to find some solitude, which, I must add, sounds like a very good idea." Some of the audience laughed quietly, and Leslie joined them. "All of this will be resolved shortly. In the meantime, we're pressing ahead and know that we will be successful in July at the convention."

Other questions came from the press section, but one of Leslie's press aides quickly came to the microphone, waved his hand, and said, "Sorry, Mrs. Ewald has another appointment. Thank you very much."

A loud voice from a reporter asked, "What will your priority as First Lady be?"

Leslie, who'd started to leave the podium, leaned back to the microphone and said, "Day care. The right of every mother to know that her children are in a safe and enriching environment when it's necessary for her to work outside the home . . . or simply because she wants to work."

Leslie's aides and Secret Service agents led her from the podium and out of the ballroom. Outside, in the lobby, another small knot of reporters waited. As Leslie passed them, a young woman in jeans with long, matted blond hair pushed close to her, shoved a microphone in her face, and asked, "Will you be the first First Lady to be divorced while in the White House?"

Leslie stopped and looked at the reporter as though she'd spoken a foreign tongue.

The reporter added, "Everyone knows that you and Senator Ewald have been estranged for years."

The aides tried to move her on, but Leslie stood firm. She looked the reporter in the eye and said, "First of all, I find you personally offensive. Second, I respect your right as a journalist to ask anything you wish. Third, my private life is exactly that, private. And fourth, you are talking to a happily married woman, whose husband is a fine and decent man and who will be the next president of the United States, your country. Knowing my husband, I know he will defend to the death your right to be offensive and boring. Have I answered,your question?"

The reporter's expression was defiant, but her voice was weak. "Yes," she said, backing into the crowd.

After the Ewald entourage had left the hotel, a veteran campaign reporter from the *Washington Post* joined a colleague for a drink in the Mayflower's refurbished Town-and-Country bar. "She talks like Ewald does," he said as the bartender served him a shot of rye and a glass of seltzer. "They don't even try to change the quotes. Jack Kennedy gave that speech about America treating everybody and their kids the way they want to be treated during the civil-rights movement. Almost word for word. Doesn't anyone remember Joe Biden's campaign?"

His friend, who'd ordered a beer, laughed. "Hey, it could be worse. They could be quoting James Watt or Jimmy the Greek."

"True." He downed the rye and waved for another. "I just wish there were some goddamn basic honesty. The kid who asked about their relationship was on the money. 'Happily married woman,' my ass."

Mac Smith watched Leslie's confrontation with the young reporter on a newscast an hour later. He was in a TV room in the Ewald house in Georgetown. "Nice work," he said to Leslie on the TV screen as she told off the reporter. He did admire the way they'd forged ahead despite the brewing scandal about Paul. They conducted themselves with dignity, and without apology. He liked that. At the same time, he knew that their statements that what had happened to them personally would have little effect on Ken's bid for the White House were at best naive, or, more likely, planned bravado. The campaign had to have suffered, and he wondered what kind of strategy was being planned at the moment.

The door to the TV room opened, and Marcia Mims asked Smith if he would like something to eat or drink.

"No, thank you, Marcia."

She lingered in the doorway, as though she wanted to say something else but wasn't sure she should. Before Smith could encourage her to speak, she backed out and closed the door.

Marcia Mims had been with the Ewald family for twenty-two years. She'd come to Los Angeles from Martinique as a young woman, after a charlatan beauty-contest promoter there convinced the beautiful and shy Marcia—as well as her mother—that he had arranged a screen test at a major Hollywood studio for the newly crowned "Miss Fort-de-

France." Marcia's mother forked over every cent they had in savings, and Marcia headed for Hollywood, the family's future riding on her certain rise to screen stardom. Of course, there was no screen test, nor was there money to return to Martinique. Prostitution? Domestic work? Marriage? She had tried them all, and after two divorces, instead of becoming a star and rich, settled for running a household of a possible political star who was rich—an aspiring California politician named Kenneth Ewald.

Aspirations then turned to reality for Ewald, and Marcia Mims was promoted to the Ewald Washington house in Georgetown when he became a United States senator. "La-dee-da," her friends said when she announced she was leaving for the nation's capital. "Just don't let massa get his hands on your butt. He looks like he likes 'em all shades," they joked. A lot of giggling. And envy. In fact, Marcia had hit it off pretty well from the start with the Ewalds. They liked her and showed it in many generous ways, gradually promoting her. She was reluctant to express too much appreciation lest she seem to be playing the house-slave role, but she knew that considering who she was and where she'd come from, there were worse things than being surrogate mother, wife, and chairman-of-the-board in a wealthy and exciting household, with gardeners, two chauffeurs, kitchen workers, and serving staff under her managerial thumb. "I don't know what I'd do without you," Leslie Ewald often said—said too often—and Marcia never failed to return the compliment, probably with as much sincerity as she perceived the lady of the house possessed.

Now, it seemed possible that she would be promoted again, this time to the White House, and the thought of it frightened her. She had begun to read books on what the White House was like, and wondered what extra demands would be placed on her, what additional duties she would be called on to perform once she was there. The White House! Serving the president of the United States! Someday, *she* would write a book and be famous. What stories she'd have to tell! Her diary was already a treasure.

Ed Farmer, Ken's campaign manager, poked his head in. "Sorry, Mac, didn't realize you were here," he said.

"No problem, Ed. I was just watching Leslie on television. She handled herself beautifully."

Farmer, whose expression was consistently dour, raised his eyebrows and leaned against the door frame. He fiddled with his bow tie as he said, "Between you and me, Mac, they're performing a lot better than the situation really is. We're in trouble. Some of the faithful are losing faith, even whispering defection."

Smith nodded. "I suppose we couldn't expect anything else, considering the serious nature of what's happened. What's the term—'damage control'?—how is that coming?"

The question brought forth a rare smile from Farmer. "The water has started pouring in, and we're trying to bucket it out as fast as possible. Sorry, I have to run." And he was gone.

Smith spent the next few minutes consulting notes he'd made on a legal pad, and added more. There was a knock on the door. "Come in." Marcia Mims reappeared. "Mr. Smith, you have a telephone call."

"Who is it?"

"The gentleman says his name is Mr. Greist, Herbert Greist, and he's calling from New York."

Smith glanced around the TV room in search of a phone. Marcia said, "Why not take it in the second-floor office?"

Smith went to the office on the second floor, which was fully equipped with fax and copying machines, an IBM computer and printer, two multiline phones, dictating equipment, and a broadcast-quality cassette tape recorder on a shelf high above the desk. He picked up the lighted extension and said, "This is Mackensie Smith."

Greist, whoever he was, seemed surprised to hear a voice on the other end of the phone. He coughed, excused himself for a moment, and Smith could hear papers being shuffled in the background. "Ah, thank you, Mr. Smith. I had to find Mrs. Feldman's file."

"Mrs. Feldman? What is this about?"

"I've been retained by Mae Feldman, regarding the murder of her daughter, Andrea." He had the tired voice of a person whose successes were few and far between, or never.

There had been some mentions in the press coverage of Andrea Feldman's murder that attempts to reach her only known family member, her mother, had been unsuccessful. Frankly, Smith hadn't given much thought to that. Damn. Dumb. Now, he would. "Go on," he said.

"We intend to file suit over the loss of Andrea Feldman's civil rights, and to ask for substantial damages from your client for my client's pain and suffering in losing her only daughter."

Smith said nothing. Greist asked if he were still on the line.

"Yes."

"And so, Mr. Smith, I think it would be in the best interest of both parties for you and me to meet to see whether there is some accommodation we could reach that would avoid further embarrassment and pain to Senator Ewald and his family."

The words "cheap hustler" ran through Smith's mind. What would it cost to not further embarrass a man running for president? Lots. Smith's inclination was to politely tell Mr. Greist to get lost. But he was no longer a free man. He couldn't. Andrea Feldman's mother certainly had the right to sue over her daughter's death. No matter what might happen in any criminal proceeding, there was lately the chance to sue for the loss of an individual's "civil rights," i.e., life. If Greist were any good—which Smith doubted—they might mount a compelling case. But Greist obviously wasn't interested in filing cases or going to court. His message was clear. Come up with enough money and they'd go away.

"When will you be in Washington, Mr. Greist?"

"My, ah, plans will keep me here in New York for some time, Mr. Smith. Perhaps you could come here for a conference."

"I'll consider it."

"I would suggest that you not wait too long. Mrs. Feldman is . . . well, she's most anxious to put this behind her, as you can well imagine."

Translation: Get money now.

"I'll be in touch, Mr. Greist. By the way, it was my understanding that Mrs. Feldman hadn't been located."

"She travels."

"She lives in San Francisco?" Smith asked.

He cleared his throat. "Well, yes, but New York is a second home for her."

"Because of her profession? Which is?"

"We can discuss that when we meet. I repeat, Mr. Smith, time is of the essence."

"Yes, I'm sure it is, Mr. Greist. By the way, I assume you're the attorney handling the disposition of whatever estate Andrea Feldman left."

"That is correct."

"She had a will?"

"Well, she . . . her affairs are in good order, Mr. Smith."

"I'm sure they are. You'll hear from me . . . or from someone on my staff. Good-bye."

Smith hung up and left the room, never noticing that the tape recorder on the shelf above him had begun recording the moment he lifted the receiver.

Downstairs, Smith checked his watch; he wanted to run home before going to the gathering at Roger Gerry's house. He'd asked Annabel to go with him, but she was busy, which was okay with him. He didn't intend to stay long, wasn't in the mood for polite parties.

He strolled to the rear of the house and found Marcia Mims in the kitchen. "I'm leaving now, Marcia. Thank you for everything."

She looked up from salmon filets she was garnishing for dinner that night and said, "Anytime, Mr. Smith."

"How are you holding up under all of this, Marcia?"

She looked down at the glistening pink flesh beneath her hands and slowly shook her head. "I don't know, Mr. Smith, how all this will end up, but I know this household is full of mess. There's serious trouble here."

Initially, Smith thought she was referring to the trouble caused by Paul's arrest, complicated by Janet's disappearance. But then he realized she was referring to something beyond that. He asked what she meant.

"It just makes me so sad to see this mess—and a wonderful family destroyed."

"Because of what happened with Paul?"

"Yes, and . . ."

"And what, Marcia?"

"And lots of other things that most folks just don't know about." She didn't give Smith a chance to press the question. "Excuse me, Mr. Smith, I have a lot of work to do."

Smith stared at her until she looked at him again. "I'll be back, Marcia. Maybe we could find some quiet time to talk."

She went back to working the fish.

Smith sat with his dean, Roger Gerry, in a comfortable study in Gerry's home. The sound of the guests mingling in the other rooms was agreeably muffled.

"I need time off," Smith told him.

Gerry, whose round, pink, and pleasant face belied a leg-trap intellect and rock-hard convictions, raised his white eyebrows. "A leave of absence?"

"Maybe not that formal, Roger. Without going into too many details at this stage, let's just say that my involvement with the Ewald family is going to keep me occupied for a period of time."

"How long do you anticipate this will go on?" Gerry asked.

Smith shrugged. "Could be a couple of months. I possibly can handle an occasional class, but I can't be bound to it. How about Tony Peet covering for me when I can't make it?" Peet was the youngest member of the law school faculty, a brilliant Harvard scholar who made no attempt to hide his aspirations to one day become a justice of the Supreme Court. Few doubted he'd achieve his goal, except those who knew what a roulette wheel court appointments were.

"All right, Mac, but you discuss it with him. If it's okay with him, it's okay with me. I need you both. Tell me, is the Feldman murder something you really want to be involved in?"

Smith laughed. "I've been asking myself that question ever since she was killed, and Ken and Leslie Ewald asked me to advise them. Annabel has been asking that question, too, and I'm not sure we've come to the same conclusion. She says she understands why I feel compelled to do this, but I don't think she really does. We both left the active, hectic practice of law to pursue things that were gentler and longer term. I suppose I can view this as a momentary digression, sort of keeping my hand in something. Besides, I've known Ken and Leslie for years. And . . ."

Gerry's white eyebrows peaked again like mountaintops, and a smile crossed his face. "And Mackensie Smith was getting bored, needs a little action in his life, sort of like an older man taking up with a young woman. Just remember one thing, Mac—old men who have flings with young women enjoy it for a brief period of time, but find that if it lasts for any duration, against all odds, it loses its appeal. And I'm not speaking legally."

"I'll keep that in mind, and please refrain from using that analogy with Annie next time you see her." Smith checked his watch. "I really can't stay long, Roger. It was kind of you to take time from your guests for this discussion."

"You will have something to eat with us?"

"Would you be offended if I didn't?"

"Of course not. I know you have many things to do, all of them undoubtedly due yesterday. Go on. Just say good-bye to Charlotte, and promise me one thing."

"What's that?"

"To keep me informed on all the sordid, inside details as they develop. I may be a law school dean, but I haven't lost my interest in the hectic, active practice—or in gossip."

"I'll give you a regular report, Roger. And thanks again. I appreciate your understanding."

Mac took Rufus for a long walk. Such a pleasant and easy conversation with Gerry seemed out of place, almost perverse. The son of the man likely to become the Democratic presidential nominee was a prime murder suspect, and he, Mac Smith, had accepted the responsibility of trying to keep *suspect* from becoming *accused.*

As he headed back toward the house, he said to himself, Pull out, pull out before it's too late.

That was as long as the thought lasted. He wouldn't pull out. The surge of purpose—and, yes, he admitted to himself, importance—would override any cautious evaluation of the situation in which he'd placed himself. He was in, all the way in, and there was a lot of work to do, the contemplation of which was full of mess, as Marcia put it, but also of an odd, fulfilling pleasure.

15

"ARE YOU AWAKE?" Smith asked Annabel, looking over at her. The sight of her copper hair strewn over a pillow never failed to delight him.

She mumbled and buried her head a little deeper in the pillow.

"It's important."

"What's important?"

"We should have made coffee last night," Smith said.

"Uh-huh."

They'd decided to stay at her place Saturday night to avoid the constant ringing of the telephone in Smith's house.

"I'll get up and make some," he said.

"Good," she said, and sank into sleep again.

He kissed a small exposed portion of her cheek, rolled out of bed, and went to the kitchen, where he prepared the coffee using the various blends that he had made certain were always stocked there. He found fresh eggs, scrambled them expertly, popped oatmeal bread into the toaster, poured orange juice, and when everything was ready, shouted, "Get up! Eat. Breakfast is ready. The world is waiting."

They finished breakfast by eight, and sat at the dining room table drinking second cups of coffee and reading the Sunday paper, enjoying an interlude both sensed must be brief. There was a long feature on the Feldman murder, including pictures of Paul, his mother and father, and the deceased. There was also a shot of Mac Smith taken outside the Ewald home.

Annabel giggled. "I never knew you had a double chin, Mac."

"Shadows from the lighting," he said.

She laughed again. "Since you're going to be the subject of media attention, maybe you should hire a media adviser, like politicians do."

"Or a surgeon, for a tuck or tug." Smith went to the funnies. He was reading *Doonesbury* when Annabel said, "Mac, time to fill me in on everything."

Which he did, in as much detail as he could summon. He told her about the call from the New York shyster Herbert Greist, replayed his interview with Paul Ewald, his conversations with Ken and Leslie Ewald, what had transpired during his meeting with Joe Riga at Riga's office, and his brief talk with Ken Ewald in which Ewald had said he hadn't stayed in his office the night of the murder but had instead gone to the Watergate Hotel for a tryst with an unnamed woman.

"Interesting, that he would tell you about that but not tell you who she is," Annabel said.

"Dumb but not unusual," Smith commented. "It's known that Ken has had a proclivity for pretty faces other than Leslie's, but he's always been mostly a model of discretion, thank God for her sake."

"Aren't you curious about who she is?"

"Yes, I'd like very much to know who she is. I need to know everything so we are not surprised, caught off base. I've learned too much from the radio so far. I'll have to know eventually. Unfortunately, so will too many other people."

"Think he would tell you if you asked him again?"

"Yes. I will—ask him, I mean. I also want to ask you a favor."

She cocked her head and raised her eyebrows. "My dear . . . asking for my favors on this Sunday morning?" Sunday mornings were a favorite time with them for making love, like the rest of the world, with the alarm clock turned off.

"That's favor number two," he said. "First, I want to set up a meeting in New York with this Greist character as quickly as possible. I thought I'd try to call him today and see if he's available sometime tomorrow. His type can be in the office Sundays—not always working. My problem is that I *have* to spend time here getting organized, hiring a temporary secretary to work out of the suite, lease some word-processing equipment, get a couple of extra phones in there, a copying machine, all the things I used to take for granted when I had the office. Would you go to a meeting with Greist in New York?"

"Mac, I own an art gallery, remember? I *used* to be a lawyer."

"Once a lawyer, always a lawyer, and you know it. Look, if you're really jammed up at the gallery, I'll try to figure out something else, but if you could go to New York as a representative of my . . ." His voice took on a certain pomposity. "As an associate in my law firm"—his voice returned to normal—"I would be forever grateful."

She poured them more coffee, and the sight of her voluptuous body beneath her robe, hair hanging loose and natural, pretty bare feet with red-tipped toes on white terra-cotta tiles, took his mind off murder for the moment. When she sat down, he repeated his request, adding, "I'll make it up to you."

"How?"

A shrug. "I don't know, a long trip somewhere exotic once this is over."

She sat back and looked at him. What she saw was a different man. Always intelligence itself, he now had the look of someone with a large commitment, almost religious in intensity. He was very much alive. She liked what she saw, even if she didn't like the reason for it. "How are things going with Tony Buffolino?" she asked.

He laughed. "He's as big a character as ever, but no matter what Tony is or isn't, he's a damned good investigator, very creative." He told her of how Tony had used the movie-star photo.

She shook her head. "You're an amazing man, Mac Smith. You have Ken Ewald, who, if he were to become president, would want you as his attorney general. You've counseled the rich and famous, and you've become a distinguished professor of law at a leading university. At the same time, you hire a foul-ball ex-cop, put him up in a suite at Watergate, and pay him probably a lot more than he, or any other private investigator, is worth, I'm sure. What's next, a limo and dancing girls?"

"I hadn't thought of that, Annabel. I will . . . think about it . . . the dancing girls part. For Tony. In the meantime, will you go to New York and talk to Greist for me? I'm going to get Tony moving tomorrow on checking into Andrea Feldman's past. I think I'll send him to San Francisco."

She assumed a pout. "He gets to go to San Francisco, and I end up in New York talking to some sleaze?"

"Do it for me and do a good job, and we'll go to San Francisco together. Soon."

"When?"

"As soon as . . ."

"All right," she said. "James can handle things at the gallery while I'm gone. He's working out very nicely."

"Good."

"I'll stay an extra day or two in New York. There are some pieces I'd like to track down, and I may as well do it on your generosity."

"Of course." She was having fun at his expense, and he found it amusing.

"You will put *me* up in fancy digs, of course."

"Of course. The Y on Forty-seventh Street. No, seriously, Annabel, you name it. Then you'll go as my associate?"

She flashed a wide and warm smile. "I'll go as your *partner.* I'll name the hotel—and my fee. Count on it."

With favor number one out of the way, they proceeded to favor number two, fell asleep in each other's arms for a half hour, then showered and went about their individual projects for the day. For Annabel, it was to sort out clothing to get ready for Washington's infamous heat and humidity, a season that would surely arrive soon. Smith settled by a phone in the living room and called the number he had for Herbert Greist. He thought he might get an answering machine, but Greist answered.

"I'm impressed, Mr. Greist," Smith said. "This is Mac Smith. You must have a heavy caseload to be working on a Sunday."

Smith's attempt at conciliatory chitchat fell on deaf ears. Greist said only, "Yes, I do."

"Mr. Greist, one of my associates"—he glanced at the bedroom— "my partner, Annabel Reed, will be in New York tomorrow on other business. I thought it might be a good time to make contact with you and to see whether there is some field of understanding that could be established."

"I'd rather see you, Mr. Smith."

"Well, as you can imagine, being the Ewalds' attorney in this matter is going to keep me anchored to Washington for quite a while. You seemed anxious to move on this. Ms. Reed has my total confidence and can speak for me." He wanted to add, "Take it or leave it."

"Yeah, I suppose so. Will four o'clock be convenient?"

"Yes, I'm sure it will be. Her other appointments are in the morning." They made the date, and Greist gave Smith his address on Manhattan's West Side.

Smith picked up the phone and called an old friend in Connecticut, Morgan Tubbs, a partner in a Wall Street law firm. He reached Tubbs at his home, and after the smallest of small talk, got to the point. "Morgan, could you have someone up there run a background check for me tomorrow morning on a New York attorney named Herbert Greist?"

"Happy to, Mac. What's his connection with Ewald?"

"No connection."

"I was really shocked, I have to tell you, when I heard you had agreed to represent the Ewald son. I thought you were out of litigation for good."

"Nothing is forever, as they say."

Tubbs laughed. "I heard a rumor that you were doing this for Senator Ewald to try and keep his campaign on track. I'd like to think that was an altruistic act on your part, but rumor also goes on to say that if Ewald becomes president, I'm talking to our next attorney general."

"No, you're speaking with an old friend who's taken some time off to help another friend, and who will be scurrying back to academia as soon as possible."

"As you wish, Mac. I'll be happy to see what I can come up with on Greist. Where can I reach you tomorrow morning, at home?"

Smith started to affirm that, then said, "No, Morgan, I've established an office in the Watergate Hotel. It's suite 1117. I should be there by late morning."

"Talk to you then."

Smith told Annabel that he would call her in New York before her meeting and fill her in on what he'd learned about Greist from Tubbs. Then he called Tony Buffolino at the Watergate, but there was no answer.

That afternoon, they went to Smith's Foggy Bottom house, where he prepared a list of things he wanted to accomplish the next day and fed Rufus. Later he suggested, "Let's take a nice, long, leisurely walk. It might be the last time for a while we can just do nothing together."

"Were we doing nothing together this morning?"

"No," he said, smiling, "we were doing everything."

They ended up at the Mall, where they strolled through the Museum of American History, had an early dinner at Clyde's in Georgetown, and spent the rest of the evening at Annabel's. She finished reading the newspapers, and he skimmed through a copy of *The A.B.C. Murders,* an old Agatha Christie novel that he found on Annabel's bookshelves, and that set his mind toward detection, discovery, and looking twice at the obvious.

He returned to his house at eleven, walked Rufus, and immediately went to bed.

16

AFTER DROPPING ANNABEL off at National Airport to catch the crowded 8 A.M. shuttle, he went to a business machine store and arranged to have necessary office equipment delivered to the Watergate. He made another stop at an office supply store and ordered basic supplies.

Buffolino was at the suite when Smith arrived shortly before eleven.

"Nice suit," Smith said.

"Thanks. I needed some new threads if I'm going to be hanging around a place like this."

"Where did you get it?"

"Downstairs. They got a men's shop."

Smith raised one eyebrow.

"It was on sale."

"I see. Are you comfortable enough here, Tony?"

"Jesus, sure I am. I really appreciate you going for this, Mac." Buffolino looked around the living room. "Brings back old memories."

"Unpleasant ones, I assume," said Smith. "Frankly, I was surprised . . . no, shocked is more like it, that you actually chose this suite to stay in."

Buffolino shrugged. "Yeah, well, I figured I'd relive the crime, like. Know what I mean? You see, I was afraid of this place. My life went south here. Actually, it's not as unpleasant as I figured it might be. Funny, when I walked in here, I could almost see that dirtbag Garcia sitting in the chair. That's one thing I'd like to do before I pack it in, Mac."

"What's that, Tony?"

"Find him and settle the score."

"Tony, that case is closed. Still, when this one is over, you'll have enough money to buy a plane ticket to Panama, if you want. He went back, didn't he?"

"That's what I heard."

"You'd be on his turf."

"That's okay," Tony said grimly. "He was on mine."

Smith told Tony about the things to be delivered that day, and also said that there was the possibility he'd have to go to San Francisco, not only to dig a little further into Andrea Feldman's background, but to find her mother, too.

"Hey, great," Buffolino said. "Always wanted to see Frisco. Good thing I bought this suit. Maybe I should get another."

"That one looks like it will travel well, Tony."

The message sank in, and Buffolino made a mental note not to bring up any further mentions of personal expenditures. He said, "You know, Mac, you're okay, putting me up in a place like this. I never figured you'd pop for it, but . . . well, I just want you to know I appreciate everything you've done for me. Including what you done for me when IA set me up in here. I didn't much go for it then, but I know you did right by me."

Smith was becoming slightly embarrassed, and was relieved when the phone rang. He picked it up.

"Mac, Morgan Tubbs."

"Good morning, Morgan. Come up with anything on Greist?"

"An interesting, albeit unsavory, character," said Tubbs. "Let's see, Herbert Greist is fifty-eight years old, a graduate of City College Law at the age of thirty. After passing the Bar, he worked for the public defender for four years after which he became deeply involved with the ACLU, but only for a year. He's been in private practice ever since. There seems to have been a series of offices, the latest of which is on West Seventy-eighth."

"Yes, I have that address," Smith said. "So far, I fail to see why you consider him to be unsavory—or even interesting."

"Well, Mac, here's what led me to say that. Herbert Greist seems to have a penchant for affiliating with what some would see as our less patriotic element."

" 'Less patriotic'?"

"Yes. Of course, none of this comes from official sources, but as it happens, we have a young attorney here whose uncle was once involved with Greist through—well, none of that matters. What our young associate tells me is that he called his uncle, and his uncle informed him that Greist's practice is rather restricted to lower-echelon socialist and Communist sympathizers who run afoul of authorities. According to the uncle, the FBI and CIA have dossiers on Greist several yards in length and continue to add to them."

Buffolino motioned to Smith across the room that there was a carafe of fresh coffee. Smith nodded—yes, he wanted a cup—and said, "The FBI and CIA run files on anyone who subscribes to *The Nation* and who drinks pink lemonade. That doesn't mean Greist is a fellow traveler." His use of that old-fashioned, McCarthy-era term made him smile.

"True, but there is more juice here than pink lemonade, Mac."

"Being facetious," Smith said.

Tubb's voice suddenly turned jarringly proper. "I certainly hope so."

Smith asked, "Any indication that Greist ever practiced law in San Francisco?"

"As a matter of fact, there is. He evidently was general counsel for a little more than a year to the Embarcadero Opera Company." Tubbs laughed. "Pornographic opera, no doubt, being in San Francisco."

"Wrong," Smith said. "It's a small, ambitious, and pretty damn good opera company. General counsel? Doesn't make sense. Performing companies like that are lucky to get a young opera-buff attorney to look over their lease. They don't have general counsels."

"Well, that's what I was told. That's right, I forgot you were an inveterate opera lover. You must miss New York."

"Not at all," Smith said. "The Washington Opera Company is first-rate. You say he was general counsel to the Embarcadero group. When was he out there?"

"Three years ago, I believe."

"Hmmm," Smith said, thinking back to a benefit performance for the Embarcadero Company he had attended in that same year at which an impressive array of singers had appeared. He'd had that same thought during Roseanna Gateaux's performance at the Ewald gala the night Andrea Feldman was murdered: She'd been one of the stars who'd lent her name and talent to the fund-raising event for the struggling San Francisco company.

"Anything else interesting?" Smith asked.

"No, Mac, that's about it. There were some Bar Association complaints against him, but action was never taken other than a few talks. Just your average, run-of-the-mill lowlife barrister." He gave forth with a hearty laugh.

Smith winced at the characterization. It was undoubtedly true, but Morgan Tubbs made such characterizations of anyone who hadn't graduated from an Ivy League school, and who dealt in any aspect of the law other than corporate high finance. "Thanks, Morgan, I appreciate your help."

"My pleasure, Mac, but you have to promise to fill me in on all the intrigue the next time you get to New York."

Smith managed not to commit to that before hanging up.

He sipped from the cup of coffee Buffolino had handed him, found a phone number on a scrap of paper in his pocket, and called it. Moments later, he was connected to Annabel's suite at the Plaza. "How was the flight?" he asked.

"Fine. The suite is lovely."

"Glad to hear it." He filled her in on what he'd learned about Herbert Greist.

"Mac."

"What?"

"I just had a chill."

"Turn up the heat," he said.

"Not that kind of chill, Mac, one that comes from inside. I can't explain it, but something tells me this is about to become a lot more complicated than you anticipated."

Smith laughed. "I think it will all be considerably simpler when you've had a chance to hear what Greist is really after. By the way, Annabel, see if you can get a handle on where Mrs. Feldman is."

"I have that on my list of questions. Where will you be when I'm done with him?"

"Hard to say. I might be here at the Watergate." He told her of steps he'd taken that morning to equip the place. "I want to get over to Ken and Leslie's house sometime today. I know they're about to hit the campaign trail again, and there are questions I need to have answered. I also want to stop in and see Paul, and to keep looking for Janet. In the rush of things, I've almost forgotten I have a client. Try me at home if you can't get me at either of those two places. I'll be anxious to hear how it goes."

Smith had no sooner hung up when there was a knock on the door. Buffolino, who was reclining on the couch, jumped up and said, "Hey, must be lunch. I forgot I ordered it." He opened the door and a young man in a starched white jacket, white shirt, and black bow tie wheeled in a serving cart covered with pristine linen. He removed metal covers from dishes, and took pains to make sure all the elements were in perfect order.

"Yeah, thanks, looks great," Buffolino said, handing him some bills.

Smith came over to see what was on the table. There was a large shrimp cocktail, filet mignon, shoestring potatoes, an arugola-and-endive salad, hot rolls, and a shimmering, undulating crème caramel.

Buffolino gave Smith a sheepish grin. "Want some?" he asked. "I can't eat all of this."

"No, but thanks anyway, Tony. Go ahead and eat before it gets cold."

Buffolino wedged the linen napkin between his shirt collar and neck and started in.

"What are your plans for the rest of the day?" Smith asked.

"I got some calls in around town, and out on the Coast. I figure I'll concentrate on trying to find Ewald's wife, Janet, unless you got something else for me to do."

"Nothing specific. Be here when they deliver the equipment and supplies, if that won't inconvenience you."

Smith's sarcasm was sharper than the knife Buffolino was using to cut his steak. He shook his head. "Hell, Mac, I'm yours. You can count on me."

Smith left for the Ewald house. Tony Buffolino wiped his mouth, got up, and called the house where his second wife and two daughters lived. One of them, Irene, answered. "Hey, babe, it's Daddy," Buffolino said.

"Hello, Daddy." Her response was pointedly cold, but Tony knew better than to mention it. He was a lousy father, and he'd never denied it. He hadn't seen Irene or her younger sister, Marie, in over six months. "Hey, look, Irene," he said, keeping his tone upbeat, "your old man's made a score, a big one, big names, the biggest. You know them all, you read about them in the paper. They're paying some good dough, and I'm set up here at a suite in the Watergate Hotel like some rich Arab in with the oil money." He waited for a response, received none. "I want you and your sister to come up for a little party. Mom, too. It'll be nice to spend a little time together. They got swimming pools inside and out, the best food you ever ate, the works. It's a suite, a real big suite with more than one room. The furniture is all leather. What do you say?"

"I'll have to ask Mommy."

"Her, too, remember. Dinner's on me, for her, too."

His daughter put down the phone, and Buffolino heard soft female voices in the background. When she came back on the line, Irene asked, "When?"

"I was thinking about tonight, if you guys can make it. I think I'll be heading for Frisco—San Francisco—in a day or two, maybe be gone a week, who knows? Yeah, how about tonight?"

His ex-wife took the phone from her daughter. "Tony, what is this crap?"

"No crap, babe. Come see for yourself. Please, you and the girls."

"You're sure?"

"Yup, I'm sure. Seven o'clock, suite 1117. Make it seven-thirty. I got to run some errands."

"Tony, if this ends up some . . ."

"Trust me, babe, and everybody dress up. Remember how you always wanted to try caviar?"

"Yes." She couldn't help but laugh.

"You tasted it since we split?"

"No, but everything else has tasted better ever since."

He let the comment slide. "Tonight's the night, babe, all the caviar you want, and buckets a' champagne. *Ciao!*"

As Buffolino finished his lunch at the Watergate, a limousine carrying Senator Jody Backus and Ken Ewald's campaign manager, Ed Farmer, pulled up in front of Anton's Loyal Opposition Bar and Restaurant. Since opening a few years earlier, on First Street NE, on Capitol Hill, it had become a favorite hangout for members of Congress. Backus hadn't been there since deciding to run against Ewald, but he'd been announcing to his staff lately that he missed it, needed "someplace normal where this ol' boy is comfortable." His staff knew that his real need was Anton's blackened redfish. He'd been expressing a yen for it for the past three days.

"What a pleasure to see you again, Senator," a tuxedoed host said at the door.

"Same here, Frank," Backus said. "Trouble with runnin' for office is that everybody wants you in places you damn well don't want to be. You've got the black redfish ready?"

Frank laughed. "Of course. The minute your office called, I made sure we did. Your usual table?"

"That'll be fine."

They were led through the restaurant, where Backus, to the trailing agent's chagrin, stopped to shake hands. Farmer watched the senator from Georgia with intense interest. Despite being overweight and crass, and with a tendency to sweat even in the blast of an air conditioner, there was an unmistakable dignity to the man. He almost looked elegant, which, Farmer rationalized, was the result of the power he wielded. Power seemed to iron out wrinkles in suits, and to assign a certain charm to crude behavior.

They moved past two large glass panels on which a donkey and elephant were etched, and to a banquette in the rear. Etched-glass panels along the back of each bench created a relatively private setting. Backus struggled to maneuver his bulk into the banquette. Across from him, the lithe Farmer slid easily into place.

Backus was sweating as he said to the host, "Bring me my usual Blanton's on the rocks and a side a' soda water. What are you drinkin', Mr. Farmer?"

"Perrier, please."

Backus's laugh was a low rumble. "Someday, Mr. Farmer, somebody will give a satisfactory explanation to this simple ol' farm boy why people pay for water in a fancy bottle when it's free out of a' any ol' tap."

"Marketing, Senator," Farmer said.

"Like sellin' a politician, huh?"

"I suppose you could draw the analogy." Farmer's small face was particularly tight above his yellow-and-brown polka-dot bow tie. His glasses were oversized on the bridge of an aquiline nose. He glanced quickly across the room to where the Secret Service agents sat in their own banquette. He said to Backus, "I would have preferred to meet in an office."

"I know you would prefer that, Mr. Farmer, but I had to get out of offices, settle in a public place where real people congregate. I need that like a drug addict needs his daily fix." Farmer started to say something, but Backus continued. "Your boss could use a little of that, too, you know. He's an insular fella, I'll say that for him. Likes to be alone too much. Sometimes, I see a little Richard Nixon in him." Backus's fleshy face sagged. His smile was gone. He leaned as far forward as his girth would allow and said, "I worry about Kenneth Ewald. He's like a son to me. I think the rigors of this campaign"—a slight smile returned —"and the rigors of an active social life, to say nothin' of fulfilling his role as a family man and havin' to stand tall where his son is involved, are takin' their toll. You agree?"

"No, sir, I don't. Senator Ewald is holding up quite nicely."

"Damn shame what happened to that Feldman girl the other night."

"A tragedy."

"Certainly for her. Have you seen Paul?"

"Since his arrest? No."

"Awful thing for a mother and father to have to face, havin' your only son a murder suspect."

"That's all he is at this point, Senator, a suspect."

"Don't think he did the evil deed, huh?"

"I don't know."

Backus sat back and slapped beefy hands on the dusty rose tablecloth. "Take a look at the menu, Mr. Farmer. I recommend the blackened redfish, but everything's pretty good here."

A waiter brought their drinks. Backus raised his glass filled with rich, amber bourbon, and said, "To the next four years of a Democratic administration. A-men!"

Farmer sipped his water and stared at Backus. Personally, Farmer found Backus to be everything he despised in politics. But one thing Ed Farmer never wanted to be accused of was naiveté. Personal responses meant little in Washington and politics. More important was the aura of power that Backus exuded, his crass style be damned. The big southern senator's body count topped that of everyone else in Congress, and he knew the location, width, and depth of every grave.

Backus locked eyes with Farmer as he downed his drink and waved for a waiter to bring him another.

"Sir?" the waiter asked Farmer.

"A small bottle of Château Giscours Margeaux, '83, please."

"That's what I like to see," said Backus. "I don't much care for wine, but—"

"Senator, could we get to the point of why we're here?"

Backus swallowed his annoyance at being interrupted. "That would be sincerely appreciated, Mr. Farmer. Proceed. This is your meeting."

"And your check?"

"If you insist. I suppose Ken Ewald doesn't pay you a hell of a lot."

"Money didn't motivate me into politics. Public service did."

"Just like me," Backus said. "What'll Ken Ewald toss you if he makes it, Mr. Farmer, chief a' staff? Press secretary? Health, Education and Welfare? I'd heartily endorse the latter. You'd be damn good givin' out welfare to the shiftless nonproducers of this society."

Farmer sniffed the wine, tasted it, nodded to the waiter, and returned his attention to the large man across from him. "Some people are suggesting it might be time to talk about a coalition."

"Coalition? With who?"

"You and him."

Backus laughed. "I figured that'd be comin' up. Senator Ewald must be a mite nervous these days about the way things are goin'."

"There's some truth to that," Farmer said flatly.

"No wonder. I heard him say in that speech he gave last week that the Republicans have had a lock on the White House all these years, and that he is the one who has what it takes to pick that lock. Nice phrase your speechwriters came up with, but the fact is, I don't think your master, Ken Ewald, is in a position to pick anybody's lock these days, not with havin' one of his staff members murdered with his own weapon, and havin' most fingers pointin' at his own son. Tell me, Ed, what's your honest evaluation of the possibility that Paul Ewald killed that poor young thing?"

Farmer hesitated before saying, "I don't think Paul Ewald killed Andrea Feldman."

"You don't sound like you're brimmin' over with conviction, Ed."

"No one knows what happened," Farmer said.

"And from Ken Ewald's perspective, just as well nobody does know, least not till after November." Backus cocked his head and smiled smugly. "Know what, Ed? I don't think your boss is goin' to make it at the convention. What do you think?"

Farmer sipped his wine.

"Just how nervous is your man?" Backus asked.

"Probably not as nervous as you hope," Farmer replied. "He's ignoring any pressure to offer you the vice-presidency up front."

"That's about the only thing I agree with him about. I don't intend to be anybody's vice-president. You hear me? You make sure Senator Ewald hears me."

"Yes, I heard you," Farmer said, touching the end of his bow tie, then examining a class ring on his finger.

"I suggest we eat," Backus said, "unless you've got more to say."

"No, I have nothing more to say, Senator Backus, except that your toast to a Democratic administration won't mean much if Ken Ewald doesn't make it at the convention."

"I don't read it that way. Seems to me that all he has to do is keep on the course he's takin', and this country might be proposin' a toast to this ol' southern boy on November nine. That wouldn't upset you too much, would it, Ed?" Backus's moonlike face was quiescent; the liquor had added a touch of color.

"I suppose not," Farmer said, "although having you as president, Senator Backus, wouldn't represent much of a change from the past eight years, a donkey instead of an elephant, but not much else different."

Backus looked above Farmer's head to the etched donkey and elephant on the glass behind him. He smiled, said, "At least we'd have a president who's in the mainstream of American thought."

"Like President Manning," Farmer said.

"Manning's not a bad fella, just handin' out favors to the wrong people."

"Like Colonel Morales and the Reverend Kane?"

"Hell, no. Morales is fightin' for freedom in Panama, and the last I heard, the American people stand up for freedom. As for the Reverend Kane, he tends to people's souls."

"Unless they're Panamanian. Then he tends to their stockpile of weapons."

"You sound like your boss, Ed," Backus said.

"I'm supposed to sound like him. I'm his campaign manager."

Backus nodded and narrowed his eyes. "I like you, Ed. I like a man who says what he's supposed to say even though it don't necessarily represent what he thinks."

"I believe in what Ken Ewald stands for," Farmer said.

"Unless he's not sittin' in a chair where he can put his ideas into action."

Farmer's smile was thin. "Like you, Senator Backus, proclaiming your wholehearted support of Ken if he gets the nomination."

"I'm a Democrat. I owe my allegiance to whoever comes out of the convention as the candidate. I just hope it isn't Ken Ewald. I got grave doubts about where he might lead this country."

"And you would prefer someone, Democrat or Republican, who espouses the Manning doctrine."

Backus leaned forward and his voice became slightly fatherly. "Ed, we've still got us a two-party system, Democrats and Republicans, but that doesn't mean a hell of a lot anymore. What matters today is political vision, not party labels."

Farmer listened silently to the quiet speech he was given by Backus. The southern senator was right, of course. There had been a shift from a two-party system in which Democrats and Republicans competed for elected office, to one in which conservatives and liberals did the vying, Democrats and Republicans sometimes joining forces on the Right, against Democrats and Republicans hooking up together in an equally uneasy alliance on the Left. Philosophy or ideology had supplanted party politics. "The cause," no matter what it was, had been elevated above allegiance to party which, some claimed, represented a positive step in that it caused the men and women of Congress and the executive to act according to their consciences, rather than along strict party lines. Under the old system, it would have made sense to pair people like Ewald and Backus together to combine the liberal and conservative voters. North and South. Big-city guy and rural American representative. But such coalitions were no longer viable. Ewald and Backus were polar opposites. The fact was—and Farmer knew it—Ken Ewald, despite his seemingly immense popularity, and his victory in a majority of the primaries, did not represent the mainstream of American thought. He was too liberal, too linked to big-budget social programs, perceived as being too soft on crime and national defense. Ewald's nomination could end up yet another example of the Democrats' penchant for self-destruction, a candidate who stood for the principles of the party but not the principles of the majority of the American voters. McCarthy. McGovern. Carter. Dukakis. Ewald.

After they ordered, Backus said, "You're obviously an ambitious fella, Ed."

"Yes, I have ambition."

"Seems like everybody in Washington has ambition."

"You aren't critical of that, are you, Senator? I'd say Senator Jody Backus has demonstrated a fair amount of ambition in his career."

"A different thing, Ed. A politician's ambitions are based upon his desire to serve the public. Then there are all those ambitious men and women lookin' to grab onto his coattails. That's how some politicians get in trouble, havin' the wrong young men and women hangin' on their coattails."

Farmer's thin nostrils flared. "Are you including me in that category, Senator Backus? It seems to me you ought to be more respectful of my ambition."

Backus gave him a conciliatory smile. "Don't take personal offense, Ed. I just call it like I see it. Your level of ambition certainly hasn't been lost on me."

Farmer said nothing.

"You see, Mr. Farmer, I *like* ambition in young men, big dreams, feet gettin' bigger along with the head, climbin' and stretchin' and sniffin' around the ones who can do them the most good. Of course, I'm not talking about loyalty here. Lots a' times, loyalty and ambition don't go hand in hand."

"I'm not sure I appreciate the tone this conversation is taking," Farmer said.

"Now ain't that too bad."

"I happen to be a very loyal person, Senator."

"Depends on how you define it, Ed. What do you figure got that nice young woman killed—too much ambition, too much loyalty, or not enough common sense when it came to the people she chose to run with?"

"I wouldn't know," Farmer said in a low voice.

The waiter arrived with their appetizers. Farmer touched his mouth with his napkin, slid out of the booth, and said to the restaurant host, "I just remembered an important appointment." He turned to Backus and said as pleasantly as possible, "I really hate to leave, Senator. Enjoy your blackened redfish, and thank you for the wine. It was palatable."

Mac Smith waited a long time in the study before Ken Ewald came through the door. "Sorry, Mac, but things get crazier every day."

When they were seated, Smith asked Ewald a number of questions that had been on his mind. Then he said, "Ken, we are alone in this room. You mentioned to me that the night Andrea Feldman was murdered, you'd left your office to meet with a woman at the Watergate Hotel."

Ewald glanced nervously at the door.

"I'm not in the habit of informing wives about husbands' indiscretions, Ken, but I have to know everything that occurred that night, with every*one.*"

"I don't see why."

"Because you've brought me into this situation. You've asked me to be Paul's attorney if he's charged, and although he hasn't been yet, there is every possibility that he will be, depending on what MPD manages to come up with. You can't bring me in and then stonewall me."

"Yes, of course, you're right, Mac, but what contribution could revealing this woman's identity possibly make to your defense of Paul, if it comes to that?"

"I don't know, Ken, but I learned long ago not to censor myself until I had the facts. When I have the facts, I can make a determination whether it contributes or not. I do not intend to be surprised at answers the DA may come up with."

Ewald sighed and said, "Okay." He cast another quick look at the door, lowered his voice, and asked, "What is it you want to know?"

"Simple. Who was the woman at the Watergate?"

Ewald frowned. "Mac, I really don't think . . ."

Smith stared at Ewald across the small space separating them. "Who was it?" he asked again.

"All right. But I'm putting tremendous trust in you."

"You have to. Do it with confidence."

"I worked in my office until about two in the morning," Ewald said. "And then . . ."

He'd called his home before leaving the office, got Marcia Mims, and said to her, "Tell Mrs. Ewald I'll be here quite late. A last-minute meeting has come up."

"Yes, sir," Marcia said.

His unmarked blue Cadillac was at the curb in front of the office building. The driver opened a rear door for the presidential candidate and his bodyguard, Agent Jeroldson. "To the Watergate," Ewald told the driver. "Go in the garage."

The driver made a U-turn, and a few minutes later came to a stop in front of a small service elevator beneath the Watergate. "I'll be back here soon," Ewald said as he and Jeroldson got out of the car and pushed a button next to the elevator. They stepped in and rode to the twelfth floor, where Jeroldson fell behind Ewald as they walked down the hushed, carpeted corridor until reaching the door to a suite at the far end. Ewald poised to knock, then looked back at Jeroldson, who momentarily locked eyes with him, then looked away at an elaborate flower arrangement on a table. "Meet me downstairs at four," Ewald said. "You're free until then."

Jeroldson nodded, which angered Ewald. Every other Secret Service agent who'd been assigned to him was courteous, would have said, "Yes, sir." Ewald almost said so, but stopped himself. Another time. "You're relieved," he said. "Please go." He watched the square-shouldered, thick-necked agent slowly turn and walk toward a bank of public elevators. He waited until Jeroldson had punched the button before knocking.

"Ken?" a voice asked from behind the door.

Ewald looked to where Jeroldson stood. The elevator had arrived, but Jeroldson hadn't entered it. He was looking at Ewald, motionless, his eyes conveying one final, mute message. He stepped into the elevator.

An eye confirmed the identity of the visitor through the peephole. The door was unlocked and opened. Ewald stared at the thick, loose black hair flowing over the shoulders of the white silk robe she wore. A large diamond suspended on a gold chain rested on the upper ivory reaches of her stunning breasts. Her fingers, bright crimson nail polish at their tips, were laden with rings. Her bare toes were tipped in the same red. A heavy scent of Joy filled the doorway, the perfume causing an instant and involuntary physical reaction in him. Leslie used only an occasional dab of Mitsouko, or L'Air du Temps, preferring the smell of soap. Ewald liked that smell, too . . . on her. But this—this you could swim into. . . .

Roseanna Gateaux stepped back, a smile on her lips. Ewald gave one final glance at the hallway, stepped over the threshold, embraced the voluptuous, warm, and welcoming body of the famous diva, and gently kicked the door shut.

"Satisfied?" Ewald asked.

"Nothing to be satisfied about, Ken, but at least the question has been answered."

"I assume you know the great faith I have in you to have told you."

"Yes, okay." Smith stood. "I really have to go. We'll keep in touch."

As they stood at the front door, Ewald said, "I just want you to know, Mackensie Smith, how much Leslie and I appreciate what you're doing for us. I don't think there is another person in this country we could turn to with such confidence."

Smith grunted. "I'm doing it for you and for Paul. I'll be in touch."

17

ANNABEL REED SAT in a closet-sized, sparsely furnished office on West Seventy-eighth Street in Manhattan. A small sign on the door read HERBERT GREIST ATTORNEY-AT-LAW. He had no receptionist or secretary. If there had been one, she wouldn't have had a place to sit.

Greist was a big but stooped man with flowing gray hair. He wore a rumpled black sharkskin suit; a tailor's nightmare, Annabel thought. His right shoulder was considerably lower than his left, and his right arm noticeably longer than his left. It gave the overall effect of a man about to fall to one side. His face was sallow and loose. Sunken eyes were surrounded by circles the color of forest mushrooms.

"Sit down, Ms. Reed, please sit down." He held out his hand and she took it, glad she was wearing gloves. "You'll have to forgive this office. I'm in the process of moving to quarters in midtown and am using this temporarily."

Sure you are, Annabel thought.

She sat in a rickety cane chair while Greist went back behind a cheap wooden desk, the veneer chipped off in places, the edges scarred from too many unattended cigars. "Mind if I smoke?" he asked as he drew one from his inside jacket pocket.

"No, not at all," she said, knowing that to protest would have been futile. She watched him light up and drop the dead match in a large once-amber ashtray overflowing with ashes.

"Frankly, Ms. Reed, I would have preferred to speak directly with Mr. Smith," Greist said, exhaling smoke.

"That may be," Annabel said, "but Mr. Smith is terribly busy in Washington. I'm completely familiar with the content of your telephone conversation with him, and have full authority to act on behalf of Mr. Smith, and our clients."

"Clients. The Ewald family. It's a fortunate law firm that has as a client the man who could be the next president of the United States."

"We were involved with the Ewald family long before Senator Ewald chose to run for the presidency. Now, Mr. Greist, could we get to the point? You indicate that Mrs. Feldman intends to file a federal suit for the loss of her daughter's civil rights."

Another cloud of blue smoke left his mouth as he leaned back and thought for a moment. "Yes. She is thinking of doing so. And certainly with justification."

"We would debate that. Still, you indicated that your client, Mrs. Feldman, was open to the idea of a settlement. Settlement is probably out of the question. But if it were a question, what kind of numbers are you talking about?"

Greist placed the cigar on the heap already in the ashtray, leaned forward on his elbows so that his chin rested in the palms of his hands, and managed a weak smile. "Directly to the point, I see," he said, with little energy behind his words.

"Yes, I don't see anything to be gained by sitting here stringing out this discussion. How much money does your client feel will adequately compensate her for the loss of her daughter?"

"That is hard to say, Ms. Reed."

Annabel smiled. "I would suggest it become easier soon, or we have nothing to talk about, Mr. Greist."

He retrieved his cigar and leaned back again. "Let me see," he said. "Would a half-million dollars shock you?"

"I don't shock easily," she said. "The fact that it is a ludicrous number probably has more effect on you. You are, of course, joking."

"Not at all." Smoke clouded his face. He coughed and rubbed his eyes.

She stood and waited until he could again speak. Looking down at him, she said, "Mr. Greist, you have wasted my time and my law firm's money in arranging this meeting. I would like to speak with your client. Perhaps we could arrange it while I'm in New York."

"My client is not in New York."

"Then why are you representing her?"

"I, too, go back a long way with my client's family. Of course, I don't have the luxury of representing rich and powerful political figures as you and Mr. Smith do, but I assure you our resolve is no less adamant." He stood, taller than she'd remembered when he first greeted her. He said, "I suggest that there are other, mitigating circumstances that might cause you and Mr. Smith to reconsider the amount of compensation with which we can be comfortable. There are aspects of Senator Ewald's life that came to be known to my client, and to her daughter. Those 'things' have a certain intrinsic value—once you are aware of the nature of them, I'm sure you will agree."

Reed wasn't sure how to react. "You are suggesting blackmail of Senator Ewald and his family."

It was the first wide smile Greist had exhibited, and it revealed teeth that had been tortured or neglected. "Blackmail? That is a terrible word. I prefer to view the sale of information as being simply that, a commercial transaction. My client has information that your client would benefit from, and I am suggesting it has a certain worth."

"More than the loss of your client's civil rights, I assume."

"As you wish."

"What is this information that Senator Ewald would want to pay a great deal of money to retrieve?"

"That, Ms. Reed, is for another day, another meeting. You'll be here a few days?"

"Yes. I'm staying at the—I'm at a hotel."

"Are you free tomorrow evening?"

"No, I am not, and I must say that I resent the entire tone of this meeting."

"Might I suggest, then, that you call Mr. Smith and tell him what has transpired at this *distasteful* meeting. As counsel to the next president of the United States, he might put a more liberal interpretation on it than you exhibit. I can be reached here tomorrow between one and three in the afternoon. Thank you for coming."

She walked back to the Plaza, her mind racing, her anger barely under control. There was a nip in the air; she pulled her gloves from the pocket of her raincoat, and in her annoyance, one of them fell to the pavement. She stopped quickly and turned to pick it up. The man behind her seemed startled at her abrupt halt and change of direction. He looked away, then pretended to peer at items in a store window. Lingerie. Reed picked up her glove, glanced back at him one more time, and walked quickly to the hotel, where she took a shower—which seemed symbolic—ordered a bottle of white wine to be sent to the room, and called Smith at the Watergate. She got the new answering machine. She had the same luck with his home number. Finally, with some hesitation, she dialed the Ewald house. The phone was answered by the head housekeeper. "Yes, ma'am," Marcia Mims said, "he was here, but he's left."

Annabel gave the housekeeper the same message she'd left on both of Smith's answering machines, that he was to call her in New York as soon as possible. She gave Marcia Mims her number at the hotel, and hung up as room service arrived.

Glass in hand, she stood at the window and looked down over the street where people were heading home from their jobs. How routine our lives are so much of the time, she told herself. Then she was forced to smile. She could understand a bit better why Mac Smith had accepted the offer to defend Paul Ewald. It broke the sought-after routine of the college professor, just as coming to New York to meet with Greist had broken her routine at the gallery. Maybe she should ease up on Mac a little. Maybe not.

She sat on the housing that covered the suite's heating system and shook her head. Herbert Greist trying to blackmail the next president. Tony Buffolino going to San Francisco to find the mother of a slain girl. Politics. Adultery. Blackmail. Murder.

"Hey, kids," she said softly to the passersby below, "you don't know what you're missing."

By the time Mac Smith returned to the suite at the Watergate, all deliveries had been made and the living room had begun to look like a working office. There was a note on the table: "Be back around six—I got something to talk to you about. Tony."

Smith called Annabel in New York, and she recounted for him her conversation with Herbert Greist. Smith took notes while she talked. When she was finished, he said, "He told you that there was damaging information about Ken that both Andrea Feldman *and* her mother had?"

"Yes, that's what he said, Mac. I made notes after I got back to the hotel."

"No idea what information that might be, or how the Feldman ladies got it?"

"No. I should have asked more questions, but frankly, I was anxious to get out of there. He's a communicable disease."

Smith considered telling her what he'd learned about Ewald's liaison with Roseanna Gateaux at the Watergate the night of the murder, but decided not to do it over the telephone.

"Greist wants to get together with me again tomorrow night," Annabel said.

"Are you?"

"I told him I couldn't, but I'm thinking now it might be a good idea. He gives me the creeps, but maybe I can find out more."

"Do whatever you think is right, Annabel, but be careful. Somebody murdered Andrea Feldman, and I don't think it was Paul Ewald."

"I'll watch myself," she said. The man who'd been behind her when she dropped her glove suddenly flashed across her mind. She didn't mention him. Overactive imagination.

"Good luck with whatever it is you're going after for the gallery," he said.

"I almost forgot about that," she said, laughing with relief. "I'll fill you in when I get back. Or sell it to you."

Smith had just poured himself a well-watered drink when Buffolino returned.

"Where've you been?" Smith asked.

"Having a pop with an old friend of mine from the IRS."

Smith smiled. "Not a bad friend to have."

"Yeah, he's come in handy over the years. I got him out of a jam when I was still on the force, one of those personal sex things that would have blown him out of the water. Anyway, he owes me, and every once in a while I remind him."

"Having tax problems, Tony?"

"Me? Nah. I don't make enough to have tax problems."

Smith raised his eyebrows.

"Well, until now. I mean, I wasn't doin' as good as I told you I was."

Smith said nothing.

Buffolino sat in a leather chair and put his feet on the coffee table. "I had my friend check out tax returns for Feldman and her mother."

Smith cocked his head. "And?"

"And they file every year, only there isn't a lot of money to account for. Andrea Feldman never got paid much working for causes. Her mother lists some income from work, but she basically is on Social Security and some interest from small investments. Nothing major league."

"What kind of work does the mother do?"

"My friend says she lists herself as a consultant."

"What kind of consultant?"

"Like all consultants, unemployed."

"Any leads on where the mother might be?"

"Disappeared, like Janet Ewald. I checked a friend at the PD. He tells me no one was ever able to make contact with the old lady to tell her her daughter was dead."

"She knows, Tony."

"How could she miss it, with all the stories on the tube and in the papers?"

Smith had been debating with himself about how much to tell Buffolino. As a good lawyer, he knew he could only be as effective as information given him by a client, and the same tended to be true for an investigator. Yet he was reluctant to reveal too much of the Ewald family's private affairs. He decided to tell Buffolino about the blackmail attempt by Herbert Greist, but keep Ken Ewald's liaison with Roseanna Gateaux to himself.

When he was finished recounting what had transpired with Greist and Annabel in New York, Buffolino said, "Weird family."

"Certainly not conventional."

"Maybe the old lady doesn't want to be found because her daughter was murdered."

"I don't follow," Smith said.

"Why else would she lie low? People who get murdered make their families feel guilty somehow. Like they were all victims—or all at fault, know what I mean? You got any better answers?"

"No, I don't. Except that I think you'd better get out to San Francisco as quickly as possible and see if you can track her down. You might also try to find out where she did her banking, whether there were any accounts for her or for her daughter. Since you seem to have friends everywhere, I assume that extends to California."

Buffolino smiled. "Mac, I got friends in every state, including a good one with Wells Fargo in Frisco. When do you want me to go?"

"How about tomorrow?"

"On my way."

"Nothin' new on our other missing person? I came up dry so far," Buffolino admitted as he went to the kitchen to make himself a drink.

"No, nothing. That's really the most pressing matter to be resolved. If it weren't for this Greist character in New York, I wouldn't be so concerned with finding Mae Feldman. Any ideas on how we can push the police to find Janet?"

"They don't take any push from me," Buffolino said. The phone rang. "I'll get it," he offered. "It's for you, Mac."

"Mr. Smith, this is Marcia Mims."

"Yes, Marcia, how are you?"

There was a long pause. ". . . Mr. Smith, I really think we should talk."

Smith heard music and voices in the background. He also heard both the urgency and the hesitation in her voice. "I'll be happy to talk to you any time, Marcia," he said.

"There are things you have to know, Mr. Smith, and I really have to talk to somebody I can trust."

"Fine. When would you like to get together?"

"I was hoping . . ."

"You were hoping we could do it right away. I don't see any reason why not. I have a suite here at the Watergate. Maybe you could—"

"Mr. Smith, I know you're very busy and I don't want to inconvenience you, but I'm not in the city. Tomorrow is my day off, and I came to Annapolis to stay with my cousin Tommy tonight. He owns a crab-cake restaurant in the Market House."

"What's the name of his place?"

"Tommy's."

"Of course. I can head over there in a little while."

"I'll be here waiting for you, and thank you, thank you very much."

"Just sit tight, Marcia. See you in about an hour."

"What was that all about?" Buffolino asked after Smith hung up.

"The Ewalds' housekeeper, Marcia Mims. Wants to meet with me about something. I'm driving over to Annapolis."

"I'll go with you."

"No, that might put her off. She's very delicate right now. You get ready for your trip, make a reservation, get set to go tomorrow. Here, copy this down and use it." He handed Buffolino his gold American Express card. Tony noted the account number.

"Where are you going to be in Annapolis, in case I need you?" Buffolino asked.

"A crab-cake restaurant called Tommy's, in the Market House."

"Sure you don't want me to come with you? I love crab cakes."

"I'll bring you a doggie bag."

Buffolino smiled, looked at his watch, then slapped the side of his head. "Jesus, I forgot."

"Forgot what?"

"I forgot I'm havin' a party up here tonight."

"A *party?*"

"Well, not really a party. I invited my wife and daughters up here for a little dinner, a quiet thing, you know?"

"Tony, I—"

"Hey, Mac, I owe 'em. This is on me. I'll pick up the tab."

"That's generous of you, Tony. And I won't bother with that doggie bag. I'm sure you'll make do."

18

HE FOUND A parking spot near the distinctive harbor that forms the center of Annapolis, and a few minutes later walked into Tommy's Crab Cake House. Business was good; there was a wait for tables, and a lively group was congregated in the small barroom.

A handsome black man wearing a perfectly fitted double-breasted gray suit came from the dining room and nimbly made his way to a podium near the front door. Smith asked, "Are you Tommy?"

The man nodded.

"My name is Mackensie Smith. I was supposed to meet your cousin, Marcia Mims, here."

"Oh, yes, Mr. Smith, Marcia told me you were coming." He looked around before leaning close and saying, "I'm glad you're here. She's very upset. If you'll give me a minute, I'll take you to her."

Tommy seated a party of six, told one of the waiters to cover the front, and motioned for Smith to follow him. They walked through the dining room, entered the kitchen, went through a door leading to a short, narrow hallway, and stepped into Tommy's cramped and cluttered office, where Marcia Mims sat on a couch, obviously having made room by pushing piles of paper and magazines aside. She stood up when she saw Smith.

"Hello, Marcia," he said.

Marcia looked at Tommy, who gave her a reassuring smile. "Relax, honey, everything's going to be all right." He said to Smith, "I have to get back. Just yell if you need anything."

"Please, Marcia, sit down," Smith said. He pulled a folding metal chair close to the couch. They said nothing for a few moments, just sat and looked at each other. Smith broke the silence. "I haven't been to Annapolis in a long time. I guess the last time was a football game at the Naval Academy. Must be three years ago."

"I come here whenever I can," Marcia said. "Tommy and his wife are very good to me."

"Seems like a nice fellow, and it looks like he's made a smiling success out of crabs."

Marcia laughed, and Smith was glad to see it. She'd been as taut as a violin string when he first came through the door. Now, she relaxed slightly, the tightness in her body visibly falling away into the soft cushions.

"Mr. Smith, I . . ."

"Yes?"

"I called you because . . . I called you because I don't know what to do. It's about Janet."

Smith sat up straight. "Janet?"

"Yes."

"Do you know where she is?"

"Yes."

"How do you . . . I mean, did Janet call you, or have you known all along?"

"She called me two days ago. She's very frightened."

"Frightened of what?"

"Of what will happen to her if she comes back."

"I don't understand, Marcia. What would she have to be frightened about? Does she think someone would hurt her?"

"She doesn't know what will happen to her, that's all. Mr. Smith, Janet has never been comfortable in the Ewald family. She's always considered herself an outsider."

Smith shrugged. "That's not uncommon for daughters-in-law. It's not a reason to be really frightened. Why did she call you, Marcia?"

"Janet has always turned to me, Mr. Smith. She says I'm the only one she feels she can trust and confide in."

"That's flattering to you, and deserved, I imagine. Where is she?"

The tension returned, and she looked away.

"I want to help, and I assume you called me because you thought I could help Janet. She certainly shouldn't be frightened of me."

The housekeeper looked at him again. "I know that, Mr. Smith. I think she knows that. It's just that I'm not sure what to do. I told her she should come back and face whatever is going to happen with Paul, but she's too confused at this point."

Smith decided that to press for Janet's whereabouts would be counterproductive. But he had to get more out of Marcia. He said, "Well, Marcia, at least she's safe. I was beginning to wonder whether something terrible had happened to her." He stood. "I suppose you'll have to make your own decision about what to do with Janet. I agree with you that she should come back, but she can't be forced to. Is there anything else you want from me at this point?"

"Please, sit down, Mr. Smith."

Smith resumed his seat and waited for her to say what was on her mind.

"I told Janet I would talk to you, and if I thought things were right, I would take you to her."

"Is she here in Annapolis?"

Marcia nodded.

"Well, here I am," he said. "Frankly, I'm going to leave one way or the other, either by myself or with you to see Janet. The smell of crab cakes is getting to me. I haven't had dinner yet."

She smiled. "I'm sorry, Mr. Smith, but I just want to do the right thing by her."

"Of course. That's why she trusts you."

"Tommy has a little apartment here in town that he only uses occasionally. Janet is there."

"Has she been there the whole time?"

"No, she stayed in a motel in Virginia before she called me."

"Let's go," Smith said. He could see that she was grappling with the decision she'd made, and he reached out and touched her hand. "Everything will work out, Marcia, for Janet and for everyone."

They stopped at the front of the restaurant to tell Tommy they'd be back, then walked slowly along the edge of the harbor, in which small boats of every description were anchored. The night was humid; a fog had begun to roll in off Chesapeake Bay. They went up a narrow street lined with shops until they reached a two-story building at the end of it. The ground level was a men's clothing store. A separate door provided access to the second floor. Marcia pulled a key from her purse and opened the door, and they proceeded up a narrow flight of stairs. There was a single door off the landing. Marcia knocked.

"Who is it?"

"It's Marcia, honey, and Mr. Smith." They waited, long enough for Smith to wonder whether Janet had decided to not let them in. Then there was the turn of a lock, and the door opened.

Tommy's apartment consisted of a living room–bedroom combination, a pullman kitchen, and a bathroom. If it weren't for the kitchen, it would have looked like any moderately priced hotel room. Tommy must put his money into clothing.

Marcia immediately went to Janet and hugged her, then stood at her side. Janet had always been frail, her features thin and birdlike, but at this moment she looked absolutely fragile. There was virtually no color in her face. The yellow sweater and black skirt she wore had undoubtedly fit her a week ago, but now hung loosely on her. She was considerably shorter than Marcia; oddly, had it not been for their color difference, they could have been mother and child.

"How have you been, Janet?" Smith asked.

Janet played with her bony white fingers. "All right, Mac. No, not all right. Not good at all."

He wondered if she might collapse, and he suggested they sit down. "Would anyone like something to drink?" Marcia asked.

"Anything cold, a soft drink," Smith said, not taking his eyes off Janet, who sat on the edge of a chair and continued to pull at her fingers.

As Marcia went into the tiny kitchen and opened the refrigerator, he said to Janet, "Marcia says you're afraid to come back, Janet. Do you know that I'm handling Paul's defense in the event he's charged with Andrea Feldman's murder?"

She looked at him with wide eyes. "Yes, I heard that. I mean, I read that." Smith started to say something, but Janet added, "Marcia told me, too. She said you've been helping everyone."

"I'm trying."

"How is Paul?"

"Doing quite well, considering the circumstances." He thought of Paul's indifference to her disappearance, said instead, "He's been frantic about you. It would be very helpful to him if he knew you were safe and if you were there at his side."

She quickly shook her head. "I can't."

"Why? What made you run the way you did?"

Marcia returned with three glasses of diet soda. Smith repeated his question to Janet.

"I had no choice. I knew they would think it was me."

"Think it was you what?"

"Who killed Andrea Feldman."

"Kill Andrea—you?"

"Yes, or they'd make it seem as though I did."

"Who would do that, Janet?"

"Ken and Leslie."

Smith looked at the floor, then back at her. "Janet, I don't know the kind of relationship you've had with your in-laws, but I don't think they're the kind of people who would falsely accuse someone of murder."

Marcia said, "Mr. Smith, there is a great deal that goes on in that house that most people wouldn't dream of."

"Like what?" he asked.

"Like . . ." She and Janet looked at each other before Janet said, "Paul wasn't the only one who had an affair with Andrea."

Smith measured his words. "Ken did, too." So Ken might have had a motive to murder Andrea himself. He looked at Marcia Mims and asked, "Is that true, Marcia? Do you know that Senator Ewald had an affair with Andrea Feldman?"

"I don't think it's my place to—"

Smith said loudly, for the first time, "Marcia, let's not play games. Can you confirm that he had an affair with her?"

"Yes."

"Quite a young woman," Smith said, more to himself than to them.

Smith pondered the situation. According to Ken's claims about what he'd done the night of the murder, he'd spent time with Roseanna Gateaux in the Watergate; she could certainly confirm that, assuming she was forced to be honest about it. Secret Service agent Jeroldson was with Ewald the rest of the night. Smith had to ask Joe Riga what had come out of his interview with Jeroldson.

As Smith looked at the two women across from him, he thought of other possibilities: Either of *them* could have killed Andrea. If Paul Ewald had gone to the Buccaneer Motel after the party and before Andrea was killed, he could have dropped her back at the Kennedy Center, left . . . and someone else could have killed her. Paul had denied having gone to that motel with her after the party. Had he or hadn't he? If he had, why lie about it? If he hadn't, and she'd gone there with someone else, that would make the motel owner, Wilton Morse, either a liar or severely mistaken because of poor eyesight. No, according to what Tony said, Morse's eyesight wasn't *that* bad. That left lying. Why would Morse lie? Had he been paid to? And, if so, who would have that much to gain by pinning Murder One on Paul Ewald?

"Janet," Smith said, "do you think your father-in-law had a motive for killing Andrea Feldman? Was Andrea blackmailing Senator Ewald?"

Another look between the two women. Marcia Mims said, "*I* don't know anything about motives, Mr. Smith, and I really don't want to be involved. All I know is that Janet means a lot to me and I want to help *her,* nobody else. That's why I called you."

"Yes, of course, and I think Janet is fortunate to have a caring friend like you. But she's opened this whole line of conversation, to which I have to respond. After all, I am her husband's attorney, and he's a prime suspect in the murder. I don't believe he did it, and if his father is the murderer, the ramifications of that are clear enough."

Smith turned to Janet. "I was brought here by Marcia to help you, Janet, and I thought perhaps to offer some advice. Well, my advice is for you to come back to Washington with me and face this thing head-on."

Janet's nervousness returned, and she shook her head. "I can't do that. I'm too afraid."

"That they'll say *you* killed Andrea Feldman? It won't happen, believe me."

"No, Mac—I'm afraid that they might kill me, too."

Smith's laugh was involuntary.

Janet's face hardened.

"I'm not laughing at *what* you're saying, Janet, but the idea is simply too farfetched for me to give much credence to it. Will you come back with me? If your physical safety is a legitimate concern, I can arrange to have you protected."

"How?"

"Leave that to me. Will you come?"

She shook her head.

Smith stood. "Well, you put me in a difficult situation. The police are looking for you, because they must talk with you as they have with everyone else. I know where you are now, and if I fail to make that known to them, I'm obstructing justice, something no one, especially an attorney, is supposed to do."

Janet turned to Marcia and said, "See, I told you this was a mistake." Marcia put her arm around her and said, "It wasn't a mistake. I trust Mr. Smith. He won't tell anyone."

"Don't place that burden on me, Marcia," Smith said sternly.

"Please, Mac, don't tell them where I am. Oh, go ahead, I won't be here anyway." She jumped up from her chair and paced the room, her thin arms wrapped around herself as though an arctic blast had hit.

"Look, Janet," Smith said, "let's leave it this way: Think about it. I won't tell anyone that I've seen you and had this conversation, no one. I promise you that. Think about it for twenty-four hours, and then let's talk again. I'll come back here tomorrow night. Promise you'll be here."

She turned and said angrily, "I don't trust anyone connected with that family."

"Suit yourself, but I'll keep my part of the bargain. I'll be here tomorrow night at the same time. I hope you'll be here, too." He looked at Marcia. "Are you coming with me?"

She shook her head. "No, I'll stay with her a while."

"Fine. You know where to reach me. Good night."

Smith was angry, and the speed at which he drove back to Washington reflected it. He went to the Watergate suite, where Tony Buffolino sat alone watching television.

"Where're your wife and kids?" Smith asked.

"Ah, they came up here, but I got into a hassle right away with my wife and they took off. Typical, man—I want to do good, but I shoot off my mouth and we end up in a brawl. I'll make it up to them. What was your trip all about?"

"Nothing, wasted time. Anything new here aside from a near-homicide fight with your wife?"

"I made my reservation to go to Frisco tomorrow."

"Good." Smith picked up the phone and dialed Joe Riga's number. To his surprise, he reached him immediately. "Joe, Mac Smith, I need to talk to you."

"Now?" Riga said.

"Now, or in the morning."

"Let's make it tomorrow, Mac."

"As early as possible. Will you be in at eight?"

"Yeah, I'll be here."

"Sorry your party didn't work out, Tony," Smith said as he prepared to leave for home.

"Story of my life, Mac. Have a good night. I'll keep in touch from Frisco."

19

"YOU WANT SOME tonsil varnish, Mac?" Joe Riga asked. Smith laughed and shook his head. It was apt slang for station-house coffee and, for a coffee snob like Mac Smith, it was even worse than that.

Riga fussed with paperwork on his desk before asking, "What can I do for you?"

"Tell me what's going on with the Andrea Feldman investigation."

Riga crumpled a piece of paper into a ball and tossed it over his shoulder. It missed the wastebasket. "Just plodding ahead, Mac. Lots of players, but no scorecard yet. Why do you ask? Your boy Ewald hasn't been charged with anything."

"True," said Smith, "but he's spending his days waiting for the proverbial second shoe to drop. Is he still your prime suspect?"

Riga smiled, exposing yellowed teeth. "Let's just say that we haven't crossed his name off the list."

"When can we expect the autopsy report?"

Riga took a sip of his coffee, made a face, and said, "We? You don't have any official connection. You don't even have a client."

"Not necessarily true, Joe. Yes, Paul Ewald has not been charged with the murder, but I'm on tap with the Ewald family. I just want to be ready in case you decide to send a couple of wee-hours visitors to his house again. Only for questioning, of course."

Riga threw a couple more spitballs at the wastebasket. "If I didn't know you better, Mac, I'd think you were ambulance chasing."

"Careful, Joe."

Riga's smile was big enough to assure Smith he was half kidding.

"What about the autopsy?" Smith repeated.

"Nothing's come down on it yet."

"Any preliminary findings?"

"Just scuttlebutt."

"Any determination whether she'd had sex that night?"

"Check Forensics."

"I will."

Riga leaned forward and said, "Look, Mac, let me level with you. All of us . . . me, the DA, a couple of others . . . wanted to break this case fast. We figured Paul Ewald did it, and we brought him in hoping he'd decide to make it easy for us, 'fess up. We figured with the circumstantial we had, plus the ID by the motel owner in Rosslyn, we could shake Mr. Ewald up enough to get a confession out of him."

"You could go to jail for that kind of police procedure," Smith said sternly.

"Why, because you claim I told you this? Come on, Mac, I'm being up front with you because we go back a ways, huh? We got a little pressure on us to solve this thing."

"I can imagine. You must have been disappointed when Paul Ewald didn't hand you a written, notarized confession when you knocked at his door in the middle of the night."

A grin from Riga. "Yeah, that would have been nice. Look, we took a shot and it didn't work, so we let him go. You came on strong with Kramer, and your client took a walk. Wanna know something, though, Mac?" Riga asked, leaning even more forward and staring at Smith.

"Life is a continuing education, Joe. Go ahead."

"I still think he did it. We've interviewed more than a hundred people so far, and when I line everybody up in my mind, I keep seeing Paul Ewald stepping forward, raising his hand, and saying, 'I did it!' "

"Not a very open-minded way to conduct a murder investigation," Smith said.

"That's for juries, Mac, not for cops. I go into an investigation with my mind closed against all the distractions, you know? My gut tells me who the major players are, and I keep the spotlight on them."

Smith went to the window and leaned against the sill. He'd come to Riga's office hoping to learn whether MPD's questioning of Secret Service agent Robert Jeroldson had revealed Ken Ewald's rendezvous with Roseanna Gateaux the night of the murder. He was reluctant to ask, but decided that if he didn't, he wouldn't learn anything. "A hundred people, you say. Everybody had an alibi except Paul Ewald?"

Riga shook his head.

"Any of the others people I might know?"

Riga nodded. "Yeah, Senator Ewald for one."

Smith raised his eyebrows and looked surprised. "Why do you say that?" he asked.

"Your senator buddy cut out of his office that night for a couple of hours."

"Oh?"

"Yeah, he and the Secret Service agent, Jeroldson, went to the Watergate Hotel."

"What did they do there?"

"Beats me, but it's on my list of questions the next time I talk to Ewald. Jeroldson says Ewald insisted they split up, and Ewald went into a room at the hotel."

"Whom did he see?" Smith asked.

"Damned if I know, but I will." Riga leaned back in his wooden swivel chair, bringing forth a loud groan from its metal tilting mechanism. "I got a feeling you're not leveling with me, Mac, and that means we're playing with two sets of rules here this morning. I showed you mine, now you show me yours."

Smith laughed and came to the desk, perched on the edge of it. "What is this, a game of doctor-nursey? Why do you want to know whom he saw that night? Maybe it was personal."

"I assume it was. Last I heard, Senator Ewald wasn't up for any Husband of the Year awards."

"Looking for gossip, Joe?"

"I got no use for gossip. What I got is a murder to solve."

"Is Senator Ewald high on your list of suspects?"

"He's part of the crowd. Anything else you want to discuss, Mac—the baseball season, Star Wars, spring fashions?"

"No, Joe, I just wanted to touch base with you. As I said, I'm on retainer to the Ewald family, and would like to avoid being blindsided. By the way, the motel owner in Rosslyn. He's a liar. Paul Ewald wasn't at that motel that night."

"I know that. Well, maybe he's not a liar, just a guy who likes to cooperate with the law to keep the law off his back. Besides, he's not what you'd call a prize witness for the prosecution. I don't think he could pass a driver's test eye exam."

As Smith went to the door, Riga asked, "How's the senator's campaign going?"

"All right, I guess. I'm not involved much in his political life."

"This kind of thing could hurt him, huh?"

"Depends on what you decide to do, Joe."

"What *I* decide to do?"

"Yes. Think of the awesome responsibility you have. Accuse anyone in the Ewald family of murder, and you potentially blow Ken Ewald's campaign for president away in smoke. You're a regular king-maker. Thanks for the time, Joe. I'm still looking forward to having that drink with you."

A long black limousine carrying Colonel Gilbert Morales, his aides, and bodyguards, passed through the Lincoln Tunnel and moved slowly in clogged Manhattan noontime traffic until it went past the front of the Waldorf, turned right at the corner, and stopped at the smaller entrance to the Waldorf Towers. The sidewalks had been barricaded by New York City police, and a cadre of uniformed officers lined the length of them. A group of onlookers strained to see who was arriving by limo.

"Who's that?" a man from Cleveland with a large video camera around his neck asked his wife.

"It's that Morales from Panama, the one fighting Communism there."

"Good thing we have Manning in the White House," the husband said gravely. "If that jerk Ewald becomes president, all Central America will go Commie."

Morales and his entourage were greeted in the small lobby of the Waldorf by a representative from a public-relations agency that had been retained to promote Morales's cause in the United States.

They all went up to a large and ornately furnished two-bedroom suite, where, after food and drinks had been delivered, they discussed Morales's scheduled appearance that night on Ted Koppel's *Nightline*.

When that discussion was concluded, one of Morales's aides and a bodyguard were assigned to escort the securely girdled, long-lashed Mrs. Morales for two hours of shopping. Everyone departed, leaving Morales alone to go over answers he'd prepared to questions that Koppel was likely to ask.

A half hour later, the phone rang.

"¿Sí?"

"It is Miguel," the voice on the other end said. "I am downstairs."

"Bueno. Come up."

A few minutes later, Morales opened the door to admit a rapier-thin young Panamanian wearing an expensive, tightly tailored blue pinstripe suit. His silk tie was the exact color of the suit. His shirt was medium blue; the collar stood high above his jacket neck, and his cuffs were below its sleeves. He wore a plain gold wedding band; a thin gold chain dangled from his left wrist.

"Come in, come in, sit down," Morales said, continuing in Spanish.

Miguel went to a sideboard, where he poured himself a glass of tomato juice. He turned and looked at Morales, who had resumed his seat.

"Sit down," Morales repeated, gesturing to a chair next to him.

Miguel sat. Morales looked into his youthful face and smiled. "So young," he said.

There was no response from Miguel, who simply took a tiny sip of the juice and placed the glass on a table in front of them.

"So young to be so good at your craft," Morales said.

"Good *because* I am young," Miguel said in an evenly modulated voice.

"Sí, sí," Morales said. "You are ready?"

Miguel narrowed his eyes and said, "I am always ready."

"Bueno. Then let us go over this again."

20

TONY BUFFOLINO retrieved his .22 revolver from Security at San Francisco International Airport. He was licensed to carry the weapon, and had checked it with airline security in New York before boarding the flight. Revolver securely nestled beneath his arm, he pulled the new suitcase he'd bought at a Watergate luggage shop from the baggage carousel and went out front to take the shuttle bus and pick up the Hertz Continental he'd reserved.

"Nice, nice," he said aloud as he settled behind the Lincoln's steering wheel and adjusted the seat and mirrors. He read over the printout he'd gotten from the Hertz direction-giving computer, and carefully studied a map of San Francisco, placing an "X" on Santiago Street, in the Sunset district. He'd intended to go to the hotel first, but changed his mind. He started the engine and headed for the "X" on the map, reaching it almost an hour later after a series of frustrating, obscenity-producing wrong turns.

The house he was looking for was nondescript, on a nondescript street, in a nondescript neighborhood. Still, there was a refreshing neatness and cleanliness to the area. The houses were all painted in pastels, as was most of the city; a shower of sun gave them a recently washed look. He parked across the street from number 21, got out of the Lincoln, spent a moment taking in more of his surroundings, then crossed to a two-family house; the numbers were 21A and 21B. The only number he'd been given by Mac Smith was 21—no letters. He took a chance on 21A and rang the bell. When there was no immediate response, he rang again, longer this time. Eventually, he heard an interior door open and close, and a female hand with chipped red nail polish pulled a flowered green curtain aside. Half her face was visible.

Buffolino flashed his biggest nonthreatening smile. The half-face continued to stare at him. "I need some help!" he yelled through the glass. The curtain returned to its original position, a key was turned, and the door opened as far as its chain would allow.

"Mrs. Feldman?"

"Next door." She had a deep booze-and-cigarette voice.

"Thank you," Buffolino said.

"She's not here."

"Do you expect her back soon?"

"No. She's gone away."

"Is that so? Has she gone away for good?"

"She still pays the rent."

"Then I suppose she'll be coming back," Buffolino said, annoyed at the crabbed conversation and the narrow opening through which it was being conducted.

"Are you a friend of Mrs. Feldman?" the low voice asked.

"Yeah, I am, from New York."

"I used to live in New York."

"Yeah?"

"Yes. Are you with a company?"

"Huh? No, I work by myself."

"An opera company."

"Opera company? No, ah . . . I dabble, if you know what I mean. Opera! Hey, are you an opera singer?" Before the low voice behind the door could answer, Buffolino said, "Opera is my chief love in life. What a coincidence. How about a cup a' coffee and some opera talk?"

She looked him up and down.

"I mean, just open the door and let's talk for a minute." The chain was released and the door opened, revealing a tall, full-bodied woman with dyed red hair and an imposing bosom that threatened the thin fabric of a pink housecoat.

"Anthony Buffolino," he said, extending his hand.

"A pleasure to meet you, Mr. Buffolino. I am Carla Zaretski."

"Pleased, I'm sure. Gee, I'm sorry I missed Mae. Any idea when she'll be back?"

Carla slowly shook her head. "She had family business to attend to."

"That so?"

"Yes. There has been a tragedy in her life."

Buffolino looked serious and said, "Andrea being murdered. I guess Mae had to make a lot of arrangements."

Carla placed her hands over her bosom and sighed. "A terrible thing to lose your only daughter. It devastated Mae, absolutely devastated her. Poor thing. Andrea was her only child . . . and such a good daughter. She visited often, always bringing things. And then *that* news. So tragic."

"Like opera," said Buffolino.

Carla glared at him.

"I mean, it's just that opera is always . . . tragic . . . the plot, I mean."

Carla's sudden flash of anger subsided as quickly as it had flared. "Great tragedy is what opera is made of."

"That's what I was saying. Where do you figure Mae went?"

"To New York."

"How come New York?"

"To find solace with her many friends. You say you are a friend?"

Buffolino shrugged and shifted from one foot to the other. "Actually,

I was more a friend of Andrea's. We were . . . well, we were pretty close once."

The expression on Carla Zaretski's face was sheer horror. "Then you, too, have suffered a great loss. Were you there when . . . when it happened?"

Buffolino looked at the ground and slowly shook his head. "No, and that makes it even harder. If I had been, maybe I could have done something. I can't get that out of my mind, you know, always wondering if I could have done something to prevent it."

Carla, who was a few inches taller than Buffolino, looked down into his eyes and asked, "Would you like a drink?"

Buffolino gave her his best aren't-you-a-wonderful-person-for-thinking-of-it look, and broke into a smile. "That's very kind of you. Yes, I would enjoy a drink, but only if you'll join me." He had no doubt that she would.

A few minutes later, he stood in the middle of her modest living room, a glass of warm whiskey in his hand. The walls were filled with photographs, all of them featuring Carla Zaretski. A badly scratched recording of Mozart's *Marriage of Figaro* came from small, cheap speakers.

"Memories," Carla said from where she'd arranged herself on a chaise longue that bore the scratch marks of four cats that roamed the room.

"You were a star, huh?" Buffolino said.

"No, never a star, but I sat on the threshold of stardom. The voice is such a fickle slave. I lost my portamento prematurely."

Buffolino stared at her. "Jesus, I'm sorry to hear that. What'd you have, an accident?"

"Accident?" She started to laugh. "You are absolutely charming. Portamento, you know, is when the singer is no longer able to smoothly transverse the octaves."

Buffolino joined her laughter. "Yeah, right, *that* portamento." He quickly turned his attention to the photographs on the wall. "Who's this with you?"

"My dear friend and one of the world's great divas, Roseanna Gateaux. Surely you recognize her."

Buffolino had certainly heard of Gateaux, and remembered Mac Smith mentioning her as part of his blow-by-blow description of the events at the Kennedy Center the night Andrea Feldman was murdered. "Sure," he said, "but that picture must have been taken years ago."

"She is here now, singing Leonora in *Il Trovatore*. How sad Mae can't be present."

"Yeah, I know. Let's talk about that. Talking eases the pain sometimes."

An hour later, Buffolino decided it was time to leave. His hostess had lapsed into a nonstop recounting of her failed operatic career, which, the more she talked, Buffolino realized had never amounted to much except unrealistic dreams and empty, childish artistic pretensions. Still, he knew that Miss or Mrs. Zaretski represented the sort of direct link to Mae Feldman that he needed. Mac Smith had told him to find out everything he could about Andrea Feldman's mother. This was paydirt.

He told her he had to leave, but added, "I'll be staying in town a few days. How would you like to have dinner with me?"

"Dinner? On such short notice?" She fluffed her hair. "You mean tonight?"

"Let's make it tomorrow night," Buffolino said lightly. "Hey, you were some knockout. I can see from the pictures. You haven't lost much as far as I'm concerned."

She giggled like a schoolgirl.

"Come on, I don't know anything about San Francisco. Dinner's on me, and you show me the sights. Whattaya say?"

When she didn't immediately accept, he asked, "Are you going to see your friend Roseanna while she's here?" He knew the answer; Roseanna Gateaux was not her friend, and she probably didn't have enough money to buy a ticket. "I'd sure like to hear her sing," Buffolino said. *"Traviata.* That's one of my favorites. What do you say we go together?"

"Trovatore," she said, but there was no hesitation now. They made a date for dinner the next night. She suggested he buy tickets to the opera, but he reached into his pocket and tossed a hundred dollars on the table. "You do it, pick some good seats. Is that enough?" She frowned. He tossed down another hundred. "Get the best."

"I will."

"Great, I'll be staying at a hotel called the Mandarin Oriental, down in the financial district. Maybe you could call me there tomorrow and we'll set it up."

She walked him to the door. "You are a very sensitive and kind man," she said.

"Well, I . . . hey, I'll level with you, I just happen to have taken a shine to you, you know? And opera, a chance to see Roseanna Gateaux. My lucky day."

21

THE LUNCH AT the Four Seasons was pleasant, but turned out to be mission impossible. Annabel spent the lunch negotiating with a collector of pre-Colombian art for a sculpture of were-jaguar. The collector was a prissy little man who wouldn't budge on the price, which, Annabel knew, was far in excess of the piece's worth. They parted and agreed to keep in touch, although she decided the only way that would happen was if he called to announce he'd cut his price in half.

She had time to kill; the appointment she'd made with Herbert Greist wasn't until six. It was a lovely day in New York, sunny and mild but with enough nip in the air to remind you that summer wasn't here yet.

She decided to take a leisurely walk, and chose upper Fifth Avenue. Although she'd dismissed the notion that she'd been followed yesterday, the thought had come back to her a few times that morning, causing her to look behind in search of the same man. He was never there, and by the time she'd reached the Four Seasons, she'd put him out of her mind again.

Now, as she took her post-lunch stroll up Fifth and over to Madison to browse shop windows, she stopped to admire a good collection of antique jewelry in a small store. The light was such that Annabel could clearly see her reflection in the window, and she moved to avoid it to see the jewelry more clearly, and saw instead the reflection of a man across the street. It wasn't the same man as the day before, but he was dressed similarly in a tan raincoat, and seemed to be reading the pick-up times on a corner mailbox. She wouldn't have thought much of it except that she wondered how much information could be on the box to keep him engaged so long. Either the entire Constitution was pasted there, or he was illiterate.

She went to the corner and waited for the light to change, looking straight ahead but seeing in her peripheral vision that he'd crossed the street against the light and now lingered on the far corner. This time, he looked down at what appeared to be a map in his hands.

The light changed in her favor. She started to cross, quickly reversed herself, and walked east on the cross street, stopping halfway down the block in front of a restaurant. She looked inside. There was a bar by the window with one man sitting there. She entered and went to a bar stool that placed her in front of the window.

"Yes, ma'am?" the bartender asked.

Annabel, who had swiveled on the stool to look out the window, said without turning, "Club soda with lime, please."

She saw the tan raincoat pass on the opposite side of the street. He didn't seem to be looking for her; he'd probably seen her enter the restaurant. He never looked in her direction as he passed from her view. She paid for her drink, stood at the window, and looked up the street. He was gone.

She left the restaurant and scanned the block. No sign of him. He'd either decided to keep going, or had found a spot from which he could observe without being seen.

"Damn," she said as she retraced her steps to Fifth and continued uptown. She stopped occasionally to see if he'd fallen in behind her, but saw no more of him.

Greist had wanted to meet at his office again, but Reed insisted they meet in a public place. His office was just too stifling and tawdry. They agreed on the Oak Bar in her hotel.

When Greist arrived, Annabel sensed he'd already been drinking— nothing overt, just that tendency to reach for the floor with his feet rather than finding it naturally. He was also outwardly more pleasant, which, she assumed, went hand in hand with whatever he'd consumed. He joined her at the small corner table she occupied.

"Did you talk to Mr. Smith?" Greist asked after he'd been served a scotch and soda.

"Yes, I did. His attitude matches mine, Mr. Greist. Unless there is some specific indication of the nature of the information you wish to sell, and proof, we couldn't even begin to consider it."

He sat back and held his drink in both hands, staring into it as though seeking his next line from the quietly bubbling liquid. He said to the glass, "That's a shame."

Annabel's laugh was sardonic. "You wouldn't expect us to recommend to our client that he pay half a million dollars for something we haven't seen, would you?"

"Faith, Ms. Reed. There is no such thing anymore as faith and trust."

"There certainly isn't in this situation, and I think you're absurd to expect it."

A tired smile formed on his lips. "Ms. Reed, this is a treacherous world. Information can be its salvation, or its ultimate destruction."

The word "crackpot" crossed her mind. She had the feeling he was about to give a speech, something vaguely political and filled with clichés about the state of the world as he perceived it. She could do without that, did not want to waste time being on the receiving end of it. He slowly turned to her and said, "The information I offer your client, the honorable senator from California Kenneth Ewald, could change the course of events in this country, perhaps in the world, if it were to get into the wrong hands."

Annabel couldn't help but laugh. "Mr. Greist, you're not making any sense at all. I think we'd get a lot further if you would be specific instead of talking in grandiose terms about world change."

"You get what you pay for, Ms. Reed."

She asked, "How did your client come into possession of this so-called world-shaking information?"

"Irrelevant."

Should I say "overruled"? she wondered. "Maybe to you, but not to me or to Mackensie Smith. Is your client here in New York now?"

"Ms. Reed, I did not agree to meet you again to answer *your* questions."

"Fine," she said. "Then you'll just have to go ahead and file your suit on behalf of Mrs. Feldman for the loss of her daughter's civil liberties, and for her pain and suffering." She motioned for the check.

Although Greist had had a drink on top of what he'd earlier consumed, he seemed more sober than when he'd walked in. He stood and said through slack lips, "You and Mr. Smith are making a grave mistake, and obviously do not have your client's best interests at heart."

"I take it the drink is on me," Annabel said.

"I'm sure your wealthy client provides you with a large expense account. Good evening, Ms. Reed."

She watched him disappear into the lobby. Was this all one grand bluff on his part, a transparent shakedown, or was there even a modicum of truth behind his threat? The waitress brought the check; Annabel quickly laid more than enough money on top of it and went to the lobby. Greist was gone. She moved to the street and saw, far in the distance, a man across Fifth Avenue, beyond the fountain. It might have been Greist. She ran to the corner, crossed, slowing to a walk as she reached the figure. It was Greist. He was walking east, and didn't seem to be in any hurry.

She fell in behind him at what she considered a safe distance, thinking of the men that she now was convinced had followed her and vowing to do a better job than they had. While waiting for a light to change at the corner of Park Avenue and Fifty-first Street, she looked over her shoulder and wondered whether the follower was being followed.

Greist went south on Park Avenue, past the barricaded entrance to the Waldorf Astoria, and took a left on Forty-eighth Street. Reed kept pace with him until he turned into the main entrance of the Inter-Continental Hotel. She quickened her pace until she reached the entrance, checked to make sure he wasn't lingering inside the door, and entered. Her heart tripped; Greist had stopped by the massive bird cage that dominated the lavish lobby. He was six feet from her. She turned and bent over as though searching in her purse. When she thought enough time had passed, she looked in the direction of the cage. He was gone. She quickly scanned the large, two-level lobby. The raised portion to her left was half-filled with men and women enjoying cocktails while a tuxedoed pianist played show tunes.

Annabel used the bird cage as a screen and looked through it. Greist had joined someone at a table, a woman wearing a black raincoat whom Annabel judged to be in her early sixties, with gray-blond hair cut short. Annabel couldn't see her full face because of the angle at which the woman sat, and she had absolutely no reason to assume anything, but only one thought came to mind: Mae Feldman.

She lingered a few seconds more, couldn't hear or read lips, and concentrated on remembering everything she could about the woman. Then she went back out to Forty-eighth Street, keeping her back to where Greist and his companion sat, and made tracks for the Plaza and a chance to get on the telephone.

22

MAC SMITH DROVE slowly along Route 50 to Annapolis. He wasn't at all certain whether Janet Ewald would be there, could only hope that she would. He'd tried to call Marcia Mims at the Ewald house but was told it was her day off, which he already knew. Would she be there, too? Again, all he could do was speculate.

He wondered how Annabel's second meeting with Herbert Greist had gone. Maybe it was still in progress. That was the first call he would make once he'd finished in Annapolis.

This time, he found a parking space close to the building that housed the store and Tommy's apartment. He looked up at the windows and saw that there was a light on—a positive sign. He got out of the car, locked it, and walked slowly toward the door, realizing that without Marcia and her key, he had no way of entering. He searched for a buzzer but found none, and rapped on the one small window in the exterior door. There was no reply.

Baloney, he thought as he crossed the street and looked up at the windows again. The light was low-wattage. He waited for ten minutes for some sign of life, a shadow, the movement of someone across the room. Nothing.

He decided to leave his car where it was and walked to Tommy's. The restaurant was as busy as it had been the previous night. Tommy spotted Smith as he walked through the door, immediately came over to him, put his hand on his arm, and guided him back outside.

"Something wrong?" Smith asked.

"I think so," said Tommy. "Marcia told me you were coming back tonight. She seemed uncertain whether you'd meet her here at the restaurant or at my apartment, and she decided to wait for you here."

"Where is she?" Smith asked.

"I don't know. She had a drink at the bar just before the rush began. I was busy with paperwork in my office. When I came out, she was gone."

"Where did she go, to the apartment?"

"No. My bartender told me she received a phone call. She hung up and left."

"You haven't heard from her since?"

"No."

"What about the apartment, Tommy? Is . . . ." He wondered whether Tommy knew that Janet Ewald was being hidden there by Marcia. He decided it didn't make any difference whether he knew or not. "Do you know whether Janet Ewald is still in the apartment? I swung by there and saw a light, but no one answered."

Tommy shook his head. "Marcia told me why she needed the apartment, but I haven't heard any more about Ms. Ewald. I don't know whether she's still there or not."

"Look," said Smith, "will you give me a key to the apartment so I can let myself in?"

"Sure." He handed the key to Smith.

"Thanks. Be back soon."

Smith returned to the small building, let himself in downstairs, and knocked on the door to the apartment. There was no answer. He tried it; it swung open easily. The light he'd seen came from an overhead fixture in the small bathroom.

He stood in the middle of the room and turned in a circle, his eyes taking in everything. There was no sign that anyone had *ever* been there. Everything was neat; a small suitcase he'd noticed the previous night, and had assumed belonged to Janet, was gone.

Then he looked at a table near the door. A manila envelope rested on it. He picked up the envelope and read what was written on it: "Mr. Smith. Take this and keep it safe. Please do not open what is in this envelope unless something happens to me. Thank you. Marcia Mims."

He left the apartment, got into his car, turned on the overhead light, and opened the envelope. Inside was a book with a blue leather cover. Stamped on it in gold leaf was DIARY. He put it back in the envelope, slid the envelope beneath the front seat, and drove back to Tommy's Crab Cake House.

"Anyone there?" Tommy asked.

"No." He handed Tommy the key and thanked him. "I'd like to talk to the bartender."

"Sure."

Smith introduced himself to Tommy's bartender and asked if he had any idea who'd called Marcia.

"No idea at all. It was a woman."

"You answered the phone?"

"Yes."

"What did the woman say?"

The bartender laughed and shrugged. "Just asked me if Marcia Mims was here. I told her to wait a minute, put down the phone, and told Marcia she had a phone call."

"Did Marcia seem upset when she got off the phone?"

"I never noticed. She was gone in a flash, left most of her drink sitting on the bar."

Smith thanked the bartender and Tommy, and drove back to Washington. He put his car in the garage, took the envelope from beneath the seat, and sat in his recliner in the study, the envelope on his lap. The temptation to open it and begin reading was strong, but he decided he'd be stronger. He placed the envelope beneath papers in the bottom right drawer of his desk and hoped there would never be reason to read it.

Then he sat looking at the drawer.

Senator Kenneth Ewald was winding up a speech in the ballroom of the Willard Hotel to a five-hundred-dollar-a-plate dinner of party movers-and-shakers. Always handsome, he was even more so in his tuxedo. Leslie, dressed in a simple but elegant white dinner dress, sat at his side and looked up adoringly. There was an unmistakable renewal of energy in his face and voice as he said, "This is a particularly happy day for Leslie and me. Recently, we've had a tremendous personal tragedy enter our lives. A talented and decent young woman was murdered in cold blood, a young woman who served me and the things I stand for so admirably as a member of my staff. Then, as you all know, our only son, Paul, was taken in and questioned about that brutal murder. You can imagine what that did to us as parents. That situation naturally had to take center stage in our lives, disrupting my run for the Democratic nomination. Leslie and I seriously considered dropping out, putting public service on the shelf, and devoting all our energies to helping our son. Fortunately, that wasn't necessary. Paul was released almost immediately because the police realized he had nothing to do with the murder."

There was long and sustained applause. Ewald waited until it had subsided before holding up his hands and saying, "Life, as we all know, seldom goes the way we would like it to go. Wilson Mizner said that life's a tough proposition, and the first hundred years are the hardest." He looked at Leslie. "We've lived our first hundred years this past week, and now that this terrible cloud has been lifted from our lives, are ready to devote our second hundred to winning the nomination in July, the White House in November, and to restoring this nation to one of equity for all, prosperity for all, and a return to the sort of values that the Democratic party has always stood tall and proud for. Thank you so

much, and God bless every one of you." Everyone in the ballroom
stood. The applause, cheers, and whistles lasted many minutes. Ken
took Leslie's hand and drew her up next to him. They waved to the
crowd, a preview, many thought, of what the scene would be at the
Democratic National Convention in San Francisco in July.

Mac Smith, who'd been watching the news on TV, called Annabel at
the Plaza. She told him of her second meeting with Greist, and that
she'd followed him.

"What the hell did you do that for? Who do you think you are,
Jessica Fletcher?"

"It was a whim, an impetuous act. Our talk was unsatisfactory. I'm
glad I did."

"Why?"

"He went into the Inter-Continental Hotel and had a drink with a
woman."

"So?"

"I think it was Mae Feldman."

"How would you know that? Have you ever seen a picture of her?"

"No, but the woman he was sitting with is exactly the way I picture
Mae Feldman. Don't ask me to explain, Mac, I just have this feeling."

"Did you see them leave?" Smith asked.

"No, I didn't want to take the chance of being seen by him, so I came
back here to the hotel."

Smith fell silent.

"Mac?"

"What?"

"Are you still there?"

"Yes, sorry, my mind wandered for a moment. Look, Annabel, I
think you ought to get back here as quickly as possible."

"I intend to, first thing in the morning."

Smith glanced at a pendulum wall clock. There were no more shut-
tles between New York and Washington that night. He said, "All right,
but grab the first shuttle in the morning. I'll meet you at the Watergate
suite. I have a temp secretary coming in."

"Fine. Have you heard from Tony?"

"No, but I haven't checked the machine at the Watergate. I'll do that
after we're through. Annabel, don't take any chances. Stay in the room
tonight, and keep the door locked."

"Do you think I'm in danger?"

"I'm sure you aren't, but I'm becoming an advocate of the better-
safe-than-sorry school."

He told her about having met Janet Ewald, and what had happened
when he went back for their second meeting.

"Where do you think she's gone now?"

"I have no idea. Frankly, I'm more concerned about Marcia Mims."
He filled her in on that story.

"Have you tried to call her?" Reed asked.

"No. I won't tonight. She's still on her day off, but if I can't reach her first thing in the morning, I'll start worrying."

"Well, Mac, we obviously have some pieces to fit together tomorrow."

"Yes, I'd say that. Okay, my dear, get some sleep. Thanks for getting involved for me. I love you."

"I love you too, Mac. Oh, by the way, I think I've been followed ever since I got to New York. Two men."

"Jesus, Annabel, why didn't you tell me earlier?"

"Because I keep forgetting about it. It happens, and then my mind gets on to other things and I just forget."

"Describe them to me."

She did, stressing the fact that they looked somewhat alike, but beyond that were without any unusual characteristics as far as she could see.

"Just blend into the background, huh? Double-lock the door, Annabel. I'll see you in the morning."

He called the Watergate answering machine. There was a long message from Tony Buffolino: "You owe me a bonus, Mac, a big one. I'm going out to dinner tomorrow night and to the opera with this fruitcake, Carla Zaretski. Whatta they call it, 'Beyond the call of duty'? That's what's happening here. Anyway, this Mandarin Oriental Hotel is some classy joint. They even give me slippers and a robe. *Ciao!*"

Annabel Reed got into *her* robe and turned on the television news on ABC. There was a promo for the appearance of Colonel Gilbert Morales on *Nightline* that night; she decided she would stay up to watch it. Then there was coverage of the activities of both Democratic candidates. The first item concerned Jody Backus, who'd spent the day in North Dakota, kissing babies and eating fried chicken. He was his usual jovial public self, and Reed had to admit he had a potent, albeit rough-hewn charm.

Next came footage of the Ewalds following the speech Ken had made. They stood together in the lobby of the Willard, he resplendent in his tuxedo, she lovely and silent as she stood at his side. They'd stopped to answer impromptu questions from reporters. The camera zoomed close on Leslie's face. A tiny tear came from one eye as she said, "Of course we knew that our son didn't kill anyone."

What the camera didn't show was the slender young Panamanian in a blue suit who stood in a corner of the lobby, far from the Ewalds. There was no expression on his face, no sign of the intensity with which he watched the scene across the lobby. As Senator and Leslie Ewald, accompanied by Ed Farmer, other aides, and Secret Service agents left the knot of reporters and headed toward the door, they passed close to the man Miguel, who'd flown back from New York late that afternoon.

"I NEVER SAW such a view in my whole life," Tony Buffolino told Carla as they sat at a window table in the Top of the Mark. Outside, a setting sun stained San Francisco gold. The city's fog had begun to roll in over the Bay as if a curtain call; the Golden Gate Bridge was being wrapped in it, adding to its compelling beauty.

"Such beauty is always better when shared," she said. She'd started speaking with an accent that hadn't been there the previous day.

Buffolino observed her closely. She'd obviously gone to great lengths to get ready for the evening. Her red hair had been curled and redyed; less black showed at the roots. Her nails had been done, and her makeup was heavy enough to border on the outlandish. Green eye shadow flecked with gold sparkles covered broad, swollen eyelids, and the weight of long black false lashes threatened to pull her eyes closed at any moment. Her lipstick was as crimson as her nails, and she'd created too large a mouth with it. Pendulous gold-plated earrings hung from the lobes of her ears to her broad shoulders, and multiple strands of costume jewelry ringed her neck. The aqua caftan she wore swept the floor as she made her entrance into the Top of the Mark. Buffolino had been embarrassed that he was the one she sought, but reminded himself that he'd better shed such feelings. It promised to be a long night.

She'd ordered a perfect Manhattan. He ordered a screwdriver. They sipped their drinks and made small talk about the splendor of San Francisco, theirs to admire through the window.

"You got the tickets?" Buffolino asked.

"Yes, and with great difficulty, I might add."

"How come?"

"Because this is San Francisco. We love our opera here. The performance has been sold out for months."

"How'd you get tickets then?" he asked, not really caring.

"Friends, sir. This lady has friends."

"I bet you do. Good thing, too."

She placed her thick hands on top of his and looked deep into his eyes. "Strange, isn't it, how one person's misfortune can benefit another?"

"Yeah?"

"Poor Mae. Poor Andrea. Lucky Carla."

She squeezed his hands hard, and he forced a smile. "I know what you mean," he said. Heavy, cheap, and very sweet perfume wafted across the table. He freed his hands, sat back in his chair, raised his drink to his lips, stared out the window, and pretended to be seduced into silence by the view. Actually, he was thinking about life's little ironies.

He'd been headed for certain juvenile delinquent status as a teenager. Born to poor parents in an even poorer section of Brooklyn, he hung around with a bunch of wise guys. By the time he was sixteen, he'd been arrested twice, once for car theft, the second time for assault on a black man who'd wandered by mistake into the neighborhood. Then along came Father Benternagel, Brooklyn's boxing priest, who told the judge he'd take responsibility for "this kid who thinks he's tough."

Buffolino became a good amateur boxer, and made it to the finals in the New York Golden Gloves, losing to a southpaw from the Bronx who threw right jabs so fast, and so often, that Buffolino never saw them coming. It didn't matter that he lost, however, because two years in the gym and the Gloves with Father Benternagel had given him a different perspective on life, and what he wanted from it.

He even thought about college, but knew that wasn't to be. While his friends drifted into various criminal pursuits, Tony went in the other direction. He applied for the New York City Police Department, didn't stand a chance because of his juvenile record, realized he wanted to be a cop more than anything else in the world, and checked into other cities whose requirements weren't as stringent, who had more openings on their force, and who might not scrutinize his teenage years with as keen an eye as the NYPD had. Washington was it. He took the tests, passed, and lived in a boarding house during his training at the D.C. Police Academy.

He loved it; he wore his uniform with peacock pride, and devoted countless off-duty hours to representing the department in community activities. He didn't labor under any delusions. He knew he would never rise to management ranks within the department, but his promotion to detective and his assignment to the special narcotics squad represented the cap of his career.

Then, of course, there developed the acute need for money, and the selling out to Garcia, the Panamanian drug dealer; the expulsion from the force; the disgrace; the embarrassment; the countless nights buying sleep with bottles of booze; the lack of self-worth he felt and, worse, assumed everyone else felt about him. How many years since that fateful night in the Watergate? How many years of hiring out as a night watchman at local companies? How many years of avoiding contact with his children from both marriages because he couldn't stand the look in their eyes, couldn't deal with the scorn they must feel for him.

In a sense, Mac Smith represented another Father Benternagel, another "priest." Buffolino had argued long and hard with Smith about the disposition of his case. Smith had said he could make a deal with the local prosecutor: no criminal charges if Buffolino would accept departmental punishment. "No deal," he told Smith a hundred times. Finally, Smith had thrown up his hands and told him to find another lawyer, which Buffolino intended to do. But he knew down deep that Smith was right, that he was lucky to escape a jail term. He left his dream with his head bowed, and his belief in himself, and in mankind, on a par with his belief in Santa Claus and the tooth fairy.

Now things had come full circle again, even if temporarily. He was living better than he'd ever lived before. A thousand a week. A suite in the Watergate, where, if he could keep his mouth shut, he could entertain his ex-wives and children in a style that had to make a statement to them—Tony Buffolino was somebody again. He was needed by one of the top legal minds in the land, and was being paid accordingly. He had new clothes (Smith had seen only one of three suits he'd bought in the fancy men's shop downstairs at the Watergate). The frozen dinners and cans to which he'd become so accustomed had been replaced by beef Wellington, crab cocktail, chocolate mousse, and caviar. The cheap whiskey with which he used to lull himself to sleep had been replaced by top-shelf bottles, although because he didn't want to appear too greedy, he'd settled for the Watergate's own brand of liquor instead of the Beefeater, Stolichnaya, etc., that headed the room-service menu.

Here he was in San Francisco, staying in a fantastic hotel, money in his pocket, the jewel of a city spread out before him. . . .

He looked at Carla Zaretski, who seemed about to cry. This time, *he* joined hands and asked, "Hey, babe, what's the matter? How come so sad?"

She answered with regal dignity, "One who has lost a promising career in the opera is not destined to be happy." That prompted a fifteen-minute encore of the story of her failed operatic career, most of it going back to high school musicals. If she ever did have a portamento, it was gone by her first year of college.

When she was finished, Buffolino said, "Well, I'm ready for dinner. Got any ideas?"

"Yes, I have given it considerable thought. A man of your taste would be satisfied with nothing less than the best."

Even though Buffolino knew it was a silly thing for her to say, it puffed him up a little. "It's your city, my dear," he said.

"And it shall be yours," she said, standing and slowly turning so that those at adjacent tables would see her. She led him through the room, down to the lobby, and into a cab.

Minutes later, they entered a restaurant on Montgomery Street that immediately reminded Buffolino of every movie he'd ever seen in which the action took place in a Barbary Coast bordello. It was called Ernie's. Carla had told him during the short cab ride that it represented San Francisco's finest dining experience. Buffolino had his doubts, based on his theory that as opulence increased, so did prices, with a corresponding decrease in portions.

They swept in and were led to a table in the smoking section to accommodate Carla. The table was set with silver and crystal. Surrounding them were walls covered with mahogany paneling, red silk tapestries, and huge, gilt-edged mirrors. Carla stayed with Manhattans and chain-smoked as they studied the elaborate menu.

"What's good here?" Buffolino asked.

She took his hands across the table, something she would do with repeated frequency throughout the evening. "Allow me to order for the both of us, dear man."

She outdid even Buffolino at the Watergate. They dined on an hors d'oeuvre of preserved black turnips under foie gras in a port wine sauce; sliced loin of lamb with breast of rabbit garnished with eggplant and roasted garlic cloves; a salad of chilled slices of Maine lobster and squab with black truffles and vinaigrette spiked with Dijon mustard and green herbs; and, for dessert, a frothy lime soufflé flavored with a dash of acacia honey. He had been in the mood for a hamburger and fries, but had to admit everything tasted good, if a little operatic.

Over coffee and cognac, Buffolino made another attempt to bring the conversation around. "What a shame Mae isn't here to enjoy dinner and the opera with us," he said.

Carla, who had begun to show the effects of the wine, clutched her bosom. "Oh, my God, how true. Poor darling, she's had so much trouble in her life."

"Yeah, that's what Andrea told me. Funny, I never could get Andrea to talk about her father. It was like he didn't exist."

Carla's face turned serious as she again touched his hands. "Oh, yes, that is exactly what happened. He doesn't exist."

Buffolino laughed. "Some miracle," he said. "Second time. Does the Church know about it yet?"

She shook her finger at him as though he were a naughty boy in school who'd used a four-letter word. "It wasn't funny."

"Sorry, I—"

"Not what you said, dear man, but the circumstances surrounding Andrea's birth."

"Do you go back that far with Mae Feldman?"

"Yes. We were friends in college."

"You were friends back then, but you don't know who Andrea's father was?"

Carla sadly shook her head. "No, Mae refused to tell anyone. They weren't married, you know, and she didn't want the poor fellow to suffer the embarrassment of fathering a child out of wedlock."

"What about *her* embarrassment?" Buffolino asked.

"Mae, embarrassed?" She laughed. "Mae was never embarrassed about anything. She proudly carried that child through nine months, three days without a whimper, and brought her up as though Andrea had been born into a normal family."

Buffolino shook his head and finished his espresso. "I still don't understand how you could go nine months and never know anything about the man who knocked up your best friend."

"Nothing strange about that, dear man. I told you, Mae did not want to identify him. Oh, I know she met him in New York. He was . . ."

"Was what?"

"Was a young law student, I believe, passionate and impetuous. Mae was such a beautiful young woman. They fell head-over-heels in love. Then, as such things will happen, passion bred pregnancy. What time is it?"

Buffolino checked his watch and told her.

"Good Lord, we'll be late for the overture. Quickly, dear, pay the bill."

Buffolino had eaten in some fancy restaurants in his life, especially lately, but nothing equaled this one. The tip alone was bigger than his previous month's food bill. He used his VISA card, grumbled as he signed the receipt, and nodded curtly at everyone as they left the restaurant, severing all diplomatic relations.

"The War Memorial Opera House," Carla told the young taxi driver, "and please be quick about it."

She snuggled next to Tony in the backseat. He put his arm around her shoulders because he didn't know what else to do. She cooed in his ear, "You are so handsome. Many women must have told you that."

"Well, yeah, one or two." He thought of his two ex-wives and the women he'd dated since his second divorce, not counting the one-night flings that came with the territory of a cop. He was glad when the driver pulled up in front of the opera house and he could disengage from Madame Zaretski.

They were ushered to their seats just as the lights dimmed, and the orchestra began the opening bars of *Il Trovatore.*

So, that's Roseanna Gateaux, Buffolino thought as scene two began with the diva performing the role of Leonora. Great-looking woman, he said silently as, to his surprise, he slowly lost himself in the powerful and poignant music of the soprano's first aria.

At intermission, Carla insisted on having drinks at a small bar in the lobby. "You sure you want another?" Buffolino asked.

"From my father, I inherited an enhanced capacity for spirits," she said imperiously.

They stood off to the side observing the crowd. Most of the men wore tuxedos, the women formal dresses, although there was a contingent in jeans. One group in a corner dominated everyone's attention, a dozen people who were obviously being shielded from the rest of the crowd. "Who's the hero?" Buffolino asked a security guard.

"That's Senator Witmer."

Buffolino turned to Carla. "You know who he is?"

"Yes, he's one of our senators from California." She stood on the toes of her purple satin heels to get a better look at the senator.

"Your other senator is Ewald, the one Andrea worked for."

"Yes, I know."

"Did Andrea ever talk about the campaign, about Ewald?"

"Not to me, although she probably did with her mother. Mae was very interested in politics."

"They say Andrea had an affair with Ewald's son."

"Filthy lies, garbage," she snapped. "Andrea was a sweet girl, not the type to sleep around."

"Yeah, well, that's what they say. The son admits it."

"A liar, too, like his father. Fetch me another drink," she said from her tiptoe perch.

"Fetch you . . . ? You've had enough. Come on, let's get back to our seats."

She came down off her toes. "You darling man," she said, "caring about my health."

"Huh?"

"You are absolutely right. The time for drinking is after the performance. We shall go to Tosca and extend this glorious night."

Buffolino followed dejectedly behind her as she reentered the auditorium and slowly walked down the aisle, her caftan gliding silently over the carpeting, her head held unnecessarily high, looking left and right, a queen entering her castle. Enough of you, lady, Buffolino thought as he held his head low, eyes to the floor, and slipped into his seat with a sigh of relief.

"It was great," he said when they left the opera house. A cab took them to Columbus in the North Beach section. The Tosca Cafe was crowded, noisy, and festive, and it took some deft maneuvering to get a place at the bar, where Carla ordered cappuccino laced with brandy for both of them. An ancient jukebox played familiar arias, and individuals burst into song in every corner of the room. Buffolino nursed two cappuccinos, while Carla downed hers as though they were soft drinks.

An hour later, the evening took its final toll. Carla leaned heavily on the bar with one elbow, put her arm around Buffolino's neck, pulled him close, and said with a thick tongue, "The time for us to exit has come."

Buffolino helped her outside and directed the driver to take them to the public garage in which he'd parked his rented Lincoln. Once in it, Carla immediately fell asleep, leaving Buffolino to find Santiago Street on his own. He had better luck than he anticipated, parked in front of her house, and helped her inside, tripping over cats before allowing her to sink with great flourish onto the tattered chaise. He looked down into her blotched and weary face, makeup askew, one eyelash partially off, and, oddly, felt a profound sadness. She'd fallen asleep again, her mouth an open, crooked chasm, a series of snorts and snores coming from it. He was pleased the evening had ended this way—that there was no need to continue it. He debated attempting to get her into the bedroom, but thought better of it. "Sleep it off here, baby," he whispered as he slowly went to the front door, cast a final glance back, and returned to his car.

He sat behind the wheel and contemplated what he'd managed to learn that evening. It wasn't much, but in one way it was more than he'd planned on.

Staring at the adjoining house that was Mae Feldman's home, Buffolino was gripped with an overwhelming urge. First, he analyzed the situation: Carla Zaretski was passed out next door and likely to stay that way for a while. It was late; a few houses on the block had interior lights on, but not the ones on either side. He looked up and down the street, saw no one, started the engine, drove around the block, and parked a dozen houses removed from number 21.

He sat quietly again with the lights off until he was satisfied that no one was paying attention to him, got out of the car, pressed the driver's door closed, and casually walked up the street until arriving at the door marked 21B. He cast a final glance to the right and left before going around to the rear of the house, where a small, unkempt yard served both sides of the dwelling. There were two first floor rear windows on Mae Feldman's side. Buffolino chose the one to his right, the one furthest from where Carla Zaretski slept. He tried to look inside, but the window was covered by heavy drapes. He surveyed the glass for signs of a security-system tape, saw none, placed his fingers beneath the top sash bar, and pushed. Nothing. He almost laughed aloud for thinking he'd be lucky enough to find it unlocked.

Squatting, he ran his hand over the ground until his fingers came to rest on a small rock. He wrapped his handkerchief around it and gently tapped against one of the panes. The second time, he hit it a little harder. His third attempt succeeded. The glass shattered, shards of it falling at his feet, the stillness of the night magnifying for him the sounds of the glass hitting the ground. He gingerly reached inside, turned the simple window lock, raised the window as high as it would go, and pulled himself over the sill.

He stood in blackness and waited until his eyes adjusted. Soon the outline of a bed was visible in a shaft of moonlight slicing through where the drapes had parted. The last thing he wanted to do was to turn on a lamp, but it hadn't occurred to him to pack a flashlight to go to the opera. He closed the drapes as tightly as he could, found a small table lamp on a dresser, and turned the switch. Perfect, he thought; the three-way bulb put out minimal brightness at its lowest setting. Now, everything in the room was visible.

He opened the door to a small closet and peered inside. A few pieces of clothing hung from the rod, most of it male, including two men's suits. An assortment of shoes was on the floor. Again, the majority of them were men's.

Buffolino pulled a jacket from one of the hangers and held it up in front of him. "Must be a damn gorilla," he mumbled. He replaced the jacket, ran his hand along the empty shelf at the top of the closet, and closed the door.

He got on his knees and looked under the bed for boxes. Nothing there. He quickly went through the dresser drawers and discovered that, like the closet, they contained a mixture of clothing, mostly male.

He quietly opened a door and stepped into the living room. He was reluctant to turn on a light that would be visible from the front of the house, but he didn't have a choice. Drapes were drawn across the front picture window; that would help. He turned on a floor lamp in a corner and quickly surveyed the room, which presented him with nothing of immediate interest.

An archway led to a small foyer. Buffolino passed through it and opened a closet door. There was just enough light from the living room for him to see a metal chest about eighteen inches wide, a foot deep, and fifteen or sixteen inches high, with a handle on either end. He slid the box toward him, and was surprised at how heavy it was—some sort of fireproof metal container. He returned to the living room and placed the box on a chair beneath the lamp. The box was locked. He reached in his pants pocket for a small pocket knife and tried to jimmy the lock. No luck. He thought for a moment, then decided to take the box with him, find a way to open it in the car, check its contents, and, if all still looked peaceful, return it to the house.

He'd just switched off the lamp when he heard a noise outside the front door. He stiffened and cocked his head. Someone was inserting a key in the lock. Buffolino quickly positioned himself just inside the door, drew his .22, and waited, watched, as the lock was released and the doorknob turned.

A man, small in stature, stepped into the foyer. He held a revolver in his hand. Buffolino struck, the weight of his right hand and weapon coming down squarely on the back of the man's neck. The intruder fell to the floor, and Buffolino leaped on top of him, twisted the arm that held the revolver and brought it up sharply behind the man's back, causing the revolver to fall, and the intruder to shout in pain.

Buffolino never saw the second person come through the door, only felt the thud of a heavy object against the base of his skull. He pitched forward, semiconscious, his .22 sliding across the tile foyer floor. He desperately reached for it, but the second man drove his foot into his temple. A sudden burst of brilliant white pinpoints of light preceded blackness.

He was out for only a few minutes. He sensed that, got to his hands and knees, blinked against the pain in his head, and was aware that his revolver was gone.

He pulled himself to his feet and made a quick decision to leave the way he'd entered, through the back, reasoning that whoever had attacked him didn't know he'd come through a broken window in the rear. He passed through the living room, saw that the metal box was no longer where he'd left it, and cursed every step that sent a spasm through his skull. He entered the bedroom and listened at the window. It occurred to him how lucky he was. Whoever they were, they were armed. They could have shot him instead of just roughing him up. Small blessings. "Count 'em, Tony," he muttered as he placed his left leg through the window. Once that foot was secure outside, he dragged his right leg behind him, the one whose injury had almost prematurely ended his career as a cop. He'd hit the floor in the foyer pretty hard, and that knee ached.

Now he was outside, maybe not with what he'd gone in for, but he was out—and alive—aching knee and head be damned.

He placed his hands on the windowsill, drew a deep breath, and slowly exhaled. It was when all the breath was out of him that he became aware of someone behind him. He slowly turned to see the moon's rays reflecting off the barrel of a shotgun. "Hey, wait a minute," he started to say as the face belonging to the shotgun came into focus.

Carla Zaretski stood there, the gun shaking in her hand, her face the same weary, swollen mess it had been when he'd brought her home.

"Carla, it's me, I—"

The shotgun discharged with a roar, the pellets from the shell tearing into the flesh of his right thigh from just below his crotch to his knee. Her second blast, which resulted from an uncontrollable spasm in her fingers, missed him and sprayed the wall with pellets. The force of the first shot blew his right leg out from under him and spun him around. He fell against the house and slid down it, a broad crimson smear tracing his descent. His only words before passing out were, "Not the knee, not the goddamn knee . . ."

Fifteen minutes later, two uniformed policemen and two paramedics placed Tony Buffolino on a stretcher after taking emergency measures to stop the bleeding. Carla Zaretski sobbed between swallows of straight rye from a tall kitchen glass. "I heard noise and went into the backyard," she said for the tenth time. "I saw the broken window and called the police. I didn't know who it was."

"Will he make it?" one of the cops asked a kneeling medic.

"Yeah, but he's lost more blood than the four of us own. Come on, let's move."

"You have any idea why he'd break in like this?" one of the cops asked Carla. "You live next door, right?"

"Yes. No, I don't know. Maybe it was . . ." Had he been after her in a fit of passion? That question comforted her long after Buffolino had been taken away and the police had completed their questioning.

24

MAC SMITH and Annabel Reed sat together on the terrace outside the Watergate suite. Coffee and Danish pastries were on a table between them. Directly in front and below was the Potomac; the John F. Kennedy Center for the Performing Arts was visible to their left.

They'd just started discussing their recent experiences when a ringing phone interrupted them. They both started to get up, but Smith was quicker. Annabel listened from the terrace, heard him say, "Yes, this is Smith. I'm sorry, your name is . . . ? Dr. Thelen, Max Thelen? Yes, I can hear you better now, Dr. Thelen. You're with Moffitt Hospital? Yes, I understand, part of the University of California Medical Center. What can I do for you, Doctor?"

Annabel entered the room as the expression on Smith's face changed from simple interest to shock.

"He's alive, you say. He *is* expected to survive."

Smith listened to the caller's answer and said, "Yes, yes, I'm relieved to hear that. Please, Dr. Thelen, one moment." He put his hand over the mouthpiece and said to Annabel, "Tony's been shot. He lost a lot of blood. It was his leg. He's okay." He returned to his conversation with the doctor. "Do you have any details on who shot him? I see. Yes. Well, thank you, Doctor, thank you very much."

"Who shot him?" Annabel asked when he hung up.

"The doctor wasn't certain about that. Let me make a call."

Smith reached Joe Riga at MPD, told him what had happened to Buffolino, and asked if he could get any information from the San Francisco police.

"Yeah, I'll make a call, Mac. I'll get back to you."

Riga called fifteen minutes later and told Smith that Buffolino had broken into a home owned by one Carla Zaretski, who'd shot him as an intruder.

"He broke into *her* house? He told me he was taking her out to dinner and to the opera."

"Mac, I'm telling you what I got from a detective I know in Frisco. Here's the number, if you want to find out more. Hey, don't be so shocked. Tony's elevator doesn't always reach the top. Likable, maybe, but a whack job."

Smith poised to argue the point but didn't.

Mac and Annabel returned to the terrace and sat quietly. She asked him what he intended to do next.

"Well, Annie, there are now two people missing, Janet Ewald and Marcia Mims. I'm going to make some calls concerning Marcia. I also want to stop in at MPD and . . ."

"And what?"

"I've got to go to San Francisco. Can you come with me?"

"Yes, of course."

"What about the gallery?"

"I've already been drawn into this by your màgnetic and persuasive personality, Mr. Smith, and I may as well stay in for the duration. I'll spend time with James at the gallery this afternoon. When do you want to leave?"

"I'm tied up tomorrow. How about Saturday?"

"Fine. I'll book us a flight. By the way, one of the men who I think was following me in New York was on my shuttle yesterday."

Smith turned to her and said sternly, "And you tell me this as an afterthought? I wonder if I'll ever get anybody on my side to speak out fully. Did you get a better look at him?"

"Yes. No long, jagged scars on the cheek, no shaved head. Looked like all the other businessmen on the flight."

They rode down together in the elevator and stood outside the main entrance to the hotel. "Do you know what I think I'll do this afternoon?" he said.

"What?"

"I think what I need is exercise. I'll hit the gym later this afternoon. Dinner tonight?"

"Sure. In or out?"

"In. A quiet evening at home with Nick and Nora Charles."

Smith's attempts to reach Marcia Mims were unsuccessful. He called the Ewald house and was told that Marcia had called in and said she would be taking a couple of additional days off. "Do you know where she's gone?" Smith asked. No.

He called Marcia's cousin Tommy, in Annapolis, and asked the same question. Tommy hadn't heard from her since she left the bar so suddenly.

When he couldn't reach Joe Riga, either, Smith decided to act on his plan to get in some exercise that afternoon. He wasn't devoted to physical activity, had never become one of what a friend termed "health Nazis," suddenly allergic people who sniff out smokers in restaurants like bounty hunters, drink only a little white wine despite serious cravings for gin, and run marathon miles each day in pursuit of eternal youth while turning their knees into centenarian joints. But because he had been an athlete, and because he did enjoy the mental clarity that usually followed physical activity, he did his best to work some form of it into his routine.

He'd been a member of the Yates Field House at Georgetown University for years, and even though he'd joined the faculty at George Washington University and had access to facilities there, he preferred to stick with familiar surroundings. He changed into shorts and a T-shirt in the club's locker room, and began to a slow trot around the indoor running track. He was the only person on the track when he started, but by the time he'd gone halfway around, a familiar face came through the door, waved, and caught up to him. It was Rhonda Harrison. "Hello, Mac," she said. "Burning off major-league dinners?"

Smith laughed. "Always a need to do that, but this has nothing to do with calories." They jogged next to each other. "This is for the mind today," he said. "I need to clear it out."

"Same here," Rhonda said. "I don't know where I'm going to find the time, but my agent just got me a good fee to do a piece for *Washingtonian* on Andrea Feldman."

Smith stopped running, and Rhonda halted a few feet ahead. She turned to him. "You look spooked, Mac."

"That name does tend to get my attention these days."

She leaned against a railing and wiped beads of perspiration from her forehead. "Yes, I guess it should. I was going to call you in a day or two. I have a list of dozens of people to interview, and you're high up on it."

Smith gave her a friendly smile.

"And, Mac, don't tell me that you can't talk to me because you're defense counsel for Paul Ewald. He's out, which means you don't have a client anymore."

"True."

"Let me ask you a question."

"Shoot."

"I'm slanting the article along the lines of a young, attractive woman with a law degree hooks up with some political heavy hitters in Washington, and gets herself killed as a result. Her mother immediately disappears, doesn't even come forward to claim the body. The son of a leading candidate for the White House is the prime suspect. This young woman, who meets an unfortunate end, is killed with a weapon belonging to this potential president of our country. Still, no one knows who killed Andrea Feldman."

Smith shrugged. "Sounds like an interesting human-interest piece. I'm sure you'll do your usual bang-up job."

"Funny choice of words. I intend to. I've talked to Feldman's associates. Not many of them, Mac. She defined 'loner.' No buddies, no steady boyfriends, no family. If it weren't for the Ewald family paying to bury her out in San Francisco, she'd be planted in the District Cemetery along with the tombs of the unknown winos and druggies. How come?"

"I'm listening, Rhonda, you're talking. Keep going."

"Damn." Rhonda said, laughing. "The more I talk about it, the better it gets. Andrea Feldman sleeps with Senator Ewald's son. Do you figure she was carrying information about Ewald out to his enemies—you know, pillow talk from Paul?"

"I wouldn't know." He hoped she would have the answer. Knowing what a good reporter she was, Smith wondered whether she'd uncovered anything about Andrea's affair with not only Paul Ewald, but with his father, too. He thought she might mention that next, but she didn't. Instead, she asked, "Do you have any idea where to find Andrea Feldman's mother?"

"No, I don't."

"I checked the birth records at Moffitt Hospital in San Francisco where Andrea was born. No father-of-record. A real mystery woman. Her last known address is in the Sunset district. I talked to her landlady, a flaky former opera singer who told me the mother left."

"Didn't know where she went?"

"Not according to her. The whole family is shrouded in mystery."

"Evidently."

They continued to jog, but without words. A man and a woman sprinted past them. Smith realized how long it had been since he'd done any running. He was getting winded quicker than usual. As they approached the door, Rhonda punched him on the arm and said with a grin, "That's it for me. See you around the quad, Mac. Can I call you in a few days about this?"

"Sure. Happy to talk to you again, Rhonda." He watched her disappear through the doors, did another lap, and headed for the gymnasium, where he lifted weights, did a series of stretching exercises that he knew he should have done before he started running, showered, dressed, and returned home. There he changed into a gray sweatshirt from his university, baggy khaki pants and Docksiders, and took Rufus for a long walk through the neighborhood.

He walked back into the house and made himself a cup of coffee. As he sat at the table, Rufus looked up with soft, watery eyes. Smith looked down into the dog's trusting face and said to him, "Doesn't make any sense to you, either, huh? Well, think about it. We'll talk more tonight." He went to his study and made notes until he realized Annabel would be there for dinner. He ran to a local market and bought the ingredients—pâté, swordfish, salad makings, new potatoes, and French bread—and made whatever preparations he could before she arrived.

After they had consumed and saluted Smith's culinary gestures, they made a gesture of another sort at each other.

Now, an hour later, they sat together in bed, naked, watching a documentary on television.

"We'll take a ten o'clock shuttle," she said. "The noon flight to San Francisco out of Kennedy on Saturday was the only one open."

"That sounds fine. We pick up three hours going in that direction anyway."

The commercials ended, and they watched the next section of the documentary. When it was again time to move into a commercial break, Ted Koppel's face came on the screen and he announced his guest for that evening's *Nightline.*

Annabel asked whether he had watched Colonel Gilbert Morales Tuesday on the Koppel show.

"Some," he said. "I really didn't focus on it."

"He mounts a convincing argument," Annabel said.

"In substance or in style?"

"A little of both."

"I think he and his cause are frauds. The Manning White House makes continual public proclamations of the drug epidemic in this country, but they keep wrapping their arms around Morales, who, everybody knows, was one of the leading drug pushers in Central America."

"He *was* an ally."

"Allies like that we don't need."

"You are such a liberal, which, I must admit, is part of your charm. An old liberal. Hubert Humphrey found old liberals to be sad. I don't. I ended up in love with one."

Smith laughed. "I probably should have taken up with an eighteen-year-old Georgetown hippie instead of a middle-aged, relatively conservative beauty. We could have protested together."

"And died prematurely in bed. Think of the embarrassment to family and friends. Besides, you're dating yourself. They're not called 'hippies' anymore."

"That's one thing I'm damned enthusiastic about with Ken's campaign," he said.

"Dying in bed with young girls?"

"No, wench. If he *does* become president, I think he'll take quick and decisive steps to cut off all aid to that fraud Morales, as well as that charlatan evangelist Garrett Kane, who claims he's set up ministries in Panama. Bull."

"We promised ourselves we would never discuss politics, remember?"

"Sure, and for good reason." He looked over at her beautiful breasts above the comforter that covered her legs, reached to touch a pink tip, and growled.

Rufus raised his head from the floor at the sound, then put it back down.

"Mac, what are you doing?"

"Something apolitical."

"Are you suggesting twice in one night?"

"As you say, Annabel, you're in love with a liberal. I can't think of anything more liberal . . ."

Her eyes widened, and a wicked smile crossed her mouth. "And I'm not nearly as conservative as you think I am when it comes to matters of the flesh. I just thought that—"

"That this *old* liberal isn't capable of repeating a triumph? Remember FDR."

"So long ago. But."

She kicked the covers off, moved her leg over to straddle him, and looked down into his eyes. "On second thought, no buts."

After a moment, she said, "My God, Smith—do you think a third term is out of the question?"

25

EARLY SATURDAY MORNING, Smith took Rufus to the local kennel, where the Dane was enthusiastically welcomed. "Don't worry about Rufus, Mr. Smith," the owner said, "just view it as him taking a nice vacation at a fancy dog hotel." The owner always said that when Smith delivered Rufus, but Smith always responded as though he were hearing it for the first time; he was very appreciative of the good care his friend received there.

Heavy weather had hit the East Coast overnight, delaying flights in and out of Washington and New York. They made their American Airlines flight from JFK to San Francisco with only minutes to spare.

"Did you talk to Ken or Leslie?" Annabel asked after they'd settled in their first-class seats and had been served Bloody Marys.

"Yes. I talked to Leslie yesterday. She kept thanking me for all I did for Paul, and I kept reminding her I didn't do anything."

"Maybe you did more than you think."

"In the meantime, we have this business with Greist to iron out."

"Well, Mr. Greist is probably nothing but a bumbling con man looking for a fast buck. Funny, but I'm anxious to meet Tony. I can't say he's my favorite person, based on the stories you've told."

"He's all right. What I want to hear from him is why the hell he was breaking into this Carla Zaretski's house after he'd taken her to dinner and the opera. His message on my machine indicated that she was a real—"

" 'Dog'? Don't use that word, Mac."

"I wouldn't dream of it. She was not the sort of female that particularly appealed to him. Better?"

"Much."

"So, I wonder why he was breaking into her house. Something must have developed during the evening that turned her into the girl of his dreams."

Annabel giggled. "You think he was breaking in to rape her?"

"No, just anxious to continue communing on a philosophical level. We'll find out soon enough."

After the flight to San Francisco, they got into a cab driven by a portly gentleman in his sixties with a swooping walrus mustache, a tweed jacket, and an Irish tweed cap. When everyone was settled inside, he turned to them, but failed to ask the expected "Where to?" Instead, he said, "And what political persuasion might you two be?"

Annabel and Smith looked at each other and stifled laughter. Smith said, "A Roosevelt Democrat."

"And you?" the driver asked Annabel.

"A conservative who has whatever it takes to make Roosevelt Democrats happy."

26

AS MAC SMITH and Annabel Reed were winging their way west, Senator Jody Backus was finishing a speech to a group of supporters in the Antrim Lodge in Roscoe, New York, a little more than two hours from New York City and known as the trout capital of the world.

"Great speech, Senator," an aide said as the corpulent candidate for president climbed down from a platform at the end of the large dining room. A hundred people had paid twenty-five dollars each to break bread with him at lunch and to hear him call for a return to decency, family values, and morality in the media. He'd been warmly received. The "morality in media" issue had only recently been injected into his otherwise-standard canned speech.

He'd ended with, "And I'll tell you one more thing. When I'm president of these United States, you'll see a president with a total commitment to the environment. They don't call Roscoe the trout capital of the world for nothin', and I'll see to it that these beautiful waters, and these big, fat trout, are around for years to come." The crowd had erupted in applause. Backus added, "As a matter of fact, as soon as we break this up, I'm headin' for Zach Filler's lodge, where I'm intendin' to spend the rest of this day and tomorrow morning haulin' 'em in."

The limo, followed by a string of cars in which press rode, turned onto the quiet little main street of Roscoe and stopped in front of a sporting goods store. "Be back in a minute," Backus said as he pulled himself out of the limo. "Got to see what the local folks are catchin' them on these days." He disappeared into the store followed by an aide and Secret Service agents.

The luncheon, like the fishing trip itself, had been decided on at the last minute by Backus. An old friend from Georgia, Zach Filler, owned a small fishing lodge in the area, and Backus's staff knew their boss needed such days. They just wished he'd plan ahead a little better.

Usually, his press aides were able to turn these sudden deviations into something positive. Ewald might seem to have the nomination wrapped up, but Backus's boys were going to take him into the convention with strength. There would have to be some dealing. The staff had managed to bring in enough upstate New York Democrats for the luncheon, and made plans to take photographs of Backus fishing, which they would release to fishing magazines and sports pages. "Fly fishing's hot these days," one of them said. "Might as well sell the old man to those fanatics, too." When they announced their plans to Backus, he dampened their assiduity by telling them this was to be pure relaxation, with only a few close advisers and a single Secret Service agent accompanying him. One of the aides mounted an argument. Backus snapped, "Damn it to hell, I am sick and tired of people and press and pressing the flesh! I need a day with the fish, just me and some big, fat ol' trout." And when a senior aide questioned whether they should run the change of schedule through Backus's campaign braintrust, he erupted. "I don't need to clear nothing through nobody, and it's time people around here got to understand that! Jody Backus is his own man."

Lodge owner Zach Filler was waiting when the limousine and two accompanying vehicles pulled up to the main house. Backus was shown to the largest cabin on the grounds. It contained two bedrooms; Agent Jeroldson was assigned to the second.

"You really threw me a curve, you rascal," Filler told Backus as the senator settled into a rocking chair and accepted a glass of bourbon from his friend. A roaring fire took the chill off the room. There were bottles of bourbon, buckets of ice, and a large tray with cheeses, breads, cold shrimp, and smoked salmon and trout. "I had to shift some good regular customers around to fit you and your people in."

"And I appreciate it, Zach. Hope it wasn't too much of an imposition. The fish bitin'?"

"Yes, they are, mostly on black ants and nymphs."

"Damn it, Zach, the fella in the store said they were risin' to mayflies and caddis. I bought myself a whole bunch a' nice flies tied by Walt and Winny Dette." The Dettes, who lived in Roscoe, were considered among the world's leading dry-fly-tying experts.

Filler laughed. "Beauty . . . and what catches fish are in the eye of the beholder. Don't worry, Jody, I'll take care of you. You'll catch yourself a fish." Filler closely observed his old friend. Obviously, running for president took its toll. Backus looked considerably older, more fatigued, and less healthy than he had the last time they'd been together, a year ago in Georgia. He asked, "How is it going, Jody?"

Backus scowled at him and drew on his drink. "Could be better, Zach."

Filler asked whether Jody wanted another drink. "Not right away, Zach. I got some heavy thinking to do, and I'd better get on the phone. You heard any news today about my opponent, Senator Ewald?"

Filler laughed. "Can't say that I have, but that's why I bought this place. The rest of the world doesn't exist up here, which suits me fine."

Backus grunted and yawned. "I may have a visitor in the morning, Zach, a special one. I'd just as soon keep that between us."

"Absolutely. You ready for a good dinner? I brought in a fine Indian cook for you. I let my regular one go last week. Son of a bitch was stealing me blind, not money, but food, which comes down to the same thing."

"I figure I can put off dinner for a while." Backus tapped his large stomach and grinned, which pleased Filler. It was the first demonstration since he'd arrived that his friend was relaxing. "Look, Zach, anybody calls for me, I'm not available, hear? The others'll take calls. I got to get as far away as possible from them."

"I can understand that, Jody," Filler said, laughing. "I only keep a phone here for city guests who can't seem to be out of contact with their businesses. Some of them spend more time on the phone than on the stream. Don't know what they catch—but they can have it."

Backus closed his eyes.

"Let me get back and see how dinner's shaping up," Filler said. "There's five of you?"

"Right. I appreciate this, Zach. I feel better already."

"Always glad to help a good friend, Jody. I'll be back."

Backus sat alone in the cabin, the flames of the fire casting a ruddy, healthy glow over his round face. He'd shed his coat, tie, and shoes, and felt himself sink into the rocking chair's well-worn cane seat. Then, as though he'd suddenly forgotten something, he looked in the direction of the room assigned to Jeroldson and shouted, "Bobby, come out here."

Jeroldson, who'd been reclining on the bed reading a copy of *Service Star,* the Secret Service's employee publication, got up and stood in the doorway.

"Come, sit, Bobby, and let's talk while we got the chance."

The dour agent took a straight-back chair near the fireplace.

"Help yourself," said Backus, gesturing toward the platter of food.

"I'm not hungry."

"Then have yourself a drink."

"Not on duty."

Backus started to laugh, but it turned into a sputter. "You are some strange breed, Bobby," he said. "Duty? The only duty you have right now is to relax and talk to me. Go on now, have a drink. You don't like bourbon? Go on up to the house and tell Zach what it is you do want— gin, beer, moose piss, whatever."

"I'll have bourbon." Jeroldson poured a small amount of it into a glass filled with ice cubes, popped a shrimp in his mouth, and returned to his chair.

"Well, now, Mr. Bobby Jeroldson, tell me how the senator and Mr. Farmer felt when you were transferred over to me last week."

Jeroldson shrugged. "They didn't say anything."

"Seems to me the senator from California would be pleased. I heard he wasn't especially fond a' you."

The comment brought a small smile to Jeroldson's wooden face.

"You want to say the feelin's mutual, don't you?"

A shrug.

"All I can say, Bobby, is that you've done a fine job keeping this ol' boy up to date on what my friend and colleague Senator Ewald has been up to. I'm sincerely appreciative. I figure you're smart enough to know that whether it's me in the White House, or Vice-President Thornton, you've got yourself a fat job up on top of the Uniformed Division. Be a nice spot for you, Bobby, about a thousand men under you, respect, make a real name for yourself." He was referring to the Secret Service's special uniformed unit charged with protecting the White House, embassies, consulates, and chanceries. Although it had been the subject of considerable criticism because of its use of extensive manpower and excessive money to patrol Washington's safest streets and best neighborhoods—while the MPD had to deal with the city's worst crime areas—it had been considered a political sacred cow ever since Richard Nixon established it in 1969.

"I didn't do much."

"More than maybe you know, Bobby. Is he still sleepin' around with that opera star, Gateaux?"

"Yes."

Backus laughed. "Wonder if she's as good at shatterin' glasses in bed as she is on the stage."

"I don't think much about things like that," Jeroldson said.

Backus yawned and scratched his sizable belly through a gap in his shirt. "You see, Bobby, although Senator Ewald and I are colleagues in the Senate, we never seem to see eye-to-eye on certain things that I feel this country vitally needs. People like Senator Ewald, even though they might think they're patriotic, seem to be hell-bent on selling this country out to the Commies and their friends. I won't mince words with you. Havin' Ken Ewald in the White House could mean the end of this beautiful democracy of ours, and you have made a fine contribution to preserving this country I know you love as much as I do."

"Thank you." He said it with a lack of expression that matched his face. Jeroldson's evaluation report at the completion of his training at the Federal Law Enforcement Training Center in Brunswick, Georgia —where Backus first met him—and at the Secret Service's own academy in Beltsville, Maryland, had noted, "Agent Jeroldson possesses all the physical and mental attributes to become a useful agent. He is, however, a young man with unbending ideals and principles, which, perhaps, will have to be tempered if he is to develop into an agent with growth potential."

"I figured now that we're smack dab in the middle of the end of this campaign, it was better for you to be with me. Now, all you have to do is keep an eye on this fat ol' Georgia boy and make sure some crackpot doesn't mistake me for a moose."

"I'll make sure that doesn't happen, Senator."

"Good, good. Best you take a walk now, go on up to the main house and read a magazine. I'll let you know when to come back. Nice country up here, isn't it?"

"Beautiful."

"A little chilly. Keep the fire goin'."

After Backus had dined with Zach Filler on fresh bass, vegetables, and corn bread, the two friends took a walk. Backus wore old, wrinkled Sears work pants, a nubby green sweater over the dress shirt he'd worn that day, and a heavy black-and-red wool jacket.

They crossed a bridge, went up a lonely road, and stopped on a bridge from which they could see the famed trout streams of Roscoe. The night was crystal clear, and chilly. The black sky above was blistered with millions of bright white stars.

"Good dinner, Zach," Backus said, staring out at the stream.

"Joey's a good cook, when he's sober."

"Sometimes it's better not to be sober, Zach. Sometimes it's better for man to miss what's going on around him."

"You feel that way these days?"

"Sometimes. My daddy always told me that when things get too complicated, all you've got to do is to stand back, give it some room, and it'll all clear up. He was right, only he wasn't dealing with the problems of keeping this country free. That's a little more complicated. You see, Zach, sometimes a man has to do things that are personally distasteful to him. He has to do those things because there is somethin' a lot bigger at stake, and in this case, it's the future security of these United States."

Filler, too, gazed out over the stream, where light from an almost full moon caught the ripples and sent them dancing. He said, "I've never pried, Jody, not where I'm not wanted, and I won't start now, but you look like a man with the weight of the world on his shoulders. If I can help . . ."

"You already have, Zach. Comin' up here is what my daddy said to do when things get rough."

"Ewald?"

"Yup."

"I could never understand how anybody could consider him for president, especially compared to you."

Backus let out a gruff laugh. "That, my old friend, is a gross understatement, and I won't pretend modesty. I have to hand it to Mr. Ewald, though, I really thought this country was finished with his kind of politics, and that I wouldn't have a hell of a lot of trouble whuppin' him in the primaries. The man proved me wrong. I gave it my best shot, Zach, and now that the handwriting is pretty much up there on the wall, I . . ." He shook his head. "Even though I'm a Democrat, I truly question what this country will be like if he ends up our president. Of course, I've got to go around sayin' I'll back him if he wins." He slowly turned and looked at Filler, who had been staring at him. "That a bad thing for me to be thinkin' and sayin'?"

"Not to me, Jody, but you're not the only one faced with that dilemma. Think of voters like me, who truly care about this country and sure as hell don't want the likes of California Ken Ewald in the White House."

"You understand, then."

"Of course I do, but all I have to do is vote. I wouldn't be in your shoes."

"I don't want to be in my shoes, either."

Filler didn't have any words for a few moments. Then he asked, "Do you think you can somehow still win the nomination?"

Backus's grin was illuminated by the moon. "Well, things have been better lately, Zach, only you never know. I know one thing."

"What's that?"

"I know that it's either goin' to be me or Raymond Thornton in the White House. Either way, this country will sail an even course."

Filler looked at his large friend with admiration in his eyes. "This country was built by people like you, Jody, and thank God we still have your breed."

The next morning, another limousine arrived at Filler's lodge. Two men wearing chest waders, bulging fishing vests, peaked hats, and large polarized sunglasses stepped from it and immediately got into a Voyager minivan that was waiting for them. The driver, Secret Service agent Jeroldson, left the parking lot and drove the new visitors, along with Jody Backus, to a point on the stream where it curved, and where a deep trout pool existed. Backus and his visitors went down a gentle bank and stepped with care into the fast-flowing water, using wading staffs for support. They'd said nothing from the moment the men got into the van. Now, after they cast their flies into the water and stood silently for several minutes, Backus said, "I think we might be goin' a little too far."

The older of the two men who'd arrived that morning said agreeably, "I think everything is going just fine, Jody. Perfect, you might say."

"I don't know, there's a point where—"

"If there's a *point,* Senator, it's that we could come close as a fly is to a tippet to losing this country, to losing democracy all over the world."

"I couldn't live with that," said Backus.

"You won't have to. God is all-giving."

"God? Seems like a few of us mortals have done a speck more, of late."

The older man made another cast. As the line snapped forward after looping behind him, the hook on the small fly caught in the fabric of his hat. He removed his hat and glasses, and worked to disengage the barb.

Zach Filler, who'd strolled down to the stream and watched the action on it from a distance, narrowed his eyes and focused on the older man as he attempted to remove the hook. Filler hadn't had any idea who Senator Backus's visitors were, nor did he care. Now, nonetheless, he knew. There was no mistaking him—the flowing silver hair, the handsome tanned face, the smile. He'd been on television too many times to not be recognized as America's most famous television evangelist.

27

"Dr. Thelen, I'm Mackensie Smith. This is Ms. Reed."

"Oh, yes, Mr. Smith, Ms. Reed. You didn't waste time getting here."

"No, Mr. Buffolino is—"

"He's told me how close you are. You're partners, I understand."

"Partners? Well, it's more a matter of . . ." He could see Annie grinning. "Yes, we're partners. How is he?"

"Doing very well, considering the amount of blood he lost. His right thigh looks like it went through a meat grinder, but I'd say the prognosis is good. He'll heal nicely, won't lose too much leg function."

" 'Lose leg function'?" Annabel said. "We didn't realize it was so serious."

"Let's just say he won't be winning any medals for the high hurdles, but he won't need a cane, either," Thelen said. "He's lucky. That previous injury to his right knee was very severe. If he'd been hit *there* again . . . No, no, I think he'll do just fine."

"Can we see him?" Annabel asked.

"Of course. He's still under sedation, but he's fairly alert, sitting up, as a matter of fact. The woman who shot him, a Ms. Zaretski, is with him."

"She is . . . *with* him?"

"Yes." The doctor winked. "Been here almost every minute since he was brought in. An obvious accident. She thought he was a burglar."

"So I heard," Smith said.

"She was an opera star," Thelen said.

"Really?" Smith said. "Maybe if she thought he was a burglar, she thought she was an opera star."

Thelen laughed. "No, she's actually had quite a career. She told me all about it."

"I'm sure she has. We won't stay long."

Tony was dozing in a chair when they entered his room. His leg was bandaged from hip to foot. A dying old man was in the other bed, his eyes fluttering, his frail body hooked up to a variety of high-tech medical equipment.

Carla Zaretski sat next to Tony, holding his hand. When she was aware of Smith and Annabel, she looked up. "You must be Mr. Smith." She said to Buffolino, "Tony, your partner is here."

Buffolino opened his eyes and focused on Smith's face. "Mac." He freed his hand from Carla's grasp and reached up to Smith, who gripped it firmly. "How's it going, Tony?"

"Not bad. At least it wasn't the goddamn knee."

"Hello," Annabel said as Tony shifted his eyes to her.

"Well, the famous Annabel Reed." He smiled. "He drag you out here? How do you put up with this guy?" he asked. He started to laugh, which sent him into a painful coughing spell. When he regained control, he introduced Carla to them, and they chatted about Tony's condition. Smith asked, "Would you mind if I had a few words alone with him?" He indicated to Annabel with his eyes that she should accompany Carla out of the room.

Smith sat in Carla's chair. "I'm glad you're going to be okay, Tony. You're lucky she didn't aim a few inches higher."

"Or lower. The knee means more to me these days."

"Why were you breaking into her house?"

"I wasn't. She owns the house, but it's a two-family place. Mae Feldman rents one side from her." He grimaced in pain.

"Are you all right?" Smith asked. "I'll get a nurse."

"No, it's okay. I figured I might as well take a look inside Feldman's place, so I came through a back window."

"And she caught you."

"No. She was in her place sleeping off too much hooch. I found this locked box in a closet in Feldman's foyer and was going to take it out to the car when two guys came through the front. I didn't know there were two of them. The second one nailed me."

"Recognize them?"

"No. The first one had a piece. He was a little guy."

"Little guy? Very little?"

"Not big. I didn't see either of them good, Mac. Anyway, I come to and go back out the rear window, only the queen wakes up when she hears me getting it, figures somebody's rippin' off next door, grabs a freakin' shotgun, and does me. She didn't know who I was till it was too late. She's okay, a pain in the butt, but okay. Drinks too much."

Smith said, "I'll bet. Did the little guy and his partner take the box?"

"Yeah. When I come to, it was gone." He sounded angry.

"That's all right, Tony. The only thing you should be thinking about is getting better." Smith could see that Buffolino was drowsy. He asked, "Anything else in Mae Feldman's apartment? See anything interesting besides the box?"

"No, she must have a guy lives with her. Either that or she's a dyke. Most of the clothes are men's clothes, cheap stuff, cut funny. Maybe she lives with King Kong."

"King Kong?"

"Yeah, the sleeves on the jacket I looked at were funny, long, hung down. Know what I mean?"

"Yes, I think so." Smith thought of the description of Herbert Greist Annabel had given him when she returned from New York. He asked, "Does your friend out there know where Mae is?"

"No. She said she goes away a lot. I guess she really took off this time."

Smith frowned. "Tony, does Carla know that the men who beat you up also took a box from Feldman's side of the house?"

"Ask her."

"No, I'm not sure I want to do that. You say there was a lot of men's clothing?"

"Right, suits, shirts, underwear, shoes."

Smith looked over at the dying old man and hoped *he* wouldn't end up that way, frail, alone, tied to machines. "Tony, I would love to get back into Mae Feldman's side of that house."

"Shouldn't be hard. Carla will let you in."

"She will?"

"I don't see why not."

"I'd rather get in there without her knowing about it. Any ideas?"

Buffolino closed his eyes and moved his tongue over his dry lips. He opened his eyes and looked at Carla's purse on the floor next to Smith's chair. "Take her keys," he said.

Smith had to smile. He was not anxious to be arrested in San Francisco for illegal entry. It wouldn't look good when he returned to teaching law at the university. Still, the temptation was strong. "Tony do you think she'll hang around here for the rest of the day?"

"Probably. That's one favor I want from you. Get the queen off my back, huh?"

"I'll do my best, but I want a favor from you, too. Keep her here for three or four hours. Make nice with her."

"You ask a lot for a grand a week, Mac."

"I'll give you a bonus. For war wounds, and double-time for Carla."

"Okay. Hey, another favor for me. Call my wife—wives—and let 'em know what happened to me, only don't make it sound too bad. And don't tell 'em about the queen out there. Maybe you could say I got gunned down by some mafioso, something glamorous, and tell 'em I'm still on the case and that they don't have to worry about money. Okay?"

"Of course. It's true. You are still on the case, and you don't have to worry about money. Anything else I can do for you in return for this great sacrifice you've made on my behalf with the lady out there?"

"Get me back to Washington. This is a nice place, and the doctors arc great, but it's too far away, Mac, too far away."

"I'll arrange it. George Washington University has an excellent hospital and staff."

There was no further need for words. Tony looked at the closed door, reached over, slipped his hand into Carla's purse, and came out with a set of keys. He handed them to Smith.

"Here. Now you didn't take 'em."

Smith said, "We'll have these back in a few hours. Remember, keep your opera-singing friend happy *and here*. I'll check in with you later."

When the women returned, Smith asked Carla, "Will you be staying with my partner a while?"

"Yes, I could never leave this dear man alone in such strange and threatening surroundings."

"You're a very good person, Ms. Zaretski." It suddenly dawned on Smith: She was more than attracted—Carla had fallen in love with Tony. Tony deserved an even bigger bonus than Smith had planned. He kept his smile to himself.

"Well, Ms. Reed and I have some business to attend to," he said. "We'll be back later today."

"A pleasure to meet both of you," Carla said.

"The feeling is entirely mutual, Ms. Zaretski," Smith said as he took Annabel's elbow and guided her out of the room.

Downstairs, Smith handed Annabel the keys from Carla Zaretski's purse.

"What are these?"

"The keys to Carla's house. I assume one of them fits the door to the side Mae Feldman lives in. I want you to go there, Annabel, and take a good look through Feldman's side."

"Mac, where did you get these?"

"Tony took them from her purse. He's going to make sure she stays here until you get back."

"Oh, Mac, I don't think that I should be . . ."

"You have to."

"Why do I have to?"

"Because you're a breed of woman who will do anything for the man she loves. Grab a cab, look around out there, get back here as soon as you can, go up to Tony's room, figure out a way to get Carla out of it, and he'll replace the keys in her purse. Nobody will know the difference."

"Why don't we go together?"

"Because I have other things to do. We'll meet up at the hotel."

"All right, Mac, but I want you to know that behind that distinguished, pleasant facade lurks your real self."

"Which is?"

"A devoted second-story man and con artist." She kissed his cheek and went outside to where a line of cabs waited.

At the end of the day, Smith went to their hotel, the Raphael on Union Square, and ordered up a bucket of ice, bottles of vodka and scotch, and two club sandwiches. He stripped off his clothes, took a hot shower, turned on the television, and poured himself a drink. He took a halfhearted bite from one of the sandwiches, turned down the TV's volume, and dialed the telephone. One of the staff answered; a few moments later, Ewald was on the line.

"This is Mac. I'm calling from San Francisco."

"What are you doing out there?"

"Running down some leads."

"Leads to what?"

"To what seems to be an evolving scenario that gets more tangled with every step."

"I don't understand. Paul is home. The charges have been dropped. What scenario are you talking about?"

"I'll be back in Washington tomorrow night. We have to talk Monday morning."

"About what?"

"Do you know a New York attorney named Herbert Greist?"

"Never heard of him."

"Well, you're about to. Ken, this is not for the phone. I only called to let you know that I think we should talk as soon as possible."

Ewald's sigh was audible. "All right, but my schedule is really getting jammed. The polls are looking up again—and I want to keep them that way. Is there something I should be especially concerned about?"

"We can explore that when we get together. Say hello to Leslie."

Annabel arrived an hour later. "How'd it go?" Smith asked.

"Better than it went for you, I think. Are you drunk?"

"Don't be ridiculous."

He refilled his glass as she kicked off her shoes, discarded her suit jacket, and flopped on the bed. He handed her a drink.

"Mac, did you get the impression at the hospital that Madame Zaretski has fallen for our Tony?"

Smith laughed. "I plan to be best man at the wedding. What did you find at Mae Feldman's house?"

"Not much. There's a lot of male clothing in the closets."

"Yes, Tony told me that."

"As I was looking around, I kept thinking of what you'd told me about Andrea Feldman's apartment in Washington, sparse, looking as though it weren't really lived in. Her mother's place is the same. It's so Spartan, very little personal around."

"Like mother, like daughter. Did you notice anything unusual about the male clothing, particularly the suits?"

"I didn't look very closely at them. I felt them. Cheap fabric."

"You didn't pull out a jacket and look at it?"

"No, why would I do that?"

"I'm not saying you should have, but Tony did."

"He did? Why?"

"Because he's been an investigator a long time, I suppose. Remember the description you gave me of Herbert Greist?"

"Of course."

"You said his arms were especially long, and that one arm was longer than the other."

"That's right."

"Funny, Tony said the jacket he examined in Mae Feldman's apartment looked like it would fit King Kong."

She laughed. "Are you saying . . . ?"

"I'm suggesting that it's possible that Herbert Greist at least uses Mae Feldman's closets for winter storage."

"Or had a relationship with her that was a little closer than that."

"Exactly."

Annabel went into the bathroom, whistling on her way. Smith sat in the chair and observed her looking into the mirror and correcting a fault with her eyebrow that only she could see. Strange, he thought, that she would react in such a cavalier manner to the possibility he'd just raised about Greist.

She returned to the main room and changed channels on the television.

"Annabel, did you hear what I said?"

She looked at him and opened her eyes wide. "Yes, I heard you."

"And?"

"I think you'll need more tangible proof that the suits in the closet belong to Herbert Greist."

"Of course I need more tangible evidence, but don't you think it's . . ."

She got up, came to him, and touched him lightly on the nose with her index finger. Her smile was playful. "Would you like more tangible evidence?"

"Wait a minute, what are you holding back from me?"

She pulled something from her purse and handed it to Smith. "This was buried beneath clothing in one of the drawers."

Smith looked down at a photo of a man he judged to be in his early twenties. "Who is this?" he asked.

"Herbert Greist."

"This is Greist? This is a young man."

"Mae Feldman was obviously a young woman when she had Andrea. Sure, Greist is a lot older now, but this is him, Mac, the young Herbert Greist, Communist sympathizer, blackmailer, Mae Feldman's lover, and, probably, the father of a dead daughter named Andrea Feldman."

Smith scrutinized the photograph more carefully, looked at Annabel, and said, "You're sure this is Greist?"

"Yes. Young, old, it's his face."

Annabel started to remove her clothing in the center of the room.

"Good job, Annie."

"As good an investigator as Tony?"

Smith sighed. "Yes."

"I only did it because I am the breed of woman who will do anything for the man she loves."

"Enough," Smith said. "You got the keys back in Carla's purse?"

She looked sternly at him. "Of course. I also follow orders very well. By the way, Tony hopes we'll arrange to get him out of here and back to Washington."

"I've already put that in motion. I made some calls after you left the hospital."

She was now naked. "You are a beautiful breed of woman, Annabel Reed."

"Thank you."

He stood and removed what little clothing he wore, crossed the room, and embraced her.

"Hard feelings seem to have suddenly developed between us," she said.

He said into her ear, "We can't have that, can we?"

They resolved it shortly thereafter.

28

SMITH AND ANNABEL flew back to Washington on Sunday. He called Ken Ewald first thing Monday morning.

"I'm on my way to St. Louis for a fund-raising luncheon," Ewald said.

"I told you it was necessary we talk as soon as I got back," Smith said. "What time is your flight?"

"Eleven," Ewald said.

"I'll meet you at the airport," Smith said. "Get there early."

Ewald agreed, without enthusiasm. The Clipper Club at ten. My enthusiasm for all this is waning, too, Mac Smith thought. Too many lies, evasions, unanswered questions. I still think I should help this man, he still seems to want my advice, but he's also always off and running. In class this morning, there are probably unanswered questions and evasions, too, but those I could handle . . .

As Smith was about to leave, his phone rang. It was an attorney named James Shevlin, who'd been with the FBI and with whom Smith had had dealings when he was in active practice.

"Pleasant surprise, Jim," Smith said.

"Yes, Mac, it's been a while. How've you been?"

"Fine, just fine. Busy, but . . ."

"Yes, I imagine, based on what I read in the papers and hear on television."

Smith laughed. "Well, it's winding down. Look, Jim, I've got to run out to an important meeting. Hate to be impolite."

"Any chance of getting together this afternoon?"

"Sure."

"Two o'clock, my office?"

"Sounds good to me."

Shevlin had been with the Bureau for sixteen years. Then, unexpectedly, he had resigned to open a private law practice in Washington. His resignation didn't make sense to most people; he had only a few years to go to retirement, and by resigning had presumably tossed it out the window.

Those more intimately familiar with the workings of the FBI, however—including Mac Smith—knew that Shevlin hadn't lost a thing by resigning. Although such moves were never confirmed, those in the know counted Shevlin among other agents who'd been "allowed" to resign, their pensions paid through a separate fund, in return for their continued cooperation with the Bureau. There were lawyers scattered across the country functioning in that capacity, just as there were accountants, also former agents, who fed financial information to the Bureau on candidates for tax-evasion charges.

Ewald was waiting in the Clipper Club with Ed Farmer, a Secret Service agent, and two senior advisers when Smith came through the door. "Can we talk alone?" Smith asked Ewald.

The others walked away.

"Ken, I have questions I'd like to have answered."

"Such as?" Ewald said flatly.

"I mentioned to you on the phone an attorney from New York named Herbert Greist."

Ewald shrugged. "I told you I never heard of him."

"That doesn't matter. Greist claims to be representing Andrea Feldman's mother, Mae Feldman. He says her mother wants to bring an action against you and the family for the loss of her daughter's civil rights."

"Preposterous. Paul has never been charged."

"Yes, that's true, but there's more to this. The fact is that Greist really doesn't want to bring a suit at all. That was his initial approach, when he suggested we discuss an out-of-court settlement. I sent Annabel to New York to meet with him, and she got a very different story. To put it bluntly, he's in the process of trying to blackmail you through me. He wants a half-million dollars."

Smith expected Ewald's face to reflect confusion and surprise. That's not what he got. Instead, Ewald sat back in his chair and slowly shook his head.

"Any idea what information he might have that would prompt him into such action?"

Ewald sat forward again. "No, no idea whatsoever."

"Ken, has Roseanna Gateaux ever mentioned Herbert Greist?"

"Why do you ask that?"

"Has she?"

"No."

"Annabel and I went to San Francisco to follow up on this. Actually, my investigator, Tony Buffolino, went out there first, and ended up in the hospital. That's a long story, and I won't get into it now. While we were out there, I made contact with an old friend who's involved with the Embarcadero Opera Company. It's small and struggling, but good. According to my information on Greist, he spent time in San Francisco. While he was there, he functioned in some legal capacity for Embarcadero. At the same time, Roseanna Gateaux was doing a considerable amount of fund-raising for the company. It seems to me that there is every possibility that they might have met under those circumstances."

"So what?"

"Well, you have had an intimate relationship with Roseanna Gateaux, and as we all know, pillow talk sometimes leads us to reveal things we wouldn't reveal under other conditions."

Ewald laughed; it was forced. "Mac, what the hell do you think I did, give Roseanna state secrets, the technical plans for SDI, the names of CIA agents? This is silly."

"It may be, Ken, but I have an obligation to you to tell you everything I know about this. Greist is serious. At least that's the way Annabel and I read him. Let me take another tack. How much do you know about Andrea Feldman's background?"

"Mac, I . . ."

"This is important, Ken. What did you know about her background?"

Ewald thought for a moment. "Very little."

"Do you have any idea who her father was?"

"No. Are you suggesting that . . . ?"

Smith shook his head. "Ken, I am suggesting nothing except that Greist must have *something* that he feels is of sufficient interest to you that you would pay to have it returned or forgotten."

"I have no idea what this Greist character thinks he has to sell about me, and I don't care." He looked at his watch. "I have to go. I appreciate what you've been doing, but, frankly, Greist sounds like an opportunistic crackpot to me."

"That may be," Smith said, "but he's been involved over the years with various Communist causes. The FBI and CIA have long dossiers on him."

Ewald stood and extended his hand. "Thanks, Mac. I know you're looking out for my best interests. It's just that I don't see much significance to any of this."

Smith srutinized Ewald's face. Somehow, as convincing as his words sounded, Smith had the feeling there was more going on in his mind than a simple dismissal of Greist and his threats. Ewald, uncomfortable with Smith's hard stare, leaned close and said, "Mac, Roseanna and I may have slept together, but I assure you, the only words exchanged between us were the sort heard in bed between lovers, hardly the stuff national security is made of. We made love, not war."

Smith said, "I'm sure that's true, but do you think there's a possibility that the very fact that you slept with Roseanna Gateaux is what Greist knows, and is willing to hush up for a price?"

That hadn't occurred to Ewald. His face sagged, and his tone was somber. "I hope not, Mac. It would devastate Leslie."

Ed Farmer waved from across the room. "We have to go, Senator." Ewald said, "Sometimes Ed is a pain, but he's efficient." He started to walk away, but Smith grabbed his arm. "Ken, before you go. Did you have an affair with Andrea Feldman, too?"

"What the hell have you been doing, peeping through my windows?"

"No need to. There have been enough other people willing to do that. What about it, Ken? Did she have access to sensitive materials through you?"

"No."

"You did have an affair with her?"

"No, I did not. My son took care of any sexual servicing of Ms. Feldman."

Smith decided to press. He quickly told him about Tony Buffolino's evening with Mae Feldman's friend and landlady, about his being shot, and about a box being taken from Mae Feldman's home.

Ewald could not suppress the frustration and anger he felt. "What the hell does that have to do with me?" he asked in too loud a voice.

"I was hoping you could answer that."

"A locked box? Maybe it contained her will and cemetery deed."

"I hope that's all it contained. Look, Ken, I know you're busy, but everything I've laid out for you here could have ramifications for your candidacy, and you know it. I suggest you not dismiss it out-of-hand."

"Is that legal advice?"

"No, that's advice from a friend who cares about whether you make it to the White House."

A sadness came over Ewald's face. "I'm sorry, Mac. I guess I'm just on edge these days. Let's talk again when I get back."

"When will that be?"

"Tonight. I'll call you."

Smith watched Ewald join the group and start to leave the club, and was suddenly compelled to tell Ewald that he'd seen Janet. He caught up with them and said, "Ken, sorry, just one more private moment, please."

They moved to the side of the corridor. "I've seen Janet," Smith said.

"You did? When?"

"A few nights ago. She's disappeared again. She'd promised to meet me a second time, but she didn't show up. She says she's too frightened to come back."

Ewald guffawed.

"I just thought you ought to know. Safe trip."

Smith showed up promptly at two o'clock at Jim Shevlin's law office. "How's your caseload?" Smith asked once they'd been seated and Shevlin had poured them coffee.

"Could be busier, but then I'd have to expand." Shevlin smiled. "I like being a one-man operation."

Smith smiled, too. When your major client—maybe the only one— was the FBI, you couldn't be anything *but* a one-man operation, unless your client sent you a cleared partner.

"So, what prompts you to invite me here?" Smith asked.

Shevlin lowered his voice and said, "Mac, what do you know about an attorney in New York named Herbert Greist?"

Smith told Shevlin what he'd learned from his friend in New York, Morgan Tubbs. Shevlin listened quietly, and the expression on his face led Smith to believe that Shevlin already knew everything he was saying. When he was done delivering his thumbnail on Greist, he asked, "What's your interest in him?"

Shevlin removed his glasses, rubbed his eyes, and placed the glasses back on his nose. "Mac, a more important question is, what's *your* interest in Herbert Greist?"

"Why do you assume I have any?"

Shevlin's voice lowered even more. "Mac, I really appreciate your coming here. I don't know whether you're aware that I maintain friendly ties with my former employer, have a few occasional contacts."

Nice understatement, Smith thought.

"Sometimes, when an important issue comes up, they'll ask me to do them a favor. It doesn't happen often, but I usually try to oblige."

I'm sure I would, too, under the circumstances, thought Smith. Did Shevlin realize that Smith knew that what he was saying was false, a boilerplate speech he'd probably made hundreds of times since leaving the Bureau and setting himself up as an unofficial link to that organization? Smith raised his eyebrows as though he were hearing something for the first time.

Shevlin hesitated, as though deciding whether to continue. Smith had no doubt that he would. He did. "This attorney, Greist, has had a long history of links with Soviet sympathizers, but then you already know that, according to what you just told me about him."

"Yes, I understand your former employer and the Central Intelligence Agency have been keeping tabs on him for some time."

"Exactly. Are you still the opera lover you were when you were in practice?"

"Yes. Why?"

"Well, I thought you might have run into Greist somewhere along the line. He was plugged into the opera crowd."

"Really?" Smith was glad he'd come; ideally, he would learn more than he'd be asked to give.

"Greist was involved with a group out in San Francisco called the Embarcadero Opera Company. My information is that he was general counsel to that group. Undoubtedly a fancied-up title."

"Undoubtedly. Jim, I don't know Greist personally, have never met him. I had occasion to check into his background concerning a threatened legal action but . . ."

"Mac, my contact at the Bureau, with whom I occasionally touch base, asked me how well I knew you. I told him we'd always had a friendly relationship. Right?"

"Right."

"So, my contact—"

"With whom you have only occasional contact."

Shevlin's smile started small, and ended up bursting across his face.

"Yes, my contact felt that you might help us learn a little more about Mr. Greist."

"Help *us?*"

"Slip of the tongue. Help *them.*"

"I have a feeling that my associate, Annabel Reed, and I have not been skipping through life these days unnoticed. Fair statement?"

A shrug.

"Annabel was recently in New York and noticed a few nondescript gentlemen exhibiting interest in her on the street. Now, I recognize that she is an extremely beautiful woman, and thousand of men have undoubtedly cast their eyes in her direction on many streets. But this was different. Have we been followed?"

"How would I know? I'm just a lawyer."

"And I'm just a college professor. Have I . . . have we been followed?"

"I think it's probably safe to assume that."

"And because my associate, this beautiful woman, made a visit to the law office of the distinguished Herbert Greist, these people with whom you have occasional contact were naturally interested."

"Sounds that way, doesn't it?"

"Why are you interested in whether Greist has a connection with opera?"

"I'm not. My friends are."

"Why don't your *friends* simply go talk to Greist?"

"They'd like to. In fact, they intended to do that yesterday, but they can't find him."

Another missing person, Smith thought. He said, "Annabel was with him last week."

"A week is a long time. Evidently, Mr. Greist has decided to abandon his law office on the West Side and to maintain an even lower profile. By the way, Mac, as long as we're having this friendly chat, can I toss another question at you?"

"I suppose so."

"You're pretty tight with the Ewald family, aren't you?"

"Yes, as everyone knows. We go back a long way."

"I really enjoyed that show put on for Senator Ewald the other night. Tragic what happened after it, the death of that young woman. I was very upset to hear it."

"You and a lot of other people."

"I admire many things about Senator Ewald, including the fact that he's a jazz lover. I am, too, you know."

"I wasn't aware of that."

"Oh, yes, I have an extensive record collection. One of the things I found interesting about the show was that all kinds of music were represented. Probably a good indication of Ewald's determination to appeal to a wide variety of voters. I assume you enjoyed Roseanna Gateaux, loving opera as you do."

Smith started to confirm that he had enjoyed the performance when it dawned on him that this portion of the conversation had nothing to do with the Kennedy Center gala for Ken Ewald. He decided to be direct. "Why are you mentioning Roseanna Gateaux? Do your *friends* have an interest in her, too?"

Shevlin laughed and stood. "No, of course not. Somebody brought up her name at lunch the other day."

"In what context?"

"I don't remember. Forget it. I don't even know why I asked. Thanks for dropping by, Mac, and please give my best to that beautiful woman who turns heads on city streets."

"I certainly will, and tell your *friends* they ought to go back to Surveillance 101."

29

SMITH MADE HIMSELF a drink when he got home, and spread left-over country pâté on stone crackers. He sat in his recliner and stared at his desk. Should he? He'd always prided himself on upholding agreements. A deal was a deal. No one had ever been burned by confiding in Mac Smith.

But he decided that this might be the time to violate his principles. Marcia Mims may have wanted him to open the diary only if something happened to her, but maybe something was happening to her and what was in it would preclude that *something* from a sad result. A weak rationalization, perhaps but it would do.

He took the envelope from the desk drawer and returned to his chair. It wasn't one of those diaries with a lock, but he had trouble opening it—not because of any physical problem, but because of the guilt he felt. Guilt? He silently reprimanded himself for assigning something as decent as guilt to what he was about to do. He knew why his fingers fumbled: What kept him from immediately opening the diary was fear at what he might find.

Two hours later, he'd finished skimming the diary's pages. The phone hadn't rung once. Now, as he closed the cover, a succession of calls came.

The first was from Annabel. She was at the gallery, and wondered how his day had gone.

"Damned interesting. I caught up with Ken at the airport, and spent an hour with Jim Shevlin, ex—or almost-ex—FBI. And I've been sitting here for the past two hours reading a remarkable document."

"What document?"

"One I would like very much to share with you, but not over a telephone. Were you planning to come here tonight?"

"Sure, unless you want to go out for dinner."

"No, I think I'd rather stay here. Spend the night. I think we're in for a good long evening of reading and discussion."

"Fine. I'll swing by home and pack my bag. What's for dinner?"

"You. That's the main course. As for the rest, your choice. Bring something from the American Cafe."

He'd no sooner hung up when Rhonda Harrison called. She said she'd just left WRC and was calling from a booth. "Are you alone, Mac?"

"For the moment. Annabel is coming over."

"I really need to speak with you."

"About your article on Andrea Feldman?"

"Yes, but it won't be one-way. I have something you might be interested in."

Should be quite an evening, he thought. "Sure, come over any time. Annabel is bringing in dinner. I'll call and suggest she bring a third dish."

"No need for that, Mac."

"Time the two of you met anyway. I've been talking about you to her for years. She's bringing in from the American Cafe. Any favorites?"

"Oh, anything will do. Make it chicken tarragon with almonds on a croissant. I'll be there in an hour."

Another call, this one from Tony, still in his hospital room in San Francisco.

"Tony, how are you? How's the leg?"

"Good, Mac, yeah, really good. Feeling better every minute. I can't wait to get on that plane tomorrow."

"It will be good to see you. I've arranged for a car to meet your flight. Look for it. The driver will hold up a sign with your name on it."

"Make sure he spells it right, with an *o* instead of an *a.*"

"I'll do my best."

"Mac, I came up with something interesting out here."

"From the hospital?"

"Yeah, it's boring here. The old guy next to me died, and they haven't brought me a new roommate yet. I've been waiting for some dynamite chick to be brought in who's just had her tubes tied, but no luck so far. Mac, I got hold of that friend I mentioned at Wells Fargo Bank."

"And?"

"The old lady—Mae Feldman—did pretty good."

"You found her account?"

"Yeah, but it wasn't easy. My friend is in charge of a lot of accounts, including Mrs. Feldman's. What made it tough was that the account isn't just under her name."

"Whose name is it under?"

"My buddy."

"Which buddy?"

"Carla. Carla Zaretski. My friend, who shall remain nameless so that he doesn't end up a *former* Wells Fargo employee, told me that the account was opened a little more than a year ago, and that the deposits into it were pretty regular."

"If it's in Carla's name, how did Mae Feldman get to use it?"

"Because she's one of the signatures on the account. It was kind of a joint thing. But now it's cleaned out."

"How much was in it?"

"Two hundred thou."

Smith grunted. "Any connection between the account and Mae's daughter, Andrea?"

"I wouldn't know. At least, my friend didn't say anything."

"And you say the account was cleaned out?"

"Yup."

"Who did the cleaning, Carla Zaretski or Mae Feldman?"

"Ms. Zaretski. She took every cent out in cash."

"Cash. That's a lot of money to be carrying around. Have you seen her lately?"

"No, and that's kind of funny. She's been hanging around here like she was my mother. The nurses were ready to strangle her. A real pain in the ass. Then, yesterday, she says she has to run an errand and that's the last I see or hear from her."

Smith looked down at the blue diary in his lap. "Good job, Tony. I want you to do nothing now but concentrate on getting back here tomorrow. Forget about this case until you're settled here and we can talk. There's a lot happening on this end that I'll fill you in on."

"Great. Did you call my wives?"

"Damn it, no, I forgot. I'll do that right now. Give me their numbers."

After Buffolino got off the line, Smith tried both numbers, reached the second wife, Barbara, and told her Tony had been shot but was recovering nicely. She was sincerely upset and asked if there was anything she could do.

"No, I don't think so. I understand you and Tony and the kids were to have a party at the Watergate suite."

She sounded embarrassed. "Yes, but Tony and I had a fight and . . ."

"Don't bother to explain. All I want to say is that once Tony has recovered, we'll all have a party at that suite to celebrate."

"That's . . . that's a wonderful idea, Mr. Smith. Tony told me what a fine man you are and—"

Embarrassed himself, Smith mumbled something about having to take another call and got off the phone.

Now he had a decision to make. Should he show Marcia Mims's diary to Rhonda Harrison? It would only be fair, he told himself. She'd been open with him, and obviously was coming to the house that night to share even more information. Had the diary dealt only with Marcia and her family and the Ewald family, he wouldn't have considered it, but there were many provocative entries concerning Andrea Feldman, the subject of Rhonda's article for *Washingtonian.*

He was still grappling with that decision when his doorbell rang. He slid the diary into the middle drawer of his desk and greeted Rhonda at the door.

"Oh, my God," she said as Rufus stood on his hind legs, which put his head above hers.

"Get down, Rufus," Smith barked. "She's a beauty but not your type." The Dane reluctantly obeyed his master, but every muscle in his huge, powerful body twitched with the desire to continue greeting this new visitor.

"Come in, Rhonda, and make yourself comfortable. Annabel should be here soon."

"What a lovely house," Rhonda said as they moved through it.

"Yes, it's very comfortable, especially for one person, and it puts me within walking distance of the university, Kennedy Center, and the Foggy Bottom Cafe. Drink?"

"Sure. White wine?"

"You've got it."

Smith joined her with the drink he'd previously made for himself. "Well, you sounded as though you had some exciting revelations," he said.

"Yes, I might have, Mac. Do you remember a year or so ago when *Washingtonian* did an exposé on that San Diego-based group, the Democratic Action Front?"

"No, I don't think so, although I have heard of it. Holds itself out as a staunch anti-Communist organization, if I'm not mistaken."

"Yes, that's the one. The writer who did that investigation was Kyle Morris. He was from California and had wormed his way into DAF. He did a hell of a good investigative job, linked a lot of DAF's activities right back here to Washington, which was why the magazine commissioned the piece." She looked at him for a reaction. He didn't give her one. She continued, "Not long after the article was published, Kyle died."

"A young man?"

"Yes. The official report was that he was drunk and ran his car into a tree in California."

"Drinking and driving never mix," Smith said, fighting off a fleeting, terrible image of the night his wife and son died on the Beltway.

"If you believe he'd been drinking."

"You don't?"

"They said so—but Kyle didn't drink. Besides, it struck more than a few people as strange that right after he does this exposé on DAF, he dies, like all those people who had something to say about the Kennedy assassination and ended up falling out of hotel windows or drowning."

"All right, let's say that this young man, Morris, paid the ultimate price for exposing the group. I'm sad to hear it. But why would that necessarily interest me?"

Rhonda sat back, sipped her wine, and smacked her lips. The look of a contented cat was painted on her pretty face. Her audience was now hanging on every word, and she seemed to be reveling in that moment of undivided attention.

Smith said, "I'm all ears, Rhonda."

She leaned forward. The smile was gone, and her eyes formed narrow slits. "Mac, Andrea Feldman was paid a lot of money by DAF."

Now it was Smith's turn to lean forward and to narrow his eyes. "By DAF? Andrea Feldman supposedly was a champion of liberal causes," he said. "That's why she went to work for Ken Ewald. Why would she be taking money from a right-wing organization?"

They sat silently and looked at each other. If their thoughts were printed out on paper, they would have read almost identically.

"She was being paid to spy on Ewald," he said.

"Has to be, right?"

"Not that it's set in stone, but it makes sense. The DAF organization supports the current administration."

"Sure. They've also contributed—undoubtedly under the table—to various campaigns of Senator Jody Backus, whose political persuasions have never been out of sync with theirs."

"I just learned from Tony Buffolino, my investigator, that Andrea Feldman's mother had a sizable account that was recently cleaned out."

Rhonda asked, "Did he come up with any evidence that the money came from the Democratic Action Front, and was paid to Andrea Feldman?"

"He didn't mention anything about that. No, in fact, I asked whether he knew the source of the money and he said he didn't. How did you come up with it?"

"I got pretty friendly with Kyle Morris when he was working on the piece. He shared a lot of things with me, especially the information he never used because he couldn't prove it to the point of satisfying his editors that they wouldn't be hit with a nasty libel suit."

Smith raised his eyebrows. "Are you telling me that you were told a year ago by this writer, Kyle Morris, that Andrea Feldman was being paid by them?"

"No, Mac, but Kyle did tell me that he knew DAF was an extension of the Garrett Kane Ministries. He couldn't prove it, but he knew it, said to me that there wasn't any doubt in his mind that Kane funded DAF."

"Which would mean that if Andrea Feldman was being paid by the DAF, the money really came from the Garrett Kane Ministries."

"Exactly."

"Back up a second, Rhonda. How did you come up with the information that Andrea was, in fact, receiving money from DAF?"

"Kyle Morris's sister lives in Washington. I got to know her, too. I called her yesterday, and we got together. She has everything of Kyle's, all the articles he'd written during his short life, his research, his notes, his tapes, and other materials an investigative journalist turns up. One of the things she had were two bank statements from DAF. Lord knows how he got hold of them. His sister didn't know. But there they were in a neatly labeled file folder."

"And?"

"And I browsed through them. There were two checks that had been issued to Andrea Feldman, endorsed over to her mother, and deposited in the Wells Fargo Bank of San Francisco."

There was the sound of a key in the front door. "Must be Annabel," Smith said, going to the hallway. "Hi, Mac," Annabel said as she stepped into the house, a large shopping bag from the American Cafe dangling from her arm.

He kissed her lightly on the lips and took the bag from her. Rufus tried to shove his nose into it, but Smith deftly swung the bag away from him and put it in the kitchen. As Annabel passed the entrance to the living room, she saw Rhonda Harrison, stepped into the room, and extended her hand. "He certainly has spoken of you a great deal, Ms. Harrison, and always in glowing terms. And, of course, I've been a fan of yours for a long time."

"Thank you," Rhonda said. "You're no stranger to me, either. He uses the same kind of terms when he talks about you."

Annabel looked at Smith. "Do you really?"

Smith said, "Usually, unless you've done something to upset me. Then . . ." He smiled. "Then I make sure I don't talk about you at all. Drink?"

"Love one. Make it out of real liquor and make it dark."

A few minutes later, the three of them sat in the living room. "Annabel has been working on every aspect of this case with me, Rhonda." He told her about Annabel's meetings in New York with Herbert Greist, and then mentioned the photograph she'd found in Mae Feldman's house of Greist when he was a young man.

Smith enjoyed the wide-eyed expression on Rhonda's face. It's called getting even, he told himself. "Can you top this?" as a parlor game.

Rhonda asked questions about the Greist connection with Andrea Feldman, and Mac and Annabel answered them. Now, Smith made an instant decision. He would no longer choose what information to give her. She deserved better than that, and time was running out. They had to pool information. "Excuse me," he said. He returned carrying

Marcia Mims's diary. "I received this from Ken Ewald's housekeeper, Marcia Mims," he said, handing it to Annabel.

Annabel asked, "Why did she give it to you?"

"I have no idea. We have to keep it confidential for now. I'd do a dramatic reading of the entire work, but I think that would bore everyone. I don't know how long you two want to sit around reading, but we have the night. I'll put the food on plates. Why don't you huddle on the couch and dip into the world of the rich, famous, and messed up?"

Smith served their food on a coffee table in front of them and took his plate to his study, where he reviewed shorthand notes he'd made while reading the diary. He checked in on them a few times. They'd hardly eaten anything.

A few hours later, Annabel had moved to a chair, leaving Rhonda alone on the couch to digest the final few pages.

"Well?" Smith asked when Rhonda had finished.

"I don't know what kind of upright president Ken Ewald will make," Rhonda said with forced lightness in her voice, "but he sure must be good horizontally. His bedside reputation isn't exaggerated."

Smith said, "Frankly, I don't think his reputation is deserved, although I suppose it depends on what church you go to. Janet Ewald was the one who first told me that she thought her father-in-law was having an affair with Andrea Feldman. Marcia confirmed it that night in Annapolis, although not with much conviction. Now, in the diary, she seems to make a more substantial case for it. If you read those sections carefully, however, you'll see that she deals from a certain base of supposition. The fact that Ken brought Andrea Feldman into the house on many occasions, and that she even remained there overnight on a few of them, doesn't prove they slept together. At least, it wouldn't hold up in court."

"It holds up with this juror," Annabel said. "Whether Ken Ewald and Andrea Feldman actually slept together or not isn't the issue. What is important is that Ken brought her into his inner circle, which meant she had access to a lot of information that would be of interest to his enemies, including his competitors for office."

"True," Smith muttered. "That means that there is the likelihood that Andrea Feldman was selling secrets out of the Ewald camp."

"Selling them to whom?" Rhonda asked.

"According to what you told me before Annabel arrived, Rhonda, she was being paid by the DAF, which, according to your sources, is funded by Garrett Kane Ministries. By extension, Colonel Morales and, possibly, Raymond Thornton could also be involved."

"What about Greist?" Annabel asked. "He claims to have something of great importance he wishes to sell to Ken Ewald, or at least is willing to hush up in return for a large payment."

"You'd have to nail down a link between Andrea Feldman and Greist," Rhonda said.

"I think we can do that," Smith said. He told them of the

conversation he'd had with Tony Buffolino in the hospital in San Francisco. Buffolino had briefly filled him in on the content of his conversation with Carla Zaretski the night he was shot. She'd said that Andrea Feldman had been born out of wedlock to Mae Feldman, and that the father, whom Mae Feldman steadfastly refused to name, had been a young attorney in New York. That matched up with what Smith had learned from his friend Morgan Tubbs about Greist's beginnings. Then, too, there was the similarity between Greist's physical makeup, as described by Annabel, the size and shape of suits found in Mae Feldman's closet, and the photograph Annabel had pulled from a drawer in Mae Feldman's room.

"Herbert Greist was Andrea Feldman's father," Rhonda said.

"Looks that way to me," said Smith. "I'm not a gambler, but I'd put money on that."

Annabel sat up straight in her chair and became more animated. "If we follow through on this, Mac, it means that Andrea was selling secrets either to the DAF or to Herbert Greist."

"Or to both," Smith said.

"Why would she do that?" Rhonda asked.

"Maybe that's at the root of who killed her. Let's say she was supposed to deliver information to one of those two 'employers', but delivered it to the other instead. That could get people pretty mad at her."

"The same information? If you're saying that she was selling inside information from the Ewald camp to the Soviet Union through Herbert Greist—and, bear in mind, we can't be positive that he is her father— what the Soviets would be interested in is hardly the same thing that would interest the DAF, Kane, and Morales."

"Maybe, maybe not," Smith said. "If I were a Soviet intelligence agent, I would find great use for information that might link DAF and Kane to the funding of Morales's troops in Panama. Don't forget that the Soviet Union is supporting the regime in power in Panama. If they could come up with something substantial that proved that DAF and Kane Ministries were funneling money illegally to Morales's troops, they could leak it to the Western press, which would, I'm sure you agree, put a hell of a lot of pressure on those people to stop."

Rhonda Harrison shook her head and said, "Somehow, from what I've learned about Andrea Feldman, which, I admit, isn't much, I have trouble accepting the scenario that she would deliberately sell information to the Soviet Union, even if her father is a Communist sympathizer."

"I tend to agree with you, Rhonda," Smith said. "Don't forget, there was a locked box in Mae Feldman's apartment that evidently contained material sufficiently important to cause two men to break in and steal it."

"Maybe it was just money," Annabel said. "Tony said Mae Feldman had cleaned out the bank account."

"Carla Zaretski, to be more precise," Smith said.

"What if it wasn't money?" Rhonda asked. "What if it was material Andrea Feldman had stolen from Ken Ewald?"

"Certainly a possibility," Smith said. "Marcia Mims says in her diary that she observed Andrea removing papers from Ken's files."

"What would be unusual about that?" Annabel asked. "Andrea Feldman was a trusted member of the Ewald staff. It would be only natural for her to pull things out of files."

"That's something we'll have to ask Marcia when—and if—we see her again." Smith looked at Rhonda. "I agree with you, Rhonda. Seems unlikely that Andrea Feldman would sell secrets to an enemy of this country. She might have given whatever she stole from Ewald to her mother for safekeeping. In that case, Mae Feldman could have turned over that same material to Herbert Greist, which would have cut Andrea out of the picture as far as DAF and Kane are concerned. And by the way, let's not forget to include President Manning and Raymond Thornton when we mention Kane and Morales."

Annabel sat up even straighter now. "If Greist ended up with whatever it was Andrea stole, and was passing that on to a Soviet contact, that would be motivation enough for him to suddenly disappear as he has, and for the FBI to have a heightened interest in him beyond simple dossier-building. From what you've told me, Mac, Greist has always been nothing more than a Communist sympathizer, and, as far as I know, we haven't harassed Communist sympathizers since Joe McCarthy."

"At least not as overtly," Smith said glumly.

"Why didn't Marcia Mims just go to Ken Ewald and tell him what she'd observed about Andrea Feldman?" Rhonda asked. "I get the impression from what you've said about her that she's an extremely loyal and dedicated employee."

Annabel laughed. "That's probably true, except she keeps a diary filled with intimate details about her employer's extracurricular sexual life. Sounds to me as though she intended to write a book."

"Whatever her motivations," Smith said, "she certainly has been a keen observer. I was interested in her references in the diary to Ed Farmer."

"You mean how he picked Andrea Feldman up on the mornings after she'd stayed overnight at the house?" Rhonda asked.

"Yes," Smith replied. "She says she observed this from an upstairs window, and found it strange that Farmer did not drive through the gate and up to the front of the house, as he otherwise did. Each time he picked up Andrea, he waited outside on the street. Why?"

"Why was he picking her up, or why out on the street?" Annabel asked. "I certainly see nothing untoward about him picking her up. Ed Farmer is a young man with ambition, and people like that get called on to perform all sorts of services for their political masters, including covering up affairs. Besides, he and Andrea worked closely together. Maybe he just wanted to get her into work on time."

"Nothing unusual about him picking her up, Annabel, but why out in the street? According to Marcia, that broke his usual pattern."

Annabel slouched back in her chair. "Who has the answers?" she asked. "Marcia Mims has vanished. So has Janet Ewald. Andrea Feldman is dead. I suppose you could ask Ed Farmer about his habit of picking her up at the house."

"Yes, and I may do that," Smith said. "First, though, I want another conversation with Ken. I'll try to catch up with him tomorrow and put some of these questions to him."

"Want me with you?" Annabel asked.

"No, not necessary. By the way, Tony is returning on Thursday, and I would appreciate some help in seeing that he's settled. I made an appointment for him on Friday with Dr. Kroger at the university." He turned to Rhonda. "I made a last-minute decision to include you in on everything we've come up with, Rhonda, including Marcia Mims's diary. I know you've been very open with me." If Smith had expressed what he was thinking, he would have gone on to say that he'd lost his sense of propriety, maybe even lost his head. He'd breached a confidence by Marcia Mims and knew he should not have shown her diary to anyone, or even read it himself, despite his earlier rationalization. Was his involvement in this case beginning to undermine his character? Too late now, he told himself. To Rhonda, he said, "All I ask is that until we clear this up, you use whatever material that comes out of it for the article, and not to develop any fast-breaking stories for WRC. I realize that's putting a restraint on a good journalist and, Lord knows, I've stood up enough times in my career for the First Amendment. But can you live with that, Rhonda?"

She got up and placed her hand on his shoulder, looked into his eyes, and said, "Don't agonize over showing me the diary, Mac, and don't worry. You have my word that I won't do anything with what's been discussed here tonight until I get the go-ahead from you."

30

SMITH CALLED the Ewald house on Tuesday morning.

"Hello, Leslie, it's Mac. Is Ken there?"

"No, he's not." She didn't sound happy. "He's in a series of meetings all day."

"I see. I am anxious to talk with him. Any idea when I might be able to catch him?"

"Well . . . he's meeting with party bigwigs at the Willard at four. They think the nomination's okay, or almost, but they also want peace with Backus. I'm meeting Ken at the Watergate at six to go over plans for the upcoming testimonial dinner."

"I see. Maybe I could steal a little of his time between meetings. Think you can arrange that?"

"I'll try. The Watergate meeting is in suite 1110. Why don't you stop by at five-thirty."

"I'll be there. Thanks."

At four-thirty that afternoon, in one of the Willard Hotel's renovated suites, Ken Ewald sat in a meeting with the chairman of the Democratic party, Matt Blair, and Blair's staff.

"Ken, I think it's wonderful that things have been sorted out with your son," said Blair. "It must have been a difficult time for the family."

"Very difficult," Ewald said. "We're all thankful it's over."

"Frankly, you had us worried," Blair said. "Primary results aside, having that charge of murder hanging over your family's head would have . . . well, a lot of rethinking would have been necessary."

Ewald nodded. "Let's just say I'm glad rethinking won't be necessary. You've seen the latest poll we commissioned."

"Yes. Impressive. It was, of course, directed at those groups who are predisposed to support Ken Ewald."

Ewald laughed. "Has there ever been a candidate-sponsored poll that *wasn't* 'directed'?"

The secretary of the party, a former representative from Missouri, Jacqueline Koshner, said, "Senator, polls aside, we'd be less than honest if we didn't express certain concerns we have with your candidacy."

"My son? He's never been charged with anything."

"No, unless that flares up again between now and the convention. I'm talking about the irrefutable shift in this country toward a more conservative posture."

Ewald narrowed his eyes. "What I see is the pendulum swinging back."

"Maybe," Blair said, "but Jackie is right. If the pendulum has begun to return to center, it has, in our judgment, a long trip ahead of it. This is *now,* Ken. If you are the party's candidate—and it looks as though you have a good shot at it—we feel you'll need balance on the ticket."

"Jody?"

"Impossible. Oil and water."

"I prefer to see it as sweet and sour," said Jacqueline Koshner, "the palate being satisfied in all ways."

Ewald said lightly, "I hope you consider me the sweet in that recipe." His comment did not generate smiles. He said, "I will not run with Jody Backus."

Blair glanced at his staff, looked at Ewald, and said, "It's possible you won't run at all."

Ewald's anger was evident. "You aren't suggesting that the party . . . you . . . would attempt to deny me the nomination, are you?"

"Of course not. If the delegates give you the votes you need, you'll be our candidate. However, Ken, your candidacy is not without obvious problems. Jacqueline is right. We are still a country that for a long time has gone to the right of center, and that will be the case in November. We want the White House this time around, Ken, and we are not about to let it slip out of our grasp. This is the year. Manning has run his string, and Thornton represents only four more years of the same, or worse. You are extremely popular in some segments, unpopular in others. This thing with your son and the murder of one of your staff members, even though it seems to have been buried for the time being, hasn't helped. Do you . . . do you see any other such incidents looming between now and the convention?"

"Another murder that my son will be suspected of committing? No."

The expression on Blair's face said that he was not pleased with Ewald's flippancy. "I think all that's left to be said at this juncture is that if you win the nomination, the party will support you in every way. But also know that if you are our candidate for president, the choice of your running mate will not be yours to make unilaterally."

Ewald nodded and stood. "I'll be happy to confer on my choice of vice-president, but strike Jody from the list."

The others remained seated as Blair walked Ewald to the foyer. He slapped him on the arm. "Keep one thing in mind, Ken."

"I'm listening."

"Backus. Even though he lost to you in a majority of the primaries, he comes into San Francisco with a hell of a lot of clout. It may not be as easy for you as it appears at this moment."

"Nothing is ever easy, Jack."

"One last thing between friends."

"Shoot."

"Is there anything else, *anything* that might explode between now and the convention?"

"About me personally?"

"Yes."

"Do you know something I don't?"

"No, just . . ."

"Just what?"

"Just rumors. Things good at home?"

"Things are very good at home, Jack. Thanks for the time. I have to meet Leslie to plan the testimonial dinner for me. Looking forward to seeing you there."

"Yes, it should be a lovely evening. Thanks for coming by."

Smith arrived at the Watergate suite precisely at five-thirty and was surprised to find Ken there. He and Leslie were alone. "My good luck," Smith said, "to have both of you here at the same time."

Ewald shook Smith's hand. He was obviously not in a pleasant mood. He spoke in short sentences, and the ready smile that endeared him to millions of voters across the country seemed to have been put on a shelf, at least for the moment.

"Look, I know you're terribly busy, Ken, and I wouldn't dream of getting in the way of your schedule, but I have some important information to share with you. In fact"—he looked at Leslie—"I think it's probably best shared with both of you."

Ewald perched on the arm of a stuffed chair and said, "Go ahead, what is this information?"

Smith filled a glass from a pitcher of orange juice, came to the center of the room, and said, "As I told you on the phone, Ken, we've been pursuing this Herbert Greist thing."

"Who's *we?*" Ewald asked gruffly.

"Various people I've brought into this, including Annabel, Tony Buffolino, my investigator, and a journalist who's been doing some pretty serious digging on her own." Smith's expression now matched Ewald's, made to seem all the more serious by dark stubble that had sprouted over the course of the day.

Leslie sat on the chair's other arm. "Go on, Mac, please."

Smith said, "I told Ken a little of this on my call from California, but let me fill you in quickly, Leslie." He told her about Tony having been shot in California, and that Tony had discovered a locked box in Mae Feldman's apartment but hadn't had a chance to ascertain its contents because of the intrusion of the two unidentified men. He said to Ewald, "We think that box might have contained material stolen from you."

Ewald looked nervously at his wife before saying, "You told me about this mysterious box, Mac, and I told you it couldn't have contained anything stolen from me."

Smith hesitated, then said, "What you told me, Ken, was that you never kept anything of significant interest in the house, at least from a national-security point of view."

"I said that because it's true."

Leslie asked, "Why are you asking this, Mac?"

"I'm just trying to put all the pieces together, Leslie. Let me continue. Ken, I assume you've told Leslie about the blackmail threat from Herbert Greist."

Ewald displayed his first smile, and directed it at his wife. "No, in the frenzy of everything I forgot to tell lots of people lots of things. Go ahead, Mac, fill her in."

Smith looked into Leslie's angry face and told her the salient facts about Greist and his threats. When he was done, she asked, "Who is this Greist? He sounds like a lowlife, a cheap blackmailer."

"Yes, he probably is those things, Leslie, but he also is probably Andrea Feldman's father."

Their mutual silence was palpable.

"How did you find that out?" Ken asked. Before Smith could answer, he added, "Can you prove it? What is this, speculation by this investigator you've hired, or some yellow journalism by this reporter? By the way, who is this journalist?"

"Rhonda Harrison, from WRC. She's not doing this for the station, however. She has an assignment from *Washingtonian* to do a piece on Feldman. She's good at her trade. Between Rhonda and Tony, they've discovered that Andrea had been receiving sizable amounts of money from an organization known as the Democratic Action Front."

Leslie's face registered a lack of recognition at the name. Ken's face was another matter. Smith waited for him to say something. Before he did, he walked to the window and looked outside. Rain had started to fall, and gusts of wind splashed it over the glass. He turned and said, "Okay, Mac, let's open this whole thing up. Not that that represents a decision on my part. You've already done it."

"Ken, what's this about?" Leslie asked.

Ken held up his hands and said, "Relax, Leslie, and you'll find out. Years ago, when I decided to make a run for president, I started building my base. That involved all the usual activities, lining up financial and political support around the country, seeking high visibility, taking stands on national issues beyond those I had taken before, the textbook approach to getting ready.

"I figured that my opponent would come out of the incumbent administration, which probably meant Raymond Thornton. Thornton would be tough, because the Manning administration has made everything seem hale and hearty in the country, manipulating economic statistics, calling tax raises something else, proclaiming a prosperity that, in reality, is built on a foundation of sand. I figured I ought to know everything I could about Thornton, and started digging." He laughed without mirth. "Funny, I used investigators, too."

"You did?" Leslie asked.

Smith looked at her. "You didn't know any of this, Leslie?"

She shook her head. "Not about investigators looking into Thornton's life." She asked her husband, "Did it result in anything worthwhile?"

"Yes, it certainly did. One of the investigators I hired was well connected in Southern California politics. He hooked up with a man named Stuart Lyme. Remember him?"

"Yes, I do," Smith said. "Stuart Lyme was a leading right-wing figure in California for years, a real back-room power player."

"You have a good memory, Mac," Ewald said.

"I also seem to remember that he died under mysterious circumstances, a fall from a window, something like that."

Ewald said, "He drowned off Baja. It happened shortly after Stuart had delivered to me, through this investigator, a report loaded with political explosives."

"Why would someone like Lyme, a dyed-in-the-wool conservative, work with you, help you out?"

"Because Stuart's son had been killed. The crime was never solved, probably because those in power didn't want it to be solved. Stuart knew his son had died at the hands of Garrett Kane."

"Kane?" Smith and Leslie said together.

"Yes. Not Kane himself, of course, but members of his inner sanctum. Stuart's son had become deeply involved in Kane's ministry. He eventually rose high enough in its structure to know what was really going on, and documented every scrap of it, including Kane's use of fronts through which to launder money, and to channel it to his pet causes, like Morales's activities in Panama. There were other fronts and causes, of course, but Panama and Morales have always been Kane's favorite.

"Lyme's son broke from Kane. I don't know why, but he did. He took the material with him. Kane eventually found out and ordered the son murdered. But before the killing could be carried out, Lyme's son had passed the material to his father.

"At first, Lyme didn't know what to do with the material. He knew that Kane was close to President Manning, and that Morales was being supported by the president and his national-security people but, as they say, blood runs thicker than water, and Lyme broke from them. That was when he decided to give me the material his son had given him. He had one request, that I use it to put Kane out of business. I've sat on it ever since."

"Why?" Smith asked. "If the material was that damaging, you could have used it to launch a Senate investigation."

Ewald's discomfort with the question was evident. He sat up a little straighter and said, "I decided to wait until I really needed it."

"Which was when you made your run for president."

"Yes. I didn't want to waste it in the Senate, where I was already comfortable and secure. I decided I'd use it against Thornton when the time was right."

"The material Lyme gave you implicates Thornton with Kane and Morales?" Leslie asked.

"In no uncertain terms," Ewald answered. "Everything was laid out —names, places, people, bank accounts, correspondence, the works. *That's* what was stolen from the house."

"Andrea Feldman?" Leslie asked.

Ewald shrugged. "I suppose so. Who else could it be? It all makes sense now, this business of Andrea receiving money from Kane through this phony organization—what's it called, Democratic Action Front?"

"Yes," Smith said.

Leslie asked, "When did you know it was missing, Ken?"

"A while ago."

"Why didn't you—"

Ewald cut her off by saying to Smith, "Sure, it all makes sense. Andrea stole it, and if this character Greist *is* her father, she gave it to him."

Smith shrugged. "Bear in mind, Ken, that Greist has been connected with Communist causes. I suppose it is possible that Andrea gave it to Greist for him to try and sell back to you, but we think it's more likely she stole it at DAF's behest. It might have ended up with Greist, but it probably wasn't Andrea's original intention to give it to him."

Ewald stood and paced the room.

"We have a theory, Ken," Smith said, "although we have no idea whether it holds water. We think Andrea might have stolen the material for Kane and Thornton, but left it with her mother for safekeeping. Her mother in turn brought in the father. They figured they could get big bucks out of you because you'd pay anything to get it back. Does that play?"

"I suppose," Ewald said. "Christ, all this would have to happen at such a crucial time."

"Well," said Smith, "at least you've confirmed that something tangible was stolen from your house." He was tempted to bring up Roseanna Gateaux. Jim Shevlin's mention of her had stayed with him. Why was the FBI interested in Gateaux? He decided he would raise the issue when he and Ewald were alone. Otherwise, it would only hurt Leslie and accomplish nothing. He said, "I know you're both terribly busy and I'll get out of your hair, but I would like something else cleared up for me. Paul indicated that he'd met Andrea at a party, and that she convinced him to put in a good word with you. Is that true?"

Ewald nodded. "It was obvious to me that Paul was infatuated with her, and that concerned me. I had reservations, but Ed Farmer tipped the scale in her favor."

"He did? He knew Andrea well enough to make such a judgment?"

"He seemed to. He told me that she would be a real asset to the campaign and urged me to hire her. I did."

"Paul must have been pleased," Smith said.

"Yes, too much so. I sensed something was going on between them long before Janet found out. I probably should have followed my gut instincts and not hired her, but with both Paul and Ed in her corner, I went with it."

He glanced anxiously at Leslie, who'd fixed him in a challenging stare. "Go on, Ken, finish the story for Mac," she said.

"What do you mean?"

"Tell Mac how Paul brought Andrea Feldman into the house and the campaign and how . . . how Daddy ended up sleeping with her."

Ewald leaped to his feet. "That's a lie, Leslie! I may have . . ."

Leslie laughed. "Little too quick with the tongue, Ken. What were you about to say, that you may have slept with others but not with her? Let's face it, Ken, your overactive glands have led this family into trouble it doesn't deserve. You had clear sailing to the White House, and look what's fallen on our son—suspicion of murder. And now you're being blackmailed because you couldn't control your libido."

She looked at Mac, who hadn't expected this eruption when he brought up Andrea's name again. He was distinctly and visibly uncomfortable. "Mac," she asked, "did you happen to see a confrontation I had with a young reporter a week or so ago?"

"The one who asked whether you would be the first divorced First Lady?"

"Yes. She nailed it—which is why I nailed her. We are not a happily married couple, and haven't been for quite a while. We are Ken and Barbie, but only for the voters. I suppose I really don't have to tell you this, Mac. You're astute enough, and have been around long enough, to have picked up on it."

Smith sighed and rubbed his eyes. "Whether I did or not, Leslie, doesn't seem to be terribly important. This isn't really my business."

"I disagree. I think it is very much your business. You have taken a leave from the university to help us, and if I remember correctly, the rule always was that your attorney must know everything."

"I'm no one's attorney, Leslie," Smith said. "I'm just a friend." He stood. "I have to leave, but there is another thing I would like to air before I do." He was happy to have something else to talk about other than their personal problems. "Lots of people presumably had reason to kill—or at least could rationalize killing—Andrea Feldman. If she were double-dealing Kane, he certainly wouldn't be a fan. Do you think she might have been murdered by someone at Kane's command, as you say Stuart Lyme's son was?"

"I wouldn't know," Ewald said, still glaring at his wife.

Smith took them both in slowly before asking, "Is there anyone within *your* circle—family, friends, household staff, campaign staff— who you think might have killed Andrea Feldman?"

"No," Leslie said without hesitation.

"Ken?" Smith asked.

"No, of course not. It was obviously someone connected with that madman Kane, maybe somebody from Morales's band of thugs, maybe even the Manning White House."

There was a knock at the door. Three members of the Watergate's catering staff had arrived for the meeting. "Come in, please," Leslie said pleasantly, a large and winning smile on her face, a triumph of muscle control.

"Thanks for your time," Smith said.

"Are you going home?" Leslie asked.

"No, I think I'll stop in the suite we've taken here in the Watergate. I have some details to take care of."

She stepped close to him and said, "I don't know why you're staying involved, but I am very glad you are." She kissed his cheek. He looked at Ken over her shoulder and saw a stone face. "I'm staying involved, Leslie, because I want to know what happened. Just that simple. I *need* to know what happened."

As Smith left the suite and waited for an elevator to take him to his floor, the young Panamanian sat alone in yet another suite in the Watergate, booked and paid for by the Reverend Garrett Kane. Earlier, Colonel Gilbert Morales had been there. Now, Miguel sat on the couch, a soft drink on the table in front of him. Around the glass were various pieces of metal. He picked up a few and began to assemble them. The Pachmayr Colt Model 1911 modular pistol had been delivered to him earlier in the day by one of Morales's aides. It had cost four thousand dollars, and could be configured to handle .45, .38 Super, or .9 mm ammunition. This model was set up for .38 Super.

He'd taken the sophisticated weapon apart and put it back together again a number of times. Each time it was fully assembled, he couldn't help but smile at the feel of it. It weighed only sixty-four ounces. The trigger had a light, crisp pull.

"*Bueno,*" he said. As he slowly began to take it apart again. "*Guapo.* Beautiful, beautiful."

31

"SURE YOU'LL BE all right?" Annabel Reed asked Tony Buffolino after he'd settled into the Watergate suite late Thursday afternoon.

"Yeah, I'm fine. Where are you guys going, out to dinner?"

"No, I think we'll have dinner at my house, make it an early night," Smith said. "Are you sure you're well enough to stay here alone?"

"Hey, come on, take a look." Buffolino pushed himself up from the chair, slipped his crutches beneath his arms, and moved quickly—too quickly—across the vast living room, losing his balance near the kitchen table and grabbing it to keep from falling. Smith and Annabel started toward him, but he said, "No sweat, just have to go a little slower."

"Why don't you call one of your ex-wives and invite her up for dinner?" Smith said.

"That's not a bad idea. Yeah, maybe I'll do that."

"Well, good to see you back, Tony," Annabel said. "Don't forget you have a doctor's appointment tomorrow."

"I won't forget. You'll be by here in the morning?"

"No, I'd better put in some serious time at the gallery." Smith said he'd drop by first thing.

They were almost at the door when the phone next to Buffolino rang. "Hey, Joe, great to hear from you. How goes it? Yeah, great, I'm doin' fine. You heard about what happened to me in Frisco. You're where, downstairs? Sure, come on up. Love to see you."

He hung up and told them that Joe Riga had stopped by to see him.

"That's nice," Annabel said, pleased that he would have company. She didn't have much faith in his ability to coax his ex-wives there on such short notice.

"See you tomorrow," Smith said.

Minutes later, Buffolino and Joe Riga sat on the terrace, drinks in their hands. Washington was clear and balmy.

"How long you figure this will go on?" Riga asked.

"What, this case?"

"Yeah, and everything that goes with it. You've got a good deal here."

"You're telling me. This is the best gig I'll ever have in my life. They broke the mold when they made Mac Smith, believe me."

"Oh, I believe you, Tony. I always got along good with Mac. He was a tough defense attorney, but he played fair, gave the profession some class. You should see some of the whack jobs we deal with now. Tell me more about this crazy woman who shot you. You say she was Mae Feldman's landlady?"

"Yeah, old buddies. Feldman's probably as flaky as Madame Zaretski."

"Madame?"

"That's what I call her. She acts like a queen, only she ain't. She says she had this big opera career going till she lost her portamento."

"Her what? Who did it?"

Buffolino explained as though the term were old hat to him.

Riga said, "Oh, portamento. *That* portamento."

"Yeah, that one."

"So, Tony, things are good with you," Riga said.

"Yeah. You?"

"Nothing changes with me, Tony. The sun goes down, the honest citizens skip the city and the cockroaches come out. You pick up a bunch of the cockroaches, and the DA or a judge tells you to let 'em go. So you let the cockroaches go, the sun comes up and they sleep, the good people come back into the city, and sun goes down and it starts all over again."

Buffolino laughed. "Yeah, I guess nothin' does change."

"I heard how you pulled that old photo routine with Morse out at the Buccaneer Motel," Riga said. "What'd you show him, a picture of Mickey Mouse?"

"Van Johnson."

"Who's he?"

"An actor. Come on, Joe, you heard of Van Johnson."

"Nah, I don't go in much for the movies. Sometimes a good cop movie, something like that."

"How come you showed the old guy a picture of Paul Ewald?" Buffolino asked.

"Why not? She had a key to the motel in her purse, and Ewald was the prime suspect. We figured they might have been out there together, so I asked Glass in Rosslyn to run a photo by the owner."

"He lied, right?"

Riga screwed up his face. "No, he didn't lie. A cop shows him anything, he agrees. We could've shown him a picture of Hitler and he would have agreed Hitler shacked up there that night with the deceased."

Buffolino laughed. "You still looking close at Paul Ewald?"

Riga nodded.

"I don't think he done it."

"Well, that settles it then. We'll drop him from the list."

"Don't be a wise-ass with me, Joe. Hey, whatever happened to Garcia, that dirtbag who set me up?"

Riga shifted position in his chair. His brow furrowed. He touched

Tony on the knee and said, "You know, Tony, I never had anything to do with that. It was IA all the way."

"I know that, Joe. You never did nothin' to me but good. What about Garcia? He went back to Panama, I heard."

"Right. After you took the fall, some of us decided that Mr. Garcia was a stud who shouldn't be left walking around. We put the arm on him and convinced him he ought to get out of the country, get out of the business. Between you and me, he left in a lot worse shape than you're in. Last I heard, he was still in Panama."

"Too good for him. Guys like that, even if you bust them up, keep the dough and live the good life, while we . . ."

Riga grabbed Tony's arm and shook it. "Hey, you look like you're doing pretty good. This ain't exactly skid row."

"No, but I'll be going back to skid row, Joe. This thing can't last long. Why should Smith hang in?"

Riga thought for a moment. "There is still the question of who murdered Andrea Feldman. Knowing Mac Smith, I figure he wants to be the one who finds out before he packs it in."

Riga's words seemed to buoy Tony's spirits, which had visibly sagged. "Yeah, I bet you're right. Besides, you know what he told me before I went to Frisco?"

"What?"

"He told me that when this is over, he'd try to get me a good job. How about that?"

"That'd be nice," said Riga. "You know, Tony, I don't have much more time till I retire. Maybe he could help me out, too. Maybe you put in a word for me. Would you do that?"

Tony silently resented what Riga was asking. He wasn't proud of what he was feeling, but it was there. Just like Washington, he thought, everybody always looking out for themselves. He mumbled something unintelligible and sipped his drink.

After Riga left, Tony sat on the terrace until he fell asleep in the chair, his heavily bandaged leg propped on the table. Riga had made him another drink, and that empty glass joined others on the green Astroturf beneath his chair. He awoke at midnight to the sound of a low-flying commercial jetliner on its approach to National. He was drunk, but managed to make his way to the bedroom, where he flopped on the bed, fully clothed, and fell back into a fitful sleep.

Rufus, giant blue Dane, stretched out across the foot of Mac Smith's bed, forcing the human animals in it to retract their legs into the fetal position. Smith grumbled, got up, and went to the kitchen, where he turned on the coffee, squeezed fresh orange juice, retrieved the paper from the front steps, brushed his teeth, assured Rufus he'd be walked in short order, and climbed back into bed. "Coffee's ready in a minute."

Annabel stretched, cooed, and turned over. Smith smiled as he looked down at that mass of hair covering her pillow. He was filled with love, which soon blossomed into lust. Moving over her, he transmitted his feelings, but she said through a yawn, "Mac, be civilized. Go get the amaretto gop you call coffee."

He swung out of bed again, went to the kitchen, and returned with their breakfast on trays, flipping on the TV as he passed. "Breakfast is served."

"Oh, God, you are a brute," she said, pushing up against the headboard and running long fingers through her hair. "Turn off the TV. TV is for nighttime."

"Morning TV is important," he said. "The world might have blown up overnight."

"Good."

"You wouldn't say that if we were blown up with it."

"We weren't. We're here, in bed, with the world's biggest dog."

They watched the news before the entertainment portion of the Friday edition of the morning show resumed. As a young, pretty actress whom neither Mac nor Annabel knew chatted with the host about starring in her latest motion picture, Smith said, "I've been doing some thinking, Annie."

"About what?"

"About this whole adventure we've been on. I thought about it a lot last night. I think it's time to get out of it."

She was gripped with a set of immediate and conflicting feelings. On the one hand, she was relieved. On the other, she was disappointed. She said, "Why this sudden change of heart?"

"I don't know, I just wonder what's to be gained by hanging in. Leslie Ewald asked me last night why I was still involved, and I gave her one of those precious existential answers—you know, an I-want-to-climb-the-mountain-because-it's-there kind of thing. Who am I kidding? I realized last night that I've been staying with this because it makes me feel important. I don't need something outside of myself to feel important, never did. It's time to wind things down and get back to the life of the unimportant college professor."

"I wouldn't argue with you about that, Mac. Whatever you say is fine with me, and you know it." She kissed him gently on the lips. "Tony will take this hard," she said.

"I know. I told him I'd do my best to find him a job when this was over, a job where he's not expected to scale tall buildings. Maybe at the university. Besides, he's made some decent money already, and I'll see to it that he gets a healthy bonus out of what Leslie has paid me."

They watched television until Annabel asked, "Are you sure this is what you want to do?"

"No, I'm not sure, but a decision has to be made. As they say, any action is better than no action."

"Okay, then let's get the morning going," she said, jumping out of bed and touching her toes. "I have to get to the gallery, and you told

Tony you'd be by to see him. Shall we have dinner out tonight to celebrate our return to the mundane?"

He started to say yes, but hesitated. She picked up on it; he wasn't
sure whether he wanted to drop everything, and she could understand
his ambivalence. She wouldn't press. Let the day go by and see what it
brings.

32

HERBERT GREIST STOOD at the dirt-crusted window of a room in
a hotel on West Forty-seventh Street. He wore his black suit pants and
a sleeveless undershirt. His socks were light gray silk; a large hole allowed one of his toes to protrude.

He looked at Mae, who was awake but still in bed. A succession of
noisy encounters in the next room between a prostitute and her Johns
had kept them awake most of the night. Mae was on her back, her eyes
fixed on the peeling ceiling. Greist picked up a cigar butt from a full
ashtray and, with some difficulty, lighted it and looked out to the street
again.

"It won't work," Mae said, only her lips moving.

"You never know," he said. "We asked too much. He doesn't want
this kind of thing spread around, not with running for president. A
hundred thousand, that's all. We can leave the country, go somewhere
safe and have enough to live on for a while."

Mae Feldman pushed herself up against the leatherette headboard
and said, "You always say things will work. You always say not to worry,
that you have it figured out. It doesn't work. It never works."

He slowly turned and fixed his eyes on her, the cigar firmly wedged in
the middle of his mouth. He removed it and said, "Things end. Nothing
is forever. We're still free, still with a chance. They don't know where
we are. We need money, that's all. We can get it from Ewald."

"How? Call that attorney, Smith? Waste of time."

"I don't need advice from you. Look what you did to us."

"What did I do? All I did was put the money in a box, and somebody
stole it. That isn't my fault, Herbert. I didn't do anything wrong."

"You *always* do things wrong, Mae. You should have hidden the
money in different places, spread it out. That would have been the
smart thing to do. The files and papers, too. All in one place so they
could pick it up and walk off. You're so stupid."

There was pleading in her voice. "I tried to do the right thing, Herbert. Don't be mad at me. I hate it when you're mad at me."

"That money and those files were ours."

"That money was blood money, our daughter's blood money."

"She's dead. She can't use the money."

Mae Feldman slumped back against the headboard and closed her eyes against the tears that seemed always to be forming.

Greist said, "We call Ewald direct. We call and tell him that if he doesn't hand us the money in cash, we go to the press, we tell them that he was screwing Roseanna and our daughter, too, for Christ's sake, who's now dead because of him. You don't think he'll pay a hundred thousand dollars to keep that quiet?"

She sat up in bed again and said, "Herbert, if we go to the press and tell them this, they'll quote us, run our pictures, and then the FBI will take us away for the rest of our lives, maybe even hang us for treason." Before, she'd been talking with sleepy slovenliness. Now that Mae was fully awake, her words had a sharper edge. "The one good thing that ever came out of my meeting you is dead. All she did was to come to me with information from Ewald. She left it with me so that it would be safe and so that she could secure her own future. What did you do when you heard about it? You said, 'Give it to me, and I'll make us rich.' How? Sell what Andrea worked so hard to get to your supposed friends, the losers you've hung with all your life? Get rich how, Herbert, by trying to blackmail a U.S. senator for a half-a-million dollars? Oh, my God, Herbert, you may be a lawyer, but that doesn't mean you're always smart."

He hurled the cigar at her. It bounced off the wall and fell to the threadbare rose-colored rug. "You'll set the place on fire," she said, leaning over and picking it up.

"Let it burn. Call him."

"Why should I call him? *You* call him, or get your tootsie to call him."

"You're sick, Mae."

"No, I am just tired of being used by you. I've loved you ever since the day I met you, and I've never done anything to hurt you. But you hurt me every day. You have that blond pig here in New York and you flaunt her, make sure I know you have other women."

"She's smart."

"Then go to her for money."

"She doesn't have any money."

She went to the bathroom. When she returned, she said defiantly, "Why should I call him? You're the lawyer, the negotiator, the one who is going to make everything work and everybody rich. Why should I call him, put my neck out, get linked up with you? As far as everybody knows, I don't even exist, because that's the way you wanted it."

"Shut up, just shut up and let me think," he said, turning once again to the window.

* * *

An hour later, they left the hotel. She went first, stepped out onto Forty-seventh Street, and casually looked up and down the block. Few people were up this early on a Saturday morning. She gave him a motion with her head and he joined her. They walked half a block to a coffee shop and had Spanish omelettes, French fries, and coffee.

"Maybe we should just get on a plane and go," she said. "I have enough for tickets."

"No. Ewald is the one who should bankroll us. He owes. You're so sad about Andrea? She's dead because of him. Let him pay."

"You're talking about our daughter in these terms? You never cared about her. You left your sperm in me and walked away. I had her. I brought her up. She is my daughter, not ours. How dare you think you can—"

He reached across the grimy Formica table and gripped her wrists. "Don't push me more, Mae."

Fear flooded her eyes. She winced against the pain of his fingertips and pulled away, striking the back of her seat, causing people in the adjoining booth to turn and glare. He relaxed his grip and sat back. He now wore the black suit jacket, a soiled white shirt, and green tie. He brushed the lapels of his jacket. "I need a good cigar. You won't call Ewald? I will."

"And I am going to leave," she said. "You're crazy, don't you know that? We don't need money from Ewald or anyone else. Let's make our own way."

He grinned and picked a glob of green pepper from between two front teeth. "Suit yourself. You've always been a loser, Mae, and the only decent things you've ever had are what I gave you."

He stood at the side of the booth. She continued to sit, her fingers laced together as she tried to keep from crying. He was right. She'd never been anything, a pathetic and weak woman who failed at almost everything she did. Except, she thought, giving birth to and raising that beautiful young woman who went on to graduate from law school, and to work with powerful political figures. No one could ever take that away from her.

She looked up and watched him ogle a short, shapely Hispanic waitress who wiggled past them. She wanted to ask, she'd wanted to ask a thousand times since that night, whether he'd killed Andrea. Each time, she stopped herself because she reasoned that a father would not kill his own flesh and blood. No father would.

Mac Smith was about to head for the Yates Field House for some exercise when the phone rang. It was Ewald. "Catching you at a bad time, Mac?"

"No, I was going to the gym. That's always easy to put off. What's up?"

"Two things. First, I received a call from Herbert Greist."

"Greist called *you?* The FBI is looking for him."

"I know. He told me that he desperately needs a hundred thousand dollars. In return, he's promised not to . . ." Smith knew the sudden silence was Ewald making sure he wasn't being overheard. "He threatens to tell the public about Roseanna and me. He also claims I slept with his daughter."

"Andrea. Greist *is* her father. Where was he calling from?"

"He didn't say. He told me to give it some thought for an hour and that he would call back."

Smith leaned against the edge of his desk and sighed. "I wonder how Greist knows about your affair with Roseanna Gateaux," he said. "A few days ago, he was trying to sell back to you the information on Garrett Kane that Andrea stole from your house. Now, he's not offering that, just a simple request for money to keep his mouth shut about Roseanna and Andrea." Ewald said nothing. "Okay, we'll try to figure that out later. You said there were two things. What's the second?"

"Marcia is gone. She came back after taking some days off, then disappeared again."

"Yes, I'm listening."

"Leslie was concerned about her this morning. We hadn't heard a peep from her. She went to Marcia's room and found that Marcia had packed a bag. One of the gardeners said he'd seen her leave the house early this morning. She was picked up by a cab."

"Ken, I think I'd better come over right away. Is that all right with you?"

"Yes, of course, but please continue to use discretion with this Roseanna thing. Leslie's out now, but she may return while you're here."

"You don't have to worry about that with me, Ken. I almost had the feeling that . . . I had the feeling during our conversation last night that Leslie might already know about Roseanna."

"Suspects, doesn't know for sure. No smoking handkerchief with lipstick on it."

"I'll be there as quickly as possible."

As Smith walked into Ewald's study, Ewald said, "You look like you're ready for the big game, Mac." Smith hadn't bothered to change out of his gray sweats and white sneakers. He wore a George Washington University windbreaker, and a rumpled tan rainhat that was a particular favorite. Ewald was dressed in a beautifully tailored Italian-cut gray suit, white shirt, and burgundy tie.

"Well, the saga continues," Ewald said as he carefully sat on a chair and made sure the crease in his trousers wasn't in danger of being crushed. "What do you think?"

"Let me find out first what *you* think, Ken. How do you feel about this?"

Ewald sat back and stretched his neck as though to work out a kink. He said, "I just wish the bastard would go away so I could focus on the campaign. The convention is in front of us, the National Committee is on my neck. If it isn't one thing, it's another."

"Wishing Greist away won't do the job," Smith said. "Still, my instincts tell me he's bluffing. Think about it. He's being hunted by the FBI for traitorous acts. Someone like that isn't likely to go to the media to tell a story about a presidential candidate having slept with a woman other than his wife."

"I was thinking the same thing," said Ewald, seemingly relieved at Smith's corroboration.

"On the other hand," Smith said, "you never can predict what people like Greist will do. The chances are good that he's with Mae Feldman, Andrea's mother. She could be the one behind this desperate grab for money, and she may be willing to do anything. We've found out that Mae Feldman had a sizable bank account, and that it was closed down the other day by a close friend in San Francisco. I wonder why they're not getting money from *her*."

Ewald pressed his lips together in anger. "If Greist knows about my affair with Roseanna, that means he must know her, or someone who fed that information to him. That's cause for real concern, wouldn't you say?"

Ewald got up and paced. "Well, learned counsel, what do I do now?"

"Greist hasn't called again?"

"No. If he sticks to his promise to call within an hour, the phone should ring any minute."

"Obviously, Ken, you can't pay blackmail or runaway money to a fugitive from the FBI. It seems to me your only course of action is to turn him down and take your chances."

"Or try to reason with him."

Smith laughed. "Greist isn't the kind of creature you reason with. Annabel tried that on two occasions. Obviously, we should be on the phone right now to the FBI letting them know we might be able to help them find Greist and Mae Feldman. If you make a date with him to hand over money, that establishes where he is in New York. The Bureau can move in and arrest him."

Ewald walked across the room. As he stood at the window, and Smith sat in a chair observing him, the phone rang. Ewald turned quickly. "Could be him."

"I'd like to listen in."

"Go upstairs to the small office on the second floor. It's—"

Smith stood, "Yes, I know where it is. Is it open?"

"Probably not. Here." He handed Smith a key.

The door to the study opened, and a secretary informed Ewald that he had a call from Mr. Greist.

Smith bounded up the stairs, opened the door, and entered the small office. He waited a moment to give Ewald time to pick up, then gently lifted the handset and heard their voices. As he listened, the reel of tape on the top shelf silently began to turn.

"Mr. Greist, you put me in a very difficult position," Ewald said.

"Yes, I know that, which is why I'm confident you will do what I say. Have you considered my offer?"

"Yes, I have. It goes against everything I stand for, but I am willing to meet your request in return for your total silence."

Greist's sigh of relief was audible. "Good. Here's what you do." He started to outline a meeting strategy when Ewald interrupted. "Mr. Greist, I have a few questions first."

"No idle talk here. I'm no fool. This call could be monitored. Here's the way it works, no questions asked."

"Go ahead."

"I want you to meet me tomorrow night in New York."

"Don't be ridiculous," Ewald said. "I'm not exactly an unfamiliar face. I'll send someone."

"Just as long as that someone has the money in cash."

"Don't worry, Mr. Greist, you will have your cash. Now, where and when?"

Greist gave him the address of a hotel in the theater district of Manhattan. Ewald's emissary was to come to room 7 at precisely nine o'clock Sunday night.

"You'll be in that room?" Ewald asked.

It was a low rumble of a laugh. "Don't take me for a fool, Senator. I won't be there for the same reason you won't be there. There will be someone waiting to accept the money."

"What assurances do I have that you will live up to your part of the bargain, Mr. Greist?"

"You don't, except that I have bigger things on my mind than tattling on you and your mistresses. I need the money. That's it."

"Fine, you'll have it."

The conversation ended, and Ewald and Smith met up once again in the downstairs study.

"What do you think?" Ewald asked.

"I think you handled it well. The question now is whether to bring in the FBI at this point and have them go to that room. If they do, you're going to have to tell them why you're being blackmailed by this cheap hustler. You may not want to do that."

"I'd give anything not to have to do that, but I don't see any choice. If I don't, I'm withholding information from the FBI. If I do . . . that could mean my affair with Roseanna getting out, maybe not to the public, but the Bureau would know."

"The FBI doesn't care about who you sleep with," Smith said.

"That's a little naive, isn't it, Mac?"

Smith smiled ruefully. "Yes, guess it is. The old FBI, Hoover's, would smack their lips. Even now, the Bureau works for whatever administration is in power. I suppose that kind of information would be of interest to Raymond Thornton."

"And/or to Jody Backus."

"Yes, to him, too."

"A rock and a hard place."

"Afraid so. Look, Ken, my advice is to let me handle things from this point forward."

"I can't let you do that, Mac. This is my mess. I made it."

"And I think I know how to get you out of it. I mean it, Ken, just get on with your campaign and let me handle it."

"That's a generous offer, Mac. What do you intend to do?"

"Leave it to me. There's no need for you to know everything. I'll keep you informed, especially if something might kick back on you. Fair enough?"

Ewald extended his hand. "Mac, you are a remarkable friend. I don't have any idea how to thank you properly."

"I don't need thanks, Ken. What I do need is to resolve this thing so I can get back to teaching law, something I miss a lot more than I thought I would. Don't tell Leslie about any of this. I also think it would be wise for you to . . ."

Leslie Ewald and Ed Farmer came into the study. "Looks like you've been out for a run," Leslie said to Smith.

"I'm just about to do that, Leslie. I was on my way to the gym and decided to stop in to see Ken." To Farmer, he said, "How are you, Ed? Things going well for the good guys?"

"Things are in good shape," Farmer said, "and should stay that way. As long as nothing stupid raises its ugly head between now and the convention."

"Let's hope that 'stupid' things are buried forever," Smith said. "Excuse me. I have to run, literally."

Smith left the house and sprinted until his breath gave out, and silently cursed a stitch in his side that slowed him to a walk. His mind told him he didn't have much time, but his body refused to cooperate. He cursed that, too, and the sages who said you were only as old as you thought. The bones and muscles always told the truth.

33

NOT LONG AGO, Washington's famed Akebono cherry trees, a gift in 1912 from Japan, had been in full bloom, attracting hundreds of thousands of tourists to witness their splendor. Now, the blossoms were gone, and this early Sunday morning at the Tidal Basin was quiet, except for a dozen joggers running their weekend route around the basin.

Smith stood in front of the Jefferson Memorial, dressed in his sweats, windbreaker, and squashed rainhat. The sky was a pristine blue; no rain forecast for that day.

A few minutes past seven, Jim Shevlin, dressed in running shorts and a sweatshirt, bounded up the stairs to Smith's side. He glanced up at the nineteen-foot bronze statue of Jefferson and said, "Good morning, Tom." Smith looked at him and said, "The same to you, Jim. Did I get you out too early?"

"For a Sunday morning, yes. Sunday mornings were made to sleep late. Anyway, you sounded like what you wanted to talk about was urgent, and I figured since you weren't suggesting breakfast, and insisted on meeting beneath the shadow of our third president, I'd better show. What's up?"

"We've had a run, let's take a walk."

They came down the steps of the rotunda and walked along the eastern edge of the basin, passing the Bureau of Engraving and Printing, and proceeding down along the treelined western edge of the water. Smith stopped abruptly and said, "Jim, I think I can deliver Herbert Greist to you."

Shevlin looked at him quizzically. "Deliver to me? Why would you say that?"

"Look, Jim, let's not play cloak-and-dagger. I don't have time. Let's just say that because of your previous employment with the FBI, you obviously know people within that organization who would be interested in knowing where Herbert Greist is. I thought I'd pass along the information to a fellow attorney as a favor, as a friend."

"As long as it's on that basis, proceed."

They moved on again, Smith talking as they walked. "I'm being blackmailed by Greist."

That stopped Shevlin in his tracks. *"You're* being blackmailed? What the hell for?"

"For nothing. Greist seems to think he has some deep, dark secret from my past that is worth money to me. He doesn't. Besides being an alleged Communist sympathizer and probable spy, he's a cheap hustler. The point is that I've agreed to pay him the money."

"Why would you do that?"

"So I can ascertain exactly where he is tonight and pass that information on to you, so that you can pass it on to your former employer."

"I see. You say tonight. Where?"

"New York. Actually, I'm not personally going to meet him. Let me back up a second. He's not going to be there, either. He's arranged to have a bagman waiting in a hotel in New York City. I'm sending Tony Buffolino with the money. I thought some of your friends back at the Bureau might enjoy accompanying him."

"Who the hell is Tony Buffolino?"

"An old friend of mine. He's—"

"That guy you defended, that foul-ball cop?"

"All in the past, Jim. Mr. Buffolino is now a respectable private investigator, and, I might add, a damn good one. Could we stop these diversions?"

"Go ahead."

By the time they had circumnavigated the basin and once again stood on the steps of the memorial, Smith had filled Shevlin in on what was to happen that night. "Interesting?" Smith asked.

"Very."

"Will you pass it along to your friends?"

"Yes, I think I will. Let's see, I seem to remember somebody who might be interested in getting involved in this little exercise this evening. Where will you be for the rest of the day?"

"Home until noon. Annabel, Tony, and I are flying to New York this afternoon. We'll be at the Waldorf."

"Okay, Mac. I, or someone from the Bureau, will get in touch with you either before you leave or in New York. Tell me, though, about this Buffolino. You really feel secure in sending him?"

"Yes. He's on crutches. Had an accident out in California about a week ago, but he's pretty good at getting around on them, at least good enough to get out of the way of another accident. Anything else you need to know?"

"Nope. Going for a run?"

"Yes, I'll jog back to the house. You?"

"Heading straight home for a good breakfast, a couple of hours with the papers, and a phone call or two, not necessarily in that order. Talk to you soon."

Annabel had packed and taken a cab to Smith's house. It was noon; Smith made salad. She sat at the kitchen table reading the papers while he put the dishes in the dishwasher. He said, "Do you know what's interesting about all of this, Annie? Greist is blackmailing Ewald in return for keeping quiet about his affair with Roseanna Gateaux. That tells me that neither he nor Mae Feldman have the stolen files on the Kane Ministries."

"You're right," she said. "Or he could be just looking for enough money to get out of the country—*with* the files—and use them later to go after bigger stakes."

Smith shook his head. "I don't think so. Those files have ended up in the hands of someone else, maybe the people who roughed up Tony and took the box from Mae Feldman's house."

"Who, in turn, undoubtedly turned them over to whomever they're working for," she said.

"Exactly. The point right now is that Greist doesn't have them."

Tony's cab arrived an hour later, and Smith helped him in with his small suitcase. The doctors at the university had redressed his wounds with a less cumbersome bandage; he was now able to wear his suit pants over it. To the surprise of Mac and Annabel, he was no longer on crutches. He had a cane.

"Are you steady enough on that?" Smith asked.

"Yeah, no problem."

"You look very distinguished," Annabel said. "A gentleman with his cane. Impressive."

"All you need is a bowler hat, and you'd be right at home in London," Smith said.

"I always wanted to go to London," Tony said. "Why don't you get somebody murdered, get us a British client, and send me there?"

Mac and Annabel looked at each other. There would be no new clients once this was over. They both knew it, but no sense dashing Tony's hopes.

Their three o'clock shuttle landed on time at La Guardia. Smith had arranged for a car to meet them, and they were driven to the Waldorf. New York City was so pleasant on Sunday, Smith thought, without the traffic jams and hordes on the streets. Very pleasant indeed. For five minutes. The rain began and was soon heavy; Annabel quietly hummed "April Showers" as the hired car pulled up in front of the hotel. They were taken to their rooms, which were across the hall from each other, and spent an hour in Tony's room going over plans for the evening.

"When do you figure they'll call?" Tony asked.

"The FBI? I don't know. They might not call us at all, just show up at the hotel without telling us. It really doesn't matter, although I would be more comfortable knowing their plans."

"Who do you figure will be in the room?" Tony asked.

"I have no idea, some crony, some gofer. Maybe even Mae Feldman."

"I'd like it to be Mae Feldman," Tony said. "Nothing I'd like more than to finally lay eyes on that woman. She damn near lost me my leg."

"Have you heard from Carla Zaretski?" Annabel asked.

"Yeah, she calls all the time. She keeps threatening to come to Washington, and I keep telling her I'm goin' out of town."

"Has she ever mentioned the money she took from Mae Feldman's bank account?"

"Nope, and I don't mention it. Should I have?"

Smith shook his head, "No, not yet."

An aluminum Samsonite camera case sat next to Tony's chair. Smith had taken it from his closet at home, removed the camera and accessories that were nestled into cutouts in the foam lining, and given it to Tony as the case he would use to carry the money. In it was a few thousand dollars Smith always kept in a safe at home. Annabel had arranged it in a layer to cover pieces of blank paper beneath. With luck, the person on the receiving end wouldn't dig too deeply.

"Where will you be?" Tony asked.

"Right here. Get this thing over with and come back as quickly as possible. Ready, Tony?"

Buffolino reached under his suit jacket and patted the bulge beneath his arm. He nodded. "Yeah, I'm ready. Any last-minute instructions?"

"Just protect your flanks," Smith said. Annabel kissed him on the cheek.

"Hey, I like that," Tony said. He looked at Smith warmly. "Don't worry, Mac, I respect you too much ever to make a move on your woman."

She had been in room 7 for the past two hours. She hadn't bothered to remove her raincoat because she was cold, and because she wanted an extra layer of protection while sitting in the dirty and only chair in the room, or on the edge of a bed covered with a soiled, torn bedspread. She smoked; an overflowing ashtray and half-filled empty coffee container held the stubbed-out results.

She checked her watch: eight o'clock. One hour to go. She'd considered leaving many times since arriving early in the afternoon, but knew she couldn't. Herbert would be furious. No telling what he would do to her. Because there was no phone in the room, she went down to the shabby lobby and called him from the pay phone. He snapped at her, "Why did you leave the room?"

"It's ours until—"

"Go back to the room, Mae. You never know. They might come early."

She hung up, went outside, and bought three packs of cigarettes and a cup of coffee to bring back with her.

When she heard the groan of the stairs fifteen minutes later, she knew someone was approaching the door. She'd been sitting on the edge of the bed; she tensed, stood, and went to the door, placed her ear against it. As she did, the person knocked, the sharp sound reverberating through her head. She pulled back. Another knock. She moved closer to the door and asked in a voice that broke, "Who is it?"

"It's Herbert," Greist said.

"Herbert?" Why was *he* here? They were to meet later, a few blocks away in a bar. "Herbert, is that really you?"

"Damn it, Mae, open the door."

She was both confused and relieved. Maybe he'd changed his mind and would replace her, or stay with her. That would be good. She hated being the one in that dingy room waiting to accept blackmail money.

Greist hit the door with his fist. "Open it, Mae."

She drew a deep breath and turned the knob. Greist carried a battered brown leather valise in his left hand. His right hand was in the pocket of his topcoat. "Thank God you're here," she said, standing back to allow him to enter.

He stepped into the room and closed the door behind him. "Herbert, I think we should leave," she said. "We don't need Ewald's money. We can find our own way, be together and not have to worry about—Oh, no." He'd brought his right hand out of his pocket. In it was a revolver. "Herbert, what are you doing? Why would you . . . ?" She began to retreat, her hands in front of her face, back and back until she bumped against the room's only window, which she'd opened to allow smoke to escape. "Dear man, please don't hurt me. We've shared so much, and there's so much to do together in the future if . . . if you don't . . . hurt . . . me." She whimpered like a puppy about to be hit with a rolled-up newspaper for soiling the rug, and cowered, shook, and said words to God.

Greist slowly crossed the room, the revolver still aimed at her face. When he was close to her, he raised his right arm and brought the full weight of the weapon against the side of her head. She fell to her knees; blood trickled from her left ear. He brought the weapon down on the top of her skull, and she pitched forward, her face landing on one of his shoes. He quickly replaced the revolver in his pocket, dropped the bag, and managed, with difficulty, to raise her up from the floor. She was unconscious. He leaned her against the window, and while holding her semi-erect by the front of her coat, opened the window with his other hand. The space outside was almost black, an air shaft, covered with years of the city's grit and grime. He slowly allowed her to sink back until her head and shoulders were out the window. Then he pushed her the rest of the way until she disappeared from view. Seconds later, the thud of her body hitting ground came back at him through the open window.

He looked down and saw her at the bottom of the shaft. Light from a first-floor window illuminated the body. She'd landed on her back, arms and legs akimbo. Her eyes were open, and there was what might be construed as a smile on her large red lips.

Greist picked up his bag and went to the door. He peered out onto the landing. There was no one there, and no sign of anyone coming up the stairs. He slowly closed the door, locked it, and sat in the room's only chair, waiting for the arrival of the money. He felt relief at what he'd just done. The woman was an albatross, always complaining, always second-guessing him. She'd lost the money and lost the files that were his ticket to retirement. Everything was gone now—everyone—his daughter and the mother of his only child, and that was good. It was better to be alone. Fewer problems, less worry. Now, all he had to do was accept the money, find a way to elude the FBI dragnet that had been cast for him, and get out, go to where he would be appreciated, maybe Cuba, or Panama, the Soviet Union itself, or Hungary, someplace where he and the money would go a long way.

A weary smile crossed his gray face. It would work now that they couldn't complicate his life. It was always someone else who caused trouble.

Tony Buffolino said to the desk clerk, who'd just awakened from a nap, "I got to see somebody upstairs." The clerk shrugged and opened a magazine featuring naked couples. Tony cursed the lack of an elevator as he slowly went up the stairs, his leg throbbing with every step. When he reached the fourth-floor landing, he stared at the door to number 7, went to it, listened, then knocked. There was no response. He knocked again. Nothing. Had this all been a joke? Had whoever was there decided it might be a trap and left? Had Greist made that decision?

"Who is it?" a voice asked through the door.

"Tony Buffolino. I got something for you from the senator."

There was silence again.

Buffolino knocked. "Hey, open up. I got what you want, and I ain't gonna stand out in this hall much longer." Something smelled bad to Buffolino, and it wasn't the urine versus the cheap disinfectant that permeated the hotel. Why the delay in opening the door? This was to be a simple transaction. He pulled his .22 from beneath his arm and concealed it behind the aluminum Samsonite case.

Inside, Greist was going through his own set of concerns. It hadn't occurred to him until that moment that the person in the hallway might not be delivering money. It could be a trap, the FBI, the New York police. Ewald might have set him up. He put his mouth close to the door and said, "Identify yourself."

"For Christ's sake, I already told you my name is Tony Buffolino and I got the money you're waiting for. Password, Ewald. Five seconds, no more. Five seconds or you can go whistle."

A lock was undone, the handle was turned, and the door opened slowly. The gray man backed up to the center of the small room and stood at the foot of the bed. Tony stepped over the threshold. Greist held a leather bag in his left hand; his right hand was in his topcoat pocket.

"Here," Buffolino said, making a little move toward Greist with the aluminum case. "Here's your money."

Greist backed up further until he was almost to the window. "Put it on the bed," he said. "Just put it on the bed and get out."

"Yeah, sure, no sweat." Tony kept his eyes on Greist's right-hand coat pocket. You've got a piece in there, he thought. Because his weapon was already drawn and hidden behind the metal case, he wouldn't have a problem getting the drop on the man, whoever he was.

Buffolino slowly walked to the foot of the bed. He realized that the moment he tossed the case on it, his revolver would be exposed. That's okay, he told himself. Dump the case, hold him in place with the gun, and back out. No sweat. But then his eyes went to a red smear on the windowsill, to Greist's left. No question about it. Why would there be blood on the windowsill? Who was this guy? Had he killed someone else? Buffolino noticed that the window behind the man was fully open.

"I got a question for you," Buffolino said.

"No questions. Leave the money," Greist snapped, his right hand stirring.

"Somethin' ain't kosher here," Buffolino said. "Are you Greist?"

"I said no questions." The guy was obviously on the edge now. His hand started to come out of his pocket. Buffolino didn't hesitate. He tossed the metal case into Greist's chest. Buffolino's cane had been dangling from his left wrist. He grabbed the curved handle, held it out, and threw himself at Greist, the point of the cane catching him in the chest and driving him back and halfway out the window. Buffolino was instantly on top of him. He pressed the snout of his revolver tight against Greist's left temple. "You move that right hand, loser, and you're dead meat."

He yanked Greist up straight by the front of his coat and threw him against the wall, knocking a lamp to the floor. He rammed his revolver against the back of Greist's neck and said, "Okay, creep, you pull that right hand out real slow."

Greist did as he was told, his revolver dangling from his index finger. "Lay it on the table nice and easy," Buffolino said. "Do it my way, or I'm gonna leave a lot of you on this wall."

Greist lowered the weapon to the table and deposited it with a clunk.

"Nice, you take instructions real good," Buffolino said. "Turn around, slow, very slow."

Greist followed instructions and stood with his back to the wall, his arms raised above his head. There was a wild, frightened look on his face. Buffolino realized for the first time how old he was. At least he looked old, sickly, all gray and pasty, breath coming hard.

"What's your name?" Buffolino asked.

"This is wrong," Greist said. "Don't you know what you've done? I'll tell what I know about Senator Ewald."

"You know nothin'," Buffolino said. He nodded toward the windowsill. "Whose blood is that?"

"Blood?"

"Yeah, don't play dumb with me. You stay right here, don't move, don't even blink. You blink, you're a former human being." He slowly backed to the windowsill, his .22 leveled at Greist's chest. He ran a finger over the red blotch and examined what came off the sill.

"You don't understand," Greist said, trying to inject calm and reason into his voice. "We can make a deal. Believe me, I—"

"Shut up!" Buffolino leaned out the window, dividing his attention between Greist and the air shaft. He quickly looked down and saw the body at the bottom. He checked Greist and looked down again, longer this time. "Oh, damn it to hell," he said, "no." Looking up at him, with her heavily made-up eyes and garish red mouth formed into a twisted smile, was Carla.

"What'd you do that for?" he said to Greist.

"Please, listen to me. We can split the money you have. Give me half. Just give me a quarter of it, so I can leave. Take the rest. I won't say anything to anyone."

Buffolino came up close to Greist once again and shoved his revolver up under Greist's chin. Greist whimpered, whined, "No, please, don't."

"What the hell did you kill her for? What'd she ever do to you?"

"She was . . ." He had trouble speaking because of the iron pressure under his chin. "She was stupid. Let's talk. I know we can . . ."

Buffolino took a few steps back. His face was a mask of rage and frustration. What he did next was pure reflex, no thought directing the movement. He brought his cane up off the floor and smashed the end of it against the right side of Greist's face. Greist slowly slipped to his knees. He'd begun to cry.

"You cockroach. Come on, stop your bawlin' and get up."

Greist preceded Buffolino out of the room and they slowly made their way down the narrow stairs, Buffolino somehow carrying both cases and his cane in his left hand, his right hand steadying his revolver at the back of Greist's head. His leg throbbed, and he misstepped. Greist began to run. Buffolino found his balance and stumbled after him through the lobby. The desk clerk looked up from his magazine, and when he saw the gun in Buffolino's hand, threw up his magazine and ducked so that he was below the level of the counter. Greist made it through the front door.

Across the street, two men in raincoats came at him. Tony looked left and right; men dressed similarly closed in from the sides. Greist was surrounded and held. One pulled out a badge. "Simmons, FBI."

"Yeah, I knew you guys were coming. Tony Buffolino. This is the shyster Herbert Greist. There's a body at the bottom of an air shaft. Mr. Greist pushed a nice older woman out the window."

"You don't understand," Greist wailed. "It was an accident. She jumped."

"And hit her head on the windowsill going out," Buffolino said with disgust. Simmons, the leader of the group, dispatched two of his men to confirm what Tony had said. They returned and reported that there was, indeed, a dead woman at the bottom of the air shaft.

"So, here he is, your Commie spy. You don't mind if I leave him with you? I got to check in with my boss. And here's his bag. Empty, like him."

"You have to come with us," one of the agents said.

"No, let him go," said Simmons. "You're going to meet with Mackensie Smith at the Waldorf?" he asked.

"Yeah."

"We'll contact you there. Nice job."

"Yeah," Tony muttered. "Nice job." He looked at Greist. "I should've done you up there, creep. She was a nice lady—a little kookie maybe, but nice. You shouldn't've done that to her. She didn't deserve it."

He limped painfully up the street, the brushed aluminum Samsonite case in his left hand, the cane in his right, supporting his weight. A rare Sunday night in the rain, a yellow cab stopped at a corner and discharged a passenger. Tony slid into the backseat and laid his leg across it. "The Waldorf Astoria," he said painfully, "and don't step on it."

34

SPECIAL AGENT SIMMONS came to the Waldorf the next morning and took a deposition from Buffolino. He thanked Smith for his help in setting up Herbert Greist, and told him they'd keep in touch.

The three of them caught an early shuttle to Washington. The hired car dropped Annabel off at her home, and took Smith and Buffolino to the Watergate.

"What's that you're humming?" Buffolino asked as he and Smith waited for the elevator.

Smith smiled. "I didn't realize I was humming anything. It's 'Celeste Aida' from Verdi's *Aida*."

"Sounds nice."

"Yes, it's a love song, one of my favorites."

"Yeah, nice. I was learnin' to like opera."

They stepped out on their floor. Directly in front of them was a large mirror over a marble-topped table. A bouquet of red and yellow fresh flowers dominated it. A young man, who'd been standing by the table, quickly turned his back to them and examined the flowers.

"That guy don't smell right to me," Buffolino said as they walked down the hall.

"I didn't notice," said Smith. "He might be part of the hotel security staff."

Smith called Ken Ewald at home and was told by a secretary he'd be back in two hours. He hung up and said to Tony, "With Greist out of the way, I'd say we're getting close to winding things up."

"Yeah, maybe, except we still got to find Janet Ewald."

"Yes, that's true, and Marcia Mims, too. Why don't you get on the phone and see what you can accomplish. I'm going back to the house. See you at four."

In a motel room in Miami Beach, Florida, Janet Ewald sat alone. It was a small motel that catered to young people; signs outside heralded free drinks for women between 4:00 and 7:00 P.M., wet T-shirt contests on Wednesday nights, and chug-a-lug competitions every Friday. The fierce Florida sun threatened to burn through purple drapes Janet had drawn tightly across the window. The television set was on but without sound. A game show was in progress.

She sat in a purple vinyl chair, her arms tightly wrapped around herself; she was wearing a cardigan sweater because the blast of the air conditioner, even turned low, chilled her. She rocked forward and back. The chair was stationary; she created the rocking motion with her own body. She continued moving until a painful whine from deep inside came through her lips and nose and caused her to violently throw her head forward, then back against the chair.

She looked across the bed at a table and a white telephone. She'd reached for that phone many times since arriving at the motel the previous afternoon, had actually picked up the receiver on occasion, but never dialed.

Standing unsteadily, she went around the bed, sat on it, and read the instructions about how to dial. She was confused by them. She opened her purse, removed a small address book, slowly turned its pages until coming to the C section, and squinted at the handwritten number next to Geoffrey Collins's name. She dialed.

"Dr. Collins's office," his receptionist said.

The sound of a voice on the other end startled Janet.

"Hello, Dr. Collins's office."

"Hello. This is . . . this is Janet Ewald."

"Oh, Mrs. Ewald. Where are you calling from?"

The question threw her. Did the receptionist know she'd been missing? Could she trust her? Could she trust anyone?

"Mrs. Ewald?"

"Yes . . . is the doctor in?"

"Yes, he's in session, but . . . please hold on."

A few moments later, Collins came on the line. "Janet, how are you? Everyone has been worried about you."

"Yes, I know they have. Dr. Collins, I . . ."

"Are you all right?"

"Yes, no . . . Oh, Doctor, I just want to die."

"Why would you want to do that, Janet? You're young. Nothing can be so bad that we need death to resolve it."

"You don't understand. I know so much . . . I know things . . . I'm afraid."

"Where are you?"

"I'm in Florida."

Collins's laugh was professional. "I wish I were there. Is the weather good?"

"Yes, very nice . . ."

"Janet, will you come back, come directly to me? Surely, you're not afraid of me. I've always been your friend, and I'll make sure nothing happens to you."

She was silent.

"Janet. Are you there?"

"Yes. I know I should come back. I have to talk to someone. I talked to Mr. Smith, but then I got scared again and ran away."

"Mr. Smith?"

"Mackensie Smith, my father-in-law's friend."

"Oh, Mac Smith. Why don't you come back and let the two of us help you through this?"

"All right. I mean, I might."

"Here's what I suggest, Janet. Enjoy the sun, have a good rest tonight, and take a plane first thing tomorrow morning. Call now and make a reservation. When you get to Washington, come directly to my office. Call and let me know what time you'll be here."

"All right."

"Do you want me to call Mac Smith?"

"No, that's—yes, call him. I trust him. I trust you." She hung up.

Smith returned to the Watergate at four and asked Buffolino, "How's the leg?"

"Pretty good. What are you up to tonight?"

"Annabel and I promised Ken Ewald that we'd attend a fund-raiser tonight at the Four Seasons Hotel. The arts crowd is throwing a party for him."

"Should be fun. I'll come along."

"No, you stay here and rest. After what you went through in New York, you could use a little relaxation."

"I don't know how to relax. Hey, Mac, let me ask you a straight question."

"What is it?"

"Are we gonna stay on this thing for a while? I mean, if this job is about to end, I'd better start making some plans."

"To be honest with you, Tony, I don't know how much longer we'll stay involved. Outside circumstances will determine that, I suppose. In the meantime, don't worry about it. You're still on the payroll, and I'll give you plenty of notice. Fair enough?"

Buffolino grinned. "You're always fair, Mac. Thanks."

Before leaving the suite, Smith dialed his answering machine at home. There was an urgent message from Dr. Geoffrey Collins. Smith returned the call.

"Good to hear your voice again, Mac," Collins said. "It's been a while."

"Good to hear you, too, Geof. I got your message. What's up?"

"I just got off the phone with Janet Ewald."

"You did? Where is she?"

"She said she was in Florida. I think I've convinced her to fly back here tomorrow morning and to come to my office. She mentioned she'd seen you, and when I asked whether she wanted me to call you, she said she did."

"This is good news, Geof. Do you think she'll actually show up?"

"I have no idea, but I would like you to be here if she does."

"Of course. Keep me informed, call anytime."

Smith said to Tony Buffolino, "That was the psychiatrist who's treated Janet Ewald. She called him from Florida and said she's coming back tomorrow. I'd just as soon she return of her own volition, but I don't have much faith in that. Can you put out some tracers in Florida? Let's assume she's in the Miami area, although she could be anywhere in the state."

"Sure. I got a friend in the airlines who owes me. They don't give out passenger manifests, but he's broken that rule for me a couple a' times. If she used her own name, I can get it. I'll give Joe Riga a call, too, and see if his pals can come up with something."

"Good. I'll check back in with you after the party."

Smith and Annabel went to a suite in the Georgetown Four Seasons where a cocktail reception for Ken and Leslie Ewald was in progress. This was a smaller gathering of a half-dozen movers-and-shakers in Washington's artistic community. A hundred lesser lights would be downstairs later.

"Any prepared remarks for me?" Ewald asked Ed Farmer.

"Prepared remarks for these people? All they want to do is shake your hand and hear you tell them how much their support means to you. Your Senate record on funding the arts makes you a hero to them. Just play hero." Smith smiled at Farmer's comment, although the campaign manager had delivered it, as usual, without any levity of tone. Farmer frowned at Smith and walked away.

Ewald and his entourage went downstairs to the larger affair where Smith and Annabel were introduced to a few people at the door, then drifted to a corner to watch Ewald work the room. Smith had considered telling Ken and Leslie about the possible return of Janet, but thought better of it. Wait for a quiet moment, when no one had to be onstage.

It was just another party until Ed Farmer captured the attention of most of the people by saying in a loud voice, "Ladies and gentlemen, I know the next president of the United States, Ken Ewald, would like to say a few words."

The whoops and hollers rose to a crescendo, and then died as Ewald said, "Ladies and gentlemen, I can say honestly to you that I've been to a lot of rubber-chicken-and-rice dinners. I've shared times like this with hundreds of thousands of people in many states, and will have to do the same in the months ahead, but never have I enjoyed an hour more than this." Applause. Ewald's hands held high in the air, Leslie beaming at his side. "As I stand here, what keeps running through my mind is the adage that many of you, especially in theater, live by. 'The show must go on.' This campaign—this *show* we are in the process of producing— has run into many out-of-town trials and tribulations. We've had to rewrite as we went, change scenes, juggle adversity—to say nothing of unexpected and unhappy surprises—but here we are ready for the con- vention, and I can tell you that *this* show is now ready for a long run, thanks to creative, caring people like you."

Smith looked at Annabel and smiled. "Prepared remarks?" he said. "He's better on his feet."

Ewald continued. "We took some battering a while back because of circumstances beyond our control. Now we have control again, and everyone in this room who cares about the cultural aspects of this soci- ety we share can rest assured that not only do I intend to win the Democratic nomination in July, I intend to become the next president of these United States. And as president, I will do everything in my power to help shift this society from one of hate and prejudice and misunderstanding to one in which the beautiful music can be heard once again, the magnificent words of our writers and poets can be heard, and the gentler aspirations that a society rich in culture fosters will be with us for at least four years and, hopefully, far into the fu- ture." He waited until the applause had ebbed, and concluded with, "This beautiful woman at my side has been my inspiration throughout the difficulties of this campaign. My main opponent is a gentleman with whom I've served for many years in the Senate. Senator Backus is a good man who loves this country as much as I do. The difference is that in an administration such as we now have in Washington, there is no room for beauty and culture, because most of the attention and most of the money are focused on destructive things. Don't misunderstand. We must have a strong and secure nation in order for the beautiful things to grow, to blossom, but there must be something else in a society if it is to be judged generations from now as one of compassion and love. Senator Backus represents an anachronistic view of how we take Amer- ica and move it forward into the light, rather than into the shadows. What more can I say, except to say thank you from me and from Leslie and from every man and woman who has worked so hard to see their dreams—and your dreams—become reality once again. When November eighth is over, I promise you one thing . . . we will all gather again, only this time it will be in the White House, and we will raise a toast to the future of this free industrial, agricultural, commercial *and* cultural giant . . . the United States of America!"

Many of those in the room tried to reach Ewald as he and Leslie made their way to the door, preceded by Farmer and Secret Service agents. Mac and Annabel didn't try to catch up with them. They lingered, watched, and, once the Ewalds and official followers were out of the room, made their own way to the lobby.

"What do you think?" she asked.

Smith shrugged. "I have my reservations about Ken, but I keep coming back to the conviction that he's a hell of a lot better than the alternative. Yes, I'd like to see him in the White House. I think some good things must come out of it."

When they returned to the Watergate suite, Buffolino told them that his airline friend found no passenger between Washington and Miami by the name of Janet Ewald. "Funny thing, though," he added. "Riga called me. His people have been checking manifests, too, and he said they ran across a passenger flying to Miami from D.C. by the name of Andrea Feldman."

Smith said, "The Andrea Feldman we know isn't taking trips anywhere these days."

"Yeah. Kind of spooky though, huh?"

"Try checking it through," Smith said.

Annabel turned on the TV. Buffolino said, "I think I'll go downstairs and get a drink. I'm getting cabin fever here."

Buffolino went to the lobby, which was bustling with well-dressed people—a typical Watergate crowd, he thought. There was a group of Japanese tourists, a familiar sight in every city in America. An aristocratic couple with regal bearing waited at the elevator, he in a tuxedo, she in a floor-length ball gown bursting with sequins. He then saw the same slender, nicely dressed Hispanic young man they'd seen on their floor earlier in the day. He thought of Smith's comment, that he was probably a member of hotel security, and decided Smith was right. He acted like a plainclothes security guy, his eyes taking in everything and everyone. Still, Tony didn't like it. Then again, all Hispanics made him uneasy since the night he'd been set up by Garcia. He had to admit that, and he did as he went to the bar and enjoyed a leisurely drink by himself. I hope this booze goes right to my thigh, he thought; it's killing me.

35

MAC SMITH HAD never believed in the observation that the great leveling factor was putting on pants one leg at a time. For him, it was paying bills, and that unpleasant task, long neglected the past weeks, was what he focused on the next morning. It seemed a good chore to undertake while waiting for a phone call from Geof Collins about whether or not Janet Ewald had arrived.

Annabel called him from her gallery to see if he'd heard. "No. I think I'll call him," he said, looking up at the clock. It was noon.

"You'll let me know as soon as you find out anything."

"Of course. How are things this morning with your little stone friends?"

"My little friends are fine. I've missed them. They've gotten dusty, poor things. James is an asset, but I suspect he doesn't do windows, and I *know* he doesn't dust. Talk with you later."

Smith's call to Collins was disappointing. Not a word from Janet. "No idea where in Florida she called from?" Smith asked.

"None whatsoever, Mac. She's very fragile, very enigmatic. I'll be relieved when we do hear from her. *If* we do."

"You and a lot of other people. Mind if I call again in a couple of hours?"

"Not at all."

He was writing out a check against his monthly tab at the Foggy Bottom Cafe when the phone rang. It was Buffolino, who wanted to know what the plans were for the rest of the day.

"Frankly, Tony, I haven't made any. Annabel and I are going to the testimonial for Ken Ewald tonight at the Watergate." Smith laughed. "How do politicians stand it, one dinner after another, plaques that never get hung up on the wall, bone-crushing handshakes, fattening foods, and having to suffer fools always looking for something from you?"

"Takes a certain kind a' guy."

"Yes, it certainly does. Anyway, there is that dinner tonight we're going to. We'll stop up at the suite before."

The last of the bills paid, and after a lunch of two hard-boiled eggs, sliced tomatoes, Bermuda onion, and breadsticks, Smith headed for the Yates Field House for a workout. During the drive, he thought about the contest between Ewald and Backus for their party's nomination. He also admitted to himself for the first time that he'd begun to question Ewald's ability to lead the nation. Did his friend lack the necessary strength of character? Smith had never viewed it that way, preferring to chalk up any perceived weakness in Ewald as representing simple human frailty, a concept that was dear to Smith's heart. As he got older, he'd become more tolerant of his fellow man (and woman, of course), and of the human dilemma.

But running for president of the United States demanded less "humanity," didn't it, someone with fewer foibles than the pack? Ken Ewald was *very* human—good enough for a friend, but was that good enough to lead the greatest nation on earth? Smith puffed his cheeks and expelled the air in a burst. "Who knows?" he muttered. "Who knows anything?"

He thought of Backus, whose political views were anathema to him yet who seemed to possess those traits necessary, perhaps, to lead effectively. Ironic, he thought as he pulled into the parking lot, that his kind of human being might be the best qualification for the White House.

While Smith ran and lifted weights and thought about him, Senator Jody Backus reached Washington, Virginia, after slightly more than an hour's drive. There were few cars parked in front of the Inn at Little Washington, and they were what one would expect to see there—two Jags, two BMWs, and a Mercedes limousine.

He paused at the main entrance to the inn and looked back at the empty road. This was the first time since he'd announced his candidacy that there wasn't at least one other vehicle trailing behind, usually filled with Secret Service agents. He'd really had to put his foot down to get them off his tail today. Thank God for Jeroldson, who took the responsibility for letting him go off on his own for a couple of hours.

Backus knocked on the door of the largest suite in the ten-room inn. It was opened by a young man who said, "Come in, Senator. We've been expecting you."

Backus had met this boy before and didn't like him. His name was Warner Jenco. A head of carefully arranged blond curls formed a helmet above his placid face. His suit, shirt, and tie were as bland as the rest of him.

Backus stood in the middle of the living room. "Where is he?" he asked.

"On the phone, Senator. He'll be with you in a minute."

"Tell him I don't have all day."

Jenco disappeared into a bedroom. Backus went to the window and looked out over the Blue Ridge Mountains; they might have been painted there for the visual entertainment of guests, who paid top dollar for the suite. A profound sadness came over him. The mountains reminded him of his home in Georgia, where as a boy he'd spent countless days roaming them. How long ago that seemed; he saw himself—a chubby, barefoot kid with the bottoms of his overalls rolled up—wading

in a crystal-clear trout stream, a sort of Mark Twain–Norman Rockwell
kid. Those were good days, when he was a good kid.

The moment of reflection calmed him. Now, as he paced the large
room, waiting, his anger returned. Easy, he told himself. You'll have a
heart attack. He took deep breaths. His face was red; he could feel his
heart pumping in his large chest.

Just as he was about to go to the door and bang on it, it opened, and
the Reverend Garrett Kane entered the living room. The smile that
lighted up millions of television sets across America was in place as he
said in his deep, cultured voice, "Jody, how good to see you." He closed
the gap between them and extended his hand. Backus looked at it, and
a sour expression crossed his face. Kane kept his hand extended, the
smile never dimming. Backus finally took it, pumped once, let go.

"Please, sit down, Jody. Bourbon? I had it ordered up just for you,
your favorite brand." He crossed to a small bar and held out a bottle
for Backus's approval, like a wine steward presenting the evening's
choice.

"Yeah, I'll have me some of that. I need a belt of something."

Kane carefully measured the drink with a shot glass, poured it over
ice, and handed it to the senator, who had begun to perspire. "Turn on
some AC," Backus said, downing the drink. "Hot as hell in here."

"I find it quite comfortable," Kane said, pulling up a straight-back
chair. "Refill?"

"I'll get it myself." Backus poured directly from the bottle.

"Do you ever worry that you drink a tad too much, Jody?" Kane
asked.

Backus looked at him with watery eyes. "What in hell business is that
of yours?" He consumed half the drink, and added, "There's nothin'
like men of the cloth who raise hell against sin, then go out and do all
the sinnin' they damn well please." He sank into an oversized leather
chair.

"I hate to see you this upset, Jody," Kane said. "No need to be upset
about anything. It seems to me that things in general are very well in
control, very well indeed."

"I don't see it that way, Garrett. I told you up at Zach Filler's lodge
that I had a feelin' things had gone too far, and I'm here to tell you it's
got to stop!"

Kane raised his head, an amused look on his face, the fingers of one
hand gently touching his chin. It was a pose Backus had seen him adopt
too many times before, a posture of superiority and scorn. Backus
wanted to lunge at him, beat a fist into his smooth, tanned face, see his
perfect white caps fall on the floor like little ice cubes.

"Jody, I only ask about your drinking habits because a man who
drinks too much often finds his judgment clouded, his lips becoming
unnecessarily loose. Do you understand me?"

"Look, drinking has nothing to do with this, and you know it. I didn't
get to where I did with bad judgment and a mouth that flaps." He fixed

Kane in a steely stare and, for the first time, saw the minister's cocky, arrogant expression change—not much, but enough to give Backus control. "What's happened here, it seems to me, is that like with a lot of good things, some people go too far, ruin it, turn somethin' good into somethin' bad, somethin' that starts to smell. I see it all the time. You could see it on the Iran-Contra committee. Riled the hell out of me that good people like North and Poindexter took a worthwhile project and turned it into somethin' stupid and illegal. I saw it when Nixon resigned in disgrace, and when Kennedy pulled his goddamn Bay of Pigs. Happens all the time in government, because people get swelled heads and think they know everything, think they are above everybody else. That's when good things go to hell in a handbasket, Garrett, and that's what I see happening here."

Kane had listened intently. When Backus's short speech was over and he returned to polishing off his drink, Kane pointedly looked at his watch. "Are you finished?" he asked.

"No, I don't think I am. I want your promise that the things I'm speaking of are goin' to stop. Listen closely to me, Garrett. If I don't get your promise, you lose this U.S. senator, and you need him."

"I think you might have it backward, Jody. The fact is, you need me more than I need you. That's probably hard for a man like you to accept, wheeling and dealing in the Senate for so many years, handing out favors, collecting your share, buying votes, and burying bodies." He strung out the last two words, said them with careful and precise emphasis. There was silence as they looked at each other.

Backus said, "You're the one with clouded judgment and loose lips, Reverend."

"And you're the one with the blood of a dead girl on your hands."

Backus rose to his full height and shouted, "Don't you say anything like that to me ever again, you hypocritical, sanctimonious bastard!"

Kane flinched at the power in Backus's voice. He quickly opened the bedroom door and said, "Come in here." Jenco and another young man stood in the doorway. Kane said to Backus, who still shook with rage, "I thought we might have the next president of the United States as a friend. You want to know the truth, Jody? You're a loser—a big, fat, drunken slob of a loser, who's going to end up shining Ewald's shoes and making speeches on his behalf. At least, that's what would be the case if I weren't here to think clearly, to understand what's at stake and to have the guts to stop it. Now, I suggest you leave and continue to go through the motions of seeking the Democratic nomination. It looks good that you do that, even though none of it makes any difference. Raymond Thornton will be the next president of the United States, and you will continue to slap backs and make promises in coatrooms until, one night, you've had too much to drink and run your car into a telephone pole. The nation will mourn the death of Senator Jody Backus." That famous smile suddenly lit up his face, and his eyes widened. "And I will be honored to officiate at the funeral. Get out!"

Backus started to say something, but the two young men came around to either side of Kane. Backus seemed unsure of what to do. He held up the glass that now contained only ice cubes, and for a second poised to hurl it at the Reverend Garrett Kane. Instead, he dropped it to the floor and slowly crossed the room, pausing at the door. He turned and said, "I've had a distinguished career as a United States senator. I may have played the political game rough at times, but I never lost sight of why. I love this country, Garrett, and I have given to it the best years of my life. You may think what you want of me, but if there is one thing this fat ol' Georgia politician is *not,* it's a party to assassination." He slammed the door behind him.

Backus had left for his meeting with Kane from his Senate office. Now, he drove directly home. His wife, Lorraine, was baking biscuits for dinner. "What are you doin' home so early?" she asked, her southern accent as thick as his. Lorraine Backus was a short, round woman whose reservoir of energy seemed never to run out. She was one of the most popular Senate wives in Washington.

Backus crossed the kitchen and kissed her on the cheek. "Those biscuits smell good," he said.

"Made them especially for you, Mr. Senator. You go take your shoes off and get comfortable, and I'll bring you a drink. I have some news for you."

Backus lumbered from the kitchen, heavy with a fatigue that threatened to pin him to the floor. He went to his study and did exactly as he was told, removed his shoes, slipped his feet into a pair of slippers, and sat in a favorite chair by a bow window. A window seat in front of the window was used as a ledge for many framed family photographs. Backus leaned forward and looked at them, as he often did. There was something wonderful about a family, something sustaining. Backus had two sons and two daughters, all grown and married, and five grandchildren. Nothing gave him more pleasure than being with his grandchildren. He'd taught them all how to fish. The youngest, Paula, had caught the biggest bass of the five; a picture taken on Jody's boat in Georgia showed a proud Paula holding her catch, almost as big as she was. Behind her, and beaming from ear to ear, was Backus.

Lorraine Backus came into the study, handed her husband a glass of bourbon, and sat on a hassock at his feet. "Well, now, what brings you home at this hour?"

"I've got to do some serious thinkin', Lorri, and I got to do it fast. I figured I could think better here than someplace else. What's this news you have for me?"

"You are about to have yourself another fishing student."

"What in hell does that mean?"

"Winnie is expecting again. She called me just a couple of hours ago. Isn't that wonderful?"

Backus sat back and clasped his hands on his chest. Tears formed in his eyes. Few people knew that Jody Backus, all 260 rough-and-ready pounds of him, was capable of crying. He made sure he did it privately, but the tears were real in solitude.

"Jody, are you all right? You look very tired today, or very worried, or both."

He managed to smile, reached out and took one of her hands in both of his. "Just a little pooped, Lorri," he said. "I think it's time for you and me to get away, take a nice vacation, maybe go to Paris, where you've always been wantin' to go, then come back and spend a little time fishin' with the kids. That sound good to you?"

"Sounds wonderful."

"Sure does to me." He patted her hand and released it. "Now, you get back in that kitchen and make sure those biscuits don't burn. I need to be alone for a bit."

Mac Smith had just slipped on his tuxedo pants and was pulling the suspenders over his shoulders when the phone rang. Annabel, he assumed, whom he'd be picking up in a half hour. "Hi," he said.

"Mac, this is Tony."

"I thought it was Annabel. What's up?"

"Mac, I think you'd better get here right away."

"What's wrong?"

"We've got a couple of visitors."

"Who?"

"Two lovely ladies. One is named Janet Ewald, the other Marcia Mims."

"I'm on my way."

36

"I WANT TO apologize for all the trouble I've put you through, Mr. Smith," Janet Ewald said. She sat in the Watergate suite with Smith, Annabel, Tony Buffolino, and Marcia Mims.

"That isn't important, Janet, although I appreciate the sentiment. I'm just glad to see you here."

"Because of Marcia." She managed a weak smile at her friend before saying to Smith, "I was going to go to Dr. Collins's office, but Marcia convinced me to come here. I called Dr. Collins and told him I was back. I'll call him again tomorrow and make an appointment. I think I could use it."

"What name were you traveling under?" Smith asked. He knew.

Janet glanced at Marcia before opening her purse and pulling out a VISA card. She handed it to Smith.

"Where did you get this?" he asked, passing it to Annabel.

"In Ken and Leslie's house."

Annabel said, "I assume—and please pardon me if I sound insensitive—I assume you found this because of Paul's affair with Andrea."

If Janet considered the comment insensitive, her face didn't say it. There was some strength there now as she said, "No. Mr. Farmer had that card. He left it in an unlocked desk drawer, and I just took it when the need arose."

"Ed Farmer? Why would he have it?" Smith asked.

"Because he and Andrea were close, *very* close."

"Are you saying that Ed Farmer had an affair with Andrea Feldman, *too?*" Annabel asked.

"I didn't say that," Janet said. "I said they were close, in a business sense. Mr. Farmer approved the credit cards for staff members. Andrea had a lot of them."

"What do you mean by a lot?" Smith asked.

"More than the others. Mr. Farmer gave her cards to department stores, house accounts at restaurants, American Express, VISA, MasterCard, all of them."

"He was the one who approved the use of them?" Annabel asked.

"Yes. He never questioned Andrea's charges."

"Go on," said Smith.

"I was in the house once when Andrea stayed overnight. She didn't know I was there. I'd been sick and decided to spend the weekend at my in-laws' house. I used the spare bedroom next to that small office on the second floor."

"Where was Paul?" Annabel asked.

"Away on business. I forget where. It doesn't matter. Sometimes when Paul is away and I'm not feeling well, I stay there to be close to Marcia."

Smith smiled at Marcia. "Go on, Janet, continue."

"That night, I heard them fighting. Andrea and Farmer. They were in the small office."

"Where was Senator Ewald?" Annabel asked.

"Out somewhere. I know he came back later because I heard him, but he wasn't there when the fight was going on."

"What were they fighting about?"

"About . . ." She looked at Marcia and suddenly went back into the shell that Smith recognized.

"Go ahead, honey, tell them," Marcia said, patting her arm.

"Remember what we talked about, that you would come back and tell everything you know, get it over with."

"They were arguing about files that Mr. Farmer had stolen from Ken."

"That *Farmer* had stolen from Ken? We thought Andrea stole files."

"I think she did, along with him. I mean, I think what happened was that they did it together. I didn't pay much attention at first, and I didn't make any kind of notes, but when they really started yelling, I sat up and listened as closely as I could. She was threatening him. She said she was going to tell Ken what he'd done, and that he had better be good to her if he didn't want that to happen."

" 'Good to her'?" Annabel said. "Do you know what she meant by that?"

"No."

Smith asked, "Did you get any hint of why the files might have been taken, who they stole them for?"

"No. They kept talking about 'they,' but they never mentioned any names."

"Janet, there must have been something else said. Didn't they discuss why they'd done it, how they got started, who had the idea?"

Janet shook her head. "No, they didn't. I learned more from Paul than from what I heard that night."

"What did Paul tell you?"

"We were arguing one night about his affair with Andrea, and he told me that he hated her and was sorry he ever brought her into his father's life. He said she was no good, evil, cared only about money and her own success. He told me that files his father kept had been stolen, and he said she did it."

"I thought you said Farmer did it with her," Annabel said.

"Yes, that's what I heard that night, but Paul didn't know that."

"Didn't you tell him?" Smith asked.

Janet looked sheepishly at her lap. "No, I didn't. I wanted him to think it was all Andrea. I *wanted* him to hate her, so that he wouldn't see her again."

Smith took a walk around the room to stretch his legs—and his mind. When he took his chair again, he said, "You told me in Annapolis that your father-in-law had slept with Andrea." He looked at Marcia. "And you agreed with her, Marcia." He almost mentioned the diary, but didn't want to bring it up in Janet's presence.

Janet sat folded into herself, a blank expression on her face.

"Well, didn't you tell me that, Janet?"

"Yes, I did."

Smith waited for more. When it didn't come, he asked, "Were you lying to me?"

"Yes," she said in a low voice.

"Why?" Annabel asked.

"Because I've always hated him. I talked about it with Dr. Collins, and he said I loved Paul so much that I actually wanted to shift the blame to his father, to make it seem that the only Ewald who'd been with Andrea was him, not my husband. I know better, of course, always did, but I suppose I was playing some kind of game with myself." She sighed and stood, a person purged, rid of a poison. "I'm sorry," she said. "I know I've caused a great deal of trouble. I never meant to, but I suppose people like me always do."

Smith said, "I think you ought to stop considering yourself unworthy, Janet. You're a good person, and I'm glad we're all here."

He asked Marcia why she'd gone along with Janet's story about Ken Ewald having slept with Andrea Feldman. Her answer was, "I suspected he did, but never knew for sure. When Janet said he had slept with her, I believed her. I'm . . . sorry."

"You said you were afraid to come back," Smith said, "that something terrible would happen to you. Who are you afraid will do something to you?"

"Mr. Farmer."

"Afraid Ed Farmer will physically hurt you?"

"I don't know what he would do. I don't like him, don't trust him, never did. I think Paul's father made a big mistake in trusting him. And when Marcia told me about the tape and what happened the night Andrea was murdered, I knew I had to get away."

"Wait a minute," Annabel said, "are you suggesting that . . . Ed Farmer murdered Andrea?"

"Yes."

"What tape?" Smith asked. "What happened the night of the murder?"

"Here." Marcia pulled a reel of tape from her purse and handed it to Smith. "There's a tape recorder in the second-floor office that goes on automatically every time the phone is picked up. Mr. Farmer had it installed. This is the tape that was on the machine the night Ms. Feldman was killed."

Smith weighed the tape in his hands, asked, "What's on it?"

Marcia said, "The telephone conversation I had with Ms. Feldman. She'd called looking for Senator Ewald. I told her he wasn't there. She said to me that she would wait outside the Kennedy Center for exactly an hour, and that I was to tell him when he came home to meet her there. She said it was urgent. She sounded very angry, very upset."

"Did you give Senator Ewald the message?" Buffolino asked. It was the first thing he'd said since Smith and Annabel arrived.

"No, he didn't come home. He'd called from his office to say he had an appointment. I told Mrs. Ewald that, but I never had a chance to give him the message from Ms. Feldman."

"That was all?" Annabel said. "I don't understand why her conversation with you is so important."

"Because after I hung up on Ms. Feldman, I saw Mr. Farmer go into the upstairs office, and heard him listening to the conversation on tape."

"What did you do then?" Smith asked.

"*I* didn't do anything, but Mr. Farmer left the house immediately."

"To meet Andrea Feldman," Annabel said.

Janet Ewald just looked straight ahead.

"Marcia, why didn't you come forward with this, especially when Paul was taken in as a suspect?" Smith asked.

"I wasn't sure what to do. When Janet disappeared, I decided to wait to discuss it with her before doing anything else. I told her about it, and she told me about the fight she'd heard between Mr. Farmer and Ms. Feldman."

"And neither of you did anything," said Buffolino.

Both Janet and Marcia shook their heads. "We were afraid," Janet said.

"I didn't even write it in my diary," Marcia added.

Smith looked at his watch. "I want the two of you to stay here. Will you do that?"

"Yes, we will," Janet said.

"Forgive me for being skeptical, Janet," Smith said, "but you've promised me things before. I want you to trust me, to know that the advice I'm giving you is good, that you won't be hurt, and that you have nothing to fear. Annabel and I are going to be leaving shortly, but Tony will stay with you." He said to Buffolino, "I'd like to talk to you for a few minutes."

They went into the bedroom, where Smith told Buffolino not to let either woman out of his sight, and to do anything short of shooting them to keep them in the suite.

They returned to the living room. "Janet, Marcia, just relax," Smith said. "Order up room service if you'd like. Just let Tony know what you want. He knows the menu by heart. We'll be back."

"Is Mr. Farmer downstairs?" Janet asked.

"I assume so, but don't worry. Whether you're correct or not about him, I assure you he won't have the opportunity to do you any harm."

Smith and Annabel went to the cocktail party, spotted and cornered Leslie. "Leslie, we need additional seating tonight."

"Mac, I can't do that at this late date."

"It's important. I have special guests with me. Can you arrange for a separate table for us at the rear of the room?"

Leslie sighed. "I'll try. Who are these 'special' guests?"

"I wish to bring my investigator, Tony Buffolino, to the dinner. He'll be joined by your daughter-in-law, Janet, and your housekeeper, Marcia Mims."

The shock value of his words registered on her face. She composed herself quickly. "You can't do this to me, Mac. I mean, I'm delighted

Janet is back, but having her at dinner under these circumstances will
. . . well, I mean, everyone knows she's been missing. It will take away
from Ken, from the focus of the dinner."

Smith smiled, although without complete sincerity. "Leslie, let me
invoke the saying of Hollywood agents. Trust me. It's important that
they be at the dinner."

She was angry, no doubt about that, but she backed off. She nodded.
But her parting words were, "Please, don't allow anything to spoil this
evening. We've worked so hard. How *is* Janet?"

"Fine. She wants very much to be part of this evening, part of this
family again."

"I wish Paul were here."

"Why isn't he?"

"He's in Taiwan. An unnecessary trip. He's distancing himself from
us. People! Families! Life would be so simple without them."

Smith half grinned. "And dreadfully empty. Thanks, Leslie."

When Mac and Annabel returned to the suite, it was clear that Tony
Buffolino hadn't wasted time in entertaining his guests. He'd ordered
up shrimp cocktails, chicken liver pâté, an obscene mound of beluga
caviar, spareribs, and an assortment of sandwiches. Janet seemed considerably more relaxed than when she'd arrived.

"Looks like you're taking good care of everyone," Smith said to Buffolino. "Expecting the Cabinet, too?"

"Just trying to be a good host," he said. "Help yourself. I think I
overdid it."

"How are you feeling, Janet?" Annabel asked.

Janet managed a small, wan smile. "Better, thank you. He's funny."
She looked at Buffolino.

"Yes, he can be amusing," said Smith.

"I was just tellin' 'em some of the old war stories from when I was on
the force. That's one good thing about being a cop, huh, you always got
a good story."

Unlike Janet, Marcia Mims was visibly on edge as she stood at a
window and vacantly looked through it. "Marcia, could we talk for a
minute?" Smith asked.

She followed him to the bedroom, where, the moment the door was
closed, he asked, "Why did you give me your diary?"

"To protect myself," she answered.

"From what?"

"From the same things Janet is afraid of, the same people. Mr.
Smith, because I've been with Senator Ewald and his family for many
years, I know a great deal. I'm always there. I see, I hear. I never
thought much about what that meant until Ms. Feldman was murdered.
Then I knew it had to be because she knew something, too. I thought
that if I gave the diary to someone else, people wouldn't have any

reason to kill me. I could tell them you had it, knew everything. Does that make sense?"

Smith sat on the edge of the bed, his elbows on his knees, and rubbed his eyes. "From what you and Janet have told me, Marcia, it's very possible that Ed Farmer murdered Andrea Feldman. But there are others who had reason to kill her, powerful people, powerful organizations whose goals could be damaged by some of the things Senator Ewald has learned over the years and that he kept in his files. People like that stop at nothing, allow no one to get in their way. They justify what they do by claiming a 'greater good.' "

"Are you speaking of the DAF?"

"How do you know about that organization?" Smith asked.

Marcia took a deep breath. She walked across the room, leaned against a desk, and said, "I've made a mess of my life, Mr. Smith, and almost made a mess of everyone else's life around me. It's time to explain." She paused, then continued with what was obviously a difficult tale. "I tell you this for the same reason I gave you my diary. I think you're the only person I can really trust, aside from Janet and my cousin."

"Go ahead, I'm listening."

"Before I came to work for the Ewalds in California, I had lived a shabby life. I was many things, including a whore. I was a whore because it helped me survive. I used drugs when they weren't even common, except in the jazz musicians' world. I was married twice—no children, thank God—and I assaulted one of my husbands with a knife. He almost died, and I didn't care. The drugs saw to that." She drew in more oxygen to keep the fire going. "I reached the end, I suppose. I saw it that way, the end of my life. But I was lucky. A few good things happened to me, and I began to realize my life didn't have to end, that it could begin with something new, and decent, and clean."

"From the years I've known you, Marcia, I'd say that's exactly what did happen with your life. You know how respected you are by the Ewalds. They obviously place tremendous faith in you."

"Not deserved, I'm afraid."

"Why do you say that?"

"When I was so low, I naturally spent my time with others like me. Then I began meeting people in California who seemed to offer me the kind of support I needed. These were people who understood what it was like to be lonely and black and strung out in a strange place. One of the people who was so good to me was a man from Panama named Garcia."

"Garcia?"

"Yes, Hilton Garcia. Like the hotels."

The first name of the Garcia who'd set up Tony for his fall was Hilton. How many Hilton Garcias could there be?

"He was very kind to me. People said he was involved in drugs, but he never displayed that side to me, never offered any to me. He loaned me money, even found me an apartment. Then, one day, he disappeared, and I heard nothing from him again."

"Marcia, are you aware that the man in the next room, Tony Buffolino, was forced to resign from the police department because of a drug dealer named Hilton Garcia?"

She lowered, then opened her eyes. "Yes, I knew when I heard about that case that it must have been the same man. I was so uncomfortable in the other room with Mr. Buffolino. He doesn't know that I was friends with the man who hurt him."

Smith said, "I don't see how what you've told me so far would cause you to feel you've betrayed Senator Ewald."

"There is more, Mr. Smith. When I was hired by Mrs. Ewald in California, you can't imagine how happy I was, how joyous. It didn't mean that my past did not exist, but I *felt* different. All of a sudden, I was part of a regular and important *American* household, and I liked it. It made *me* feel important."

Smith felt considerable compassion for her. Marcia Mims was obviously an intelligent and decent woman who'd made some serious mistakes but had managed to rise above them. Certainly, nothing she'd said caused him to think less of her.

"One day—it was maybe a year, a year and a half ago—I got a call from a man who said that Hilton Garcia had suggested he contact me. His name was Miguel. He was Panamanian, too." She looked to Smith for a reaction; he gave her none. The name meant nothing to him.

"He seemed very nice, said he was alone in the United States and wondered if I would meet him for lunch. I remembered back to how I felt in California, and so we met on my next day off. He said he worked for a Colonel Gilbert Morales."

"That means he worked for a very controversial figure."

"Yes, I know that now, but I didn't know it then. I have read about Colonel Morales and the debate that surrounds him. Even though I work for a United States senator, I've never followed politics very closely. I don't know whether Colonel Morales's cause is the right one or not."

"I don't suppose it really matters, in a sense. What did this Miguel do for Colonel Morales?"

"He said he was an administrative assistant to him, that he was helping him return to power. He was very convincing, and during that lunch I did form an opinion of the colonel's goals. I started believing in them."

Smith looked at his watch. "Marcia, I'm going to have to get ready for Senator Ewald's dinner. Did you continue to see Miguel, become friends?"

"Yes. We met a number of times, maybe four, for lunch, dinner, or just a cup of coffee. Then . . ."

"Then what?"

"Then he said he wanted me to tell him things about Senator Ewald."

"What sort of things?"

"Things about conversations I might hear the senator having about Colonel Morales, telephone calls, people who met with Senator Ewald about Colonel Morales."

"He wanted you to *spy* on Senator Ewald."

"Yes."

"Anything else?"

"Yes. He asked me if I would look through any files Senator Ewald might keep in the house about Colonel Morales. He wanted me to make copies and give them to him."

"Did you?" Smith asked.

"No, I never gave him files, but I told him things about what went on in the house."

"Why did you do that to Senator Ewald? He's always been generous and good to you."

If Marcia were going to cry during this confession, it was now. Her lower lip trembled. She said, "I did it because Miguel knew everything about me from Hilton, about my whoring, what I did to my husband, the drugs. He threatened to destroy me with the Ewalds. I took that seriously. Can you understand that?"

Smith stood and put his hand on her shoulder. "Yes, Marcia, I understand it very well. The only important thing now is that you tell me the sort of information you gave Miguel that might have hurt Senator Ewald."

Her eyes were wet. "I never gave him much. I even lied, told him about things that never happened. I tried very hard not to hurt the senator, but at the same time did what I thought I had to do to protect myself." She almost smiled. "I became very good at that back in California, on the street."

Smith stepped back. "Have you been talking to Miguel recently? Has this been an ongoing relationship?"

"No. I mean, yes, we did talk recently. He stopped contacting me about six months ago. I was relieved, and assumed I would never hear from him again. Then he called me on Friday."

"This past Friday?"

"Yes. He wanted to know whether I knew Senator Ewald's plans for today."

"What did he mean, 'plans'?"

"Whether I had access to an itinerary, knew where the senator would be at every minute."

"Did you tell him what the senator's schedule was?"

"No, because I didn't know."

"Why do you think he wanted to know that, Marcia?"

"I have no idea. Well, I did think that . . ."

"You thought he possibly wanted to know those things because he intended to harm Senator Ewald. Is that what you were thinking?"

"Yes."

"You obviously know what this Miguel looks like."

"Of course."

"I'm glad you're coming to the dinner with us tonight."

"Mr. Smith, I couldn't do that. I'm the housekeeper. I . . ."

"You may become a housekeeper who saves a senator's life. Do you have any dressy clothes with you?" She was wearing a wrinkled lavender polyester pantsuit.

"Yes, I have a suitcase in the other room. I don't know if I have nice-enough clothes for a fancy dinner, but . . ."

Smith said, "Marcia, you are a very beautiful woman. You must know that. Remember it. Whatever you choose to wear will be just fine."

They arrived downstairs as the last guests from the cocktail party were entering the ballroom for dinner. Leslie Ewald stood at the ball-room door. She saw Smith and his group enter and went to them, stopping directly in front of Janet. She seemed to be struggling with what to say, then did the human thing that needs no words. She wrapped her arms around Janet and said, "I am very glad to see you, Janet. Welcome home."

"I'm sorry, Leslie," Janet said. "I've been a fool. I'm happy to be here."

"Come on. The catering staff here is marvelous. They've set up the table you asked for, Mac." She led them into the ballroom.

Their table had obviously been hastily set; the tablecloth and napkins were pink; the rest of the room was in red, white, and blue. "I did the best I could," Leslie said to Smith after they'd been seated.

"You did fine, Leslie, thank you. We can make do with pink."

Smith had instructed Marcia Mims to keep her eyes open for Miguel. He whispered it to her again as he excused himself and made his way to the front of the room, where he recognized a Secret Service agent, Robert Jeroldson. "May I speak with you for a moment?" Smith said.

Jeroldson scowled. Smith ignored his expression and said, "I'm Mackensie Smith, legal adviser to Senator Ewald. I have reason to believe that an attempt will be made on his life, either tonight or in the near future."

"Where did you get that?" Jeroldson asked.

"I really don't have the time, or the inclination, to explain." Smith now placed Jeroldson as the agent Ken Ewald didn't like. He asked, "Who's in charge of the Secret Service detail here tonight?"

"I am," said Jeroldson.

"Then listen to me. There is a young Panamanian named Miguel in the vicinity, probably in the hotel. My information is that he might be here to attempt an assassination of the senator. I haven't told Senator Ewald about this, nor do I intend to until the dinner is over." Smith pointed across the room to his table. "The black woman with me knows what Miguel looks like, and she's keeping her eyes peeled for him. I suggest you and your men stick especially close to the senator and his family until they're safely out of here. At that time, I'll get together with you and make a fuller report."

Smith didn't know whether Jeroldson resented being told what to do by someone outside his service or was simply a surly, unresponsive individual. Either way, Smith now shared Ewald's dislike for him. "Well?" Smith said.

"I'll discuss it with my superiors."

"I thought you were in charge."

"I have to call them. Excuse me." Jeroldson walked away from Smith and left the ballroom.

Dessert was served, and when it had been consumed the evening's MC stepped to the podium. "Ladies and gentlemen, please give a very warm reception to the next president of the United States, Senator Kenneth Ewald."

The room erupted into an ovation as Ewald came to the microphone. He held his hands high until the guests, most of whom were now standing, resumed their seats and quieted down.

"Ladies and gentlemen, you apparently think I'm okay, but *you* are wonderful!"

The applause started all over again, and most people jumped to their feet. Funny, Smith thought, how a simple declaration could trigger a reaction in a crowd. Politics. Strange game.

After the guests were again seated, Ewald began to speak spiritedly of his unbridled optimism for America, of the value of restraint in foreign affairs. He was well into it when Smith, whose back was to the main door to the ballroom, sensed that someone had entered. He turned and saw Jody Backus. Smith quietly left the table and went to where Backus was standing. "Senator Backus, Mac Smith," Smith whispered.

Backus acknowledged Smith's greeting but did not take his eyes off Ewald at the podium. The smell of liquor was heavy on his breath, but he wasn't drunk. Intense was more like it.

Why was he here? Smith wondered. What would bring Ewald's leading opponent to a fund-raiser? Smith slipped his hand in the crook of Backus's elbow and led him to the darkness against the rear wall. "What a surprise to see you, Senator. What brings you here?"

"Conscience."

"Conscience about what?" Smith asked in a whisper.

"About your friend up there, Mr. Ewald. I came up with some information—it doesn't matter where I got it—that says to me that your friend might get himself killed. Lots a' people don't like him much, includin' me. The difference between them and me is that I believe in the system."

"We've been alerted to a possible threat on Ken's life tonight," Smith said. "I've primed the Secret Service, and I intend to tell Ken the minute his speech is over."

"That's good, Mac. You tell your friend up there to watch his ass. You know, I've played lots a' political games in my life, and nobody's ever been better at it. I've made lots of deals, sold out to lots of people because I believed the result was good for America. But every man has his limit, and I reached mine today. You know what I think?"

"What?"

"I think Mr. Ewald is goin' to be the next president of these United States. I don't like that idea much, and I've made no bones about it, but if he's the one the party and the people want, then I'll work my fat ol' Georgia butt off to help him, hear?"

"Yes, Senator, I hear," Smith said. "Please, join us at that table over there."

Smith took a chair that was against the wall and brought it to the table for Backus. Everyone at the table recognized him, but no one said anything. They were all tuned in to what Ken Ewald was saying at the front of the room.

When Ewald's speech ended, on a rare quiet note, and the room had again applauded at length, Smith said into Backus's ear, "Please, don't leave, Senator. I'll be right back." He skirted tables until reaching the dais where Ken and Leslie sat. Smith motioned for Ken to lean forward. "Ken, Jody Backus is sitting with me."

"What is he doing here?"

"I won't go into it now, but I believe, and so does he, that someone is about to make an attempt on your life tonight."

Ewald's face turned ashen.

"Ken," Smith continued, "I don't know what your plans are for the rest of the evening, but change them immediately. Take another route, leave this dinner early, and get to somewhere safe. I've told the Secret Service about it."

"Who?"

"All that later, when you and the family are safe. By the way, Janet is with me."

"Christ, is she involved with . . . ?"

"Ken, Janet is back because she wants to be. I'll see you later. Come to our suite upstairs, room 1117." He repeated it.

The band began a two-beat medley for dancing. Ewald, his face expressing his mixed emotions, turned and deftly handled the swarm of well-wishers flocking around the dais, each anxious to press important flesh.

Smith returned to his table. "What are your plans for the rest of the evening, Senator?"

"To tell Ken Ewald I think he'll make a fine president."

"I'm sure he'll be delighted to hear that, especially from you, but how about delivering that message up in our suite? I want him out of here as fast as possible. We can all go up together. I've told Ken about the possibility of an attempt on his life, and he's trying to wrap this up faster than usual."

"You know somethin', Mac Smith, Kenny-boy is right. You'd make a hell of an attorney general, maybe even chief of staff in his White House."

Smith's proclamation that he was committed to returning to teaching law was on the tip of his tongue, but he decided it was the wrong time and place to make it. He smiled, said, "We'll all be leaving in a minute."

"You say the Secret Service has been alerted?" Backus asked.

"Yes." Smith saw Jeroldson standing with a colleague and pointed to him. "He's in charge," Smith said to Backus.

"That don't necessarily mean anything, Mac."

"What do you mean?"

"He's . . . well, not to be trusted."

"I don't understand."

"Just believe me. We goin'?"

"Yes."

Smith told Tony Buffolino to stay as close as possible to Ewald, and to keep his eye on Marcia. If she showed any sign of recognition, he was to act.

"My piece is upstairs," Buffolino said.

"Then you'll have to do without it. I'll be with you every step of the way."

Smith took Janet's arm, and with the others from the table, including Jody Backus, melded into the flow of people surrounding Ken and Leslie Ewald, moved them through the large doors, crossed the room in which the cocktail party had been held, and entered the lobby. A large crowd was waiting. The sight of Ewald, who stood taller than most of those surrounding him, triggered applause. Smith glanced at Ewald; he was doing his best to smile, but there was unmistakable concern on his face. A wedge of Secret Service agents led the way, and slowly, gently but firmly, parted the crowd.

They were halfway across the lobby when Marcia Mims stiffened. "There he is, over there," she said.

Smith stood on his toes and looked in the direction she was pointing. It was the same slim young man he'd noticed waiting for an elevator and lingering in the hallway upstairs. Of course.

Tony Buffolino saw what was going on and asked Smith, "Who's that?"

"I think it's our man."

Buffolino moved quickly, his cane leading the way. "Excuse me, sorry," he said, pushing people aside. "Come on, come on," he said to those impeding his progress. "Move, Tony, move," he heard Smith say from behind.

Buffolino was no more than twenty feet from Miguel when he saw the slender Panamanian remove his hand from his jacket, the modular Pachmayr Colt in it. Tony glanced back, saw Ken and Leslie Ewald moving quickly as the agents opened up a straight path for them to the elevators—and directly toward Miguel.

"Hey, dirtbag!" Tony yelled as loud as he could. He shoved a matronly woman to the floor, pushed two men aside, and flung himself at Miguel, knocking up the arm with the weapon. A shot shattered dozens of small pieces of crystal dangling from a chandelier. Tony rammed the tip of his cane into Miguel's midsection. The Panamanian doubled over, and the revolver discharged again, this bullet kicking back up off the marble floor and passing through an agent's shoulder.

With his cane in both hands, Buffolino brought it down sharply across the back of Miguel's neck. He crumpled to the floor, and Tony held him there. The revolver had slid away, stopping at the feet of a hysterical woman. Secret Service agents and uniformed security guards stood over Tony as he pinned Miguel to the ground. Tony looked up. "How 'bout this guy? This guy wasn't goin' to vote for the next president of the United States."

37

THE ATMOSPHERE IN the suite was charged with confusion and horror.

"Who was he?" Ewald asked Smith.

"His name is Miguel, Ken, and he works for Colonel Gilbert Morales."

Ewald looked at Smith. "Morales put a hit out on me?"

"It looks that way. He must have taken your speeches seriously, about trying to avoid returning tyrants to power. Even 'our' tyrants. We can thank Marcia for recognizing Miguel."

Ewald looked across the room to where Marcia stood with Leslie, Janet, and Tony Buffolino. He then spotted Jody Backus standing alone in the opposite corner, glass in hand. Ewald said to Smith, "I need some quick explaining, Mac. Let's go into the other room."

They started to make their way through a cluster of people when Ed Farmer stopped them, locked eyes with Smith, and said, "I want to talk to you."

"Yes, I'm sure you do," said Smith.

"What's going on?" Ewald asked.

"Ed and I will talk first, Ken," Smith said. "I don't think we'll be long."

Smith and Farmer entered the empty bedroom, and Smith closed the door. "I think I know what you want to say, Ed."

"Yes, I suppose you do, Mac. Interesting cast you assembled tonight. I can see we have the missing neurotic daughter-in-law with us, and the faithful minority housekeeper. They must be filling you with tantalizing stories."

"Tantalizing? That's tabloid talk. I prefer to think of what they've told me as useful, illuminating."

Farmer smiled. "Mac, obviously I'm going to need your help."

"For what?"

"To defend me, of course."

Smith looked steadily at the man. "For the murder of Andrea Feldman."

"I wouldn't use the word 'murder.' To me, murder is an act that accomplishes nothing more than the death of an individual. I did not *murder* Andrea Feldman."

"I've never been a fan of semantic games, but go ahead, Farmer, use your definition. You did *kill* her."

"Yes, but it certainly wasn't premeditated."

·"You took Ken's gun with you when you went to meet her."

"Only because it was handy."

"Why take a gun at all if you didn't intend to use it?"

"For emphasis." He smiled again, which rankled Smith. "Andrea was bright enough, but sometimes didn't get the point. Do you know what I mean? She'd latch onto a way of thinking about something, and nothing, not even the most reasoned argument, could get her to see it differently."

"And she didn't see things your way when you met her outside the Kennedy Center."

"Exactly." The expression on Farmer's face seemed to indicate that he thought Smith not only understood what he was saying, but was sympathetic to it.

"What was it you were trying to get across to her?" Smith asked.

"That I was not somebody to threaten."

"What did she threaten you with, Farmer, that she would tell your boss, Senator Ewald, that you were selling him out?"

"Come on, Mac, nobody sells anybody out at this level of politics. You evaluate, read the tides, and take the boat that will get you there the fastest."

At least he hadn't used sports metaphors, Smith thought.

"Mac, Andrea was a slut, a user. She was capable of selling anyone out for personal gain. She called Ken's house after the gala that night. Ken wasn't there because he was shacked up with the opera singer. Marcia took the call. Andrea told Marcia to tell Ken to meet her behind the big German relief across from the Kennedy Center's main entrance."

"And you heard the conversation on the tape in the second-floor office."

"Yes. Who told you that?"

"It doesn't matter. What was Andrea going to tell Ken?"

"That I'd stolen sensitive files having to do with Morales and the Kane Ministries."

"Why would she say that? Did you steal them? My information is that *she* stole them."

"To be precise, Mac, I never physically took the files from the house, although I did make their contents known to certain people."

"What people? Garrett Kane?"

"No, the distinguished senator in the other room."

"Jody Backus?"

"Yes."

Smith stood and leaned on the back of a chair. "Why would you help Ken's major competitor for the nomination?"

"Ken Ewald won't win the White House," Farmer said.

"And you think Jody Backus can?"

Farmer shook his head. "No, Raymond Thornton will be our next president."

"So what did you have to gain by passing secrets along to Backus?"

"Assurance of a job. Backus might be a Democrat, but he's much more wired into the Manning administration and Raymond Thornton than anyone really knows."

Smith sighed. "Then the ideas that Ken Ewald stands for mean nothing to you."

"Ideas? Of course not. There are no ideas or ideals in politics. The only thing that matters is winning. Hanging in with blind faith and loyalty to a loser doesn't get you very far."

Smith felt, at once, disgust and pity. The young man with the bow tie, tweed jacket, and penny loafers was like so many young people in Smith's law classes, void of ideals, of dreams other than wealth and power; there were no causes that they would fight for unless there were tangible gains, nothing for which they would stand on a soapbox and preach, only a pragmatic sense of self. God help you, Mr. Farmer, God help us all, Smith thought. He said, "You brought me in here and said you might need my help. Do you really think I would defend you?"

"Why not? He's not going to win, which means you'll never become attorney general. I think you and I are very much alike, Mac. We're both good players in this game, and we're both dependent on how the voters see Ken Ewald versus Raymond Thornton. They'll go for Thornton. Trust me. There's nobody better at analyzing a political situation than me."

"That may be," Smith said, "but why did you have to kill her?"

"I didn't intend to. As I said before, I just wanted to emphasize my point. Funny, but it occurred to me just before I pulled the trigger that even if she told Ken Ewald what I'd done, it really shouldn't affect my future. But then the irony, the reality, of the situation became clear to me. There isn't a politician in this country who doesn't try to gain damaging information about opponents, and most of them are happy to pay for it. But the minute you're the one who sells it to them, they become self-righteous and brand you as a person who can't be trusted. What garbage, huh, Mac? I looked at Andrea that night and realized the difference. She'd sold out only for money. As far as I'm concerned, that's intolerable."

"You consider your own motives loftier?"

"Of course I do. Don't you see it that way?" He became uncharacteristically passionate. "I see wonderful things ahead for this country, and I see people like you and me helping to shape them. I can't do that standing at Ken Ewald's side when he gives his concession speech in November." A small smile crossed Farmer's lips, and Smith felt himself begin to tremble.

"When I saw Backus arrive tonight, saw Marcia Mims and Janet Ewald here, I knew you'd put it together. Was I wrong, Mac? You knew I was the one who killed Andrea."

"Not with any certainty, but yes, I knew."

"They'll have trouble proving it."

"I don't think so. I'll certainly testify to our conversation here tonight."

Farmer guffawed. "You can't."

"Why not?"

"Because you're my lawyer. Attorney-client privilege."

"I'm not your attorney, Farmer. You were willing to let Paul Ewald take the rap, weren't you?"

Farmer's eyes opened wide, and a smug expression crossed his face. "Of course. I really thought I was off the hook when they focused on Paul as the prime suspect. Seemed perfect. There he was having an affair with her, fighting with Janet all the time, disappearing the night of the murder, and having easy access to his father's gun. Then you came into the picture and the spotlight on Paul dimmed. You were one of the best criminal attorneys this city has ever seen, and I know you'll pull out all the stops for me. Believe me, Mac, someday I'll be in a position to return the favor."

Smith sprang from his chair, grabbed Farmer by the lapels, lifted him from the chair, and slid him across the desk into the wall. Farmer's glasses fell off, and his smile was replaced by an expression of terror.

"You slimy bastard, comparing me to you, sitting here calmly while you talk about all the good reasons you had for killing someone. Defend you? I'll do everything I can to see that you spend the rest of your pathetic life in jail." He released his grasp, opened the door, and stepped into the living room. Ken Ewald and Jody Backus were in the corner talking. People became aware of Smith and turned to him. Conversation dwindled, then stopped.

Smith motioned to Tony Buffolino to come to him. He said quietly, "Call the police and tell them we have Andrea Feldman's murderer."

Buffolino looked toward the open door to the bedroom. "Him? Joe Bow Tie?"

"Yes."

Farmer appeared in the doorway. He'd replaced his glasses and was straightening his tie. He smiled at Smith as he crossed the room to where Ewald and Backus stood. "Well, Senator Backus, telling your esteemed colleague how you tried to sell him out?"

Backus glowered at Farmer through watery eyes. He said to Ewald, "You've had yourself a Judas in your own house all along, Ken. You know what this weasel tried to do?"

Ewald look quizzically at Farmer.

"This little weasel tried to make a deal with me to sell secrets out of your campaign," Backus said. "How 'bout that?"

Smith joined them as Farmer said, "Don't listen to him, Ken. He'd do anything to make sure you never become president, including murder."

"What's he saying, Jody?"

Farmer continued, "Your good friend, the esteemed senator from Georgia here, arranged to have Andrea Feldman killed to cover up the fact that she was selling your files on Kane and Morales to him."

Backus was about to reach for Farmer when Smith stepped between them. He said to Ewald, "Ken, this will all be resolved and explained in short order. Let me just say that your trusted campaign manager Mr. Farmer is the one who murdered Andrea Feldman to cover his own tracks. The two of them, Andrea and Farmer, had been selling you out all along."

Ewald's face was sheer bewilderment. He shook his head and said, "I just don't understand what's going on this evening."

"You don't know who your friends are, Ken," said Farmer. "I'm glad you'll never be president of this country. You've made too many messes in your life, and you won't have me anymore to clean up after you." He looked at Leslie Ewald, who'd come up to them. "Your whole family is pathetic," he said.

Farmer slowly turned and started for the door.

"Tony, don't let him leave," Smith said to Buffolino, who was on the phone with the MPD. Tony dropped the phone and started to get up, but Smith said, "No, don't bother. Let him go. He won't disappear." Or maybe he'll kill himself, Smith thought, not at all pleased at his casual acceptance of that possibility.

Smith looked at Leslie, who was obviously as confused as her husband. He said, "I think a lot of nasty things are behind you and Ken now." To Ken, he added, "I'll give you details another time. It's time for you to nail down the nomination, Ken, and for me to get back to teaching law."

Backus, whose glass was empty, slapped Ewald on the back, which brought a wince to Ewald's face. "It's been a tough campaign, Ken, and I bow to the better man. You've got my support one hundred percent, and you can count on it from this moment forward."

38

"I HAVE NOTHING more to say today, except that I hope at least a few of you will occasionally take time away from your pursuit of fees and partnerships to do something with your legal education that benefits others." Smith surveyed the faces of the students in his advanced criminal-law class. It was the final day they would be together before graduation.

"Professor Smith."

"Yes?"

"Are you going to the convention in San Francisco?"

"Yes," Smith answered.

"Do you think Senator Ewald will be the Democratic nominee?"

"I would imagine so, now that Senator Backus has dropped out and has given his full support to Senator Ewald."

"If he wins in November, will you become his attorney general?"

"Why would that be of interest to you?" Smith asked.

"Well, sir, it would be . . ." She laughed nervously. "It would be a nice credential to have been taught by an attorney general of the United States."

"Frankly, Ms. Mencken, I don't see that as representing any particular advantage to a law student. People who become attorneys general are like some doctors who become chiefs of staff at their hospitals—and exhibit far more interest in politics than in healing the sick, or, in the case of your intended profession, in defending the unjustly accused or convicting the accurately accused. Not only that, they don't have time to practice their profession because they are always too busy running for office, one kind of office or another. If you must have surgery in the future, Ms. Mencken, I suggest you not seek the services of any medical chief of staff. Based on that thesis, it would be to your advantage that I *do not* become attorney general."

The red-faced young man next to her quickly raised his hand and said, "You've evaded the question, Professor Smith. Will you be the next attorney general if Senator Ewald becomes president?"

Smith smiled, slid his notes into his briefcase, and snapped it shut.

He looked at the class and said, "Next November, I will be at this university teaching this course to other students. You will have graduated and begun your careers. I will be flattered if you drop in from time to time, or send me a brief note letting me know how you're progressing." He was about to end the class with his usual, "Good day, ladies and gentlemen." Instead, he waved to them and said, *"Ciao!"*

United States Senator Kenneth Ewald had been receiving people all day in his suite at the Compton Court Hotel in San Francisco. The final roll call was that night. Things were looking good, although there had been a last-minute move to position a more conservative senator from Texas as a serious contender. But that ploy seemed designed as much for four years in the future as for the moment. The die-hard conservatives in the party determined to deny Ewald the nomination had been busy rallying elaborate support for the Texas legislator, but according to Ewald's new campaign manager, Paul Ewald, they were falling considerably short of their goal.

Still, Ken Ewald was worried, would be until the final votes were counted. He sat alone after a long meeting with leading delegates committed to him. A glass of club soda with a wedge of lime was at the table next to him. He looked at his watch: an hour before his next appointment. He had scheduled it that way. Ewald needed time to think, something he'd decided to do more of in the future.

Outside the closed door, in the living room, secretaries and staff members fielded phone calls. "No, the senator is unavailable at this moment." "Yes, he will be attending the meeting in two hours." "No, he has no intention of releasing a statement before tonight."

One of his secretaries, whose nerves were becoming frazzled from the pace of the day, answered a call with an abrupt, "Yes?"

"This is Roseanna Gateaux. Would it be possible for me to speak with Senator Ewald?"

The secretary placed her hand over the mouthpiece and said to a young aide next to her, "Roseanna Gateaux? Isn't that the opera singer?"

"Yeah. She's an old friend of the senator."

"She wants to speak with him."

The male aide shrugged. "He said not to disturb him, but I think I'd better with this one." He winked, went to the door, and knocked. Ewald told him to come in. "Senator, a Ms. Gateaux wishes to speak with you on the phone."

The mention of her name hit Ewald physically. He realized the aide was waiting for an answer. He said, "Put her through."

"Roseanna?" he said after the aide was gone.

"I know I shouldn't be calling you like this but . . ."

"It's all right." He didn't say he was aware that she was the one person capable of ruining his chances for the presidency, and ruining his marriage, which was, Lord knew, shaky enough.

"Ken, could I possibly see you for a few minutes? I promise it won't take me long to say what I have to say."

He wanted to say no, but he was afraid to. They hadn't had any contact since the events of a month ago, and he knew it had to be that way. Still, there was a part of him that thought it better to resolve problems face-to-face, and in this case to make it plain that there could never be a relationship again. He took into consideration the fact that he had scheduled this private time, and that Leslie would not be back for at least another two hours. "Yes," he said, "but I only have a few minutes. Where are you?"

"Downstairs in the hotel."

"All right, please come up."

His secretary ushered Roseanna into the room. Ewald was aware of a questioning look on the secretary's face and quickly dismissed her, saying, "It's okay. Five minutes."

"You look very good," Roseanna said, not moving from just inside the door.

"So do you. You do know, Roseanna, that this will be the last time we will ever be alone together. It has to be that way."

"I understand. I only came here to tell you that you need never worry about me, need never wake up in the middle of the night and wonder whether what we shared together will ever become public knowledge. No kiss-and-tell books, no talk-show interviews, no articles in the *National Enquirer*."

He smiled. The smile represented relief at her words, as well as certain sadness at what they meant. "Come, sit," he said.

"No, I know you don't have the time, and—"

"Sit down, Roseanna, just for a minute."

They sat in the armchairs that were side by side and looked at each other. She was the most inordinately beautiful woman he'd ever known, possessing a beauty so different from Leslie's; a difference that was, after all, part of the attraction.

She said, "You will become president."

"I don't know, Roseanna. I'm trying very hard to be, although I'm not sure I should."

"Why do you say that?"

"Because . . . because I'm not sure any longer that I'm the man to sit in such a position of power, of life and death."

Her hand poised in midair as though having a mind of its own, then decided to come down on top of his hand, lightly, fingertips only. Her eyes filled as she said, "I think this country will be very fortunate to have you leading it, and I consider *myself* very fortunate to have been able to touch you, to know you."

He was embarrassed, and looked away.

She stood. "Ken, what we had was very special to me. I know we will never have it again, and that is a sorrow. At the same time, I celebrate, rather than mourn, what I've lost. Good luck tonight. I'll be watching."

Before he could say anything, she went to the door, opened it and paused as though about to deliver an exit line, then went through it, and was gone.

Mac Smith, Annabel Reed, and Tony Buffolino had taken the afternoon to ride the cable car to Fisherman's Wharf, where they'd browsed the eclectic wares of sidewalk artisans, bought chocolate in Ghirardelli Square, eaten crab and calamari out of small paper bowls purchased from vendors along Jefferson Street, walked out of the famous Boudin Bakery with loaves of sourdough bread, and returned to the Raphael Hotel footsore and happy.

They sat in Buffolino's room and toasted their good day with champagne.

Eventually, the conversation got around to the events that had brought them together in this place. Buffolino asked Smith what he thought of Ed Farmer's chances in his trial. Farmer had pleaded not guilty, and had hired a top D.C. lawyer, Morris Jankowski.

"Jankowski is good," Smith said. "He'll find plenty of holes in the prosecution's case, including my testimony, which, I'm sure, Jankowski will paint as unimportant, create an atmosphere in which I had a personal grudge against Farmer, misunderstood what he was saying."

"Can you believe this about Greist?" Annabel said, picking up that day's San Francisco *Examiner* and tossing it back on a table. "Ridiculous!" Herbert Greist had suffered a fatal heart attack. The story in the *Examiner* was based on charges by a left-wing group that the Bureau might have killed him.

Smith laughed. "Tomorrow we'll read that a right-wing group is accusing the Communists of killing him to keep him quiet."

"Ya know, Greist looked like a guy with a bum ticker," Buffolino said.

"Anybody hear anything new about the Miguel person?" Annabel asked.

Buffolino said, "They'll never get him to admit any connection to Morales."

"Or to Kane," Smith said.

"Or to Backus," said Buffolino.

"Or to Thornton," Annabel said.

"Possibly because he didn't have a connection to any of them except Morales," Smith said.

"Getting soft in your old age," Annabel said.

"No, just getting less cynical as I enter into *middle age.* More champagne?" Smith asked. He refilled their glasses.

Buffolino asked, "Do you believe your buddy, Shevlin, about the box in Mae Feldman's house?"

·

Smith grunted, nodded. "Yes, I don't see any reason for him to lie to me. The FBI has wanted those files for a long time. They figured out where they might be and took them. They just also ended up with a couple of hundred thousand dollars in cash. What they didn't figure out was that Mae Feldman and Carla Zaretski were one and the same. Sorry you had to learn it under such nasty circumstances, Tony."

Buffolino scowled. "And I got cold-cocked in her house by a couple of Bureau guys." He looked up as though to commune with God. "Jesus, there I was with a box with all Ewald's files and all that cash." He laughed. "You never would have seen me again."

"I doubt that," Smith said. "You're a man of honor, Tony."

"Yeah, that's me, the honorable Anthony Buffolino." He raised his glass. "A toast to Mackensie Smith, who did good by me. I hope you know how much I appreciate everything, Mac."

"My pleasure." Smith had paid Tony a bonus, and arranged a security job for him at the university.

"A toast to you, Tony," said Annabel. "You're a lot nicer than what Mac said you'd be."

"Hey, Mac, what did you tell her? No matter. To you, Annabel, a real classy lady."

"Ready for an announcement?" Smith asked.

"What kind a' announcement?"

"We've decided to get married."

"No kidding?"

"Yes," Annabel said, giggling. "Isn't it wonderful? Two can live as cheaply as one, if you cut down on the takeout dinners. We're going to London on our honeymoon."

"Hey, congrats. If you have any problems, married-people problems, any questions, just ask me. I got experience."

"Up to being best man, Tony?" Smith asked.

"I thought I was all along." He stood and twirled his cane in the air. "London. I can't wait."

Mac and Annabel looked at each other.

"I'm goin' with you, right?"

"No," Smith said.

"No," Annabel said.

"No?"

"No," they said in unison.

"I guess you mean no."

"Yes, we mean no."

Tony Buffolino was invited to remain in San Francisco for a few days after the convention as the personal guest of Ken Ewald. He was put up in a penthouse suite at the Mark Hopkins, for, as Ewald said, "your heroism in the lobby of the Watergate Hotel on my behalf." Tony was delighted; he'd fallen madly in love with Alicia, a cocktail waitress at the Top of the Mark, and told Mac Smith that if he moved fast enough, there might be a double wedding.

Mac and Annabel shook their heads and flew back to Washington the day after the convention. Newspapers on their laps said it all: EWALD DEM CHOICE BY ACCLAMATION. BACKUS HIS VEEP. A large photograph of Ewald and Backus with their hands clasped and raised, their families at their sides, dominated the front pages.

"I'm proud of you," Annabel said, after their flight had taken off.

"For what?"

"For the way you turned Ken down when he asked you to manage his campaign, and to become attorney general."

"What else could I do with a redheaded honey badger standing within striking distance behind me?"

"For a second, I thought you might say yes."

"Not a chance. My brief moment in the political arena will last me a lifetime. Ken Ewald and Jody Backus. Strange bedfellows, as the saying goes."

"Incredible more than strange," Annabel said.

"I suppose so," said Smith. "I believe Ed Farmer when he says that it was Backus who made the deal with him to buy Ken's files on DAF, Morales, and Kane. But Ken doesn't believe it, which is just as well I suppose."

"Not if Backus sells him out in some way when he's the VP."

"I don't think that will happen, Annabel. This is politics, not real life. Hell, Germany and Japan tried to kill us in World War Two, and as a reward we've helped them kill us economically. No, Backus will be a loyal and useful VP, for whatever that's worth."

"Ken Ewald and Jody Backus, our next president and vice-president."

"Probably."

"Will we go to the inaugural? I'll need a new gown."

"We'll watch on TV. When it's over, we'll become not-so-strange bedfellows, and fool around a little."

"Yeah?"

"Yeah. Any objections?"

"Only one."

"What is it?"

"That we not have to wait until January twentieth. I propose we celebrate our own upcoming inaugural the minute we get back, provided that animal you call a dog will give us the bed."

"I miss Rufus already."

She growled. He laughed. And they clinked glasses, settled back, and fell asleep as if on schedule.

MURDER
IN THE
CIA

1

The British Virgin Islands, November 1985

HER NAME WAS BERNADETTE, eighteen, tall, a classic island "smooth skin," as they say there—very dark and with a velvety texture —hair the color of ink and falling to her shoulder blades, a full, rounded body defined beneath a clinging maroon jersey dress, a truc *mantwana*, the island word for voluptuous woman.

They'd been teasing her since the launch left Anguilla Point on Virgin Gorda for its morning run to Drake's Anchorage on Mosquito Island. She'd started seeing a popular young man from Virgin Gorda, which prompted the gentle ribbing. Although she protested, she enjoyed it. She was proud of her new boyfriend and knew the other girls were jealous. "Gwan tease me, marrow deh," she said, a defiant smile on her lips. Tease all you want; tomorrow will be my day.

There were fifteen of them on board; waiters and waitresses, the bartender, kitchen help, chambermaids, and gardeners. Most of the help lived on Virgin Gorda and were brought in by launch. Drake's Anchorage was the only resort on Mosquito Island (named for a Colombian Indian tribe, not the dipterous insect), and there was only one house for staff, which was occupied by two engineers.

Bernadette was the assistant manager. Her English was excellent; so were her number skills. Her father, a bone fisherman, waded out into the shallow flats of Murdering Hole at dawn each morning in search of the indigenous fish, the so-called ladyfish. Her parents had a hard life, one they hoped she wouldn't inherit. She was their only child.

She turned her face into the wind and thought of last night with her new love. Spray from the intensely blue water stung her face. Life was good now. Last week she'd been depressed, wondered whether she would have to spend the rest of her life in this one place, as beautiful as it might be. Now, *he* was there and the glass was half full again.

The resort had been booked exclusively for two days by a Canadian businessman who'd done the same thing three months earlier, to hold seminars for key people, his assistant had said. The top echelon stayed in two magnificent villas overlooking Lime Tree Beach. Lesser managers occupied ten white-clapboard oceanfront cottages built on stilts and facing Gorda Sound. They all ate together in the thatch-roofed, open-air restaurant where the chef served up vol-au-vent stuffed with escargots, dolphin baked with bananas, West Indian grouper done with spices, herbs, and white wine, and deeply serious chocolate mousse from a guarded recipe.

Bernadette remembered the rules that had been laid down by the Canadian the last time he'd been there. The two villas were to be off-limits to everyone except his people, and resort workers were to come to them only when specifically invited. The villas were to be cleaned while their occupants were breakfasting. Always, the younger men who occupied the smaller cottages would be present in the villas when the chambermaids cleaned, or when busboys delivered food and whiskey.

Although secrecy had been the byword during the Canadians' first visit on Mosquito Island, there were those inevitable, human moments when the shroud was lifted, like the day on the beach when Bernadette saw one of the younger men sitting in a brightly striped canvas chair while cleaning a handgun. When he realized she was watching, he returned the weapon to its holster and quickly entered his cottage.

After that, Bernadette's friends noticed that others in the party carried revolvers in armpit holsters, although they took pains to conceal them. "Businessmen," the chef had said to her. "Serious business, I would say."

While the Canadian and his three senior colleagues had met in the villas, the younger men, always dressed in suits, sat on terraces surrounding the villas, saying nothing, their eyes taking in everything. They seemed pleasant enough men but kept to themselves. One had been a little more open and Bernadette had had a few friendly conversations with him. He was handsome and had a nice smile. Bernadette assumed he was in charge of communications because he frequently talked into a small portable radio to two yachts anchored offshore. Three of the four older men had arrived on those yachts. A float plane had delivered the fourth.

The radioman seemed to enjoy talking to Bernadette and she'd openly flirted with him. Once, she'd asked why there was so much secrecy surrounding a business meeting. She'd asked it lightly, giggled actually, and touched his arm. He'd smiled and said quietly, matter-of-factly, "We're about to launch a new product that our competitors would love to learn more about. That's all. Just taking precautions."

Bernadette didn't ask about the guns because it was none of her business, but she and other staff gossiped about them, speculated, eventually came to the conclusion that big mucky-mucks from up north attached more importance to themselves and to what they did than was necessary. "Silly boys," they said. One thing was certain: The silly boys tipped big. Everyone from Drake's Anchorage was happy to see them return.

On this day, a single yacht carrying three of the group's leaders arrived a few minutes past two. The float plane touched down a half hour later and slowly taxied toward the long, thin dock.

Bernadette had greeted those who'd disembarked from the yacht, and had been disappointed when the handsome young radioman wasn't among them.

Now, as she waited for the float plane's three passengers to step onto the dock, she saw his face through a window. He was the last one out of the aircraft, and she gave him her biggest welcome. He simply nodded and got into a motorized cart with the two older men. The native driver pulled away from the dock and proceeded along a narrow path that followed the contour of the sea. Bernadette watched it disappear around the curve of a hill and wondered why he'd been so curt. "Strange people," she told herself, happy that she had her new boyfriend back on the bigger island.

The arrival of the yacht and plane had been witnessed, and generally ignored, by people on yachts in the surrounding waters. Yachts in the British Virgins are as common as yellow cabs on New York City streets. One man, however, watched the comings and goings through a telescope from his 46-foot Morgan. He'd been anchored a mile offshore since early morning and had cooked breakfast on board. He had sandwiches for lunch accompanied by a Thermos of rum punch, and had just put on a pot of coffee. A pad of paper at his side was filled with notes. He wore cut-off jeans, brown deck shoes, a T-shirt that said EDWARDS YACHT CHARTERS, and a white canvas hat with a large, floppy brim on which was sewn a blue, red, and yellow patch—BRITISH NAVY: PUSSER'S RUM

He looked up and checked wind conditions. It'd be slow going back to base on Tortola. No sense raising the sails. It'd be engine all the way. He debated staying longer, decided there was nothing to be gained, hauled in the anchor, took a last look toward Mosquito Island, and headed home on a course that took him past a tiny island on which a single structure stood, an imposing, three-story concrete house surrounded by a tall chain-link fence. Two Doberman pinschers ran on the beach. A float plane and a pair of large, fast powerboats bobbed in a gentle swell against a private dock.

The man on the Morgan with his name on his T-shirt smiled as his boat slowly slid by the island. He poured rum into his coffee, lifted the cup toward the island, and said, *"Za vashe zdarov'ye!"* He laughed, put his cup down, and extended the middle finger of his right hand to the island.

2

Washington, D.C., October 1986

"WHAT'S NEW WITH the audio rights on Zoltán's new book?" Barrie Mayer asked as she entered her office on Georgetown's Wisconsin Avenue.

Her assistant, David Hubler, looked up at her from a desk piled high with manuscripts and said, "Not to worry, Barrie. We'll have contracts this week."

"I hope so," Mayer said. "You'd think we were negotiating for a million the way they drag their feet drawing papers. A lousy thousand bucks and they treat it like they were buying rights to Ronald Reagan's guide to sex after seventy."

She entered her inner office, tossed her attaché case onto a small couch, and opened the blinds. It was gray outside, threatening. Maybe a storm would clear out the hot, humid Washingtonian weather they'd been having the past few days. Not that it mattered to her. She was on her way to London and Budapest. London was always cool. Well, *almost* always cool. Budapest would be hot, but the Communists had recently invented air conditioning and introduced it to their Eastern bloc countries. With any luck she could spend her entire stay inside the Hilton.

She sat behind her desk and crossed long, slender, nicely molded legs. She wore a favorite traveling outfit: a pearl gray pants suit that had lots of give and barely wrinkled. Sensible burgundy shoes and a shell-pink button-down blouse completed the ensemble. Hubler poked his head through the door and asked if she wanted coffee. She smiled. Not only was he remarkably talented and organized, he didn't mind serving his boss coffee. "Please," she said. He returned a minute later with a large, steaming blue ceramic mug.

She settled back in her leather chair, swiveled, and took in floor-to-ceiling bookcases that lined one wall. The center section contained copies of many books written by the writers she represented as literary agent. There were twenty writers at the moment; the list swelled and ebbed as their fortunes shifted, but she could count on a hard core of about fifteen, including Zoltán Réti. Réti, the Hungarian novelist, had recently broken through and achieved international acclaim and stunning sales due, in no small part, to Barrie Mayer's faith in him and the extra effort she'd put into his latest book, *Monument*, a multi-generational novel that, according to the *New York Times* review, "touches the deepest aspects of the Hungarian, indeed the human, spirit."

Timing had been on the side of Réti and Mayer. The Soviets had recently loosened restrictions on Hungarian writers and artists, including travel. While Réti's manuscript had gone through a review by officials of the Hungarian Socialist Workers' Party under the leadership of János Kádár, it had emerged relatively unscathed. Réti had skillfully wrapped criticism of Hungary since its "liberation" in 1945 by the Soviet Union into innocuous passages, and reading between the lines said more than his Socialist readers had caught.

Monument was snapped up by publishers around the world and sat on best-seller lists for weeks. It was gratifying to Barrie Mayer because she'd put her all into the book. Now the major dilemma was what to do with the large sums of money Réti was earning from its success. That problem was still being addressed, and one of the reasons for Mayer's trip to Budapest was to confer with Réti and with a ranking member of the Hungarian Presidium who, according to Réti, "could be persuaded" to bend some rules.

Barrie had to smile when she thought of what "could be persuaded" meant. It translated into graft, pure and simple, money under the table to the right Hungarian officials, New York City style, a capitalist solution to a Socialist problem.

On a previous trip to Budapest, Barrie had been introduced to the Presidium member with whom she would meet again this time. He'd sustained a hard, incorruptible façade throughout most of that initial confab, referring to Réti as "a writer for the Hungarian people, not motivated by commercial success." To which Barrie had responded, "If that's the case, sir, we'll keep his millions in our account until there is a shift in policy."

"We have restrictions on foreign currency entering Hungary," said the official.

"A shame," said Mayer. "We're potentially talking millions of U.S. dollars. That would be good for your economy—*any* economy."

"Yes, a good point, Miss Mayer. Perhaps . . ."

"Perhaps we can pursue this another time." She got up to leave.

"I might be able to think of a way to create an exception in this case."

Barrie smiled. What did he want for himself, one of the new condos going up in the Buda hills that only went to Hungarians with a fistful of hard currency, a new car in months instead of the usual four-year wait, a bank account of his own in Switzerland?

"When will you return to Budapest?" he asked.

"Whenever you've . . . 'created your exception.' "

That meeting had taken place a month ago. The official had informed Réti that he'd "smoothed the way for Réti's funds to reach him in Budapest." He'd added, "But, of course, Mr. Réti, there must be some consideration for the time and effort I have expended in your behalf, to say nothing of the risk in which I place myself."

"Of course," Réti said.

"Of course," Barrie Mayer said to Réti when he relayed the official's message.

"Of course," she said to herself, grinning, as she sipped the hot, black coffee in her Washington office and allowed her eyes to wander to other books on the shelves written by foreign authors. Funny, she thought, how things in life take their own natural course. She'd never intended to become a literary agent specializing in foreign writers, but that's what had happened. First one, then another, and soon a blossoming reputation as an agent especially sensitive to the needs of such artists. She enjoyed the status it gave her within the publishing industry and in Washington, where she'd become a "hot name" on party invitation lists, including foreign embassies. There was the extensive travel, which, at times, was fatiguing but stimulating as well. She seemed to live out of suitcases these days, which displeased people like her mother who made no effort to conceal her disappointment at seeing so little of her only child.

Barrie's mother lived in a town house in Rosslyn, far enough away for Barrie's sanity, but close enough to see each other occasionally. Mayer had stayed at her mother's last night, an accommodation because of the trip she was about to begin that morning. They'd had a pleasant dinner at Le Lion d'Or, then sat up talking at her mother's house until almost 2:00 A.M. Barrie was tired; it would be good to get on the Pan Am flight from New York to London, sink into a first-class seat, and nap.

She pulled a box of scented pink notepaper from her desk and wrote quickly in broad, bold strokes:

I know I shouldn't bother writing because in the frame of mind you've been in lately, the sentiment behind it won't register. But, that's me, always willing to take another shot and lay *me* on the line. You've hurt me again and here I am back for more. The only reason you're able to hurt me is because I love you. I also suspect that the *reason* you hurt me is because you love me. Fascinating creatures, men and women. At any rate, I'm about to leave and I wanted to say that when I get back we should book some private time, just the two of us, go away for a few days and talk. Maybe this time the words won't get in the way. London and Budapest beckon. Be good, and miss me, damn you.

Hubler came in again. "Got everything?"

"I think so," Mayer said, putting the pages in an envelope, sealing and addressing it, and slipping it into her purse. "Thanks to you."

"You'll be gone a week?"

"A day shy. I'll be at Eleven, Cadogan Gardens in London, and the Hilton in Budapest."

Hubler laughed. "So, what else is new?"

Mayer smiled and stood, stretched, blinked green eyes against sleepiness. "Is the car here?"

"Yeah." The agency had a corporate account with Butler's Limousine, and a stretch was waiting downstairs. "Barrie, a question."

"What?"

"You uncomfortable with this meeting with the Commie big shot in Budapest?"

"A little, but Zoltán says 'Not to worry.' " They both laughed. "He's been talking to you too much, David."

"Maybe he has. Look, I know *you* know your business, but greasing palms in a Socialist country might not be the smartest thing to do. You could be set up. They do it all the time."

Mayer grinned, then picked up her attaché case from the couch, came to where Hubler stood, and kissed him on the cheek. "You, David, are a dear. You also worry more than my mother does, which puts you in the Guinness class. Not to worry, David. Call me if you need me. I'll check in with you a couple of times. By the way, where's Carol?" Carol Geffin was one of two secretaries at the agency. The other, Marcia St. John, was on vacation. The only other two people on Mayer's staff were away on business, one in Hollywood following through on film rights to Réti's novel, the other in New York attending a conference.

"Must have been another heavy night at the Buck Stops Here," Hubler said. Carol Geffin's favorite disco closed at 6:00 A.M., sometimes.

Mayer shook her head. "You tell Carol that she's got to make a choice between working and dancing. One more late morning and she can dance all day on her money, not mine. Give me a hand, huh?"

Hubler carried her briefcase and a suitcase Mayer had dropped off in the reception area to the waiting limo. "See you in a week," she said as she climbed inside the back of the Fleetwood Brougham. The driver closed the door, got behind the wheel, and headed for National Airport and the shuttle to New York. She glanced back through the tinted glass and saw Hubler standing at the curb, his hand half raised in a farewell. One of many things Mayer liked about him was his disposition. He was always smiling, and his laugh was of the infectious variety. Not this day, however. His face, as he stood and watched the limo become smaller, was grim. It bothered her for a moment but quickly was displaced by thoughts of the day ahead. She stretched her legs out in front of her, closed her eyes, and said to herself, "Here we go again."

Her suitcase had been checked through to London, leaving her free to grab a cab from La Guardia into the city, where she was let off at the corner of Second Avenue and 30th Street. She walked toward the East River on 30th until she reached a brownstone with a series of physicians' names in black-on-white plaques.

JASON TOLKER—PSYCHIATRIST. She went down the steps and rang the
bell. A female voice asked through an intercom, "Who is it?"

"Barrie Mayer."

A buzzer sounded and Barrie opened the door, stepped into a small
carpeted reception area, and closed the door behind her. She was the
only person there except for a young woman who came from an office
in the rear and said, "Good morning."

"Good morning," Mayer said.

"He's not here, you know," the nurse said.

"I know, a conference in London. He told me to . . ."

"I know. It's here." The nurse, whose face was severely chiseled and
whose skin bore the scars of childhood acne, reached behind a desk and
came up with a black briefcase of the sort used by attorneys to carry
briefs. Two straps came over the top, and a tiny lock secured the flap to
the case itself.

"He said you'd been told about this," the nurse said.

"That's right. Thank you."

The nurse's smile was a slash across her lower face. "See you again,"
she said.

"Yes, you will."

Mayer left, carrying the new briefcase as well as her attaché case, one
in each hand. She checked into a room at the Plaza that David had
reserved from Washington, had lunch sent up, and perused papers from
her attaché case until three, when she placed a wake-up call for five,
stripped naked, and took a nap. She got up at five, showered, dressed
again, took a cab to Kennedy Airport, and checked in at the Clipper
Club, where she had a martini and read a magazine before boarding
Pan Am's seven o'clock 747 to London.

"Can I take those for you?" a flight attendant asked, indicating the
two briefcases.

"No, thank you. Lots of work to do," Mayer said pleasantly.

She slid both cases under the seat in front of her and settled in for
the flight. It left on time. She had another martini, and then caviar and
smoked salmon, rare beef carved at her seat, and blueberry cheesecake;
Cognac to top it off. The movie came on, which she ignored. She put on
slippers provided by the flight attendant and a pair of blue eyeshades
from a toiletry kit given to each first-class passenger, positioned a pillow behind her head, covered herself with a blue blanket, and promptly
fell asleep, the toes of her left foot wedged into the handle of the
briefcase she'd picked up at Dr. Jason Tolker's office.

The cabbie from Heathrow Airport to her hotel was an older man
who took more delight in chatting than in driving. Mayer would have
preferred silence but he was a charming man, as all the older London
cab drivers seemed to be, and she thought of the difference between
him and certain New York cabbies, who not only were rude and uncar-
ing but malicious, nervous, opinionated, hyperactive, and who curbed
any tendency toward humanity by driving insanely.

"Here we are, ma'am," the driver said as he pulled up in front of a row of brick houses on Cadogan Gardens. There was no indication of a hotel on the block. Only the number 11 appeared above a polished wooden door that Mayer went to. She rang a bell. Moments later a hall porter in a white jacket opened the door and said, "Welcome, Miss Mayer. Splendid to see you again. Your room is ready."

She signed the guest book and was led to the suite she usually reserved—Number 27. It consisted of a living room, bedroom, and bath. The white ceilings were high, the walls of the living room bloodred. Victorian furniture was everywhere, including a glass-fronted bookcase, an armoire, a dressing table in front of French windows in the bedroom that overlooked a private park across the street, and a gracefully curved chaise and chairs upholstered in gold.

"Would you like anything, ma'am?" the porter asked.

"Not this minute, thank you," Barrie said. "Perhaps tea at three?"

"Of course."

"I'll be leaving tomorrow for a few days," she said, "but I'll be keeping the room for my return."

"Yes, ma'am. Tea at three."

She slept, and later watched BBC-TV while enjoying scones with clotted cream and jam with her tea. She had dinner at seven at the Dorchester with a British agent, Mark Hotchkiss, with whom she'd been exploring a business link for the past few months, and was back in bed at the Cadogan by ten.

She arose at seven, had breakfast sent up to the room, dressed and left the hotel at eight. She arrived at Heathrow's Terminal Number 2 and joined a long line of people waiting to go through a security section leading to a vast array of flights by smaller foreign airlines, including Malev, the Hungarian National Airline.

She'd been through this before. How many trips had she taken to Budapest in the two or three years? Fifteen, twenty? She'd lost track. Only her accountant knew for certain. The line at Terminal 2 was always impossibly long and slow, and she'd learned to be patient.

She glanced up at a TV departure monitor. Plenty of time. An older man in front of her asked if she'd "protect" his place while he went to buy a pack of cigarettes. "Of course," she said. A woman behind her ran the wheel of a suitcase caddy into Mayer's heel. Mayer turned. The woman raised her eyebrows and looked away.

The line moved in spurts. Mayer carried her briefcases, and pushed her suitcase along the ground with her foot.

A loud voice to her right caused Barrie, and everyone else in the line, to turn in its direction. A young black man wearing an open white shirt, black trousers, and leather sandals had gotten up on a trash container and began screaming a protest against British policy in South Africa. Everyone's attention remained on him as two uniformed airport-security officers pushed through crowds of people in his direction.

"Barrie."

She didn't immediately react. Because she, and everyone else in the line, had turned to her right, her back was to a row of counters. The mention of her name had come from behind her.

She turned. Her eyebrows went up. She started to say something, a name, a greeting, when the hand came up beneath her nose. In it was a metal tube that might have held a cigar. The thumb on the hand flicked a switch on the tube and a glass ampule inside it shattered, its contents blown into Mayer's face.

It all happened so quickly. No one seemed to notice . . . until she dropped both briefcases to the floor and her hands clutched at her chest as a stabbing pain radiated from deep inside. She couldn't breathe. The airport, and everyone in it, was wiped away by a blinding white light that sent a spasm of pain through her head.

"Lady, are you . . . ?"

Her face was blue. She sank to her knees, her fingers frantic as they tried to tear open her clothing, her chest itself in search of air and relief from the pain.

"Hey, hey, over here, this lady's . . ."

Mayer looked up into the faces of dozens of people who were crouching low and peering at her, in sympathy or in horror. Her mouth and eyes opened wide, and rasping sounds came from her throat, pleas without words, questions for the faces of strangers so close to her. Then she pitched forward, her face thudding against the hard floor.

There were screams now from several people who saw what had happened to the tall, well-dressed woman who, seconds before, had stood in line with them.

The man who'd gone to get cigarettes returned. "What's this?" he asked as he looked down at Mayer, sprawled on the floor of Terminal Number 2. "Good God," he said, "someone do something for her."

3

"I JUST CAN'T BELIEVE IT," Collette Cahill said to Joe Breslin, as they sat at an outdoor table at Gundel, Budapest's grand old restaurant. "Barrie was . . . she'd become my best friend. I went out to Ferihegy to meet her flight from London, but she wasn't on it. I came back to the embassy and called that hotel in Cadogan Gardens she always stays at in London. All they could tell me was that she left that morning for the airport. Malev wouldn't tell me anything until I got hold of that guy in operations I know who checked the passenger manifest. Barrie was listed as a reservation, but she hadn't boarded. That's when I really started worrying. And then . . . then, I got a call from Dave Hubler in her Washington office. He could barely talk. I made him repeat what he'd said three, four times and . . ." She'd been fighting tears all evening and now lost the battle. Breslin reached across the table and placed a hand on hers. A seven-piece roving Gypsy band dressed in bright colors approached the table but Breslin waved them away.

Collette sat back in her chair and drew a series of deep breaths. She wiped her eyes with her napkin and slowly shook her head. "A heart attack? That's ridiculous, Joe. She was, what, thirty-five, maybe thirty-six? She was in great shape. Damn it! It can't be."

Breslin shrugged and lighted his pipe. "I'm afraid it can, Collette. Barrie's dead. No question about that, sadly. What about Réti, her writer?"

"I tried his house but no one was there. I'm sure he knows by now. Hubler was calling him with the news."

"What about the funeral?"

"There wasn't any, at least nothing formal. I called her mother that night. God, I dreaded it. She seemed to take it pretty well, though. She said she knew that Barrie wanted immediate cremation, no prayers, no gathering, and that's what she had."

"The autopsy. You say it was done in London?"

"Yes. They're the ones who labeled it a coronary." She closed her eyes tightly. "I will not buy that finding, Joe, never."

He smiled and leaned forward. "Eat something, Collette. You

haven't had a thing for too long. Besides, I'm starved." Large bowls of goulash soup sat untouched in front of them. She took a spoonful and looked at Breslin, who'd dipped a piece of bread in the hearty broth and was savoring it. Cahill was glad she had him to lean on. She'd made many friends since coming to Budapest, but Joe Breslin provided a stability she needed at times like this, perhaps because he was older, fifty-six, and seemed to enjoy the role of surrogate father.

Breslin had been stationed with the American Embassy in Budapest for just over ten years. In fact, Collette and a group of friends had celebrated his tenth anniversary only last week at their favorite Budapest night spot, the Miniatur Bar on Budai Läszlö Street, where a talented young Gypsy pianist named Nyári Károly played a nightly mix of spirited Hungarian Gypsy melodies, American pop tunes, Hungarian love songs, and modern jazz. It had been a festive occasion and they'd closed the bar at three in the morning.

"How's the soup?" Breslin asked.

"Okay. You know, Joe, I just realized there's someone else I should call."

"Who's that?"

"Eric Edwards."

Breslin's eyebrows lifted. "Why?"

"He and Barrie were . . . close."

"Really? I didn't know that."

"She didn't talk about it much but she was mad about him."

"Hardly an exclusive club."

The comment brought forth the first smile of the evening from her. She said, "I've finally gotten old enough to learn never to question a relationship. Do you know him well?"

"I don't know him at all, just the name, the operation. We had some dispatches from him this morning."

"And?"

"Nothing startling. Banana Quick is alive and well. They've had their second meeting."

"On Mosquito?"

He nodded, frowned, leaned across the table, and said, "Was Barrie carrying anything?"

"I don't know." They both glanced about to make sure they weren't being overheard. She spotted a table four removed at which a heavyset man and three women sat. She said to Breslin, "That's Litka Morovaf, Soviet cultural affairs."

Breslin smiled. "What is he now, number three in the KGB here?"

"Number two. A real Chekist. Drives him crazy when I call him Colonel. He actually thinks not wearing a uniform obscures his military rank. He's a pig, always after me to have dinner with him. Enough of him. Getting back to Barrie, Joe, I didn't always know whether she was carrying or just here on business for her agency. She'd tightened up a lot lately, which made me happy. When she first got involved, she babbled about it like a schoolgirl."

"Did she see Tolker before leaving?"

"I don't know that, either. She usually contacted him in Washington but she had time to kill in New York this trip, so I assume she saw him there. I don't know anything, Joe—I wish I did."

"Maybe it's better you don't. Feel like dinner?"

"Not really."

"Mind if I do?"

"Go ahead, I'll pick."

He ordered *Fogasfile Gundel Modon*, the small filets of fish accompanied by four vegetables, and a bottle of Egri Bikavér, a good red Hungarian wine. They said little while he ate. Cahill sipped the wine and tried to shake the thoughts that bombarded her about Barrie's death.

They'd become friends in college days. Collette was raised in Virginia, attended George Washington University, and graduated from its law school. It was during her postgraduate work that she met Barrie Mayer, who'd come from Seattle to work on a master's degree in English literature at Georgetown University. It had been a chance meeting. A young attorney Cahill had been seeing threw a party at his apartment in Old Town and invited his best friend, another attorney who'd just started dating Barrie Mayer. He brought her to the party and the two young women hit it off.

That they became close friends surprised the attorneys who'd introduced them. They were different personalities, as different as their physical attributes. Mayer, tall, leggy, had a mane of chestnut hair that she enjoyed wearing loose. She seldom used makeup. Her eyes were the color of malachite and she used them to good advantage, expressing a variety of emotions with a simple widening or narrowing, a partial wink, a lift of a sandy eyebrow, or a sensuous clouding over that she knew was appealing to men.

Cahill, on the other hand, was short and tightly bundled, a succession of rounded edges that had been there since adolescence and that had caused her widowed mother sleepless nights. She was as vivacious as Mayer was laid-back, deep blue eyes in constant motion, a face punctuated by high cheekbones that belied her Scottish heritage, a face that seemed always ready to burst apart with enthusiasm and wonder. She enjoyed using makeup to add high color to her cheeks and lips. Her hair was black ("Where did that come from, for heaven's sake?" her mother often asked), and she wore it short, in a style flattering to her nicely rounded face.

Their initial friendship was rooted in a mutual determination to forge successful careers. The specific goals were different, of course. For Mayer, it was to eventually head up a major book-publishing company. For Cahill, it was government service with an eye toward a top spot in the Justice Department, perhaps even becoming the first female

Attorney General. They laughed often and loudly about their aspirations, but they were serious.

They remained close until graduation, when the beginning stages of their work moved them away from each other. Cahill took a job with a legal trade journal published in Washington that kept tabs on pending legislation. She gave it a year, then took a friend's advice and began applying to government agencies, including Justice, State, and the Central Intelligence Agency. The CIA was first with an offer and she accepted it.

"You *what*?" Barrie Mayer had exploded over dinner the night Cahill announced her new job.

"I'm going to work for the CIA."

"That's . . . that's crazy. Don't you read, Collette? The CIA's a terrible organization."

"Media distortion, Barrie." She had smiled. "Besides, after training, they're sending me to England."

Now Mayer's smile matched Collette's. "All right," she said, "so it's not such a terrible organization. What will you be doing there?"

"I don't know yet, but I'll find out soon enough."

They ended the dinner with a toast to Collette's new adventure, especially to London.

At the time of Collette Cahill's decision to join the Pickle Factory, as CIA employees routinely referred to the agency, Barrie Mayer was working at a low-level editorial job with *The Washingtonian*, D.C.'s leading "city" magazine. Her friend's decision to make a dramatic move prompted action on her part. She quit the magazine and went to New York, where she stayed with friends until landing a job as assistant to the executive editor of a top book publisher. It was during that experience that she took an interest in the literary agent's side of the publishing business, and accepted a job with a medium-size agency. This suited her perfectly. The pace was faster than at the publishing house, and she enjoyed wheeling and dealing on behalf of the agency's clients. As it turned out, she was good at it.

When the founder of the agency died, Mayer found herself running the show for three years until deciding to strike out on her own. She ruled out New York; too much competition. With an increasing number of authors coming out of Washington, she decided to open Barrie Mayer Associates there. It flourished from the beginning, especially as her roster of foreign authors grew along with an impressive list of Washington writers.

Although their careers created a wide geographical distance between them, Barrie and Collette kept in touch through occasional postcards and letters, seldom giving much thought to whether they'd ever renew the friendship again in person.

After three years at a CIA monitoring station in an abandoned BBC facility outside of London, where she took raw intercepts of broadcasts from Soviet bloc countries and turned them into concise, cogent reports for top brass, Cahill was asked to transfer to a Clandestine Services unit in the Hungarian division, operating under the cover of the U.S. Embassy in Budapest. She debated making the move; she loved England, and the contemplation of a long assignment inside an Eastern European Socialist state did not hold vast appeal.

But there was the attraction of joining Clandestine Services, the CIA's division responsible for espionage, the *spy* division. Although space technology, with its ability to peek into every crevice and corner of the earth from miles aloft, had diminished the need for agents, special needs still existed, and the glamour and intrigue perpetuated by writers of spy novels lived on.

What had they said over and over during her training at headquarters in Langley, Virginia, and at the "Farm," the handsome estate a two-hour drive south of Washington? "The CIA is not essentially, or wholly, an espionage organization. It has only a small section devoted to espionage, and agents are never used to gain information that can be obtained through other means."

Her instructor in the course "Management of the Espionage Operation" had quoted from British intelligence to get across the same point. "A good espionage operation is like a good marriage. Nothing unusual ever happens. It is, and should be, uneventful. It is never the basis of a good story."

Her cover assignment would be the embassy's Industrial Trade Mission. Her real responsibility would be to function as a case officer, seeking out and developing useful members of Hungary's political, industrial, and intelligence communities into agents for the United States, to "turn" them to our side. It would mean returning to Washington for months of intensive training, including a forty-four-week language course in Hungarian at the Foreign Service Institute.

Should she take it? Her mother had been urging her to return home from England and to put her law training to the use for which it was intended. Cahill herself had been considering resigning from the Pickle Factory and returning home. The past few months in England had been boring, not socially but certainly on the job as her routine became predictable and humdrum.

It was not an easy decision. She made it on a train from London after a weekend holiday of good theater, pub-crawling with friends she'd made from the Thames Broadcasting Network, and luxuriating in a full English tea at Brown's.

She'd take it.

Once she'd decided, her spirits soared and she enthusiastically prepared for her return to Washington. She'd been instructed to discuss it with no one except cleared CIA personnel.

"Not even my mother?"

An easy, understanding smile from her boss. "*Especially* your mother."

* * *

"You will hear two things from Hungarians," her language instructor at Washington's Foreign Service Institute told the class the first day. "First, they will tell you that Hungary is a very small country. Second, they will tell you that the language is *very* difficult. Believe them. Both statements are true."

Friday.

Cahill's first week of language classes had ended, and she'd made plans to spend the weekend with her mother in Virginia. She stopped in the French Market in Georgetown to pick up her mother's favorite pâté and cheese, and was waiting for her purchases to be added up when someone behind her said her name. She turned. "It can't be," she said, wide-eyed.

"Sure is," Barrie Mayer said.

They embraced, stepped apart, and looked at each other, then hugged again.

"What are you doing here?" Mayer asked.

"Going to school. I'm being transferred and . . . it's a long story. How are you? The agency's doing well? How's your . . . ?"

"Love life?" A hearty laugh from both. "That, too, is a long story. Where are you going now? Can we have a drink? Dinner? I've been meaning to . . ."

"So have I. I'm going home for the weekend . . . I mean, where my mother lives. God, I can't believe this, Barrie! You look sensational."

"So do you. Do you have to go right now?"

"Well, I—let me call my mother and tell her I'll be late."

"Go tomorrow morning, early. Stay with me tonight."

"Ah, Barrie, I can't. She's expecting me."

"At least a drink. My treat. I'm dying to talk to you. This is incredible, bumping into you. Please, just a drink. If you stay for dinner, I'll even send you home by limo."

"Things are good, huh?"

"Things are *fantastic*."

They went to the Georgetown Inn where Cahill ordered a gin and tonic, Mayer an old-fashioned. There was a frenetic attempt to bring each other up to date as quickly as possible, which resulted in little information actually being absorbed. Mayer realized it and said, "Let's slow down. You first. You said you were here to take classes. What kind of classes? What for?"

"For my job. I'm"—she looked down at the bar and said sheepishly— "I can't really discuss it with . . . with anyone not officially involved with the Company."

Mayer adopted a grave expression. "Heavy spy stuff, huh?"

Cahill laughed the comment away. "No, not at all, but you know how things are with us."

"*Us?*"

"Don't make me explain, Barrie. You know what I mean."

"I sure do."

"Do you?"

Mayer sat back and played with a swizzle stick. She asked, "Are you leaving jolly old England?"

"Yes."

"And?"

"I'll be . . . I've taken a job with the U.S. Embassy in Budapest."

"That's wonderful. With the embassy? You've left the CIA?"

"Well, I . . ."

Mayer held up her hand. "No explanations needed. I read the papers."

What had been an exuberant beginning to the reunion deteriorated into an awkward silence. It was Cahill who broke it. She clutched Mayer's arm and said, "Let's get off the cloaks and daggers. Barrie, your turn. Tell me about *your* agency. Tell me about, well . . ."

"My love life." They giggled. "It's stagnant, to be kind, although it has had its moments recently. The problem is that I've been spending more time on airplanes than anywhere else, which doesn't contribute to stable relationships. Anyway, the agency is thriving *and*, coincidentally, you and I will probably see more of each other in Budapest than we have for the past five years."

"Why?"

She explained her recent success with foreign authors, including the Hungarian, Zoltán Réti. "I've been to Budapest six or eight times. I love it. It's a marvelous city despite Big Red Brother looking over your shoulder."

"Another drink?"

"Not for me. You?"

"No. I really should be heading off."

"Call your mother."

"All right."

Cahill returned and said, "She's such a sweetness. She said, 'You spend time with your dear friend. Friends are important.'" She delivered the words with exaggerated gravity.

"She sounds wonderful. So, what is it, dinner, stay over? You name it."

"Dinner, and the last train home."

They ended up at La Chaumière on M Street, where Mayer was given a welcome worthy of royalty. "I've been coming here for years," she told Cahill as they were led to a choice table near the center fireplace. "The food is scrumptious and they have a sense of when to leave you alone. I've cut some of my better meals and deals here."

It turned into a long, leisurely, and progressively introspective evening, aided by a second bottle of wine. The need to bombard each other with detailed tales of their lives had passed, and the conversation slipped into a comfortable and quiet series of reflective thoughts, delivered from their armchairs.

"Tell me more about Eric Edwards," Cahill said.

"What else is there to say? I was in the BVI meeting with an author who'd recently hit it big. Besides, never pass up a chance at the Caribbean. Anyway, he took me on a day cruise, and the charter captain was Eric. We hit it off right away, Collette, one of those instant fermentations, and I spent the week with him."

"Still on?"

"Sort of. It's hard with my travel schedule and his being down there, but it sure ain't dead."

"That's good."

"And . . ."

Cahill looked across the candlelit table and smiled. "That's right," she said, "there was something you were dying to tell me."

"Eric Edwards isn't enough?"

"Only if you hadn't hinted that there was something even bigger. Lay it on me, lady literary agent. That last train home isn't far off."

Mayer glanced around the restaurant. Only two other tables were occupied, and they were far away. She put her elbows on the table and said, "I joined the team."

Cahill's face was a blank.

"I'm one of you."

It dawned on Cahill that her friend might be referring to the CIA but, because it didn't make much sense—and because she had learned caution—she didn't bring it up. Instead, she said, "Barrie, could you be a little more direct?"

"Sure. I'm working for the Pickle Factory." There was mirth in her voice as she said the words.

"That's . . . how?"

"I'm a courier. Just part time, of course, but I've been doing it fairly regularly now for about a year."

"Why?" It was the only sensible question that came to Cahill at the moment.

"Well, because I was asked to and . . . I like it, Collette, feel I'm doing something worthwhile."

"You're being paid?"

Mayer laughed. "Of course. What kind of an agent would I be if I didn't negotiate a good deal for myself?"

"You don't *need* the money, do you?"

"Of course not, but who ever has too much money? And, finally, some earnings off the books. Want more specifics?"

"Yes and no. I'm fascinated, of course, but you really shouldn't be talking about it."

"To *you?* You're cleared."

"I know *that*, Barrie, but it's still something you don't chit-chat about over dinner and wine."

Mayer adopted a contrite expression. "You aren't going to turn me in, are you?"

Collette sighed and looked for a waiter. Once she'd gotten his attention, she said to Mayer, "Barrie, you have ruined my weekend. I'll spend it wondering about the strange twists and turns my friend's life has taken while I wasn't around to protect her."

They stood outside the restaurant. It was a crisp and clear evening. The street had filled with the usual weekend crowds that gravitated to Georgetown, and that caused residents to wring their hands and to consider wringing necks, or selling their houses.

"You'll be back Monday?" Mayer asked.

"Yup, but I'll be spending most of my time out of town."

"At the Farm?"

"Barrie!"

"Well?"

"I have some training to take. Let's leave it at that."

"Okay, but promise you'll call the first moment you're free. We have a lot more catching up to do."

They touched cheeks, and Collette flagged a cab. She spent the weekend at her mother's house thinking about Barrie Mayer and the conversation at the restaurant. What she'd told her friend was true. She *had* spoiled her weekend, and she returned to Washington Monday morning anxious to get together again for another installment of Barrie Mayer's "other life."

"This restaurant isn't what it used to be," Joe Breslin said as he finished his meal. "I remember when Gundel was . . ."

"Joe, I'm going to London and Washington," Cahill said.

"Why?"

"To find out what happened to Barrie. I just can't sit here and let it slide, shrug and accept the death of a friend."

"Maybe you should do just that, Collette."

"Sit here?"

"Yes. Maybe . . ."

"Joe, I know exactly what you're thinking, and if what you're thinking bears any relationship to the truth, I don't know what I'll do."

"I don't know anything about Barrie's death, Collette, but I do know that she assumed a known risk once she got involved, no matter how part time it might have been. Things have heated up since Banana Quick. The stakes have gotten a lot bigger, and the players are more visible and vulnerable." He added quickly, in a whisper, "The schedule's been moved up. It'll be sooner than planned."

"What are you saying, Joe, that this could have been a Soviet wet affair?" She'd used Russian intelligence slang for blood, for an assassination, which had been picked up by the intelligence community in general.

"Could be."

"Or?"

"Or . . . your guess. Remember, Collette, it might have been exactly what it was labeled by the British doctors, a coronary pure and simple."

A lump developed in Cahill's throat and she touched away a tear that had started down her cheek. "Take me home, Joe, please. I'm suddenly very tired."

As they left Gundel, the Soviet intelligence officer at the table with three women waved to Collette and said, "*Vsyevó kharóshevo*, Madam Cahill." He was drunk.

"Good night to you, too, Colonel," she responded.

Breslin dropped her at her apartment on Huszti ut, on the more fashionable Buda side of the Danube. It was one of dozens of apartments the U.S. government had leased to house its embassy personnel, and although it was extremely small and three flights up, it was light and airy and featured a remodeled kitchen that was the best of all the kitchens her embassy friends had in their subsidized apartments. It also came with a telephone, something Hungarian citizens waited years for.

A flashing red light indicated Cahill had two messages on her answering machine. She rewound the tape and heard a familiar voice, his English heavily laden with his Hungarian birthright. "*Collette, it is Zoltán Réti. I am in London. I am shocked at what I have heard about Barrie. No, shocked is not the word to describe my feelings. I read about it in the paper here. I am attending a conference and will return to Budapest tomorrow. I am sorry for the loss of your good friend, and for my loss. It is a terrible thing. Goodbye.*"

Cahill stopped the machine before listening to the second message. London? Hadn't Réti known Barrie was coming to Budapest? If he hadn't—and if she knew he wouldn't be here—she had to be on CIA business. But that broke precedent. She'd never traveled to Budapest without having him there as the reason for her visit which, in fact, was legitimate. He was a client. The fact that he happened to be Hungarian and lived in Budapest only made it more plausible and convenient to perform her second mission, carrying materials for the Central Intelligence Agency.

She started the second message:

"*Collette Cahill, my name is Eric Edwards. We've never met, but Barrie and I were quite close, and she talked about you often. I just learned about what happened to her and felt I had to make contact with someone, anyone who was close to her and shares what I'm feeling at this moment. It seems impossible, doesn't it, that she's gone, like that, this beautiful and talented woman who . . .*" There was a pause, and it sounded to Cahill as though he were trying to compose himself. "*I hope you don't mind this long and convoluted message but, as I said, I wanted to reach out and talk to her friend. She gave me your number a long time ago. I live in the British Virgin Islands but I wondered if . . ."* The line went dead. He was cut off, and the machine made a series of beeping noises.

His call set up another set of questions for her. Didn't he know that *she* would know who he was, that he lived in the British Virgins, was a CIA operative there whose primary mission had to do with Hungary? Was he just being professional? Probably. She couldn't fault that.

She made herself a cup of tea, got into her nightgown, and climbed into bed, the tea on a small table beside her. She decided three things: She would request time off immediately to go to London and Washington; she would look up everyone who was close to Barrie and, at least, be able to vent her feelings; and she would, from that moment forward, accept the possibility that her friend Barrie Mayer had died prematurely of a heart attack, at least until there was something tangible to prove otherwise.

She fell asleep crying silently after asking in a hoarse, low voice, "What happened, Barrie? What *really* happened?"

4

COLLETTE: *Please see me as soon as you come in. Joe.*

The note was taped to the telephone in her office on the second floor of the embassy. She got a cup of coffee and walked down the hall to Breslin's office. "Come in," he said. "Close the door."

He took a sip of his coffee which, Cahill knew, contained a healthy shot of akvavit, compliments of a buddy in the U.S. Embassy in Copenhagen who always included a bottle in his diplomatic pouch. "What's up?" she asked.

"Feel like a walk?"

"Sure." He wasn't suggesting it because he needed exercise. What he had to say was important and private, and Breslin was a notorious paranoid when it came to holding such conversations inside the embassy.

They went down a broad staircase with worn red carpeting, through a door tripped electronically by a young woman at the front desk, past a Hungarian Embassy employee who was running a metal detector over a visitor, and out into bright sunshine that bathed Szabadság ter and Liberation Square.

A group of schoolchildren gathered at the base of a huge memorial obelisk dedicated to Soviet soldiers who'd liberated the city. The streets were bustling with people on their way to work, or heading for Váci utca and its parallel shopping boulevard from which all vehicles were banned. "Come on," Breslin said, "let's go down to Parliament."

They walked along the Danube's shoreline until they reached the domed, neo-Gothic Parliament building with its eighty-eight statues depicting Hungarian monarchs, commanders, and famous warriors. Breslin looked up at it and smiled. "I would have liked being around here when they really did have a Parliament," he said. Since the Soviets took over, the Parliament continued to function, but in name only. The *real* decisions were made in an ugly, rectangular building farther up the river where the MSZMP—the Hungarian Socialist Workers' Party—sat.

Cahill watched boat traffic on the Danube as she asked, "What do you want to tell me?"

Breslin pulled his pipe from his jacket, tamped tobacco into its bowl, and put a wooden match to it. "I don't think you'll have to ask for time off to chase down what happened to your friend Barrie."

"What do you mean?"

"Based upon what Stan told me this morning, you're going to be asked to do it officially." Stanley Podgorsky was chief-of-station for the CIA unit operating out of the embassy. Of two hundred Americans assigned there, approximately half were CIA people reporting to him.

"Why me?" Cahill asked. "I'm not a trained investigator."

"Why not? How many Company investigators have you known who were trained?" It caused her to smile. "You know how it works, Collette, somebody knows somebody who's been compromised and they get the assignment, instant investigator. I think that's you this time around."

"Because I knew Barrie?"

"Exactly."

"And it wasn't a heart attack?"

"Not from what I hear."

They approached a construction crew that was using jackhammers to tear out an old dock. When they were close enough so that even sophisticated, long-range microphones would fail to distinguish their words from the din, Breslin said, "She *was* carrying, Collette, and evidently it was important."

"And it's gone?"

"Right."

"Any ideas?"

"Sure. It was either us or them. If it was them, they have the material and we're in a panic. If it was us, one of our people has what she had in her briefcase and maybe is looking to sell it to the other side." He drew on his pipe and said, "Or . . ."

"Or wanted what she had for other reasons, personal maybe, incriminating, something like that."

"Yes, something like that."

She squinted against the sun that popped out from a fast-moving cloud and said, "Joe, we're down here for more than just a preliminary warning to me that Stan might ask me to look into Barrie's death. He told you to feel me out, didn't he?"

"Not in so many words."

"I'll do it."

"Really? No hesitation?"

"None. I wanted to do it on my own time anyway. This way I don't blow what leave I have coming to me."

"That's pragmatic."

"That's working for the Pickle Factory too long. Do I go back and tell him, or do you?"

"You. I have nothing to do with this. One final bit of advice, Collette. Stan and the desk people back at Langley really don't give a damn how Barrie died. As far as they're concerned, she had a heart attack. I mean, they know she didn't but *she* doesn't count. The briefcase does."

"What was in it? Who was it from?"

"Maybe Stan will tell you, but I doubt it. Need-to-know, you know."

"If I'm trying to find out who ended up with it, I'll need to know."

"Maybe, maybe not. That's up to Stan and Langley. Let them lay out the rules and you stay within them." He looked over half-glasses to reinforce his point.

"I will, and thanks, Joe. I'll go see Stan right now."

Podgorsky occupied an office that had a sign on the door that read TYPEWRITER REPAIR. Many CIA offices within the embassy had such signs which, the thinking went, would discourage casual visitors. They usually did.

He sat behind a battered desk with a row of burn marks from too many cigars perched on the edge. Stanley was short and stocky, with a full head of gray hair of which he was inordinately proud. Cahill liked him, had from the first day she arrived in Budapest. He was shrewd and tough but had a sentimental streak that extended to everyone working for him.

"You talked to Joe?" he asked.

"Yes."

"Make sense to you?"

"I guess so. We were close. I was supposed to meet her flight."

He nodded and grunted, rolled his fingertips on the desk. "Were you meeting her for us?"

"No, strictly personal. I didn't know whether she was carrying or not."

"She ever talk to you about what she was doing?"

"A little."

"Nothing about this trip."

"Nothing. She never got specific about any trip she took here. All she ever got into was her meetings with her agency clients like Zoltán Réti."

"He's not here."

"I know. He called me last night from London and left a message on my machine."

"You find it strange he isn't here?"

"As a matter of fact, yes."

"She was supposed to meet with him and a Party big shot about clearing Réti to get the money his books are making in the West."

"How much was *that* going to cost?"

Podgorsky laughed. "Whatever the *papakha* needed to buy one of those condos up on the hill, or to get himself a fancy new car quick."

"Palms are all the same."

"So's the grease and the way it goes on." His face became grim. "We lost a lot, Collette."

"What she was carrying was that important?"

"Yeah."

"What was it?"

"Need-to-know."

"*I* need to know if I'm going to be digging into what led up to her death."

He shook his head. "Not now, Collette. The assignment is clear-cut, no ambiguities. You go home on leave and touch base with everybody in her life. You're grieving, can't believe your good friend is dead. You find out what you can and report it to a case officer at Langley."

"How cynical. I really do care what happened to my friend."

"I'm sure you do. Look, you don't have to do this. It's not in your area, but I'd suggest you think six times before turning it down. Like I said, the stakes are big here."

"Banana Quick?"

He nodded.

"Am I really taking leave?"

"It'll be on the books that way in case somebody wants to snoop. We'll make it up to you later. That's a promise from me."

"When do you want me to start?"

"Leave in the morning."

"I can't. You know I have a meet set up with Horgász."

"That's right. When?"

"Tomorrow night."

Podgorsky thought for a moment before saying, "It's important?"

"I haven't seen him for six weeks. He left word at one of the drops that he had something. It's been set, can't be changed."

"Then do it, leave the next morning."

"All right. Anything else?"

"Yeah. Go easy. Frankly, I tried to veto having you assigned to this. Too close. Good friends usually get in the way. Try to forget who she was and concentrate on business. A briefcase. That's all anybody cares about."

She stood and said, "I really do hate this place, Stan."

"Gay ol' Budapest?" He laughed loudly.

"You know what I mean."

"Sure I do. Everything set for Horgász?"

"I think so. We're using the new safehouse."

"I still don't like that place. I should have stuck to my guns and killed it when it was suggested. Too close to too many other things."

"I'm comfortable with it."

"That's good. You're a trouper, Collette."

"I'm an employee. You said I'll be on leave, which means no official status. That makes it tough."

"No it doesn't. The only thing having status would give you is access to our people. You don't need them. They don't have any answers. They're *looking* for answers."

"I want to retrace Barrie's steps. I'll go to London first."

He shrugged.

"I want to talk to the doctors who did the autopsy."

"Nothing to be gained there, Collette. They used cleared personnel."

"British SIS?"

"Probably."

"How was she killed, Stan?"

"Beats me. Maybe prussic acid if it was the Soviets."

"We use it, too, don't we?"

He ignored the question by going through a slow, elaborate ritual of clipping, wetting, and lighting a cigar. "Forget the British doctors, Collette," he said through a cloud of blue smoke.

"I still want to go to London first."

"Nice this time of year. Not many tourists."

She opened the door, turned, and asked, "How's the typewriter repair business?"

"Slow. They make 'em too good these days. Take care, and keep in touch."

She spent the remainder of the day, much of the night, and all of the next day preparing for her meet with a man, code name Horgász, Hungarian for "Fisherman." He represented Collette Cahill's coup since being in Budapest. Horgász, whose real name was Árpád Hegedüs, was a high-ranking psychologist within the KGB's Hungarian intelligence arm.

Cahill had met Árpád Hegedüs the first week she was in Budapest at a reception for a group of psychologists and psychiatrists who'd been invited to present papers to a Hungarian scientific conference. Three Americans were among the invited, including Dr. Jason Tolker. Cahill's dislike for Tolker was instantaneous, although she hadn't thought much about it until Barrie Mayer confided in her that he was the one who'd recruited her into the part-time role of CIA courier. "I didn't like him," Cahill had told her friend, to which Mayer replied, "You're not

supposed to like your shrink." Mayer had been his patient for a year
before hooking up with Central Intelligence.

Árpád Hegedüs was a nervous little man, forty-six years old, who
wore shirt collars that were too tight and wrinkled suits that were too
large. He was married and had two children. Most of his training in
psychology had been gained at the Neurological and Psychiatric Clinic
on Balassa utca, near the Petöfi Bridge linking the Pest and Buda sides
of the Grand Boulevard. He'd come to the attention of Soviet authorities after he'd developed and instituted a series of psychological tests
for workers in sensitive jobs that were designed to flag personality traits
that could lead to dissatisfaction, and perhaps even disloyalty. He was
taken to Moscow, where he spent a year at VASA, the Soviet military
intelligence school that constitutes a special department of the prestigious Military Diplomatic Academy. His intellect shone there and he
was brought into the Sovetskaya Kolonia, the KGB's arm responsible
for policing the loyalty of the Soviet's colonies abroad, in this case its
Hungarian contingent. That was the job he held when Cahill met him at
the reception, although his official position was with the teaching staff
of his Hungarian alma mater.

Cahill bumped into him a few more times over the ensuing months.
One night, as she ate dinner alone in Vigadó, a downtown brasserie on
Vigadó Square, he approached the table and asked if he might join her.
They had a pleasant conversation. He spoke good English, loved opera
and American jazz, and asked a lot of questions about life in the United
States.

Cahill didn't attach any significance to the chance meeting. It was
two weeks later that the reason for his approach became obvious.

It was a Saturday morning. She'd gone for a run and ended up at the
former Royal Palace on Castle Hill. The palace had been completely
destroyed during World War II. Now the restoration was almost completed and the baroque palace had been transformed into a vast museum and cultural complex, including the Hungarian National Gallery.

Cahill often browsed in the museum. It had become, for her, a peaceful refuge.

She was standing in front of a huge medieval ecclesiastical painting
when a man came up behind her. "Miss Cahill," he said softly.

"Oh, hello, Mr. Hegedüs. Nice to see you again."

"You like the paintings?"

"Yes, very much."

He stood next to her and gazed up at the art work. "I would like to
speak with you," he said.

"Yes, go ahead."

"Not now." He looked around the gallery before saying so softly she
almost missed it, "Tomorrow night at eleven, at the St. Mary Magdalene Church in Kapisztrán ter."

Cahill stared at him.

"In the back, behind the tower. At eleven. I will wait only five minutes. Thank you. Goodbye." Cahill watched him cross the large room, his head swiveling to take in the faces he passed, his short, squat body lumbering from side to side.

She immediately returned to her apartment, showered, changed clothes, and went to Stan Podgorsky's apartment.

"Hi, Lil," Cahill said to his wife when she answered the door. "Sorry to barge in but . . ."

"Just a typical Hungarian Saturday at home," she said. "I'm baking cookies and Stan's reading a clandestine issue of *Playboy*. Like I said, just your run-of-the mill Hungarian weekend."

"I have to talk to you," Cahill told him in the crowded little living room. "I've just had something happen that could be important."

They took a walk and she told him what had transpired in the museum.

"What do you know about him?" he asked.

"Not much, just that he's a psychologist at the hospital and . . ."

"He's also KGB," Podgorsky said.

"You know that for certain?"

"I sure do. Not only is he KGB, he's attached to the SK, the group that keeps tabs on every Russian here. If he's making an overture to us, Collette, he could be playing games—or he could be damn valuable. No, Christ, that's an understatement. He could be gold, pure gold."

"I wonder why he sought me out," she said.

"It doesn't matter. He liked the way you looked, sensed someone he could trust. Who knows? What matters is that we follow up on it and not do anything to scare him off, on the long shot that he might be turned—or *has* turned." He looked at his watch, said, "Look, go on home and pack a small overnight bag. I'll meet you at the embassy in two hours, after I get hold of some others we need on this. Take a circle route to the embassy. Make sure nobody's tailing you. Anybody look interested in your conversation with him at the museum?"

"I really wasn't looking for anyone, but he sure was. He was a wreck."

"Good. And for good reason. Okay, two hours, and be ready for a marathon."

The next thirty-six hours were intense and exhausting. By the time Cahill headed for the square of St. John Capistrano, she'd had a complete briefing on Árpád Hegedüs provided by the station's counterintelligence branch, whose job it was to create biographical files on everyone in Budapest working for the other side.

A gray Russian four-door Zim with two agents was assigned to follow her to the street-meet with Hegedüs. The rules that had been laid down for her were simple and inviolate.

She was to accept nothing from him, not a scrap of paper, not a matchbook, *nothing*, to avoid being caught in the standard espionage trap of being handed a document from the other side, then immediately put under arrest for spying.

If anything seemed amiss (*"Anything!"* Podgorsky had stressed), she was to terminate the meeting and walk to a corner two blocks away where the car would pick her up. The same rule applied if he wasn't alone.

The small Charter Arms .38-caliber special revolver she carried in her raincoat pocket was to remain there unless absolutely necessary for her physical protection. If that need arose, the two agents in the Zim would back her up with M-3 submachine guns with silencers.

She was to commit to nothing to Hegedüs. He'd called the meet, and it was her role to listen to what he had to say. If he indicated he wished to become a double agent, she was to set another meeting at a safehouse that was about to be discarded. No sense exposing an ongoing location to him until you were sure he was legit.

Cahill lingered in front of a small café down the street from the Gothic church. She was grateful for its presence. Her heart was beating and she drew deep breaths to calm down. Her watch read 10:50. He said he'd wait only five minutes. She couldn't be late.

The gray Zim passed, the agents looking straight ahead but taking her in with their peripheral vision. She walked away from the café and approached the church, still in ruins except for the meticulously restored tower. She had a silly thought—she wished there were fog to shroud the scene and to give it more the atmosphere of spy-meeting-spy. There wasn't; it was a pristine night in Budapest. The moon was nearly full and cast a bright floodlight over the tiny streets and tall church.

She went behind the church, stopped, looked around, saw no one. Maybe he wouldn't show. Podgorsky had raised that possibility. "More times than not they get cold feet," he'd told her. "Or maybe he's been made. He's put his neck way out on a limb even talking to you, Collette, and you may have seen the last of him."

She had mixed emotions. She hoped he wouldn't show up. She hoped he would. After all, that's what her new job with the CIA in Budapest was all about, to find just such a person and to turn him into a successful and productive counterspy against his own superiors. That it had happened so fast, so easily, was unlikely, was . . . "Life is what happens while you're making other plans," her father had always said.

"Miss Cahill."

His voice shocked her. Although she was expecting him, she was not ready for his voice, any voice. She gasped, afraid to turn.

Hegedüs came out of the shadows of the church and stood behind her. She slowly turned. "Mr. Hegedüs," she said in a shaky voice. "You're here."

"*Igen*, I am here, and so are you."

"Yes, I . . ."

"I will be brief. For reasons of my own I wish to help you and your country. I wish to help Hungary, my country, rid itself of our most recent conquerors."

"What sort of help?"

"Information. I understand you are always in need of information."

"That's true," she said. "You realize the risk you take?"

"Of course. I have thought about this for a very long time."

"And what do you want in return? Money?"

"Yes, but that is not my only motivation."

"We'll have to talk about money. I don't have the authority to . . ." She wished she hadn't said it. It was important that he put his complete trust in her. To suggest that he'd have to talk to others wasn't professional.

It didn't seem to deter him. He looked up at the church tower and smiled. "This was a beautiful country, Miss Cahill. Now it is . . ." A deep sigh. "No matter. Here." He pulled two sheets of paper from his raincoat pocket and thrust them at her. Instinctively, she reached for them, then withdrew her hand. His expression was one of puzzlement.

"I don't want anything from you now, Mr. Hegedüs. We'll have to meet again. Is that acceptable to you?"

"Do I have a choice?"

"Yes, you can reconsider your offer and withdraw it."

It was a rueful laugh. "Pilots reach a point in their flight that represents no return. Once they pass it, they are committed to continuing to their final destination—or crashing. It is the same with me."

Cahill pronounced slowly and in a clear voice the address of the safehouse that had been chosen. She told him the date and time: exactly one week from that night, at nine in the evening.

"I shall be there, and I shall bring what I have here to that meeting."

"Good. Again, I must ask whether you understand the potential ramifications of what you're doing?"

"Miss Cahill, I am not a stupid man."

"No, I didn't mean to suggest that. . . ."

"I know you didn't. You are not that kind of person. I could tell that the moment I met you, and that is why it was you I contacted."

"I appreciate that, Mr. Hegedüs, and I look forward to our next meeting. You have the address?"

"Yes, I do. *Viszontlátásra!*" He disappeared into the shadows. Somehow, his simple "Goodbye" was inadequate for Collette.

If the meet went smoothly, she was not to get into the Zim but return to her apartment by public transportation. A half hour after she'd arrived, there was a knock on the door. She opened it. It was Joe Breslin. "Hey, just in the neighborhood and thought I could buy you a drink."

She realized he was there as part of what had gone on at the church. She put on her coat and they went to an outdoor café, where he handed her a note that read, *"Tell me what happened without mentioning names or getting specific. Use a metaphor—baseball, ballet, whatever."*

She recounted the meeting with Hegedüs as Breslin lighted his pipe and used the match to incidentally ignite the small slip of paper he'd handed her. They both watched it turn to ash in an ashtray.

478 Margaret Truman

When she was done, he looked at her, smiled his characteristic half-smile, touched her hand. "Excellent," he said. "You look beat. These things don't take a hell of a lot of time, but they drain you. So drain a *hosszúlépés* and I'll take you home. If anyone's tail is on us, they'll think we're having just another typical, torrid, capitalistic affair."

Her laugh caught, became almost a giggle. "After what I've been through, Joe, I think we should make it a *fröccs*." Two parts wine to one part soda, the reverse of what he'd suggested.

Now, two years later, she prepared for another meet with the Fisherman. How many had there been, fifteen, twenty, maybe more? It had gotten easier, of course. She and "her spy" had become good friends. It was supposed to end up that way, according to the handbook on handling agents-in-place. As Árpád Hegedüs's case officer, Cahill was paid to think of everything that might compromise him, threaten him, *anything* that conceivably could jeopardize him and his mission. So many rules she had to remember and remind herself of whenever a situation came up.

Rule One: The agent himself is more important than any given piece of information he might be able to deliver. Always consider the long haul, never the immediate gain.

Rule Two: Never do anything to jog his conscience. Never ask for more than his conscience will allow him to deliver.

Rule Three: Money. Small and steady. A change in basic lifestyle tips off the other side. Make him come to depend upon it. No bonuses for delivering an especially important piece of information, no matter how risky it was to obtain. Among other reasons, don't reveal how important any one piece of information might be.

Rule Four: Be alert to his moods and personal habits. Be his friend. Hear him out. Counsel when it's appropriate, hear his confessions, help him stay out of trouble.

Rule Five: Don't lose him.

This meet had been arranged like all the others. When Hegedüs had something to pass on, he left a red thumbtack in a utility pole around the corner from his home. The pole was checked each day by a Hungarian postman who'd been on the CIA payroll for years. If the tack was there, he called a special number at the American Embassy within ten minutes. The person answering the phone said, "International Wildlife Committee," to which the postman would respond, "I was thinking of going fishing this weekend and wondered about conditions." He would then abruptly hang up. The person who'd taken the call would inform either Stan Podgorsky, Collette Cahill, or the station's technical coordinator and second-in-command, Harold "Red" Sutherland, a hulk of a man with sparse red hair, feet that had broken down years ago beneath his weight, and who was fond of red suspenders and railroad handkerchiefs. Red was an electronics genius, responsible for video and audio eavesdropping for the Budapest station, including an elaborate recording operation in the safehouse where Cahill and Hegedüs met.

It was understood that a meet would take place exactly one week from the day the tack was found, at a predetermined time and place. Cahill had informed Hegedüs at their last get-together of the change in safehouses, which was acceptable to him.

Cahill arrived an hour before Hegedüs. The recording and photographic equipment was tested, and Cahill went over a set of notes she and others at the station had developed. Hegedüs's desk officer back at Langley, Virginia, had transmitted a series of "RQMs," intelligence requirements, that they wanted met from this most recent meet. They all involved the operation known as Banana Quick. Primarily, they needed to know how much the Soviets knew about it. Cahill had given the requirement to Hegedüs at their last meeting and he'd promised to come up with whatever he could.

When Árpád Hegedüs walked into the room, he chuckled. A table was set with his favorite foods, which had been brought in that afternoon—*libamáj*, goose liver; *rántott gombafejek*, champignon mushroom caps that had been fried in the kitchen by Red Sutherland shortly before Hegedüs's arrival; a plate of cheeses, Pálpusztai, Márványsajt, and a special Hungarian cream cheese with paprika and caraway seeds known as *körözött*. For dessert there was a heaping platter of *somlói galuska*, small pieces of sponge cake covered with chocolate and whipped cream—they were a passion for Hegedüs. Everything would be washed down with bourbon. He'd been served vodka early in the game, but one night he expressed a preference for American bourbon and Red Sutherland arranged for Langley to ship in a case of Blanton's, the brand Sutherland, a dedicated bourbon drinker, claimed was the best. An hour-long meeting on the subject of which bourbon to sneak into Hungary had been held behind embassy closed doors and, as often happened, it became a project with a name—"Project Abe," referring to Abraham Lincoln's pre-political career as a bourbon distiller.

"You look well, Árpád," Cahill said.

He smiled. "Not nearly as good as you, Collette. You're wearing my favorite outfit." She'd forgotten that at a previous meeting he'd complimented her on the blue and gray dress she had on again this night. She thanked him and motioned toward a small bar in the corner of the room. He went to it, rubbed his hands, and said, "Splendid. I look forward to these evenings for seeing Mr. Blanton almost as much as for seeing you."

"As long as I'm still the most important, the highest proof, you might say" she said. He seemed puzzled; she explained. He grinned and said, "Ah, yes, the proof. The proof is always important." He poured himself a full glass and dropped an ice cube from a silver bucket into it, causing the amber liquid to spill over the sides. He apologized. Cahill ignored him and poured herself an orange juice, almost as rare in Budapest as bourbon.

"Hungry?" she asked.

"*Always*," he answered, his eyes lighting up as if there were candles on the table. He sat and filled a plate. Cahill took a few morsels and sat across from him.

Hegedüs looked around the room, as though suddenly realizing he was in a new place. "I like the other house better," he said.

"It was time to change," Cahill said. "Too long in one place makes everyone nervous."

"Except me."

"Except you. How are things?"

"Good . . . bad." He waved his pudgy hand over his plate. "This will be our last meeting."

Cahill's heart tripped. "Why?" she asked.

"At least for some time. They are talking of sending me to Moscow."

"What for?"

"Who knows how the Russian mind works, what it's for? My family packs now and will leave in three days."

"You won't be with them?"

"Not immediately. It had occurred to me that sending them has other meanings." He answered her eyebrows. "It has been happening to others recently. The family is sent to Russia and the man stays behind expecting to join them but . . . well, he never does." He devoured two of the mushrooms, washed them down with bourbon, put his elbows on the table, and leaned forward. "The Soviets become more paranoid every day here in Hungary."

"About what?"

"About what? About security, about leaks to your people. Having the families in Russia is a way to control certain . . . how shall I say? . . . certain questionable individuals."

"Are you now considered 'questionable'?"

"I didn't think so, but this move of my family and talk of moving me . . . Who knows? Do you mind?" He indicated his empty glass.

"Of course not, but put the ice in first," she said lightly. She'd been growing increasingly concerned about his drinking. Almost the entire bottle had been consumed last time, and he was quite drunk when he left.

He returned to the table and sipped from his fresh drink. "I have news for you, Collette. What did you call your request last time—an RQM?"

"Yes, a requirement. What is the news?"

"They know more than your people perhaps realize."

"About Banana Quick?"

"Yes. That island they've taken has been doing its job. The surveillance equipment on it is their best, and they've recruited native people who have been passing on information about your activities."

The Russians had leased the private island in the British Virgins from its owner, a multimillionaire British real estate developer who was told it was to be used as a rest-and-recreation area for tired, high-ranking Soviet bureaucrats. The U.S. State Department, upon learning of this and after hurried conferences with the CIA, approached him and asked that he reconsider. He wouldn't. The deal went through and the Russians moved in.

A further assessment was made then by State and Central Intelligence. Their conclusion: The Soviets could not move in enough sophisticated equipment and staff in time to effectively monitor Banana Quick, nor had they enough agents in place to build an effective corps of citizen-spies.

"Can you be more specific?" Cahill asked.

"Of course." He pulled papers from his rumpled black suit jacket and handed them to her. She laid them flat on the table and started reading. When she was done with the first page, she looked up at him and allowed a tiny whistle to come through her lips. "They know a lot, don't they?"

"Yes. These dispatches arrived from the island outpost. It was all I felt I could safely take—and bring with me. I return them in the morning. However, I have seen many more and have done my best to commit them to memory. Shall I begin?"

Cahill looked to the wall that concealed the cameras and recorders. Hegedüs knew they were there and often joked about them, but they remained shielded from his view, the sight of such instruments providing neither inspiration nor incentive. She prompted him to start before more of the bourbon disappeared and his memory with it.

He talked, drank, ate, and recalled for three hours. Cahill focused on everything he said, making notes to herself despite knowing every word was being recorded. Transcripts seldom provide nuance. She pushed him for details, kept him going when he seemed ready to fade, complimented, cajoled, stroked, and encouraged.

"Anything else?" she asked once he'd sat back, lighted a cigarette, and allowed a permanent smile of satisfaction to form on his thick lips.

"No, I think that is all." He suddenly raised his index finger and sat up. "No, I am wrong, there is more. The name of a man you know has come up."

"What man? I know him?"

"Yes. The psychiatrist who is involved with your *Company*."

"You mean Tolker?" She was instantly furious at herself for mentioning the name. Maybe he didn't mean him. If so, she'd given the name of a CIA-connected physician to the other side. It was a relief to hear him say, "Yes, that is the one. Dr. Jason Tolker."

"What about him?"

"I'm not really sure, Collette, but his name was mentioned briefly in connection with one of the dispatches from our island listening post about Banana Quick."

"Was it positive? I mean, were they saying that . . . ?"

"They said nothing specific. It was the tone of the voices, the context in which it was said that led me to believe that Dr. Tolker might be . . . *friendly*."

"To you. To the Soviets."

"Yes."

Cahill had forgotten about Barrie during the session. Now her image filled the room. She wasn't sure how to respond to what Hegedüs had said, so said nothing.

"I am afraid I am becoming an expensive friend to you and your people, Collette. Look, the bourbon is all but finished."

She resisted mentioning that it always was, said instead, "There's always more to replace it, Árpád. But not to replace you. Tell me, how are things with you personally?"

"I shall miss my family but . . . perhaps this is the time to bring up what is on my mind."

"Go ahead."

"I have been thinking, I have been feeling lately that the time might be approaching for me to consider becoming one of you."

"You are. You know that. . . ." She observed him shaking his head. He was smiling.

"You mean time to defect to our side?"

"Yes."

"I don't know about that, Árpád. As I told you when that subject came up before, it isn't something I deal with."

"But you said you would talk to those in charge about the possibility."

"Yes, I did." She didn't want to tell him that the discussion with Podgorsky and with two people from Langley had resulted in a flat denial. Their attitude was that Árpád Hegedüs was valuable to them as long as he remained ensconced in the Hungarian and Soviet hierarchy and could provide information from the inner councils. As a defector, he was useless. Of course, if it meant saving him in the event he'd been uncovered by his superiors, that would create a different scenario; but Cahill had been instructed in no uncertain terms that she was to do everything in her power to dissuade him from such a move, and to foster his continued services as an agent.

"It was not met with enthusiasm, I take it," he said.

"It isn't that, Árpád, it's just that—"

"That I am worth more where I am."

She drew a breath and fell back in her chair. It was naive of her to think he wouldn't know exactly the reason without being told. He worked for an organization, the KGB, that played by the same rules, operated from the same set of needs and intelligence philosophies.

"Don't look worried, Collette. I do understand. And I intend to continue functioning as I have. But, if the need arises, it would be comforting to me and my family to know that the possibility was there."

"I appreciate your understanding, Árpád, and I shall bring it up with my people again."

"I am grateful. Well, what do you say, 'One for the road'? I shall have one, and then the road, and then home."

"I'll join you."

They sat in silence at the table and sipped from their drinks. His smile was gone; a sadness that pulled down the flesh of his face had replaced it.

"You're more upset about your family going to Moscow than you want to admit," she said.

He nodded, eyes on his glass. He grunted, looked up, and said, "I have never told you about my family, about my dear children."

Collette smiled. "No, you haven't, except that your daughter is very beautiful and sweet, and that your son is a fine boy."

There was a flicker of a smile, then gloom again. "My son is a genius, a very bright boy. He is sensitive and loves artistic things." He leaned forward and spoke with renewed animation. "You should see how the boy draws and paints, Collette. Beauty, always such beauty, and the poetry he writes touches me so deeply."

"You must be very proud," Collette said.

"Proud? Yes. And concerned for his future."

"Because—"

"Because in Russia, he will have little chance to develop his talents. For the girl, my daughter, it is not so bad. She will marry because she is pretty. For him . . ." He shook his head and finished his drink.

Cahill was tempted to come around and hug him. Any initial thoughts of the chauvinistic attitude he'd expressed were tempered by her understanding of the society in which he, and his family, functioned.

She thought, then said, "It would be better for your son here in Hungary, wouldn't it?"

"Yes, there is more freedom here, but who knows when that will end? America would be best. I am not a religious man, Collette, but I sometimes pray to someone that my son will be allowed to grow up in America."

"As I said before, Árpád, I'll try to . . ."

He wanted to continue, and did. "When I first came to you and offered my services, I talked about how my beloved Hungary had been destroyed by the Soviets. I talked of disgust with their system and ways, of how this wonderful country has been forevermore changed by them." He sighed deeply, sat back, and nodded in agreement with whatever he was thinking at the moment. "I was not completely honest, Collette. I came to you because I wanted to find a way to see my family—my son—reach America. Instead, he goes to Moscow."

Cahill stood. "Árpád, I will make every effort to help bring that about. No promises, but a decent effort."

He stood, too, and extended his hand. She took it. "Thank you,

Collette. I know you will do what you say. I have been here a long time. I must go."

He was paid and she escorted him to the door. She said, "Árpád, be careful. Don't take risks. Please."

"Of course not." He looked back to the center of the room. "The tape and camera are off?"

"I assume they are. The main show is over."

He motioned her into the hall and spoke in a whisper, so close to her ear that his lips touched it. "I am in love."

"In . . . love?"

"I have met a wonderful woman recently and . . ."

"I don't think that's a good idea," Cahill said.

"Good idea, bad idea, it has happened. She is very beautiful and we have commenced . . . an affair."

Collette wasn't sure what to say, except, "What about your family, Árpád? You say you love them so much and . . ."

His grin was sheepish, a little boy caught in a quandary. His eyes averted her and he shuffled his feet. Then he looked at her and said, "There are different forms of love, Collette. Surely, that reality is not a Socialist aberration." He cocked his head and waited for a response.

Cahill said, "We should meet again soon and discuss this. In the meantime, take extra care. Discuss what you're doing with no one. No one, Árpád."

"With her?" His laugh was guttural. "We have so little time together that discussion is the last thing on our minds. *Köszönöm*, Collette."

"Thank *you*, Árpád."

"Until the next time a tack appears in the pole. *Viszontlátásra!*"

Rule Six: Do anything you can to keep your agent from having an affair —at least with anyone else.

5

COLLETTE CAHILL got off a Malev flight in London, went to a phone booth, and dialed a number. A woman answered, "Eleven, Cadogan Gardens."

"My name is Collette Cahill. I was a close friend of Barrie Mayer."

"Oh, yes, what a tragedy. I'm so sorry."

"Yes, we were all terribly shocked. I've just arrived in London for a few days' vacation and wondered if you had any available rooms?"

"Yes, we do, a few suites as a matter of fact. Oh, goodness."

"What?"

"Number 27 is available. It was Miss Mayer's favorite."

"Yes, that's right, she always talked about it. That would be fine with me."

"You wouldn't mind . . . ?"

"Staying where she'd stayed? No, not at all. I'll be there within the hour."

She spent the first hour sitting in the Victorian living room and imagining what Barrie had done the last day and night of her life while in London. Had she watched television, gone across to the private park, read, called friends, napped, walked the pretty, quiet streets of Chelsea and Belgravia, shopped for relatives back home? It eventually became too sad an exercise. She went downstairs to the main drawing room and flipped through an array of magazines and newspapers, then caught the attention of one of the hall porters. "Yes, ma'am?" he said.

"I was a very good friend of Miss Mayer, the lady who'd stayed in Number 27 and who recently died."

"Poor Miss Mayer. She was one of my favorite guests whenever she was here, a real lady. We're all terribly sad at what happened."

"I was wondering whether she did anything special the day she arrived, the day before she died?"

"Special? No, not really. I brought her tea at three . . . let me see, yes, I'm quite certain it was three o'clock the afternoon she arrived. We made a reservation for her that evening at the Dorchester for dinner."

"For how many people?"

"Two. Yes, for two. I can check."

"No, that's all right. Did she take a taxi, or did someone pick her up?"

"She took the limousine."

"*The* limousine?"

"Ours. It's available to our guests twenty-four hours a day."

"Did the limousine pick her up at the Dorchester?"

"I don't know, madam. I wasn't here that evening when she returned, but I can ask."

"Would you mind?"

"Of course not."

He returned a few minutes later and said, "To the best of recollection, Miss Mayer returned a little before ten that evening. She arrived by taxi."

"Alone?"

He looked at the floor. "I'm not sure, madam, whether that would be discreet to comment upon."

Cahill smiled. "I'm not snooping. It's just that we were such good friends and her mother back in the States asked me to find out what I could about her daughter's last hours."

"Of course. I understand. Let me ask."

He returned again and said, "She was alone. She announced she was going straightaway to bed and left an early call. That was the morning she was leaving for Hungary, I believe."

"Yes, that's right, to Budapest. Tell me, didn't the police come and ask questions about her?"

"Not to my knowledge. They came and took her things from the room and . . ."

"Who's *they*?"

"Friends, business colleagues, I think. You'd have to ask the manager about that. They spoke to her. They took everything and were gone within ten minutes. The other one . . . there were three chaps . . . he stayed behind for at least an hour. I remember he said he wanted to sit where Miss Mayer had spent her last hours and think. Poor chap, I felt terrible for him."

"Did any of them have names?"

"I feel like I'm getting a proper interrogation," he said, not angrily but with enough of an edge to cause Cahill to back off. She smiled. "I guess so many people knew and loved her that we're not behaving in our usual manner. Sorry, I didn't mean to ask so many questions of you. I'll check with the manager a little later."

He returned the smile. "No problem, madam. I understand. Ask me anything you wish."

"Oh, I think I've asked enough. Did they have names, the men who came here and took her things?"

"Not that I recall. They might have muttered something or other but . . . Yes, one of them said he was a business associate of Miss Mayer. I believe he said his name was Mr. Hubler."

"David Hubler?"

"I don't think he used a first name, madam."

"What did he look like? Was he fairly short, dark, lots of black curly hair, handsome?"

"That doesn't quite fit my memory of him, madam. Tall and sandy would be more like it."

Cahill sighed and said, "Well, thank you so much. I think I'll go back upstairs and take a nap."

"May I bring you anything? Tea at three?"

Like Barrie, Cahill thought. "No, make it four," she said. "Yes, madam."

She called David Hubler a few minutes before tea was scheduled to arrive. It was almost eleven in the morning in Washington. "David, Collette Cahill."

"Hi, Collette."

"I'm calling from London, David. I'm staying in the same hotel Barrie always used."

"Eleven, Cadogan. What are you doing there?"

"Trying to sort out my mind about what happened. I took a vacation and am heading home, but thought I'd stop here on the way."

There was silence.

"David?"

"Yeah, sorry. I was just thinking about Barrie. Unbelievable."

"Have you been here in London since she died?"

"Me? No. Why?"

"Someone at the hotel thought you might have been the one who picked up her things from the room."

"Not me, Collette."

"Were any of her things sent back to you at the office?"

"Just her briefcase."

"Her briefcase. Was it the one she usually carried?"

"Sure. Why?"

"Oh, nothing. What was in it?"

"Papers, a couple of manuscripts. Why are you asking?"

"I don't know, David. My mind just hasn't functioned since you called me with the news. What's happening back there? The agency must be in chaos."

"Sort of, although not as bad as you might think. Barrie was incredible, Collette, but you know that. She left everything in perfect order, right down to the last detail. You know what she did for me?"

"What?"

"She had me in her will. She left me insurance money, one of those key-man policies. In effect, she left me the agency."

Cahill was surprised, enough so that she wasn't quite sure what to say. He filled the gap with, "I don't mean she left it all to me, Collette. Her mother benefits from it, but she structured things so that I'm to run it for a minimum of five years and share in the profits. I was flabbergasted."

"That was wonderful of her."

"Typical of her is more like it. When will you be back in Washington?"

"A day or two. I'll stop by."

"Please do, Collette. Let's have lunch or dinner. There's a lot we can talk about."

"I'd like that. By the way, do you have any idea who she might have seen here in London before . . . before it happened?"

"Sure, Mark Hotchkiss. They were scheduled for dinner the night she arrived."

"Who's he?"

"A British literary agent Barrie liked. Why, I don't know. I think he's a swine and I told her so but, for some reason, she kept talking to him about linking up. With all Barrie's brights, Collette, there were certain people who could con her, and Hotchkiss is one."

"Know how I can reach him while I'm here?"

"Sure." He gave her an address and phone number. "But watch out for him, Collette. Remember, I said swine, *cochon*."

"Thanks, David. See you soon."

She replaced the phone in its cradle as the porter knocked. She opened the door. He placed the tea tray on a coffee table and backed out of the suite, leaving her sitting in a gold wingback chair. She wore a light blue robe; shafts of late-afternoon sunlight sliced through gaps in the white curtains and across the worn Oriental rug that took up the center of the room. One beam of light striped her bare foot and she thought of Barrie, who was always so proud of her feet, gently arched and with long, slender toes that were perfectly sized in relation to each other. Cahill looked at her own foot, short and stubby, and smiled, then laughed. "God, we were different," she said aloud as she poured her tea and smeared clotted cream and black cherry jam over a piece of scone.

She caught Mark Hotchkiss just as he was leaving his office, introduced herself, and asked if he were free for dinner.

"Afraid not, Miss Cahill."

"Breakfast?"

"You say you're Barrie's friend?"

"Yes, we were best friends."

"She never mentioned you."

"Were you that friendly that she would have?"

His laugh was forced. He said, "I suppose we could meet for something in the morning. You have a decent place near you on Sloane Street, right around the corner. It's a café in back of the General Trading Company. Nine?"

"Fine. See you then."

"Miss Cahill."

"Yes?"

"You do know that Barrie and I had entered into a partnership arrangement just prior to her death?"

"No, I didn't know that, but I was aware it was being discussed. Why do you bring it up now?"

"Why not bring it up *now*?"

"No reason. You can tell me all about it in the morning. I look forward to it."

"Yes. Well, cheerio. Pleasant evening. Enjoy London. The theater season is quite good this year."

She hung up agreeing with David Hubler. She didn't like Hotchkiss, and wondered what aspect of him had seduced Barrie into entering a "partnership agreement," if that claim were true.

She called downstairs and asked if they could get her tickets to a show. Which one? "It doesn't matter," Cahill said, "something happy."

The curtain went up on *Noises Off* at seven-thirty, and by the time the British farce was over, Cahill's sides hurt from laughing, and the unpleasant reason for her trip had been forgotten, at least for the duration of the show. She was hungry, had a light dinner at the Neal Street Restaurant, and returned to the hotel. A porter brought Cognac and ice to her room and she sat quietly and sipped it until her eyes began to close. She went to bed, aware as she fell asleep of the absolute quiet of this street and this hotel, as quiet as the dead.

6

CAHILL ARRIVED on time at the General Trading Company, whose coat of arms heralded the fact that it had provided goods to at least one royal household. She took a table in the rear outdoor area. The morning had dawned sunny and mild. A raincoat over a heather tweed suit made her perfectly comfortable.

She passed the time with a cup of coffee and watching tiny birds make swooping sorties on uncovered bowls of brown sugar cubes on the tables. She glanced at her watch; Hotchkiss was already twenty minutes late. She'd give it ten more minutes. At precisely nine-thirty, he came through the store and stepped onto the terrace. He was tall and angular. His head was bald on top, but he'd combed back long hair on the sides, giving him the startling appearance of—not swine, David, she thought, duck—he looked like a duck's rear end. He wore a double-breasted blue blazer with a crest on its pocket, gray slacks, a pair of tan Clark's desert boots, a pale blue shirt with white collar, and a maroon silk tie. He carried a battered and bulging leather briefcase beneath his arm. A similarly well-worn trench coat was slung over his shoulder.

"Miss Cahill," he said with energy. He smiled and extended his hand, his teeth markedly yellow, and she noticed immediately that his fingernails were too long and needed cleaning.

"Mr. Hotchkiss," she said, taking his hand with her fingertips.

"Sorry I'm late but traffic is bastardly this hour. You've had coffee. Good."

Cahill stifled a smile and watched him ease into a white metal chair with yellow cushions. "Not chilly?" he asked. "Better inside?"

"Oh, no, I think it's lovely out here."

"As you wish." He made an elaborate gesture at one of the young waitresses, who came to the table and took their order for coffee and pastry. When she'd gone, he sat back, formed a tent beneath his chin with his fingers, and said, "Well, now, we're obviously here to discuss Barrie Mayer, poor dear, may she rest in peace. You were friends, you say?"

"Yes, close friends."

"She never mentioned you, but I suppose someone like Barrie had so many friends or, at least, acquaintances."

"We were close *friends*," Cahill said, not enjoying his inference.

"Yes, of course. Now, what was it you wished to discuss with me?"

"Your relationship with Barrie, what she did the night before she died, anything that might help me understand."

"Understand? Understand *what*? The poor woman dropped dead of a heart attack, coronary thrombosis, premature certainly but Lord knows what life has in store for any of us."

Cahill had to remind herself of her "official" role in looking into Mayer's life. She was a grieving friend, not an investigator, and her approach would have to soften to reflect that. She said, "I'm actually as interested for Barrie's mother's sake as I am for my own. We've been in contact and she asked me to find out anything that would . . . well, comfort her. I'm on my way to Washington now to see her."

"What do you do for a living, Miss Cahill? I know that's hardly a British question, more what you Americans seem always to ask at first meeting, but I am curious."

"I work for the United States Embassy in Budapest."

"Budapest! I've never been. Is it as gray and grim as we hear?"

"Not at all. It's a lovely city."

"With all those soldiers and red stars."

"They fade into the background after a while. You had dinner with Barrie the night before she died."

"Indeed, at the Dorchester. Despite the Arabs, it still has London's finest chef."

"I wouldn't know."

"You must let me take you. Tonight?"

"I can't, but thank you. What mood was Barrie in that night? What did she say, do? Did she seem sick?"

"She was in the pink of health, Miss Cahill. May I call you Collette? I'm Mark, of course."

"Of course." She laughed. "Yes, call me Collette. You say she seemed healthy. Was she happy?"

"Irrepressibly so. I mean, after all, we forged a partnership that evening. She was bubbling."

"You mentioned on the phone that you'd become partners. I spoke with David Hubler in Barrie's Washington office. He had no idea it had gone that far."

"David Hubler. I dislike being indiscreet but I must admit Mr. Hubler is not my favorite person. Frankly, I thought he was a stone about Barrie's neck, and I told her so."

"I like David. I always understood from Barrie that she was extremely fond of him, and had great professional respect for him."

"Besides being a consummate businesswoman, Barrie Mayer was also gullible."

Cahill thought of Hubler saying the same thing. She said to Hotchkiss, "Mark, are you aware of Barrie's will and what it contains relative to David Hubler?"

"No." He laughed loudly, revealing the yellowed teeth. "Oh, you mean that nonsense about ensuring that Hubler runs the Washington office if she should die. A bone, that's all, a bone tossed at him. Now that the agency . . . *all of it* . . . passes to me, the question of Mr. Hubler's future has little to do with a piece of worthless paper."

"Why?"

"Because the agreement Barrie and I entered into takes precedence over what was decreed before." He smiled smugly and formed the finger tent again. The waitress delivered their coffee and pastry and Hotchkiss held up his cup. "To the memory of a lovely, talented, and beautiful woman, Barrie Mayer, and to you, Miss Collette Cahill, her dear friend." He sipped his coffee, then asked, "Are you truly not free this evening? The Dorchester has a very nice dance band and, as I said, the chef is without parallel in London these days of mediocre food. Sure?" He cocked his head and elevated one bushy eyebrow.

"Sure, but thank you. You signed a paper with Barrie that night?"

"Yes."

"May I . . . I know this is none of my business, but . . ."

"I'm afraid it would be inappropriate at this time for me to show it to you. Are you doubting me?"

"Not at all. Again, it's just a matter of wanting to know *everything* about her just before she died. Did you go to the airport with her the next morning?"

"No."

"I just thought . . ."

"I dropped Barrie back at the hotel. That was the last time I saw her."

"In a taxi?"

"Yes. My goodness, I'm beginning to feel as though you might have an interest beyond that of a close friend."

Cahill grinned. "The hall porter at the hotel said the same thing. Forgive me. Too many years of asking stranded American tourists where they might have lost their passports."

"Is that what you do at the embassy?"

"Among other things. Well, Mark, this was extremely pleasant."

"And informative, I trust. I'll be coming to Washington soon to tidy up things at the agency. Do you know where you'll be staying?"

"With my mother. She lives outside the city."

"Splendid. I shall call you there."

"Why not contact me through David Hubler? I'll be spending considerable time with him."

"Oh, I think I've placed one foot in one very large mouth."

"Not at all." She stood. "Thank you."

He stood, too, and accepted her hand. They both looked down at the check the waitress had placed on the table. "My treat," Cahill said, knowing it was what he wanted her to say.

"Oh, no, that would be . . ."

"Please. I initiated this. Perhaps I'll see you in Washington."

"I certainly hope so."

Hotchkiss left. Cahill stopped on her way through the large store to buy her mother a set of fancy placemats, and a book for her nephew. She walked around the corner to the hotel, where she made a series of calls to the physicians who'd performed the autopsy on Barrie and whose names she'd gotten from Red Sutherland before leaving Budapest. The only one she reached was a Dr. Willard Hymes. She introduced herself as Barrie Mayer's closest friend and asked if she could arrange to meet with him.

"Whatever for?" he asked. He sounded young.

"Just to put my mind, and her mother's mind, at rest."

"Well, Miss Cahill, you know I'm not at liberty to discuss autopsy findings except with designated authorities."

Pickle Factory authorities, Cahill thought. She said, "I understand that, Dr. Hymes, but it wouldn't breach any confidences if you were to tell me the circumstances of the autopsy, your informal, off-the-record reactions to her, what she looked like, things like that."

"No, Miss Cahill, that would be quite out of the question. Thank you for calling."

Cahill said quickly, "I was concerned about the glass that was found in her face."

"Pardon?"

Cahill continued. She'd read up on past cases in which prussic acid had been used to "terminate" agents on both sides. One of the telltale signs was tiny slivers of glass blown into a victim's face along with the acid. "Dr. Hymes, there was glass in her face."

She was guessing, but had drawn blood. He made a few false starts before getting out, "Who told you about the glass?"

That was all she needed, wanted. She said, "A mutual friend who'd been at the airport and saw her just after she died."

"I didn't know there was a friend with her."

"Were you at the airport?"

"No. She was brought here to clinic and . . ."

"Dr. Hymes, I really appreciate the chance to talk with you. You've been very generous with your time and I know Barrie's mother will appreciate it."

She hung up, sat at a small desk near the French windows, and wrote a list of names on a piece of the hotel's embossed buff stationery:

KNEW BARRIE CARRIED FOR THE CIA

Dr. Jason Tolker
Stanley Podgorsky
Red Sutherland
Collette Cahill
Langley Desk Officer
Dr. Willard Hymes
Mark Hotchkiss ???
David Hubler ???
Barrie's mother ???
Eric Edwards ???
Zoltán Réti ???
KGB ???
Others ??? Other boyfriends—Others at literary agency—Others at Budapest station—The World.

She squinted at what she'd written, tore the paper into tiny pieces and ignited them in an ashtray. She called downstairs and told the manager on duty that she'd be leaving the following morning.

"I hope you've enjoyed your stay," the manager said.

"Oh, yes, very much," Cahill said. "It's every bit as lovely as Miss Mayer always said it was."

7

THE TWIN-ENGINE turboprop Air BVI plane from San Juan touched down on Beef Island and taxied to the small terminal. Thirty passengers deplaned, including Robert Brewster and his wife, Helen. Both looked tired and wilted. There had been a delay in San Juan, and the Air BVI flight had been hot; tiny fans installed in the open overhead racks had managed only to stir the warm, humid cabin air.

The Brewsters passed through passport control and Customs, then went to a yellow Mercedes parked behind the terminal. Helen Brewster got in. Her husband said to the native driver, "Just a few minutes." He went to a pay phone, took out a slip of paper, and dialed the number on it. "I'm calling Eric Edwards," he told the woman who answered. "He's dining with you tonight."

A few minutes later, Edwards came on the line.

"Eric, it's Bob Brewster."

"Hello, Bob. Just get in?"

"Yes."

"Pleasant trip?"

"Not especially. Helen isn't feeling well and I'm beat. The heat."

"Well, a nice week's vacation down here will straighten you out."

"I'm sure it will. We're looking forward to seeing you again."

"Same here. We must get together."

"I was thinking we could catch up for a drink this evening. We'll go to the hotel and freshen up and . . ."

"I'm tied up this evening, Bob. How about tomorrow? I have a free day. We'll take a cruise, my treat."

Brewster didn't bother, nor did he have the energy to argue. He said, "I can't speak for Helen. Call me in the morning. We're staying at Prospect Reef."

"Give my best to the manager there," Edwards said. "He's a friend, might even buy you a welcoming drink."

"I'll do that. Call me at eight."

"It'll have to be later. I'm in for a long evening."

"Eric."

"Yes?"

"Life has become very complicated lately."

"Has it? That must be why you and Helen are so tired. Simplicity is far less fatiguing. We'll talk about it tomorrow."

Eric Edwards returned to a candlelit table in the Sugar Mill Restaurant, part of a small and exclusive resort complex on Apple Bay. Across from him sat a tall, stately blond woman of about thirty-five who wore a low-cut white silk dress. Because her skin was deeply tanned, it contrasted sharply with the white dress, like teeth against the natives' dark skin. It had taken her many hours in the sun to become that color. Her skin, especially the tops of her breasts, hinted at the leathery texture it would turn to by sixty.

Her nails were long and painted an iridescent pink. Her fingers held large rings, and ten slender gold bracelets covered each wrist.

Edwards was dressed in white duck slacks, white loafers sans socks, and a crimson shirt worn open to his navel. His hair—sun-bleached blond with gray at the temples so perfectly blended that it might have come from a Hollywood makeup expert—swirled casually over his forehead, ears, and neck. The features on his tanned face were fine and angular, yet with enough coarseness to keep him from being pretty. There was sufficient worldly weariness and booze in his gray eyes to give them substance and meaning.

Eric Edwards was a handsome man, no matter what the criterion. Ask Morgana Wilson who sat across from him. Someone had, recently. "He's the most sensuous, appealing male animal I've ever known," she told a friend, "and I've known a few in my day."

Edwards smiled up at the waiter as he removed bowls that had contained curried banana soup, a house specialty. Edwards ordered another rum punch, reached across the table, and ran his fingers over the top of Morgana's hand. "You usually look beautiful. Tonight, you look spectacular," he said.

She was used to such compliments and simply said, "Thank you, darling."

They said little as they enjoyed their entrees—pasta with lime cream and red caviar, and grilled fish with fennel butter. There was little to say. Their purpose was not to exchange thoughts, only to establish an atmosphere conducive to the mating game. It wasn't new to them. They'd spent a number of intimate evenings together over the past four or five years.

She'd met Edwards during a trip to the BVI with her husband, a successful New York divorce lawyer. They'd chartered one of Edwards's yachts for an overnight cruise. Her husband returned to New York after only a few days in the islands, leaving Morgana behind to soak up a few additional days of sun. She spent them with Edwards on one of his yachts.

Six months afterward, she was divorced, and Edwards was cited as having been caught in *particeps crimini*—a corespondent to the action. "Ridiculous," he'd told her. "Your marriage was damn near over anyway." Which was true, although his powerful attraction had certainly played a role.

They saw each other no more than three or four times a year, always when she visited him in the BVI. As far as she knew, he never came to New York. In fact, he never called her when he was there. There were others to contact on those trips.

"Ready?" he asked, when she'd finished the soursop fruit ice cream and coffee.

"Always," she said.

The alarm clock next to Edwards's bed buzzed them awake at six the next morning. Morgana sat up, folded her arms across her bountiful bare breasts, and pouted. "It's too early," she said.

"Sorry, love, but I've got a charter today. I have to provision it and take care of some other things before my guests arrive." His voice was thick with sleep, and raspy from too many cigarettes.

"Will you be back tonight?"

"I think so, although you never know. Sometimes they fall in love with the boat and decide to stay out overnight."

"Or fall in love with you. Can I come?"

"No." He got out of bed and crossed the large bedroom, tripping over her discarded clothing on the floor. She watched him as he stood before one of two large windows with curved tops, the first rays of sunrise casting interesting patterns over his long, lean naked body.

"I have to leave tomorrow," she said in a little girl's voice that always grated on him.

"Yes, I know. I'll miss you."

"Will you?" She joined him at the window and they looked down from his hilltop villa to Road Harbor, the site of his chartering operation. Edwards Yacht Charters was a small company compared to the Moorings, the reigning giant of island chartering, but it had managed to do well, thanks to some innovative PR a one-man agency in New York had conceived and implemented for it. Edwards currently owned three yachts—a Morgan 46, a Gulfstar 60, and a recently purchased, Frers-designed 43-foot sloop. Finding customers in season for them wasn't difficult. Finding experienced, trustworthy captains and mates was.

She turned him so they faced and wrapped her arms about his body. She was tall; the top of her head reached his nose, and he was over six feet. The warmth of her naked body, and the damp, sweet smell of sex in her hair radiated powerfully in surges through him. "I really have to go," he said.

"So do I. I'll be back in a flash," she said, heading for the stone bathroom that was open to the sky. When she returned, he was back in bed and ready for her.

Edwards's mechanic, a skinny Tortolian named Walter who was capable of fixing anything, was on board when Edwards arrived. Native *kareso* music blared from a large portable cassette recorder. As Edwards poked his head down into the engine room, Walter said, "*Laam*, I work on this engine all night long."

Edwards laughed and mimicked him. "*Laam*, I really don't care, and I'm not paying you extra. How about that, my conniving friend?"

Walter laughed and closed a cover over the engine. "How about the boat don't run so good today, huh? How about that, my rich boss?"

"*Laam*, or Lord, or whatever it is you say, don't do that to me, and turn down the bloody radio."

The good-natured banter was standard. Edwards knew that Walter would turn himself inside out to please him, and Walter knew that Edwards appreciated him, and would slip him extra pay.

Edwards had called Robert Brewster and arranged to meet him at the dock at ten. Brewster arrived wearing madras Bermuda shorts, a white button-down shirt, high-top white sneakers, and black ankle socks. He carried a canvas flight bag. His legs were white; this would be the first exposure to sunlight they'd received all year.

"No snorkeling equipment today, huh?" Walter said to Edwards after observing the new arrival.

"No, not today," Edwards said. "Where's Jackie?"

"I see her at the coffee shop. She be down." Jackie was a native girl Edwards sometimes used to crew smaller charters. She was willing, energetic, a good sailor, and almost totally deaf. They communicated through a pidgin sign language they'd developed. She arrived a few minutes later and Edwards introduced her to Brewster, who seemed distinctly uncomfortable standing on the deck. "She doesn't hear anything," Edwards said. "If her father only owned a liquor store I'd be tempted to . . ."

"Could we get on with it?" Brewster said. "I want to get back to Helen."

"Sure. She still under the weather?"

"Yes. The heat."

"I like heat," said Edwards. "It makes you sweat—for the right reasons. Let's get going."

Fifteen minutes later, after they'd cleared the channel, Edwards hoisted sail with Jackie's help. Once everything was trimmed, he turned to Brewster, who sat next to him at the helm, and said, "What's up? What did you mean things are getting complicated?"

Brewster smiled at Jackie as she delivered a steaming cup of coffee from the galley. Edwards shook his head when she offered one to him and told her with his hands that he and his guest needed time to be alone. She nodded, grinned at Brewster, and disappeared down the galley ladder.

Brewster tasted his coffee, made a face, and said, "Too hot and too strong, Eric . . . and I don't intend to say it reflects you. All right, what's going on down here?"

"With what?"

"You know what I mean. With Banana Quick."

"Oh, *that*." He laughed and turned a winch behind him to take up slack in a sail. "As far as I'm concerned, everything's just wonderful with Banana Quick. You hear otherwise?"

"It isn't so much what I hear, Eric, it's more a matter of what's blatantly visible. The death of Miss Mayer has a lot of people upset."

"None more than me. We were close."

"Everyone knows that, and that's exactly what has people back at Langley wondering."

"Wondering about what? How she was in bed?"

Brewster shook his head and shifted on his seat so that his back was to Edwards. He said over the gentle rush of wind and whoosh of water over the keel, "Your cuteness, Eric, doesn't play well these days."

Edwards had to lean close to him to hear. Brewster suddenly turned and said into his face, "What was Barrie Mayer carrying to Budapest?"

Edwards leaned back and frowned. "How the hell would I know?"

"It's the opinion at Langley, Eric, that you damn well might know. She'd been down here to see you just before she died, hadn't she?"

Edwards shrugged. "A couple of days, something like that."

"One week exactly. Would you like her itinerary?"

"Got videos of us making love, too?"

Brewster ignored him. "And then *you* disappeared."

"Disappeared where?"

"You tell me. London?"

"As a matter of fact I did pop over there for a day. I had a . . ." He smiled. "I had an appointment."

"With Barrie Mayer?"

"No. She didn't know I was there."

"That's surprising."

"Why?"

"It's our understanding that you had become serious."

"You understand wrong. We were friends, close friends, and lovers. End of story."

Brewster chewed his cheek and said, "I don't want to be the rude guest, Eric, but you'd better listen to what I have to say. There is considerable concern that Banana Quick might have been compromised by Barrie Mayer, with your help."

"That's crap." Edwards pointed toward the private island on which the Russians had established their supposed R & R facility. "Want to stop in and ask them what's going on?"

Brewster moved to the side of the yacht and peered at the island. Edwards handed him a pair of binoculars. "Don't worry," he said, "they're used to me looking down their throats. See all that rigging on the roof? They can probably hear us better than we can hear each other." He laughed. "This game gets more ridiculous every day."

"Only for people like you, Eric." Brewster held up the binoculars and watched the island slip past. He lowered them, turned, and said, "They want you back in Washington."

"What for?"

"For . . . conversation."

"Can't do it. This is the busy season down here, Bob. How would it look if I . . . ?"

"The end of the week, and don't give me 'busy season' dialogue, Eric. You're here because you were put here. This wonderful boat of yours, and the others, are all compliments of your employer. You're to be back by the end of the week. In the meantime, they want us . . . you and I . . . to spend a little time together going over things."

"What things?"

"What's been going on in your life lately, the status of your mission here, the people you've been seeing . . ."

"Like Barrie Mayer?"

"Among others."

"How come they sent you down, Bob? You're a desk jockey . . . what's it called, employee evaluation or some nonsense like that?"

"Helen and I decided to come here on vacation and they thought—"

"No, they thought you and Helen should come here on vacation and, while you're here, have these little talks. More accurate?"

"It doesn't matter. The fact is that I'm here, they want, and you are expected to give. What do you think, Eric—that the Company set you up here in the British Virgin Islands because it likes you, felt it owed you something? You pulled off what I consider the biggest coup . . . no, let's call it what it is, the biggest scam anyone has ever pulled on the agency."

Edwards's laugh was more forced this time.

"What did they put up to get you started, Eric, a half a million, three quarters of a million?"

"Somewhere around there."

"It hasn't been cost-effective."

"Cost-effective?" Edwards guffawed. "Name me one agency front that's cost-effective. Besides, how do you measure the return?"

Brewster stared straight ahead.

"Whose idea was it to use the BVI as headquarters for Banana Quick?" He didn't wait for Brewster's reply. "Some genius up there at Langley decides to direct an Eastern European operation from down here. Talk to me about cost-effective. The point is that once that decision was made, there had to be a surveillance unit in place, and that's me."

"You were here before Banana Quick."

"Sure, but I have to figure it was already in the planning stages when the deal was made to send me here. What was the original reason, to make sure that these idyllic islands weren't infiltrated by the bad guys? I had to laugh at that, Bob. What they really wanted was to keep tabs on our British cousins."

"You talk too much, Eric. That's something else that has them worried. You operate too loose, get close to too many people, drink too much. . . ."

"What the hell have they appointed you, Company cleric? I do my job and I do it well. I did twelve years of dirty work while you guys basked in air conditioning at Langley, and I keep doing my job. Tell them that."

"Tell them yourself at the end of the week."

Edwards looked up into a scrim of pristine blue sky, against which puffs of white clouds quickly moved across their bow. "You had enough?" he asked.

"I was just beginning to enjoy it," Brewster answered.

"I'm getting seasick," Edwards said.

"Want a Dramamine? I took one at breakfast."

"You're getting sunburned, Bob."

"Look at you, a prime candidate for skin cancer." The two men stared at each other before Edwards said, "Tell me about Barrie Mayer."

"What's to tell? She's dead."

"Who?"

"Mother Nature. A clogged artery to the heart, blood flow ceases, the heart cries out for help, doesn't get it, and stops pumping."

Edwards smiled. Jackie came up from the galley and gestured. Did they need anything? Edwards said to Brewster, "You hungry? I stocked a few things."

"Sure. Whatever you have."

"Lunch," Edwards said to the slender native girl, using his hands. "And bring the Thermos." He said to Brewster, "It's full of rum punch. We can get drunk together and get candid."

"Too early for me."

"I've been up a while. Barrie Mayer, Bob. Why did you ask me what she was carrying? Her principal's the one to ask. It's still that shrink, Tolker."

"That bothers me."

"What bothers you?"

"That you know who her principal was. What else did she tell you?"

"Damn little. She never said a word about signing on as a courier until . . ."

"Until what?"

"Until somebody told her about me."

"That you're Company?"

"Yeah."

"Who was that?"

He shrugged.

* * *

Edwards thought back to the night Barrie Mayer told him she was aware that he was more than just a struggling charter boat owner and captain.

She'd come to the BVI for a week's vacation. Their affair had been in progress for a little more than a year and they'd managed to cram in a considerable amount of time together, considering the physical distance that separated them. Mayer flew to the BVI at every opportunity, and Edwards made a few trips to Washington to see her. They'd also met once in New York, and had spent an extended weekend together in Atlanta.

Seeing her get off the plane that day jolted him with the same intense feelings she always raised in him. There had been many women in his life, but few had the impact on him she did. His first wife had had that effect. So did his second, come to think of it, but none since . . . until Barrie Mayer.

He recalled that Barrie was in a particularly giddy mood that day. He asked her about it in his car on their way to his villa. She'd said, "I have a secret to share with you." When he asked what it was, she said it would have to wait for a "very special moment."

The moment occurred that night. They'd gone out on one of his yachts and anchored in a cove where they stripped off their clothes and dove into the clear, tepid water. After their swim—more aquatic embracing than swimming—they returned to the yacht and made love. After that he cooked island lobsters and they sat naked on the bleached deck, legs crossed, knees touching, fingers dripping with melted butter, a strong rum swizzle burning their bellies and tripping the switches that cause incessant laughter.

They decided to spend the night on the yacht. After they'd made love again and lay side by side on a bundle of folded sails, he said, "Okay, what's this big, dark secret you have to share with me?"

She'd dozed off. His words startled her awake. She purred and touched his thigh. "Eurosky," she said, or something so softly that he couldn't catch it. When he didn't respond, she turned on her side, propped her head on her elbow, looked down into his face, and said, "You're a spy."

His eyes narrowed. Still, he said nothing.

"You're with the CIA. That's why you're here in the BVI."

He asked quietly, "Who told you that?"

"A friend."

"What friend?"

"It doesn't matter."

"Why would anyone tell you that?"

"Because . . . well, I told . . . this person . . . about you and me and . . ."

"What about you and me?"

"That we've been seeing each other, that I . . . really want to hear?"

"Yes."

"That I'd fallen in love with you."

"Oh."

"That seems to upset you more than my knowing about what you do for a living."

"Maybe it does. Why would this *friend* even bring it up? Does he know me?"

"Yes. Well, not personally, but knows of you."

"Who does your friend work for?"

She started to feel uncomfortable, hadn't expected the intense questioning from him. She tried to lighten the moment by saying with a laugh, "I think it's wonderful. I think it's silly and wonderful and fun."

"What's fun about it?"

"That we have a mutual interest now. You don't care about my literary agency, and I don't care about your boats, except for enjoying being on them with you."

His raised eyebrows asked the next question. Mutual?

"I work for the CIA, too."

His eyebrows lowered. He sat up and looked at her until she said, "I'm a courier, just part time, but it's for the Company." She giggled. "I like the Pickle Factory better. It's . . ." She realized he was not sharing her frivolity. She changed her tone and said, "I can talk about it to you because . . ."

"You can talk about it to nobody."

"Eric, I . . ."

"What the hell do you think this is, Barrie, a game, cops and robbers, an exercise to inject more excitement into your life?"

"No, Eric, I don't think that. Why are you so angry? I thought I was doing something worthwhile for my country. I'm proud of it and I haven't told anyone except you and . . ."

"And your friend."

"Yes."

"And your friend told you about me."

"Only because she knew I was seeing you."

"It's a woman?"

"Yes, but that doesn't matter."

"What's her name?"

"I think under the circumstances that . . ."

"Who is she, Barrie? She's breached a very important confidence."

"Forget it, Eric. Forget I even mentioned it."

He got up and sat on the cabin roof. They said nothing to each other. The yacht swayed in the soft evening breeze. The sky above was dark, the stars pinpoints of white light through tiny holes in black canvas. "Tell me all about it," Edwards said.

"I don't think I should," she said, "not after that reaction."

"I was surprised, that's all," he said, smiling. "You told me you had a big surprise to share with me at an appropriate time and you weren't kidding." She stood next to him. He looked into her eyes and said, "I'm sorry I sounded angry." He put his arm around her and kissed her cheek. "How the hell did you end up working for the CIA?"

She told him.

8

San Francisco

DR. JASON TOLKER sat in his suite at the Mark Hopkins and dialed his Washington office. "Anything urgent?" he asked his receptionist.

"Nothing that can't wait." She read him a list of people who'd called, which included Collette Cahill.

"Where did she call from?" he asked.

"She left a number in Virginia."

"All right. I'll be back on schedule. I'll call again."

"Fine. How's the weather there?"

"Lovely."

It was two in the afternoon. Tolker had until six before his meeting in Sausalito. He put on a white cable-knit sweater, comfortable walking shoes, tossed his raincoat over his arm, posed for an admiring moment before a full-length mirror, then strolled down California Street to Chinatown, where he stopped in a dozen small food shops to peruse the vast array of foodstuffs. Among many of his interests was Chinese cooking. He considered himself a world-class Chinese chef, which wasn't far from true, although, as with many of his hobbies, he tended to overvalue his accomplishments. He also boasted a large collection of vintage jazz recordings. But, as a friend and devoted jazz buff often said, "The collection means more to Jason than the music."

He bought Chinese herbs that he knew he'd have trouble finding in Washington, or even in New York's Chinatown, and returned to the hotel. He showered, changed into one of many suits he had tailored by London's Tommy Nutter, went to the Top of the Mark, sat at a window table with a glass of club soda, and watched the fog roll in over the Golden Gate Bridge on its way to obscuring the city itself. Nice, he thought; appropriate. He checked his watch, paid, got into his rented Jaguar, and headed for the bridge and his appointment on the other side.

He drove through the streets of Sausalito, the lights of San Francisco across the bay appearing, then disappearing through the fog, and turned into a street that began as a residential area, then slowly changed to light industry. He pulled into a three-car paved parking lot next to a two-story white stucco building, turned off his engine and lights, and sat for a moment before getting out and approaching a side door that was painted red. He knocked, heard footsteps on an iron stairway, and stood back as the door was opened by an older man wearing a gray cardigan sweater over a maroon turtleneck. His pants were baggy and his shoes scuffed. His face was a mosaic of lumps and crevices. His hair was gray and uncombed. "Hello, Jason," he said.

"Bill," Tolker said as he stepped past him. The door closed with a thud. The two men walked up a staircase to the second floor. Dr. William Wayman opened a door to his large, cluttered office. Seated in it was a woman who Tolker judged to be in her mid-thirties. She was in a shadowed corner of the room, the only light on her face coming through a dirty window at the rear of the building.

"Harriet, this is the doctor I told you about," Wayman said.

"Hello," she said from the corner, her voice small and conveying her nervousness.

"Hello, Harriet," Tolker said. He didn't approach her. Instead, he went to Wayman's desk and perched on its edge, his fingers affirming the crease in his trousers.

"Harriet is the person I told you about on the phone," Wayman said, sitting in a chair next to her. He looked at Tolker, who was illuminated by a gooseneck lamp.

"Yes, I was impressed," Tolker said. "Perhaps you'll tell me a little about yourself, Harriet."

She started to talk, then stopped as though the tone arm on a turntable had been lifted from a record. "Who are you?" she asked.

Waymen answered her in a calm, patient, fatherly voice. "He's from Washington, and is very much involved in our work."

Tolker got up from the desk and approached them. He stood over her and said pleasantly, "I think it's wonderful what you're doing, Harriet, very courageous and very patriotic. You should be extremely proud of yourself."

"I am . . . I just . . . sometimes I become frightened when Dr. Wayman brings other people into it."

Tolker laughed. It was a reassuring laugh. He said, "I'd think you'd find that comforting, Harriet. You're certainly not alone. There are thousands of people involved, every one of them like you, bright, dedicated, *good* people."

Tolker saw a small smile form on her face. She said, "I really don't need a speech, Dr. . . . what was your name?" Her voice was arrogant, unfriendly, nothing like the sweet quality it had when they'd been introduced.

"Dr. James. Richard James." He said to Wayman, "I'd like to see the tests, Bill."

"All right." Wayman placed his hand on Harriet's hand, which was on the arm of her chair. He said, "Ready, Harriet?"

"As ready as I'll ever be," she said in a voice that seemed to come from another person. "It's showtime, Dr. J-a-m-e-s."

Wayman glanced up at Tolker, then said to her in a soothing voice, "Harriet, I want you to roll your eyes up to the top of your head, as far as you can." He placed his forefinger on her brow and said, "Look up, Harriet." Tolker leaned forward and peered into her eyes. Wayman said, "That's right, Harriet, as far as you can." Her pupils disappeared, leaving only two milky white sockets.

Tolker nodded at Wayman and smiled.

Wayman said, "Now, Harriet, I want you to keep your eyes where they are and slowly lower your eyelids. That's it . . . very slowly . . . there you are. You feel very relaxed now, don't you?" She nodded. "Now, Harriet, your arm, the one I'm touching, feels light, buoyant, as though a dozen helium-filled balloons were attached to it. Let it rise, let it float up. That's it, that's wonderful." Her arm drifted into the air and hung there as though suspended by an invisible wire.

Wayman turned to Tolker and said, "She's a perfect 'five,' the best I've ever seen."

Tolker grunted and leaned close to her face. "This is Dr. James, Harriet. How do you feel?"

"I feel good."

"I have something I want to ask you to do."

"I . . . I won't."

Wayman said, "She responds only to me. What do you want her to do?"

"Learn a phrase, and be told I'm the one she's to repeat it to."

"All right. Harriet, I want you to remember what I'm about to say to you. You'll never repeat it to anyone else except someone who says to you, 'The fog is thick.' All right?"

"Yes," she said in a dreamy voice.

"I want you to remember, 'There are four people. Two of them are good, and two of them are bad. The bad ones are Bill and Sally.' Do you understand?"

"Yes."

"When I tell you to come out of the pleasant, relaxed state you're enjoying now, you'll remember that phrase and only repeat it to someone who says, 'The fog is thick.' "

"Yes."

"I'm going to count backwards from five to one. When I reach one, you'll open your eyes and feel very good, very relaxed. Ready?"

"Yes."

"Five—four—three—two—one."

She blinked open her eyes and a placid smile crossed her face.

"Feel good?" Wayman asked.

"Yes. I feel good."

"You look very relaxed, at peace," Tolker said.

"Who are you?" she asked.

Tolker laughed. "You know who I am. I was introduced to you only a few minutes ago."

"Yes, I remember. You're Dr. James."

"That's right. I was wondering, Harriet, about the four people we've been discussing."

She looked at Wayman and frowned.

"You know who I mean," Tolker said, "the four people we're concerned about. We want to know which ones we can trust and which ones we can't trust."

"I don't understand," she said.

"Of course you don't," Wayman said. He looked at Tolker and said, "Go ahead."

Tolker said to her, "Harriet, the fog is thick."

She closed her eyes, opened them, and blinked rapidly.

"Did you hear me, Harriet? I said the fog is thick."

Her eyes continued to flutter. They rolled up in her head, and her arm began to tremble. She said in a halting, tentative voice, "There are . . . four people. Some of them are good and . . . two of them are bad. The bad ones are . . . Bill . . . and . . . Sally."

"Excellent," Wayman said. He sat back and looked to Tolker for approval. Tolker returned to the desk and resumed his seat on its edge.

Wayman said to Harriet, "That was very good, Harriet. You're not in your relaxed state anymore. You can open your eyes now. You've done a very good job."

Tolker watched her come out of her hypnotic state. She shook her head and rubbed her eyes.

"What do you remember?" Wayman asked her.

"I remember . . . I was feeling very good. Is there something else I should remember, *Doctor*?" It was the same angry, scornful voice she'd used earlier.

"No," Wayman said. He stood and held out his hand to her. "Why don't you wait in the other room. I won't be long. I just want to talk to my colleague for a few moments."

She got up and ran her hands over the front of her dress. Tolker observed that she was attractive, a little overweight but with a frank sensuality she was used to displaying. She watched him, openly inviting him as she crossed the room, opened a door, and went out.

"Impressed?" Wayman said. He'd gone to his chair behind the desk and lighted a cigarette.

"Yes. She's good. I'm not sure she's a five, though."

"I test her that way," said Wayman.

"I'd have to look again. Her upgaze is, but the eye roll might not be."

"Does it really matter?" Wayman asked, not bothering to mask the amusement in his voice. "This search for the perfect five is probably folly, Jason."

"I don't think so. How long have you been working with her?"

Wayman shrugged. "Six months, eight months. She's a prostitute, or was, a good one, highly paid."

"A call girl."

"That is more genteel. We came across her by accident. One of the contacts arranged for her to bring men to the safehouse. I watched a few of the sessions and realized that what I was seeing in *her* was far more interesting than the way the men were behaving under drugs. I mentioned it to the contact and the next time she was up, we were introduced. I started working with her the next day."

"She was that willing?"

"She's bright, enjoys the attention."

"And the money?"

"We're paying her fairly."

Tolker laughed. "Is this the first time she's been put to the test?"

It was Wayman's turn to laugh. "For heaven's sake, no. I'd started planting messages with her and testing the recall process within the first month. She's never failed."

"I'll have to see more."

"Tonight?"

"No." Tolker walked to a window that was covered by heavy beige drapes. He touched the fabric, turned, and said, "There's something wrong with using a hooker, Bill."

"Why?"

"Hookers are . . . Christ, one thing they're *not* is trustworthy."

Wayman came up behind and patted him on the back. "Jason, if one's basic morality were a criterion for choosing subjects in this project, we'd all have abandoned it years ago. In fact, we'd all have been ruled out ourselves."

"Speak for yourself, Bill."

"Whatever you say. Shall I continue with her?"

"I suppose so. See how far you can take her."

"I'll do that. By the way, I was sorry to hear about Miss Mayer."

"I'd rather not discuss it."

"Fine, except it must rank as a loss, Jason. If I understood you correctly the last time we met at Langley, she represented one of your best cases."

"She was all right, a solid four, nothing special."

"I thought she was . . ."

"Just a solid four, Bill. I couldn't use her to carry mentally. She worked out as a bag carrier."

"Just that?"

Tolker glared at him. "Yes, just that. Anything else for me to see while I'm out here?"

"No. I have a young man in therapy who shows potential, but I haven't made up my mind yet."

Wayman showed Tolker out of the building and to his car. "You drive her home?" Tolker asked.

"Yes."

"She live in San Fran?"

"Yes."

"She still turn tricks?"

"Only for us. We have a session set up for tomorrow night. Care to join us?"

"Maybe I will. Same place?"

"Yes. Good night, Jason."

"Good night, Bill."

Dr. William Wayman closed the door behind him and muttered "Slime" as he climbed the stairs.

Tolker returned to the city, called his wife from the room at the Hopkins, had a brief conversation. Their marriage had deteriorated to an accommodation years ago. He called another number. A half hour later a young Oriental girl wearing a silk dress the color of tangerines knocked at the door. He greeted her, said, "It's been too long," and sprawled on the bed as she went into the bathroom. When she returned, she was nude. She carried a small plastic bag of white powder, which she placed on the bed next to him. He grinned and absently ran his hand over her small breast.

"I brought the best," she said.

"You always do," he said as he rolled off the bed and started to undress.

At eleven o'clock the next night Jason Tolker stood with Dr. William Wayman and two other men in a small apartment. A video camera was positioned against an opening through the wall into the adjoining apartment. A small speaker carried audio from the other apartment.

"Here we go," one of them said, as what had been a static picture of the next room on the monitor suddenly came to life. The door to the next room opened. Harriet, the woman from Wayman's office the night before, led a rotund man through the door. She closed and locked it, turned, and started to undo his tie. He was drunk. A large belly hung over the front of his pants, and his suit jacket was visibly wrinkled even in the room's dim light.

"Drink?" she asked.

"No, I . . ."

"Oh, come on, join me in a drink. It gets me in the mood."

She returned from the kitchen with two glasses.

"What's she using?" Tolker asked.

"That new synthetic from Bethesda," Wayman said.

It turned out to be a wasted evening, at least scientifically. The man

Harriet had brought to the apartment was too drunk to be a valid subject, the effects of the drug she'd placed in his drink compromised by the booze. He was too drunk even to have sex with her, and fell asleep soon after they'd climbed into bed, the sound of his snoring rasping from the speakers. The men in the next room continued to watch, however, while Harriet pranced about the room. She examined her full body in a mirror, and even hammed for the camera after a cautious glance at the sleeping subject.

"Disgusting," Tolker muttered as he prepared to leave.

"Harriet?" Wayman asked.

"The fat slob. Tell her to pick better quality next time." He returned to the hotel and watched Randolph Scott in a western on TV before falling asleep.

9

Virginia, Two Days Later

IT WAS GOOD to be home.

Collette Cahill had slept off her jet lag in the room that had been hers as she grew up. Now she sat in the kitchen with her mother and helped prepare for a party in her honor that night, not a big affair, just neighbors and friends in for food and drinks to welcome her back.

Mrs. Cahill, a trim and energetic woman, had gone to an imported food store and bought things she felt represented Hungarian fare. "That's all I eat now, Mom," Collette had said. "We get a lot of Hungarian food."

To which her mother replied, "But we don't. It's a good excuse. I've never had goulash."

"You still won't have had it, Mom. In Hungary, goulash is a soup, not a stew."

"Pardon me," her mother said. They laughed and embraced and Collette knew nothing had changed, and was thankful for it.

Guests began to arrive at seven. There was a succession of gleeful greetings at the door: "I can't believe it." "My God, it's been ages!" "You look wonderful." "Great to see you again." One of the last guests to arrive was, to Collette's surprise, her high school beau, Vern Wheatley. They'd been "a number" in high school, had dated right through graduation when they promptly went their separate ways, Collette staying in the area to attend college, Wheatley to the University of Missouri to major in journalism.

"This is . . . this is too much," Cahill said as she opened the door and stared at him. Her first thought was that he'd grown more handsome over the years, but then she reminded herself that every man got better-looking after high school. His sandy hair had receded only slightly, and he wore it longer than in his yearbook photo. He'd always been slender, but now he was sinewy slim. He wore a tan safari jacket over a blue button-down shirt, jeans, and sneakers.

"Hi," he said. "Remember me?"

"Vern Wheatley, what are you doing here? How did you . . . ?"

"Came down to Washington on assignment, called your mom, and she told me about this blast. Couldn't resist."

"This is . . ." She hugged him and led him to the living room where everyone was gathered. After introductions, Collette led him to the bar where he poured himself a glass of Scotch. "Collette," he said, "you look sensational. Budapest must be palatable."

"Yes, it is. I've had a very enjoyable assignment there."

"Is it over? You're coming back here?"

"No, just a leave."

He grinned. "You take leaves, I take vacations."

"What are you doing these days?"

"I'm an editor, at least for the moment. *Esquire*. It's my fifth . . . no, seventh job since college. Journalists have never been known for stability, have we?"

"Judging from you, I guess not."

"I do some free-lancing, too."

"I've read some of your pieces." He gave her a skeptical look. "No, I really have, Vern. You had that cover story in the *Times* magazine section on . . ."

"On the private aviation lobby helping to keep our skies unsafe."

"Right. I really did read it. I said to myself, 'I know him.' "

"When."

"Huh?"

"I knew him when. I'm still in my when stage."

"Oh. Do you like New York?"

"Love it, although I can think of other places I'd rather live." He sighed. "It's been a while."

"It sure has. I remember when you got married."

"So do I." He chuckled. "Didn't last long."

"I know, Mom told me. I'm sorry."

"I was, too, but then I realized it was good it fell apart so soon, before there were kids. Anyway, I'm not here to talk about my ex-wife. God, I hate that term. I'm here to celebrate Collette Cahill's triumphant return from behind the Iron Curtain."

She laughed. "Everybody thinks Hungary is like being in the Soviet Union. It's really very open, Vern. I suppose that bothers the Soviets, but that's the way it is, lots of laughter and music, restaurants and bars and . . . well, that's not entirely true, but it's not as bad as people think. The Hungarians are so used to being conquered by one country or another that they shrug and get on with things."

"You're with the embassy?"

"Yup."

"What do you do there?"

"Administration, dealing with trade missions, tourists, things like that."

"You were with the CIA."

"Uh-huh."

"Didn't like it?"

"Too spooky for me, I guess. Just a Virginia country girl at heart."

His laugh indicated he didn't buy it but wasn't about to debate.

Collette drifted to other people in the room. Everyone was interested in her life abroad and she did her best to give them capsule responses.

By eleven, just about everyone had gone home, except for her Uncle Bruce who'd gotten drunk, a next-door neighbor who was helping Collette's mother to gather up the debris, and Vern Wheatley. He sat in a chair in the living room, one long leg casually dangling over the other, a beer in his hand. Collette went to him and said, "Nice party."

"Sure was. Feel like escaping?"

"Escaping? No, I . . ."

"I just figured we could go somewhere, have a drink and catch up."

"I thought we did."

"No we didn't. How about it?"

"I don't know, I . . . just a second."

She went to the kitchen and said she might go out for a cup of coffee with Wheatley.

"That's nice," said her mother, who then whispered, "He's divorced, you know."

"I know."

"I always liked him, and I could never understand what he saw in that other woman."

"He saw something—a ring, a marriage, a mate. Sure you don't mind?"

"Not at all."

"I won't be late. And, Mom, thanks for a wonderful party. I loved seeing everyone."

"And they loved seeing you. The comments, how beautiful you are, what a knockout, a world traveler . . ."

"Good night, Mom. You're spoiling me." She said goodbye to the neighbor and to her Uncle Bruce, who was hearing or feeling nothing, but would in the morning, and she and Wheatley drove off in his 1976 Buick Regal.

They went to a neighborhood bar, settled in a corner booth, ordered beers, and looked at each other. "Fate," he said.

"What?"

"Fate. Here we are, high school sweethearts separated by fate and together again because of fate." ·

"It was a party."

"Fate that I was here when the party was thrown, fate that you came home at the right time, fate that I'm divorced. *Fate*. Pure and simple."

"Whatever you say, Vern."

They spent two hours catching up on their lives. Cahill found it awkward, as usual, that there was much she couldn't talk about. It was one of the limitations to working for the CIA, particularly in its most clandestine division. She avoided that aspect of her recent life and told tales of Budapest, of the nights at the Miniatur and Gundel, of the Gypsy bands that seemed to be everywhere, of the friends she'd made and the memories she'd developed for life.

"It sounds like a wonderful city," Wheatley said. "I'd like to visit you there someday."

"Please do. I'll give you a special tour."

"It's a date. By the way, your former employer made a pass at me not too long ago."

Cahill tried to imagine someone she'd worked for doing that. A homosexual former boss?

"The Pickle Factory."

"The CIA? Really?"

"Yeah. Journalists used to be big with them. Remember? Then all the crap hit the fan back in '77 and it was 'cool it' for a while. Looks like they're back with us."

"What did they want you to do?"

"I was heading off for Germany on a free-lance assignment. This guy in a cheap suit and raincoat got to me through a friend who lives in the East Village and sculpts for a living. This guy wanted me to hook up with a couple of German writers, get to know them, and see what they knew about the current situation in Germany."

Cahill laughed. "Why didn't they just ask them themselves?"

"Not enough intrigue, I guess. Besides, I figured that what they really want is to have you in their pocket. Do them one favor, then another, collect a little dough for it and start depending upon more. You know what?"

"What?"

"I'm glad you aren't with them anymore. When I heard you'd taken a job with the CIA, all I could think of was what I wrote in your yearbook."

She smiled. "I remember it very well."

"Yeah. *'To the one girl in this world who will never sell out.'*"

"I really didn't understand it then. I do now."

"I'm glad." He sat up, rubbed his hand to signal that that phase of the conversation was over, and asked, "How long will you be home?"

"I don't know. I have . . ." She had to think. "I have two weeks' leave, but I'm spending a lot of it trying to run down what happened to a very dear friend of mine."

"Anybody I know?"

"No, just a good friend who died suddenly a week or so ago. She was in her mid-thirties and had a heart attack."

He made a face. "That's rough."

"Yes, I'm still trying to deal with it, I guess. She was a literary agent in Washington."

"Barrie Mayer? I didn't know you were friendly."

"You know about it?"

"Sure. It made the New York papers."

"I didn't read anything about it," Cahill said with a sigh. "I know her mother real well and promised her I'd try to find out as much as I could about what Barrie was doing right up until she died."

"Not a great way to spend a vacation. Leave. I forgot."

"Holiday. I like the British approach."

"So do I, in a lot of things. I'm sorry about what happened to your friend. Having friends die is for . . . for older people. I haven't started reading the obits yet."

"Don't. You know, Vern, this was great but I'm pooped. I thought I was slept out but my circadian rhythms are still in chaos."

"Is that like menopause?"

"Vaguely." She laughed. "I should get home."

"Sure."

They pulled up in front of her mother's house. Wheatley turned off the engine and they both looked straight ahead. Cahill glanced over and saw that he was grinning. She thought she knew what he was thinking, and a grin broke out on her face, too, which quickly turned into stifled laughter.

"Remember?" he said.

She couldn't respond because now laughter took all her breath. She tried. "I . . . I remember that you . . ."

"It was you," he said with equal difficulty. "You missed."

"I did not. You had your coat collar turned up because you thought it was cool and when I went to kiss you good night, all I hit was . . . the . . . coat collar."

"You ruined the coat. I never could get the lipstick off."

They stopped talking until they'd gotten themselves under control. She then said to him, "Vern, it was great seeing you again. Thanks for coming to my party."

"My pleasure. I'd like to see you again."

"I don't know if . . ."

"If we should, or if you'll have time while you're home?" She started to reply but he placed his finger on her lips. "I've never forgotten you, Collette. I mean . . . I'd like to see you again, go out, have dinner, talk, just that."

"That'd be nice," she said. "I just don't know how much time I'll have."

"Give me whatever you can spare. Okay?"

"Okay."

"Tomorrow?"

"Vern."

"Are you staying here?"

"At the house? Another night, I think. Then I'm going to stay in the city. I really should have dinner with Mom tomorrow."

"Absolutely. I remember what a hell of a cook she is. Am I invited?"

"Yes."

"I'll call you during the day. Good night, Collette."

He made a deliberate gesture to flatten his jacket collar. She laughed and kissed him lightly on the lips. He tried to intensify the kiss. She resisted, gave in, resisted again, and opened the door. "See you tomorrow," she said.

10

JASON TOLKER'S Washington office was located in a three-story detached house in Foggy Bottom, next to the George Washington University campus and with a view of the Kennedy Center from the third floor.

Cahill arrived precisely at 6:00 P.M. Tolker's secretary had told Cahill that he would see her after his last patient.

She rang, identified herself through an intercom, and was buzzed through. The reception area was awash in yellows and reds, and dominated by pieces of pre-Columbian and Peruvian art. Her first thought was to wonder whatever happened to the notion of decorating therapists' offices in soothing pastels. Her second thought was that Dr. Tolker was a pretentious man, not the first time she'd come to that conclusion. Her only other meeting with him, which occurred at the scientific conference in Budapest a week after she'd arrived there, had left her with the distinct impression that his ego was in direct proportion to the outward manifestations of his personality—movie-star handsome (Tyrone Power?), expensive clothing on a six-foot frame built for designer suits, money (it was as if he wore a sandwich board with a large green dollar sign on it). But, and probably more important, there was a self-assuredness that many physicians seemed to carry with them out of medical school but that was particularly prevalent with those who dealt with a patient's emotions and behavior, a godlike view of the world and fellowmen, knowing more, seeing through, inwardly chuckling at how the "others" live their lives, scornful and bemused and willing to tolerate the daily brush with the human dilemma in fifty-minute segments only, payment due at conclusion of visit.

The receptionist, a pleasant, middle-aged woman with a round face, thinning hair, her coat and hat on, ready to leave, told Cahill to be seated: "Doctor will be with you in a few minutes." She left, and Cahill browsed a copy of *Architectural Digest* until Tolker came through a door. "Miss Cahill, hello, Jason Tolker." He came to where she was sitting, smiled, and offered his hand. Somehow, his gregarious greeting didn't match up with what she'd remembered of him from Budapest. She stood and said, "I appreciate you taking time to see me, Doctor."

"Happy to. Come in, we'll be more comfortable in my office."

His office was markedly subdued compared to the waiting room. The walls were the color of talcum; a soothing pastel, she thought. One wall was devoted to framed awards, degrees, and photographs with people Cahill didn't recognize at first glance. There was no desk; his wine leather swivel chair was behind a round glass coffee table. There were two matching leather chairs on the other side of the table. A black leather couch that gracefully curved up to form a headrest was against another wall. A small chair was positioned behind where the patient's head would lie.

"Please, sit down," he said, indicating one of the chairs. "Coffee? I think there's some left. Or maybe you'd prefer a drink?"

"Nothing, thank you."

"Do you mind if I do? It's been an . . ." A smile. "An interesting day."

"Please. Do you have wine?"

"As a matter of fact, I do. Red or white?"

"White, please."

She watched him open a cabinet, behind which was a bar lighted from within. Her reaction to him was different than it had been in Budapest. She began to like him, finding his demeanor courteous, friendly, open. She also knew she was responding to his good looks. For a tall man, he moved fluidly. He was in shirtsleeves; white shirt, muted red tie, charcoal gray suit trousers, and black Gucci loafers. His dark hair was thick and curly, his facial features sharp. It was his eyes, however, that defined him: large, saccadic raven eyes that were at once soothing and probing.

He placed two glasses of wine on the coffee table, sat in his chair, lifted his glass, and said, "Health."

She returned the salute and took a sip. "Very good," she said.

"I keep the better vintages at home."

She wished he hadn't said it. There was no need to say it. She realized he was staring at her. She met his gaze and smiled. "You know why I'm here."

"Yes, of course, Mrs. Wedgemann, my secretary, told me the nature of your visit. You were a close friend of Barrie Mayer."

"Yes, that's right. To say I was shocked at what happened to her is one of those classic understatements, I suppose. I've been in touch with her mother who, as you can imagine, is devastated, losing her only daughter. I decided to take . . . to take a vacation and see what I could find out about things leading up to Barrie's death. I promised her mother I'd do that but, to be honest, I would have done it for myself anyway. We *were* close."

He pressed his lips together and narrowed his eyes. "The question, of course, is why come to me?"

"I know that Barrie was in therapy with you, at least for a while, and I thought you might be able to give me some hint of what frame of mind she was in before she died, whether there was any indication that she wasn't feeling well."

Tolker rubbed his nose in a gesture of thoughtfulness before saying, "Obviously, Miss Cahill, I wouldn't be free to discuss anything that went on between Barrie and me. That falls under doctor-patient confidentiality."

"I realize that, Dr. Tolker, but it seems to me that a general observation wouldn't necessarily violate that principle."

"When did you meet Barrie?"

The sudden shift in questioning stopped her for a moment. She said, "In college. We stayed close until we each went our separate ways for a number of years. Then, as often happens, we got back in touch and renewed the friendship."

"You say you were close to Barrie. How close?"

"Close." She thought of Mark Hotchkiss, who'd exhibited a similar skepticism of the depth of her relationship with Mayer. "Is there some element of doubt about my friendship with Barrie or, for that matter, my reason for being here?"

He smiled and shook his head. "No, not at all. I'm sorry if I gave you that impression. Do you work and live in the Washington area?"

"No, I . . . I work for the United States Embassy in Budapest, Hungary."

"That's fascinating," said Tolker. "I've spent some time there. Charming city. A shame the Soviets came in as they did. It certainly has put a lid on things."

"Not as much as people think," Cahill said. "It's got to be the most open of Soviet satellite countries."

"Perhaps."

It dawned on Cahill that he was playing a game with her, asking questions for which he already had answers. She decided to be more forthright. "We've met before, Dr. Tolker."

He squinted and leaned forward. "I thought we had the minute I saw you. Was it in Budapest?"

"Yes. You were attending a conference and I'd just arrived."

"Yes, it comes back to me now, some reception, wasn't it? One of those abominable get-togethers. You're wearing your hair different, shorter, aren't you?"

Cahill laughed. "Yes, and I'm impressed with your memory."

"Frankly, Miss Cahill, when more than a year has passed since meeting a woman, it's always safe to assume she's changed her hair. Usually, it involves the color, too, but that isn't the case with you."

"No, it isn't. Somehow, I don't think I was born to be a blonde."

"No, I suppose not," he said. "What do you do at the embassy?"

"Administration, trade missions, helping stranded tourists, run-of-the-mill."

He smiled and said, "It can't be as dull as you make it sound."

"Oh, it's never dull."

"I have a good friend in Budapest."

"Really? Who is that?"

"A colleague. His name is Árpád Hegedüs. Do you know him?"

"He's . . . he's a colleague, you say, a psychiatrist?"

"Yes, and a very good one. His talent is wasted having to apply it under a Socialist regime, but he seems to find room for a certain amount of individuality."

"Like most Hungarians," she said.

"Yes, I suppose that's true, just as you must find room for other activities within the confines of your run-of-the-mill job. How much time do you devote to helping stranded tourists as opposed to . . . ?"

When he didn't finish, she said, "As opposed to what?"

"As opposed to your duties for the CIA."

His question startled her. Early in her career with Central Intelligence, it would have thrown her, perhaps even generated a nervous giggle as she collected her thoughts. That wasn't the case any longer. She looked him in the eye and said, "That's an interesting comment."

"More wine?" he asked, standing and going to the bar.

"No, thank you, I have plenty." She looked at her glass on the table and thought of the comment Árpád Hegedüs had made to her during their last meet in Budapest: "Jason Tolker might be friendly to the Soviets."

Tolker returned, took his seat, sipped his wine. "Miss Cahill, I think you might accomplish a lot more, and we might get along much better, if you practiced a little more candor."

"What makes you think I haven't been candid?"

"It isn't a matter of thinking, Miss Cahill. I *know* you haven't been." Before she could respond he said, "Collette E. Cahill, graduated cum laude from George Washington University Law School, a year or so with a legal trade journal, then a stint in England for the CIA and a transfer to Budapest. Accurate? Candid?"

"Am I supposed to be impressed?" she asked.

"Only if your life to date impresses you. It does me. You're obviously bright, talented, and ambitious."

"Thank you. Time for me to ask you a question."

"Go ahead."

"Assuming the things you've said about me were correct, particularly my supposed continuing employment with the CIA, how would you know about that?"

He smiled, and it quickly turned into a laugh. "No argument, then?"

"Is that Shrink School 101, answer a question with a question?"

"It goes back further than that, Miss Cahill. The Greeks were good at it. Socrates taught the technique."

"Yes, that's true, and Jesus, too. As a learning tool for students, not to evade a reasonable question."

Tolker shook his head and said, "You're still not being candid, are you?"

"No?"

"No. You know, either through Barrie or someone else in your organization, that I have, on occasion, provided certain services to your employer."

Cahill smiled. "This conversation has turned into one with so much candor that it would probably be upsetting to . . . to our employers, *if* we worked for them."

"No, Miss Cahill, your employer. I simply have acted as a consultant on a project or two."

She knew that everything he'd said up to that moment was literally true, and decided it was silly to continue playing the game. She said, "I'd love another glass of wine."

He got it for her. When they were both seated again, he looked at his watch and said, "Let me try to tell you what it is you want to know without you having to ask the questions. Barrie Mayer was a lovely and successful woman, as you're well aware. She came to me because there were certain aspects of her life with which she was unhappy, that she was having trouble negotiating. That, of course, is a sign of sanity in itself."

"Seeking help?"

"Of course, recognizing a problem and taking action. She was like most people who end up in some form of therapy, bright and rational and put together in most aspects of her life, just stumbling now and then over some ghosts from the past. We worked things out very nicely for her."

"Did you maintain a relationship after therapy was finished?"

"Miss Cahill, you know we did."

"I don't mean about what she might have done as a courier. I mean a personal relationship."

"What a discreet term. Do you mean did we sleep together?"

"It would be indiscreet for me to ask that."

"But you already have, and I prefer not to answer an indiscretion with an indiscretion. Next question."

"You were telling me everything I need to know without questions, remember?"

"Yes, that's right. You'll want to know whether I have any information bearing upon her death."

"Do you?"

"No."

"Do you have any idea who killed her?"

"Why do you assume someone killed her? My understanding is that it was an unfortunate, premature heart attack."

"I don't think that's really what happened. Do you?"

"I wouldn't know more about that than what I've read in the papers."

Cahill sipped her wine, not because she wanted it but because she needed a little time to process what had transpired. She'd assumed when she called and asked for an appointment with Tolker that she would be summarily turned down. She'd even considered seeking an appointment as a patient but realized that was too roundabout an approach.

It had all been so easy. A phone call, a brief explanation to the secretary that she was Barrie Mayer's friend—instant appointment with him. He'd obviously worked fast in finding out who she was. Why? What source had he turned to to come up with information on her? Langley and its central personnel files? Possible, but not likely. That sort of information would never be given out to a contract physician who was only tangentially associated with the CIA.

"Miss Cahill, I've been preaching candor to you without practicing it myself."

"Really?"

"Yes. I'm assuming that you're sitting here wondering how I came up with information about you."

"As a matter of fact, that's right."

"Barrie was . . . well, let's just say she didn't define close-mouthed."

Cahill couldn't help but laugh. She remembered her dismay at her friend's casual mention of her new, part-time job as courier.

"You agree," Tolker said.

"Well, I . . ."

"Once Barrie agreed to carry some materials for the CIA, she became talkative. She said it was ironic because she had this friend, Collette Cahill, who worked for the CIA at the American Embassy in Budapest. I found that interesting and asked questions. She answered them all. Don't misunderstand. She didn't babble about it. If she had, I would have ended the relationship, at least that aspect of it."

"I understand what you're saying. What else did she say about me?"

"That you were beautiful and bright and the best female friend she'd ever had."

"Did she really say that?"

"Yes."

"I'm flattered." She sensed that a tear might erupt and swallowed against it.

"Want my honest opinion about how and why she died?"

"Please."

"I buy the official autopsy verdict of a coronary. If that *isn't* why she died, I'd assume that our friends on the other side decided to terminate her."

"The Russians."

"Or some variation thereof."

"I can't accept that, not today. We're not at war. Besides, what could Barrie have been carrying that would prompt such a drastic action?"

He shrugged.

"What *was* she carrying?"

"How would I know?"

"I thought you were her contact."

"I was, but I never knew what was in her briefcase. It was given to me sealed, and I would give it to her."

"I understand that but . . ."

He leaned forward. "Look, Miss Cahill, I think we've gotten off onto a tangent that goes far beyond the reality of the situation. I know that you're a full-time employee of the CIA, but I'm not. I'm a psychiatrist. That's what I do for a living. It's my profession. A colleague suggested to me years ago that I might be interested in becoming a CIA-approved physician. All that means is that when someone from the agency needs medical help in my specialty, they're free to come to me. There are surgeons and OB-GYN men and heart specialists and many others who've been given clearance by the agency."

She cocked her head and asked, "But what about being a contact for a courier like Barrie? That isn't within your specialty."

His smile was friendly and reassuring. "They asked me somewhere along the line to keep my eye out for anyone who might fit their profile of a suitable courier. Barrie fit it. She traveled often to foreign countries, particularly Hungary, wasn't married, didn't have any deep, dark secrets that would jeopardize her clearance, and she enjoyed adventure. She also appreciated the money, off-the-books money, fun money for clothes and furniture and other frills. It was a lark for her."

His final words hit Cahill hard, caused her to draw a deep breath.

"Something wrong?" Tolker asked, observing the pain on her face.

"Barrie's dead. 'Just a lark.' "

"Yes. I'm sorry."

"Do you feel any . . . any guilt about having recruited her into a situation that resulted in her death?"

For a moment, she thought his eyes might mist. They didn't, but his voice had a ring of pathos. "I think about it often. I wish I could go back to that day when I suggested she carry for your employer and withdraw my offer." He sighed and stood, stretched, and broke his knuckles. "But that's not possible, and I tell my patients that to play the what-if game is stupid. It happened, she's dead, I'm sorry, and I must leave."

He walked her to the office door. They paused and looked at each other. "Barrie was right," he said.

"About what?"

"About her friend being beautiful."

She lowered her eyes.

"I hope I've been helpful."

"Yes, you have, and I'm appreciative."

"Will you have dinner with me?"

"I . . ."

"Please. There's probably more ground we could cover about Barrie. I feel comfortable with you now. I didn't when you first arrived, thought you were just snooping around for gossip. I shouldn't have felt that way. Barrie wouldn't have a very close friend who'd do that."

"Maybe," she said. "Yes, that would be fine."

"Tomorrow night?"

"Ah, yes, fine."

"Would you mind coming by here at seven? I have a six o'clock group. Once they're gone, I'm free."

"Seven. I'll be here."

She drove home realizing two things. One, he'd told her everything that she would have known anyway. Two, she was anxious to see him again. That second thought bothered her because she couldn't effectively separate her continuing curiosity about Barrie Mayer's death from a personal fascination with him as a man.

"Have a nice night?" her mother asked.

"Yes."

"You're staying in the city tomorrow night?"

"For the next few nights, Mom. It'll be easier to get things done. I'm seeing Barrie's mother tomorrow for lunch."

"Poor woman. Please give her my sympathy."

"I will."

"Will you be seeing Vern?"

"I don't know. Probably."

"It was fun having him at dinner last night, like when you were in high school and he used to hang around hoping to be invited."

Cahill laughed. "He's nice. I'd forgotten how nice."

"Well," said her mother, "the problem with pretty girls like you is having to pick and choose among all the young men who chase you."

Cahill hugged her mother and said, "Mom, I'm not a girl anymore, and there isn't a battalion of men chasing me."

Her mother stepped back, smiled, and held her daughter at arm's length. "Don't kid me, Collette Cahill. I'm your mother."

"I know that, and I'm very grateful that you are. Got any ice cream?"

"Bought it today for you. Rum raisin. They were out of Hungarian flavors."

11

CAHILL DROVE A rented car into the city the next morning and checked into the Hotel Washington at 15th and Pennsylvania. It wasn't Washington's finest, but it was nice. Besides, it had a sentimental value. Its rooftop terrace restaurant and bar offered as fine a view of Washington as any place in the capitol. Cahill had spent four glorious Fourth of Julys there with friends who, through connections, had been able to wangle reservations on the terrace's busiest night of the year, and were able to view the spectacular festivities that only Washington can provide on the nation's birthday.

She went to her room, hung up the few items of clothing she'd brought with her, freshened up, and headed for her first appointment of the day: CIA headquarters in Langley, Virginia.

The person she was seeing had been a mentor of sorts during her training days. Hank Fox was a grizzled, haggard, wayworn agency veteran who had five daughters, and who took a special interest in the increasing number of women recruited by the CIA. His position was Coordinator: Training Policy and Procedures. New recruits often joked that his title should be "Priest." He had that way about him—ignoring his five issue, of course.

She whizzed along the George Washington Memorial Parkway until reaching a sign that read CENTRAL INTELLIGENCE AGENCY. It hadn't always been marked that way. In the years following its construction in the late 1950s, a single sign on the highway read BUREAU OF PUBLIC ROADS. Frequent congressional calls for the agency to be more open and accountable brought about the new sign. Behind it, little had changed.

She turned off the highway and onto a road leading to the 125-acre tract on which the Central Intelligence Agency stood. Ahead, through dense woods, stood the modernistic, fortress-like building surrounded by a high and heavy chain-link fence. She stopped, presented her credentials to two uniformed guards, and explained the purpose of her visit. One of them placed a call, then informed her that she could pass through to the next checkpoint. She did, submitted her identity again to scrutiny, and was allowed to proceed to a small parking area near the main entrance.

Two athletic young men wearing blue suits and with revolvers beneath their jackets waited for her to approach the entrance. She noticed how short their hair was, how placid the expression on their faces. Again, a show of credentials, a nod, and she was escorted through the door by one of them. He walked slightly in front of her at a steady pace until coming to the beginning of a long, straight white tunnel that was arched at the top. Royal blue industrial-grade carpeting lined the floor. There was nothing in the tunnel except for recessed lights that created odd shadows along its length. At the far end was an illuminated area where two stainless-steel elevator doors caught the light and hurled it back into the tunnel.

"Straight ahead, ma'am."

Cahill entered the tunnel and walked slowly, her thoughts drifting back to when she was a new recruit and had first seen this building, had first walked this tunnel. It had been part of an introductory tour and she'd been struck by the casualness of the tour guide, a young man who demonstrated what Cahill, and others in her class, considered strangely irreverent behavior considering the ominous image of the CIA. He'd talked about how the contractor who'd built the building wasn't allowed to know how many people would occupy it, and was forced to guess at the size and capacity of the heating and air-conditioning system. The system turned out to be inadequate, and the CIA took him to court. He won, his logic making more sense to the judge than the "national security" argument presented by the agency's counsel.

The guide had also said that the $46-million building had been approved in order to bring all agency headquarters personnel under one roof. Until that time, the CIA's divisions had been spread out all over Washington and surrounding communities, and Congress had been sold on the consolidation because of problems this created. But, according to this talkative, glib young man, whole divisions began moving out shortly after moving in when construction was completed. When this came to the attention in 1968 of then director Richard Helms, he was furious and decreed that no one was to make a move without his personal approval. Somehow, that didn't deter division chiefs who found being under one roof to be stifling and, if nothing else, boring. The exodus continued.

Cahill often wondered how you ran an organization with that kind of discipline, and whether the young tour guide's loose tongue had cut short his agency career. It wasn't like the FBI, where public relations and public tours were routine, conducted by attractive young men and women hired solely for that purpose. The CIA did not give tours to outsiders; the guide was obviously a full-fledged employee.

She reached the end of the tunnel where two other young men awaited her. "Miss Cahill?" one asked.

"Yes."

"May I see your pass?"

She showed him.

"Please take the elevator. Mr. Fox is expecting you." He pushed a button and a set of the stainless-steel doors slid open quickly and silently. She stepped into the elevator and waited for them to close. She knew better than to look for a button to push. There weren't any. This elevator knew its destination.

Hank Fox was waiting for her when the doors opened a floor above. He hadn't changed. Though older, he'd always looked old, and the changes weren't quickly discernible. His craggy face broke into a smile and he extended two large, red, and callused hands. "Collette Cahill. Good to see you again."

"Same here, Hank. You look terrific."

"I feel terrific. At my age you might as well or, at least, lie. Come on, Fox's special blend of coffee awaits you." She smiled and fell in step with him down a wide hallway carpeted in red, its white walls providing a backdrop for large, framed maps.

Fox, Cahill noticed, had put on weight and walked with a slower, heavier gait than the last time she'd seen him. His gray suit, its shape and material testifying to its origins in a Tall and Big (read Fat) Man's clothing shop, hung gracelessly from him.

He stopped, opened a door, and allowed her to enter. The corner office's large windows looked out over the woods. His desk was as cluttered as it had always been. The walls were covered with framed photos of him with political heavyweights spanning many administrations, the largest one of him shaking hands with a smiling Harry S. Truman a few years before the President's death. A cluster of color photographs of his wife and children stood on his desk. A pipe rack was full; little metal soldiers stood at attention along the air-conditioning and heating duct behind the desk.

"Coffee?" he asked.

"If it's as good as it used to be."

"Sure it is. The only difference is that they told me I have a fast and irregular pulse. The doc thought I was drinking too much coffee and said I should use de-caf. I compromised. I mix it half and half now, half the amaretto from that fancy coffee and tea shop in Georgetown, the other half de-caf. Never know the difference." Hank Fox's special blends of coffee were well known throughout the agency, and being invited to share a pot carried with it the symbolism of acceptance and friendship.

"Sensational," Cahill exclaimed after her first sip. "You haven't lost your touch, Hank."

"Not with coffee. Other things, well . . ."

"They moved you."

"Yeah. That's right, the last time I saw you was when I had that office in with Personnel. I liked it better there. Being up here in Miscellaneous Projects is another world. The director said it was a promotion, but

I know better. I'm being eased out, which is okay with me. Hell, I'm sixty."

"Young."

"Bull! All this crap about being only as old as you think is babble from people who are afraid of getting old. You may feel young, but cut you open and the bones and arteries don't lie." He sat in a scarred leather swivel chair, propped his feet on the desk, and reached for a pipe, leaving Cahill staring at the soles of his shoes, both of which sported sizable holes. "So one of my prize pupils has returned to see the aging prof. How've you been?"

"Fine."

"I got a BIGOT from Joe Breslin saying you were coming home." Fox often used intelligence terms from his early days, even though they'd passed out of common usage over the years. "BIGOT" stemmed from secret plans to invade France during World War II. Gibraltar had been established as a planning center, and orders for officers being sent there were rubber-stamped "TO GIB." BIGOT was the reverse, and the term came into being: sensitive operations were known to be *bigoted*, and personnel given knowledge of them were on the *bigot list*.

"Any reason for him doing that?" she asked.

"Just an advisory. I was going to call but you beat me to it. This your first leave from Budapest?"

"No. I took a few short ones to Europe, and got back home once about a year ago for a favorite uncle's funeral."

"The boozer?"

She laughed. "Oh, God, what a memory. No, my hard-drinking Uncle Bruce is still very much with us, rotted liver and all. Having him in the family almost blew my chances here, didn't it?"

"Yeah. That prissy little security guy raised it during your clearance investigation." He belched and excused himself, then said, "If having an alky in the family ruled you out for duty around here, there'd only be a dozen temperance-league types running intelligence for the good ol' U.S. of A." He shook his head, "Hell, half the staff drinks too much."

She laughed and sipped more coffee.

"Let me ask you a question," he said in a serious tone. She looked up and raised her eyebrows. "You here strictly for R & R?"

"Sure."

"The reason I ask is that I thought it was strange . . . well, maybe not strange, but unusual for Joe to bother using a BIGOT to tell me you were coming."

She shrugged. "Oh, you know Joe, Hank, the perpetual father figure. It was nice of him. He knows how fond I am of you."

" 'Fond.' Pleasant term to use on an old man."

"*Older* man."

"Thank you. Well, I'm fond of you, too, and I just thought I'd raise the question in case you were involved in something official and needed an inside rabbi."

"Rabbi Henry Fox. Somehow, Hank, it doesn't go with you. Priest, yes. They still call you that?"

"Not so much anymore since they shifted me."

His comment surprised Cahill. She'd assumed he'd only been physically moved, but that his job had remained the same. She asked.

"Well, Collette, I still keep a hand in training, but they've got me running an operation to keep track of the Termites and Maggots. It's an Octopus project."

Cahill smiled, said, "I never could keep it straight, the difference between Termites and Maggots."

"It really doesn't matter," Fox said. "The Termites are media types who don't carry a brief for the Communists, but who always find something wrong with *us*. The Maggots follow the termites and do whatever's popular which, as you know, means taking daily shots at us and the FBI and any other organization they see as being a threat to their First Amendment rights. Between you and me, I think it's a waste of time. Take away their freedom to write what they want and there goes what the country's all about in the first place. Anyway, we've got them on the computer and we plug in everything they write, pro or con." He yawned and sat back in his chair, his arms behind his head.

Cahill knew what he'd meant by it being an "Octopus project." A worldwide computer system to track potential terrorists had been termed Project Octopus, and had become a generic label for similar computer-rooted projects. She also thought of Vern Wheatley. Was he a Maggot or a Termite? It caused her to smile. Obviously, he was neither, nor were most of the journalists she knew. It was a tendency of too many people within the CIA to apply negative terms to anyone who didn't see things their way, a tendency that had always bothered her.

She'd debated on her way to Langley whether to open up a little to Fox and to bring up Barrie Mayer. She knew it wasn't the most prudent thing to do—Need-to-know coming to the fore—but the temptation was there, and the fact that Joe Breslin had alerted Fox to her arrival gave a certain credence to the notion. There were few people within the Pickle Factory that she trusted. Breslin was one; Fox was another. Mistake! Trust no one, was the rule. Still . . . how could you go through life viewing everyone with whom you worked as a potential enemy? Not a good way to live. Not healthy. In Barrie Mayer's case, it had worked the other way around. Whose confidence had she trusted that turned against her? Had Tolker been right, that her death might have been at the hand of a Soviet agent? It was so difficult to accept, but that was another rule that her employer instilled in every employee: "It's easy to forget that we are at war every day with the Communists. It is their aim to destroy our system and our country, and a day must never pass when that reality isn't at the forefront of your thinking."

"You know what I was just thinking, Collette?" Fox asked.

"What?"

"I was thinking back to when this whole organization was started by

President Truman." He shook his head. "He'd never recognize it today. I met Truman, you know."

She glanced at the photograph on the wall before saying, "I remember you talked about that during training." He'd talked about it often, as she recalled.

"Hell of a guy. It was right after those two Puerto Ricans tried to assassinate him in 'fifty. They did their best to do him in, botched it, got death sentences, and then Truman turns around at the final minute and commutes their sentences to life. I admired him for that."

Along with cabinet building, winemaking, jewelry design and crafting, and a dozen other interests, Hank Fox was a history buff, especially the Harry Truman presidency. During Cahill's training, it was obvious that the Truman hand in creating the CIA in 1947 was being deliberately glossed over. She hadn't understood the reasons for it until Fox had sat down with a few favorite recruits over dinner at Martin's Tavern in Georgetown and explained.

When Truman abolished the OSS following World War II, he did so because he felt that such wartime tactics as psychological warfare, political manipulation, and paramilitary operations that had been practiced during the war by the OSS had no place in a peacetime, democratic society. He did, however, recognize the need for an organization to coordinate the collection of intelligence information from all branches of government. As he said, "If such an organization had existed within the United States in 1941, it would have been difficult, if not impossible, for the Japanese to have launched their successful attack on Pearl Harbor."

And so the Central Intelligence Agency was born—to collect, assimilate, and analyze intelligence, not to engage in any other activity.

"He got snookered," Fox had told his handful of students that night at dinner. "Allen Dulles, who ended up running the CIA six years later, thought Truman's views on intelligence were too limited. Know what he did? He sent a memo to the Senate Armed Services Committee undercutting Truman's view of what the CIA was supposed to be."

Fox had produced a copy of that memo for his students:

Intelligence work in time of peace will require other techniques, other personnel, and will have rather different objectives. . . . We must deal with the problem of conflicting ideologies as democracy faces communism, not only in the relations between Soviet Russia and the countries of the West but in the internal political conflicts with the countries of Europe, Asia, and South America.

Dulles went on to contribute a concept to what would eventually become intelligence law, and which gave the CIA its ultimate power. It called for the agency to carry out "such other functions and duties related to intelligence as the National Security Council may from time to time direct." This took it out of the realm of congressional control and helped establish the atmosphere under which the CIA could function autonomous from virtually all control, including manpower and financing. The director had only to sign a voucher and the funds were there, something President Truman had never envisioned happening.

Cahill and the other students at that dinner with Hank Fox later discussed his somewhat irreverent view of the agency and its history. It was refreshing; everyone else with whom they'd come into contact seemed rigidly bound to a party line, no room for deviation, no patience with frivolity or casual remarks that could be construed as less than sanctified.

"Well, on to other functions and duties," Cahill said. "I lost a very good friend recently."

"I'm sorry. Accident?"

"No one is sure. It's been ruled a heart attack but she was only in her thirties and . . ."

"She work with us?"

Cahill hesitated, then said, "Part time. She was a literary agent."

He removed his feet from the desk and replaced them with his elbows. "Barrie Mayer."

"Yes. You know about her, about what happened?"

"Very little. The rumor mill swung into full gear when she died, and the word was that she did some part-time carrying for us."

Cahill said nothing.

"Did you know she was affiliated?"

"Yes."

"Did she carry to you in Budapest?"

"Not directly but yes, she carried to Budapest."

"Banana Quick."

"I'm not sure about that, Hank."

"Is that what you're on these days?"

"Yes. I turned someone."

"So I heard."

"You did?"

"Yeah. Whether you know it or not, Miss Cahill, your Hungarian friend is viewed around here as the best we've got at the moment."

She resisted a smile of satisfaction and said, "He's been cooperative."

"That's a mild way to put it. Your girlfriend's demise has a lot of people reaching for the Tums bottle."

"Because of Banana Quick?"

"Sure. It's the most ambitious project we've had since the Bay of Pigs. Unfortunately, it has about half as much chance of succeeding, and you know how successful the Cuban fiasco was, but the timetable's been pushed up. Could be anytime now."

"I wouldn't know about the overall project, Hank. I get information from my source and I feed it back. One spoke. I'm not privy to what the wheel does."

"Operation Servo?"

"Pardon?"

"Haven't heard of it?"

"No."

"Just as well. Another act of genius by our army of resident geniuses. I hope death is final, Collette. If it isn't, Harry S. Truman has been twisting and turning ever since he left us the day after Christmas, 1972." He drew a deep breath and his face seemed to sink, to turn gray. He pressed his lips together and said in a low voice lacking energy, "It's no good here anymore, Collette. At best, it's disorganized and ineffectual. At worst, it's evil."

She started to respond but he quickly said, "You'll have to pardon a tired, disgruntled old man. I don't mean to corrupt your enthusiasm with my jaded grumbling."

"Please, Hank, no apologies." She glanced around the office. "Are we secure?"

"Who knows?"

"You don't care?"

"No."

"Why?"

"It's a perk of becoming old. Lots of things don't matter anymore. Don't get me wrong. I do my job. I give them my best effort and loyalty for the check. I want to retire. Janie and I bought a pretty house on some land down in West Virginia. Another year and that's where we head. The kids are doing nicely. We bought another dog. That's three. The five of us, Janie, me, and the canine trio, need West Virginia."

"It sounds great, Hank," Cahill said. "Should I leave now?"

"You have to?"

"I have a luncheon appointment in Rosslyn."

" 'Appointment.' " He smiled. "Not a date?"

"No. I'm meeting Barrie Mayer's mother."

"Only kid?"

"Yes."

"Tough."

"Yes."

"Come on. I'll walk you out. I need fresh air."

They stood next to her small red rented car and Fox looked up at the building, then out over the woods that shielded other buildings from view. "Rosslyn? I spend a lot of time over there."

"Really?"

"Yeah. One of the Octopus computer centers moved to Rosslyn. Half this joint is empty now."

Cahill laughed as she thought of the tour guide who'd talked about that. She mentioned him.

"I remember him," Fox said. "He was an idiot which, we've all come to realize, doesn't preclude you from working here. He was a running joke around here, and his boss was told to get him out. He hit him with fifty demerits in a week, and you know what that means. Fifty in a *year* is automatic dismissal. The kid was really broken up. He came to me and begged for another chance. I felt sorry for him but he *was* an idiot. I told him I couldn't do anything and he slunk away. He's probably a millionaire four times over now."

"Probably. Hank, it was wonderful seeing you, touching base like this."

"Good to see you, too, kid. Before you take off, listen carefully to me."

She stared at him.

"Watch that pretty little rear end of yours. The Barrie Mayer thing is hot. So's Banana Quick. It's trouble. Watch who you talk to. Banana Quick is a mess, and anybody associated with it goes down the tube along with all the rest of the dirty water." He lowered his voice. "There's a leak in Banana Quick."

"Really?"

"A big one. Maybe that's why your friend isn't with us anymore."

"Oh, no, Hank, she'd never . . ."

"I didn't say she'd do anything, but maybe she got too close to the wrong people. Understand?"

"No, but I have a feeling you're not about to continue my education."

"I would if I could, Collette. I've been kicked upstairs, remember? Need-to-know. I don't have that need anymore. Be careful. I like you. And remember Harry Truman. If they could screw the President of the United States, they can screw anybody, even bright, pretty girls like you who mean well." He kissed her on the cheek, turned, and disappeared inside the building.

12

"IT WAS SWEET of you to come," Mrs. Mayer said as they sat at a window table in Alexander's III in Rosslyn, just over the Key Bridge from Georgetown. Rosslyn had grown rapidly. Their view of Georgetown and Washington from the penthouse restaurant was partially obscured by the latest in a series of high-rise office and apartment buildings.

"Frankly, I dreaded it, Mrs. Mayer," Collette said, running a fingernail over the starched white linen tablecloth.

Melissa Mayer placed her hand on Collette's, smiled, and said, "You shouldn't have. It means a great deal to me that one of Barrie's closest friends cared enough to see me. I've felt very lonely lately. I don't today."

Her words boosted Cahill's spirits. She smiled at the older woman, who was impeccably dressed in a light blue jersey suit, white blouse with lace at the neck, and mink stole. Her hair was white and pulled back into a severe chignon. Her face had a healthy glow, aided by makeup that had been expertly applied. She wore a substantial strand of pearls around her neck and pearl earrings with tiny diamond chips. Her fingers, gnarled by arthritis, supported heavy gold and diamond rings.

"I had all sorts of things I'd planned to say when I saw you but . . ."

"Collette, there really is very little to say. I'd always heard that the saddest thing in life was to have a child predecease a parent and I never debated it. Now I *know* it's true. But I am also a believer in the scheme of life. It was never meant to be perfect. The odds are that children will outlive their parents, but it certainly isn't set in stone. I've grieved, I've cried, I've cried a great deal, and now it's time to stop those things and continue with my life."

Cahill shook her head. "You're an amazing woman, Mrs. Mayer."

"I'm nothing of the sort, and please call me Melissa. 'Mrs. Mayer' creates too wide a gap."

"Fair enough."

A waiter asked whether they'd like another drink. Cahill shook her head. Mayer ordered a second perfect Manhattan. Then Collette said, "Melissa, what happened to Barrie?"

The older woman frowned and sat back. "Whatever do you mean?"

"Do you believe she died of a heart attack?"

"Well, I . . . what else am I to believe? That's what I was told."

"Who told you?"

"The doctor."

"Which doctor?"

"Our family doctor."

"He examined her, did an autopsy?"

"No, he received confirmation from a British physician, I believe. Barrie died in . . ."

"I know, in London, but there's . . . there's some reason to question whether it really was her heart."

Mayer's face hardened. She said in a voice that matched her expression. "I'm not sure I understand what you're getting at, Collette."

"I'm not sure what I'm getting at either, Melissa, but I'd like to find out the truth. I simply can't buy the notion that Barrie had a coronary at her age. Can you?"

Melissa Mayer reached into an alligator purse, took out a long cigarette, lighted it, seemed to savor the smoke in her lungs and mouth, then said, "I believe that life revolves around accepting, Collette. Barrie is dead. I must accept that. Heart attack? I must accept that, too, because if I don't, I'll spend the rest of my days in torment. Can't you accept *that*?"

Cahill winced at the intensity in her voice. She said, "Please don't misunderstand, Melissa, I'm not trying to raise questions that would make Barrie's death more painful to you than it is right now. I realize losing a friend is not as traumatic as losing a daughter, but I've been suffering my own brand of torment. That's why I'm here, trying to lessen my own pain. I suppose that's selfish, but it happens to be the truth."

Cahill watched the older woman's face soften from the hard mask it had become, for which she was thankful. She was feeling an increasing amount of guilt. There she was sitting with a grieving mother under false pretenses, pretending only to be a friend but, in actuality, functioning as an investigator for the CIA. That damned duality, she thought. It was the thing that bothered her most about the work, the need to lie, to withhold, to be anything but the basic person that you were. Everything seemed based upon a lie. There was no walking in the sunshine because too much was conducted in shadows and safehouses, messages written in code instead of plain English, strange names for projects, a life of looking over your shoulder and watching your words, and suspicions about everyone with whom you came in contact.

"Melissa, let's just have a pleasant lunch," Cahill said. "It was wrong of me to use this occasion to salve my own feelings about losing my friend."

The older woman smiled and lighted another cigarette. "Barrie was always chiding me for smoking. She said it would take ten years off of my life but here I sit, very much alive, smoking like a chimney and talking about my health-conscious daughter who's very much dead." Collette tried to change the subject but Mrs. Mayer shook her off. "No, I would like to talk about Barrie with you. There really hasn't been anyone since it happened that I could turn to, be open with. I'm very glad you're here and were close to her. There didn't seem to be many people close to her, you know. She was so outgoing, yet . . . yet, she had so few friends."

Cahill looked quizzically at her. "I would have thought the opposite was true. Barrie was so gregarious, full of life and fun."

"I think that was more show than anything, Collette. You see, Barrie had a lot of nasty things to deal with."

"I know she had occasional problems but . . ."

The smile on Melissa Mayer's face was a knowing one. She said, "It was more than just normal problems, Collette. I'm afraid I'll go to *my* grave regretting those aspects of her life in which I played a part."

Cahill felt uncomfortable at what seemed to be Mayer's apparent intention to delve into some cavern of secrets about Barrie and her. Yet she was as curious as she was uncomfortable, and did nothing to hinder the conversation.

Mayer asked, "Did Barrie ever mention her father to you?"

Cahill thought for a moment. "I think so but I can't remember in what context. No, I'm not even sure she did." In fact, it had struck Cahill a few times during her years of friendship with Barrie Mayer that she didn't mention her father. She remembered a conversation during college with Barrie and some other girls about fathers and their impact on daughters' lives. Barrie's only contribution to the conversation had been sarcastic comments about fathers in general. Later that night, Cahill asked about her own father and was met with the simple response, "He's dead." The tone of Barrie's voice had made it plain that the conversation was over.

Cahill told Melissa Mayer about it and the older woman nodded. Her gaze drifted across the dining room as though in search of a place to which she could anchor her thoughts.

"We don't have to talk about this, Melissa," Cahill said.

Mayer smiled. "No, I was the one who introduced the subject. Barrie's father died when Barrie was ten."

"He must have been a young man," said Cahill.

"Yes, he was young and . . . he was young and not missed."

Cahill said, "I don't understand."

"Barrie's father, my husband, was a cruel and inhuman person, Collette. I wasn't aware of that when I married him. I was very young and he was very handsome. His cruelty started to come out after Barrie was born. I don't know whether he resented that a child came between us or whether it just represented a warped aspect of his character, but he was cruel to her, abusive physically and psychologically."

"That's terrible," Cahill said.

"Yes, it was."

"It must have been terrible for you, too."

A pained expression came over Mrs. Mayer's face. She bit her lip and said, "What was terrible was that I did so little to stop it. I was afraid of losing him and kept finding reasons for what he was doing, kept telling myself that he would change. All that did was to prolong it. He . . . *we* virtually destroyed Barrie. She had to find ways to escape the pain of it and went into her own private little world. She didn't have any friends then, just as she didn't as an adult—except you, of course, and some love interests—so she created her own friends, imaginary ones who shared her private world which was, Lord knows, better than her real one."

Collette felt a lump develop in her throat. She thought back to spending time with Barrie and tried to identify some sort of behavior that would indicate such a childhood. She came up empty, except for Barrie's tendency sometimes to drift off into her own thoughts, even in the middle of a spirited conversation with a group of people. But that hardly constituted strange behavior. She'd done it herself.

Melissa Mayer interrupted Cahill's thoughts. "Barrie's father left on her ninth birthday. We had no idea where he went, didn't hear from him again until Barrie was ten and we received a call from the police in

Florida. They told me that he'd died of a stroke. There wasn't even a funeral because I didn't want one. He was buried in Florida. I have no idea where." She sighed. "He certainly lived on in Barrie, though. I've carried the guilt and shame of what I allowed to be done to my daughter all these years." Her eyes filled up and she dabbed at them with a lace handkerchief.

Collette felt a twinge of anger at the woman across from her, not only because of her admission that she did nothing to help her daughter, but because she seemed to be looking for sympathy.

She quickly told herself that wasn't fair and motioned for a waiter. They both ordered lobster bisque and Caesar salads.

The conversation took a decided upturn in mood. Melissa wanted Cahill to talk about experiences she'd had with Barrie, and Collette obliged her, some of the stories making Melissa laugh heartily, aided, in Cahill's mind, by the second drink.

When lunch was over, Cahill brought up the subject of the men in Barrie's life. Her question caused Barrie's mother to smile. She said, "Thank God the experience with her father didn't sour her on men for the rest of her life. She had a very active love life. But you must know more about that than I do. It's not the sort of thing daughters routinely share with their mothers."

Cahill shook her head. "No, Barrie didn't tell me about her male friends in great detail, although there was one, a yacht charter captain from the British Virgin Islands." She waited for a response from the mother but got none. "Eric Edwards. You didn't know about him?"

"No. Was it a recent relationship?"

Cahill nodded. "Yes, I think she was seeing him right up until the day she died. She shared her feelings about him with me. She was madly in love with him."

"No, I didn't know about him. There was that psychiatrist she was seeing."

Cahill almost said the name but held herself in check. "Seeing professionally?" she asked.

The mother made a sour face. "Yes, for a while. I was very much against it, her going into therapy where she'd have to bear her soul to a stranger."

Cahill said, "But, considering Barrie's childhood, that might have been the best thing she could do. Hadn't she had any professional help up until seeing this psychiatrist? You said his name was . . . ?"

"Tolker, Jason Tolker. No, I never saw the need for it. I think I was the one who should have had therapy, considering the grief it caused me all these years, but I don't believe in it. People should be able to handle their own emotional lives. Don't you agree?"

"Well, I suppose . . . I gather from what you've said that Barrie saw him socially as well."

"Yes, and I found that appalling. Imagine going to someone like that for more than a year and telling your most intimate secrets and then going out with him. He must have considered her a fool."

Cahill thought for a moment, then said, "Was Barrie in love with this psychiatrist?"

"I don't know."

"Did you meet him?"

"No. Barrie kept her personal life very separate from me. I suppose that goes back to her childhood needs to escape her father."

"I really don't know of any other men in Barrie's life," Cahill said, "except for fellows she dated in college. We fell out of touch for a while, as you know."

"Yes. There is that fellow at the office, David Hubler, who I think she was interested in."

That was news to Cahill, and she wondered whether the mother had it straight. She asked whether Barrie had actually dated Hubler.

"Not that I know of, and I suppose the fact that she freely introduced him to me means there was not romantic interest." She suddenly looked older than she had at the beginning of lunch. She said, "It's all water over the dam, isn't it, now that she's dead? All so wasted." She sat up straight, as though she'd suddenly realized something. She looked Cahill in the eye. "You really don't believe Barrie died of a heart attack, do you?"

Cahill slowly shook her head.

"What, then? Are you saying someone killed her?"

"I don't know, Melissa, I just know that I can't accept the fact that she died the way they say she did."

"I hope you're wrong, Collette. I know you're wrong."

"I hope so. I'm glad we could get together for this lunch. I'd like to keep in touch with you while I'm back here in Washington."

"Yes, of course, that would be lovely. Would you come for dinner?"

"I'd like that."

They went to the basement parking garage and stood next to Melissa Mayer's Cadillac. Cahill asked, "When was the last time you saw Barrie?"

"The night before it happened. She stayed with me."

"She did?"

"Yes, we had a nice quiet dinner together before she took off on another journey. She traveled so much. I don't know how she managed to keep her sanity with all the trips."

"It was a hectic schedule. Did she have her luggage with her at your house?"

"Her luggage? Yes, she did, as a matter of fact. She was going to go directly to the airport but decided to stop at the office first to take care of some things."

"What kind of luggage did Barrie have?"

"Regular luggage, one of those hang-up garment bags and a nice leather carry-on. Of course, there were always the briefcases."

"Two of them?"

"No, only the one that she always used. I bought it for her birthday a few years ago."

"I see. Did she act different that night at your house? Did she complain about feeling ill, display any symptoms?"

"Goodness, no, we had a delightful evening. She seemed in very good spirits."

They shook hands and drove off in their respective automobiles. A third car left the garage at the same time and fell in behind Cahill.

She returned to the hotel and called David Hubler. They made a date for drinks at the Four Seasons at four. She then called the British Virgin Islands, got the number of the Edwards Yacht Charter Company, and reached a secretary who informed her that Mr. Edwards was away for a few days.

"I see," Cahill said. "Do you have any idea when he'll be back? I'm calling from Washington and . . ."

"Mr. Edwards is in Washington," said the young woman, whose voice had an island lilt.

"That's wonderful. Where is he staying?"

"At the Watergate."

"Thank you, thank you very much."

"What did you say your name was, ma'am?"

"Collette Cahill. I was a friend of Barrie Mayer." She waited; the name didn't trigger a response from the girl.

She hung up, called the Watergate Hotel, and asked for Mr. Edwards's room. There was no answer. "Would you like to leave a message?"

"No, thank you, I'll call again."

13

CAHILL SAT IN the lavish lobby of Georgetown's Four Seasons Hotel waiting for David Hubler. A pianist played light classics, the delicate notes as muted as the conversations at widely spaced tables.

Cahill took in the faces of the well-dressed men and women. They were the faces of power and money, cause and effect, probably in reverse order. Dark suits, furs, highly polished shoes, minimal gestures, and comfortable posture. They belonged. Some people did and others didn't, and nowhere was the distinction more obvious than in Washington.

Were the people around her involved in politics and government? It was always assumed that everyone in Washington worked in its basic industry, government, but that had changed, Cahill knew, and for the better.

It had seemed to her during her college days that every eligible young man worked for some agency or congressman or political action committee, and that all conversation gravitated toward politics. It had become boring for her at one point, and she'd seriously considered transferring to another college in a different part of the country to avoid becoming too insular. She didn't, and ended up in government herself. What if? A silly game. What was reality for her was that she worked for the Central Intelligence Agency, had lost a friend, and was now in Washington trying to find out what had happened to that friend, for herself and for her employer.

She realized as she waited for Hubler that she'd been forgetting or, at least, ignoring that second reason for being there.

Her official assignment to take "leave" and to use it "unofficially" to find out more about Barrie Mayer's death had been handed her so casually, as though it really didn't matter what she discovered. But she knew better. Whatever underlying factors contributed to Mayer's death, they had to do with Banana Quick, perhaps the most important and ambitious clandestine operation the Company had ever undertaken. The fact that it had been compromised in some way by Mayer's death, and its implementation had been accelerated, added urgency— an urgency that Cahill now felt.

She lost track of time, and of the Four Seasons as she reflected on what had transpired over the past few weeks, especially what had been said to her by her Hungarian agent, Árpád, and what Hank Fox had said that morning about a leak in Banana Quick.

Tolker? Hegedüs had hinted that he might be "friendly" to the other side. But, she wondered, what information could he have on Banana Quick that would threaten the project and, if he did, where did he get it?

Barrie Mayer? It was the only source that made any sense to her, but that raised its own question—where would Mayer have learned enough about the project?

Eric Edwards? Possible. They were lovers, he was CIA, and he lived in the British Virgins.

If Mayer *was* killed because of what she was carrying that pertained to Banana Quick, who had the most to gain, the Soviets, or someone working with or within the CIA with something to hide?

She checked her watch. Hubler was a half hour late. She ordered a white wine and told the waitress she had to make a phone call. At Barrie's agency, Marcia St. John answered. "I was supposed to meet David at the Four Seasons a half hour ago," Collette said.

"I don't know where he is," St. John said. "I know he planned to meet you but right after you called, he got another call and tore out of here like an Olympic sprinter."

"He didn't say where he was going?"

"No. Sorry."

"Well, I'll wait another half hour. If he doesn't show and checks in with you, ask him to call me at the Hotel Washington."

"Shall do."

As Collette resumed her seat in the Four Seasons and quietly sipped her wine, David Hubler parked his car in front of a hydrant in Rosslyn, got out, locked the door, and looked up the street. He had to squint, finally to shield his eyes with his hand from the harsh, direct rays of a blazing setting sun that was anchored at the far end of the busy road. There was a heavy, dirty haze in the air that compounded the blinding effect.

He said aloud the address he'd been given by the caller who'd prompted him to run from the office, and to break his date with Collette. He checked his watch; he was ten minutes early. Street signs at the corner told him he was within half a block of his destination, an alley between two nondescript commercial buildings.

A group of teenagers passed, one carrying a large portable radio and cassette player from which loud rock 'n' roll blared. Hubler watched them pass, turned, and started for the corner. The sidewalk was busy with men and women leaving their jobs and heading home. He bumped into a woman and apologized, circumvented a young couple embracing, and reached the corner. "What the hell," he said as he turned left and walked halfway down the block until reaching the entrance to the alley. He peered down it; the sun was anchored at its end, too. He cocked his head, focused his eyes on the ground, and took a few steps into the narrow passageway. It was empty, or appeared to be. Steel doors that were rear entrances to businesses were closed. Occasional piles of neatly bagged garbage jutted out into the alley; two motorcycles and a bicycle were securely chained to a ventilation pipe.

Hubler continued, his eyes now searching walls on his left for a large red sign that would say NO PARKING. He found it halfway into the alley, above a bay of sorts. A narrow loading dock with a roll-down corrugated door was below the sign. Large drums, probably having contained chemicals or some other industrial product, were stacked three high and five deep, creating a pocket invisible to people on the streets at either end.

He looked at his watch again. It was time. He skirted the drums and went to the loading dock, placed his hands on it, and listened. The alley was a silent refuge from the distant horns of the streets, the boom boxes, and the animated conversations of people happily escaping nine-to-five.

"On time," a male voice said.

Hubler, hands still on the loading dock, raised his head and turned in the direction of the voice. His pupils shut down as his eyes tried to adjust from shadows to the stream of sunlight pouring into the alley. The man to whom the voice belonged took three steps forward and thrust his right hand at Hubler's chest. A six-inch, needle-thin point of an ice pick slid easily through skin and muscle and reached Hubler's heart, the handle keeping it from going through to his back.

Hubler's mouth opened wide. So did his eyes. A red stain bloomed on the front of his shirt. The man withdrew the pick, leaned his head closer to Hubler, and watched the result of his action, like a painter evaluating an impetuous stroke of red paint on his canvas. Hubler's knees sagged and led his body down to the cement. His assailant quickly knelt and pulled Hubler's wallet from his pants pocket and shoved it into his tan rain jacket. He stood, checked both ends of the alley, and walked toward the sun, now in the final stage of its descent.

When Hubler didn't arrive, Cahill paid for her drink and returned to her hotel. There were two messages, one from Vern Wheatley, the other from the British literary agent, Mark Hotchkiss. She tried Dave Hubler at home. No answer. Hotchkiss, the message said, was staying at the newly renovated Willard. She called; no answer in his room. Vern Wheatley was staying in his brother's apartment on Dupont Circle. She reached him.

"What's up?" she asked.

"Nothing much. I just thought you might be free for dinner."

"I'm not, Vern, wish I were. Rain check?"

"Tomorrow?"

"Sounds good. How's the assignment going?"

"Slow, but what else is new? Trying to pin down bureaucrats is like trying to slam a revolving door. I'll give you a call tomorrow afternoon and set things up."

"Great."

"Hey, Collette?"

"Huh?"

"You have a date tonight?"

"I wouldn't call it that unless the fact that I'm having dinner with a man makes it so. Business."

"I thought you were home to relax."

"A little relaxation, a little business. Nothing heavy. Talk to you tomorrow."

She hung up and chided herself for the slip. As she took off her clothes and stepped into the shower, she found herself wishing she were on a vacation. Maybe she could tack on a week of leave when she was done snooping into Barrie Mayer's death. That would be nice.

After her shower, she stood naked in front of a full-length mirror and looked herself over from head to toe. "Strictly a salad, no bread," she said to her reflection as she pinched the flesh at her waist. She certainly wasn't overweight, but knew the possibility was always there should she neglect her sensible eating habits and go on a binge.

She chose one of two dresses she'd brought with her from home, a mauve wool knit she'd had made for her in Budapest. Her hair had grown longer and she debated with herself whether she liked it that way. It didn't matter at the moment. She wasn't about to get a haircut that evening. She completed her ensemble with tan pumps, a simple, single-strand gold necklace, and tiny gold pierced earrings, a gift to her from Joe Breslin on the first anniversary of her assignment to Budapest. She grabbed her purse and raincoat, went to the lobby, and told the doorman she needed a cab. She wasn't in the mood to drive and have to search for parking spaces.

It had started to rain, and the air had picked up a chill from a front that was passing through Washington. The doorman held a large golf umbrella over her as he opened the door to a taxi that pulled up. She gave the driver Jason Tolker's address and, a few minutes later, was seated in his reception area. It was six forty-five; Tolker's group session was still in progress.

Fifteen minutes later, the participants in the group filed past her. Tolker emerged moments later, smiling. "Spirited group tonight. You watch them argue with each other over trivialities and understand why they don't get along with colleagues and spouses."

"Do they know you're that cynical?"

"I hope not. Hungry?"

"Not especially. Besides, I've put on a few pounds and would just as soon not compound it tonight."

He looked her up and down. "You look perfect to me."

"Thank you." He didn't waste time, she thought. She'd never responded to men who came up with lines like that, found them generally to be insecure and immature. Vern Wheatley flashed through her mind, and she wished she hadn't accepted Tolker's dinner invitation. Duty! she told herself, smiled, and asked what restaurant he had in mind.

"The best in town, my house."

"Oh, wait a minute, doctor, I . . ."

He cocked his head and said in serious tones, "You're stereotyping me, Miss Cahill, aren't you, assuming that because I suggest dinner at my place the seduction scene is sure to follow?"

"It crossed my mind."

"Mine, too, frankly, but if you'll come to dinner at my house, I promise you that even if you change your mind, you'll get no moves by me. I'll throw you out right after coffee and Cognac. Fair enough?"

"Fair enough. What's on the menu?"

"Steaks and a salad. Skip the dressing and you'll lose a pound or two."

His champagne-colored Jaguar was parked outside. Cahill had never been in one; she enjoyed the smell and feel of the leather seats. He drove swiftly through Foggy Bottom, turned up Wisconsin Avenue and passed the Washington Cathedral, then took smaller streets until reaching a stretch of expensive houses set back from the road. He turned into a driveway lined with poplar trees and came to a stop on a gravel circle in front of a large stone house. A semicircular portico decorated with egg-and-dart detail protected the entrance. There were lights on in the front rooms that shed soft, yellow illumination through drapes drawn over the windows.

Tolker came around and opened Collette's door. She followed him to the front door. He pushed a buzzer. Who else was there? she wondered. The door opened and a young Chinese man wearing jeans, a dark blue short-sleeved sweatshirt, and white sneakers greeted them.

"Collette, this is Joel. He works for me."

"Hello, Joel," she said as she entered the large foyer. To the left was what looked like a study. To the right was a dining room lighted by electrified candelabra.

"Come on," Tolker said, leading her down a hall and to the living room. Floor-to-ceiling windows afforded a view of a formal Japanese garden lighted by floodlights. A high brick wall surrounded it.

"It's lovely," Cahill said.

"Thanks. I like it. Drink?"

"Just club soda, thank you."

Tolker told Joel to make him a kir. The young man left the room and Tolker said to Cahill, "Joel's a student at American University. I give him room and board in exchange for functioning as a houseboy. He's a good cook. He's been marinating the steaks all day."

Cahill went to a wall of books and read the titles. They all seemed to be on the field of human behavior. "Impressive collection," she said.

"Most of them pop garbage, but I wanted them all. I'm a collector by nature." He came up beside her and said, "Publishers have been after me to write a book for years. Frankly, I can't imagine spending that much time on anything."

"A book. I imagine that would be an ego-booster, not that . . ."

He laughed and finished her sentence. "Not that I need it."

She laughed, too, said, "I sense you're not lacking in it, Doctor."

"Ego is healthy. People without egos don't function very well in society. Come, sit down. I'd like to learn more about you."

She wanted to say that she was the one who wanted to learn something from the evening. She sat on a small, gracefully curved Louis XV sofa upholstered in a heavy bloodred fabric. He took a seat on its mate, across an inlaid leather coffee table. Joel placed their drinks in front of them and Tolker said, "Dinner in an hour, Joel." He looked to Cahill for approval, and she nodded. Joel left. Tolker lifted his glass and said, "To dinner with a beautiful woman."

"I can't drink a toast to that, but I won't argue."

"See, you have a healthy ego, too."

"Different from yours, Doctor. I would never toast myself. You would."

"But I didn't."

"It wouldn't have offended me if you had."

"All right, to a beautiful woman *and* to a handsome, successful, bright, and impossibly considerate gentleman."

She couldn't help but laugh. He got up and started a tape that sent soft sounds of a modern jazz trio into the room. He sat again. "First of all, how about calling me Jason instead of Doctor?"

"All right."

"Second, tell me about your life and work in Budapest."

"I'm on leave," she said.

"Spoken like a true Company employee."

"I think we ought to drop any conversation along those lines."

"Why? Make you nervous?"

"No, just aware that there are rules."

"Rules. I don't play by them."

"That's your choice."

"And your choice is to rigidly adhere to every comma and period. I'm not being impudent, Collette. I just find it amazing and wonderful and damned ironic that you and Barrie and I have this uncommon common bond. Think about it. You and your best friend both end up doing work for our country's leading spook agency, you because of a sense of patriotism, or the need for a job with a pension and a little excitement, Barrie because she became close to me, and I, as I've already acknowledged, have been a consultant to the spooks a time or two. Remarkable when you think of it. Most people go through their lives not knowing the CIA from the Audubon Society and never meeting a soul who works for them."

"Small world," she said.

"It turned out that way for us, didn't it?"

He arranged himself comfortably on his couch, crossed his legs, and asked, "How well did you know Barrie?"

"We were good friends."

"I know, but how well did you know her, *really* know her?"

Cahill thought of her luncheon conversation with Mayer's mother and realized she didn't know her friend well at all. She mentioned the lunch to Tolker.

"She was more disturbed than you realize."

"In what way?"

"Oh, what we call a disturbed myth-belief pattern."

"Meaning?"

"Meaning that she lived by a set of troublesome beliefs caused by childhood myths that were not tied to normal childhood patterns."

"Her father?"

"Her mother mentioned that to you?"

"Yes."

He smiled. "Did she indicate her role in it?"

"She said she felt guilty for not putting a stop to it. She was very candid. She admitted that she was afraid to lose her husband."

Another smile from him. "She's a liar. Most of Barrie's adult problems stemmed from her mother, not her father."

Cahill frowned.

"The old lady's a horror. Take it from me."

"You mean from Barrie. You've never met the mother."

"True, but Barrie was a good enough source. What I'm suggesting to you, Collette, is that you become a little more discriminating about who in Barrie's life you turn to for information."

"I'm not looking for information."

"You said you were trying to find out what went on with her just before she died."

"That's right, but I don't consider that 'looking for information.' I'm curious about a friend, that's all."

"As you wish. More club soda?"

"No, thank you. You obviously aren't including yourself in that restricted list."

"Of course not. I was the best friend she had . . . excluding you, of course."

"You were lovers, too."

"If you say so. Barrie didn't have any trouble attracting men."

"She was beautiful."

"Yes. Her problem was she couldn't tell the white hats from the black. Her choice in men was terrible, self-destructive to say the least."

"Present company excepted."

"Right again."

"Eric Edwards?"

"I wondered whether you knew about Barrie's macho yacht captain."

"I know a lot about him," Cahill said. "Barrie was very much in love with him. She talked about him a great deal."

"Excuse me, I need a drink." He returned a few minutes later. "Joel's started the steaks. Let me give you a quick tour before dinner."

The house was unusual, an eclectic assortment of rooms, each decorated in a different style. The master bedroom had been created from three rooms. It was huge. While the other rooms in the house smacked of an Early American influence, this room was modern. The thick carpet was white, as was the bedspread on a king-size round bed that stood in the middle of the room like a piece of sculpture, spotlights in the ceiling focusing all attention on it. One wall housed a huge projection screen television and racks of state-of-the-art sound equipment. Besides a black lacquered nightstand that held controls for the audio and video equipment, the only other furniture was black leather director's chairs scattered about the room. There wasn't a piece of clothing, a shoe, or a magazine.

"Different, isn't it?" he said.

"From the rest of the house, yes." She pictured Barrie Mayer in the bed with him.

"My apartment in New York is different, too. I like different things."

"I suppose we all do," she said, walking from the room at a pace just under a run.

Dinner was relaxed, the food and talk good. The subject of Barrie Mayer was avoided. Tolker talked a great deal about his collections, especially wine. When dinner was finished, he took Cahill to the basement where thousands of bottles were stored in temperature-controlled rooms.

They came upstairs and went to his study, which had the look of a traditional British library, books on three walls, polished paneling, carpet in warm earth tones, heavy patinated furniture, pools of gentle light from floor lamps next to a long leather couch and leather armchairs. Tolker told Joel to bring them a bottle of Cognac, then told him he was finished for the night. Cahill was glad the young Chinese man wouldn't be around any longer. There was something unsettling about him, and about the relationship with Tolker. Joel hadn't smiled once the entire evening. When he looked at Tolker, Cahill could see deep anger in his eyes. When he looked at her, it was more resentment she sensed.

"Brooding young man, isn't he?" she said, as Tolker poured their drinks.

Tolker laughed. "Yes. It's like having a houseboy and guard dog for the price of one."

They sat on the couch and sipped from their snifters. "Do you really think you're overweight?" Tolker asked.

Cahill, who'd been staring down into the dark, shimmering liquid, looked at him and said, "I know I can be if I'm not careful. I love food and hate diets. Bad combination."

"Ever try hypnosis?"

"No. Oh, that's not true. I did once, in college. So did Barrie."

It had been a fraternity party. A young man claimed to know how to do hypnosis and everyone challenged him to try it on them. Cahill was reluctant. She'd heard stories of how people can be made to act foolish at the hands of a hypnotist. It represented giving up control and she didn't like the idea.

Mayer, on the other hand, eagerly volunteered and convinced Cahill to give it a try. She eventually agreed and the two of them sat next to each other on a couch while the young man dangled his fraternity ring from a string in front of their eyes. As he talked about how they would begin to feel sleepy and relaxed, Cahill realized two things: She was feeling anything except sleepy, and was finding the whole situation funny. Mayer, on the other hand, had sagged into the couch and was actually purring. Cahill diverted her eyes from the ring and glanced over at her friend. The hypnotist realized he'd lost Cahill and devoted all his attention to Mayer. After a few more minutes of soothing talk, he suggested to Mayer that her hands were tied to helium balloons and would float up. Cahill watched as Mayer's arms began to tremble, then slowly drifted toward the ceiling. They remained there for a long time. Others in the room were watching intently. They were quiet; only the hypnotist's voice invaded the silence.

"I'm going to count from one to five," he said. "When I reach five, you'll be awake, will feel real good, and won't remember anything from the last few minutes. Later, someone will say to you, 'The balloons are pretty.' When you hear that, your arms will feel very light again and they'll float up into the air. You won't try to stop it because it will feel good. Ready? One—two—three—four—five."

Mayer's eyes fluttered open. She realized her arms were high in the air, quickly stretched them, and said, "I feel so good and rested."

Everyone applauded and the beer keg became the center of attention again.

Twenty minutes later, a friend of the hypnotist who'd been prompted casually said to Mayer, "The balloons are pretty." Others at the party knew it was coming and were watching. Barrie Mayer yawned. A contented smile crossed her face and her arms floated up toward the ceiling.

"Why are you doing that?" someone yelled.

"I don't know. It just . . . feels good."

The hypnotist told her to lower them. "No," she said, "I don't want to."

He quickly went through the induction again, then told her that her arms were normal and that there weren't any balloons filled with helium. He counted to five, she shook her head, and that was the end of it.

Later, as Collette and Barrie sat in a booth in an all-night diner drinking coffee, Collette said, "You're such a phony."

"Huh?"

"That business with hypnosis and your arms being light and all. You were going along with it, right?"

"I don't know what you mean."

"You were acting. You weren't asleep or hypnotized."

"No, I really was hypnotized. At least I *think* I was. I don't remember much about it except feeling so relaxed. It was great."

Collette sat back and looked closely at her friend. "The balloons are pretty," she said softly.

Barrie looked around the diner. "What balloons?"

Collette sighed and finished her coffee, still convinced that her friend had been playacting for the sake of the hypnotist.

When she was finished telling the story to Jason Tolker, he said, "You shouldn't be so skeptical, Collette. Just because you weren't receptive doesn't mean Barrie wasn't. People differ in their ability to enter an altered state like hypnosis."

"Barrie must have been *very* receptive. It was incredible what that student was able to get her to do unless . . . unless she was just going along with it for fun."

"I don't doubt you're not hypnotizable, Collette," Tolker said, smiling. "You're much too cynical and concerned about losing control."

"Is that bad?"

"Of course not, but . . ."

"Did you ever hypnotize Barrie?"

He paused as though thinking back, then said, "No, I didn't."

"I'm surprised," Cahill said. "If she was that susceptible and . . ."

"Not susceptible, Collette, receptive."

"Whatever. If she was that receptive, and you use it in your practice, I would have thought that . . ."

"You're crossing that line of doctor-patient confidentiality."

"Sorry."

"You might be more hypnotizable than you think. After all, your only brush with it was with a college amateur. Want me to try?"

"No."

"Could help you resist fattening food."

"I'll stick to willpower, thank you."

He shrugged, leaned forward, and said, "Feel like turning on?"

"With what?"

"Your choice. Pot. Coke. Everything I have is the best."

An invitation to drugs wasn't new to Cahill, but his suggestion offended her. "You're a doctor."

"I'm a doctor who enjoys life. You look angry. Never turn on?"

"I prefer a drink."

"Fine. What'll you have?"

"I don't mean now. I really should be going."

"I really *have* offended you, haven't I?"

"Offended? No, but I am disappointed you choose to end the evening this way. I've enjoyed it very much. Would you take me home now?"

"Sure." His tone was suddenly surly, his expression one of annoyance.

They pulled up in front of her hotel and shut off the engine. "You know, Collette, Barrie wasn't the person you thought she was. She enjoyed drugs, used them with some frequency."

Cahill turned and faced him, her eyes narrowed. "One, I don't believe that. Two, even if it's true, it doesn't matter to me. Barrie was tall, slender, and her hair was sandy. I'm short, could be chubby, and have black hair. Thanks for a nice evening."

"I kept my promise, didn't I?"

"Which one?"

"Not to put moves on you. Can I see you again?"

"I don't think so." It swiftly crossed her mind that maybe she should keep in touch with him as a potential source of information. She had learned things about Barrie that were previously unknown to her and that, after all, was the purpose for her being in Washington. She softened her rejection with, "Please don't misunderstand, Jason. I'm a little confused these days, probably a combination of lingering jet lag, still grieving about Barrie's death, and a lot of other things. Let me see how my schedule goes the next few days. If I'm free, I'll call you. All right?"

"Don't call us, we'll call you."

She smiled. "Something like that. Good night."

"Good night." His face was hard and angry again, and she could see a cruelty behind his expression that caused her to flinch.

She stepped from the car—he didn't bother getting out to open the door for her this time—and started toward the hotel's entrance where the doorman, taken by surprise by her sudden exit, quickly pushed open the door for her. Across the lobby, she could see Vern Wheatley. He was seated in a wing chair facing the door. When he spotted her, he jumped up and met her just inside.

"Vern, what are you doing here?" she asked.

"I have some news, Collette, and I think we'd better discuss it."

14

CAHILL SAT WITH Vern Wheatley the next morning in his brother's apartment. "Good Morning America" was the program on television. The morning paper sat on a coffee table. The lead story on page one seemed to be set in gigantic type; it virtually sprang off the page at Cahill.

D.C. LITERARY AGENT MURDERED

David Hubler, 34, a literary agent with the Georgetown firm of Barrie Mayer Associates, was found murdered last night in an alley in Rosslyn. A spokesman for the Rosslyn Police Department, Sergeant Clayton Perry, said that the cause of death appeared to be a sharp object driven into the victim's heart.

According to the same police spokesman, robbery was the apparent motive. The victim's wallet was missing. Identification was made from business cards in his pocket.

The story went on to provide sketchy details about Hubler. Barrie Mayer's death was mentioned in the final paragraph: "The agency for which Hubler worked suffered another recent loss when its founder and president, Barrie Mayer, died in London of a coronary."

Collette sat on a couch in the living room. She wore Wheatley's robe. Her eyes were focused on the newspaper. Wheatley paced the room.

"It could be a coincidence," Cahill said in a monotone.

Wheatley stopped at the window, looked out, rolled his fingertips on the pane, turned, and said, "Be reasonable, Collette. It can't be. Both of them within such a short period of time?"

A local news cutaway came on TV and they turned their attention to it. It was the second lead story. Nothing new. Just the facts of Hubler's death—apparent robbery—a thin, sharp object the weapon. No suspects. "Back to Charles Gibson in New York and his guest, a former rock star who's found religion."

Collette clicked off the set. They'd been up all night, first in her room at the hotel, then to the apartment at 4:00 A.M. where Wheatley made coffee. She'd cried, much of it out of sympathy for David Hubler, some of it because she was frightened. Now her tear tank, she thought, was empty. All that was left was a dry throat, stinging eyes, and a hollow feeling in her stomach.

"Tell me again how you found out David was dead."

"That's a *real* coincidence, Collette. I happened to be over at Rosslyn police headquarters trying to run down some leads for this assignment I'm on. I was there when the report came in about Hubler. Because of you, I knew right away who he was. You talked a lot about him the night of your party, how that guy Hotchkiss claims he ended up owning the agency and what it would mean to Hubler."

"You just happened to be there?" There was disbelief in her voice.

"Yeah. The minute I heard, I came looking for you at the hotel."

She blew a stream of breath through her lips and pulled on a clump of her hair. "It's scary, Vern, so scary."

"You bet it is, which is why you can't go around viewing it as some dumb coincidence. Look, Collette, you don't buy the fact that your friend Barrie dropped dead of a heart attack. Right?"

"I never said that."

"You didn't have to. The way you talked about it said it all. If you're right—if she was killed by someone—Hubler's death means a hell of a lot more. Right?"

"I don't know how Barrie died. The autopsy said . . ."

"What autopsy? Who did it, some London doctor, you said? Who's he? Did anybody back here connected with her family confirm it?"

"No, but . . ."

"If Barrie Mayer didn't die of natural causes, who do you think might have killed her?"

"Damn it, Vern, I don't know! I don't know anything anymore."

"More coffee?" Wheatley asked.

"No."

"Let's view it rationally," Wheatley said. "Whoever killed Hubler might have killed Barrie, right? The motive could have to do with the agency, with a client, a publisher, or with this character Hotchkiss. What do you know about him?"

"That I didn't particularly like him, that he had dinner with Barrie in London the night before she died, and that he claims to have entered into a partnership agreement with her."

"Did he show you papers?"

"No."

"Do you know where he lives, where his office is in London?"

"I have it written down. He's not there, though. He's in Washington." Wheatley's eyes widened. "He's here."

"Yes. He left a message for me. He's at the Willard."

"You talked to him?"

"No. He wasn't there when I returned his call."

Wheatley started pacing again. He paused at the window. "Let me talk to Hotchkiss," he said.

"Why would you want to do that?"

"I'm interested."

"Why? You didn't know any of these people."

"I feel like I did because of you." He sat next to her and put his hand on her arm. "Look, Collette, you check out of the hotel and come stay here with me. My brother won't be back for another couple of weeks."

"I thought . . ."

"So did I, but he called from Africa yesterday. He finished the photo assignment but he wants to do some shooting for himself."

She pondered his suggestion. "You seem to think *I* might be in danger," she said.

He shrugged. "Maybe, maybe not, but you're a link, too, to both of them. You've met Hotchkiss. He knows you were close to Barrie and that you know about Barrie's will that sets Hubler up to run the agency. I don't know, Collette, I just think being safe is better than being sorry."

"This is all silly, Vern. I could go back to Mom's house."

"No, I want you here."

She looked up into his slender, chiseled face and realized he was giving an order, wasn't suggesting anything. She got up, went to the window, and watched people on the street below scurrying to work, briefcases and brown paper bags of coffee and Danish in their hands. There was something comforting about seeing them. It was normal. What was happening to her wasn't.

Wheatley said, "I'm going to take a shower. I have some appointments this morning. What are you up to?"

"I don't have any definite plans. I have some calls to make and . . ."

"And we check you out of the hotel. Right?"

"Okay. Can I use the phone?"

"Use anything you want. And let's get something straight right now, up front. You stay here, but it doesn't mean you have to sleep with me."

She couldn't help but smile. "Did you really think I'd assume that?" she asked.

"I don't know, but I just want it understood."

"Understood, sir."

"Don't be a wise guy."

"And don't you be a male chauvinist."

"Yes, ma'am. I'll do my best."

She heard the shower come on, picked up the phone in the living room and called her mother.

"Collette, where have you been? I tried you many times at the hotel and . . ."

"I'm okay, Mom, just a change of plans. I'll tell you all about it when I see you. Is anything wrong with you?"

"No, but Mr. Fox called. He was the one you liked so much, wasn't he?"

"Yes. What did he want?"

"He said it was very important that you call him. I promised I'd get the message to you but I couldn't reach you."

"That's okay, Mom. I'll call him this morning. Anything else new?"

"No. Your Uncle Bruce fell last night. He broke his arm."

"That's terrible. Is he in the hospital?"

"He should be but he wouldn't stay. That's the problem with drinking like he does. He can't go to the hospital because he can't drink there. They set his arm and sent him home."

"I'll call."

"That would be nice. He's such a good man except for all the drinking. It's a curse."

"I have to go, Mom. I'll call you later in the day. By the way, I'll be staying at Vern's brother's apartment for a few days."

"With him?"

"Vern? Well . . ."

"His brother."

"Oh, no. He's in Africa on a photo assignment. Vern will be here but . . ."

"You be careful."

"Of Vern?"

"I don't mean that, I just . . ."

"I'll be careful."

"Give him my best. He's a nice boy."

"I will." She gave her the apartment phone number.

Wheatley came from the shower wearing a big, fluffy red towel around his waist. His hair was wet and fell over his forehead. "Who'd you call?" he asked.

"My mother. She says hello."

"The bathroom's all yours."

"Thanks."

She closed the bathroom door, hung the robe on the back of it, and turned on the shower. A radio inside the stall was tuned to a light rock station. She reached through the water and steam and found WGMS-FM, where Samuel Barber's *Adagio for Strings* was being performed by the New York Philharmonic. She turned up the volume, withdrew her hand, stood in front of the mirror, wiped condensation from it with her palm, and peered at herself.

"Out of control," she said. "Everything's out of control."

The poignancy of the music drew her into the shower, where she eased herself under the torrent of hot water until her body had acclimated, then thrust her face beneath it. As fatigue was driven from her by the pulsating stream, she thought of her decision—*his* decision—to stay with him. Maybe she shouldn't. There was no need. She wasn't in any danger.

She absently wondered why Wheatley was so interested? Of course . . . how stupid not to realize it immediately. There's a story in it, possibly a big one. He wanted her close in case she could contribute to it by knowing Mayer and Hubler. She'd undoubtedly be finding out more about their deaths, and he could use that knowledge. It didn't anger her that she might be used by him. In fact, it set her mind at ease.

She took a plastic bottle of shampoo from a white wire rack, poured some into her hand, and vigorously worked it into her hair. It relaxed her; she felt ready to start the day. She'd call Hank Fox, then go to Barrie Mayer's agency where she'd find out what she could from her associates. There was Mark Hotchkiss to call, and Eric Edwards. It would be a busy day but she welcomed it. She'd been floundering too long, flopping between the role of concerned, grieving friend and unofficial investigator. It was time to pull everything together, accomplish what she could, grab a legitimate week's vacation and get back to Budapest where, no matter how much intrigue existed, there was a sense of order and structure.

She didn't hear the door open. It was only an inch at first, then wider. Wheatley stuck his head inside the bathroom and said softly, "Collette."

The water and music blotted out everything for her.

"Collette," he said louder.

She sensed rather than heard him, looked through the glass door and saw him standing there. She gasped; hot water instantly filled her throat and caused her to gag.

"Collette, I have some clean jockey shorts if you want a pair. Socks, too."

"What? *Shorts?*"

"Yeah. Sorry to barge in." He backed out and closed the door.

She quickly finished showering, stepped out and stood immobile, her heart pounding, her lips quivering. "Shorts," she said. "Jockey shorts." She began to calm down and started to laugh as she dried her hair. He'd left a clean pair of shorts and white athletic socks on a hamper. She put them on, slipped the dress she'd worn the night before over her

head, and went to the bedroom where he was finishing dressing in
jeans, a turtleneck, and a corduroy sport jacket.

"Thanks for the shorts and socks," she said. "They don't exactly go
with the dress, but they'll do until I can get back to the hotel."

"We'll go right now," he said. "Hope I didn't scare you?"

"Scare me? Of course not. I thought you were making a move."

"I promised, remember?"

She thought of Jason Tolker's similar promise. She tried to slip her
pumps over the heavy socks, gave up, and slipped bare feet into them.
"Can't use these," she said, tossing the socks on the bed.

They drove to the hotel in her rented car, checked out, and an hour
later were back in the apartment. "Got to go," Wheatley said. "Here's
an extra key to the place. Catch up later?"

"Sure."

"Who are you seeing today?"

"I'm going over to Barrie's agency."

"Good idea. By the way, who was that guy you were with last night?"

"Just a friend. A doctor, friend of the family."

"Oh. We're on for dinner tonight, right?"

"Right."

"Take care. Maybe I'm being paranoid but I'd move easy," he said.
"Don't take chances."

"I won't."

"Not worth it. After all, murder isn't your business. You help
stranded tourists, right?"

"Right." There was a playful, disbelieving tone in his voice, and it
irked her.

After he'd gone, she picked up the phone and called Hank Fox in
Langley.

"You took your time," he said.

"I just got the message. My mother couldn't track me last night."

"One of those nights, huh?"

"Not in the least. Why did you call me?"

"A need to talk. Free now?"

"Well, I . . ."

"Be free. It's important. You have a car?"

"Yes."

"Good. Meet me in an hour at the scenic overlook off the G.W.
Parkway, the one near the Roosevelt Bridge. Know it?"

"No, but I'll find it."

"An hour."

"I'll be there."

15

COLLETTE DRESSED IN a gray skirt, low shoes, red-and-white striped button-down shirt and blue blazer. She went to a coffee shop around the corner from the apartment and had bacon and eggs, then got in her car and headed for her rendezvous with Hank Fox.

She kept to the speed limit on the George Washington Memorial Parkway, but her mind was going faster. Had Fox found a link between Barrie Mayer's and David Hubler's deaths? That possibility opened up another avenue of thought—David Hubler might have been involved with the CIA, too. That hadn't occurred to her before but, now that it had, it didn't seem far-fetched. Hubler and Mayer worked closely together at the agency. Mayer's frequent trips to Budapest, and the constant contact with authors like Zoltán Réti, could easily have opened up areas of discussion between them. Even if it hadn't, there had to be some tangible vestige of Mayer's part-time work for the CIA kicking around the office. Maybe she'd actually recruited Hubler into her second life. If that were the case, Cahill hoped she'd done it with agency blessing. Taking others into the fold without being ordered to do so was bound to cause major trouble, big enough, she realized, to have caused their deaths. She'd heard of agents who'd been "terminated" by the CIA itself, not for revenge or punishment as with the Mafia, but as an expedient means of closing leaks on a permanent basis.

Traffic was light this morning, so light that she noticed a green sedan that had fallen in behind her as soon as she turned onto the parkway. It stayed a considerable distance from her, but occasional glances in the rearview mirror confirmed that it was still there. She decided not to proceed to the location given her by Hank Fox until the green sedan was no longer an issue. She reached the scenic overlook Hank Fox had mentioned but passed it, her eyes quickly surveying the area. There were two cars, one a four-door pale blue Chevrolet Caprice, the other a white station wagon with paneling. A young woman holding a baby on her hip walked a dalmatian on a leash. A pit stop for the dog, Cahill thought, as she got off at the next exit and made a series of sharp turns on local streets until finding her way back onto the parkway. She checked her watch; she was ten minutes early but that time would be eaten by having to exit the parkway again and circling back. She checked behind her in the mirror. No green sedan. So much for that.

Precisely an hour after she'd talked to Fox she turned into the parking area. The woman, baby, and dog were gone, leaving the Caprice sitting by itself. Cahill pulled up next to it, put her car into PARK, turned, and peered into the Caprice. Hank Fox looked back at her through the glass. She noticed there was someone else in the car. She stiffened; why would he bring someone else? Who was it? She tried to see, but glare on the window left only a vague image in the passenger seat.

Both doors on the Caprice opened. Hank Fox stepped out of the driver's side, Joe Breslin the other. Collette breathed a sigh of relief, and surprise. What was Breslin doing there?

Fox slid in next to her and Breslin got in the rear.

"Joe, what a surprise," Cahill said, turning and smiling.

"Yes, for me, too," Breslin said, slamming the door.

"Let's go," Fox said.

"Where?" asked Cahill.

"For a ride, that's all. Head out toward the airport."

Cahill did her turnaround again and headed south on the parkway, along the Potomac, until reaching National Airport. Fox told her to pull into the metered parking area. When she was at a meter and had turned off the engine, he said, "You two go inside. I'll stay with the car."

They entered the terminal and Breslin led the way to the observation deck entrance. They paid, went through the door, and stood at a railing. Below them was the aircraft ramp area and active runways. A brisk wind whipped Collette's hair. She gently pressed her middle fingers against her ears to muffle the whine of jet engines.

"Just right," Breslin said.

"What?"

"Just the right amount of ambient noise." He moved closer to her, turned, and said inches from her ear, "Plans have changed."

Cahill looked quizzically at him.

"How would you like a little time in the sun?" he asked.

"Sounds nice. I was going to ask about a vacation."

"It's not a vacation. It's an assignment."

When he didn't say more, she asked.

"They want you in the BVI."

"Why?"

"To get to know Eric Edwards. They want you to get close to him, see what he's up to."

Cahill looked to the runway where a Boeing 737 was slicing into a gray sky. Breslin, his hands shoved into his raincoat pockets, a dead pipe clenched in his teeth, paused for what he'd said to sink in, then removed the pipe and leaned toward her. "Banana Quick has been badly compromised, Collette. We have to know how and why."

"Edwards is in Washington, not the BVI," she said.

"We know that, but he'll be returning there in a couple of days. They want you to make contact with him here and do whatever you have to do to . . . to get inside him. See if you can wangle an invitation from him to go down there."

"Wait a minute," she said, her face reflecting her anger, "you want me to sleep with him?"

"The orders don't stipulate that. They just say . . ."

"To do anything I have to do to 'get inside him.' No dice, Joe. Hire a hooker. The Pickle Factory's ripe with them."

"You're overreacting."

"I'm underreacting," she said sharply.

"Call it what you will, the order has come down and you're it. You don't have a choice."

"Ever hear of quitting?"

"Sure, but you won't. I don't want you to. You don't have to sleep with anybody, just get to know a little about his operation and tell us about it. He's too independent, not enough controls."

"What if he doesn't invite me to the BVI?"

"Then you will have failed. Try not to let that happen."

"Where are you getting your information about the leak?"

Breslin glanced around before saying, "From your man in Budapest, Árpád Hegedüs."

"It's definitely Edwards?"

"We don't know, but he's a logical place to start. He's our eyes and ears down there. We know he's a drinker and a talker. Maybe he's been drinking and talking with the wrong people."

"The Russians know everything?"

Breslin shrugged. "They know too much, that's for sure." Some other people came onto the observation deck and stood close to them. "There are two tickets at the Concert Theater box office for some dance recital tomorrow night at the Kennedy Center," Breslin told her. "Go to it. I'll be on the terrace at intermission. Check in with me then."

Collette let out a deep sigh and placed her hands on the railing. "Why did they send you all the way from Budapest to tell me this?" she asked.

"Why do they do anything, Collette? Besides, sending me indicates how important the project is. When the stakes are big, they care enough to send their very best." He smiled.

She couldn't help but smile, too. "They sent you because they knew you could get me to do it."

"Did I?"

"I'll do my best, no promises."

"Can't ask for more than that," he said, touching her arm and turning.

A half hour later they were back at the overlook. Before Fox and Breslin got out of her car, Fox asked, "How was your evening with Jason Tolker?"

"You know about that?"

"Yes."

"It was pleasant enough. He and Barrie were close. I wanted to find out what I could from him."

"Did you? Find out anything?"

"A little."

Breslin said from the back seat, "Save it for tomorrow night on the terrace, Collette." He slapped Fox on the shoulder and said, "Let's go."

They got into Fox's car and drove off, neither man looking back. When they were gone, Cahill felt alone and vulnerable. She gripped the bottom of the steering wheel and saw her eyes in the rearview mirror. Somehow, they didn't belong to her. She tapped the mirror so that it no longer reflected her face, started the engine, and drove as quickly as she could to the apartment, remembering to check her mirror a few times. No green sedan.

16

"ERIC EDWARDS?"

"Yes."

"This is Collette Cahill, Barrie Mayer's friend."

"Hi, how are you? My secretary told me you'd called. I assume you got my message in Budapest?"

"Yes, I did. I'm sorry I didn't contact you sooner but I've been busy."

"I understand."

"I still can't believe she's dead."

"Hard for any of us to believe it. Barrie talked a lot about you. I suppose you were her best friend?"

"We were close. I was wondering if we could get together for a drink, or lunch, or whatever works for you. Will you be in Washington long?"

"Leaving tomorrow. You on vacation?"

"Yes."

"How's things in Budapest?"

"Fine, except for when I heard about Barrie. Are you free for lunch?"

"No, unfortunately I'm not. I'm on a tight schedule."

"Time for a fast drink this afternoon? I'm free all day."

"Well, I suppose . . . how about six? I have a dinner date at seven."

"That'd be fine." She realized she was not about to generate enough interest from him in an hour to result in an invitation to the BVI. "Actually," she said, "I'm not being completely honest. I do want to talk to you about Barrie, but I also would love some good advice on the BVI. I'm spending part of my vacation there and thought you could recommend a good hotel, restaurants, that sort of thing."

"Happy to. When are you leaving?"

Some quick thinking. "In a few days."

"I'll give it my best shot when we meet tonight. On a budget?"

"Sort of, but not too tight."

"Fine. Like sailing?"

Collette had never been out in a sailboat. "Yes," she said, "I love it." She knew she should qualify her answer. "I really don't know much about it, though. I've only been a few times."

"Let's see if we can't arrange a day trip for you. I'm in the yacht-chartering business."

"I know. It sounds . . ." She laughed. "It sounds wonderful and romantic."

"Mostly hard work, although it does beat a suit and tie and nine to five, at least for me. Any suggestion where to meet tonight?"

"Your choice. I've been away from Washington too long."

"Might as well come over here to the Watergate. Would make my life a little easier. Come to my room. I'll have something sent up. What do you drink?"

"Scotch and soda?"

"You got it. See you at six, Room 814."

She drove to Barrie Mayer's literary agency where Marcia St. John and Carol Geffin were behind their desks. Tony Tedeschi, one of the associate agents, was burrowing through a file cabinet in the corner.

St. John, a lanky, attractive mulatto, who'd been there the longest, greeted Cahill soberly.

"I heard," Cahill said.

St. John shook her head. "First Barrie, now David. It's incredible."

Tedeschi said, "How are you, Collette?"

"Okay, Tony. The question is how are *you*?"

"We're holding up. Have you heard anything new about David?"

"No, just the TV and newspapers. What are the funeral plans?"

"Not set yet," St. John said. "How's Budapest?"

"Fine, last I saw it." Collette looked at the door leading to Barrie's private office. It was open a crack and she saw a figure cross the room, then disappear. "Who's in there?" she asked.

"Our new leader," St. John said, raising her eyebrows.

"New leader?"

"Mark Hotchkiss."

"Really?" Cahill went to the door and pushed it open. Hotchkiss, in shirtsleeves, bow tie, and yellow suspenders, was seated behind what had been Barrie Mayer's desk. A pile of file folders were on his lap. He looked up over half-glasses, said, "Be with you in a minute, Miss Cahill," and went back to leafing through the files.

Cahill closed the door and stood at the edge of the desk. She waited a few moments before saying, "I find this arrogant, at best."

He looked up again and smiled. "Arrogant? I'd hardly call it that. Due to unforeseen circumstances, there's been a dreadful gap created at this agency. I'm being decisive. If that represents arrogance, so be it."

"Mr. Hotchkiss, I'd like to see the partnership agreement you and Barrie signed."

He smiled, exposing his yellow teeth, pushed the glasses up to the top of his head and leaned back in Mayer's chair, arms behind his head. "Miss Cahill, I have no reason whatsoever to show you anything. The partnership arrangement Barrie and I constructed is quite sound, quite legal. I suggest that if your curiosity is that strong, you contact Barrie's solicitor . . . attorney, Richard Weiner. Would you like his address and phone number?"

"No, I . . . yes, I would."

Hotchkiss found a slip of paper on the desk and copied it onto another slip. "Here you are," he said, a smug smile on his face. "Call him. You'll find that everything is quite in order."

"I'll do that."

"Now," he said, standing and coming to her, "I believe we had tentative plans for dinner here in Washington. What night is good for you?"

"I'm afraid I'm all booked up."

"Pity. I'm sure we have a great deal to talk about. Well, if you change your mind, give me a call. I suspect I'll be here day and night trying to sort things out." His face suddenly sagged into a sympathetic expression. "I am so sorry about that poor chap, Hubler. We had our differences, but to see such a personable young man snuffed out at such an early age is bloody awful. Please give my deepest sympathies to his family."

Cahill's frustration level made further talk impossible. She spun around and left the office. Tedeschi was the first to see her. "You, too, huh?"

"This is absurd," Cahill said. "He just walks in and takes over?"

"Afraid so," Tedeschi said. "He's got the piece of paper. He ran it through Dick Weiner. Weiner doesn't believe it, either, but it looks legit. Why Barrie would have hooked up with this bozo is beyond me, but it looks like the lady made a mistake."

"She made it, we live with it," said Marcia St. John, who'd overheard the conversation.

"Barrie had a will," Cahill said. "She turned things over to David in the event of her death."

Tedeschi shook his head. "The will's invalid, according to Weiner. The partnership agreement takes precedence for some legal reason, the way it was worded, who knows? It's all foreign language to me."

"I'm going to see Weiner."

"You know him?" Tedeschi asked.

"No, but I will."

"He's a nice guy and a good lawyer, but you're wasting your time. Hotchkiss has the agency as the surviving partner. Excuse me, Collette, I gotta work on my résumé."

"I just don't believe this," Collette said, shaking her head and knowing it was a pathetically ineffective statement.

"Life in the fast lane," Carol Geffin said.

"How's David's family holding up?" Collette asked.

"The way they're supposed to, I guess. God, he was young." St. John started to cry and went to the ladies' room.

Collette asked again about funeral arrangements, and was told a decision was to be made later that afternoon. She left the office and went to a phone booth from which she called the attorney, Richard Weiner. She explained her relationship, he was on the line in seconds.

"This can't be right," she said. "Barrie would never have signed an agreement with Hotchkiss making him a full partner so that he'd inherit the agency if she died."

"I feel the same way, Miss Cahill, but the papers do seem in order. Frankly, I can't take any further steps without the prompting of her family. They'd have to challenge it, go after expert handwriting analysis, probe the background of the deal."

"Her only family is her mother."

"I know that. I spoke with her earlier this morning after hearing about David Hubler."

"And?"

"She said she was too old to become involved in something like this."

"What about Dave's family? Her will took care of him. Wouldn't it be in their interest to challenge Hotchkiss?"

"Probably not. Barrie didn't leave the agency to him. She simply stipulated that he be retained on a specified compensation package for five years. She left him key-man insurance, too, fifty thousand dollars."

"Who gets that now that *he's* dead?"

"The agency."

"Hotchkiss."

"Ultimately, not directly. It goes in the corporate coffers. He's the corporation."

She banged her fist against the booth and said, "First her, now David. Do you think . . . ?"

"Think what, that Hotchkiss might have killed David? How can I think that, Miss Cahill?"

"I can. I have."

"Well, I suppose you're . . . but what about Barrie? She died of natural causes."

Cahill had to fight with herself to keep from telling him that Barrie hadn't died of natural causes, that she'd been murdered. Instead, she said, "I'm glad I had a chance to talk with you, Mr. Weiner."

"Let's talk more. If you come up with any information that bears on this, call me day or night." He gave her his home phone number. She pretended to write it down but didn't bother. She knew she wouldn't be calling him at home, or at his office again either. Barrie Mayer's business affairs really didn't interest her, unless Mark Hotchkiss were involved in both deaths. She doubted it. Weiner was right; Hotchkiss wasn't the type.

Still, there was the question of how he'd enticed Mayer into signing such a binding partnership agreement. Had he held something over her head? What could it be? Wrong road, Cahill decided. She'd pursue it later, after taking care of primary business, her initial meeting with Eric Edwards.

That brought up another whole series of thoughts as she returned to the apartment, stopping first at a bookstore to buy a travel guide to the British Virgin Islands.

Did Edwards know for whom she was working? That was one of the biggest problems in tracking Mayer's life prior to her death. Who knew what? Tolker knew. She had to assume that Edwards knew, too. He hadn't indicated it on the message he left on her answering machine in Budapest, or during their brief telephone conversation that morning. But *he knew;* she had to operate under that assumption.

It also began to lean heavily on her that she'd been hopelessly naive in this matter. She'd never once questioned the motives or activities of people like Joe Breslin, Hank Fox, Stan Podgorsky, or any of the others with whom she'd developed a "father-daughter" relationship. The fact was that they responded to a higher calling than Collette Cahill's personal needs and future. They were Company men, fully capable of selling anyone down the river to further the cause for which they'd been hired, or to perpetuate their own careers and lifestyles. "Damn it," she mumbled as she parked the car and headed for Vern Wheatley's brother's apartment, "I hate this."

Those feelings were forgotten as she spent an hour reading the travel guide and formulating questions for Eric Edwards about her "vacation." It took her into the early afternoon. She called Mayer's office and asked whether there'd been any word on funeral plans for David.

"Private," St. John told her. "Just family."

"Why?"

"Because that's the way they want it."

"Who's in the family?"

"His mother and father, a sister who's flying in from Portland, cousins, others, I guess."

"You were his family, too, at least part of it."

"Collette, I only work here. There's a man in Barrie's office with a funny way of talking and yellow fangs. One of the nicest guys I ever knew is being buried. Tony's grinding out résumés like it was the State of the Union address, and Carol is dwelling on which disco will have the best collection of hunks tonight. I miss you, David. I'd be there if they let me. Understand, Collette?"

"Sure. Sorry. I can keep in touch?"

It was a hollow laugh. "P-l-e-a-s-e," St. John said. "Make sure *I'm* alive on a day-to-day basis."

Collette hung up and wrapped her arms about herself as the meaning of St. John's final remark sent a chill through her body. Two dead out of the same office. That realization caused her to begin rethinking everything that had happened. Maybe Barrie Mayer's death had absolutely, positively nothing to do with spies and governments. Maybe it had to do with commerce, pure and simple. Maybe . . . maybe . . .

There were so many of those.

17

EDWARDS ANSWERED his door wearing a white hotel-provided terrycloth robe with a "W" on the breast pocket. "Miss Cahill, come in. I'll only be a minute. I managed to get in a little workout at the end of the day." He disappeared into the bedroom, leaving her alone in the suite's living room.

A small set of barbells rested on towels on the floor. Written on them in black was PROPERTY OF WATERGATE HOTEL. A rock station blared the day's latest hits. Clothing was strewn on every piece of furniture.

She answered a knock on the door. A young Hispanic bellhop rolled a cart into the room, opened its leaves, fussed with napkins and silverware, and handed Collette the check. "I'm not . . . Sure." She signed Edwards's name and included a dollar tip.

Edwards came from the bedroom wearing slacks. Cahill couldn't help but take immediate note of his bare upper body—heavily muscled arms and chest, trim waist, and all of it the color of copper. "It arrived," he said. "I owe you anything?"

"No. I signed."

"Good. Well, let me finish dressing. Help yourself."

"Can I pour you something?"

"Yes, please. Just gin on the rocks. The bottle's over there." He pointed to a cabinet on which a half-empty bottle of gin sat. He returned to the bedroom and Cahill fixed the drinks. When he again joined her he'd put on a monogrammed white silk shirt and yellow loafers. She handed him his glass. He held it up and said, "To the memory of Barrie Mayer, one hell of a fine lady." He drank. She did, too, the Scotch causing her mouth to pucker.

"I'm sorry to be in a rush." He cleared clothing and magazines from the couch and they sat on it. "Tell me, is there anything new about Barrie?"

"New? No. I assume you heard about her associate being murdered last night?"

"No, I didn't. Which associate?"

"David Hubler."

"I don't believe it. She really liked him. He was murdered?"

"That's what the police say. It happened in Rosslyn. Somebody rammed a sharp object into his heart."

"Jesus."

"They say robbery was the motive because his wallet and credit cards were missing, but that doesn't prove anything to me."

"No, I guess not. What irony, the two of them dying so close together."

Collette nodded.

He looked directly at her and said, "I miss Barrie. We were getting close to making it official."

Cahill was surprised. "You were planning marriage?"

"Maybe 'planning' isn't the word, but we were headed in that general direction." He smiled. It was a charming, engaging, little boy's smile. "You must have thought I was some college sophomore with that message I left on your answering machine. It took me forever to get a line to Budapest. When I did and was faced with that infernal machine, I just started babbling. I was very upset. *Very* upset."

"I can imagine," said Cahill. "When had you last seen her?"

"A week or so before. Frankly, we'd been having a few problems and were looking forward to getting away for a few days to straighten things out. She was planning a trip to the BVI when she got back from Hungary. She'll never make that trip now, will she?"

Cahill reacted by filling up. She took a deep breath and forced a smile. Her thoughts were on the situation that existed at the moment, the same old one that characterized every meeting she'd had during the past few days. Did he know she worked for the CIA? She reminded herself that *she'd* decided the answer to that earlier in the day. He knew. Still, should she bring everything up, Barrie's courier life, Jason Tolker, her job in Budapest, and her knowledge of his job in the British Virgins?

Not yet, she decided. The wrong time.

"So, to get onto a lighter note," Edwards said, "you're coming to my little part of the world for a rest."

"Yes, that's right." She'd forgotten that aspect of her visit.

"Made any plans yet?"

"Not really. It's a last-minute decision. I thought I'd go to a travel agent but then I remembered you. Barrie said you know the BVI better than anyone."

"That's not true, but I have learned a lot sailing those islands. Want to go posh? Peter Island, Little Dix, Biras Creek. Want a little more action? The Tradewinds, Bitter End. Looking for a real native feel? Andy Flax's Fischer's Cove, Drake's Anchorage on Mosquito Island. Lots of choices, with even more in between."

Mosquito Island, she thought, the site of Banana Quick's highest-level meetings. "What would you recommend?"

"There's always my place."

Would it be this easy?

"Or," he said, "one of my yachts, if one is available. I promised you a day's sailing. Might as well stay on board and save yourself some money."

"That's much too generous."

"I wouldn't be offering it to just anyone. Barrie stayed with me so many times, at my house and on the yachts. I'd really be privileged to have you, Collette. I can't promise I'll be around much. It depends on bookings, but we're still out of season down there and, at least when I left, things were slow." He stood and refilled his glass. "Another?"

She checked her watch. "You have to leave," she said, "and I have things to do. I feel as though I should be doing something to repay your generosity."

"Don't be silly," he said, walking her to the door.

"If you weren't going back tomorrow, I'd invite you to join me at the Kennedy Center. I ended up with two tickets to a marvelous performance and there's just me to use them."

"Damn, I wish I could," he said, "but it's impossible. I have appointments back home in the afternoon. You'll find somebody else."

She was glad he turned her down. It had been an impetuous offer, one she thought might help bring them closer together in a hurry. But then, she realized, it would be awkward, if not impossible, to meet with Joe Breslin at intermission. Did Edwards know Breslin, and Hank Fox? Probably by name, not by sight. Agents like Edwards operated as rogues, seldom coming into contact with administrative types. They had their single contact in Langley, some operatives in place, and that was it. The nature of the beast. Whether he knew about her was another matter, a bridge to be crossed when . . .

"How's things at the embassy?" he asked as they stood at the door.

"Fine, last I heard."

"You still with the same division?"

What division was that? She said, "Yes."

"When are you planning to come to the BVI?"

"I thought maybe . . . maybe Saturday." It was Wednesday.

"Great. Pan Am goes into San Juan and you can catch an Air BVI flight from there. There's a new direct service out of Miami, too."

"I'd rather leave from New York." She made a mental note to check out the Miami flight. "Thanks for the offer."

"I look forward to it. You have my phone number. Let me know when you're due to arrive and I'll have you picked up."

"This is all overwhelming."

"It's for Barrie. See you in the sun in a couple of days."

18

THE DANCE THEATRE of Harlem ended its first act to thunderous applause from twenty-five hundred people in Kennedy Center's concert hall. Cahill joined in enthusiastically from her twelfth-row-center seat. She picked up her raincoat from the empty seat next to her and moved with the crowd as it spilled out into the Grand Foyer, the Hall of States, and the Hall of Nations. It had been raining when the audience arrived, but had stopped during the first act.

She went to one of the doors leading to the broad terrace on the Potomac and looked out. A few people had gone outside and stood in small groups separated by puddles. She looked toward the railing on the river side and saw Joe Breslin. His back was to her. Blue smoke from his pipe drifted up into the damp night air.

She came up behind him. "Hello, Joe."

He didn't turn as he said, "Nice night. I like it just after it rains."

She joined him at the railing and they looked out over the river and toward National Airport. A jet screamed over them as it sought the solid safety of the runway, its landing gear extended like a large bird's talons reaching for a tree branch. After its engine noise had faded, Breslin asked, "Enjoying the performance?"

"Very much. You?"

"It's not my favorite entertainment but I suppose it has its place."

She started to discuss the dance troupe but knew it wasn't why they were standing there. "I made contact with Eric Edwards," she said.

"And?"

"I'm joining him in the BVI on Saturday."

He swiveled his head and stared at her, smiled, raised his eyebrows, and returned his gaze to the river. "That was fast," he said, sounding disapproving.

"It was easy," she said. "Barrie paved the way."

"Barrie?"

"The common bond between us. I didn't have to do any seducing. We're a couple of friends because of her."

"I see. Are you staying with him?"

"Yes, either at his home or on one of his yachts."

"Good. How did you meet up with him?"

"I called. He invited me for a drink at his suite at the Watergate. Actually, I invited myself. I told him I was planning a vacation in the BVI and asked for recommendations."

"Good tactic."

"I thought so. Anyway, it worked. Now, what's the next step?"

"Meaning what?"

"Meaning, what are you looking for while I'm there?"

Breslin shrugged and drew on his pipe. "I don't know, anything that looks interesting."

"It can't be that vague, Joe."

"I don't mean it to be." His sigh was deep and prolonged. He looked around at others on the terrace. The nearest people were fifteen feet away—two couples who'd come to the railing to see the river. Breslin positioned his body so that he leaned on the rail with his back to them, and was facing Cahill. "Why are you staying with your former boyfriend?"

His directness took her aback. "Vern Wheatley? How do you know about him?"

"It's not so much knowing about him, Collette, it's knowing about you."

"I'm being followed?"

"You're being protected."

"From what?"

"From harm."

"I resent this, Joe."

"Be grateful. What about Wheatley?"

"What about him? We went together in high school, that's all. When I came home, my mom threw a party and he showed up. He's down here on assignment for *Esquire* magazine."

"I know that. Why are you staying with him?"

"Because . . . Christ, Joe, what business is it of yours?"

"You're right, Collette, it's not my business. It's the Company's business."

"I'd debate that."

"Don't bother."

He looked at her and said nothing. She said, "Vern was the one who told me about David Hubler being killed."

"And he convinced you to leave the hotel and move in with him for . . . for your own safety?"

"Yes, as a matter of fact, that's exactly what happened." She shook her head and made a sound by blowing air past her lips. "Boy, I am some protected girl, huh, Joe? What are you doing now, trying to get me to distrust Vern, too? Trust nobody, right? Everybody's a spy or a double agent or a . . ."

Breslin ignored her rising emotions and said flatly, "You do know that your high school beau is in Washington researching a story on us?"

It hit her in the chest like a fist. "No, I did not know that," she said in a controlled voice.

"Hank Fox's unit has been tracking your friend."

"So?"

"Maybe he wants you close to him for information."

"I doubt that."

"Why?"

"Because . . ."

"I think you should be aware of the possibility."

"Thank you." She wasn't proud of the snippy way she answered, but it was the best she could manage.

"About Edwards. There's a possibility that he's the leak in Banana Quick."

"So I heard."

"If so, he's potentially dangerous."

"In what way?"

"Physically. To you. It's something else I thought you'd appreciate knowing."

"Of course I do."

"It's possible he's been turned."

Another fist in the chest. "I thought it was just a matter of drinking too much and a loose tongue."

"Could be those things, too, but the possibility of a turn can never be overlooked. It isn't prudent to overlook such possibilities."

"I certainly won't. Anything else you think I should know?"

"Lots of things. Your man, Árpád Hegedüs, is on his way to Russia."

"He is? They did it?"

"Yes. We had one final meeting with him before he left. It wasn't easy. He wouldn't talk to anyone except 'His Miss Cahill.' We managed to convince him that it was in his interest to talk with somebody else."

"How is he?"

"Frazzled, afraid of what's in store for him once he's back in Mother Russia. He almost bolted, came over to us."

"He wanted that."

"I know, I went over the transcript of the session with Stan. The woman he's met complicated things for him. He was ready to defect and bring her with him."

"He didn't."

"We dissuaded him."

"Because we need him." Now it was scorn she didn't intend to come from her mouth.

"We suspect he'll be all right. There's nothing to indicate he's in trouble."

"The woman?"

"She's a clerk in a Hungarian food-processing plant. No use to us."

"I don't think we'll ever see Hegedüs again."

"We'll see. What's really important is that casual, last-minute comment he made at the end of your session with him about Dr. Tolker."

"I know. I never had a chance to discuss it with anyone before I left. I figured the transcript would tell the tale."

"We think Tolker's okay."

"Why?"

"Because . . . because he's never done anything to raise anyone's doubts. Still . . ."

"Still, he was Barrie Mayer's contact, and she was intimate with Eric Edwards which, according to Logic 101, means a link with Banana Quick. Maybe Tolker's the leak."

"Maybe, maybe not. We're watching him. What concerns us more at the moment is his link with your former beau, Mr. Wheatley."

The fists to the breastbone were beginning to hurt. "What link?" she asked.

"Wheatley is digging into a program that we abandoned years ago. Project Bluebird? MK-ULTRA?"

"Means nothing to me."

"It was covered in your training. Mind control. Drug experimentation."

"Okay, I remember vaguely. Why would Vern be interested if it's past tense?"

Breslin hunched his shoulders beneath his raincoat against a sudden cool breeze that whipped in from the river. "That's what we'd like to know. Maybe you could . . . ?"

"Nope."

"Why not? He's using you as a source of information for *his* ends."

"That's your interpretation, not mine."

"Do him a favor, Collette, and ask some questions. He's swimming in deep water."

"Why do you say that?"

"Look at Mr. Hubler."

Cahill started to respond, pushed away from the railing, and took steps toward the door leading back into the Kennedy Center. Breslin said, "Collette, come here."

She stopped; lights flashed indicating the second act was about to begin. She turned, hands in her blazer pockets, head cocked, eyes narrowed.

Breslin smiled and made a small motion with his index finger for her to return to him. She looked down into a wavy reflection of herself in a large puddle on the terrace, brought her eyes back up to him, and retraced her steps. Another jet, this time taking off from National, shattered the moment with its crescendo of full throttle.

Breslin said once she was again at his side, "David Hubler came over to Rosslyn because he'd been told there was a book to be offered on an inside story about us." She started to say something but he raised his finger to silence her. "He was to meet someone on the corner where we have a facility. This unnamed person was to talk to him about selling inside information which, in turn, would be turned into a book, a best seller no doubt."

Cahill just stared at him and blinked.

"This facility in Rosslyn is the one Hank Fox directs."

Another blink. Then, the question, "And David was killed by this person who was going to sell him information?"

"David was killed by . . . we don't know."

"Not robbery?"

"Not likely."

"Us? Someone from . . . *us*?"

"I don't know. Your friend, Vern Wheatley, was there when it happened."

"He was with the Rosslyn police looking for information on a story he's doing about Washington and . . ."

"He was there." His words were stone-hard.

"Good God, Joe, you're not suggesting that Vern had anything to do with David's murder?"

"I stopped suggesting things a long time ago, Collette. I just raise possibilities these days."

"You're damn good at it."

"Thanks. By the way, one of Barrie Mayer's clients, Zoltán Réti, was in to see us." He laughed. "Talk about a poor choice of words. He contacted Ruth Lazara from Cultural Exchange at a party, said he had to talk to someone. We arranged a meet."

"What did he say?"

"He said that he was convinced that he'd been sent to London for a conference because they knew he was supposed to meet Barrie Mayer when she arrived in Budapest."

"Meaning what?"

"Meaning . . . that the Soviets evidently knew not only that she was carrying something important, but that they wanted her point man out of the way."

"You think the Soviets killed her?"

"No idea."

"Joe."

"What?"

"What was Barrie carrying?"

"As far as I can ascertain, nothing."

"Nothing?"

"Nothing."

"She was killed for *nothing*?"

"Looks like it."

"Great. That gives real value to her life."

He re-ignited his pipe.

"We have to go in," Cahill said. "It's starting again."

"Okay. One more thing, Collette. Keep these things in mind. One, choosing you to follow up on the Banana Quick leak isn't a frivolous choice. You have the perfect reasons for asking questions, and now you've got an invitation from one of our primary people. You've met Tolker. Don't drop that contact. You're living with someone who's poking his nose into our affairs, which means you have as much access to him as he has with you. Be a pro, Collette. Drop all the personal reactions and do the job. You'll be rewarded."

"How?"

He grunted. "You want figures?"

"No, I want some sense of being able to return to a routine life."

"Meeting Hungarian turncoats in secret safehouses?"

"Right now, Joe, that's like working nine to five as a switchboard operator."

"Do the job and you can have what you want. They told me."

"Who?"

"The brain trust."

"Joe."

"What?"

"I don't know you."

"Sure you do. When this whole thing settles, it'll be like old times, dinners at Gundel, the Miniatur, heartburn, out-of-tune violins. Trust me."

"They say that in L.A."

"Trust me. I'm a fan."

"I'll try."

Cahill skipped the second act and returned to the apartment where Vern Wheatley was waiting. He was in his shorts, a can of beer in his hand, his bare feet propped up on the coffee table. "Where've you been?" he asked.

"The Kennedy Center."

"Yeah? Good concert?"

"Dance recital."

"Never could get into dance."

"Vern."

"What?"

"Let's talk."

19

BY THE TIME Saturday rolled around and Cahill was settled into a seat on a Pan Am flight to San Juan, she was more than ready to escape Washington, and to spend some time on an island. She had no illusions. Her trip to the BVI was just an extension of everything else she'd been doing since returning from Budapest but, for some reason (probably the concept of hitting your foot with a hammer to make you forget a headache), there was a vacation air to the trip.

There hadn't been time to visit her mother before leaving, but she did squeeze in a frantic shopping spree in search of warm-weather clothing. She didn't buy much; sunny islands didn't demand it—two bathing suits, one a bikini, the other a tank suit, both in shades of red; a multicolored caftan, white shorts, sandals, a clinging white dress, and her favorite item, a teal blue cotton jumpsuit that fit perfectly, and in which she felt comfortable. She wore it that morning on the plane.

Once airborne, and breakfast had been served, she removed her shoes, reclined in her seat, and tried to do what she'd promised herself —use the flight to sort things out without interruption, off by herself, some time alone in her own private think tank.

She'd had one additional contact with Langley before leaving. It was with Hank Fox. During their meeting on the Kennedy Center's terrace, Breslin had verbally given her a special telephone number to call, and suggested she check in each day, saying to whoever answered, "This is Dr. Jayne's office calling for Mr. Fox." She did as instructed and Fox came on the line a moment later. All he said was, "Our friend's gone back to Budapest. You're all set to go south?"

"Yes, Saturday."

"Good. In the event you get homesick and want to talk to someone, there's always a large group of friends at Pusser's Landing. They congregate in the deck bar and restaurant. Feed the big bird in the cage between noon and three. You'll have all the conversation you need."

She'd been on the receiving end of enough double-talk since joining the CIA to understand. Obviously, they kept a bird in a cage at this place called Pusser's Landing, and if she fed it at the right time, she'd be approached by someone affiliated with the CIA. It was good to know.

"Call this number when you get back," Fox said. "I'll be here."

"Right. Thanks."

"My best to Dr. Jayne."

"What? Oh, yes, of course. He sends his regards, too."

Silly games, she used to think, until she was in the field and understood the thinking behind such codes. *Need-to-know*; unless the person receiving the call was certain to answer, there was no need for whoever else picked up the phone to know who was calling. They carried it to extremes at times, especially those who loved intrigue, but it made sense. You had to adopt that attitude, she'd reasoned during her training, or you'd never take anything seriously, and that could get you in trouble.

Had Barrie Mayer not taken it seriously enough? Cahill wondered. She had been shockingly cavalier at times, and Cahill had called her on it. Had she joked at the wrong time, when the thing she was carrying was no joke? Had she taken too lightly the need to use a code name, or failed to contact someone through circuitous routes rather than directly?

The possible link between Mayer's and Hubler's deaths remained at the top of her list of thoughts. Dave Hubler had been killed in an alley adjacent to a CIA facility in Rosslyn, the one run by Hank Fox. Supposedly, Hubler had gone there to meet with someone who'd indicated he, or she, was willing to sell inside Company information that could be used in a book. That certainly drew Hubler in enough to validate a possible *mutual reason* for both murders.

She tried to stretch her mind to accommodate all the possibilities. She was hindered in this exercise by the most pervasive thought of all, the last thirty-six hours with Vern Wheatley.

She'd returned from the dance recital and decided to force a conversation. They talked until three o'clock the next morning. It was a frustrating discussion for Cahill. While Wheatley had been open to an extent, it was clear that there was more he was holding back than offering.

Collette had started the discussion with, "I'd like to know, Vern, exactly what this assignment is you're on for *Esquire*."

He laughed; Rule Number One, he told her, was never to discuss a story in progress. "You dilute it when you do that," he said. "You talk it out and the fire's gone when you sit down to write it."

She wanted to say, "Rule Number One for anyone working for the CIA is to stay far away from journalists." She couldn't say that, of course. As far as he knew, she'd left Central Intelligence for a mundane job with the United States Embassy in Budapest.

Or *did* he believe that? If Hank Fox's insinuations were correct, Wheatley had made contact with her again not to rekindle their romance, but to get close to a potential inside source to feed the story he was working on about a program that had been dropped long ago.

There it was again, *the* dilemma. Who knew what about whom? On top of that, could she believe Hank Fox? Maybe Wheatley wasn't pursuing a story about the CIA. The agency's paranoia wasn't any secret. There were people within it who found conspiracies behind every garage door in Georgetown.

She realized as she sat with Wheatley that night in his brother's apartment that she'd have to be more direct if anything near the truth were to be ferreted out. She took the chance and said, "Vern, someone told me today that you weren't in Washington doing a story on social changes here. This person told me you were digging into a story about the CIA."

He laughed and shook his empty beer can. "I think I'll have another. Can I get you something?"

"No, I . . . sure, any Scotch in there?"

"Probably. My brother has been known to take a drink now and then. Neat?"

"A little water."

She used his absence to go to the bedroom, where she undressed and got into one of his brother's robes. Three of her could have been enfolded in it. She rolled up the sleeves and returned to the living room where her drink was waiting. Wheatley raised his beer can. "Here's to the basic, underlying distrust between man and woman."

Cahill started to raise her glass in a reflex action. She stopped herself and looked at him quizzically.

"Great scenario, Collette. Some clown tells you I'm down here doing a story on the CIA. You used to work for the CIA so you figure I showed up at your house to get close to a 'source.' That's my only interest in Collette Cahill, hoping she'll turn into a Deep Throat—hey, maybe that wouldn't be so bad—and now she confronts me with the naked facts." He threw up his hands in surrender. "Your friend is right."

Wheatley put his beer can down on a table with considerable force, leaned forward, and said with exaggerated severity, "I've come into information through a highly reliable source that the Director of the CIA is not only having a wild affair with a female member of the Supreme Court—naturally, I can't mention her name—but is, at the same time, engaged in a homosexual liaison with a former astronaut who has been diagnosed at a clinic in Peru as having AIDS."

"Vern, I really don't see. . . ."

"Hold on," he said, his hand raised as a stopper. "There's more. The CIA is plotting the overthrow of Lichtenberg, has permanently wired both of Dolly Parton's breasts, and is about to assassinate Abe Hirschfeld to get control of every parking lot in New York City in case of a nuclear attack. How's it play for you?"

She started to laugh.

"Hey, Collette, nothing funny here."

"Where's Lichtenberg? You meant Liechtenstein."

"I meant Lichtenberg. It's a crater on the moon. The CIA wouldn't bother with Liechtenstein. It's the moon they want."

"Vern, I'm being serious," she said.

"Why? You still work for our nation's spooks?"

"No, but . . . it doesn't matter."

"Who told you I'm working on a CIA story?"

"I can't say."

"Oh, that's democratic as hell. I'm supposed to bare my soul to you, but the lady 'can't say.' Not what I'd expect from you, Collette. Remember the yearbook line I wrote."

"I remember," she said.

"Good. Anything new about your friend Hubler?"

"No."

"You talk to that Englishman, Hotchkiss?"

"Yes, I ran into him at Barrie's agency. He's taken over. He owns it."

"How come?"

She explained the partnership agreement and told him of her call to Mayer's attorney.

"Doesn't sound kosher to me."

"To me, either, but evidently Barrie saw fit to make such a deal."

"She was that impetuous?"

"Somewhat, but not to that extent."

He joined her on the couch and put his arm around her. It felt good, the feel of him, the smell of him. She looked up into his eyes and saw compassion and caring. He lightly brushed her lips with his. She wanted to protest but knew she wouldn't. It was preordained, this moment, in the cards, an inevitability that she welcomed . . .

They slept late the next morning. She awakened with a start. She looked over at Vern, his face calm and serene in sleep, a peaceful smile on his lips. Are you being legit with me? she questioned silently. All thoughts of their discussion the night before had been wiped away by the wave of passion and pleasure they'd created for themselves in bed. Now sunlight came through the windows. The passion was spent, the reality of beginning another day took center stage. It was depressing; she preferred what she'd felt under the covers where, someone once said, "They can't hurt you."

She got up, crossed the room, and sat in a chair for what seemed to be a very long time. It was only minutes, actually, before he woke up, yawned, stretched, and pushed himself to a sitting position against the headboard. "What time is it?" he asked.

"I don't know. Late."

Another yawn, legs swung over the side of the bed. He ran his hand through his hair and shook his head.

"Vern."

"Yeah?"

"I loved last night but . . ."

He slowly turned his head and screwed up his face. "But *what*, Collette?"

She sighed. "Nothing. I guess I just hate having to wake up, that's all. I'll be away a few days."

"Where you going?"

"The British Virgin Islands."

"How come?"

"Just to get away. I need it."

"Sure, I can understand that, but why that place? You know people there?"

"One or two."

"Where are you staying?"

"Ah . . . probably on a chartered yacht a friend of mine is arranging."

"You have rich friends." He stood, touched his toes, and disappeared into the bathroom.

Cahill realized she was sitting in the chair naked. She picked up her robe from where she'd tossed it on the floor and started a pot of coffee.

When he returned, he'd turned cold. He'd showered and dressed. He went through papers in a briefcase and started to leave.

"Don't you want coffee?" Cahill asked.

"No, I have to go. Look, I may not see you before you leave."

"Won't you be back tonight?"

"Probably, only I may end up going out of town overnight. Anyway, have a nice vacation."

"Thanks, I will."

He was gone.

He didn't return that night, and it bothered her. What had she done to turn such a warm, loving night into a frosty morning? Because she was going away? He was jealous, imagining that she'd be sleeping with someone else, an old or current boyfriend in the BVI. She wished she could have confided in him about the nature of her trip, but as that thought caused a jolt of sadness and frustration in her, it was tempered by knowing that he probably wasn't being open with her, either.

She got up early Saturday morning and packed. At the last minute she looked for a paperback book to take with her. There were piles of them everywhere. She picked up a half dozen from a nighttable next to the bed and scanned the covers. One immediately caught her eye. Its title was *Hypnotism*, by someone named G. H. Estabrooks. She put it in a shoulder bag she intended to carry on board, called a local cab company, and was on her way to National Airport.

After the Pan Am flight attendant had served Collette a cup of coffee, she pulled the book from her bag and opened it to a page on which was a brief biographical sketch of the author. Estabrooks had been a Rhodes Scholar, held a 1926 doctorate in educational psychology from Harvard, and was a professor of psychology, specializing in abnormal and industrial psychology at Colgate University. The book she held was first published in 1943, and had been revised in 1957.

The first few pages dealt with a murder trial in Denmark in which a man had hypnotized another to commit a murder. The chief state witness, Dr. P. J. Reiter, an authority on hypnotism, stated that any man is capable of any act while hypnotized.

She continued skimming until reaching page sixteen, where Estabrooks discussed the use of hypnotism in modern warfare. She read his thesis carefully.

Let us take an illustration from warfare, using a technique which has been called the "hypnotic messenger." For obvious reasons the problem of transmitting messages in wartime, of communication within an army's own forces, is a first-class headache to the military. They can use codes, but codes can be lost, stolen or, as we say, broken. They can use the dispatch carrier, but woe betide the messages if the enemy locates the messenger. They can send by word of mouth, but the third degree in any one of its many forms can get that message. War is a grim business and humans are human. So we invent a technique which is practically foolproof. We take a good hypnotic subject in, say, Washington, and in hypnotism we give him the message which we wish transferred. This message can be long and complicated, for his memory is excellent. Let us assume the war is still on and that we transfer him to Tokyo on a regular routine assignment, say, with the Army Service Corps.

Now note a very curious picture. Awake, he knows just one thing as far as his transfer to Tokyo is concerned; he is going on regular business which has nothing whatever to do with the Intelligence Department. But in his unconscious mind there is locked this very important message. Furthermore, we have arranged that there is only one person in all this world outside ourselves who can hypnotize this man and get this message, a Major McDonald in Tokyo. When he arrives in Tokyo, acting on posthypnotic suggestion, he will look up Major McDonald, who will hypnotize him and recover the message.

With this technique, there is no danger that the subject in an off-guard moment will let drop a statement to his wife or in public that might arouse suspicions. He is an Army Service Corps man going to Tokyo, that is all. There is no danger of getting himself in hot water when drunk. Should the enemy suspect the real purpose of his visit to Tokyo, they would waste their time with third-degree methods. Consciously, he knows nothing that is of any value to them. The message is locked in the unconscious and no amount of drugs, no attempts at hypnotism, can recover it until he sits before Major McDonald in Tokyo. The uses of hypnotism in warfare are extremely varied. We deal with this subject in a later chapter.

Collette went to the chapter on using hypnotism in warfare but found little to equal what she'd read on page sixteen. She closed the book, and her eyes, and replayed everything having to do with hypnosis and Barrie Mayer. Their college experience. Mayer had been such a willing and good subject.

Jason Tolker. He obviously had delved deeply into the subject, and had been Mayer's contact. Had she been hypnotized in her role as a courier? Why bother? Estabrooks's theory sounded exactly that—a theory.

MK-ULTRA and Project Bluebird—those CIA experimental programs of the sixties and early seventies that resulted in public and congressional outrage. Those projects had been abandoned, according to official proclamations from the agency. Had they? Was Mayer simply another experimental subject who'd gone out of control? Or had Estabrooks's theories, refined by the CIA, been put to practical use in her case?

For a moment, she lost concentration and her mind wandered. She'd soon need hypnosis to focus on the subject. Her eyes misted as she thought of Vern Wheatley—and then they opened wide. Why did Vern have Estabrooks's book at his bedside? Hank Fox had said that Wheatley was digging into the supposedly defunct ULTRA and Bluebird projects. Maybe Fox was right. Maybe Wheatley was using her as a conduit for information.

"Damn," she said to the back of the seat in front of her. She took a walk up and down the aisles of the aircraft, looking into the faces of other passengers, women and children, old and young, infants sleeping on mothers' laps, young lovers wrapped around each other, businessmen toiling over spread sheets and lap-top computers, the whole spectrum of airborne humanity.

She returned to her seat, loosely buckled her seat belt and, for the first time since she'd joined the CIA, considered resigning. The hell with them and their cops-and-robbers games, hiding behind vague claims that the fate of the free world depended upon their clandestine behavior. Destroy the village to save it, she thought. The Company's budgets were beyond scrutiny by any other branch of government because it was in "the national interest" to keep them secret. President Truman had been right when he'd eventually railed against the animal he'd created. It *was* an animal, free of all restraints, roaming loose in the world with men whose pockets were filled with secret money. Buy off someone here, overthrow someone there, turn decent people against their own countries, reduce everything to code words and collars turned up in the night. "Damn," she repeated. Send her off to dig into the lives of other people while, undoubtedly, people were delving into her life. Trust no one. A Communist threat exists under every pebble on the shore.

The flight attendant asked if Cahill would like a drink. "Very much," Cahill said, "a bloody Mary."

She drank half the drink and her thoughts went to the reason for her trip to the British Virgin Islands. That was the problem, she realized. Some things were important, not only for America but for people in other parts of the world. Like Hungary.

Banana Quick.

She hadn't been allowed access to all aspects of the plan—Need-to-know—but had learned enough to realize that the stakes were enormous.

She also knew that Banana Quick had been named after a tiny BVI bird, the bananaquit, and that someone within the CIA, whose job it was to assign names to projects, had decided to change it to Banana Quick. Quit was too negative, went the reasoning. Quick was more like it, positive, promising action and speed, more in line with the agency's vision of itself. There'd been laughter and snide remarks when the story had gotten around, but that was often the case in Central Intelligence. The international stakes might be high, but the internal machinations were often amusing.

Banana Quick was designed to set into motion a massive uprising by Hungarians against their Soviet keepers. The '56 attempt had failed. No wonder. It was ill-conceived and carried out by poorly armed idealists who were no match for Soviet tanks and troops.

Now, however, with the backing of the major powers—the United States, Great Britain, France, and Canada—there was a good chance that it would succeed. The climate was right. The Soviets had lost control over Hungary in a social and artistic sense. Hungarians had been gradually living freer lives, thumbing their noses at the young men in drab uniforms who wore red stars on their caps. What had Árpád Hegedüs told her when she asked how to distinguish Hungarian soldiers from Russian soldiers? "The dumb-looking ones are Russian," he'd answered.

Hungary had slowly turned in the direction of capitalism. Graft and corruption were rampant. Pay someone off and you'd have your new automobile in a month instead of six years. Condominiums were rising in the fashionable hills, available to anyone with enough hidden, hoarded illegal cash to buy in. More shops had been opened that were owned by individual entrepreneurs. They, too, had to pay some Russian, in some department, for the privilege, and that Russian was buying his own condo in the hills.

Banana Quick. A small bird flying free in the simple, excruciating beauty of the BVI. Stan Podgorsky had told her that they'd chosen the idyllic Mosquito Island as a planning center because, in his words, "Who'd ever think of looking there for planning a major uprising in an Eastern European country? Besides, we're running out of remote places to meet, unless we go to Antarctica or Ethiopia, and I, for one, am not going to those hellholes."

Who would look to the BVI for the brain trust behind a Hungarian uprising?

The Russians, for one. They'd taken over the private island because they knew something was up, knew the gray-haired men in dark suits flying in were anything but Canadian businessmen going over marketing strategies for a new product. The Soviets were many things; dumb wasn't one of them. Something was up. They'd play the game, too, lie, claim they needed a place for their weary bureaucrats to unwind in the sun. They'd watch. We'd watch.

Eric Edwards. He was there to *watch*. To look into their telescopes through his own, eye to eye, think one step ahead, as each man reported back to the dark suits in his own country.

Games.

"Games!" she said as she finished her drink.

As she deplaned in San Juan, she'd come to peace with the fact that she was a player in this game, and would give her all. After that, she'd see. Maybe . . .

Maybe it was time to get out of the business.

In the meantime, she'd apply her father's philosophy. "You take someone's money, you owe them a decent day's work."

20

"HELLO, MY NAME IS JACKIE, I work for Mr. Edwards," the slight native girl said in a loud voice.

"Yes, he told me you'd be here," Cahill said. Edwards had also told her during the telephone conversation that the girl he was sending for her was almost totally deaf. "Talk loud and let her see your lips," he'd said.

Jackie drove a battered yellow Land Rover. The back seat was piled high with junk, so Cahill sat in front with her. Edwards needn't have bothered instructing her how to communicate with Jackie. There was no conversation. The girl drove on the left side of the road with a race car driver's grim determination, lips pressed together, foot jamming the accelerator to the floor, one hand on the wheel, the heel of the other permanently against the horn. Men, women, children, dogs, cats, goats, cattle and other four-legged animals either heeded the horn or were run over.

The ride took them up and over steep hills. The views were spectacular—water like a painter's palette, every hue of blue and green, lush forests that climbed the sides of mountains and, everywhere, white slashes in the water that were yachts, big and small, sails raised or lowered. It was, at times, so breathtaking—their perch so high—that Cahill gasped.

They came down into Road Town, skirted Road Harbor, and then headed up a steep incline that took them through a clump of trees until reaching a plateau. A single house stood on it. It was one story and pristine white. The roof was covered with orange tiles. A black four-door Mercedes stood in front of a black garage door.

Collette got out and took a deep breath. A breeze from the harbor below rippled her hair and the elephant ears, kapok, white cedar, and manalikara trees that surrounded the house. The air was heavy with hibiscus and bougainvillea, and with the sound of tree frogs. Bananaquits flew from tree branch to tree branch.

Jackie helped bring the luggage into the house. It was open and airy. Furniture was at a minimum. The floors were white and yellow tile, the walls stark white. Flimsy yellow curtains fluttered in the breeze through the open windows. A huge birdcage that stood floor to ceiling housed four brilliantly colored, large parrots. "Hello, goodbye, hello, goodbye," one of them repeated over and over.

"It's just beautiful," Cahill said from behind Jackie. She remembered, came around in front of the girl, and said, "Thank you."

Jackie smiled. "He'll be back later. He said for you to be comfortable. Come." She led her to a rear guest bedroom with a double bed covered in a white-and-yellow comforter. There was a closet, dressing table, two cane chairs, and a battered steamer trunk. "For you," Jackie said. "I have to go. He'll be here soon."

"Yes, thanks again."

"Bye-bye." The girl disappeared. Cahill heard the Land Rover start and pull away.

Well, she thought, not bad. She returned to the living room and talked to the parrots, then went to the kitchen, opened the refrigerator, and took out one of many bottles of club soda. She squeezed half a lime into it, walked to a terrace overlooking the harbor, closed her eyes, and purred. No matter what was in store for her, this particular moment was to be cherished.

She sat on a chaise longue, sipped her drink, and waited for Edwards to arrive.

It was a longer wait than she'd anticipated. He rolled in an hour later on a Honda motorcycle. He'd obviously been drinking. Not that he was overtly drunk, but there was a slur to his speech. His face glowed; he'd been in the sun.

"Hello, hello, hello," he said, taking her hand and smiling.

"As long as you don't say, 'Hello, goodbye, hello, goodbye,'" she said with a laugh.

"Oh, you met my friends. Did they properly introduce themselves?"

"No."

"Bad manners. I'll have to speak to them. Their names are Peter, Paul, and Mary."

"The fourth?"

"Can't decide. Prince, Boy George, some bloody rock-'n'-roll star. I see you've helped yourself and are well into limmin'."

"Limmin'?"

"Native for loafing. Pleasant trip?"

"Yes, fine."

"Good. I've made plans for dinner."

"Wonderful. I'm famished."

They left an hour later in his Mercedes and drove to a small local restaurant ten minutes away where they dined on native food; she passed up what he ordered as a main course, souse, a boiled pig's head with onion, celery, hot peppers, and lime juice. She chose something more conventional, *kallaloo*, a soupy stew of crab, conch, pork, okra, spinach, and very large pieces of garlic. The soup was *tannia*, their before-dinner drinks rum in a fresh coconut split open at the table.

"Delicious," she said when they were through, and after she'd tasted "bush tea," made of soursop.

"Best cure for a hangover ever invented," he said.

"I may need it," she said.

He laughed. "I think I probably spill more in a day than you drink."

"Probably so."

"Game for a little sightseeing?"

She looked through the window at darkness. Only a few flickering lights on distant hills broke the black.

"Beautiful time to be out on the water. Can't sail . . . wind's always down about now, but we can loaf along on the engine. I think you'd like it."

She looked down at the slinky white dress she was wearing. "Hardly sailing clothes," she said.

"No problem," he said, getting up and pulling out her chair. "Plenty of that on board. Let's go."

During the short drive to where Edwards's yachts were docked, Cahill pleasantly realized that she was totally relaxed, something she hadn't been in far too long a time. She was all for limmin' if it made you feel the way she felt at that moment.

The man behind the wheel, Eric Edwards, had a lot to do with it, she knew. What was it in men like him that made a woman feel important and secure? His thoroughly masculine and slightly dissipated looks contributed, of course, but there was more to it. Chemical? Some olfactory process at work? The climate, the sweet fragrances in the tropical night air, the food and rum in the belly? Who knew? Cahill certainly didn't, nor did she really care. Pondering it was just a way of intensifying the feeling.

Edwards helped her to board the Morgan 46. He started the engine and generator, and turned on a light in the cabin. "Take what you want from under that bench," he said.

Cahill picked up the bench top and saw an assortment of female clothing. She smiled; along with everything else, he was practiced at enticing women on impetuous nighttime sailings. She pulled out a pair of white terrycloth shorts and a sleeveless, navy blue sweatshirt. Edwards had gone up on deck. She quickly kicked off her shoes, slipped out of her dress, and put on the shorts and shirt. She hung her dress behind a door that led to a lavatory and joined him as he freed his dock lines.

Edwards skillfully manipulated engine and wheel and backed away from the dock, then reversed power and slowly guided the large, sleek vessel past other secured boats until reaching open water. "Here, you take it," he said, indicating the wheel. She started to protest but he said, "Just keep aiming for that buoy with the light on it. I'll only be a minute." She slid behind the wheel as he went forward and took a breath against her nervousness, then smiled and relaxed into the seat cushion.

If she'd felt relaxed before, it had been nothing compared to the euphoria she now experienced.

He came back to her a few minutes later and they settled into a leisurely sightseeing journey, moving smoothly on an eastern tack through Sir Francis Drake Channel, the lights of Tortola, and the silhouette of the "Fat Virgin"—Virgin Gorda Island—their land markers.

"What are you thinking?" he said in a soft voice.

Her smile was one of pure contentment. "I was just thinking that I really don't know how to live."

He chuckled. "It isn't always this peaceful, Collette, not when I have a charter with three or four couples all hell-bent on having a good time and guzzling booze as fast as I can stock it."

"I'm sure that's true," Cahill said. "But you have to admit it isn't always that way. Obviously, you have time to . . ."

"Time to take moonlight sails with beautiful young women? True. You don't hold that against me, do you?"

She turned and looked into his face. He was wearing a broad smile. His teeth, very white, seemed phosphorescent in the light of the moon. She said, "How could I hold it against you? Here I am enjoying it to the hilt." She was about to throw in a disclaimer that she wasn't necessarily a "beautiful woman," but she decided not to bother. She'd never felt more beautiful in her life.

They continued their cruise for another hour, then headed back, reaching the dock at two in the morning. She'd fallen asleep next to him, her head on his shoulder. She helped him secure the Morgan and they went to the house, where he poured nightcaps of straight Pusser's Rum into large brandy snifters.

"You look tired," he said.

"I am. It's been a long day . . . and night."

"Why don't you get to bed? I'll be out early, but you sleep in. The house is yours. We'll catch up when I get back. I'll leave the keys to the Mercedes in the kitchen. Feel free."

"That's generous, Eric."

"I like having you here, Collette. Somehow, it makes me feel a little closer to Barrie." He studied her face. "You aren't offended at that, are you? I don't want you to feel used, if you understand what I mean."

She smiled, stood, and said, "Of course not. Funny, but while we were out on the water I thought a lot about Barrie and realized that I was feeling closer to her, too, by being here. If there is any using, we're both guilty. Good night, Eric. Thanks for a lovely evening."

21

S HE HEARD E DWARDS leave and took his advice: rolled over and went back to sleep. When she awoke again, she didn't know what time it was but the room had become hot. She looked up into a gently revolving ceiling fan, then slipped on her jumpsuit and strolled out to the kitchen. A heavy black woman was polishing countertops. "Good morning," Collette said.

The woman, who wore a flowered dress and straw sandals, smiled and said in a singsong voice, "Good morning, lady. Mr. Edwards, he gone."

"Yes, I know. I heard him. My name is Collette."

The woman evidently did not want to extend the conversation to that level of intimacy because she turned away and went back to making circles on the counter.

Collette took a pitcher of fresh-squeezed orange juice from the refrigerator, filled a large glass, and took it to the terrace. She sat at a round white table with an orange umbrella protruding from a hole in the middle and thought about the exchange in the kitchen. Her interpretation was that Edwards had so many young women walking into the kitchen and introducing themselves that the housekeeper had decided it wasn't worth getting to know them. Chances were they never stayed around long enough to become part of the household.

The marina and harbor below bustled with activity. Cahill squinted against the sun and picked out the section of the complex where Edwards's yachts were situated. She was too far away to see whether he was there, but she assumed he'd left early to take out a charter. Then again, he hadn't specified that, so maybe he had other business on the island.

She got the Estabrooks book on hypnotism from the bedroom and returned to the terrace, settled in the chair, and picked up reading where she'd left off on the plane.

She was fascinated as she read that certain people have a heightened ability to enter the hypnotic state, and that these people, according to the author, were capable of remarkable feats while under hypnosis. Estabrooks cited examples of men and women undergoing major surgery, with hypnotism as the only anesthesia. To such special people, total amnesia about the hypnotic experience was not only possible, it was easily accomplished by a skilled hypnotist.

She also learned that contrary to popular perception, those who enter a hypnotic state are anything but asleep. In fact, while under hypnosis, the subject enters a state of awareness in which it is possible to focus most intently, and to block out everything else. Memory "inside" is enhanced; it's possible under hypnosis to compress months' worth of material into an hour and to retain virtually everything.

Collette found particularly fascinating the chapter on whether it was possible to convince someone under hypnosis to perform a degrading or illegal act. She remembered high school chatter when boys used to kid about hypnotizing girls to get them to take off their clothes. One boy had sent away for a publication advertised on the back of a comic book promising "total hypnotic, seductive power over women." The girls in school had giggled, but the boys kept trying to get them to submit to their new-found power. No one did, and it was forgotten in the wake of the next fad which was, as she recalled, the ability to "throw your voice through ventriloquism."

According to Estabrooks, it was not possible to blatantly convince people in hypnosis to act against their moral and ethical codes. It was, however, possible to achieve the same end by "changing the visual." He went on to explain that while you could not tell a moral young lady to take off her clothes, you could, with the right subject, convince that person under hypnosis that she was alone in an impossibly hot room. Or, while you could not persuade someone, even the most perfect hypnotic subject, to murder a close friend, you could create a visual scenario in which when that friend came through the door, it was not that person. Instead, it was a rabid bear intent upon killing the subject, and the subject would fire in self-defense.

Cahill looked up into the vivid blue sky. The sun was above her; she hadn't realized how long she'd been reading. She returned the glass to the kitchen, took a shower, dressed in the loosest, coolest clothing she had, and got into the Mercedes, through the wrong door. The steering wheel was on the right side. She'd forgotten that the islands were British. No problem, she thought. She'd had plenty of experience driving on the other side of the road in England.

She drove off without the slightest idea of where she was going. That

pleased her. The lack of destination or timetable would give her a
chance to leisurely explore the island and to find her own adventures
and delights.

She drove into Road Town, the BVI's only thoroughly commercial
area, parked, and strolled its narrow streets, stopping to admire classic
examples of West Indian architecture painted in vivid colors, hip roofs
glistening in the midday sun, heavy shutters thrown open to let in air
and light. She stopped in shops, many of which were just opening, and
bought small gifts to bring home.

At two, she drove on again. Once she left the town, she was lost, but
it didn't bother her. The vistas in every direction were spectacular, and
she stopped often along the side of a mountain road to drink in their
natural beauty.

Rounding a sharp curve, she looked to her right and saw a large sign:
PUSSER'S LANDING. She'd forgotten what Hank Fox had told her. She
checked her watch; it was almost three, but she reasoned that since
everything else started late on the island, lunch hour would probably
still be in progress. She parked, entered beneath the sign, passed a gift
shop, and reached the outdoor dining deck that overlooked a gentle,
protected bay.

As she headed for a vacant table near the water, she came to a large
birdcage. In it was a big, docile parrot. She glanced around. There were
perhaps twenty people on the deck, some at tables, others standing in
small clusters sipping rum drinks. She decided to go to the table first
and order, then feed the bird to see if someone approached her. She
ordered a hamburger and a beer and went to the cage. "Hello there,
fella," she said. The bird looked at her with sleepy eyes. A tray of bird
food was in front of the cage. She picked up a piece of fruit and extended her hand through the open cage door. The bird took the fruit
from her fingers, tasted it, then dropped it to the cage floor.

"Fussy, huh?" she said, picked up some seed, and extended her open
palm. The bird picked at the seed and swallowed it. "Want some
more?" she asked. She was so engrossed in feeding the bird that she'd
forgotten the real reason for doing it.

"Like him?" a male voice asked.

The voice startled her, and the snap of her head toward it testified to
that fact. So she smiled. "Yes, he's beautiful."

The man to whom the voice belonged was tall and heavy. He wore
baggy overalls and a soiled tan shirt. His black hair was thinning and
swirled over his head without direction. His round face bore the scars
of childhood acne. He was light-skinned, obviously the child of mixed
parentage, and his eyes were pale blue. An interesting-looking man,
Cahill thought.

"I call him Hank," the man said.

"He looks like a fox to me," she said intuitively.

The man laughed. "Yes, a Fox called Hank. Are you visiting the
islands?"

"Yes, I'm from the States."

"Have you found our people pleasant and helpful?"

"Very." She fed the bird more seeds.

"We have that reputation. It's important for tourism. If there's anything I can do for you while you visit us, please do not hesitate to let me know. I have lunch here every day."

"That's kind of you. Your name is . . . ?"

He grinned and shrugged. "Call me Hank."

"Like the fox."

"Look at me. Bear would be more like it. Have a good day, miss, and enjoy your stay."

"Thank you; now I know I will."

22

"HAVE A GOOD DAY?" Eric Edwards asked as he came to the terrace where Collette was sitting. She'd bathed and slipped into her caftan, found a glass pitcher in the refrigerator filled with a dark liquid and decided to try it. "What is this?" she asked Edwards as he joined her at the table.

"Oh, you found my daily supply of *maubi*. The housekeeper whips it up for me. It's non-alcoholic, but if you let it age long enough it ferments into something that knocks your socks off. It's got tree bark, ginger, marjoram, pineapple, stuff like that in it."

"It's delicious."

"Yeah, only I'm ready for a real drink. Let me get it and I'll brief you on the next couple of days of your vacation."

When he returned, he carried a large vodka martini on the rocks. "How would you like a *real* sail?" he asked.

"I'd love it," she said. "What does a *real* sail mean?"

"Two days and a night. Jackie's provisioning the boat first thing in the morning. We'll spend the day with sails up and I'll really show you the BVI. We'll find a pleasant place to anchor overnight, and spend the days catching beautiful winds and seeing one of God's gifts to the world. Sound good?"

"Sounds religious," she said. This didn't reflect what she was thinking at first. The sail would mean being out of touch, particularly with her contact at Pusser's Landing. Somehow, that brief encounter had been comforting.

Still, she knew that her job was to stay close to Edwards and to find out what she could. So far, she'd been successful only in discovering that he was handsome, charming, and a generous host.

He took her for dinner that night to the Fort Burt Hotel, and they stopped for a drink at Prospect Reef before returning to the house. She assumed this warm, pleasant evening would culminate in some attempt at seduction. Later, she had to laugh quietly in bed when she realized that the absence of any attempt at seduction left her ambivalent. She didn't want to be seduced by Eric Edwards. On the other hand, there was a side of her, part psychological and part physical, that yearned for it.

She heard Edwards walking about the house and tried to determine from her bedroom what he was doing. She heard him go outside, then return, listened to the dishwasher start and begin its cycles. She closed her eyes and focused on sounds from outside her window. The tree frogs were especially noisy. A pleasant sound. She allowed waves of contemplation of two days on that magnificent yacht to carry her into a blissful sleep.

Edwards, who'd poured himself a glass of rum over ice, sat on the terrace. The harbor below was peaceful and dark, except for occasional lights shining through tiny portholes on the yachts docked there. One of those lights came from his Morgan. Inside, Edwards's shipmate, Jackie, was putting the finishing touches on a vegetable tray she'd prepared for the sail. She covered it with plastic wrap and placed it in the galley's refrigerator along with the other food and drinks Edwards had ordered.

She went to the companionway, took two steps up, and surveyed the deck and dock. Then she returned to the cabin and went to a low door that led to a large hanging locker containing extra gear, flotation cushions, and snorkeling equipment. She opened the door. A flashlight's movement threw a sudden ray of light on her. "Are you done yet?" she asked.

A young native scrambled toward her on his knees, shone the light on his face, and nodded. She motioned for him to come. He took a final look back into the black corner of the stowage locker. She, of course, could hear nothing, but if he concentrated hard enough, he could hear the regular, rhythmic ticking in the silence of the night.

He joined her in the main cabin and they turned out the interior lights. She went up the companionway again, looked around, saw that it was clear, waved for him to follow, and they quickly climbed onto the dock. They looked at each other for a moment, then separated, Jackie heading in the direction of the main buildings, the young man following a narrow strip of wooden walkway until he reached a small beach and disappeared into the trees.

23

"GOOD JOB, JACKIE," Eric Edwards said, as the slender girl in tight shorts and a T-shirt tossed him the last line from the dock.

She smiled and waved.

Once Edwards had backed the yacht away from the dock and was proceeding toward the same water they'd traveled two nights ago, he turned over the wheel to Cahill. This time she took it with confidence, eager to guide the sleek vessel with enough proficiency to make him proud.

"I don't know how much you know about sailing," Edwards said, "but you're going to have to help me."

"I don't know much," Cahill said, raising both hands in defense, "but I'll do what you tell me to do."

"Fair enough," Edwards said. "Let's kill that noisy engine and get some sail up."

The difference between sailing up Sir Francis Drake Channel in the daytime and at night, Cahill realized, was literally as different as day and night. The sun on the water turned it into a glistening turquoise and silver fantasy. She sat at the helm and watched Edwards, who wore only white duck pants, scurry back and forth over the coach roof and foredeck adjusting halyards and running rigging. The huge white sails billowed in the wind, the sound of them flapping against the yacht's spar like a giant bird's wings. When Eric was satisfied, he stood, hands on hips, and looked up at the full white sheets pressed into perfect symmetry by the 20-knot Caribbean breeze. Like something out of a movie, Cahill thought, as she took deep breaths and raised her face to the sun. A spy movie—or a romance?

"Where are we going?" she asked as he joined her at the wheel.

"We'll go right up the channel past Beef Island—that's where you flew in—and then up through the Dogs."

"The dogs?"

"Yeah. Why they're called that depends on who you talk to. Somebody told me once Sir Francis Drake dropped his dogs off on them. Some people think the islands look like dogs. The way I figure it, they named them the Dogs the way they name most things down here. Somebody just liked the name. There's three of them. Once we're past them, we'll be up off the northwest tip of Virgin Gorda. I thought we'd come around and go into Mosquito Island."

Was he testing her? Cahill wondered. Looking for a sign of recognition when he mentioned Mosquito Island? It didn't seem that way because the minute he finished telling her of their sailing plans, he left her side and busied himself again up front.

They reached the Dogs a little after three and anchored near Marina Cay, where they took a swim in the warm, incredibly clear water and had lunch. Eating made her sleepy, but once they were under way again, her spirits and energy picked up and she threw herself into the role of mate. They sailed between West Dog and Great Dog, came around a tiny bump in the water that Edwards said was Cockroach Island, then sailed almost due east toward Anguilla Point, which jutted out from the Fat Virgin. Far in the distance was Mosquito Island.

"See that island over there?" Edwards said, pointing to his left. "That's really the dogs, or gone to the dogs." Cahill shielded her eyes and saw a small island dominated by a large house built on its highest point. Edwards handed her a pair of binoculars. She peered through them and adjusted the lenses until the island and its structure were sharp. Virtually the entire island was surrounded by a high metal fence, with barbed wire stretched along its top. Two large black Dobermans ran along the perimeter of the property. On top of the building were elaborate antennas, including a huge dish.

She lowered the binoculars to her lap. "Is that a private island?"

Edwards laughed. "Yes, privately owned. The owner leased it out to the Soviet Union not long ago."

Collette feigned surprise. "Why would the Soviet Union want an island down here?"

Another laugh from Edwards. "They say it's to provide rest and recreation for its top bureaucrats. There's some debate about that."

Cahill looked at him quizzically. "Do people think it's a military installation?"

Edwards shrugged and returned the binoculars to the clip on the taffrail. "Nobody knows for sure," he said. "I just thought you'd be interested in seeing it."

"I am," she said.

He guided the vessel around Anguilla Point and approached Mosquito Island from the south. He went below and called Drake's Anchorage, the only resort on Mosquito, on VHF Channel 16 to inform them they would be mooring in the bay and would like a launch to bring them in for drinks and dinner. The pleasant female voice asked Edwards what time he estimated dropping anchor. He looked at his watch. "About an hour, hour and a half," he said. He flicked off the microphone switch, said to Cahill, "Feel like another swim before we go ashore?"

"Love it," she said.

"Make it an hour and a half," Edwards said to the young woman on the other end of the radio.

Ordinarily, Edwards would have brought the Morgan in closer, but he wanted Cahill to see a prime snorkeling reef a few miles to the east, near Prickly Pear Island. He headed for it, dropped anchor, went below, opened the door to the stowage locker, and pulled out two sets of masks and flippers. He helped Collette fit her feet into her flippers, adjusted the mask on her face, then put on his own set. "Ready?" he asked.

She nodded.

"Let's go."

Edwards climbed up onto the stanchion and threw himself over backwards into the water. Cahill managed a minor variation on the technique and soon they were paddling along, side by side, toward the coral reef he'd pointed out.

Edwards moved in front of her and began pointing beneath the water to a spectacular staghorn reef, its multi-colored polyps beckoning as though they were millions of fingers. A thick school of yellow snapper appeared from behind the reef and crossed below them, so close that Cahill was able to probe the middle of the school with her hand.

Edwards brought his head out of the water and spit the breathing tube from his mouth. Cahill raised her head, too. He said, "Let's go around the reef that way," indicating the direction with his head. "There's a great . . ."

The sound started with a low rumble that was more felt than heard from where they were. Thunder? On such a day? They looked around, then back in the direction from which they had come. A microsecond later, Edwards's 46-foot Morgan rose into the brilliant blue BVI sky in a giant, ferocious fireball. Out of the top of the cloud came thousands of shreds and shards of what had been a magnificent sailing vessel.

The explosion was deafening, but more potent was what the impact did to the water below the surface. Cahill and Edwards were suddenly engulfed in a swirl of water gone mad. She was flipped on her back and water rushed into her mouth. Her arms and legs flailed for something to grab on to, something to help her combat the violent force in which she was trapped.

Then, as quickly as it had begun, the water's surge ebbed. Debris rained down from the sky above, flaming pieces of the yacht hitting the water with a vicious sizzle, large hunks of fiberglass and wood, steel and plastic falling like meteorites. A piece of burning material struck Cahill on her back, but she quickly turned over and the pain was gone.

She'd now regained enough of her senses to begin to think about what had happened, and about what to do next. She looked for Edwards, saw him close to the reef. He was on his side. One hand reached into the sky as though looking for a hook to grasp. There was blood coming from the exposed side of his face, and his mouth was open like that of a dying fish.

Cahill swam to him. "Are you all right?" she asked foolishly, her hand instinctively going to the wound on his temple.

His whole body heaved as he discharged water from his mouth and throat. He shook his head and said, "I think my arm is broken."

Cahill turned in the water and looked back to where the yacht had been. All that was left were random pieces, smoke drifting lazily from them. A large motor launch pierced the smoke, skirted the debris, and came directly at them.

The three young natives in the launch helped Cahill into it, then carefully brought Edwards on board. Cahill looked at his arm and asked, "Can you move it?"

He winced as he tried to extend the arm. "I think I can. Maybe it isn't broken."

Now, safe in the launch, Cahill was suddenly assaulted by the mental and physical horror of what had happened. She fell against the back of one of the wooden seats and began to breathe deeply and quickly. "Oh, my God. My God, what happened?"

Edwards didn't answer. His eyes were wide and fixed upon the remains of the Morgan.

"We take you back?" one of the natives asked.

Edwards nodded and said, "Yes, take us to the island. We need to make a phone call."

24

AFTER CAHILL APPLIED first aid to his arm and head in the manager's office of Drake's Anchorage, Edwards made a call to his office on Tortola and told them to send a motor launch to pick them up on Virgin Gorda. The Mosquito Island shuttle boat took them there and they went to a clinic where more sophisticated aid was given Edwards, including an X ray of his arm. It wasn't broken. The gash on his head, the result of a falling piece of metal, was deeper than they'd realized. It took eleven stitches to close.

They were driven to a dock where one of Edwards's native staff was waiting with a large powerboat. An hour later they were back at Edwards's house.

Throughout the return to Tortola, they said little to each other. Collette was still in mild shock. Edwards seemed to have his wits about him, but he made the journey with his face set in a pained, brooding expression.

They stood together on his terrace and looked down on the harbor.

"I'm sorry," he said.

"Yeah, sorry, me, too," she said. "I'm just glad to be alive. If we hadn't taken that swim . . ."

"There are a lot of *ifs*," he mumbled.

"What could have caused it?" Cahill asked. "A gasoline leak? I've heard about that happening with boats."

He said nothing, stared instead at the marina far below. Then he slowly turned his head and said, "It was no gasoline leak, Collette. Somebody wired the yacht. Somebody planted explosives on a timer."

She took a few steps back until her bare calves touched a metal chair. She collapsed into it. He continued looking out over the harbor, his hands on the terrace railing, his body hunched over. Finally, he turned and leaned against the rail. "You damn near lost your life because of things you don't know, and I'm going to tell you about them, Collette."

As much as she wanted to hear what he had to say, she was gripped with a simultaneous, overwhelming wave of nausea and shaking, and her head had begun to pound. She stood and used the arm of the chair for support. "I have to lie down, Eric. I don't feel well. Can we talk later?"

"Sure. Go rest. Whenever you feel up to it we'll sit down and hash out what happened."

She gratefully climbed into bed and fell into a troubled sleep.

When she awoke, she was facing the window. It was dark outside. She sat up and rubbed her eyes. The tree frogs were performing their usual symphony. They provided the only sound.

She looked toward the door, which was open a crack. "Eric?" she said in a voice that could be heard by no one. "Eric," she said louder. No response.

She'd slept in what she'd been wearing that day, removing only her shoes. She placed her bare feet on the cool tile floor, stood, and tried to shake away her lingering sleepiness and the chill that had turned her flesh into a pattern of tiny bumps. She said it again: "Eric?"

She opened the door and stepped into the hallway. A light from the living room spilled over to where she stood. She followed it, crossed the living room, and went to the open terrace doors. No one. Nothing.

She was met with the same situation when opening the front door. The Mercedes and motorcycle were there, but no sign of their owner.

She went to the car and looked inside, then walked to the side of the house where a large tree created a natural roof above a white, wrought-iron love seat.

"Sleep good?"

A burst of air came from her mouth. She turned and saw Eric standing behind the tree.

"All rested?" he asked as he approached her.

"Yes, I . . . I didn't know where you'd gone."

"Nowhere. Just enjoying the evening."

"Yes, it's . . . lovely. What time is it?"

"Nine. Feel like some dinner?"

"I'm not hungry."

"I'll put it out anyway, nothing fancy, a couple of steaks, local vegetables. A half hour okay?"

"Yes, that will be fine, thank you."

A half hour later she joined him on the terrace. Two plates held their dinner. A bottle of Médoc had been opened, and two delicately curved red wineglasses stood on the table.

"Go ahead, eat," he said.

"Funny, but I am hungry now," she said. "Some people eat when they're upset, others can't bear the thought of it. I was always an eater."

"Good."

She asked how his arm felt, and he said it was better. "A bad sprain," the doctor at the clinic had said. Edwards had been told to keep it in the sling the doctor had provided, but he'd discarded it the minute they left the clinic. There was a large compression bandage on his left temple. A spot of dried blood that hadn't washed off remained on his cheek.

Cahill pushed her plate away, sat back, and said, "You said you wanted to share something with me. Sorry I wasn't in any shape to listen before, but I'm ready now. Do you still want to tell me?"

He leaned forward, both forearms on the table, took a breath and looked down into his plate, as though debating what to say.

"You don't have to," she said.

He shook his head. "No, I want to. You almost lost your life because of me. I think that deserves an explanation."

Cahill thought: Barrie Mayer. Had *she* lost her life because of him?

He repositioned his chair so that there was room for him to cross his legs and to face her. She adopted a similar posture, her hands in her lap, her eyes trained on his.

"I really don't know where to begin." A smile. "At the beginning. That makes sense, doesn't it?"

She nodded.

"I suppose the best way to get into this, Collette, is to tell you that I'm not what I appear to be. Yes, I have a yacht-chartering service here in the BVI, but that's a front." She told herself to offer nothing, take in what he had to say and make decisions later.

He continued. "I work for the Central Intelligence Agency."

It struck her that he was being completely honest, that he had no idea that she knew about his involvement. Obviously, Barrie hadn't told him what her close friend Collette did for a living. That realization was refreshing. On the other hand, it put Cahill in a position of being the dishonest one. It made her squirm.

Her turn to say something. "That's . . . interesting, Eric. You're an . . . agent?"

"I suppose you could call it that. I'm paid to keep my eyes and ears open down here."

Cahill took a moment to appear as if she were looking for the next question. In fact, she had a list of a dozen. She said, "The CIA has people everywhere in the world, doesn't it?" She didn't want to appear too naive. After all, he knew she had once worked for the CIA. She certainly would be somewhat knowledgeable about how things worked.

"It's more than just having people plopped in places around the globe to report back on what's going on. I was sent down here for a specific purpose. Remember the island I pointed out to you, the one the Russians have taken over?"

"Yes."

When he didn't say anything else, she leaned forward. "Do you think the Russians blew up the yacht?"

"That would be the logical explanation, wouldn't it?"

"I suppose it's possible, considering you're an agent for the other side. But you don't seem convinced."

Edwards shrugged, poured more wine into each of their glasses, held his up in a toast. "Here's to wild speculation."

She picked up her glass and returned the gesture. "What wild speculation?"

"I hope you don't misunderstand why I would say something like I'm about to say. I mean, after all, we both work for the United States government."

"Eric, I'm not a recent college graduate having her first taste of bureaucracy."

He nodded. "Yeah, well, here goes. I think the CIA set the charge aboard the yacht, or arranged for someone to do it."

It hadn't occurred to her for a moment since the incident that the people *she* worked for would do such a thing. She'd thought of the Russians, of course, and also wondered whether it hadn't been the act of a competing yacht-chartering company. She'd also had to question whether anyone else *had* been involved at all. There was no more evidence to link the explosion to a plot than there was to rule out a natural cause.

But those thoughts had little value at the moment. She asked the only obvious question: "Why do you think that?"

"I think it because . . . because I know things that the CIA would prefer not be told to anyone else."

"What things?"

"Things about individuals whose motivations are not in the best interests of not only the Central Intelligence Agency but the United States as well. In fact . . ."

Collette's body tensed. She was sure he was about to say something about Barrie Mayer's death.

He didn't disappoint her. "I'm convinced, Collette, that Barrie was murdered because she knew those same damaging things." He pulled his head back a little and raised his eyebrows. "Yes, she knew them from me. I suppose that's why I'm talking to you this way. Being responsible for the death of one person is bad enough. Seeing a second person come this close"—he created a narrow gap between his thumb and index finger—"to losing her life is too much."

Cahill leaned back and looked up into a sky that had, like her mind, clouded over. Her brain was short-circuited with thoughts and emotions. She got up and went to the edge of the terrace, looked down on the harbor and dock. What he was saying made a great deal of sense. It represented the sort of thing her instincts had pointed to from the beginning.

A new thought struck her. Maybe he was wrong. Assuming that the explosion had been the result of someone's having planted a device on board, who was to say the intended victim hadn't been herself? She turned to him again. "Are you suggesting that someone from the CIA murdered Barrie?"

"Yes."

"What about Dave Hubler, her associate at the literary agency?"

He shook his head. "I don't know anything about that, unless Barrie gave him the same information she'd gotten from me."

Collette returned to her chair, took a sip of wine, and said, "Maybe I was to be the victim."

"Why you?"

"Well, I . . ." She'd almost stepped over the line she'd drawn for herself in terms of how much she would reveal to him. She decided to stay on her side. "I don't know, you were the one who toasted 'wild speculation.' Maybe somebody wanted to kill me instead of you. Maybe the engine just blew up by itself."

"No, nothing blew up by itself, Collette. While you were sleeping, the authorities were here questioning me. They're filing a report that the destruction of the yacht resulted from an accidental electrical discharge into a fuel tank because that's what I want them to think. No, I know better. It was deliberate."

Cahill was almost afraid to ask the next question but knew she had to. "What was it that Barrie learned from you that caused her death, and that prompted somebody to try to kill you?"

He gave forth a throaty laugh, as though saying to himself, "My God, I can't believe I'm doing this." Collette felt for him. Obviously, the event near Mosquito Island, and Barrie's death, had brought him to a level of candor that every bit of his training cautioned against; in fact, prohibited. Her training, too, for that matter. She touched his knee. "Eric, what was it that Barrie knew? It's terribly important for me to know. As you said, I came this close to losing my life."

Edwards closed his eyes and puffed out his cheeks. When he exhaled through his lips and opened his eyes again, he said, "There are people within the CIA whose only interest is their own *self*-interest. Ever hear of Project Bluebird?"

Back to that again. Jason Tolker. Was that what he was getting at?

She said, "Yes, I've heard of it, and MK-ULTRA, too." The minute she'd said it, she knew she'd offered too much.

His surprised look indicated she was right.

"How do you know about those projects?" he asked.

"I remember them from my training days with the CIA, before I quit and went to work for the embassy."

"That's right, they did talk about such projects in training, didn't they? You know, then, that they involved experimentation on a lot of innocent people?"

She shook her head. "I don't know the details of it, just that those projects had been operative and were abandoned because of public and congressional pressure."

Edwards narrowed his eyes. "Do you know how Barrie got involved with the CIA?"

Collette did a fast mental shuffle. Should she acknowledge knowing about Mayer's life as a courier? She decided to continue playing the surprised role.

"Did Barrie ever mention someone named Tolker?"

Cahill raised her eyes as if thinking back, then said, "No, I don't think so."

"He's a psychiatrist in Washington. He was the one who recruited her."

"Really?"

"You didn't know that? She never told you any of this?"

"No, I don't remember anyone named Tolker."

"How much did she tell you about what she was doing for the CIA?"

Her laugh was forced. "Not much. It certainly wouldn't have been professional for her to tell me, would it?"

Edwards shook his head. "No, it wouldn't, but Barrie wasn't necessarily the most professional of intelligence couriers." He seemed to be waiting for Cahill to respond. When she didn't, he said, "I suppose it doesn't matter what she told you. The fact is that she'd been seeing this guy Tolker professionally. She was a patient of his. He used that opportunity to bring her into the fold."

"That isn't so unusual, is it?" Cahill asked.

"I suppose not, although I really don't know a hell of a lot about that end of the business. The point is, Collette, that Dr. Jason Tolker was deeply involved in Operation Bluebird and MK-ULTRA—and continues to be involved in experimentation programs that spun out of those projects."

"The CIA is still doing mind-control experimentation?"

"Sure as hell is, and Tolker is one of the top dogs. He manipulated Barrie, brought her into the CIA as a courier, and that's why she's dead today. More wine?"

It seemed an absurd thing to say considering the tenor of the conversation, but she said, "Yes, please." He poured.

Collette thought about what she'd read in the book by G. H.

Estabrooks, about how people could be persuaded to do things against their will if the hypnotist changed the visual scenario. Was that what Edwards was suggesting, that Barrie had been seduced into the role of CIA courier against her will? She asked him.

"Barrie evidently was an unusual hypnotic subject," Edwards answered, "but that really isn't important. What *is* important is that when she left on her most recent trip to Budapest, she carried with her information that would hang Jason Tolker by his thumbnails."

"I don't understand."

"Tolker is a double agent." He said it flatly and matter-of-factly. It left Cahill stunned. She got up and crossed the terrace.

"He's a goddamn traitor, Collette, and Barrie knew it."

"How did she know it? Did you tell her?"

Edwards shook his head. "No, she told me."

"How did *she* learn he was a double agent?"

He shrugged. "I really don't know, Collette. I pumped her, but all she'd say was that she had the goods and was going to blow him out of the water." He grinned. "That's an apt way to put it considering our little snorkeling excursion today, huh?"

Her smile was equally rueful. She asked the next obvious question. Who was Barrie going to tell about what she knew of Tolker's supposedly traitorous acts?

He answered, "My assumption was that she'd tell somebody back in Washington. But it didn't take me long to realize that that didn't make any sense. She didn't know anybody at Langley. Her only contact with the CIA *was* Jason Tolker. . . ."

"And whoever her contact was in Budapest."

Edwards nodded and joined her at the edge of the terrace. The strains of a fungee band, with its incessant island rhythms, drifted up to them.

They stood close together, their hips touching, both lost for a time in their individual thoughts. Then Edwards said in a monotone, "I'm getting out. I don't need boats blown out from under me."

She turned and looked into his face. Lines that had always been there now seemed more pronounced. "Was the yacht insured?" she asked.

His face broke into a wide smile. "Insured by the richest insurance company in the world, Collette, the Central Intelligence Agency."

"That's something to be thankful for," she said, not meaning it. It was something to say. Money meant nothing in this scenario.

He turned grim again. "The CIA is run by evil men. I never wanted to accept that fact. I never even acknowledged it until recently. I was filled with the sort of patriotism that leads people into working for an intelligence agency. I believed in it and its people, *really* believed in what the CIA stood for and what I was doing." He shook his head. "No more. It's filled with the Jason Tolkers of this world, people who only care about themselves and who don't give a damn who gets trampled in the process. I . . . ." He placed his hands on her shoulders and drew her to him. "You and I have lost something very special in Barrie Mayer because of these people. I didn't know David Hubler, but he just joins the list of people who've had to pay with their lives because of them."

She started to say something but he cut her off. "I told Barrie to stay away from Tolker. The projects that he's involved in are at the root of what's rotten about the Company and the government. It uses innocent citizens as guinea pigs without any regard for their fate. They've lied to everyone, including Congress, about how they abandoned Operation Bluebird and MK-ULTRA. Those projects never missed a beat. They're more active today than they ever were."

Cahill was legitimately confused. "But what about funding? Projects like that cost money."

"That's the beauty of an organization like the CIA, Collette. There's no accountability. That's the way it was set up in the beginning. That was one of the reasons Truman had serious thoughts about establishing a national intelligence-gathering organization. The money is given to individuals and they're free to spend it any way they want, no matter who it hurts. There's got to be a thousand front groups like mine, shipping companies and personnel agencies, little airlines and weapons brokers, university labs and small banks that do nothing but launder Company money. It stinks. I never thought I'd get to this point but it *does* stink, Collette, and I've had it."

She stared at him for a long time before saying, "I understand, Eric, I really do. If you're right, that whoever blew up the yacht today did it on orders from people in my own government, I don't know how I can keep working for it, even in State."

"Of course you can't. That's the whole point. I'm glad to be an American, always have been, always considered it a rare privilege to have been born American, but when I end up as part of a series of systematic abuses that result in the murder of a woman I loved very much, it's time to draw the line."

The band down the hill began a slow, sensuous rendition of an island song. Edwards and Cahill looked at each other until he said, "Care to dance?"

Again, the absurdity of the request, considering the circumstances, caused her to burst out laughing. He joined her, slipped his right arm around her waist, took her left hand in his, and began leading her across the terrace.

"Eric, this is ridiculous."

"You're right, it is so ridiculous there is only one thing left to do—dance."

She stopped protesting and gracefully followed his lead, thinking all the while of how ludicrous it was yet at the same time how romantic and beautiful. The feel of his hardness against her sent a succession of tiny sexual electric bursts through her body. He kissed her, tentatively at first, then with more force, and she returned his hunger.

As they danced by the table, he deftly took the wine, led her through

the open doors and into the bedroom. There, he released her and his
fingers began opening the bottons on the front of her blouse. She knew
it was the last opportunity to protest, or to step away, but she moved
closer. They made love, and soon her intensely pleasurable response
merged with his, and with visions of the fireball in the blue skies of the
British Virgin Islands.

The next day, Edwards was out early. He said he had a number of
officials on the island with whom he had to speak about the explosion.

After he was gone, Cahill grappled with conflicting thoughts. What
he'd said last night had caused her to rethink everything she'd done
since coming to work for Central Intelligence. She certainly didn't
share his passionate disgust with the CIA. She wasn't even sure that
what he'd said was true. All she knew was that it was time to do some
serious thinking, not only about this assignment, but about who she
was.

She considered placing a call to Hank Fox in Washington but was
afraid of breaching security. Phone calls from the islands went to the
United States via satellite; conversations were open to the world, including the Russians on their small, private island.

Pusser's Landing.

She drove Edwards's Mercedes there at noon, took a table, ordered a
sandwich and a Coke, then went to the birdcage where she fed the
parrot. She'd noticed the big man from the day before. He was down on
the dock repairing an outboard engine on a small runabout. Soon, he
had casually made his way to her side.

"I thought I'd come back for lunch again," she said. "It was so pleasant last time."

"It is a pleasant place, miss," he said. He looked about to ensure no
one was near them before adding, "It is even nicer in Budapest. You
should go there immediately."

"Budapest? Who . . . ?"

"As quickly as possible, miss. Today."

Cahill asked, "Does my travel agent know about this?"

The big man smiled and said, "Ask him yourself. You are to go to
Washington first."

She left Pusser's Landing, telling the waiter that an emergency had
arisen, found her way back to Edwards's house, quickly packed, and left
him a note.

DEAR ERIC,

I won't even try to explain why I've rushed away but I assure you
it's urgent. Please forgive me. There are so many things I want to

say to you about last night, about feelings it generated in me, about
—well, about a lot of things. There's no time now. Thank you for
providing a wonderful vacation in your beloved BVI. I hope I'll be
able to share it with you again soon.

COLLETTE

25

CAHILL GOT OFF the plane at Dulles Airport, rented a car, and
drove directly to her mother's house where she was met with a barrage
of questions about where she'd been and why she was running off again
in such a rush. Cahill explained, "They're having some kind of a budget
crisis at the embassy at Budapest and I have to get back right away."

"What a shame," her mother said. "I thought I might get to see you
for at least a day."

Collette stopped rushing for a moment, hugged her, said she loved
her and yes, she would have coffee, and ran upstairs to pack.

She shared the next hour with her mother in the kitchen and felt a
desperate yearning to stay, to retreat into childhood where the world
was wondrous and the future bright when viewed from the protective
custody of family and home. She had to force herself to say goodbye,
leaving her mother standing at the front door with a poignant expression on her face. "I'll be back soon," Cahill yelled through the open car
window. She knew her mother's smile was forced but she appreciated
the effort.

She drove back to Washington, went to a phone booth, and dialed
the special number Hank Fox had given her. When a young woman
answered, Cahill said, "This is Dr. Jayne's office calling for Mr. Fox."
The woman told her to hold. A minute later Fox came on the line and
said, "I heard about the accident. I'm glad you're all right."

"Yes, I'm fine. I made friends with someone at Pusser's Landing. He
told me . . ."

Fox said sharply, "I know what he told you. The Fisherman is restless
in Budapest."

"The Fisherman?" Then, it dawned on her. Code name Horgász—
Árpád Hegedüs. She said, "I thought he went to . . . ?"

"He didn't, and he wants to talk to his friend. It's important that he
see her as soon as possible."

"I understand," she said.

"How is your boyfriend in the British Virgin Islands?"

"He's . . . he's not my boyfriend."

"How is he?"

"Fine." She started to think of the last conversation she'd had with Edwards but Fox didn't give her enough time to complete the thought.

"You can leave tonight?"

Cahill sighed. More than anything she didn't want to get on a plane for Budapest. What she really wanted was to return to the BVI and be with Eric Edwards, not only because of the intimacy that had developed between them, but because she wanted to talk more about this thing she was doing, this organization she'd placed so much trust in. That trust wasn't there anymore. Now she knew: She wanted out, too.

"I'll be hearing from Joe," Fox said. Breslin.

"I'm sure you will. I have to go. Goodbye." She slammed the receiver into its cradle, gripped the small shelf beneath the phone and shook it, muttering as she did, "The hell with you, the hell with it all."

She caught a flight out of Washington to New York and barely made the Pan Am flight to Frankfurt, Germany, where she could make a direct connection for Budapest. She'd called Vern Wheatley at his brother's apartment but there was no answer. She needed to talk with him. Somehow, she had the sense that if she didn't talk to someone outside the organization, someone who wasn't intrinsically bound up in its intrigues, she'd go to pieces. And that, she knew, would be the worst thing that could happen.

By the time she left the plane in Budapest she was exhausted but, at least, more in control of herself and her circumstances. She realized as she went through Customs that she was now back in her official status as an employee of the United States Embassy. It didn't matter that her real employer was the CIA. What *did* matter was that things were familiar now; not quite as comforting as the bosom of her mother, but certainly better than what she'd been through the past week.

She took a cab to her apartment and called Joe Breslin at the embassy.

"Welcome back," he said. "You must be beat."

"I sure am."

"It's five o'clock. Think you can stay awake long enough for dinner?"

"I'll make myself. Where?"

"Légrádi Testvérek."

Cahill managed a smile despite her fatigue. "Going fancy, are we? Is this in honor of my return?"

"If it makes you feel good thinking that, then that's what it's for. Actually, my stomach is in need of a good meal, and I get a kick out of the chubby little violin player."

"I'll consider it in my honor. What time?"

"I prefer late but, considering your condition, maybe we should make it early. How's eight sound?"

"Eight? I'll be dead to the world by then."

"Okay, tell you what. Take a good long nap and meet me there at ten."

She knew there was little sense in trying to negotiate a different time. He said he'd make a reservation under his name. She opened the door of her small refrigerator and remembered she'd cleaned it out before leaving. The only thing in it was two bottles of Szamorodni, the heavy dessert white wine, a half dozen bottles of Köbányai világos beer, a tin of coffee, and two cans of tuna fish her mother had sent in a "care package" a month ago. She opened the tuna fish, realized she was out of bread, ate it directly from the can, stripped off her clothing, set her alarm clock, climbed into bed, and was asleep in seconds.

They sat across from each other in a small room at Légrádi Testvérek. The oval table between them was covered with a white lace tablecloth. Their chairs were broad, had high backs covered in a muted tapestry. A single silver candle epergne with ruffled glass dishes on two protruding arms dominated the center of the table. One of the dishes held fresh grapes and plums, the other apples and pears. The walls were stark white, the ceiling low and curved. Gypsy music emanated from a short, fat violinist and a tall, handsome cimbalom player who used tiny mallets to delicately strike the strings on his pianolike instrument.

"You look good," Breslin said, "considering the schedule you've been on."

"Thank you. Nothing like a can of American tuna fish and a nap to put color back in a girl's cheeks."

He smiled and looked up at the owner, who'd come to take their order. They decided to share a dish of assorted appetizers—caviar, tiny shrimps on salmon mousse stuffed into an egg, three kinds of pâté, and marinated oysters. Breslin ordered beef with pâté as his entrée; Cahill opted for chicken layered with a paprika sauce and little pools of sour cream. They skipped wine; Breslin had a Scotch and soda, Cahill mineral water.

"So?" he asked.

"So?" she mimicked. "You don't want a litany here, do you?"

"Why not?"

"Because . . ." She made a small gesture with both hands to indicate the public nature of the restaurant.

"Skip the names, and I don't need details. First, what about your boyfriend in the pretty place?"

She shook her head and sat back. "Joe, what do you and Hank do, talk every twenty minutes?"

"No, just two or three times a day. What about him? Did you enjoy your vacation?"

"Very much, except for a minor mishap out in the water."

"I heard. What were you doing, snorkeling or something?"

"Exactly, and that's why I'm sitting here tonight. As for my so-called boyfriend, he's terrific. Want to know something? A lot of our *friends* have said bad things about him. . . ." She raised her eyebrows and adopted an expression to reinforce she was talking about her employer. "People are wrong. If there's a problem, it's not with my 'boyfriend.' "

"I see," Breslin said, scratching his nose and rubbing his eyes. "We can discuss that at length another time. Did you see your shrink while you were back?"

"My— Oh, you mean Dr. Jayne."

"Who?"

"Don't worry, Joe, we're talking about the same person. I didn't see him again after I saw you in Washington. I felt no need to. My mental health is getting better all the time."

He narrowed his eyes as he scrutinized her across the flickering candle. "Something up with you, Collette? You okay?"

"I think I'm beginning to be more than okay, Joe. I think I grew up this past week."

"What does that mean?"

"It means . . ." She realized she was on the verge of tears and told herself that if she cried, she would never forgive herself. She looked around the restaurant. A waiter brought the appetizers on a white china platter. He filled their glasses with water and asked if they needed anything else.

"No, *köszönöm szepen,*" Breslin said politely. The waiter left and Breslin gave his attention to Cahill. "You're not happy, are you?"

Cahill shook her head in wonder and laughed. She leaned forward so that her face was inches from the candle's flame and said, "What the *hell* am I supposed to be happy about, Joe?"

He held up his hands and said, "Okay, I won't press it. You've been under a lot of strain. I realize that. Come on, enjoy the food. It's costing me a month's salary."

Throughout the meal, Cahill was on the verge a dozen times of telling him how she felt. She resisted the temptation and contented herself with light conversation.

The doorman got Breslin's car for him. When he and Cahill were in it, Breslin asked, "Feel up to a little nightlife?"

"Joe, I . . . the Miniatur?"

"No, I ran across another spot while you were away. Change is good for the soul, right?"

"If you say so, Joe. Might as well catch up on what's new in Budapest, but not too late, huh? One drink and get me home."

"Trust me."

She always had, but wasn't so sure anymore.

He drove slowly through the narrow, winding streets of the Pest side of the city until reaching Vörösmarty ter, with its statue of the famed Hungarian poet for whom the square was named. They passed a succession of airline offices and government buildings until they reached Engels Square and its large bus terminal. Ahead of them was St. Stephen's basilica. Breslin made a sharp turn north and, five minutes later, entered an especially narrow street made worse by cars hanging off their sidewalk parking spots. He found a place, wedged his small Renault between two other cars, and they got out. Cahill looked up the street to the huge red star atop the Parliament Building. She was back. Hungary. Budapest. Red stars and Soviet tanks. She was glad. Oddly, it was as close to home as she'd ever be outside of her mother's house in Virginia.

The bar wasn't marked, no sign, no windows. Only the faint tinkling of a piano heralded its location, and that was confused by a dozen dark doors set into the long concrete wall that formed the front of the street's buildings.

Breslin rapped with a brass knocker. The door opened and a large man in a black suit, with long greasy black hair and sunken cheeks, scrutinized them. Breslin nodded toward Cahill. The man stepped back and allowed them to enter.

Now the music was louder. The pianist was playing "Night and Day." Female laughter in the air mingled with his notes.

Cahill looked around. The club was laid out much like the Miniatur —bar as you entered, a small room just off it in which customers could enjoy the piano.

"*Jó napot* (How are you?)," Breslin said to an attractive woman with hair bleached white, wearing a tight red satin dress.

"*Jó estét* (Good evening)," she said.

"*Fel tudya ezt váltani?* (Can you change this?)," Breslin asked, handing her a Hungarian bill of large denomination.

She looked at the bill, at him, then stepped back to give them access to a door hidden in shadows beyond the bar. Breslin nodded at Cahill and she followed him. He hesitated, his hand poised over the knob, then turned it. The door swung open. Breslin indicated that Cahill should enter first. She took a step into a small room lighted only by two small lamps on a battered table in the middle. There were no windows, and heavy purple drapes covered all walls.

Her eyes started to adjust to the dimness. A man, whose face was vaguely familiar, was the first object she focused on. He had a thick, square face. Bones beneath bushy eyebrows formed hairy shelves over his cheeks. His black hair was thick and curly and streaked with gray. She remembered—Zoltán Réti, the author, Barrie Mayer's author.

Next to Réti sat Árpád Hegedüs. One of his hands on the table covered a female hand. A plain, wide-faced woman with honest eyes and thin, stringy hair.

"Árpád," Cahill said, the surprise evident in her voice.

"Miss Cahill," he said, standing. "I am so happy to see you."

26

COLLETTE LOOKED ACROSS the table at Hegedüs and Réti. Hegedüs's presence was the more easily understood. She'd known that the purpose of her return to Budapest was to meet with him. Réti was another matter. She'd forgotten about him in the rush of the past weeks.

"Miss Cahill, allow me to introduce you to Miss Lukács, Magda Lukács," Hegedüs said. Cahill rose slightly and extended her hand. The Hungarian woman reached out tentatively, then slipped her hand into Cahill's. She smiled; Cahill did too. The woman's face was placid, yet there was fear in her eyes. She wasn't pretty, but Cahill recognized an earthy female quality.

"I mentioned Miss Lukács to you the last time we were together," Hegedüs said.

"Yes, I remember," said Cahill, "but you didn't mention her name." She again smiled at the woman. Here was Hegedüs's lover, the woman Cahill had fervently hoped would not deter him from continuing to provide information. Now, as she observed the happiness in Hegedüs's face, she was glad he'd found Magda Lukács. He was happier and more relaxed than Cahill could ever remember seeing him.

As for Réti, she knew him only from photographs, and from having seen him on Hungary's state-controlled television network. Barrie had often spoken of him but they'd never met. "I'm glad to finally meet you, Mr. Réti," she said. "Barrie Mayer spoke so often and enthusiastically of you and your work."

"That is flattering," said Réti. "She was a wonderful woman and a fine literary agent. I miss her very much."

Cahill turned to Breslin. "Joe, why are we here?"

Breslin glanced at the others before saying, "First of all, Collette, I should apologize for not telling you up front how the evening would play. I didn't want to lay a lot of tension on you at dinner. From what I've heard, there's been enough of that in your life already."

She half smiled.

"Mr. Hegedüs has come over to our side."

Collette said to Hegedüs, "You've defected?"

He gave her a sheepish smile. "Yes, I have. My family is in Russia and I am now one of you. I am sorry, Miss Cahill. I know that was not what you or your people wished."

"No need to apologize, Árpád. I think it's wonderful." She looked at Magda Lukács. "You have defected, too?"

Lukács nodded. "I come with Árpád."

"Of course," said Cahill. "I'm sure that . . ." She swung around to Breslin. "But that isn't why we're sitting here, is it?"

Breslin shook his head. "No, it's not. The defection has already taken place. What we *are* here for is to hear what Mr. Hegedüs and Mr. Réti have to tell us." He smiled. "They wouldn't say a word unless you were here, Collette."

"I see," Cahill said, taking in the table. "Well, go ahead. Here I am, and I'm all ears."

When no one spoke, Breslin said, "Mr. Hegedüs."

Now Hegedüs seemed more like his old nervous self. He cleared his throat and squeezed his lover's hand. He ran a finger beneath his shirt collar and said with a forced sense of gaiety, "We are in a bar, yes? Could I possibly have some whiskey?"

His request visibly annoyed Breslin, but he got up with a sigh and went to the door, opened it, and said to the woman in the red satin dress who was seated at the bar, "Could we have a bottle of wine, please?"

Hegedüs said from behind Breslin, "Would bourbon be all right?"

Breslin turned and screwed up his face. *"Bourbon?"*

"Yes, Miss Cahill always . . ."

Breslin shook his head and said to the woman in red, "A bottle of bourbon." He then laughed and added, "And some Scotch and gin, too." He closed the door and said to Cahill, "Never let it be said that Joe Breslin didn't throw as good a defector party as Collette Cahill."

"You're a class act, Joe," Collette said. She looked at Zoltán Réti and asked, "Have you defected too, Mr. Réti?"

Réti shook his head.

"But have you . . . ?" She checked Breslin before continuing. His expressionless face prompted her to go ahead. "Have you been involved with our efforts all along, Mr. Réti, through Barrie Mayer?"

"Yes."

"Were you Barrie's contact here in Budapest?"

"Yes."

"She would hand you what she was carrying for us?"

He smiled. "It was a little more complicated than that, Miss Cahill."

There was a knock at the door. Breslin opened it and the woman in red carried in a tray with the liquor, a bucket of ice and glasses. After she'd placed it on the table and left, Collette cocked her head and listened to the strains of piano music and the laughter of patrons through the wall. Was this place secure enough for the sort of conversation they were having? She was almost ashamed for even questioning it. Breslin had a reputation of being the most cautious intelligence employee within the Budapest embassy.

"Maybe I'd better lead this conversation," Breslin said.

Cahill was momentarily taken aback, but said, "By all means."

Breslin pointed a finger across the table at Zoltán Réti and said, "Let's start with you." To Hegedüs, "You don't mind, do you?"

Hegedüs, busy pouring a tall glass of bourbon, quickly shook his head and said, "Of course not."

Breslin continued. "Mr. Réti, Miss Cahill has been back in the United States trying to find out what happened to Barrie Mayer. I don't know if you're aware of it, but they were best of friends."

"Yes, I know that," said Réti.

"Then you know that we've never believed that Barrie Mayer died of natural causes."

Réti grunted. "She was assassinated. Only a fool would think otherwise."

"Exactly," said Breslin. "One of the pieces we've had trouble with has to do with what she could have been carrying that was important enough for her to have been murdered. Frankly, we weren't even aware of her final trip to Budapest until after the fact. We expected nothing from Washington. But you evidently knew she was coming."

Réti nodded, and his heavy eyebrows came down even lower over his eyes.

Cahill said, "But you weren't *here*, Mr. Réti. You were in London."

"Yes, I was sent there by the Hungarian Arts Council to make an appearance at an international writers' conference."

"Didn't Barrie know that you wouldn't be here to meet her?" Cahill asked.

"No, I had no time to contact her. I was not allowed access to any means of communication with her before she left the United States."

"Why?" Cahill realized she had taken the meeting from Breslin. She cast a glance at him to see if he were annoyed. The expression on his face showed that he wasn't.

Réti shrugged. "I can only assume that they . . . the government had become aware that she and I were more than simply agent and author."

Cahill processed what he'd said, then asked, "And they didn't do more to you than just keep you from telling Barrie that you wouldn't be here to meet her? They knew that you were involved in some sort of activity on our behalf, but only kept you from calling her?"

Réti smiled, exposing a set of widely spaced teeth. He said, "That is not so surprising, Miss Cahill. The Russians . . . and my government . . . they are not so foolish to punish someone like myself. It would not look so good in the world, huh?"

His explanation made sense to Cahill, but she said, "Still, if Barrie *had* arrived and didn't find you here, what would she do with what she was carrying? Who would she hand it to?"

"This time, Miss Cahill, Barrie was not to hand me anything."

"She wasn't?"

"No."

"What was she to do, then?"

"She was to tell me something."

"Tell?"

"Yes. This time what she carried was in her head."

"Her mind, you mean."

"Yes, in her mind."

The room was hot and stuffy, yet a chill radiated through Collette that caused her to fold into herself. Was it all coming true now—Jason Tolker, Estabrooks's theories on using hypnosis to create the perfect intelligence courier, programs like Operation Bluebird and MK-ULTRA, supposedly scrapped years ago but still going strong—everything Eric Edwards had told her, every bit of it?

She looked at Breslin. "Joe, do you know what Barrie was supposed to tell Mr. Réti?"

Breslin, who'd just lighted his pipe, squinted through the smoke and said, "I think so."

Cahill hadn't expected an affirmative answer. Breslin said to Hegedüs, "Perhaps it's time for you to contribute to this conversation."

The Hungarian psychiatrist looked at Magda Lukács, cleared his throat with a swallow of bourbon, and said, "It has to do with what I told you the last time, Miss Cahill."

Collette said it quietly, almost to the table: "Dr. Tolker."

"Yes, your Dr. Tolker . . ."

"What about him?"

A false start from Hegedüs, then, "He had given Miss Mayer information of the gravest importance to the Banana Quick project."

"What sort of information?" Cahill asked.

"The source of the leak in the British Virgin Islands," Breslin said.

Cahill raised her eyebrows. "I thought that . . ."

Breslin shrugged. "I think you're beginning to understand, Collette."

"You told me the last time we were together, Árpád, that Tolker was not to be trusted."

"That is correct."

"But now I'm to understand that he's the one who is identifying a security leak in Banana Quick."

"Right," said Breslin. "You know who we're talking about, Collette."

"Eric Edwards."

"Exactly."

"That's ridiculous," Collette said.

"Why?" Breslin asked. "Edwards has been a prime suspect from the beginning. That's why you were . . ." He stopped. The rules were being broken. Take everything you could from the other side but offer nothing.

Collette was having trouble controlling her emotions. She didn't want to mount an impassioned defense of Edwards because it would only trigger in Breslin the question of why she was doing it. She imposed calm on herself and asked Breslin, "How do you know what Barrie was carrying? Maybe it had nothing to do with Banana Quick . . . or Eric Edwards."

Breslin ignored her and nodded at Hegedüs, who said regretfully, "I was wrong, Miss Cahill, about Dr. Tolker."

"Wrong?"

"I was misled, perhaps deliberately by certain people within my professional ranks. Dr. Tolker has not been disloyal to you."

"Just like that," Cahill said.

Hegedüs shrugged. "It is not such a crime to be wrong, is it, not in America?"

Cahill sighed and sat back. "Collette," Breslin said, "the facts are written on the wall. Barrie was coming here to . . ."

She said, "Coming here to deliver a message that had been implanted in her mind by Jason Tolker."

"That's right," said Breslin. "Tell her, Mr. Réti."

Réti said, "I was to say something to her when she arrived that would cause her to remember the message."

"Which was?" Collette asked.

"That this Eric Edwards in the British Virgin Islands has been selling information to the Soviets about Banana Quick."

"How do we know that's what she was carrying?"

"Tolker has been contacted," Breslin said.

Cahill shook her head. "If Tolker can simply tell us what he knows about Eric Edwards, why did he bother sending Barrie with the information? Why didn't he just go to someone at Langley with it?"

"Because . . ." Breslin paused, then continued. "We can discuss that later, Collette. For now, let's stick to what Mr. Réti and Mr. Hegedüs can provide us."

"Well?" Cahill said to the two Hungarians.

"Miss Cahill," Réti said, "first of all, I did not know what Barrie was to tell me when I said to her the code words."

"What were those words?" Cahill asked.

Réti looked to Breslin, who nodded his approval. "I was to say, 'The climate has improved.' "

"The climate has improved," Cahill repeated.

"Yes, exactly that."

"And she was then to open up to you like a robot."

"I do not know about that. I was simply following instructions."

"Whose instructions?"

"Mr. . . ." Another look at Breslin.

"Stan Podgorsky," Breslin said. "Stan's been the contact for Barrie and Mr. Réti since the beginning."

"Why wasn't I told that?" Cahill asked.

"No need. Barrie's courier duties had nothing to do with you."

"I wonder about that."

"Don't bother. It's the way it is. Accept it."

"Árpád, who has caused you to change your opinion of Jason Tolker?"

"Friends." He smiled. "Former friends. There are no longer friends for me in Hungary."

"Collette, Mr. Réti has something else to share with us," Breslin said.

Everyone waited. Finally, Réti said in a low, slow monotone, "Barrie was bringing me money, too."

"Money?" Cahill said.

"Yes, to pay off one of our officials so that the earnings from my books could reach me here in Hungary."

"This money was in her briefcase?"

"Yes."

"Joe, Barrie received her briefcase from Tolker. Why would he . . . ?"

"He didn't," Breslin said. "The money wasn't from Mr. Réti's fund in the States. It was Pickle Factory money."

"Why?"

"It's the way it was set up."

"Set up . . . with Barrie?"

"Right."

"But she had Réti's own money, didn't she? Why would she need CIA money?"

Breslin lowered his eyes, then raised them. "Later," he said.

"No, not later," Cahill said. "How about now?"

"Collette, I think you're becoming emotionally bound up in this. That won't help clarify anything."

"I resent that, Joe."

What she was really feeling was a sense of being a woman, and disliking herself for it. Breslin was right. He'd read her; she wasn't taking in and evaluating what was being said at the table like a professional. She was bound up in protecting a man, Eric, a man with whom she'd slept and, incredibly, with whom she'd begun to fall in love. It hadn't seemed incredible at the time, but it did now.

She took in everyone at the table and asked, "Is there anything else?"

Hegedüs forced a big smile, his hand still resting on his lover's hand. He said, "Miss Cahill, I would like you to know how much I appreciate . . . how much Magda and I appreciate everything you have done for us."

"I didn't do anything, Árpád, except listen to you."

"No, you are wrong, Miss Cahill. By spending time with you, my decision to leave the oppression of the Soviets was made clear, and easier." He stood and bowed. "I shall be forever grateful."

Cahill found his demeanor to be offensive. "What about your family, Árpád, your beautiful daughter and bright young son? Your wife. What of her? Are you content to abandon them to the tenuous life you know they'll lead in Russia?" He started to respond but she went on. "You told me you wanted more than anything else for your son to have the advantage of growing up in America. What was that, Árpád, all talk?" Her voice was now more strident, reflecting what she was feeling.

"Let's drop it," Breslin said with finality. Collette glared at him, then said to Réti, "What happens to you now, Mr. Réti? The money never reached you."

Réti shrugged. "It is the same now as it was before. Perhaps . . ."

"Yes?"

"Perhaps you could be of help in this matter."

"How?"

"We're working on it, Mr. Réti," Breslin said. To Cahill, "It's one of the things I want to discuss with you when we leave here."

"All right." Collette stood and extended her hand to Magda Lukács. "Welcome, Miss Lukács, to freedom." Hegedüs beamed and offered his hand to Cahill. She ignored it, said to Breslin, "I'm ready to leave."

Breslin got up and surveyed the bottles on the table. "Souvenirs?" he asked, laughing.

"If you would not be offended I would . . ."

"Sure, Mr. Hegedüs, take it with you," Breslin said. "Thank you for being here, all of you. Come on, Collette, you must be exhausted."

"That, and more," she said, opening the door and walking into the smoky barroom. The lady in red was standing at the door.

"*Jó éjszakát,*" Breslin said.

"*Jó éjszakát,*" she said, nodding at Cahill.

Collete said "Good night" in English, walked past her, and stood in the cool, refreshing air outside the club. Breslin came to her side. Without looking at him, she said, "Let's go somewhere and talk."

"I thought you were beat," he said, taking her arm.

"I'm wide awake and I'm filled with questions that need answering. Are you up to that, Joe?"

"I'll do my best."

Somehow, she knew his best wouldn't be enough, but she'd take what she could get.

They'd driven out of the city to the Római fürdo, the former Roman baths that now constituted one of Budapest's two major camping sites. The sky had clouded over and was low. It picked up the general glow of the city's lights and was racing over them, pink and yellow and gray, a fast-moving scrim cranked by an unseen force.

"You said you had questions," Breslin said.

Cahill had opened her window and was looking out into the dark. She said into the night, "Just one, Joe."

"Shoot."

She turned and faced him. "Who killed Barrie Mayer?"

"I don't know."

"Know what I think, Joe?"

"No, what?"

"I think everybody's lying."

He laughed. "Who's *everybody*?"

"*Everybody!* Let's start with Réti."

"Okay. Start with him. What's he got to lie about?"

"Money, for one thing. I knew Barrie was supposed to pay off some government bigwig on Réti's behalf, but I didn't know until tonight that Barrie was actually carrying the money with her in the missing briefcase. Oh, that's right, you said you'd discuss with me later why the Company used its money to buy off the official, instead of Barrie using what she'd already collected of Réti's earnings. This is later, Joe. I'm ready."

He scrutinized her from where he sat in the driver's seat, ran his tongue over his lips, then pulled a pipe from his raincoat pocket and went through the ritual of lighting it. This was all too familiar to Cahill, using the pipe to buy thinking time, and tonight was especially irritating. Still, she didn't interrupt, didn't attempt to hasten the process. She waited patiently until the bowl glowed with fire and he'd had a chance to inhale. Then she said, "Réti's money. Why the Company?"

"To make sure he knew who he owed," Breslin answered.

"That doesn't make sense," she said. "Why would he owe anyone? The money is his. His books earned it."

"That's what he said, but we educated him. He's Hungarian. His big money is earned out of the country. Puts him in a tough position, doesn't it? All we did was to set up a system to help him get his hands on some of it."

"If he played the game with us."

"Sure. He thought Barrie would take care of it as his agent." Breslin smiled. "Of course, he didn't know up front that she worked for us, and would do what we told her to do. We struck a nice deal. Réti cooperates with us, and we see that he gets enough money to live like a king here."

"That is so . . . goddamned unfair. He earned that money."

"I suppose it is unfair, unless you're dealing with a Socialist writer and a capitalist agent. Come on, Collette, you know damn well that nothing's fair in what we're called upon to do."

" 'Called upon to do.' You make it sound so lofty."

"Necessary. Maybe that's more palatable to you."

She drew a sustained, angry breath. "Let's get to Hegedüs and Jason Tolker. Why do you buy Hegedüs's change of mind about Tolker?"

"Why not buy it?"

"Why *not?* Joe, hasn't it occurred to you that Árpád might have come over to feed us disinformation? What if Tolker has been cooperating with the other side? How convenient to have Hegedüs defect and get us to look the other way. No, I can't buy it. When Hegedüs told me earlier that Tolker was not be to trusted, he meant it. He doesn't mean what he's saying now. He's lying."

"Prove it."

"How do you prove anything in this stupid game?"

"Right, you don't. You look at everything you've got—which sure as hell never amounts to much—and you feel what your gut is saying and listen to what your head says and you make your decisions. My decision? We've got ourselves a defector, a good one. Sure, we'd all prefer he'd stayed in place so he could keep feeding us from the inside, but it's okay that he's with us now. He's loaded with insight into the Soviet and Hungarian psychological fraternity. You did a good job, Collette. You turned him nicely. He trusted you. Everybody's pleased with the way you've handled him."

"That's terrific. Why don't *you* trust me?"

"Huh?"

"Why can't you put some stock in what my gut feels and my head says? He's lying, Joe, maybe to protect his family back in the Soviet Union, maybe to play out his own brand of patriotism to his government. Don't you question why the Soviets have let him off the hook? He was supposed to go back to Russia because they didn't trust him. He doesn't go, and he neatly defects. He's lying. They've plopped him into the middle of us, and one of his jobs is to get Jason Tolker off the hook."

"Pure speculation, Collette. Ammunition. Give me something tangible to back it up."

She spread her hands. "I don't have any, but I know I'm right."

"What about Réti?" Breslin asked. "What's he got to lie about?"

"I don't know. But remember, he was in London when Barrie died."

"Meaning?"

"Meaning maybe he killed her because he knew her briefcase was loaded with cash."

"His cash. Why kill her for it?" A long, slow drag on his pipe.

"Did he know how much she was bringing to him?"

"Not sure. Probably not."

"Maybe Mr. Réti figured out that he was never going to get a square count from us. Maybe he figured out that he'd only get a small piece of what she was carrying. Maybe he wanted to get his hands on the money while he was outside Hungary and stash it."

"Interesting questions."

"Yes, aren't they?"

"What about Hubler back in Washington? Réti sure as hell didn't kill him, Collette."

"He could have arranged it if Hubler knew what had happened. The Soviets could have done it. Then again, maybe it was pure coincidence, nothing to do with Barrie."

"Maybe. What other theories do you have?"

"Don't dismiss what I'm saying, Joe. Don't treat me like some schoolgirl who's spewing out plots from bad TV shows she's watched."

"Hey, Collette, back off. I'm a white hat, remember? I'm a friend."

She wanted to question what he'd said but didn't. Instead, she asked if he had a cigarette.

"You don't smoke."

"I used to, back when I was a schoolgirl watching bad TV shows. Got any?"

"Yeah, in the glove compartment. Every once in a while I get the urge."

She opened the compartment and reached inside, found a crumpled pack of Camels, and pulled one from the pack. Breslin lighted it for her. She coughed, exhaled the smoke, then took another drag, tossed the cigarette out the window, and said, "You think Eric Edwards is a double agent?"

"Yes."

"Do you think he killed Barrie?"

"Good chance that he did."

"Why would he do that? He was in love with her."

"To save his skin."

"What do you mean?"

"Barrie knew he was a double agent."

"Because Tolker told her."

"No, because she told Tolker." He reached across the seat and grabbed her arm. "You ready for some heavy stuff, Collette?"

"Heavy stuff? The last week hasn't exactly been lightweight, Joe, has it?"

"No, it hasn't." He paused, used his pipe to fill a few seconds, then said, "Your friend Barrie sold out, too."

"Sold out? What do you mean? Sold out to whom?"

"The other side. She was in it with Edwards."

"Joe, that's . . ."

"Hey, at least hear me out."

She didn't, jumped in with, "If she was in it with Edwards, why would she be off to Hungary to blow the whistle on him?"

"Ever hear of the woman scorned?"

"Not Barrie."

"Why not?"

"Because . . . she wouldn't do something like that." Now there was only a modicum of conviction behind her words. What spun through her mind was the kind of control someone like Jason Tolker could exercise over a good subject like Barrie Mayer. What she'd read in Estabrooks's book was there, too, about changing the "visual" in order to get people to behave in a manner foreign to their basic personality and values.

"What if Tolker programmed her to come up with a story about Eric Edwards out of . . . I don't know, out of jealousy or pique or to save his own hide? Maybe Tolker is a double agent and used Barrie to cover up. Maybe he poisoned Barrie against Edwards."

"Yeah, maybe, Collette. Who poisoned you against Tolker?"

"I'm not . . ."

"Put another way, how come you're so hell-bent on defending Edwards?"

"I'm not doing that, either, Joe."

"I think you are."

"Think again, and get off treating me like some pathetic woman defending a lover to the death. I am a woman, Joe, and I am an agent of the CIA. Know what? I'm good at both."

"Collette, maybe . . ."

"Maybe nothing, Joe. You and Stan have wrapped everything up in what you think is a neat little package, no loose ends, no doubts. Why? Why is it so damn important to resolve Barrie's murder by laying it on Edwards?" He raised his eyebrows as though to say, "There you go again." She shook her head. "I don't buy it, any of it, Joe."

"That's a shame," he said quietly.

"Why?"

"Because that attitude will get in the way of your next assignment." She stared quizzically at him, finally asking, "What assignment?"

"Terminating Eric Edwards."

She started to speak but all that came out was breath.

"You understand what I'm saying, don't you?"

"Terminate Eric? Kill him."

"Yes."

It was hardly an accurate reflection of what was on her mind, but it happened anyway: She laughed. Breslin did, too, and continued until she stopped.

"They mean it," he said.

"They?"

"Up top."

"*They* . . . they told you to assign me to kill him?"

"Uh-huh."

"Why me?"

"You can get close to him."

"So can lots of people."

"Easier and neater with you, Collette."

"How do 'they' suggest I do this?"

"Your choice. Go by Tech in the morning and choose your weapon."

"I see," she said. "Then what?"

"What are you talking about, what happens after it's done?"

"Right."

"Nothing. It's over, the double agent in Banana Quick is no longer a problem and we can get back to normal, which can't be too soon. Banana Quick is close to popping."

"Back to normal for me, here in Budapest?"

"If you wish. It's customary for anyone carrying out a wet affair to have their choice of future assignment, even to take a leave of absence, with pay, of course."

"Joe, I'm sorry but . . ." She started to laugh again, but it did not become laughter, and this time he didn't join her. Instead, he puffed on his pipe and waited for her nervous, absolutely necessary reaction to subside.

"They're serious, Collette."

"I'm sure they are. I'm not." She paused, then said, "Joe, *they* blew up the yacht, didn't they?" When he didn't respond, she added, "Eric knew it."

Again, no reply from him.

"I was on that yacht, Joe."

"It wasn't us."

"I don't believe you."

"It was the Soviets."

"Why would they do that if he's on their side?"

A shrug from Breslin. "Maybe he started holding out for more money. Maybe they thought he was feeding them bad information. Maybe they didn't like him carousing around with a pretty CIA agent."

Cahill shook her head. "You know what's remarkable, Joe?"

"What?"

"That 'they' means the same people . . . the Soviets, the CIA . . . all the same, same morality, same ethics, same game."

"Don't give me the moral equivalency speech, Collette. It doesn't play, and you know it. We've got a system to preserve that's good and decent. Their system is evil. I'll tell you something else. If you do want to view it that way, keep it between us. It wouldn't go over too big with . . ."

"The hell with *them*."

"Suit yourself. I've given you the assignment. Take it?"

"Yes."

"Look, Collette, you realize that . . . ?"

"Joe, I said I'd do it. No need for more speeches."

"You'll really do it?"

"Yes, I'll really do it."

"When?"

"I'll leave tomorrow."

"I get the feeling that . . ."

"Take me home, Joe."

"Collette, if there's any hesitation on your part, I'd suggest you sleep on it."

"I'll do that. I'll sleep just fine."

"Why?"

"Why what?"

"Why the sudden willingness to kill Edwards?"

"Because . . . I'm a pro. I work for the CIA. I do what I'm told. It's obviously for the good of the country, *my* country. Someone has to do it. Let's go."

He pulled up in front of her apartment building and said, "Come talk to me in the morning."

"What for?"

"To go over this a little more."

"No need. You'll tell Tech I'll be by?"

He sighed, said, "Yes."

"Know something, Joe?"

"What?"

"For the first time since I joined the CIA, I feel part of the team."

27

SHE AWOKE THE next morning feeling surprisingly refreshed. There was no hangover from jet lag or from the late evening and its drinks. She showered quickly, chose her heather wool tweed suit and burgundy turtleneck, and called for a taxi. A half hour later she walked through the front door of the United States Embassy on Szabadság ter, flashed her credentials at the security guard who knew her well, was buzzed into the inner lobby, and went directly to the transportation office. There she booked an afternoon Malev flight to London, and a connecting flight to New York the following evening.

"Good morning, Joe," she said brightly to Breslin as they approached each other in the hall.

"Hello, Collette," he said somberly.

"Can we get this over with now?" she asked.

His was a deep, meaningful sigh. "Yeah, I suppose so," he said.

He closed the door to his office. "Got a cigarette, Joe?" she asked pleasantly.

"No. Don't start the habit."

"Why not? Looks like I'm about to start a whole new set of bad habits."

"Look, Collette, I talked to Stan late last night. I tried to . . ." He looked up at the ceiling. "Let's take a walk."

"No need. You've arranged for me to go to Tech this morning?"

"Yes, but . . ." He got up. "Come on."

She had little choice but to follow him out of the embassy and across Liberation Square to a bench on which he propped a foot and lighted his pipe. "I tried to get you off it, Collette," he said.

"Why? I didn't balk."

"Yeah, and that worries me. How come?"

"I thought I explained myself last night. I want to be a pro, part of the team. You join an organization like this because, no matter how much you want to—need to—deny your fascination with James Bond movies, it's always there. Right, Joe?"

"Maybe. The point is, Collette, I went to Stan's house after I dropped you and tried to persuade him to cancel the order from Langley."

"I wish you hadn't. I don't want to be treated different from anyone else because I'm a woman."

"That wasn't what I pegged my request upon," Breslin said. "I don't think you're the one to go after our friend in the BVI because of your relationship with him."

"I don't have a *relationship* with him, Joe. I went down there on business and did what I was told to do. I got close to him and damn near ended up fish food in the bargain. It makes perfect sense for me to do this."

"Hank thinks so, too."

"Fox? I'm flattered. All I seem to end up with are father figures, and want to know something, Joe?"

"What?"

"I don't need a father, and that includes you."

"Thanks."

"No gratitude necessary. All my fathers seem to do—including you— is to send their daughters into battle. New definition of fatherhood, I guess. Female liberation. I'm glad. Now, let's get back to basics. You tried to get me off, you failed. That's good because I'm committed to this. Everything is right in my mind. One thing I don't need is a set of doubts implanted." She laughed. "Besides, I'm a lousy hypnotic subject. It's a shame Barrie wasn't."

Breslin nodded toward a far corner of the square where two men in overcoats and hats stood, conspicuously not watching them. "I think we've talked enough," Breslin said.

"I think you're right," Cahill said. "I have a plane reservation for this afternoon. Better get inside and pick up my supplies."

"All right. One other thing, though." He walked away from her and toward a corner where a line of taxicabs waited for fares. He slowed down and she caught up with him. "When you get home, Collette, contact no one involved with us. No one. Understand?"

"Yes." The order didn't surprise her. The nature of her mission would preclude touching base with anyone even mildly associated with the CIA and Langley.

"But," he said, "if you need help in a real emergency, there's been a control established for you in D.C."

"Who?"

"It doesn't matter. Just remember that it's available in an emergency. You make contact any evening for the next two weeks at exactly six o'clock. The contact point is the statue of Winston Churchill just outside the British Embassy on Massachuetts Avenue. Your contact will hold for ten minutes each evening, no more. Got it?"

"Yes. Do I still have my contact in the BVI, at Pusser's Landing?"

"No."

"All right."

She had nothing more to say, just followed him back inside the embassy, went to her office, closed the door, and stood at the window peering out at the gray, suddenly bleak city of Budapest. Her phone rang but she ignored it. She realized she was in the midst of an unemotional void: no feelings, no anxiety or anger or confusion. There was nothing, and it was pleasant.

Ten minutes later she went to the embassy's basement where a closed door bore the sign TECHNICAL ASSISTANCE. She knocked; a latch was released and Harold Sutherland opened the door.

"Hi, Red," she said.

"Hi. Come on in. I've been expecting you."

Once the door was closed behind them, Sutherland said, "Well, kid, what do you need?"

Cahill stood in the middle of the cramped, cluttered room and realized he was waiting for an answer. What was the answer? She didn't know what she "needed." Obviously, there were people who did for a living what she was about to do. For a death. *They* knew what was needed in their job. She didn't. It wasn't her job to kill anyone, at least not in the lengthy job description that accompanied her embassy employment. But those specifications were a lie, too. She didn't work for the embassy. She worked for the Central Intelligence Agency, the CIA, the Company, the Pickle Factory, whose stated purpose was to gather and assimilate intelligence from all over the world and . . . and to kill when it was necessary to keep doing its job.

She'd had courses during her CIA training at the Farm that dealt with killing, although it was never labeled as such. "Self-protection," they called it. There were other terms—"Termination Techniques," "Neutralization," "Securing the Operation."

"You flying somewhere?" Sutherland asked.

His gravel voice startled her. She looked at him, forced a smile, and said, "Yes."

"Come here."

He led her past his desk, past rows of floor-to-ceiling shelving stocked with unmarked boxes and to a tiny separate room at the rear. It was a miniature firing range. She didn't even know it existed. She'd participated in firing exercises on the embassy's main range, which wasn't much bigger, just longer.

There was a table, two chairs, and a thick, padded wall ten feet away. The pads were filled with holes. She glanced up; the ceiling was covered with soundproofing material. So were the other walls.

"Have a seat," Sutherland said.

She took one of the chairs while he disappeared back into the shelves, returning moments later carrying a white cardboard box. He placed it on the table, opened it, and removed a purple bag with a drawstring. She watched as he opened the bag and lifted from it a piece of white plastic that was shaped like a small revolver. He pulled a second bag from the box. It contained a plastic barrel. The only metal item was a small spring.

"Nine millimeter," he said as he weighed the components in his large, callused hand. "It's like the Austrian Glock 17, only the barrel is plastic, too. It's U.S.-made. We just got it last week."

"I see."

"Here, put it together. Simple."

He watched as she fumbled with the pieces, then showed her how to do it. When it was assembled, he said, "You stick the spring in your purse and pack the rest in your suitcase. Wrap it in clothes, only that's not even necessary. X-ray picks up nothing."

She looked at him. "Bullets?"

He grinned. "Ammunition, you mean? Pick it up in any sporting goods store where you're traveling. Want to try it?"

"No, I . . . Yes, please."

He showed her how to load it and told her to shoot at the padded wall. She placed two hands on it and squeezed the trigger. She'd expected a kick. There was virtually nothing. Even the sound was small.

"You need a silencer?"

"Ah, no, I don't think so."

"Good. It's developed but we don't have it yet. Break it down. I'll watch."

She disassembled and assembled the small plastic weapon four times.

"Good. You've got it down. What else?"

"I . . . I'm not sure, Red." What she wanted to say was that she was about to go off on an assignment to kill someone, to kill a man she'd slept with, to terminate him for the good of her country and the free world. She didn't say anything, of course. It was too late for that. It wouldn't be professional.

"Red."

"Yeah?"

"I'd like some prussic acid and a detonator."

His eyebrows went up. "Why?" he asked.

"I need it for my assignment."

"Yeah? I ought to . . ." He shrugged and heaved his bulk to its feet. "Joe said give you anything you wanted. Sure you want this?"

"Yes, I'm sure."

It took him a few minutes to assemble her request. When he handed it to her, she was amazed at the smallness of it. "Know how to use it?" he asked.

"No."

He showed her. "That's all there is to it," he said. "You get it close to the nose and trip this spring. Make sure it's not your own nose. By the way, if it is, use this stuff fast." He handed her a package of two glass ampules. "Nitro. If you get a whiff of the prussic, break this under your nose or . . ." He grinned and patted her on the shoulder. "Or I lose a favorite of mine."

His words cut into her, but then she smiled, too, and said, "Thanks, Red. Any last words of wisdom?"

"Yeah, I got a few."

"What are they?"

"Get out of the business, kid. Go home, work for a bank, get married and raise a couple of good citizens."

She wanted to cry but was successful in fighting the need. "Actually," she said, "I was going to become the Attorney General of the United States."

"That's not much better than what you're doing now." He shook his head and asked, "You want to talk?"

She did, desperately, but what she said was, "No, I have to get going. I haven't packed. The other stuff, that is." She looked down at the white box she held in her hands. Sutherland had put the revolver, the prussic acid vial, and detonator in it, packing it carefully, like a bridal gift.

"Good luck, kid," he said. "See you back here soon?"

"Yeah, I guess so. Unless I decide to go work for a bank. Thanks, Red."

"You take care."

28

IT WAS A RUNNING joke among embassy employees—Malev airlines, the national Hungarian airline, sold a first-class section on its flights, but its seats, food, and service were identical to those in the rear of the plane. A Communist compromise with free enterprise.

It was also unusual, Cahill knew, for her to be flying first class. Company policy put everyone in coach, with the exception of chiefs-of-station. But when Cahill had walked into the Transportation Department, she was handed first-class tickets on every leg of the trip. The young woman who handled embassy travel arrangements lifted a brow as she handed the tickets to Cahill. It had amused Cahill at the time, and she was tempted to say, "No, there hasn't been a mistake. Assassins always ride first class."

Now, at thirty thousand feet between Budapest and London, it was not as amusing. It carried with it a symbolism that she would have preferred to ignore, but couldn't. Like a last meal, or wish.

She passed through Heathrow Customs and went to the approximate place where Barrie would have been standing when the prussic acid was shoved beneath her nose. She stared at the hard floor for a long time, watching hundreds of pairs of shoes pass over it. Didn't they know what they were walking on? What a horrible place to die, she thought as she slowly walked away, took a taxi outside the terminal, and told the driver to go to 11, Cadogan Gardens.

"Yes, we have a room," the manager on duty told her. "I'm afraid the room you enjoyed last time isn't available, but we have a nice single in the back."

"Anything will be fine," Cahill said. "This was a last-minute trip, no time to call ahead."

She ordered a dinner of cold poached salmon and a bottle of wine. When the hall porter had left, she securely latched the door, undressed, removed the small plastic revolver from her suitcase, did the same with the spring and prussic acid detonator from her purse, and placed everything on the table next to the tray. She tasted the white wine the porter had uncorked. It was chilled and tart.

She ate the salmon with enthusiasm, and finished half the wine, her eyes remaining for most of the meal on the mechanical contraptions of death with which she'd traveled.

The phone rang. "Was dinner satisfactory?" the porter wished to know.

"Yes, fine, thank you," said Cahill.

"Do you wish anything else?"

"No, no, thank you."

"Shall I remove the tray, madam?"

"No, that won't be necessary. In the morning. Will you arrange a wake-up call for me at ten, please?"

"Yes, madam."

"And breakfast in the room. Two eggs over easy, bacon and toast, coffee, orange juice."

"Yes, madam. Have a pleasant evening."

"Thank you."

She stood at the window and watched a brisk wind whip leaves from the trees on the street below. People walked their dogs; someone was attempting to squeeze a too-large automobile into a too-small parking space.

She went to the table and picked up the white plastic revolver, assembled its components and, with two hands, aimed at an oil of a vase of roses that hung on the far wall. There was no ammunition in the weapon; she'd have to buy it when she got to the British Virgin Islands.

She'd never bought bullets before and wondered whether she'd be able to do it with aplomb. Like a teenage boy sheepishly buying contraceptives, she thought.

She squeezed the trigger several times, sat on the couch and took the weapon apart, put it back together again, and repeated the process a dozen times. Satisfied, she carefully picked up the detonator and tested the spring, making sure before she did that the ampule of prussic acid wasn't in it.

She dialed a local number. It was answered on the first ring.

"Josh, this is Collette Cahill."

"Collette, great to hear your voice. How've you been?"

"It's good to hear your voice, too, Josh. I've been fine. I'm in London."

"Hey, that's great. Can we get together? How about dinner tomorrow? I'll round up some of the troops."

"I'd love it, Josh, but I'm here on business and have to leave early tomorrow evening. Actually, I'm calling for a favor."

"Anything. What is it?"

"I need a photograph."

"You're looking for a photographer?"

"No, I need an existing photograph of someone. I thought maybe you could pull one out of the files for me."

He laughed. "Not supposed to do that, you know."

"Yes, I know, but it really would be a tremendous help to me. I won't have to keep it, just have it for an hour or so tomorrow."

"You've got it—if we have it. Who do you want a picture of?"

"A literary agent here in London named Mark Hotchkiss."

"I don't know whether we'd have anything on a literary agent, but I'll check. You'd probably do better through a newspaper morgue."

"I know that, but I don't have time."

"I'll check it out first thing in the morning. Where can I meet up with you?"

She gave him the address of the hotel. "At least I'll get to see you tomorrow," he said. "If I come up with the photo, you owe me the chance to buy you a quick lunch."

"That'll be great. See you around noon."

Josh Moeller and Collette had worked closely together during her previous CIA assignment to the listening post in England. They'd become fast friends, sharing a mutual sense of humor and a quiet disdain for much of the bureaucratic rules and regulations under which they lived and worked. Their friendship evolved into a brief affair shortly before Cahill's reassignment to Budapest. Her move concluded the affair with finality, but they both knew it had effectively died by its own hand before that, one of those situations in which the friendship was stronger and more important to both parties than the passion. They'd initially kept in touch, mostly through letters delivered by way of the diplomatic pouch between Budapest and London. But then their correspondence tapered off, too, as will happen with the best of friends, especially when the friendship is strong enough to preclude any need for frequent contact.

Her next call was long-distance. It took ten minutes for it to go through to the BVI. Eric Edwards's secretary answered.

"Is Mr. Edwards there?" Cahill asked, glancing at her watch to reconfirm the time difference.

"No, ma'am, he is not. He is in the United States."

"Washington?"

"Yes, ma'am. Is this Miss Cahill?"

Cahill was surprised to be asked. "Yes, it is."

"Mr. Edwards told me that if you called I should inform you that he is staying at the Watergate Hotel in Washington, D.C."

"How long will he be there?"

"One more week, I think."

"Thank you, thank you very much. I'll contact him there."

One final call, this one to her mother in Virginia.

"Collette, where are you?"

"London, Mom, but I'll be coming home in a few days."

"Oh, that will be wonderful." A pause: "Are you all right?"

"Yes, Mom, I'm fine. I think . . . I think I might be coming home for good."

Her mother's gasp was audible even over the poor connection. "Why?" she asked. "I mean, I'd love for that to happen but . . . are you sure everything is all right? Are you in some sort of trouble?"

Collette laughed loudly to help make the point that she wasn't. She simply said, "Lots of things have been happening, Mom, and maybe the best of them all is to come home and stay home."

The connection was almost lost, and Cahill said quickly, "Goodbye, Mom. See you in about a week."

She knew her mother was saying something but couldn't make out the words. Then the line went dead.

She stayed up most of the night, pacing the room, picking up and examining the weapons she'd brought with her—thinking—her mind racing at top speed, one person after another in her life taking center stage—Barrie Mayer, Mark Hotchkiss, Breslin, Podgorsky, Hank Fox, Jason Tolker, Eric Edwards—all of them, the chaos and confusion they'd caused in her small world. Was it that simple to restore order, not only to her life but to so complex and important a geopolitical undertaking as Banana Quick? The ultimate solution, they said, lay on the coffee table—a white plastic revolver that weighed ounces and a spring-loaded device that cost a few dollars to make, devices whose only purpose was to snuff out life.

She could almost understand now why men killed on command. Women, too, in this case. What value has a single human life when wrapped in multiple layers of "greater good"? Besides, eliminating Eric Edwards wasn't her idea. It didn't represent what she was really all about, did it? "But wait, there's more," she told herself as she paced the room, stopping only to look out the window or to stare at the tools of the trade on the table. She was avenging the death of a good friend. Barrie had died at the hand of someone who viewed life and death from the same perspective as she was being called upon to accept. In the end, it didn't matter who the individual was who'd taken Barrie's life—a Soviet agent, a doctor named Tolker, very different characters like Mark Hotchkiss or Eric Edwards—whoever did it answered to a different god, one it was now necessary for her to invoke if she were to go through with this act.

As she continued trying to deal with the thoughts that had invaded her ever since Joe Breslin told her to kill Eric Edwards, she became fascinated with the process going on inside her, as though she were a bystander watching Collette Cahill come to terms with herself. What she'd been asked to do—what, in fact, she was actually setting out to do —represented so irrational an act that had it been suggested to her at any other point in her life, it would have immediately gotten lost in her laughter. That was no longer true. What had evolved, to the bystander's amusement and amazement, was a sense of right and reason responsive to the act of murder. More important, it could be done. *She* could do it. She hadn't thrown up her hands, raced from Breslin's car, hid in her apartment, or hopped the first flight out of Budapest. She'd accepted the mission and chosen her weapons carefully, no different from selecting a typewriter or pencil sharpener for an office job.

She was numb.

She was confused.

And she was not frightened, which was the most frightening thing of all for the bystander.

In the morning, a series of taps on her door. She'd forgotten; she'd ordered breakfast. She scrambled out of bed and said through the door, "Just a minute," then went to the living room and hastily took the tools from the coffee table and slid them into a desk drawer.

She opened the door and a hall porter carried in her tray. He was the same porter she'd talked to during her last visit to the hotel, the one who'd told her about the three men coming to collect Barrie Mayer's belongings. "Will you be on duty all day?" she asked him.

"Yes, madam."

"Good," she said. "I'd like to show you something a little later."

"Just ring, madam."

Josh Moeller arrived at a quarter of twelve carrying an envelope. After they'd embraced, he handed it to her, saying in slight surprise, "We had this in our own files. I don't know why, although there's been a push for the past year to beef up the general photo files. You'd think Great Britain had become the enemy the way we've been collecting on everybody."

Collette opened the envelope and looked into the black-and-white glossy face of Mark Hotchkiss. The photo was grainy, obviously a copy of another photograph.

Moeller said, "I think this came from a newspaper or literary magazine."

Cahill looked at him and said, "Any dossier on him?"

Moeller shrugged. "I don't think so, although I have to admit I didn't bother checking. You said you wanted a photograph."

"Yes, I know, Josh, that's all I needed. Thanks so much."

"Why are you interested in him?" he asked.

"A long story," she replied, "something personal."

"Got time for the lunch you promised me?"

"Yes, I do. I'd love it, but first I have to do one thing."

She left him in the suite and went downstairs to where the hall porter was sorting mail. "Excuse me," she said, "do you recognize this man?"

The porter adjusted half-glasses on his large nose and moved the photo in and out of focus. "Yes, madam, I believe I do, but I can't say why."

She said, "Do you remember those three men who came to collect the belongings of my friend, Miss Mayer, right after she died?"

"Yes, that's it. He was one of the gentlemen who came here that day."

"Is this a photograph of Mr. Hubler, David Hubler?"

"Exactly, madam. This is the gentleman who introduced himself as a business associate of your lady friend. He said his name was Hubler, although I can't quite recall what his first name was."

"It doesn't matter," Cahill said. "Thank you."

Cahill and Moeller had lunch in a pub on Sloane Square. They promised to keep in touch, and hugged before he climbed into a taxi. She watched him disappear around the corner, then walked briskly back to the hotel where she carefully packed, had the desk call a taxi, and went directly to Heathrow Airport for a first-class ride home.

29

CAHILL DEPLANED in New York and went to the nearest public telephone where she dialed Washington, D.C., information. "The number for the Watergate Hotel," she asked.

She placed the call and said to the hotel operator, "Has Mr. Eric Edwards changed suites yet?"

"Pardon?"

"I'm sorry. I'm here in Washington with the French contingent of Mr. Edwards's investors. When I tried to reach him before, I realized he'd changed suites. Is he still in 845?"

"Well, I . . . no, he's still in 1010 according to my records. I'll connect you."

"Oh, don't bother. I just didn't want to bring the French group to the wrong suite." She laughed. "You know how the French are."

"Well . . . thank you for calling."

Collette hung up and sighed. Hotel operators didn't give out room numbers, but there were ways. Dazzle 'em with confusion. She picked up the phone again, dialed the Watergate number, and asked whether there were any suites available.

"How long will you be staying?" she was asked.

"Three days, possibly more."

"Yes, we have two diplomat suites available at $410 a night."

"That will be fine," Cahill said. "Do you have one on a low floor? I have a phobia about high floors."

"The lowest we would have is on the eighth floor. Our diplomat suites are all higher up."

"The eighth floor? Yes, I suppose that will be all right." She gave her name, read off her American Express card number, and said she would be taking the shuttle to Washington that evening.

It took her longer to get from Kennedy Airport to La Guardia than it did for the flight to Washington's National Airport. The minute she stepped off the plane, she went to a telephone center, pulled out a Washington Yellow Pages, and scanned the listing for sporting goods stores. She found one in Maryland within a few blocks of the district line and took a cab to it, catching the owner as he was about to close. "I need some bullets," she told him sheepishly, the teenager buying condoms.

He smiled. "Ammo, you mean."

"Yes, ammunition, I guess. It's for my brother."

"What kind?"

"Ah, let's see, ah, right, nine millimeter, for a small revolver."

"Very small." He rummaged through a drawer behind the counter and came up with a box. "Anything else?"

"No, thank you." She'd expected questioning, a demand for an address, for identification. Nothing. Just a simple consumer purchase. She paid, thanked him, and returned to the street, a box of bullets in her purse.

She walked to the Watergate and checked in, her eyes scanning the lobby.

The moment she was in her suite, she unpacked, took a hot shower and, wearing a robe provided by the hotel, stepped out onto a wrap-around balcony that overlooked the Potomac River and the oversized, gleaming white Kennedy Center. It was a lovely sight, but she was too filled with energy to stand in any one place for more than a few seconds.

She went to a living room furnished with antique reproductions, found a scrap of paper in her purse, and dialed the number on it. The phone at Vern Wheatley's brother's apartment rang eight times before Wheatley answered. The minute he heard her voice, he snapped, "Where the hell have you been? I've been going crazy trying to find you."

"I was in Budapest."

"Why didn't you tell me you were leaving? You just take off and not even tell me?"

"Vern, I tried to call but there was no answer. It wasn't a leisurely trip I took. I had to leave immediately."

His voice indicated that he'd ignored her words. He said flatly, "I have to see you right away. Where are you?"

"I'm . . . why do you want to see me?"

He snorted. "Maybe the fact that we slept together is good enough. Maybe just because I want to see you again. Maybe because I have something damned important to discuss with you." She started to say something but he quickly added, "Something that might save both our lives."

"Why don't you just tell me on the phone?" she said. "If it's that important . . ."

"Look, Collette, there are things I haven't told you because . . . well, because it wasn't the right time. The right time is *now*. Where are you? I'll come right over."

"Vern, I have something I have to do before I can talk to you. Once it's done, I'll *need* to talk to someone. Please try to understand."

"Damn it, Collette, stop . . ."

"Vern, I said I have other things to do. I'll call you tomorrow."

"You won't catch me here," he said quickly.

"No?"

"I'm getting out right now. I was on my way when the phone rang. I almost didn't bother answering it."

"You sound panicked."

"Yeah, you might say that. I always get a little uptight when somebody's looking to slit my throat or blow up my car."

"What are you talking about?"

"What am I talking about? I'll tell you what I'm talking about. I'm talking about that freaky outfit you work for. I'm talking about a bunch of psychopaths who start out ripping wings off flies and shooting birds with BB guns before they graduate to people."

"Vern, I don't work for the CIA anymore."

"Yeah, right, Collette. That one of the courses down on the Farm? Lying 101? Goddamn it, I have to see you right now."

"Vern, I . . . all right."

"Where are you?"

"I'll meet you someplace."

"How about dinner?"

"I'm not hungry."

"Yeah, well I am. I'm in the mood for Greek. Like drama or tragedy. Meet me at the Taverna in an hour."

"Where is it?"

"Pennsylvania Avenue, Southeast. An hour?"

She almost backed out but decided to go through with the date. After all, she'd called him. Why? She couldn't answer. That weakness coming through, that need to talk with someone she knew and thought she could trust. Talk about *what*, that she was back in Washington to assassinate someone? No, there'd be no talk of that. He sounded desperate. It was *he* who needed to talk. Okay, she'd listen, that's all.

As she dressed, she went over in her mind what she'd been told about Vern by Joe Breslin. He'd come to Washington to do an exposé of one sort or another on the CIA, particularly its mind-control experimentation programs. If that was true—and she was sure it was, based upon their brief conversation a few minutes ago—he was to be as distrusted as the rest of them. Nothing was straightforward anymore. Living a life of simple truth must be reserved for monks, nuns, and naturalists, and it was too late to become any of those.

She rode the elevator to the tenth floor and walked past Suite 1010, her heart tripping in anticipation of running into Edwards. It didn't happen; she retraced her steps, got in the elevator, and went to the lobby. The Watergate was bustling. She stepped through the main entrance to where a long line of black limousines stood, their uniformed drivers waiting for their rich and powerful employers or customers to emerge. A cab from another line moved forward. Cahill got in and said, "The Taverna, on Pennsylvania Avenue, South. . . ."

The driver turned and laughed. "I know, I know," he said. "I am Greek."

She walked into what the cabbie had said was a "goud Grick" restaurant and was immediately aware of bouzouki music and loud laughter from the downstairs bar. She went down there in search of Wheatley. No luck. He hadn't specified where he would meet her but she assumed it would be the bar. She took the only vacant stool and ordered a white wine, turned and looked at the bouzouki player, a good-looking young man with black curly hair who smiled at her and played a sudden flourish on his instrument. She was reminded of Budapest. She returned his smile and surveyed others in the room. It was a loud, joyous crowd and she wished she were in the mood—wished she were in the position—to enjoy something festive. She wasn't. How could she be?

She sipped her wine and kept checking her watch; Wheatley was twenty minutes late. She was angry. She hadn't wanted to meet him in the first place but he'd prevailed. She looked at the check the bartender had placed in front of her, laid enough money on it to take care of it plus tip, got up and started for the stairs. Wheatley was on his way down. "Sorry I'm late," he said, shaking his head. "I couldn't help it."

"I was leaving," she said icily.

He took her arm and escorted her up the stairs to the dining room. Half the tables were vacant. "Come on," he said. "I'm starved."

"Vern, I really don't have time to . . ."

"Don't hassle me, Collette, just spend an hour while I get some food for my belly and feed you some food for your thoughts."

The manager showed them to a corner table that put them at considerable distance from other patrons. Collette took the chair that placed her back against the wall. Wheatley sat across from her.

After they'd ordered a bottle of white wine, Wheatley shook his head and grinned. "You could drive a guy crazy."

"I don't mean to do that, Vern. My life has been . . ." She smiled. "It's been chaotic lately, at best."

"Mine hasn't been exactly run-of-the-mill, either," he said. "Let's order."

"I told you I'm not hungry."

"Then nibble."

He looked at the menu, motioned for the waiter, and ordered moussaka, stuffed grape leaves, and an eggplant salad for two. After the waiter was gone, Wheatley leaned across the table and said, his eyes locked on hers, "I know who killed your friend Barrie Mayer, and I know why. I know who killed your friend David Hubler, and I know why he was killed, too. I know about the people you work for but, most of all, I know that you and I could end up like your dead friends if we don't do something."

"You're going too fast for me, Vern," she said, her excitement level rising. A large "What if?" struck her. What if Breslin and the rest of them were wrong? What if Eric Edwards was not, in fact, a double agent, had not killed Barrie Mayer? It was the first time since she left

Budapest that she acknowledged to herself how much she hoped it was the case. . . .

Wheatley said, "All right, I'll slow down for you. In fact, I'll do even better than that." He had a briefcase on the floor at the side of his chair. He pulled from it a bulging envelope and handed it to her.

"What's this?" she asked.

"That, my friend, is the bulk of an article I'm writing about the CIA. There's also the first ten chapters of my book in there."

She immediately thought of David Hubler and the call that brought him to Rosslyn and to his death. She didn't have to ask. Wheatley said, "I was the one who called Hubler and asked him to meet me in that alley."

His admission hit her hard. At the same time, it wasn't a surprise. She'd always questioned the coincidence of Wheatley having been there at the time. The look on her face prompted him to continue.

"I've been working through a contact in New York for months, Collette. He's a former spook—I hope that doesn't offend you, considering you're in the same business. . . ." When she didn't respond, he continued. "This contact of mine is a psychologist who used to do work for the CIA. He broke away a number of years ago and almost lost his life in the bargain. You don't just walk away from those people, do you?"

"I don't know," Cahill said. "I've never walked away," which was only half true. She'd left Budapest committed to never returning, not only to that city but to any job within Central Intelligence once her present assignment was completed.

"When someone tried to kill my contact, he did some fast thinking and came to the conclusion that his best protection was to offer up everything he knew for public consumption. Once he did that, why bother killing him? Eliminating him would only make sense if it were to avoid disclosure."

"Go on," she said.

"A mutual friend got us together and we started talking. That's what brought me to Washington."

"Finally, some simple honesty," Cahill said, not particularly proud of the smugness in her voice.

"Yeah, that must be refreshing for you, Collette, considering that you've been dishonest with me all along."

She was tempted to get into that discussion but resisted. Let him continue talking.

"My contact put me in touch with a woman who'd been an experimental subject in the Operation Bluebird and MK-ULTRA projects. They pulled out all the stops with her and, in the process, manipulated her mind to the extent that she doesn't know who she is anymore. Ever hear of a man named Estabrooks?"

"A psychologist who did a lot of work with hypnosis." She said it in a bored tone of voice.

"Yeah, right, but why should I be surprised? You probably know more about this than I ever imagined."

She shook her head. "I don't know much about those CIA projects from the past."

He guffawed. "From the *past*? Those projects are going on stronger than ever, Collette, and someone you know pretty well is one of the movers and shakers in them."

"Who would that be?"

"Your friend Dr. Jason Tolker."

"He's not a friend. I simply . . ."

"Simply slept with him? I don't know, maybe I've got my definition of friendship all screwed up. You slept with me. Am I your friend?"

"I don't know. You used me. The only reason you got together with me again was to get close to someone involved with the . . ."

"The CIA?"

"You were saying?"

"What you just said, about me making contact with you because you're with the CIA, is only partially true. You're acknowledging that you're with the CIA, right? The embassy job is a front."

"That doesn't matter, and I resent being put in the position of having to explain what I do with my life. You have no right."

He leaned toward her, and there was a harsh edge to his voice. "And the CIA has no right to go around screwing up innocent people, to say nothing of killing them, like your friend Barrie, and Hubler."

Collette leaned away from him and glanced about the restaurant. The sounds of the bar crowd downstairs mingled with the strains of the bouzouki music as it drifted up the stairs. Upstairs, where they sat, it was still relatively quiet and empty.

Wheatley sat back. His was a warm, genuine smile and his voice matched it. "Collette, I'll level with you one hundred percent. After that, you can decide whether you want to level with me. Fair enough?"

She knew it was.

"This woman I mentioned, the one who was a subject in the experimentation, is a prostitute. The CIA is big on hookers. They use them to entice men into apartments and hotel rooms that have been wired for sight and sound. They slip drugs in their drinks and the shrinks stand behind two-way mirrors and watch the action. It's a nasty game, but I suppose they rationalize it by saying that the other side does it, too, and that 'national defense' is involved. Whether those things are true or not I don't know, but I do know that a lot of innocent people get hurt."

Cahill started to add to the conversation but stopped herself. She simply cocked her head, raised her eyebrows, and said, "Go on."

Her posture obviously annoyed him. He quickly shook it off and continued. "I came down to Washington to see what I could find out about whether these experimental projects were still in operation. The day before Hubler was killed, I got a call from this lady, the prostitute, who told me that someone within the CIA was willing to talk to me. No, that isn't exactly accurate. This person was willing to *sell* information to me. I was told to meet him in that alley in Rosslyn. I figured the first thing I ought to do was to test the waters with a book publisher, see if I could raise the money I needed to pay the source. I knew the magazine wouldn't pay, and I sure as hell don't have the funds.

"I was trying to think of people back in New York to call when Dave Hubler came to my mind. You'd told me all about him, how Barrie Mayer put a lot of faith in him and had actually left the agency to him. I figured he was my best move, so I called him. He was very receptive. In fact, he told me that if the kind of information I was talking about was valid, he could probably get me a six-figure advance. The problem was he wanted to hear with his own ears what this source was selling. I invited him to meet with me. I knew the minute I hung up that it was a mistake. Having two of us show up would probably scare the guy off, but I figured I'd go through with it anyway. Want to know what happened?"

"Of course."

"I ran late, but Hubler got there on time. Obviously, there was nobody selling information. It was a setup, and if I'd arrived when I was supposed to and alone, I would have had the ice pick in my chest."

His story had potency to it, no doubt about that. If what he'd said were true, it meant . . . "You've got problems," she told him.

"That's right," he said. "I'm being followed everywhere I go. The other night I was driving through Rock Creek Park and a guy ran me off the road. At least he tried to. He botched it and took off. I think they've thrown a tap on my brother's phone, and my editor back in New York told me he'd received a call from a personnel agency checking my references for a job I was applying for with another magazine. I didn't apply for a job with another magazine. There's no legitimate personnel agency checking on me. These guys will stop at nothing."

"What do you plan to do?" she asked.

"First of all, keep moving. Second, I'm going to adopt the philosophy of my shrink friend back in New York, get everything I know on paper, and make sure it's in the proper hands as fast as possible. No sense killing somebody once they've spilled what they know."

Cahill looked down at the heavy envelope. "Why are you giving me this?"

"Because I want it in someone else's hands in case anything happens to me."

"But why *me*, Vern? You seem filled with distrust where I'm concerned. I'd think I'd be the last person you'd give this to."

He grinned, reached across the table, and held her hand. "Remember what I wrote in the yearbook, Collette?"

She said softly, "Yes, of course I do. I'm the girl in this world who would never sell out."

"I still feel that way, Collette. You know something else I feel?"

She looked in his eyes. "What?"

"I'm in love with you."

"Don't say that, Vern." She shook her head. "You don't know me."

"I think I do, which is why I'm throwing in with you. I want you to hold on to this, Collette," he said, tapping the envelope. "I want you to read it and look for any gaps."

She shoved the envelope back across the table at him. "No, I don't want that responsibility. I can't help you."

His face, which had settled into a slack and serene expression, now hardened. His voice matched it. "I thought you took some oaths when you became a lawyer, silly things like justice and fairness and righting wrongs. I thought you cared about innocent people being hurt. At least, that was the line you used to give. What was it, Collette, high school rhetoric that goes down the drain the minute you hit the real world?"

She was stung by his words, assaulted by hurt and anger. Had she succumbed to the hurt, she would have cried. Instead, her anger overrode the other feeling. "Don't preach to me, Vern Wheatley, about ideals. All I'm hearing from you is journalist's rhetoric. You're sitting here lecturing me about right and wrong, about why everybody should jump on your bandwagon and sell out our own government. Maybe there is justification for what an organization like the CIA does. Maybe there are abuses. Maybe the other side does it, only worse. Maybe national defense *is* involved, and not just a slogan. Maybe there are things going on in this world that you or I have no idea about, can't even begin to conceive of the importance of them to other people— people who don't have the advantages we have in a free society."

The eggplant salad had gone untouched. Now the waiter brought the stuffed leaves and moussaka. The moment he left, Collette said to Vern, "I'm leaving."

Wheatley grabbed her hand. "Please don't do that, Collette," he said with sincerity. "Okay, we've each made our speech. Now let's talk like two adults and figure out the right thing to do for both of us."

"I already have," she said, pulling her hand away.

"Look, Collette, I'm sorry if I shot off my mouth. I didn't mean to, but sometimes I do that. The nature of the beast, I guess. If spies are out in the cold, journalists need friends, too." He laughed. "I figure I have one friend in this world. You."

She slumped back in her chair, stared at the envelope, and suffered the same sensation she'd been feeling so often lately, that she had become increasingly dishonest. She was perfectly capable of taking a stand at the table, yet, more than anything, she wanted that envelope and its contents. She was desperate to read it. Maybe it contained factual answers to events that had shrouded her in confusion.

She deliberately softened as she said, "Vern, maybe you're right. I'm sorry, too. I just . . . I don't want, alone, the responsibility for that envelope."

"Fine," he said. "We'll share the responsibility. Stay with me to-night."

"Where?"

"I've taken a room in a small hotel over in Foggy Bottom, around the corner from Watergate. The Allen Lee. Know it?"

"Yes, friends who used to visit me at college stayed there."

"I figured it was low class enough that they wouldn't look for me there, although that's probably naive. I used a phony name when I checked in. Joe Black. How's that for a pseudonym?"

"Not very original," she said, realizing that she shouldn't have checked into the Watergate under her own name. Too late to worry about that now. "Vern, I think it's better if I left now and we both did some thinking on our own." He started to protest but she grabbed his hand and said earnestly, "Please. I need time alone to digest what you've said. I can use it to read your article and book. Okay? We'll catch up tomorrow. I promise."

Dejection was written all over his face but he didn't argue.

He slid the envelope back toward her. She looked at it, picked it up, and cradled it in her arms. "I'll call you at the Allen Lee, say around four tomorrow afternoon?"

"I guess that's the way it will be. I can't call you. I don't know where you're staying."

"And that's the way it will have to be until tomorrow."

He forced himself to lighten up, saying pleasantly, "Sure you don't want some food? It's good."

"So my cab driver said. He told me this was 'goud Grick.' " She smiled. "I'm not a fan of Greek food, but thanks anyway." When his expression sagged again, she leaned over and kissed him on the cheek, said into his ear, "Please, Vern. I've got a lot of thinking to do and I'll do it best alone." She straightened up, knew there was nothing more to say, and quickly left the restaurant.

A taxi was dropping off a couple. Cahill got in.

"Yeah?"

"I'd like to go to . . ." She'd almost told him to take her to Dr. Jason Tolker's office in Foggy Bottom.

How silly. Like giving the name of an obscure restaurant and expecting the driver to know it.

She spelled out Tolker's address.

30

LIGHTS WERE ON in Tolker's building. Good, she thought, as she paid the driver. She hadn't wanted to call ahead. If he weren't there, she'd go to his house. She'd find him someplace.

She rang the bell. His voice came through the intercom. "Who is it?"

"Collette. Collette Cahill."

"Oh. Yes. I'm tied up right now. Can you come back?" She didn't answer. "Is it an emergency?" She smiled, knew he was asking it for the benefit of whoever was with him. She pressed the "Talk" button: "Yes, it is an emergency, Doctor."

"I see. Well, please come in and wait in my reception area, Miss Cahill. It will be a few minutes before I can see you."

"That will be fine, Doctor. Thank you."

The buzzer sounded. She turned the knob and pushed the door partially open. Before entering, she patted her raincoat pocket. The now familiar shape of the small revolver resisted her fingers' pressure. A deep breath pumped any lost resolve back into her.

She stepped into the reception area and looked around. Two table lamps provided minimal, soft lighting. A light under his office door, and muffled voices, indicated at least two people in there. She stepped close and listened. She heard his voice, and then a woman. Their words were only occasionally audible: ". . . Can't help that . . . Hate you . . . Calm down or . . ."

Collette chose a chair that allowed her to face the office door. She'd started to pull the revolver from her raincoat pocket when the office door suddenly opened. She released the weapon and it slid back to its resting place. A beautiful and surprisingly tall young Oriental girl, dressed in tight jeans, heels, and wearing a mink jacket, came into the reception area, followed by Tolker. The woman strained to see Collette's face in the room's dimness. "Good night," Tolker said. The girl looked at him; there was hatred on her face. She crossed the room, cast a final, disapproving look at Collette, and left. Moments later the front door closed heavily.

"Hello," Tolker said to Collette.

"Hello. A patient?"

"Yes. You thought otherwise?"

"I thought nothing. It's nice of you to see me on such short notice."

"I try to accommodate. What's the emergency?"

"Severe panic attack, free-floating anxiety, paranoia, an obsessive-compulsive need for answers."

"Answers to what?"

"Oh, to . . . to why a friend of mine is dead."

"I can't help you with that."

"I disagree."

He conspicuously looked at his watch.

"This won't take long."

"I can assure you of that. Ask your questions."

"Let's go inside."

"This is . . ." He stopped when he saw her hand come out of her raincoat holding the revolver. "What's that for?"

"A persuasive tool. I have a feeling you might need persuasion."

"Put it away, Collette. James Bond never impressed me."

"I think I can . . . *impress* you."

He blew through his lips and sighed resignedly. "All right, come in, *without* the gun."

She followed him into his office, the revolver still in her hand. When he turned and saw it, he said sharply, "Put the goddamn thing away."

"Sit down, Dr. Tolker."

He made a move toward her. She raised the weapon and pointed it at his chest. "I said sit down."

"You've gone off the deep end, haven't you? You're crazy."

"That's professional."

"Look, I . . ." She nodded toward his leather chair. He sat on it. She took the matching chair, crossed her legs, and observed him. He certainly hadn't overreacted, but she could discern discomfort, which pleased her.

"Go ahead," she said. "Start from the beginning, and don't leave anything out. Tell me all about Barrie, about how she came to you as a patient, how you hypnotized her, controlled her, got her involved in the CIA and then . . . I'll say it . . . and then killed her."

"You're crazy."

"There's that professional diagnosis again. Start!" She raised the revolver for emphasis.

"You know everything, because I told you everything. Barrie was a patient. I treated her. We had an affair. I suggested she do some courier work for the CIA. She gladly and, I might add, enthusiastically agreed. She carried materials to Budapest, things she got from me, things I didn't know. I mean, I would hand her a briefcase, a *locked* briefcase, and off she'd go. Someone killed her. I don't know who. It wasn't me. Believe that."

"Why should I?"

"Because . . ."

"When Barrie made her last trip to Hungary, whatever it was she carried wasn't in a briefcase. It was in her mind, because you implanted it there."

"Wait a minute, that's . . ."

"That's the truth, Dr. Tolker. I'm not the only one who knows it. It's common knowledge. At least it is now."

"What of it? The program calls for it."

"What was the message?"

"I can't tell you that."

"I think you'd better."

He stood. "And I think you'd better get out of here."

Collette held up the envelope she'd been given by Vern. "Know what's in this?"

He tried for levity. "Your memoirs of a clandestine life."

She didn't respond in kind. "A friend of mine has been researching the projects you're involved with. He's done quite a job. Want an example?"

"You're talking about Vern Wheatley?"

"Right."

"He's in deep water."

"He's a strong swimmer."

"Not with these tides. Go ahead. I know all about him, and about you. Bad form, Collette, for an intelligence agent to sleep with a writer."

"I'll let that pass. Vern knows, and so do I, that you programmed Barrie to claim that Eric Edwards, from the BVI, was a double agent. Correct?"

To her surprise, he didn't deny it. Instead, he said, "That happens to be the truth."

"No, it's not. You're the double agent, Doctor."

The accusation, and the weight of the envelope despite neither of them knowing what was in it, stopped the conversation. Tolker broke the silence by asking pleasantly, "Drink, Collette?"

She couldn't help but smile. "No."

"Coke? The white kind?"

"You're disgusting."

"Just trying to be sociable. Barrie always enjoyed my sociability."

"Spare me that again."

"Like to spend some intimate moments with our deceased friend?"

"What?"

"I have her on tape. I'm reluctant to expose myself to you because, naturally, I'm on the tape too. But I will."

"No thanks." Collette didn't mean it. Her voice betrayed her true feelings.

He did exactly the right thing. He said nothing, simply sat back down, crossed his legs, folded his hands in his lap, and smirked.

"What kind of tape? While she was hypnotized?"

"No, nothing concerning therapy. That would be highly unprofessional of me. The tape I'm talking about is more *personal*."

"When she was . . . with you?"

"When she was very much with me, right here in this office, after hours."

"You recorded it?"

"Yes. I'm recording us, too."

Cahill's head snapped left and right as she took in the room in search of a camera.

"Up there," Tolker said casually, pointing to a painting at the far end of the room.

"Did Barrie know?"

"Shall we see it?"

"No, I . . ."

He went to bookshelves where hundreds of videotapes were neatly lined up and labeled. He pulled one from the collection, knelt before a VCR hooked up to a 30-inch NEC monitor, inserted the tape, pushed buttons, and the screen came alive.

Collette turned her head and watched the screen from an angle, like a child wanting to avoid a gruesome scene in a horror movie, yet afraid to miss it. Tolker resumed his seat and said smugly, "You came here demanding answers. Watch closely, Collette. There's lots of answers on the screen."

Cahill looked away, her eyes going to where Tolker indicated there was a camera recording them. Out of the corner of her eye, a naked form appeared on the TV monitor. She focused on the screen. It was Barrie, walking around Tolker's office, a glass in her hand. She went to where he sat fully dressed in his chair. "Come on, I'm ready." Her words were slurred; her laugh was that of a drunken woman. When he didn't respond, she sat on his lap and kissed him. His hands ran over her body . . .

"You slime," Collette said.

"Don't judge me," Tolker said. "She's there, too. Keep watching. There's more."

A new scene appeared on the screen. Barrie was seated cross-legged on the carpet, still nude. A man's naked form—presumably Tolker—was in shadows. He obviously knew where to position himself so that he was out of the camera's direct focus, and out of the lighting.

Barrie held a clear plate on which cocaine was heaped. She put a straw to her nose, leaned forward, placed the other end in the powder, and inhaled.

Cahill stood. "Turn that damn thing off," she said.

"It's not over. It gets even better."

She went to the VCR and pushed the "Stop" button. The screen went blank. She was aware that he'd come up behind her. She quickly fell to her knees, spun around, and pointed the revolver up at his face.

"Easy, easy," he said. "I'm not out to hurt you."

"Get away. Back up."

He did as she requested. She stood, was without words.

"See?" he said. "Your friend was not the saint you thought she was."

"I never considered her a saint," Collette said. "Besides, this has nothing to do with how she died."

"Oh, yes, it does," Tolker said. He sat in his chair and tasted his drink. "You're right, Collette, this is kid's stuff. Ready for the adult version?"

"What are you talking about?"

"Barrie was a traitor. She sold out to Eric Edwards, and to the Soviets." He sighed and drank. "Oh, God, she was so innocent in that situation. She didn't know a Soviet from a Buddhist monk. A great literary agent, a lousy intelligence agent. I should have known better than to get her involved. But that's water over the dam."

"She wasn't a traitor," Collette said, again without conviction. The truth was that she knew little about her close friend. The video she'd seen—so unlike the image she had of Barrie—caused anger to swell in her. "How dare you record someone in their . . ."

Tolker laughed. "In their *what*, most intimate moments? Forget the tape, think about what I just told you. She was going to turn Edwards in, and that's what got her killed. I tried to stop her but . . ."

"No you didn't. You were the one who poisoned her against Eric."

"Wrong. You're wrong a lot, Collette. Sure, she told me that Edwards was working both sides of the street, and I encouraged her to blow the whistle on him. Want to know why?" Cahill didn't answer. "Because it was the only way she had a chance to get herself off the hook. They knew about her."

"Who?"

"The British. Why do you think that buffoon, Hotchkiss, came into the picture?"

Cahill was surprised. "What do you know about him? Why . . . ?"

"You came here for answers," Tolker said, standing. "I'll give them to you, *if* you give me the gun, sit down, and shut up!" He extended his hand; his expression said he'd lost patience.

For a moment, Collette considered handing the revolver to him. She started to, but when he went to grab it from her hand, she yanked it away. Now his expression indicated he'd progressed beyond impatience. He was angry. He would do whatever he had to do. He would hurt her.

Collette glared at him; there was an overwhelming desire to use the small plastic revolver—to kill him. It had nothing to do with having determined his responsibility for Barrie's death, nor was it bound up in some rational thought process involving her job or mission. Rather, it represented what had become an obsession to take action, to push a button, place a phone call, pull a trigger to put an end to the turmoil in her life.

Then again, it occurred to her, there *was* a certain order to what was being played out, a Ramistic logic that said, "Enjoy the pragmatic role you're in, Collette. You're a CIA agent. You have the authority to kill, to right wrongs. Nothing will happen to you. You're expected to act with authority because it is your country that is at stake. You're a member of law enforcement. The gun has been given to you to use, to enforce a political philosophy of freedom and opportunity in order to keep evil forces from destroying a precious way of life."

The thoughts cleared her mind and calmed her down. "You underestimate me," she said.

"Get out."

"When I'm ready. Hotchkiss. What role did he play?"

"He . . ."

"Why are you knowledgeable about him?"

"I have nothing more to say to you."

"You said the British knew about Barrie being a . . . traitor. That's why Hotchkiss is here?"

"Yes."

"You convinced Barrie to become his partner?"

"It was best for her. It was the understanding."

"Understanding?"

"The deal. It saved her. Our people agreed with it."

"Because they believed you, that she and Eric Edwards were traitors."

"No, Collette, because they *knew* they were. They gave Barrie's mother money not to pursue any interest in the agency. Barrie's will left operating control to Hubler, but her mother was to receive Barrie's share of profits. The old bitch was happy for cash."

"How much?"

"It doesn't matter. Any amount was too much. She created the person Barrie became, a muddled, psychotic, pathetic human being who spent her adult life hiding from reality. It's not unusual. People with Barrie's high capacity for hypnotic trance usually come out of abused childhoods."

A smirk crossed Collette's face. "Do you know what I want to do, Dr. Tolker?"

"Tell me."

"I either want to spit on you, or kill you."

"Why?"

"You never tried to help Barrie get over her abused childhood, did you? All you were interested in was exploiting it, and her. You're despicable."

"You're irrational. Maybe it's a female thing. The agency ought to reconsider hiring women. You make a good case against the policy."

Collette didn't respond. She wanted to lash out. At the same time, she couldn't mount an argument against what he'd said. Somehow, defending equality between the sexes didn't seem important.

His voice and face had been cold and matter-of-fact up until now. He softened, smiled. "Tell you what," he said. "Let's start over, right now, this night. No silly guns, no nasty remarks. Let's have a drink, dinner. Good wine and soothing music will take care of all our differences. We are on the same side, you know. I believe in you and what you stand for. I like you, Collette. You're a beautiful, bright, talented, and decent woman. Please, forget why you came in here tonight. I'm sure you have other questions that I can answer, but not in this atmosphere of rancor and distrust. Let's be friends and discuss these matters as friends, the way you used to discuss things with Barrie." His smile broadened. "You *are* incredibly beautiful, especially when that anger forces its way to the surface and gives your face a . . ."

He went for her. She'd shifted the revolver to her left hand minutes before. As he lunged, she dropped Vern's envelope, stiffened her right hand, and brought the edge of it against the side of his neck. The blow sent him sprawling to the carpet. A string of four-letter words exploded from him as he scrambled to his feet. They stood facing each other, their breathing rapid, their eyes wide in anger and fear.

Collette slowly backed toward the door, the revolver held securely in two hands, its tiny barrel pointed directly at his chest.

"Come here," he said.

She said nothing, kept retreating, her attention on controlling the damnable shaking of her hands.

"You've got it all screwed up," he said. She sensed the tension in his body as he prepared to attack again, a spring being compressed to give it maximum velocity and distance when released. The restraint on the spring was disengaged. It uncoiled in her direction. Her two fingers on the trigger contracted in concert; there was an almost silly "pop" from the revolver—a Champagne cork, a dry twig being snapped, Rice Krispies.

She stepped back and he fell at her feet, arms outstretched. She picked up the envelope, ran through the door and to the street where, once she realized the revolver was still in her hands, she shoved it into her raincoat and walked deliberately toward the nearest busy intersection.

The message light on her telephone was on when she returned to her suite at the Watergate. She called the message center. "Oh, yes, Miss Cahill, a gentleman called. He said"—the operator laughed. "It's a strange message. The gentleman said, 'Necessary that we discuss Winston Churchill as quickly as possible.' "

"He didn't leave a name?"

"No. He said you'd know who he was."

"Thank you."

Collette went to the balcony and looked out over the shimmering lights of Foggy Bottom. What had Joe Breslin told her? She could make contact with someone at the Churchill statue any evening for the next two weeks at six o'clock, and that the contact would remain there for no more than ten minutes.

She returned to the living room, drew the drapes, got into a robe, and sat in a wing chair illuminated by a single floor lamp. On her lap was Vern Wheatley's envelope. She pulled the pages from it, sighed, and began reading. It wasn't until the first shaft of sunlight came through a gap in the drapes that she put it down, hung the DO NOT DISTURB sign on the door, and went, soberly, to bed.

31

SLEEP. It was what she'd needed most. The small travel alarm clock on the nightstand next to her bed read 3:45. She'd slept almost ten hours, and it had been easy. The events earlier in the evening seemed not to have happened or, at least, had happened to someone else.

It was four-thirty when she got out of the shower. As she stood in front of the bathroom mirror drying her hair, she remembered she was supposed to call Vern. She found the number for the Allen Lee Hotel and dialed it, asked for Mr. Black's room. "Sorry to be late calling," she said. "I slept all day."

"It's okay. Did you read what I gave you?"

"Read it? Yes, two or three times. I was up all night."

"And?"

"You make some remarkable accusations, Vern."

"Are they wrong?" he asked.

"No."

"Okay, talk to me. How did you react to . . . ?"

"Why don't we discuss it in person?"

He whooped. "This is called progress. You mean you're actually going to initiate a date with me?"

"I wasn't suggesting a date, just some time to discuss what you've written."

"Name it. I'm yours."

"I have to meet someone at six. How about getting together at seven?"

"Who are you meeting?" he asked. It irked her but she said nothing. He said, "Oh, that's right, Miss Cahill operates incognito. Known in high school as the girl most likely to succeed dressed in a cloak and dagger."

"Vern, I'm in no mood for your attempts at sarcasm."

"Yeah, well, I'm not in any mood for jokes, either. You ever hear of Operation Octopus?"

She had to think. Then she started to mention Hank Fox, cut off her words, and said, "No."

"It's a division of the CIA that keeps computer tabs on writers, at least the ones who don't carry briefs for the goddamn agency. I'm at the top of the list." When she didn't respond, he added, "And they take care of writers like me, Collette. Take care." He guffawed. "They goddamn kill us, that's what they do."

"Where shall we meet at seven?" she asked.

"How about picking me up here at the hotel?"

"No, let's meet at the bar in the Watergate."

"You buying? Drinks there cost the national debt."

"If I have to. See you here . . . there at seven."

She found a vacant cab and told the driver to take her to the British Embassy on Massachusetts Avenue. As they approached it, she kept an eye out for a statue. There it was, less than a hundred yards from the main entrance, set into clumps of bushes just off the sidewalk. The driver made a U-turn and let her off in front of the embassy gate. It had started to rain, and the air had taken on a distinct chill. She brought the collar of her raincoat up around her neck and slowly walked toward the statue of Winnie. It was imposing and lifelike, but the years had turned Churchill green, blending into the foliage. He would not have liked that.

Traffic was heavy on Massachusetts Ave. It was raining harder, too, which slowed the traffic. There were few pedestrians, those scurrying past her coming from jobs at the British Embassy. She checked her watch; exactly six. She looked up and down the street in search of someone who might be interested in her but saw no one. Then, across the broad avenue, a man emerged from Normanstone Park. It was too dark and he was too far away for her to see his face. His trench-coat collar was up, his hands deep in his pockets. It took him some time to cross the street because of the traffic but, eventually, there was a break and he took advantage of it with long, loping strides. Good.

She sensed someone approaching from her right, turned, and saw another man coming down the sidewalk. He wore a hat, and had hunched his shoulders and lowered his head against the rain. She'd forgotten the rain and realized her hair and shoes were soaked. She quickly looked to her left again. The man from the park was gone. Another look to the right. The man in the hat was almost abreast of her. She poised, waiting for him to look up and say something. Instead, he walked by, his head still lowered, his eyes on the sidewalk.

She took a deep breath and wiped water from her nose and eyes.

"Miss Cahill." It came from her left. She knew immediately who it was from the accent. British. She turned and looked into the long, smiling face of Mark Hotchkiss.

"What are you doing here?" she said quickly. The question represented the only thought on her mind at the moment. What *was* he doing there?

"You arrived precisely on time," he said pleasantly. "Sorry I'm a few minutes late. Traffic and all that, you know."

As difficult as it was to accept, she had no choice. The contact who was to meet her here at the Winston Churchill statue. "I suggest we get out of this bloody rain and go somewhere where we can talk."

"You left the message at my hotel?"

"Yes, who else? Let's go to my office. I have some things to say to you."

"Your office? Barrie's, you mean?"

"As you wish. It's one and the same. Please, I'm getting damn well drenched standing here. Not much of a Londoner, forgetting my umbrella this way. Too long in the States, I suppose."

He took her arm and led her back toward the entrance of the British Embassy. They passed it and turned left on Observatory Lane, the U.S. Naval Observatory on their right, and walked a hundred yards until reaching a champagne-colored Jaguar. Tolker's Jaguar. Hotchkiss unlocked the passenger door and opened it for her. She became rigid and stared at him.

"Come on, now, let's go." His voice was not quite as pleasant as earlier.

She started to bend to get in, stopped and straightened, took a few steps back, and fixed him in a hard look. "Who *are* you?"

His face testified to his exasperation. "I don't have time to answer your silly questions," he said harshly. "Get in the car."

She backed farther away, her right hand up in a gesture of self-defense. "Why are you here? You have nothing to do with . . ." He'd been standing with his hands outstretched as he attempted to convince her. Now his right hand slipped into his raincoat pocket.

"No," she said. She spun around and ran back toward Massachusetts Avenue. She stumbled; one shoe fell off but she kept going, an increasing wind whipping her face with water. She looked over her shoulder without breaking stride, kicked off her second shoe, and saw that he had started after her but had stopped. He shouted, "Come back here!"

She kept going, reached the avenue and ran, retracing her route toward the statue of Winston Churchill, passing other embasssies and racing through puddles that soaked her feet. She kept going until she was out of breath, stopped, and looked back. Hotchkiss's Jaguar came up to the corner and waited for a break in traffic to make a right. A vacant taxi approached her. She leaped into the gutter and frantically waved it down. The driver jammed on his brakes, causing others behind him to do the same. Horns blew and muffled curses filled the air. She got in the back, slammed the door, and said, "The Watergate, please, the hotel, and if a light Jag is behind us, please do everything you can to lose him."

"Hey, lady, what's the matter? What's going on?" the young driver asked.

"Just *go*—please."

"Whatever you say," he said, slapping the gearshift and hitting the accelerator, causing his wheels to spin on the wet pavement.

Cahill looked through the rear window. Vision was obscured but she could see a dozen car-lengths behind. The Jaguar wasn't to be seen.

She turned around and said to the driver, "Get off this street, go through the park."

He followed her order and soon drove up to the main entrance to the Watergate Hotel.

Cahill was drained. Once she was certain that Hotchkiss wasn't behind them, her energy had abandoned her and she slumped in the back seat, her breath still coming heavily.

"Lady, you all right?" the driver asked over the seat.

She'd closed her eyes. She opened them and managed a small smile. "Yes, thank you very much. I know it all seems strange but . . ." There was no need to explain any further. She handed him a twenty-dollar bill and told him to keep the change. He thanked her. She got out and suddenly realized the condition she was in. Her shoeless feet were bleeding from cuts on the soles. The bottoms of her stockings were in shreds.

"Evening," the doorman said from beneath the protection of a canopy.

Cahill mustered all the dignity she could and said, "Messy night," proudly walked past him and into the lobby, aware that he'd turned and was taking in her every step.

The lobby was busy as usual which, Cahill reasoned, was to her advantage. People were too engaged in coming and going and in conversations to care about a shoeless, wet woman.

She went to the elevator bank serving her floor and pushed the "Up" button. Because she was in a hurry, it was a series of eternities as she watched the lights above the elevator door indicate a slow descent from the top of the hotel. "*Damn*," she muttered as she glanced left and right to see whether there was any interest in her. There wasn't. She looked up again; the elevator had stopped at the tenth floor. She thought of Eric Edwards and Suite 1010. Had it stopped to pick him up? Coincidence but . . .

She moved away from the door so that she was not in the line of anyone's vision coming through it. She could still see the lighted numbers. The elevator had stopped at Five, had skipped Four and stopped at Three. A large party of conventioners who'd flooded the center of the lobby ever since Cahill entered moved out en masse, affording her a clear view of a cluster of small tables and stuffed chairs at which well-dressed people enjoyed pre-dinner cocktails. The sight didn't seem real at first, but it took her only a second to realize that it was. He was sitting at a table by himself, a glass in his hand, legs casually crossed, his attention directed at a woman seated at an adjacent table. Cahill quickly turned her head so that only her back was visible to him.

The sudden opening of the elevator door startled her. A dozen people filed out. Collette faced the wall and took each of them in with her peripheral vision. No Eric Edwards.

The moment the elevator was empty, she sidestepped into it, her back still to the cocktail area. She pushed Eight, then the "Close Door" button. She kept punching it, silently cursing the fact that it had no effect on what the elevator did. Like "Walk" buttons at intersections, she thought. Placebos.

A man in a tuxedo and a woman in a gown and furs joined her in the elevator. She ignored their glances at her feet and kept her eyes trained on the control buttons. The doors started to close; a man suddenly reached in and caused them to open again. He stepped in, followed by two teenage girls. One of them looked down at Cahill's shoeless dishabille, nudged her friend, and they both giggled.

The doors finally closed and the elevator made its ascent. The teenagers got off first, glancing back, then the man who'd stopped the doors with his arm. At the eighth floor, Cahill hobbled out. The man in the tux and the woman in furs whispered something unintelligible to each other. Oh, to be respectable.

She went to her door and opened it. A maid had been in and turned down the bed, leaving two small pieces of foil-wrapped chocolate on the pillow. Cahill locked the door from inside and attached the chain. She quickly got out of her raincoat, which was soaked through, and dropped it on the floor. The rest of her clothes followed. A tiny smear of blood on the carpet from her foot was dissolved by the wet clothing. She turned on the shower and, when it was as hot as she could stand it, stepped in. Ten minutes later she emerged, dried herself, found a Band-Aid in her purse and applied it to the small cut on her foot.

She hadn't noticed upon entering her room that her message light was on. She picked up the phone and identified herself. "Yes, Miss Cahill, you have a message from a Dr. Tolker. He said he was anxious to speak with you and would be in the hotel this evening. You can have him paged."

"No, I . . . Yes, thank you very much, I'll do that later, not now."

The message from Tolker was no surprise. Seeing him sitting in the lobby with a glass of wine had been. She'd assumed she'd killed him. Unless his CIA-funded research had resulted in perfect clone development, he was very much alive. She was glad for that. And frightened.

She picked up the phone again, dialed the number for the Allen Lee Hotel, and asked for Mr. Black's room. There was no answer. Then the operator asked, "Do you happen to be Miss Collette Cahill?"

"Yes, I am."

"Mr. Black had to run out but he left a message in case you called. He said he would return at ten. He said he had some urgent business that came up at the last minute."

Collette's sigh of frustration was, she was certain, audible to the operator even without the benefit of a telephone. She closed her eyes and said dejectedly, "Thank you."

Naked while on the phone, she suddenly felt cold and vulnerable. She pulled out a pair of jeans from the suitcase that she hadn't bothered to unpack, and a furry pink sweater. She got into them and slipped her feet into white sneakers.

She turned on all the lights, looked at the suitcase on the floor, hesitated, then went to it and unlocked an inside compartment. She reached in and came out with the ampules of prussic acid and nitro, and the cigar-shaped detonator. She sat in a chair beneath a lamp and assembled it, then reloaded the small white plastic revolver. She slipped everything into her purse and sat quietly, her fingers playing with the purse's shoulder strap, her ears cocked for sound, her eyes skating over every inch of the large room.

It was intensely quiet, which unnerved her. She was getting up to turn on the television set when the phone rang. The sound of it froze her in the middle of the room. Should she answer? No. Obviously, Tolker and Mark Hotchkiss knew that she was staying at the Watergate, and she didn't want to speak to either of them. Vern didn't know where she was. "How stupid," she chided herself. Why had she played it so secret with him? He loomed large as the only human being in Washington that she could trust. That was ironic, she realized, considering how deceitful he'd been up until their dinner last night.

What suddenly imbued him with trustworthiness was that of everyone in her recent life, only Vern was outside the Company. In fact, he was outside trying to break in, dedicated to exposing and harming it. So much of what he'd written was accurate, at least to the best of her knowledge. Although he hadn't stated it in so many words, the pattern that emerged from his pages gave considerable weight to the idea that it was Jason Tolker who was responsible for Barrie Mayer's and David Hubler's deaths. It all seemed so clear to her now, as though a brilliant light illuminated the truth as she stood in the center of the room.

Árpád Hegedüs *had* lied in that small bar in Budapest. What he'd told her earlier in their relationship was the truth, and what she'd suggested to Joe Breslin made sense. Hegedüs had come over as a defector in order to spread disinformation to the Americans. Tolker had been selling information to the Soviets about the results of mind-control experimentation in the United States. More than that, according to Wheatley's manuscript, he'd used various hypnotized subjects to transmit that information.

Wheatley hadn't mentioned Eric Edwards in his pages. Chances were he didn't even know about him. But Cahill quickly created a scenario in which Tolker, viewing Edwards as a threat because of his close relationship with the too-chatty Barrie, had convinced those involved in Banana Quick that Edwards was a double agent selling information to the other side. What other explanation could there be for his having been accused of double-dealing? Again, there was no tangible evidence to support her thesis, but the cumulative weight of everything that had happened, of every scrap of input she'd taken in, supported her notion.

She knew that she might be justifying her initial instincts about Tolker, but that didn't matter now. The picture she'd painted was good enough. The paramount thing in her mind at this point was to avoid Tolker and Hotchkiss, find Vern and, together, make contact with someone within the CIA who could be trusted. Who could that be? she wondered. The only name she could come up with was Eric, but that posed a risk. He was surrounded by controversy. Still, he represented for Cahill the one person besides Wheatley who seemed to deal with things in a straightforward manner. Hank Fox also came to mind but she dismissed the thought. He was too much one of *them*, despite his fatherly approach.

The phone stopped ringing. Collette returned to the chair, opened her purse, and ran her fingers over the revolver's smooth, plastic finish. Mark Hotchkiss! The confrontation with him had shaken her. What was he, MI-6? A contract agent. There were lots of them in the global system. Hotchkiss's obvious close working relationship with Tolker both puzzled and dismayed her. It made sense, in a way, she reasoned. Tolker wouldn't have physically killed Barrie and Dave Hubler. Too messy, not his style, or role. But Hotchkiss might have been the actual killer, working under Tolker's direction. Yes, that played for her.

She squeezed her eyes shut and shook her head. Why was she bothering trying to make sense out of a system that depended, to a great extent, upon being nonsensical? Too many things in the gray world of intelligence were inscrutable, begging answers, defying the common man's logic. Friends. Enemies. You needed a scorecard to tell the players on opposing teams. Hotchkiss had been in place geographically to kill both Barrie and David. Of course, it was possible that he had no connection with Tolker at all. If he'd killed Mayer and Hubler, he might have been acting strictly on behalf of British intelligence. They'd preached during her training days that there were no allies in the spy business, no forbidden, hands-off nations. The Israelis had proved that recently, and it was well known that the British had dozens of agents in place within the United States.

The phone rang again. Cahill ignored it for a second time. Then another sound intruded upon her thoughts.

Someone was knocking at her door.

32

SHE WENT SLOWLY, quietly to the door and placed her ear against it. A male voice said, "Collette?" She couldn't place it. It wasn't Hotchkiss; no trace of a British accent. "Collette."

She remained silent and motionless, the small revolver at her side, her senses acutely tuned. She pressed her eye against the peephole in the door, saw no one. Whoever had been calling her name was against a wall, out of range of the wide-angle lens. She had no way of knowing whether he was still there. The halls were carpeted; no footsteps to give a clue.

She went to the phone and called Vern again on the chance that he might have returned early. He hadn't.

Pacing the living room of her suite, she tried to sort out her next move. She was tempted to abandon the safety of the locked room, but that very safety kept her from doing it, at least for now. Still, she knew she'd have to leave sometime to go to the Allen Lee. Should she, could she wait until Wheatley returned and ask him to come to the Watergate? She answered no to both questions.

She looked down at the phone and read the instruction for calling another room in the hotel. She debated it, then picked up the receiver, dialed the required prefix, and punched in 1010. It rang a long time. She was about to hang up when Eric Edwards came on the line. He sounded out of breath.

"Eric. It's Collette."

"I don't believe it. Mystery lady surfaces. Let me get my breath. I've been working out. Where are you?"

"I'm . . . I'm in the vicinity."

"I knew you were in Washington. My secretary told me. How long will you be here?"

She wanted to say forever, said instead, "I really don't know. I'd like to see you."

"I hoped you'd want to see me," he said. "I was really upset the way you disappeared on me down in the BVI."

"I couldn't help it. I'm sorry."

"Nothing to be sorry about, and thanks for the note. I have a dinner engagement later this evening but . . ."

"I really need to see you tonight, Eric."

"Could you come by now? We can have a drink before I have to get dressed."

Collette paused before saying, "Yes, I can be there in ten minutes."

"Hope you don't mind a sweaty host."

"I won't mind that at all. Will we be alone?"

"Sure. What are you suggesting?"

"Nothing. Ten minutes."

"Fine, I'm in Suite 1010."

"Yes, I know."

After hanging up, she put on her raincoat and slipped the revolver into its pocket. She slung her purse over her shoulder and went to the door, her ear again cocked against the cool metal. There wasn't a sound outside. Then she heard the rattling of dishes and someone whistling—a hotel employee going past her room with a serving cart. She listened to the jangle as it faded into the distance, and until everything was silent again. She undid the chain as quietly as possible, turned the lock on the knob and opened the door, looking out into the hallway right and left. Empty. She made sure she had her key, stepped through the opening, and closed the door behind her.

The elevators were to her left, about a hundred feet away. She started swiftly toward them when Mark Hotchkiss stepped from around a bend in the hallway beyond the elevators. She stopped, turned, and saw Jason Tolker approaching from the opposite direction. His right arm was in a sling, that side of his suit jacket draped over his shoulder. She hadn't noticed that downstairs. "Collette," Tolker said. "Please, I want to talk to you."

"Get away," she said, backing toward the elevators, her hand slipping into her pocket.

Tolker continued to walk toward her, saying, "Don't be foolish, Collette. You're making a big mistake. You must listen to me."

"Shut up," she said. Her hand came out of the pocket holding the revolver and she pointed it at him. It stopped him cold. "I won't miss you this time."

"Miss Cahill, you're being bloody unreasonable," Hotchkiss said from behind.

She glanced over her shoulder and showed him the weapon. "I'm telling you to stay away from me or I'll kill you both. I mean it."

Both men stopped their advance and watched as she moved toward the elevators, her head moving back and forth like a spectator's at a tennis match, keeping them both in view.

"Get her," Tolker yelled.

Hotchkiss extended his arms and stumbled toward her. She waited until he was about to grab her, then brought her knee up sharply into his groin. His breath exploded from him as he sank to his knees, his hands cupping his wounded genitals.

Collette ran to the elevators and pushed the "Down" button. Almost immediately one of the doors opened. The elevator was empty. She backed into it. "Don't come after me," she said, the doors sliding closed and muffling her words.

She looked at the control panel and pushed Seven. The elevator moved a floor lower. She got out, ran along the hall, and turned a corner until she came to another bank of elevators. She frantically pushed the button until one of them arrived. In it were two couples. She stepped inside and pressed Ten.

The couples got out with her at the tenth floor. She waited until they'd entered a room, then walked past it and went directly to 1010. She knocked. The door was immediately opened by Eric Edwards. He wore blue gym shorts and a gray athletic shirt with the sleeves cut off at the shoulders. His hair was damp with perspiration and hung over his tanned forehead.

"Hello, Eric," she said.

"Hello to you," he said, stepping back so that she could enter. He closed the door and latched it.

She went to the center of the room and looked down at a pair of hotel barbells and a couple of towels tossed in a pile on the floor. She kept her back to him.

"Not even a kiss hello?" he asked from behind. She turned, sighed, lowered her eyes, and her body began to shake. Large tears instantly ran down her cheeks.

He put his arms around her and held tight. "Hey, come *on* now, it can't be that bad. Some reaction to me. I should be offended."

She controlled herself, looked up, and said, "I'm so confused, Eric, and frightened. Do you know why I'm here in Washington?"

"No, except you said you had some business to attend to."

"But do you know what that business was?"

He shook his head and smiled. "No, and unless you tell me, I never will."

"I was sent here to kill you."

He looked at her as though she were a small child caught in a lie. She said, "It's true, Eric. They wanted me to kill you, and I said I would."

"Telling you to kill me is one thing," he said as he went to a chair near the window, "agreeing to it is another. Why would you want to kill me?"

She tossed her raincoat on a couch. "I don't. I mean, I didn't. I never intended to."

He laughed. "You're incredible, you know that?"

She shook her head, went to him, and sank to her knees in front of the chair. "Incredible? No, I'm anything but. What I am is a terribly mixed up and disillusioned woman."

"Disillusioned with what, our good friends at Langley?"

She nodded. "The so-called Company, everyone in my life, life itself I guess." She took a deep breath. "They wanted me to kill you because they think you're a double agent, selling information to the Soviets about Banana Quick."

He grunted, shrugged.

"When I came to you and asked for advice about a vacation in the BVI, it was all a lie. They told me to do it. They wanted me to get close to you so that I could find out what you were doing down there."

He leaned forward, touched her cheek, and said, "I knew that, Collette."

"You did?"

"Well, not for certain, but I had a pretty strong feeling about it. It really didn't bother me for a couple of reasons. One, I fell in love with you. Two, I figured that when you almost went up with me and the yacht, you'd lost your taste for doing their dirty work. Was I right?"

"Yes."

"Having something like that happen puts things in perspective, doesn't it? You can see how little you or I mean to them. We can go out and put our necks on the line for their crazy sense of duty and patriotism, but when push comes to shove, we're all expendable. No questions asked, just 'terminate' some people and get on with the sham."

His words had considerable impact on her, as words always do when they say what you've already been thinking. She thought of Tolker and Hotchkiss and their confrontation. "There are two men in the hotel who tried to stop me in the hall."

He sat up. "Who are they? Do you know them?"

"Yes. One is Jason Tolker, the psychiatrist who was Barrie's control. He brainwashed her, Eric. The other is an Englishman named Mark Hotchkiss, the one who took over Barrie's agency."

Edwards's placid face turned grim as he looked out the window. "You know him?" Collette asked.

"I know of him. He's British intelligence, an old buck who supposedly did some hits for MI-6, the Middle East, I think."

Cahill said, "I think Tolker is the one who killed Barrie and David Hubler, maybe not directly, but I'm convinced he was behind it."

Edwards continued to stare silently at the window. Finally, he turned to her and said, "I have a proposal for you, Collette."

"A proposal?"

He managed a thin smile. "Not that kind of proposal, although maybe that's in the cards down the road. As it would have been with Barrie if . . ." She waited for him to finish his thought. Instead, he said, "For all her intelligence, Barrie didn't have one tenth the smarts you have, Collette."

"If there's one thing I don't consider myself these days, it's smart."

He placed his hands on her shoulders and kissed her gently on the forehead. "You've seen more in your lifetime than most people can only imagine. You've not only witnessed the rotten underbelly of the CIA, what they call Intelligence, you've been a victim of it, like me. Barrie didn't understand that. She never realized how she was being used by them."

Cahill sat back on her haunches. "I don't understand," she said.

"I suppose it doesn't matter anymore about Barrie. She's dead. It's different for you, though. You could . . . you could step in where she left off, sort of in her memory." His face lit up as though what he'd just said represented a profound revelation. "That's right, you could view it that way, Collette, as doing something in Barrie's memory."

"View *what* that way?"

"Doing something to right wrongs, to avenge all the things that have happened because of them, including the loss of your good friend, and that young man who worked for her. You could do something very worthwhile for the world, Collette."

"What do you mean?"

"Come in with me," he said.

She had no idea what he meant, and her face indicated it.

He hunched forward and spoke in low, paternal tones. "Collette, I want you to think carefully about everything that's happened over the past weeks, beginning with the death of Barrie Mayer." He scrutinized her face. "You know why Barrie died, don't you?"

"Sometimes I think I do, but I've never been sure. Do you know . . . for sure?"

His expression was one of bad taste in his mouth. He said in the same measured tones, "Barrie died because she wouldn't listen to me. She did in the beginning, and it was good for her, but then she started listening to others."

"Tolker?"

"Yes. He had remarkable control over her. I warned her. I tried to reason with her, but every time she'd see him, he'd capture another small piece of her mind."

"I knew that was the case, but . . ."

"But what?"

"Why would he have killed her if she were so obedient to him?"

"Because that's the flaw in their whole stupid mind-control program, Collette. They spend millions, screw up one life after the other, but still can't—and never will—create a person they can *totally* control. It's impossible, and they know it."

"But they . . ."

"Yeah, they keep spending and trying. Why? The freaks who work in those projects, like Tolker, get off on it. They exaggerate results and keep promising a breakthrough, while the ones who control funding rationalize the millions by claiming the other side is doing it, and in a bigger way. Barrie might have been manipulated by Tolker, but he didn't own her. Maybe it would have been better if he did. Or thought he did."

Collette said nothing as she thought about what he'd said.

"Tolker filled Barrie with a lot of lies that turned her against me," Edwards continued. "It was a tragic mistake on her part. She didn't know who to trust, and ended up putting all her cards in the wrong player's hand."

Cahill went to a table. She leaned her hands on it and peered down at its surface. As hard as she tried, she couldn't fully process what he was saying. Everything was so indirect, raising more questions than answers.

"Eric, why was Barrie killed? What did she know that made it necessary to murder her? Who would have been so hurt if she stayed alive that they'd be driven to such an act?"

He came closer to her. "You have to understand, Collette, that Barrie knew the risks involved in what she was doing."

"Being a courier? Occasionally carrying things to Budapest shouldn't pose that much of a risk, Eric."

"Not unless what she was carrying could be construed as being destructive to the Company."

"Why would it be destructive? She was working *for* it, wasn't she?"

"In the beginning, then . . . Look, let me level with you, Collette, the way I've been doing right along. I won't try to soften it, mince words. Barrie eventually saw the wisdom in cooperating with—the other side."

Collette shook her head. "No, I can't believe that Barrie would double-deal. No, sorry, I can't accept that."

"You have to, Collette. Open your mind. Don't automatically make it negative. What she was doing was noble in its own way."

"Noble? You're saying she was a traitor."

"Semantics. Is trying to achieve a balance of sanity in this world a traitorous act? I don't think so. Is saving the lives of thousands of innocent people, Hungarians in this case, traitorous? Of course it isn't. Banana Quick was ill-conceived from the beginning, doomed to failure, like the Bay of Pigs and the rescue attempt in Iran and all the other misguided projects we undertake in the name of freedom. If Banana Quick is implemented, it will only result in the death of innocent people in Hungary. Barrie didn't see that at first, but I eventually convinced her of it."

"*You* convinced her?"

"Yes, and I want to convince you of the same thing. This is something I've wanted to do ever since I met you, but I was never sure you'd be receptive. Now I think you will be, just as Barrie was, once she understood."

"Go ahead."

"I want you to work with me to fend off this madness. I want you to pick up where Barrie left off. I want you to . . . to help me feed information to where it will do the most good, to what you call 'the other side.' "

Cahill's stomach churned and she felt light-headed. What they'd said was true. He *was* a double agent, and had recruited Barrie. She didn't know what to say, how to respond, whether to lash out at him physically or to run from the room. She held both instincts in check. "I defended you at every turn. I told them they were wrong about you. I was the one who was wrong." She'd said it with a calm voice. Now she exploded. "Damn it, damn you! I thought Tolker was the double agent leaking information about Banana Quick. I really believed that, but now you're admitting to me that you are. You bastard! You set Barrie up to be killed, and now you want me to put myself in the same position."

He shook his head slowly. "Collette, you have a lot more to offer than Barrie did. She was so naive. That's what got her in trouble, what led to her death. When I took Barrie into my confidence, I had no idea of her potential for control by someone like Tolker. She told him everything, and he convinced her to inform on me. She'd learned too much. I never should have let her get that close, but I fell in love. I do that too easily and often for my own good."

"Love? You call it love for a woman to recruit her into selling out her country?"

"Love comes in all forms. It was a nice partnership, personally and professionally, until Tolker soured everything. Barrie made a lot of money from our partnership, Collette, a lot more than she was getting from the CIA."

"Money? That matters to you?"

"Sure. It mattered to her, too. There's nothing inherently evil with money, is there? Let me suggest something. Climb down off your high horse and hear me out. I'll cancel my date tonight and we'll have dinner right here in the room. We'll get to know each other better." He laughed. "And we can pick up where we left off in the BVI. No strings, Collette. You don't have to fall in with me. Nothing lost by talking about it."

"I don't want to talk about it," she said.

"You don't have much choice."

"What do you mean?"

"You're already in because you know too much. That makes sense, doesn't it?"

"Not at all."

He shrugged, leaned over and picked up a barbell, lifted it a few times over his head. "I'll make a deal with you. All you have to do is go back to Budapest and tell them I'm clean. I'll give you materials that make a case against Tolker as having thrown in with the Soviets. That's all you have to do, Collette, tell them you dug up this material and are turning it over like a good Company employee. They'll take care of Tolker and . . ."

"And what, terminate him?"

"That's not our concern. You knew, didn't you, that Barrie was carrying almost two hundred thousand dollars to pay off some Hungarian bureaucrat?"

She didn't reply.

"I have it."

"You took it from her after you killed her." She was amazed at how matter-of-factly she was able to say it.

"It doesn't matter how I got it. What's important is that half is yours for clearing me. After that, there'll be plenty more if you decide to help me on a long-term basis. Think about it, lots of money stashed away for your retirement." Another laugh as he did curls with the barbell. "I figure I've got maybe another year at best before it's time for me to get out. I want enough money to start my own charter service, not a front I don't own. What do you want in a year, Collette? A house in Switzerland, an airplane, enough money in a foreign bank so that you'll never have to work again? It's yours." He dropped the barbell to the floor and said, "How about it? Dinner? Champagne? We'll toast anything you want, anybody, and then we can . . ."

"Make love?"

"Absolutely. I established a rule with myself years ago that I'd never let anything get in the way of that, especially when it's a beautiful and bright woman like you who . . ." He shook his head. "Who made me fall in love again."

She went for her raincoat on the couch. He jumped in front of her and gripped the back of her neck, his fingertips pressing hard against her arteries. She could see the muscles rippling in his bare arms, and the red anger on his face. "I'm through being nice," he said, pushing her across the room and into the bedroom. He flung her down on the bed, grabbed the front of her sweater, and tore it off.

She rolled off the bed and scrambled across the floor toward the door, got to her feet, and raced into the living room. She swiped at her raincoat and tried to get behind the couch where she'd have time to retrieve the revolver. He was too quick; she'd barely managed to pull the weapon from the pocket when he grabbed her wrist and twisted, the white plastic gun falling to the floor.

"You bitch," he said. "You would kill me, wouldn't you?"

His ego was so damaged momentarily that he relaxed his grip on her wrist. She sprang loose and ran to where she'd left her purse on top of a large console television set, grabbed it, and tried to find something to get behind, a haven where she could catch her breath and ready the detonator. There wasn't any such place—her only escape route was into the master bedroom. She ran there and tried to slam the door behind her, but he easily pushed it open, the force sending her reeling toward the bed. Her knees caught it, and she was suddenly on her back, her hands frantically seeking the device in her purse.

He stood over her and glared. "You don't understand the game, do you? What did you think would happen when you decided to get some excitement in your life by joining up? What did you think, you can play spy but run home to Mommy when it hurts?"

"I'm . . . please don't hurt me," she said. Her purse had fallen to the floor, but she'd grasped the loaded detonator and cupped it in her right hand, her arms flung back over the edge of the bed.

"I don't want to," he said. "I don't hurt people for fun. Sometimes, though . . . sometimes it's necessary, that's all. Don't make it necessary for me to hurt you."

"I won't." His eyes were focused on her bare breasts. He smiled. "A beautiful woman. You'll see, Collette, we'll end up together. It'll be nice. We'll stash the money, then go away somewhere and enjoy the hell out of it—and each other."

He leaned forward and put a hand on either side of her head. His face was inches from her face. He kissed her on the lips, and she managed to return it, mimicking the memory of their night together, until he pulled his head back and said, "You're beautiful."

Then she brought her hand up and jammed the detonator against his lips. Her thumb pulled the switch and the ampule exploded, sending the acid and a thousand fine fragments of glass into his face. He gasped and fell back to his knees, his hands ripping at his sweatshirt, his face contorted.

Cahill, too, felt the effect of the acid. Her face had been too close to his. She reached down and shoved her hand into her open purse, found the small glass vial of nitro and broke it beneath her nose, breathing deeply, praying it would work.

"Me . . ." Edwards said. He was now writhing on the floor, one hand outstretched, his last living expression one of pleading. Cahill lay on her stomach, her head at the foot of the bed, her eyes wide as she watched him breathe and then, with one last convulsion, his head twisted to one side and he was dead, his open eyes looking up at her.

33

SHE MADE HER final trip to Budapest a week later, to process out and to arrange for the shipment of her things back to the United States.

Joe Breslin met her Malev flight and drove her to her apartment. "I really don't have much," she said. "It was probably silly for me even to come here."

"You didn't have to bother with packing," Breslin said, lighting his pipe. "We would have done it for you. Got a beer?"

"Go look. I don't know."

He returned from the tiny kitchen with a bottle of the Köbányai világos and a glass. "Want one? There's plenty."

"No."

He sat on a deep window bench and she leaned against a wall, her arms folded across her chest, ankles crossed, her head down. She sighed, looked at him, and said, "I'll hate you and everybody in the CIA for the rest of my life, Joe."

"I'm genuinely sorry about that," he said.

"So am I. Maybe if I grow up someday and begin to understand everything that's happened, I won't feel quite so filled with hatred."

"Maybe. You know, none of us likes doing what we have to do."

"I don't believe that, Joe. I think the agency's filled with people who love it. I thought I did."

"You did a good job."

"Did I?"

"Your handling of Hegedüs was as masterful as any I've ever seen."

"He was telling the truth about Tolker, wasn't he?"

"Yeah. I wish the Fisherman were still in place. He's no good to us now."

She made a sound of displeasure.

"What's the matter?" he asked.

" 'He's no good to us now.' That's the way it is, isn't it, Joe? People are only worthwhile as long as they have something to give. After that . . . instant discard."

He didn't respond.

"Tell me about Hotchkiss," she said.

Breslin shrugged and drew on his pipe. "MI-6, an old-timer who hung in. They—the Brits—set Hotchkiss up in the literary agency business years ago. Nice cover, good excuse to travel and get a pulse on what's happening in the literary fraternity. In most countries, literary means political. Having him in that business paid off for them. They're not talking, at least to us, but somehow they got wind that Barrie had turned, and was working with Edwards. They sicced Hotchkiss on her." Breslin's laugh was one of admiration. "Hotchkiss did a better job than they'd hoped for. He actually got Barrie to consider going into partnership."

"Consider? They did become partners."

"Not really. The papers were bogus. We figure your friend told Hotchkiss to get lost the night before she died. That eventuality had been considered for a long time. Those papers were drawn, and her signature forged, in anticipation of the deal going down the tube."

"But why . . . ?"

"Why what? Go through all that? The British have been complaining from the first day about Banana Quick. They felt we were running the show, and that they were being left in the dark about too many things. Answer? Get someone on the inside, in this case Barrie Mayer. Knowing what she was up to was as good as sleeping with Edwards."

"And Jason Tolker?"

A long draw on his pipe. "Funny about Tolker. He really was in love with Barrie Mayer, but he found himself between a rock and a hard place. The British suspected she was double-dealing, but never knew for certain. Tolker knew. He was the only one, besides Edwards, but what does he do with the information? Turn them in and destroy the woman? He couldn't do that, so he went to work on her and tried to convince her to drop Edwards, turn him in, and hope that they'd let her off the hook. He was effective, *too* effective. She finally decided to do it. Edwards couldn't allow that. That's why he killed her. All such a waste. They've scrapped Banana Quick."

Cahill stared at him incredulously, then quickly went to a closet. She would not allow him to see that her eyes were moist. She waited until she was under control before pulling out a blue blazer and slipping it on over her white blouse. "Let's go," she said.

"Stan wants to talk to you before you leave," said Breslin.

"I know. What is it, a debriefing?"

"Something like that. He'll lay down the rules. He has to do that with anyone leaving. There are rules, you know, about disclosure, things like that."

"I can live with rules."

"What about your friend, the journalist?"

"Vern? Don't worry, Joe, I won't tell him what happened, what *really* happened."

"The book he's writing."

"What about it?"

"You've seen it. Is it damaging?"

"Yes."

"We'd like to know what's in it."

"Not from me."

"Do him a favor, Collette, and get him to drop it."

"That sounds like an order."

"A strong request."

"Denied."

She started to open the door but he stopped her with "Collette, you sure you want to make such a clean break? Hank Fox told you what your options were before you came here. The outfit takes good care of those who do special service, and do it well. You could have six months anywhere in the world with all expenses paid, a chance to get your head together and for enough time to pass so that it all doesn't seem so terrible. Then a nice job back at Langley, more money, the works. People who . . ."

"People who carry out an assassination are taken care of. Joe, I didn't assassinate Eric Edwards. He tried to rape me. I was like any other woman—except I had a plastic gun, a vial of lethal acid, and the blessing of my country's leading intelligence agency. I killed him to save myself, no other reason."

"What does it matter? The job got done."

"I'm glad that makes everyone happy. No, Joe, I want ten thousand miles between me and the CIA. I know there are a lot of good people in it who really care about what happens to their country, and who try to do the right thing. The problem is, Joe, that not only are there lots of people who *aren't* like that, but the definition of 'right thing' gets blurred all the time. Come on. Let me go and have the rules explained to me, and then let's have dinner. I'm really going to miss Hungarian food."

About the Author

MARGARET TRUMAN is the author of numerous bestselling murder mysteries exposing the intricate, behind-the-scenes working of Washington, D.C., the city she knows so well, including *Murder in the White House, Murder on Capitol Hill, Murder in the Supreme Court, Murder in the Smithsonian, Murder on Embassy Row, Murder at the FBI, Murder in Georgetown, Murder in the CIA,* and *Murder at the Kennedy Center.* She has also written biographies of her parents, the late President Harry S. and Bess Truman. She and her husband, Clifton Daniel, live in New York City.